THE LAST SUMMER

THE LAST SUMMER

Judith Kinghorn

WINDSOR
PARAGON

First published 2012
by Headline Review
This Large Print edition published 2012
by AudioGO Ltd
by arrangement with
Headline Publishing Group

Hardcover ISBN: 978 1 445 89389 1
Softcover ISBN: 978 1 445 89390 7

All characters in this publication—other than the obvious historical characters—are fictitious and any resemblance to real persons, living or dead, is purely coincidental

British Library Cataloguing in Publication Data available

Printed and bound in Great Britain by
MPG Books Group Limited

To Jeremy.

What is this life if, full of care,
We have no time to stand and stare.
No time to stand beneath the boughs
And stare as long as sheep or cows.
No time to see, when woods we pass,
Where squirrels hide their nuts in grass.
No time to see, in broad daylight,
Streams full of stars, like skies at night.
No time to turn at Beauty's glance,
And watch her feet, how they can dance.
No time to wait till her mouth can
Enrich that smile her eyes began.
A poor life this if, full of care,
We have no time to stand and stare.

William Henry Davies

Part One

CHAPTER ONE

I was almost seventeen when the spell of my childhood was broken. There was no sudden jolt, no immediate awakening and no alteration, as far as I'm aware, in the earth's axis that day. But the vibration of change was upon us, and I sensed a shift: a realignment of my trajectory. It was the beginning of summer and, unbeknown to any of us then, the end of a *belle époque*.

If I close my eyes I can still smell the day: the roses beyond the open casement doors, the lavender in the parterre as I ran through; and grass, lambent green, newly mown. I can feel the rain on my face; hear my voice as it once was.

I can't recall exactly who was there, but there were others: my three brothers, some of their friends from Cambridge, a few local people, I think. Our adolescent conversation was still devoid of any faltering uncertainty, and we didn't stand on the brink, we ran along it, unperturbed by tremulous skies, sure of our footing and certain of sunshine, hungry for the next chapter in our own unwritten stories. For lifetimes—lifetimes we had only just begun to imagine—stretched out before us criss-crossing and fading into a distant horizon. There was still time, you see. And the future, all of our futures, lay ahead, glistening with promise, eternal with possibility.

I can hear us now; hear us laughing.

That morning, as clouds gathered overhead, the earthbound colours of my world seemed to me more vibrant than ever. The gardens at Deyning were always at their best during June and early July. It was then, during those few precious weeks of midsummer that the place came into its own. And though Mama had often looked anxious, complaining about the incessant battering of her roses, every well-tended bloom and leafy branch appeared to me luminous and fresh. From the flagstone terrace the lawns spread out in an undulating soft carpet, and on the mossy steps that led down to the grass wild strawberries grew in abundance.

I can taste their sweetness, even now.

Mama had predicted a storm. She'd informed us that our croquet tournament may have to be postponed, but not before people had arrived. So we'd all stood in the ballroom, which my brothers and I simply referred to as 'the big-room', looking out upon the gardens through the open casement doors, debating whether to go ahead with our game or play cards instead. Henry, the eldest of my three older brothers, took charge as usual and voted that we go ahead in our already established teams. But no sooner had we arranged ourselves with mallets upon the lawn than the heavens opened with a reverberating boom, and we all ran back to the house, shrieking, soaking wet.

'Henry wishes tea to be served in the big-room, Mrs Cuthbert. We're all back inside now,' I said, standing by the green baize door, wringing out my hair.

Mrs Cuthbert had been our housekeeper for only a few weeks at that time. Years before she'd been employed by Earl Deyning himself, not only at Deyning Park—now our home—but also at his estate in Northamptonshire. It had been lucky for us that Mrs Cuthbert had agreed to come back to Deyning after the old Earl died, and my mother was delighted to have a housekeeper who knew the place so well. 'Such pedigree,' Mama had said, and I'd immediately imagined a little dog in an apron and mobcap.

'And how many of you are there, miss?' Mrs Cuthbert asked, glancing over at me, smiling.

'Oh . . . fourteen, I think. Shall I go and count again?'

'No, that's quite all right, dear. I'll come through myself and see.' She wiped her hands on her apron. 'You've got my Tom with you today,' she said.

'Tom? *Your* Tom?'

'Yes, he came home yesterday, and your mother kindly invited him to join today's little game. Have you not been introduced?'

'No. Well, I'm not sure. I don't think so . . .'

I followed Mrs Cuthbert along the back passageway, towards the big-room, and I remember looking down at the red and black quarry-tiled floor, trying—as I'd done since childhood—not to step on the black ones. But now it was impossible. My feet were too big.

'He's not like your brothers, miss,' she said, turning to look at me. 'He's a gentle soul.'

In the big-room, everyone had already seated themselves around the four card tables pushed up together. And suddenly I was aware of a new face, dark eyed and solemn, staring directly at me. As Mrs Cuthbert introduced me to her son, I smiled, but he didn't smile back, and I thought then how rude. 'Hello,' I said, and he stood up, still not smiling, and said, 'Pleased to meet you,' then looked away.

There was no thunderbolt, no quickening of the heart, but there was a sense of recognition. A familiarity about his face: the nose, the eyes; his stature.

I opted out of whist. All three of my brothers were playing and I knew I stood no chance. Instead, I wandered to the other end of the room and sat down on the Persian rug in front of the fireplace. As I played with Caesar, Mama's Pekinese dog, I caught Tom Cuthbert looking at me. I didn't smile, but he knew I'd seen him. And, when I rose to my feet and walked back across the room, I was aware of him watching me. I sat down in an armchair, closer to the card tables, picked up a magazine and began to flick through its pages. I glanced over at him, caught his eye once more, and this time he smiled. And I knew it to be a special gesture, meant only for me. I didn't realise what it was like for him then, of course; had no idea of his discomfort as his mother served us all tea.

My upbringing had prepared me for a certain life, a life where I'd never question my role or the cast of players sharing my stage. It was a thoroughly modern idea, then, to educate a daughter, and, in my father's opinion, a pointless expense. So I'd studied at home, with Mademoiselle: a tiny bird of a woman, whose dislike of fresh air and susceptibility to draughts had rendered her pale and brittle. Her lessons in life had depended as much upon the temperature of her heart as the weather outside. Men, she had often told me—usually during arithmetic, and with a rug over her knees—were brutes; they had simply not evolved from animals, she said. However, Keats and Wordsworth appeared to bring out an entirely different side of Mademoiselle's compact and complex character, for then she would sometimes throw back the rug, rise to her feet, and tell me that life was '*nuzzeen*' at all if one had never loved. But by that summer Mademoiselle had left my life for good, for by then it was assumed I knew enough to be able to converse in polite society without appearing completely vacuous.

Like my mother's orchids, I had been nurtured in a controlled environment, an atmosphere maintained at a consistent temperature, protected from cold snaps, clumsy fingers and bitter frosts. My three brothers, on the other hand, had been allowed—even encouraged—to develop unruly tendrils, to thrive beyond the confines of any hothouse, to spread their roots, unrestrained, through that English earth they belonged to. It was different for a girl.

Marriage and children, a tidy home and a manicured garden were a foregone conclusion. And a husband with money was always a prerequisite. For how else could that life be achieved? I was a Home Counties girl, happy to be part of a family who enjoyed a sensible, uninterrupted existence, no matter the weather, the visitors, or the events beyond the white gate: the boundary between my understanding and the rest of the universe. When I was young I'd sometimes nudged that boundary: I'd walked down the long avenue of beech trees to the gate, and perched myself there, on top of it. There was little traffic on the road that bordered our land then, but occasionally an omnibus or new motor car would pass by and I would raise my hand to the unknown faces staring back at me. They were gone in an instant, but I always remembered those fleeting connections: new friends, all at once there, then gone again. Where did they go? What happened to them? Did they remember that moment too? Did they ever wonder what had become of me, the girl on the gate?

That evening, over dinner, I wanted to ask my mother about Tom Cuthbert, but she appeared abstracted. She gazed about the room with an unreadable expression on her face, and I wondered if she was thinking about the servants, again. She'd returned from London the day before, festooned with packages, and with a new hairdo, but noticeably agitated. 'It's simply *impossible*,' she'd announced in the hallway, and in a voice much louder than usual, 'to find any decent domestic staff these days. And when one does, one inevitably finds oneself replacing those months later.' I couldn't blame her for her exasperation. She had travelled to London only the previous week to interview a prospective parlourmaid, a butler, and a new chauffeur, and had stayed overnight—as she quite often did—in the comfort of her Piccadilly club. It was no wonder to me she knew the train timetable to the second and off by heart, but so much to-ing and fro-ing had, she said, left her feeling *quite frazzled*.

'I met Mrs Cuthbert's son today, Mama. He's called Tom, and he's been away . . . though I'm not sure where.'

'He attends university, dear,' she replied, without looking at me.

'But where?' I asked.

'Ha! Don't become too intrigued by Cuthbert, sis,' Henry broke in. 'Mama expects you to have your sights set *slightly* higher, I think,' he added, and then laughed.

'I wondered about him, that's all. He's seems rather shy and . . . well, he has only his mother.'

Henry looked across the table at me. 'Shy, eh? I reckon Cuthbert's probably quite a rogue—underneath that aloof exterior.'

'A rogue?' I repeated. 'I don't think so. I think he probably prefers his own company to . . . to the likes of us.'

'Aha! And she leaps to his defence! First sign, sister dear, first sign,' Henry said, and George and William both sniggered.

'Enough teasing, thank you, Henry,' said Mama, glancing to my father for reinforcement. My father cleared his throat, as though about to speak, but then said nothing.

'You're simply jealous,' I said, looking back at Henry and forcing a smile. It was one of my stock replies to him when I didn't quite know what else to say.

'And why on earth would I be jealous? He's a servant, for God's sake.'

'No, he's not. Mama's just informed us—he's at university.'

'Oh yes, learning to polish silver, no doubt,' Henry replied.

'You're jealous because he's so much more handsome than you and isn't inclined to boastfulness,' I said, staring down at my plate, and then added, 'Mademoiselle says gentlemen who feel the need to boast almost always have unusually small *cerveaux*.'

'Ha! Mademoiselle . . . hmm, well, she would know of course. And yes, that's right, I'm jealous of our housekeeper's son, for I shall never have what he has and I can never be the bastard son of—'

'Henry! That's enough,' my father intervened. 'I don't expect language like that from you or anyone else at this table. And I think you should leave your tittle-tattle and gossip at Cambridge. Do you understand?'

'Yes, sir,' my brother answered.

And that was that.

I had no doubt that my eldest brother, Henry, knew a great deal of *tittle-tattle*. And more than that: I imagined there'd be idle gossip and tittle-tattle about him, too, somewhere. For of late he seemed to have acquired new friends, and spent more time in London than at home or Cambridge. Everyone knew Henry, and he, it appeared, knew everything about everyone. But his coterie had never been confined to Cambridge. Two of his closest friends from school had gone up to Oxford, another few straight into the army. He was the most outgoing of my three brothers, confident, popular, and extremely well connected. He liked to say he had his *ear to the ground* and I often imagined him lying prostrate upon some bustling city street.

Later that same evening I quizzed my brother, asked him what he'd meant by his remark, but he'd heeded my father's warning. 'I was being flippant, dear. It meant nothing,' he said to me. But I knew there was more, and something specific: something my father did not wish to have repeated, particularly not in front of me. There was no point in my pursuing it with Henry; he'd never go against Papa, no matter how full of bravado he appeared, and I was very much aware that to him I was still a child. But as I lay in my bed that night I pondered on it all again. I wondered who paid for Tom

Cuthbert's education; and then I wondered if I'd heard Henry correctly. Had he actually used the word *bastard*?

CHAPTER TWO

My father's inheritance, though by no means insubstantial, had been built upon and added to over the years, mainly through returns on investments in the railways. Five years before I was born he'd purchased Deyning Park from the impoverished Earl, and commissioned one of England's finest architects to make it grander than ever. A ballroom and two entire wings were added to the main building, old windows and doors replaced; the old panelled library was refurbished, and an ornate carved staircase, Italian marble floor and Corinthian pillars were added to the main lobby. Almost five hundred tons of white Tuscan marble had been brought to Deyning to create my father's vision: a grand entrance hall with twenty-foot-high pillars. The oak-panelled dining room was easily big enough to comfortably seat thirty, and the sixteen bedrooms and four modern bathrooms ensured my parents could entertain *and* accommodate their house guests in style.

Later, some five or six years after my birth, electric lights were installed in a few of the formal reception rooms, their twentieth-century brilliance altering Mama's colour scheme, and causing much debate and consternation amongst the servants. At that time, a rumour drifted about the house that looking directly upon the electric light could blind a person, and one of the servants—Edna, I think, suspect now, though I have no evidence and it was a very long time ago—had told George this. My brother—in the midst of a scientific phase—had been determined to test this theory, and, as usual, appointed me his assistant. My role in this particular experiment was to stand guard as he climbed up on to the dining-room table and then, once in position, beneath the new chandelier, and only when he gave me the codeword 'eureka', to flick the wall-mounted switch. But as I stood on a chair, waiting for my cue, George became distracted by new possibilities, and as he flew along the highly polished mahogany table in his stocking feet he collided with Mama's oversized and elaborate crystal epergne, taking the thing with him on its final short journey. George and the epergne landed on the oak floor in a crash loud enough to wake the dead and within seconds half the servants and Mama were in the room. Luckily George wasn't injured, but the epergne—which, we were informed by Mama, was an *airloom*—was pronounced unrepairable. Later on, in the library, George was tried: I was called to give evidence, and he was found guilty and sentenced by Papa to twenty-four hours' solitary confinement. And that marked the end of George's interest in electricity.

Parts of our home, I'd been told, dated back to the sixteenth century, but from the outside, at least, the place appeared resolutely Georgian: built in the neoclassical style from honey-hued stone with a pleasing symmetry, perfectly balanced lines, and a multitude of tall windows. At the front of the house, in the centre, two Ionic columns framed the doorway, supporting a stone pediment with the words *Ubi bene, ibi patria* carved into it. To the east of the house, around a cobblestoned courtyard—always referred to as the stable yard—were the stables, coach house and a few servants' cottages. A warren of dark passageways and small interconnecting rooms led from the house to the coach house, where two motor cars now sat alongside the old wagonette and landau carriage of my childhood. And there, too, the sleigh: still used occasionally in the depths of winter, when the lanes around us were white and thick with snow.

Father's penchant for the neoclassical was a fitting backdrop to his and my mother's vast collection of artefacts and souvenirs from abroad: antiques, paintings, books, bronzes and sculptures from their continental tours. A delivery of crates and the unveiling of new works of art for Deyning inevitably followed each return home. In his newly furbished library my father added to his burgeoning collection of rare books; books he would never read; books no one could read in any one lifetime. And whilst he indulged himself with his love of antiquities, Mama focused on our comfort, with new fitted carpets and expensive wall coverings from Harrods and Gamages. She'd taken advice, albeit paid for, from an old friend of hers who had an interior decorating business in London.

Sumptuous would best describe Mama's style. It was what she'd been accustomed to all her life; was what she knew. Consequently, our home was as lavishly furnished and decorated as any other fine country house: each window festooned, draped in richly coloured silk brocades; looped back, tasselled and fringed; each vista—north, south, east and west—opulently framed in a colour specifically chosen to match the light of that room, and the views beyond.

From my bedroom window I looked out across the formal gardens and lake, beyond the six hundred acres of landscaped parkland to the South Downs in the distance. It was the only point in my vision that my father did *not* own, and I sometimes wondered who lived there, beyond my world, beyond Deyning. As a child I'd rarely ventured farther than the ha-ha, which separated the park from the formal gardens. Terraces, ornamented with statues, urns and fountains, led down from the house's south façade to the striped lawns and broad herbaceous borders, extravagantly stocked with Mama's prize-winning roses and peonies.

A small army of gardeners and outdoor staff were employed at Deyning then. Even now, I see their faces, and their hands, my *outside friends*. Together, they managed the parkland, the home farm and the kitchen gardens; they maintained the formal gardens, and the tennis and croquet lawns, constantly rolling and trimming the grass to perfection. They pulled, planted, chopped, clipped and snipped, like defenders of a realm, for Deyning was a kingdom, guarded by acreage and entirely self-sufficient. The walled kitchen gardens produced all manner of fruit and vegetables: asparagus, strawberries, raspberries, loganberries, currants (white, red and black), gooseberries, plums, pears, apples, rhubarb, potatoes, cabbages, carrots, cauliflowers and spinach. And in summer, up against the pink brick walls, peaches and nectarines. The home farm supplied us with all our milk, cream, eggs, butter and cheese, as well as our meat, poultry and game.

We knew no lack, experienced no want, and I knew no other way. I had never looked from the outside in; never thought about *how* we lived. Until that time: until Tom Cuthbert entered my life.

That summer we were all at home, still living a collective existence, still a family. At five years my senior, Henry had only just finished his studies at Cambridge, and William, two years younger than Henry, had completed his first year there, studying Theology. George, my closest sibling—a year younger than William and two years my senior—was at Aldershot, training to be an officer. And, at sixteen years of age, it seemed my education was complete. Mama had been keen for me to attend a fashionable finishing school in Paris before coming out. It was what she had done, what everyone did, she said. But events on the continent had made my parents anxious, and so my sojourn in Paris was indefinitely postponed.

Strange though it may seem, I had no desire at that time for a more eventful existence, or a broader vista. I filled my days with walks through the grounds, following the same paths, anticipating the same sights, content with familiarity. I lost myself in books, spent hours in my father's library, pulling out whichever title caught my eye. And it was there, in the library, that I had my first proper conversation with Tom Cuthbert. I'd seen him about the place: walking down the drive, disappearing into the distance; helping one of the under-gardeners cut logs in the stable yard; and a couple of times in the kitchen, when I'd been sent to query a menu for Mama. He'd been sitting at the table, reading a newspaper, doing nothing in particular, and he'd stood up and said, 'Hello,' without any smile.

When he appeared in the library that day I was perched at the top of the library steps, reading a volume of Emily Brontë's poems, and I can't be sure, but I think I may have been reading aloud. He cleared his throat. 'Excuse me,' he said, 'your father told me that I was welcome to borrow any books . . . I can come back later.'

'No, please, I'm idling here, do come in,' I said, looking down at him. He closed the door, and I had the faintest inkling of intimacy.

'I was reading a poem . . . do you like poetry, Mr Cuthbert?' I asked, filling the silence as he surveyed the shelves on the opposite side of the room, his back to me.

He pulled out a book. 'Yes, I like poetry,' he said, without turning to face me.

'I'm rather fond of the Brontë sisters myself . . . especially dear Emily,' I said, trying desperately to sound grown up and worldly. He made no reply but continued his inspection of the volumes immediately in front of him, occasionally bending down or stretching up. And I watched him, surreptitiously, in case he should suddenly turn.

He was tall, taller than Henry, and his dark hair longer than my brothers' or anyone else's I'd seen. It hung down over his forehead in a wave he ran his hand through from time to time. He wore dark grey flannel trousers with navy braces, a plain pale blue shirt; no tie, no jacket.

'I imagine it's rather dull for you here,' I said at last, uncomfortable with our lack of conversation and longing for a break in the deadlock.

He turned, smiled at me. 'Dull? No, not at all. Why do you say that?'

'Well, it's somewhat quiet here, especially when my brothers aren't about the place, and not everyone's partial to the peace of the countryside.'

He laughed. 'I think I may very well be *dull* then, Miss Granville. I'm happy to be amidst this peacefulness. I get quite enough noise and bustle up at Oxford.'

'Oxford?' I repeated, climbing carefully down the library steps.

'Yes, but only for another year, and then I'm done.'

'And then what?' I asked.

'I shall go to the bar, become a practising lawyer.'

'Oh, so you'll live in London, I suppose . . .'

'Yes, that's my plan.'

'Everyone seems to go to London, eventually, but I'm not so sure I shall. I rather think I prefer the country,' I said.

He stared at me, half smiling, and I pushed my hair back from my face, glanced down at the book in my hand.

'Well, you're still quite young . . . you may change your mind yet.'

'Oh no, I'll be seventeen in August. I'll be coming out soon, and then I shall have to be in London,' I said, and his smile broadened. He looked so handsome, so nonchalant at that moment, his hair hanging down over one eye. And as I felt myself blush I looked away once more. He was amused, quietly amused. I was still a child to him, naive and innocent; locked up in a modern-day fortress, talking nonsense.

'And I'm sure you'll have a gay time, and many suitors too,' he said, still smiling, still staring. 'But it's an odd ritual, is it not?' he continued, moving away from the shelves, a book gripped in his own hand now too. 'Coming out? It's about finding a husband, isn't it?'

'No, not entirely,' I said, unsure of what else to say, because I'd never really thought about it until that moment; what 'coming out' meant, its purpose.

'Oh?'

'It's more about parties . . . meeting new people, that sort of thing. I think originally, historically, it was about finding a husband, but of course it's different now.' I smiled. 'After all, this is the twentieth century,' I continued, feeling quite bold and modern, 'things have changed.' Then I added, 'Look at the suffragettes . . .'

I wasn't quite sure what I meant by that last line, but I liked the sound of it. For despite Papa's misgivings (hooligans, he called them), I'd become deeply fascinated by the recent dramatic events I'd read about taking place in London. The window-smashing women, full of passion and fury, no matter how far from my own gilded cage, had captured my imagination.

He smiled at me, and I noticed his eyes: darkest mahogany, glinting with light. 'Have times changed?' he asked. 'Are you sure about that, Miss Granville?' He frowned, looking at me quizzically. And I knew he was being provocative. Like my brothers, I thought.

'I'm used to being teased, Mr Cuthbert,' I replied. 'I have three older brothers—remember?'

'But I'm not teasing you. I'm curious, genuinely so. Do you really think times have changed? Do you truly believe that your own coming out and that of all the other debutantes isn't about finding a suitable husband?'

'Well, yes, I'll be introduced to society, and that society may well include my future husband, or not, as the case may be,' I replied, perhaps a little too quickly. He said nothing, but tilted his head to one side and looked back at me through half-closed eyes. Then he shook his head and turned away.

'I amuse you,' I said, without thinking.

'You do somewhat, but it's not so much you, it's the way . . . the way your sort operate,' he replied, and I simply couldn't understand what he meant. Was he being rude? Was he playing? I couldn't be sure, so I shrugged and then laughed myself.

'Yes, we're a strange lot, aren't we?' I said.

'You're right, of course. Things are changing, and changing fast. Look at me: the son of a humble servant, at Oxford and bound for a career in the City.'

'Yes indeed, your mother must be very proud of you,' I replied, sounding like Mama.

He laughed again. He was so handsome when he laughed; so utterly uninhibited and free. It was not a joke, but he was free enough to laugh. To laugh out loud at me, pretending to be something.

'I'm sorry,' he said. 'I don't mean to be rude or disrespectful.'

'No, I know that. I mean, I can see that.'

He fixed his eyes on me. 'Yes, yes I think you can . . . Clarissa.'

And when he said my name, it was as though I'd heard it spoken for the very first time, as though he'd placed his hand upon my bare skin. No one other than my immediate family ever addressed me so directly, so honestly, using only my first name. *Clarissa*. He'd said my name, said it slowly, looking straight at me.

I'd been released from a cage and allowed to fly.

'I think I must go now,' I said, not entirely sure of how to deal with his entrance into my life. 'I need to dress for dinner.'

'Of course,' he replied, glancing over to the clock. 'And I should get back to my studies.'

'Really, Tom,' I said, adopting his familiar style, 'you don't need to go on my account. Stay here a while, I'm quite sure no one will disturb you.'

'No, I should go. But I'll come back tomorrow,' he said, looking at me.

I smiled, nodded. 'Yes. Yes, do that.'

CHAPTER THREE

The next day, when I awoke, I remember feeling quite different. In fact, everything seemed strangely altered. It was as though a door had finally opened on to my world, letting in light so every detail appeared sharper, more focused. And from that doorway I was able to look back on my life, my family, and begin to see us as others saw us: as Tom Cuthbert saw us.

I'd slept in that morning. By the time I went down to breakfast it was after nine, and yet the house seemed unusually quiet. Henry, I knew, was away, staying with friends in Salisbury, and my father, as usual, remained up in town, attending to business. But I wondered where my mother was.

As I sat at the dining-room table, already cleared but for one setting, Mrs Cuthbert emerged through the baize door with fresh tea. She asked if I'd like Edna to cook me something. And then she reminded me that my mother had caught the 7.38 to London—to attend a horticultural exhibition with Mr Broughton, the head gardener—and wasn't expected back until late that evening. She told me that George and Will had also risen early; already set off to attend their old school Speech Day. And I felt momentarily angry that they'd all gone and left me there, alone. Why had Mama not invited me to accompany her? And why could my brothers not have taken me with them to their Speech Day reunion? It didn't seem fair. I was being treated like a child, I said to Mrs Cuthbert.

'Oh, but you have all the time in the world, your whole life ahead of you. Don't wish it away too soon.'

'I don't wish it away, Mrs C, but I'd rather like *something* to happen.'

Then I thought of Tom Cuthbert.

'And how is Tom?' I said. 'It must be lovely for you to have him back with you.'

She smiled. 'Yes, it is. And he's a good boy . . . a gentle soul,' she said, again, and then disappeared through the baize door.

For so many years, since George, the last of my brothers to be sent away to boarding school, had gone, I'd languished in a daydream at Deyning. Floating through the house and about the grounds, inventing people, places and events: a revered guest at so many glittering parties out on the lawn; an actress upon the stage of the ha-ha; an intrepid explorer cutting a swathe through the Amazon jungle of long meadow grass. And though those desultory days of my childhood, when an hour had stretched to a lifetime and time itself was of no import, lingered on, they were in fact drawing to a close.

More latterly, the fantasies of my idle hours had taken on a different hue. For now it seemed I had to be *rescued*, and, perhaps inevitably, by a dashingly handsome—albeit slightly unkempt—young man. I was often confused, irritated by these unscripted interventions. I liked to imagine myself as one of those pioneering Victorian women I'd read about: independent, brave, and resourceful. But no matter which way my dream unfolded, a swashbuckling-style hero inevitably marched on to lift me up into his arms. And, more latterly still, a struggle of sorts had usually ensued, which almost always resulted in a kiss.

The days of catching moths and butterflies were over. News of kittens in the stables or newly born lambs down at the farm no longer made my heart race. Though sometimes, particularly if Papa was present, I felt duty bound to feign that lost excitement.

But that day, I could think only of him, Tom Cuthbert. I wondered where he was, what he was doing. I floated about the house, intermittently looking in on the library hoping to find him there. I went to the kitchen three or four times on the pretext of needing to speak to Mrs Cuthbert about some sewing. I walked out to the lake, through the stable yard, past Mrs Cuthbert's cottage and back again the same way. I dawdled in the walled garden, distractedly helping a new kitchen maid pick raspberries, with one eye fixed on the gate to the yard, through which the door of Mrs Cuthbert's cottage was clearly visible. And then I dallied with Frank and John, the two youngest under-gardeners, as they sat on the bench by the greenhouse, eating the sandwiches Edna had sent out to them in a basket.

'Please, do sit down and enjoy your lunch,' I said, as they rose simultaneously to their feet.

They took their orders from Mr Broughton—a man whom I'd more than once heard described by Edna, our cook, as *a dark horse*—and were usually employed in what were still referred to as the 'pleasure gardens': keeping the borders free of bindweed and ivy, cutting back and clipping the many and various shrubs, and attending to the pathways—so easily lost and overgrown. Up a ladder or down on their knees, they were always there, together, always smiling and laughing. Frank, short and squat, with freckles and bright red curls, and John, so immensely tall and gangly, with shorn jet-black hair. Even to look at they made a comical pair, and Mama often said they should be on the stage.

That day, Frank, the same age as me and mad on cricket, blushed to the colour of a ripe tomato when I enquired how his team were doing that season, and John said, 'He wears the colour of 'is 'eart on 'is face, miss,' and then laughed. They had both worked in the gardens at Deyning since they were boys, both been part of every Christmas, birthday and celebration; and each summer, when Deyning played against the village team, Frank had no obvious conflict and always switched allegiance to bowl for Deyning Park.

The previous summer, when the days had been long, stretching late into the evening, I'd taken it upon myself to teach Frank to read—and be able to write more than just his name. (Both he and John were too old to have benefited from my father's founding of the village school. They had, they said, for a while at least, on certain days, walked the three miles to the nearest school, but there were simply too many distractions on their route, and neither of them were suited to being kept indoors.) Each evening, after dinner, I'd sat with Frank outside on the veranda, teaching him the sounds of letters and familiar words, writing them out for him to copy and practise. I read passages out loud to him from a few of my favourite books, and some poems too. And we made progress. By the end of summer Frank was able to recognise any number of words, and confident enough to attempt the pronunciation of others. With a little help from me, he'd written a letter to his mother, even though she wouldn't be able to read it, he said; would need someone to read it for her. He joined the local lending library, and I gave him a list of books I thought he might enjoy. Then Mama intervened. She said she thought Frank was becoming a little *too attached*; that I had done enough, and that it was wrong—and possibly misleading—for me to continue my *sponsorship* of him. So I told him, reluctantly, that I'd taught him as much as I could, that he'd have to go on alone; go on reading, and continue with books until he could read as well as anyone else.

'I imagine you've both met Mrs Cuthbert's son . . .' I said at last, leaning against a warm pane of the greenhouse.

'Tom?' John replied. 'He were just out here, earlier. Weren't he, Frank?'

Frank, mouth bulging with bread, glanced up at me, blushing once more, and nodded.

'Well, he seems like a jolly nice sort,' I said,

looking from one to the other, and wondering if either of them knew any more than me. 'But such a shame about his father . . .'

'What's that then?' John asked.

'Mr Cuthbert,' I replied, not sure what else to say.

'Mr Cuthbert? Thought he'd been gone long since.'

'Yes . . . yes, that's what I meant. Such a shame, for Mrs Cuthbert I mean, and for Tom. I don't suppose he ever knew his father . . .'

John turned to Frank and—in a much quieter voice—said, 'Aye, well, plenty like that round here.' And they both laughed.

Finally, late in the afternoon, as I once again half-heartedly perused my father's bookshelves, I heard footsteps in the marble hallway coming towards the open library door. I grabbed a book, and sat down just in time.

He closed the door behind him and remained perfectly still for a moment, looking over at me.

'Oh, hello, Tom,' I said, sounding surprised (even to myself).

'Hello, Clarissa, I was hoping I might find you here. And what are we reading today?' he asked, walking towards me. 'More of the Brontës?'

I glanced down at the book, noticed it was covered in plain paper, and opened it quickly. 'Ha! No, not today,' I said, searching for the title. 'No, today I'm quite lost in . . . The Life and Adventures of *dear* Miss Fanny Hill.'

'Really?'

He stood in front of me, his hands in his pockets, a quizzical look upon his face.

'Why so surprised?' I asked, looking up at him,

smiling. 'I don't limit myself to *just* the Brontë sisters, you know.'

'Clarissa . . .'

'Yes?'

'Have you actually been *reading* that book?'

'Yes . . . yes, indeed I have.' I opened the book at random. 'I was somewhere . . . about here . . .' I flicked a page or two. 'This page, I think . . . yes, this one. *She, no doubt, thought it was time to give up the argument, and that all further defence would be in vain . . .*'

I looked up again, blinking. He sat down in the chair opposite me, leant forward, resting his elbows on his knees, clasping his hands in front of him. His shirtsleeves were rolled back and I noticed the dark hair on his forearms.

'Yes, that's where I was up to.'

'Do continue . . . please, read some more,' he said.

'Are you sure? To be honest I was finding it rather dull.'

He smiled. 'No, please. I'd like to hear you read on.'

I cleared my throat. '*And he, throwing her petticoats over her face . . .*' I paused, slightly confused; '*which was now as red as scarlet, discovered . . . a pair of . . .*' I paused again, then continued, slowly, quieter, '*stout, plump, substantial thighs . . . and tolerably white; he mounted them round his hips . . .*' My mind began to swim, my face grew hot, but I continued, my voice ever quieter. '*And coming out with his drawn weapon, stuck it in the cloven spot . . . where he seemed to find a less difficult entrance than perhaps he had flattered himself with . . .*'

I looked up at him, my face stinging. I wasn't entirely sure if what I'd read was the run-up to a grisly murder or some other act of wickedness. But by Tom's expression I could hazard a guess. He reached over, eased the book from my hand and closed it.

'I'm quite certain your father wouldn't want you to be reading that particular book.'

'No,' was all I could manage. I felt my lip quiver, and for a moment I thought I might cry.

'Are you feeling quite all right?' he asked.

'No, not terribly,' I replied.

'Come, let's go outside. You look as though you need some air.' He rose to his feet and walked ahead of me through the library, placing the book upon a shelf without a second glance. I followed him across the hallway and then outside, into the garden. *Perhaps he thought I read that sort of book. Perhaps he thought I'd picked it on purpose, wanted to read it to him* . . . I stopped, closed my eyes, and shivered.

'Do you need a shawl or something?' he asked.

'No, no thank you, I'm fine.'

We walked in silence across the flagstones, past Mama's gaudy new swing-chair, down the steps and on to the lawn. It had been another indifferent overcast day, but now the garden glowed in the warmth of the early evening sun. We walked under the drooping branches of the sycamore towards the bank of rhododendrons and the ha-ha just beyond.

'Feeling better?' he asked, turning to me.

'Mm, slightly,' I said, not looking at him, a hullabaloo of unfamiliar words still echoing in my head.

I was neither able nor ready to put together a

longer sentence. But I was aware that since reading about *his drawn weapon . . . in the cloven spot* I'd barely uttered a word.

'There's a bench over here,' I managed at last. 'One can see for miles.'

'Perfect. All we need is a Singapore Sling,' he said, as we sat down upon the wooden seat.

'Singapore what?'

'It's a cocktail, all the rage up at Oxford.' He turned to me, smiling. 'Have you ever had a cocktail?'

'I had a champagne cocktail once . . . at New Year.'

'And did you enjoy it?'

'Yes. It made me feel quite . . . in love with life,' I replied, remembering my dance with Billy Robertson, a handsome under-gardener who'd since vanished from my father's employ.

He laughed. 'Alcohol does that. It loosens folk up, makes them feel freer,' he said, staring into the distance.

'Are there lots and lots of parties up at Oxford?' I asked, my equilibrium almost restored by the combination of air and conversation.

'Yes, there are. But I'm neither fashionable enough nor rich enough to be invited to some. And,' he turned to me, 'I need to work. I'm not like the other undergraduates who have a private income and are simply there because they have nothing better to do. Or want to have a wild few years before taking over the family estate. I have an opportunity, and I don't intend to throw it away.'

'It must be difficult,' I said, not sure what else to say.

'Difficult?'

'Yes, difficult for you—if you feel excluded or perhaps on the outside of something.'

'Clarissa, you are sweet. But I'm not remotely bothered about parties or socialising.'

'I think all Henry does is gallivant about—attending parties . . . and womanise,' I added, borrowing one of Mama's words.

'Well, it's different for him. Look at this,' he said, gesturing at everything in front of us. 'All this will be his one day. Whereas I,' and he turned to me again, 'I shall inherit a shoebox of mementos, if I'm lucky.'

'But you may be like Papa . . . you might *make* a fortune.'

'Yes, I intend to do that. But what about you, Clarissa? You may be married, and to an earl—or even a duke—by this time next year.'

I tried to laugh. 'I hope not. I don't wish to be married *too soon*. And I'm not sure I want to be married to either a duke *or* an earl.'

'Perhaps not, but your parents may.' He reached into his pocket, pulled out a packet of cigarettes and offered me one.

'No, thank you. I don't.'

I watched him light his cigarette, draw heavily on it, sucking in his cheeks.

'I hope they want me to be happy more than anything else,' I said. 'And I intend to be ferociously happy.'

He made no reply. But I watched him from the corner of my eye as he smoked his cigarette, staring into the distance through half-closed eyes, and I wondered what he was thinking. I longed to know his thoughts. I longed to know him. And, though it was much too warm an evening to be sitting outside in the sun, I didn't want that moment to end.

I noticed the tiny beads of perspiration glistening on the temple of his brow, above his mouth; the damp indigo patch under his arm. I watched him as he placed his lips around the cigarette, inhale, and then blow a series of smoke rings into the sultry evening air. I fiddled with the lace on the ruffle of my high-necked blouse, pushed my fingers underneath the fabric on to my own hot skin; and I wished I'd done as Mama had repeatedly told me and worn my hair up.

'We'd better go. Your brothers will probably be back by now and no doubt wondering where you are,' he said, flicking his cigarette over the ha-ha.

'I don't think so. They're not remotely interested in where I am. No one ever is.'

He turned towards me. 'If you were mine—I mean, if you were my sister—I'd be interested, and I don't suppose I'd be too happy to know you were idling with the housekeeper's son.'

'It's up to me who I choose to idle with,' I said, staring back at him, our eyes inches apart. I saw him glance to my lips then back to my eyes, then back to my lips. *Kiss me. Kiss me now*, I begged silently.

He raised his hand to my face—as though about to touch it; then, in one swift movement, pulled away. 'You know, you're quite dangerously beautiful, Clarissa Granville. Just as well you're kept locked away here,' he said, and rose to his feet. 'Come. I should take you back.'

'But it's not late. I don't need to go back, not yet.'

'I need to get back.'

'Why? Will your mother be worried?'

'Clarissa . . . it's not right for us to stay out

here—alone.'

'Why ever not? What's going to happen? I hardly think you're about to seduce me, Mr Cuthbert. No, I feel quite safe here with you.'

'Aha! But perhaps you shouldn't.'

'Why? Do you plan on seducing me?' I asked, rising to my feet, looking back at him, into his eyes. 'If so, do please tell me—as I'd like a moment to prepare.'

He pulled me to him. 'You really shouldn't say such things . . . you've no idea . . . have you?'

He held me tightly; his mouth so close I could feel the heat of his breath—in short sharp bursts upon my face.

'No idea of what?' I asked, watching his eyes on my lips.

Kiss me. Kiss me now.

'No idea,' he repeated, turning his face away, releasing his grip. He stepped back from me, thrust his hands into his pockets and looked up at the sky with a groan.

'I'm sorry . . .'

He sighed, turned to face me. 'What are you sorry for? You've no reason to apologise. Come, let's walk back,' he added, smiling at me once more.

We began to walk across the lawn in the direction of the house. 'I'm sorry if . . . if I've made you feel uncomfortable in some way,' I said. 'I'm afraid my brothers' teasing has probably blunted my sensibilities . . . made me too flippant.'

At the edge of the lawn, he stopped, looked down at the grass. 'Perhaps I'll see you tomorrow . . .'

'Yes, perhaps,' I replied, glancing away, towards the lake in the distance.

'I still need to look up a few books in your

father's library . . .'

'Of course.'

'Perhaps, later in the day . . . around four.'

I turned to him. 'Yes, around four, I'm sure that will be fine.'

He smiled, and as he began to move away—walking backwards—he said, 'Oh, and Clarissa, promise me one thing . . .'

'What's that?' I asked, intrigued.

'Promise me you won't read another word of that book.'

I laughed. 'Of course not, I promise.'

And then I went inside, to the library, pulled out the book and took it up to my room.

CHAPTER FOUR

I awoke early the following morning: catapulted back to my bed from Tom Cuthbert's arms. We'd been lying in an exotically decorated open-sided tent, on the lawn, under the sycamore tree. '*Clarissa . . . Clarissa*,' he'd repeated, holding me tightly, gazing into my eyes. Then he'd kissed me, and the passion of his kiss had woken me. I closed my eyes and returned there, to languish once more in his arms. But as I felt his hands move over my body, I realised my state of dishabille; for I was in nothing more than my flimsy summer nightgown, which he appeared to have unbuttoned. And I leapt from my bed, still breathless and hot from that imagined kiss.

I was distracted over breakfast, and Mama, too, was unusually silent. She liked to check the menu for dinner each morning and almost always read it out loud, but not today. I stood by the sideboard, staring down at my reflection in a polished silver lid. *Perhaps I should wear my hair up* . . . As I lifted the lid from a dish of devilled kidneys, my mother sighed, loudly, and then informed me that she was going out to make calls later that afternoon. Did I wish to accompany her?

'Would you mind if I didn't today? I'm quite lost in my book . . . and determined to finish it this afternoon.'

I sat down at the table next to her.

'Very well, but I think you should stay inside, out of the sun. And please do something with your hair, Clarissa,' she said, and then she rose to her feet and left the room.

I was relieved she appeared so preoccupied, and I presumed she must be tired, for she'd returned home from London very late the previous evening. I'd been in my bed, reading, but when I'd heard her arrive back I'd gone to see her, in her dressing room. She'd been in one of her dreamy moods, and told me that she'd seen the most beautiful painting she'd ever seen in her life, *at a gallery in London*.

'But I thought you went to a horticultural exhibition . . .'

'Oh . . . no,' she said, turning to me 'I left Broughton to do that. I met Venetia and we went to a gallery . . . and then out to dinner.'

Later that day, as I watched her disappear down the driveway, I thought how remarkably brave and independent she was. Unwavering and indefatigable in her commitment to her many causes, she was happy to travel about the locality on her own in the dogcart; visiting people, delivering food parcels—eggs, butter, fruit and vegetables and produce from the farm—ministering to those sick and needy, and attending to her many and various charitable causes. There seemed to be an inexhaustible list of charities with which she was affiliated, from the NSPCC to the League of Pity and the Mothers' Union; she attended drawing-room meetings, and sat on the council of the Primrose League, in my mind something to do with gardening: her one true passion.

Mama was obsessed with her garden, and not only in summer, but all year round. There was *always* something to be done, always something requiring her attention. In early summer her roses and peonies, in particular, inevitably scooped her a few first prizes at local flower shows. But sometimes she travelled further afield—to more out-of-the-way places, in order to exhibit a vividly coloured orchid from the hothouse, or a new hybrid tea rose. She'd return from these trips with a ribbon or rosette, reinvigorated, and quite obviously elated.

I wondered if I'd be like Mama one day: as poised and controlled, as elegant. She seemed to me to inhabit an aura of ineffable loveliness, gliding about the place in a cloud of tuberose, exuding a soporific maternal balm upon our senses. Taller than most other women, she held her head high, for good posture and manners were, she said, the surest and most important indicator of character. She abhorred raised voices, or aggression of any kind, and had no time for wanton displays of emotion, or—what she deemed—self-indulgent outbursts.

Papa often said that when he looked at me he saw *the perfect vision* of my mother. And I never quite knew what he meant by that. For how could anyone be more perfect than Mama? But I was like her, in appearance, at least: I had her colouring, eyes and hair. And, as I'd grown up, others had inevitably commented: *Ah, yes, Edina's daughter through and through. Quite uncanny . . .*

As a child, I'd basked in that air of perpetual calm enveloping her, mesmerised by her beauty, the luminosity of her pale skin against her dark chestnut hair, the way she sometimes closed her eyes as she spoke. In the evenings—whenever she and Papa were at home—she'd come to the night nursery and I'd gaze up at her as she read to me: her dark blue eyes following the words on the page; her perfect lips moving with mellifluous sound. She was to me the stuff of fairy tales, the embodiment of all that was good and fine.

The granddaughter of the diplomat and financier, Sir Montague Vincent, my mother's formative years had been divided between the palatial drawing rooms of London and her grandfather's vast estate in Hampshire. And there, waited on by liveried footmen in powdered wigs, she had spent some of *the happiest days* of her life. Before her own coming out, her mother had taken her to Paris to be fitted with gowns, a habit she had never grown out of. Each season she returned there—to be fitted with the latest fashions from Worth. Her jewellery drawer, my childhood treasure trove, included cuffs, collars and combs of diamonds, and endless ropes of pearls. She changed three—sometimes even four—times each day, aided by Wilson, her maid, and bathed in rose-scented bathwater. And her bedroom and dressing room—in the French style, all toile de

Jouy and soft fine lace, and scented with roses and orchids from the hothouse—were to me simply an extension of her.

But Mama had secrets. I could tell. For there was some unfathomable mystery lurking in those benevolent, smiling eyes; and tantalising but as yet unspoken words on the very edge of her soft tongue. Oh yes, Mama had secrets, and I had had a glimpse of one of them, once, many years before.

'And what are my naughty cherubs up to?' she'd asked, entering her dressing room.

We'd been playing with her jewels. And Georgie had spent a good hour dressing me up as the May Queen, with ropes of pearls around my head, tangled and fastened in my hair with brooches, diamonds galore about my neck and arms; and rings, slipping and sliding off my tiny fingers. He'd put powder and rouge on my face, though, and perhaps thankfully, I hadn't yet had a chance to check my appearance in the looking glass.

She moved towards me, slowly, and bent down, levelling her face with my own. 'This one,' she said, her eyes staring back into mine as she removed a heavy gold ring from the middle finger of my left hand, 'is *not* for playing with.'

'But that's the King's ring!' Georgie called out. 'And she's the Queen . . . and she looks so beautiful,' he added, rather appealingly.

She moved away and I watched her slip the King's ring back into the jewellery drawer, then lock it, and push the key into the top of her dress. It's a secret, I thought: the King's ring is Mama's secret. And I wondered if she'd told Papa. And if she had not, what a perfect secret it was.

When she left us to continue our game, I turned

to my brother and put my finger to my lips.

'What?' he whispered. 'What is it?'

I shook my head, for if he didn't know—I couldn't possibly tell him.

And I never did.

Sometimes I had been allowed to sit quietly and watch my mother prepare for a party or a ball. As she sat at her dressing table, straight backed and head high, I'd looked on as Wilson brushed and then carefully pinned up Mama's waist-length hair, Mama lifting and turning her head this way and that, checking her profile, tucking in a curl here and there. I'd watch her select her jewels for the evening, running her fingers over the dark red velvet-lined tray; and though I'd looked for the King's ring, I'd never again seen it. I'd sat in silence and watched Wilson fasten my mother's jewels in place, and occasionally my mother would glance at me, my reflection in the looking glass in front of her. She'd tilt her head, smile at me. 'These will be yours one day,' she'd say, raising her hand to the gems glinting upon her décolleté. She was to me, then, the personification of romance, a dazzling celebration, like Christmas, and a luxurious gift to us all. But there were so many things, rituals and habits, too plebeian for my mother; for it was not how things *were* that mattered, but how they appeared. And idolatry such as mine could never be sustained, nor survive what lay ahead.

That afternoon, I timed my arrival in the library with perfection. And I'd taken a little more time with myself. I'd had Wilson pin up my hair, and wore a favourite blouse: one made from the softest white muslin with hand-stitched pin-tucks. 'You're a picture, Miss Clarissa, a perfect picture,' Wilson said. 'Such a shame there's no young gentlemen here to admire you.'

He was already there, sitting in an armchair, his head bent, reading. And as soon as I entered, he closed his book and stood up.

'I do hope I'm not disturbing you,' I said, standing inside the doorway, unsure of what to do.

'No, no of course not. I was hoping . . . hoping I might see you.'

He remained on his feet, watching me as I ambled my way across the library, glancing to the shelves on my left. I quite wanted him to notice my hair, make a comment, compliment me, but of course he didn't.

'What are you reading?' I asked, standing opposite him, behind the other chair.

'Something very dull . . . much more dull, I think, than *dear* Fanny Hill,' he said and smiled.

I looked away.

'It's a book about the principles of company law, Clarissa. And I'm quite sure you're not remotely interested in that.'

'Hmm. Yes, that does sound awfully dull. Do you *have* to read it?'

His smile broadened. 'I'm afraid I do, if I'm to pass my exams.'

'Then I'm very pleased I shall never have to take exams.'

'But now you're here I have a most welcome distraction,' he said, putting the book down on the table beside him.

'Oh,' I replied, not quite sure how to *be* a welcome distraction, and feeling the distinct pressure to be entertaining. 'Well, I suppose we could have a game of cards . . .' I suggested.

He laughed, and I think he thought I was being funny.

'Are you allowed . . . I mean to say, would you care to take a stroll? Perhaps where we walked yesterday?'

I was a little shocked by his boldness, but it had turned into a glorious day and there was no harm in a walk.

We took a different direction to the one we'd taken the previous evening, this time venturing a little further from the house, down through the meadow known as 'lower meadow', towards the lake. It was my suggestion; I wanted to take him to my favourite place. He told me that he'd been helping out on the farm that morning, had woken early and been there by seven. I didn't mention that he couldn't possibly have been there at that hour, that we'd been lying on the lawn together, under the sycamore tree, kissing. But I imagined him walking to the farm in the early-morning sunshine as I'd been lying in my bed, and I wondered if he'd thought of me.

We stopped under the shade of the old chestnut tree.

'There should be a seat here,' he said, staring out towards the lake.

'Exactly, and I've told Papa this so many times,' I replied, staring in the same direction. 'But he's promised me faithfully that he's going to find me an Arabian tent,' I added.

He turned to me. 'An Arabian tent?'

'Yes, so that I can sleep outside, under the stars.'

'Would you really like that? Would you not be afraid?'

'Afraid? No, what's there to be afraid of? An

owl, a fox, a badger . . . or perhaps a deer? No, there's nothing to be afraid of, other than the stars, the universe, and that sense of being infinitesimal . . .'

We stood side by side and the air hummed with the sound of summer. If I'd been on my own I'd have lain down upon the dry grass, as I'd done so many times before, squinting up at a mosaic sky through branches; searching for a cloud from which I would be able to see some far-off exotic country. When I was young George had told me that those very wispy, celestial clouds, the ones which appeared to me to have faces, were not really above us, even though they seemed to be so. No, he'd explained, those ones, those particular clouds, floated in the atmosphere *hundreds of thousands* of miles above another country. 'So . . . which country is that one above?' I'd asked, pointing up to the blue yonder. 'That one . . . that one,' he'd said, scratching his head, and appearing to work out some immensely complicated mathematical equation, 'That one, Issy, is above . . . the Sahara Desert.' It was stupendous that he knew, that he was able to work this out at no more than ten years old; and the fact that I could see the cloud above the Sahara Desert enabled me to look down from it. I'd stare up at the white vapour and I was there. I could see the camels, the Arabian tents pitched next to a palm tree, an oasis.

I heard Tom's voice. 'So, is this where you like to come?' But I was adrift; lost in a blissful trance and unable come back to now, unable to answer. As though the universe for a moment held me to it, and that feeling of oneness—complete connectedness—had locked me in.

'Clarissa?'

I turned to him. He stepped towards me, raised his hand to my brow, where it hovered for a second or two. He ran his finger down the side of my face, along my jaw and on to my neck. I stared back into his dark, solemn eyes, felt my throat tighten. *Kiss me*. He glanced to my mouth, moved his head a little closer. I ran my tongue over my lips, half closed my eyes, waiting. He tilted his head towards me, his lips almost touching my own. Then he stepped back from me.

'I'm sorry,' he said, looking down at the ground.

I didn't say anything. What was there for me to say?

'I'm not sure I *can* be trusted to be alone with you after all,' he added.

'Oh, I think you can. In fact, I think you've just proved it,' I said, and walked on towards the lake.

At first I thought he wasn't going to follow me. He loitered under the tree for a moment or two, and then I heard him: coming through the long grass, purposefully striding.

'You've every right to be angry,' he began, walking alongside me, 'and I can only apologise, Clarissa. I'm sorry, truly I am. I didn't mean to compromise you. It wasn't my intention to . . .'

I quickened my pace. 'Tom, please don't go on so, you're giving me a headache with all of your apologising.'

'You're cross. I knew you were.'

'I'm not cross. Why should I be cross? You've done *nothing*.'

'But I could have . . . and I very nearly did, which is why you're quite rightly angry.'

'I'm *not* angry, Tom; I'm simply a little hot.'

'Promise me you won't say anything, Clarissa . . . to your parents, your brothers.'

I stopped. He stopped. I looked at him.

'Tom,' I began, about to tell him, assure him that I'd never breathe a word to anyone. What did he take me for? A silly girl who'd go running back to her mama as soon as the first boy made eyes at her? But then I saw his furrowed brow, his dark and anxious eyes, and I caught my breath. I reached out, placed my hand on his arm. 'Really, it was my fault as much as yours. I encouraged you.'

'You did no such thing, and now I feel even more wretched if that's what you think.'

I walked on, slowly, for I wasn't about to insist that I had encouraged him. My hope had been silent, but nonetheless heartfelt. I knew this and he did not, I reminded myself. I stopped again, and he stopped.

'Think nothing of it. It's forgotten already,' I said, and smiled.

He took hold of my hand. 'I don't want you to think of me as some hot-headed lout, Clarissa. I'm well aware that you're destined for greater things than . . . than me.'

I eased my hand out of his. I knew where we stood was visible from the stable-yard gate. 'Let's be friends then, and please believe me when I say the very last thing I think of you as is a lout, hot headed or otherwise.' And at last that worrisome look melted from his features.

Minutes later, as we sat upon the wooden steps of the boathouse, he asked me my impression of him, his character. 'But I hardly know you,' I replied.

'But you must have an impression by now, and

tell me—I'm curious.'

'Lonely, angry . . . determined,' I said. They were the three words that sprung to my mind at that moment. He raised an eyebrow, and as he pulled out his cigarettes, I said, 'So, now I've given you three adjectives, can you give me your three of me?'

He lit his cigarette, looking into the distance once more with half-closed eyes, then said, 'Beautiful, desirable . . . unattainable.'

'Unattainable?' I repeated. The first two words had made me smile as he'd said them each in turn, but that last one perplexed me.

He looked down. 'Well, unattainable to . . . someone such as me.'

I wanted to say, 'No, no, I'm not, I'm not unattainable.' But I did nothing, and I said nothing.

'Strange to think,' he went on, 'that by this time next year I'll have finished my studies, left Oxford . . . probably be living in some rather dismal lodgings in London. And you . . .' he glanced at me, 'you may be married, Clarissa, or engaged to be married, at least.'

'Nothing is certain,' I said.

'No, of course, nothing is certain, apart from a chasm which ensures our futures remain quite separate, I think.' And then he turned to me, once again smiling. 'Unless, of course, I go into domestic service, and then perhaps our paths may cross.'

I tried to laugh. I knew it was a joke, but I wasn't altogether happy with his cynicism.

'None of us knows our destiny,' I said. 'And no one knows what the future holds. But I certainly don't wish to be married. Not yet.'

'So will you marry for love?' he asked, sucking out the last dregs of his cigarette.

'Yes, of course. Why else would one marry?'

He shrugged. 'Position; to maintain a status quo, perhaps; because one's parents deem it the right and proper thing to do. And the union of new money and old titles still seems to be very much in vogue.'

I wasn't entirely sure what he meant by that, but his talk of futures being sold off made me feel nervous. I was out of my depth. Politics, social divides and the loveless marriages he alluded to were not my forte.

'I think there may be a thunderstorm later,' I said, rising to my feet.

The air was stagnant and feverishly hot in that quiet hollow by the lake, and as I walked along the jetty I could feel the fine white muslin of my blouse sticking to my skin. I longed to be able to take off my shoes and stockings, to walk in bare feet and dip my toes into the cool, clear water. And for a moment, only a moment, I wished he wasn't there—so that I could remove my shoes, lift my skirt, and dangle my legs over the side of the little pier. I looked out across the water: I could hear a dog barking somewhere in the distance, and someone calling for it; a dragonfly hovered beside me, its wings iridescent in the early evening sun; and below me spiders skimmed across the lake's flat surface. A family of moorhens took to the water in front of me: a mother followed by half a dozen red-billed, fluffy black chicks. Late chicks, I thought. And as I watched them, I pondered once more on that word: unattainable. It didn't matter what he'd meant by it, I concluded, because the other two words I understood perfectly: *beautiful . . . desirable.*

I smiled to myself, glanced over to him. He was still on the steps, leaning back, watching me. 'He desires me,' I said out loud, as quietly as I could.

There are moments too sublime to be later conjured in words. Standing on the jetty that midsummer evening so long ago, the world was perfect and I felt invincible.

* * *

My Darling T, your words made my hands shake, my heart sing out with joy, & I pray that no matter what the future holds those sentiments never change. Yesterday was heavenly, our perfect, perfect time, & I have spent the entire morning quite lost in my dream of it—& you. But today I cannot shirk my responsibilities, and oh how many I suddenly seem to have! In haste . . . YOD

CHAPTER FIVE

I met Tom the following afternoon at five, though I thought I'd spotted him earlier in the day, in the distance, by the lake, and for a moment I'd panicked, thinking one of us had confused our rendezvous. And later, when I approached the boat-house and couldn't see him, my heart sank. But he was there, beyond the trees, sitting at the end of the jetty. He stood up as I walked towards him. 'Shall we take a stroll?' he asked. 'It's much too hot here in the sun.'

We walked slowly across the meadow, cutting

a swathe through knee-high grass filled with buttercups, cornflowers, daisies and cow parsley, and continued on—into the next field. At the far side of that field we came to the stile, beyond which lay two paths, one to the farm, the other back down to the lake. From the top of the stile I could see the farmhouse, a perfectly straight silver line rising up into the blue from the chimney on its red tiled roof.

'Are you going to stay up there for long?' he asked, squinting up at me.

'If I jump will you catch me?'

He moved nearer to me. 'Of course, but I wouldn't advise it.'

I stayed exactly where I was, my hand to my brow as I surveyed and considered the options. I suggested to him that we follow the path down by the lake rather than take the path to the farm. I remembered a seat there, which Papa had often taken me to when I was younger. As I spoke, I felt something touch my ankle, and I stopped, looked down, and saw him pull away his hand. Then, as he helped me down from the stile, he turned away, as though he couldn't bear to look at me any more. I began to walk but he didn't move.

'Is something the matter?'

'Let's not take that path,' he said. 'I really should be getting back.'

'I see. Well then, you go back and I shall continue alone.'

'No. You can't possibly walk so far from the house on your own. We need to go back, Clarissa.'

I didn't say anything. He helped me back over the stile, looking away as I lifted my skirt, and we walked back through the fields in silence. As we neared the house, he said to me, 'You're so innocent, Clarissa. Innocent and beautiful, and you know, it's really not a very safe combination.'

'Oh. And what do you mean by that?'

'I mean you really shouldn't be suggesting we disappear off into the undergrowth on our own.'

I stopped. 'Ha! I did no such thing. I merely said we should take the path I know, the one I've taken with Papa.'

He stopped, closed his eyes for a moment, as though I'd already exasperated him. And right then I felt a little bit furious.

'It's perfectly all right, Tom, I can see my way from here,' I said, and marched on as fast as I could walk through the long grass.

'Clarissa . . . please, I'm telling you this for your own good,' he said, catching up with me, and sounding quite cross himself. 'You need to understand . . . you need to appreciate that . . .'

I stopped again. 'That *what*, Tom? That you're afraid you might one day lose control? Chance would be a fine thing!'

He stared at me, his jaw set, chewing his tongue.

'And I need to tell you,' I continued, pulling off my hat, 'that I shan't be able to meet you again. Ever.'

'Well, that's probably a good thing too. We have nothing in common and it seems to me that all these walks you're so fond of are a completely pointless and time-consuming exercise.'

'Good. Then we have nothing more to say to each other.'

'It seems not.'

'Goodbye then.'

'Goodbye.'

There was an awkward moment as I strode on up

was trying—trying very badly—to tell you that day was simply that I find it a little difficult, tricky, with you.'

He turned, presumably to check my expression. I raised my eyebrows, expectantly.

'What I mean is . . . you know who you are, what you are; how your life will be. It makes it hard for someone like me. Do you understand?'

'Yes,' I said, emphatically, but I had not a clue.

'I'm not really worthy of your attention or interest. And I have to remind myself of this all the time. I have to remember who I am and who you are. I have to remember that we will both be moving on . . . in quite different directions.'

He stopped there, and I waited a moment before I spoke.

'Well then, let's be friends again,' I said, and, instinctively, I reached out and placed my hand upon his arm.

He pulled his arm away. 'But this is the crux; this is the problem. I'm not sure that I can be friends with you.'

'Oh.'

He ran his hands through his hair. 'You see, I find myself . . . I find myself . . .' he went on, falteringly, then sighed.

'Tom, please. Can't we be friends? I promise that I shan't invite you on another walk,' I said. And he laughed.

'Yes. Yes, let's be friends again.' He tilted his head, looking at me sideways through a wave of almost black hair.

'Good, then it's settled, and you have nothing to fret about—and neither do I.'

He pulled out his packet of cigarettes and lit one.

'I've missed seeing you,' he said, leaning forward once more. 'You weren't at the last croquet game, and I've not seen you for . . .' he paused, 'for a while. Are you well?'

'Yes, quite well.'

He turned to me. 'You do look well.'

'Yes, I'm very well.'

'Perhaps later, if you'd like, we can take a walk—down by the lake.'

I smiled. It wasn't exactly begging for forgiveness, but it was enough.

* * *

I had never known my mother to look fretful or to frown. I'd grown up with her telling me 'girls who frown shall never wear a crown', and it was enough, when I was small, for me to run my finger between my eyebrows to check my expression. That summer, whenever I came across my mother standing in contemplative pose, looking out through open windows, I took her hand in mine, assured her that all would be well . . . her roses would survive. But there was a new look in her eyes, the clear line of a frown between her brows, and when she smiled back at me I could see she didn't quite believe me. At mealtimes, whenever the conversation turned to events taking place in Europe, she'd look at me and give me that same smile. Of course, I'd seen the newspapers, and I'd heard my brothers and my father talking, but the crisis unfolding on another continent was so far from Deyning, so far from our lives.

Weeks before, the day after Henry returned home from Cambridge, the Archduke had been assassinated, and I'd heard him say to Papa, 'This'll surely mean war.' At that time I had no notion of war, or death. God, I believed, created life, all of nature and beauty, and I had faith in Him. I loved Him. My father and brother were speaking of a strange-sounding, almost unpronounceable place, far away from us. These were modern times, civilised times; and wars—at least in my mind—belonged to history.

But events in Europe and talk of war began to take over *all* mealtime conversation. I tried to ignore these discussions, for I didn't understand them, didn't want to understand them, and they did not belong to summer. Instead, I continued to luxuriate in the reverie of the season. I walked through the walled garden, where even the curls of peeling paint upon the greenhouse door seemed unusually perfect to my eye. And where, inside, the heady aroma of ripening tomatoes and cucumbers fed my senses. I inhabited a profoundly fragrant world, where the scents of jasmine and honeysuckle mixed with sweet geranium, verbena and mint; where the incessant hum of bumblebees serenaded my thoughts and only butterflies caught my eye; where peaches and nectarines grew fat and ripe under a warm English sun. And when I looked out towards the cornfields in the distance, I saw only the glinting colour of my future. There would be no war. How could there be? Certainly not in the midst of that summer.

But the cuckoo had already begun to change his tune, and a sudden, cruel westerly wind had scattered rose heads and petals about the lawns and pathways—like snow in summer. And I began to have the queerest feeling, a slipping away sort of feeling. As though my material world was as ephemeral as the colours of that season, as though nothing was quite fixed any more. You see, I wanted time to stand still; I wanted to fasten down those days and harness every colour and shape in them.

I met Tom every evening, on what Mama referred to as my 'solitary amble'. And though we now spoke easily with each other, and had learned much of one another's characters in the preceding weeks, he seemed reluctant to move beyond a certain point. His reticence had made me bolder than I should have been, I knew this, and sometimes, alone in my room, replaying a conversation we'd had in my head, I'd find myself aghast at my own unscripted lines. There had been so many moments when he could have, should have, almost kissed me, I was beginning to wonder if perhaps he had some sort of problem—with me, or with girls. My cousin Edina (named after my mother) had explained to me the previous summer that some men simply *aren't that way inclined*. There are some men who *prefer* men, she'd told me. At that time I'd remained unconvinced; I needed evidence, I said. She'd picked on Broughton as an example, simply because he was, she estimated, over forty, and remained so very unmarried and unattached. And the idea of Broughton falling in love with another man had reduced me to a fit of giggles. But now I wondered if Tom fell into Edina's *disinclined* category, for he certainly seemed troubled.

It had been Edina who, four summers earlier, had educated me on *other matters* too. Sitting on our own in the summerhouse one afternoon she'd informed me, in her own inimitable way, how babies were conceived and born. We'd both sat in silence for a moment, each of us distracted by the image of any future husband attempting such a gross act upon us. Then, with immeasurable horror, I realised that Papa had done this to Mama—and not once, but four times!

'Oh my God! Papa . . . Mama . . .'

'I know. It's beyond belief, but I had to tell you, Issa. You need to know.'

'And the baby?' I asked, my hands still over my mouth.

'The baby grows inside its mother until it's ready to be born and then . . . are you ready for this? Prepare yourself, please dear . . . it comes out of her bottom, ripping her in two!'

'Ugh! No . . . but it can't be so . . . Mama . . . she looks fine.'

'I know. Mine too. But this is why so many women die, dear. And they bleed for up to ten years afterwards. Can you imagine?'

'No! And I don't want to.'

It had been a bittersweet moment in my life, for I'd made up my mind then that I—like Edina—would never have children. But four years had passed since that particular revelation, and now I merely smiled at my remembrance of it. And that twelfth summer, once the best and most cherished, had faded and blurred, fusing with all previous summers into a montage of shapes and colours, scents and sounds: the hot sun upon the unmoving sycamore, the dark coolness of the lawn beneath; the hum and grind of the mowing machine; the glistening water of the lake in the distance; white butterflies on lavender, sweet peas on wicker;

sun-bleached red stripes, white lines painted upon green; the hearty clank of a croquet mallet, the soft bounce of a tennis ball upon the grass.

But summer hadn't yet ended.

I sat on the bank, alone, watching them play: Henry and George against Will and Tom. It was always towards the close of day that Henry took his competitive spirit out on to the tennis lawn, and one evening he inadvertently appropriated my rendezvous with Tom by inviting him to make up the numbers for *all-male* doubles. It was another sweet-smelling, balmy evening, the brightness of the day diffused to a liquid gold and poured out across the trees; everything languid and perfectly still, but for those white-clad figures in front of me. And in that soft westering light, a light tinged with the iridescence of early evening sun, they shone: dazzling, youthful beauty, immortal vigour and vitality.

Too perfect . . . too perfect.

Then, as though hearing my doubt, the chime of the church bell in the distance, calling out across the countryside, reverberating through that palette of overlapping colour and texture and lullaby sounds. But this time interrupting, discordant, like a call to arms, stirring a sudden pang within me and reminding me once again how fleeting the moment of rapture. I lay back, flat against the earth's warm surface, listening to its rhythm, the bounce of the ball upon the grass, and those young male voices. I stared up at the empty sky and imagined myself floating up into it, higher and higher, and all the time looking down upon myself and Deyning: smaller and smaller. I could still hear the church bell, hear birds calling out from the tops of the trees, but I could no longer hear the voices from the tennis lawn. They had gone. Evaporated.

'Were you dozing?' he asked, standing over me.

I sat up. 'No, I don't think so . . . I'm not sure . . . who won?'

'Henry, of course.'

'Henry *and* George,' I corrected him.

He sat down on the bank next to me, swatting at the grass with his racquet. He'd wanted to win, I thought.

'Henry—as I think you already know—rather likes winning. It makes him feel . . . complete.'

He turned to me, smiling. 'We all like to win.'

'I've never won anything, ever,' I said. 'But it doesn't really matter.'

'It's different for you,' he said, looking away and pulling out his packet of cigarettes. 'You don't need to win at anything.'

'Oh, and you do?'

He shook his head, raised one side of his mouth. 'No, I don't *need* to . . . but I want to. All men like to compete, I think, and win. And if I'm to make anything of my life . . .'

He didn't finish his sentence and we sat in silence for a few minutes, watching George and William knocking balls about on the tennis lawn below us.

'The Granvilles . . . all destined for greatness,' he said, wistfully, still staring ahead at my brothers. I said nothing. I watched him once more from the corner of my eye. On the side of his clean-shaven face he'd missed a patch: a few dark hairs, a newly discovered imperfection, lending a perfect vulnerability.

'No . . . I think you're the one destined for greatness, Tom.'

He turned to me, looking into my eyes with that now so familiar solemn, searching gaze. And reflected in those eyes the setting sun, picking out small flecks of gold in brown.

'I see it in you . . . I see it in you quite clearly,' I added, staring back at him, anchored.

He glanced down at my hand, resting on the grass. 'And of all people . . . of everyone, you're the one I'd most like to have believe that.'

* * *

My Dearest T, did you really wait ALL night? I feel utterly wretched at the thought, but we are filled to the brim here & it's quite impossible for me to escape. Please tell me that you understand . . . Yr D

CHAPTER SIX

On August the first we enjoyed a heavenly day of croquet, and we had almost a full house. Papa was in London once again, and Mama's dear friend, and my godmother, Venetia Cooper, had come down for a few days with her son, Jimmy, and Charlie Boyd, another old friend of Henry's from his school days. All four of my cousins—Edina, Lucy, Archie and Johnnie—were with us for the week, along with their mama, my mother's sister, Maude. And William, too, had a couple of friends staying. For me, everything was as it had always been, only better, because Tom was now with us. If only Henry and some of the others hadn't been so determined to talk about the possibility of war.

It was towards the end of the day when I yelled across the croquet lawn at Henry and Tom, 'Please do stop discussing politics! You're spoiling our game!' And when I shouted that line at them for a second time, Henry immediately threw down his mallet and said, 'Someone please help me throw my baby sister into the lake and then we can all have some peace!'

I saw him striding across the lawn towards me and I screamed, dropped my mallet and took off towards the woods. I heard Edina and Lucy shrieking, the boys cheering, and as I raced through the ferns, with Henry hot on my tail, I lost my shoe, tripped and fell.

'Please don't, Henry! Please don't!'

He laughed. 'Oh, for goodness sake, Issa, do get up. Look at the state of you.'

I could barely breathe. 'I can't,' I gasped. 'I've hurt my ankle.'

As Henry shook his head and walked away, Tom appeared, holding my shoe. He bent down. 'Which ankle?' he asked.

'The left.'

He placed his hand over my white stocking. 'Here?'

I shook my head.

He moved his hand up over my ankle. 'Here?'

'Yes . . . yes there,' I replied, wiping away a tear.

'Are you able to stand?'

He took my hand and I let him pull me up. I stood on one foot as he slipped his arm about my waist. 'Hold on to me,' he said. I put my arm around his shoulder and tried to walk, but it was too painful and I cried out. 'There's only one thing for it, I'm afraid, I shall have to carry you.' He handed me my shoe, and then picked me up just as though I were a small child.

'I'm sorry,' I said, as he strode back through the ferns towards the croquet lawn.

'Don't be sorry. Henry shouldn't have chased you like that. Anyway, I get the chance to have you in my arms,' he replied, glancing down at me, smiling.

When we emerged from the woods Edina and Lucy came rushing over from the boys, who were standing in a huddle on the lawn with Henry.

Edina said, 'Oh, darling! Are you very badly hurt?'

'She's twisted her ankle,' Tom replied, in a perfectly calm and assured voice, and Edina looked up at me, raised her eyebrows, and smiled.

Then Will, George, Archie and all the others were around us, all wishing to look at my injured ankle. But Tom didn't stop. He continued walking across the lawn, then up the steps, on to the terrace, where my mother sat with Maude. When Mama saw us she stood up.

I remained silent in Tom's arms as he explained to Mama, with Maude standing next to her, exactly what had taken place, and I saw my mother look across the lawn in Henry's direction, narrowing her eyes. Maude looked at me, frowning with a tad too much concern, and then she scrunched her face up even more and said, 'Such a brave Issa.' Mama was examining my ankle, and as she rubbed her hand over it I cried out once more.

'Oh my poor child, you have hurt yourself, haven't you? He's such a beastly boy, that brother of yours.' She looked at Tom. 'Tom, would you be even more of an angel and take Clarissa up to her room? I shall fetch Mabel; she always knows exactly what's required with these sorts of injuries.'

As he carried me into the house I felt faint, almost as though I were in a dream. I couldn't quite believe that Mama had asked Tom to take me to my room. And I suppose, looking back, it was a measure of her trust in him. I watched him, his face, as we moved through the hallway, past the jardinière, with its oversized palm, across the polished marble floor; his fingers spread out around my waist, his eyes fixed ahead. I studied the line of his jaw, the dark shadow of his clean-shaven chin, the curve of his mouth: a flicker of a smile playing upon his lips. We climbed the staircase in silence, through shafts of dust-filled light, and I could feel his heart, beating in perfect time with my own.

'You'll have to direct me from here,' he said, standing at the top of the stairs.

I pointed. 'Over there.'

My door was ajar and as he carried me into the room he looked up and around, as though taking in its dimensions more than its detail: the walls, the windows, the ceiling, and then my bed.

'Beautiful room,' he said, at last. 'Strange, but it's exactly as I'd imagined.'

'Are you going to put me down? I think you've more than done your bit, Tom.'

He moved to the side of the bed, stopped and looked down at me, into my eyes, and then we finally relinquished our hold on each other as he placed me upon my bed. I shuffled up against the pillows, without thinking bent my leg and unbuttoned my other shoe. He moved over to the window, the one looking directly south over the terrace and the lake.

'Stunning view,' he said. He turned and came towards me. 'I should go. Mabel will be here in a moment and I'm sure she'll look after you.' But he seemed awkward, almost reluctant to leave me.

I looked up at him. 'Thank you, Tom, you've been most gallant.'

He smiled at me, moved nearer. 'You look like Titania,' he said, pulling a piece of green fern from my hair.

At that moment Mama appeared in the doorway, shadowed by a stony-faced Mabel, carrying a small box and a bowl.

'Thank you so much, Tom,' she said, moving past him.

He raised his hand to me and disappeared through the door.

That night I did not go down to dinner. My ankle had swollen to the size of a baby elephant's, despite Mabel bringing up towels filled with ice and insisting I rest it upon them. Edina and Lucy visited me in my room, as well as each of my brothers, and Henry apologised. Sitting on the side of my bed and taking my hand in his, he said, 'You know, I really am sorry. I thought you were feigning, Issa—like you always used to.'

Mama, too, came and fussed over me. Plumping up my pillows and straightening the bed, she said, 'Tom Cuthbert was very considerate today, very charming and kind.'

'Yes, he's a nice boy,' I replied, knowing how much the term *nice boy* meant to Mama.

She glanced at me. 'Yes, a very nice boy.'

Some time after my eleventh birthday, I'd been relocated from the nursery floor to the vast expanse of my new 'grown-up' bedroom, with its four tall windows looking out to the south and west. At first I'd hated it. The room seemed ridiculously large and much too formal with its matching wallpaper, curtains, upholstery and bedcover. I longed to return upstairs, to the gated confines of my childhood, to the sloping ceilings of my cosy attic life, and the dust and debris of a land far away from Mama's coordinated, plumped-up world. I longed for the toys I'd had to leave behind there: my brothers' toy soldiers and tattered fort; my dolls' house, my dolls; and those treasured books suddenly deemed 'too immature'. Miss Stephens, my nursemaid, departed, along with Miss Greaves—a governess (of sorts), and Mademoiselle arrived. I'd resented these changes, was quietly angry with my mother. But by now, by this time, I had grown into my room and rarely ventured upstairs. I'd moved on.

The following morning, my ankle greatly improved, I went down to breakfast. When Mama entered the dining room—accompanied by Aunt Maude—they both looked unusually troubled, and then Mama announced to us all that Germany had declared war upon Russia. All day it was all anyone could speak of, and though we continued our croquet tournament, it wasn't the same. At four, play was suspended whilst Mabel and Mrs Cuthbert once again brought out trays of fresh tea, jugs of lemonade and iced coffee, strawberries, cream and scones; and then served us from linen-covered tables set up on the edge of the lawn. For an hour or so we slumped in deckchairs on the grass under the sycamore tree, as Mama, Venetia and Aunt Maude looked on anxiously from the terrace. The boys all lay about on the lawn discussing whether and when they would enlist—if there were to be a war. And it seemed to me as though they were all set on it. From underneath my straw hat I watched Tom, even as I made conversation with Edina and Lucy. And from time to time he glanced at me, smiled, and then looked away.

Earlier that day, before our game started, when I'd been sitting on the grass with the others, Tom had sat down next to me. I'd had my hand behind me, resting flat upon the lawn, and I suddenly felt the tips of his fingers touching mine. I turned to him, but he did nothing; didn't look to me and didn't move his hand away from mine. I glanced at Edina, sitting directly opposite us, wondering if she could see, and when she smiled back at me I knew that she had, and I quickly pulled my hand away. Later, in the evening, Edina came to my room, asking if she could borrow a ribbon.

'I think you have an admirer, Issa,' she said, her back to me, as she fiddled with my comb box.

'Oh really,' I replied, with adroitly manufactured nonchalance.

'Yes, and I think you know too.' She turned to me, smiling. 'Tom Cuthbert?'

I laughed. 'Edina, really . . . Tom is Mrs Cuthbert's son.'

'That may be, but he's extraordinarily handsome and, I believe, utterly preoccupied with you.'

This, of course, was music to my ears. And I immediately recognised the potential benefit of an ally, a spy. For Edina was nothing if not an observer of people, and for as long as I could remember she'd been an unexploited expert on the subtle intricacies of character and human dynamics.

'Preoccupied with me? Do you really think so?' I

asked, looking down, playing with the ribbon in my hands.

'Completely and utterly.'

I looked up at her, unable not to smile. 'He is rather gorgeous, isn't he?'

'Divine, darling. And you appear to have captured his heart *and* his mind.'

'But how can you tell? What did you see?' I asked, eager for her to share her observations.

'Oh but, Clarissa, you hardly need me to tell you, dear heart. You must surely see yourself.' She glanced at me, smiling. 'He's completely enamoured by you; in love, I'd say. And how do I know this? Because from the moment I arrived—or rather the moment he appeared, when we all sat on the terrace that very first evening—he seemed to be . . . a little too aware of you,' she continued, moving about the room, as though conducting a talk to an audience far larger than one. 'He'd simply fail to notice any other beauty fluttering her eyelashes at him. And even when he's talking, listening to someone else, he's so obviously distracted by you, dear.' She looked at me, gave a little shiver. 'Captivated . . . totally captivated.'

It was tempting. I could have told her then that Tom Cuthbert and I had already begun a type of love affair, at least a love affair in my mind. But I decided not to. Although ten months older than me, which qualified her as indisputably worldly at that time, I knew Edina to be too easily flattered to be discreet. She'd be bound to want to disclose my secret to another, if only to be acknowledged in her role as confidante.

The following day, a little too self-conscious under Edina's scrutiny, I found myself avoiding the hill, for I realised he, too, had to walk in that direction, but he hung back and let me walk on alone. When I reached the house I ran through the hallway, up the stairs and into my room. And as I slammed the door of my bedroom, a painted plate my godmother had given me fell from the wall and split in two.

For the next week or so I simmered quietly in a daydream, imagining Tom Cuthbert begging for my forgiveness, his declaration of undying love, and then . . . his kiss. I'd seen him about the place but had managed to avoid him, and once, when Mama invited him to play in a croquet match, I feigned a headache and stayed in my room.

I was sitting on the bench by the ha-ha, my unopened journal on my lap, when he walked up to me, eight days after our fracas. It was a glorious morning with no breath of wind and I'd been sitting there for some time, looking out into the distance, listening to the hum of bumblebees on the lavender close by. Perhaps it was the aroma of the lavender, soothing my senses, making me sleepy, but I felt unusually mellow: quite at peace with the world. And thus far I'd failed to record anything of the day in my journal.

'May I sit with you?' he asked.

I smiled. 'But of course,' I replied, looking up at him from under my hat.

He sat down next to me. 'I need to talk to you.' He leant forward, fiddling with his hands. 'You see . . . you see I like you, Clarissa. You're quite different to anyone I've known before, and really . . . well, I didn't mean those things I said.'

'No, of course not. And neither did—'

'Please . . . please hear me out,' he said. 'What I

Tom's gaze altogether. He and I seemed unable to converse in front of others, and so but for the occasional 'yes' or 'no' we usually said almost nothing at all to each other during those afternoon croquet games. But later, each evening, when we met in the meadow, we compared notes, dissecting the characters of Deyning's assorted house guests.

'She's too uppity,' he said, when I asked him about Edina. 'And she watches you all the time. It's as though she's guarding you, or observing your every move for some in-depth study or other.'

'How simply fascinating,' I said. 'She must be observing us both then . . .'

'How so?'

'Oh, nothing. Edina likes to watch people, and I have to say she's really rather good at it.'

'I hadn't realised it was an art.'

'And what do you make of Lucy?' I asked.

'She's sweet. More like you . . . apart from that annoying habit of repeating the last line of everything anyone says.'

I laughed. 'She's only fifteen, Tom.'

'I think Charlie Boyd rather likes you,' he said, reaching down and pulling at a blade of grass.

'Charlie? Oh, Charlie's a dear, an absolute dear, and I've known him forever. He's like another cousin, that's all.'

He made no reply and I wanted to tell him then that I wasn't in the least interested in Charlie, but instead I moved on, to my godmother.

'And what of Venetia?' I asked. I was curious to know what he thought of my godmother; curious to know if he was drawn to her in the same way other young men seemed to be. 'Like moths to a flame,' Mama had once said.

He turned to me. 'Venetia?'

'Yes, what do you make of her? She's rather beautiful, isn't she?'

'Yes, I suppose she is rather . . . exotic,' he replied, looking away from me.

I felt a twinge. I'd like to have been described as *exotic*; but it struck me that perhaps it was something one grew into.

'Voluptuous?' I asked, referring to Venetia's unmistakable and much renowned curves.

'Hmm, yes, voluptuous . . .' he said, dreamily.

And I could feel my face flush. 'Well, you'll be pleased to know she rather likes *young* men, Tom,' I said, rising to my feet.

He looked up at me, smiling. 'And what do you mean by that?'

I hesitated. 'Oh, nothing . . . nothing at all. I must get back now.'

We walked back through the meadow in silence, maintaining our distance and separating at the stable-yard gate with a casual, 'Goodbye'. Aunt Maude—like her daughter, a keen observer—had asked me over dinner the previous evening whom she'd seen me with, walking back from the meadow. 'Oh, possibly Tom Cuthbert, or perhaps Mr Broughton,' I replied. 'I bumped into each of them on my walk. It was such a glorious evening, Aunt.'

Then Mama said, 'Clarissa does so love her solitary ambles,' and I caught the tail end of Edina's knowing smile.

I couldn't sleep that night. It was hot, too hot. And despite every window in my room being open, the curtains tied back, the air was completely still. I heard Henry on the terrace beneath my bedroom, talking to our cousins, Archie and Johnnie. And I moved over to my window seat. 'We've all got to do it,' he was saying. 'Those Huns are on the move now and they won't stop. They're after our empire . . .'

I returned to my bed and lay down upon the sheet. I thought of Tom; wondered if he was asleep. Was he dreaming of me? Henry's voice continued, and I tried to block it out and focus my mind on Tom: Tom and me under the sycamore tree. But Henry was gathering momentum, interrupting my scenes with his diatribe about whatever it was he was so impassioned about. I rose from my bed, walked over to the window and shut it, loudly and firmly.

I'm not entirely sure what woke me, or what time it was, but it was late, very late, and the voices on the terrace were much quieter. I heard giggling, female giggling, and I crept over to the window and peered down. At first I thought I must be dreaming, hallucinating, and as I looked away I could feel the sound of blood rushing through my brain. Venetia Cooper, Mama's friend, my godmother, was sitting on Henry's lap, and from what I could make out they were canoodling. I crouched down, peering over the padded cushion of the window seat. I saw Henry's hand move down her gown, then creep back up—on to her breast. I turned my head away. *I must have made a mistake* . . . I looked back, saw her stand up, take hold of his hand and lead him inside. I moved swiftly to my bedroom door, my heart pounding as I pressed my ear to it. I heard them coming up the stairs, heard them whispering as they passed by my door and headed towards the rose guest room. Then a door closed.

I sat down on my bed, contemplating the

implications of what I'd just witnessed. I felt sick. Venetia must be almost forty, I thought, *and* she was the mother of his friend! Did Jimmy know? I wondered. And what would Mama and Papa say? I remembered Papa saying that Hughie, Venetia's husband, was an 'exceptional shot', and I lay down and closed my eyes.

*   *   *

Your note did amuse me, not least your mention of the Grande Dame, but please don't be too hard on her. She has such innate charm, & I do so love her colourful displays, & her ways with 'les garcons'. Snob? I am not entirely sure what you mean. She certainly relishes her place with the 'Smart Set', as you call it, but surely that's no crime? And indeed, how could it be otherwise? As for H's devotion, I make no comment . . . YOD

CHAPTER SEVEN

The following morning, over breakfast, Mama received a telegram, and I remember thinking, praying, *please don't let this be about Henry and Venetia*. There had been more telegrams than usual arriving at Deyning, but Papa was in London and I'd supposed them to be from him.

Mama looked up.

'I'm afraid it is as we've all feared,' she began. And I looked down at my plate of kedgeree, for I knew what was coming, and I could hear the next sentence: *Henry, my eldest, has been making love to my best friend, Venetia* . . . 'Germany has invaded Belgium and declared war upon France.'

My relief was immense, and I can't be sure now, but I think I looked up and smiled at Mama.

'We have given an ultimatum . . . all we can do now is wait, and pray,' she added. Then she lifted her teacup. 'God bless England.'

'God bless England!' we all repeated, teacups in hand and in perfect unison.

I looked over at Venetia, who was staring at Henry. I glanced at Edina, who looked back at me solemnly and shook her head. And then I looked at Lucy, who—it has to be said—appeared quite mystified by the announcement.

Immediately after breakfast I walked in the grounds with Edina. And she seemed to me almost excited by the prospect of war.

'Can you believe it? We may be at war . . . at war, by this time tomorrow!' she exclaimed, wide eyed.

'No, I can't believe it . . . and I don't want to believe it. I don't want my brothers to go and fight, Edina.'

'But England is in danger, dear . . . we have to defend this island of ours,' she said, marching slightly ahead of me across the lawn, her head high. And I wondered who she'd been talking to, where she'd learnt that line.

'I hope that Germany sees sense,' I said, not at all sure what *sense* I was referring to. 'And that it doesn't come to a war. Because it will affect everything, won't it?'

'Well yes, I should say!'

'Do you suppose we'll still be able to go to Brighton?' I asked, for I was still thinking in terms of the days ahead, and our planned excursion to the coast. 'I've been *so* looking forward to it.'

'I'm not sure,' she replied. 'I suppose it all depends. Mama says if there's to be a war there'll need to be a great mobilisation of troops . . . and we'll all have to do our bit.'

'In what way? How can *we* do anything?'

'Well . . . if all the men go to war, I imagine we'll have to do all sorts of things.' She stopped. I stopped. She stared over into the trees, tapping her finger on her lips, pondering, and so I waited; waited to hear what we'd all have to do. 'Drive motor cars,' she began, 'do gardening . . . that sort of thing.'

It didn't sound like much to me, and as we moved on I said, 'But Papa doesn't garden and neither do my brothers.'

'No, but Broughton does, and think of the under-gardeners, all the outdoor servants you have here who may have to go.'

'Really? You think they'll want servants as well?'

'Yes, of course, they'll all have to go and fight, dear.'

It sounded slightly far-fetched to me. I wasn't convinced Edina had her facts right. I thought of Broughton: surely he'd not be much use. He was quite old and so gentle, only interested in flowers. And he wouldn't hurt a fly; was always rescuing injured animals. But if my cousin were right, how would we manage at Deyning without gardeners? I looked around me, across the manicured lawns to the neatly arranged borders where Frank and John were already on their knees and busy. It will all go to wrack and ruin, I thought. The whole place will become overgrown and lost in a wilderness.

I looked up towards the house, the west side, and amidst a verdant tangle of Virginia creeper, jasmine and wisteria clinging to its stone façade, there was someone up a ladder there too. There were always people everywhere—attending to something.

That day no one seemed to want to do anything at all. We simply sat about watching the minutes and hours pass by, just as though we'd all received a death sentence. Telegrams were delivered, telegrams were despatched; and Mrs Cuthbert, Mabel, Wilson and Mr Broughton wore funereal faces, as though they'd already received the bad news they had sworn to keep from us.

When I met Tom early that evening he was distracted, and as we sat upon the steps of the boathouse we had little to say to each other.

'Strange, isn't it? Summer seems to have ended already,' he said, lighting another cigarette.

I turned to him, placed my hand upon his arm. I couldn't think of anything to say at that moment and somehow a touch seemed more voluble than any words. But he simply glanced at my hand and then looked away.

I don't know how long we sat there for, but long enough. And when we rose to our feet and I began to walk back towards the house, he called after me, said my name. I turned, expecting him to say something, but he simply stared at me, frowning.

'What is it?' I asked. And I so wanted to add to that, 'my darling'.

'Don't go back yet,' he said.

'But I must go back. I have to.'

'Clarissa . . .'

'Yes?'

He looked down at the grass. 'Oh, nothing,' he

said.

When I arrived back at the house I bumped into Mama in the hallway.

'Have you seen Tom?' she asked.

I swallowed. 'No, why?'

'I thought I'd invite him to join us for dinner. It's Edna's night off and Mrs Cuthbert's cooking for us. He shouldn't be on his own at a time like this,' she added, and walked off towards the servants' hall.

I stood still; I could hear Mama asking Mrs Cuthbert if Tom would like to join us for dinner, but I couldn't quite hear Mrs Cuthbert's reply; and then I heard Mama's footsteps coming back towards the hallway and I quickly turned and hurried off up the stairs.

Half an hour or so later, when I entered the drawing room, he was there, looking extraordinarily dapper, and sitting in front of the fire with Venetia and Jimmy. He glanced over at me, nervously, and I smiled. It was strange to see him there, in that room, dressed for dinner. There he was: one of us.

I wandered over to the boys, gathered by the window around George. He'd received a telegram requesting him to be back at Aldershot by midnight. They were asking him questions, talking about the war. I glanced across at Tom, wondered what he and Venetia were discussing. I could hear her saying something about Paris. She loved talking about Paris, slipping into French here and there. I looked ahead, out of the window. Nothing stirred. Every blade of grass, each stem and flower and leaf and shrub appeared perfectly still, as though all of nature held her breath, waiting; and the sun, still above the trees, more achingly golden than ever before. I'm not sure how long I stood there, transfixed, lost in that halcyon moment, but as I turned away I wondered what tomorrow would bring. Would it all be the same? *Will it be the same?*

I walked over to Maude, Edina and Lucy, who sat playing cards next to another window.

'Would you like to join us, dear?'

'No thank you, Aunt. I'm a little bored of cards . . . or rather, bored of losing at cards,' I replied, and she laughed.

I moved on again, slowly, towards the fireplace. Above it hung the portrait of Mama by Philip de László. It had been commissioned by my father some years earlier, and was mesmerisingly beautiful. Venetia was speaking about Venice, another of her *most* favourite and yet-to-be-visited places. I caught Tom's eye, smiled. He didn't smile back at me, but I caught his gaze move from my face down over my body. And as I stood in front of the fireplace, running my finger over the contours of one of Mama's precious Meissen figurines, I sensed him watching me.

No fire had been lit that evening, which struck me as odd, because Mama usually insisted on a fire in that room each evening, even in summer. Lends the place atmosphere and warmth, she said. But the polished steel grate remained empty, and the carved marble surround—with its acanthus scrolls, swags of husk and little putti—felt colder than usual to the touch. When I turned, the sky beyond the windows was changing, the last of the sun's rays shining low into the room, throwing pale mauve jets of light across the patterned carpet and silk furnishings.

'Clarissa, darling,' Venetia began, her cigarette holder in hand, 'you're such an ongoing distraction to these poor, poor boys . . . I'm surprised they can think of war—or anything else—with such a vision of beauty in their presence.'

'Is there any news?'

She smiled. 'No, dear child, not yet. We shan't know anything until much later tonight or perhaps tomorrow morning,' she replied. 'Do sit with us.'

'You do look terribly beautiful tonight, Clarissa,' Jimmy said, as I sat down next to him on the sofa.

'And it may not be fashionable for a lady to have tanned skin, but it suits you, suits you very well,' Venetia added. 'Don't you agree, Tom?'

I looked at him. He was leaning forward in his chair, holding a glass of something. 'Yes, it does,' he replied, looking back at me, without any trace of a smile.

'Clarissa is going to be a sensation in London, an absolute sensation,' Venetia continued, with a little shiver, and a shrug of lace. She reminded me of a box of chocolates that night. Confection, sealed in tight, perfectly wrapped and tied up in ribbons. The previous evening she'd come down to dinner in a purple-plumed silver turban and opera cloak. Oh, is it fancy dress? Lucy had asked.

'I've already warned your father, warned him that he'll have to keep a gun by his bed,' she continued. 'You'll be inundated, darling, inundated, but I'm hoping that Jimmy might be able to be your chaperone about town one day,' she added, smiling at her son.

Jimmy turned to me. 'I'd be more than delighted, anytime at all,' he said, looking slightly awkward.

'Thank you, that's very kind, but I don't know when that will be, at least not now. If there's to be a war, I don't suppose there'll be many parties or balls to attend.'

'Oh but of course there'll be. Life must go on,' Venetia said, and then she looked across at Tom. 'And Tom, you must call on me next time you're up in town. I just *adore* having the young around me.'

I felt my skin bristle. I hadn't told Tom—hadn't told anyone—about Henry's affair with Venetia, and it was definitely an affair. I'd been watching them, surreptitiously noting their furtive glances and private little jokes. Only that morning, when I'd walked round to the veranda, I'd found them there, almost entwined. They'd quickly moved away from one another and Henry had stuttered something to me about looking for a tennis racquet for Venetia, but Venetia didn't play tennis, I knew that. What did he take me for? And now she was trying to lure Tom to London.

'Yes, I shall do that,' I heard him say.

I looked over to him. 'Oh, and do you go to London very often, Mr Cuthbert?'

He raised one side of his mouth. 'No, I don't, but I'll be there soon enough and I'm sure I'll be grateful for a few friends.'

I picked up one of Mama's magazines lying upon the ottoman in front of me and began flicking the pages, and then I glanced up and saw Venetia smiling at him with a worldly look about her. I glanced over at Tom. He was looking down but still smiling. I put down the magazine and stood up.

'I really must go and find Mama,' I said, and left the room.

I didn't go in search of Mama. I went outside and stood on the terrace. He's going to have an affair with Venetia, I thought, wringing my hands and feeling utterly powerless. He's going to go up to London and embark on a torrid affair with that woman. I was pleased I'd broken her plate, and as I walked towards the window I wondered if its shattering had in fact been portentous. I peeked in through the glass: he was still sitting in the same place, listening to Mama, now seated on the sofa next to Jimmy. They all looked so serious, so worried. I marched back along the terrace towards the door into the house.

'Clarissa! I was wondering where you were. Can I get you a glass of lemonade or something?'

It was Charlie Boyd.

'No, no thank you, Charlie. I was taking some air. It's so stuffy inside and . . . and all of this waiting, waiting for news, it's altogether rather depressing.'

'Hmm. Yes, it is somewhat. But you mustn't let it worry you too much, you know. You're much too pretty to wear a frown.'

'So I've been told,' I said, my head still full of Tom's impending trip to London. 'I'm sorry, Charlie,' I added, glancing back at the window. 'I've recently discovered something quite . . . quite shocking, and I'm a little distracted.'

'Oh dear, nothing sinister, I hope.'

'Well, that's just it; it could be. But I really can't say any more.'

'I see,' he said, looking at me, smiling. And I immediately wondered if he knew something.

We walked back inside and as we entered the drawing room I took hold of his arm. I was determined not to look across at Tom or Venetia, but I heard her saying something to him about a hotel, and then the gong sounded and we all made our way through to the dining room.

I was seated at the opposite end of the table to

Tom, and on the same side, so that I couldn't, even if I'd wanted to—which I didn't—see his face. And after dinner, when Mama asked the ladies to retire to the drawing room for some cards and leave the boys to enjoy a glass of port, I excused myself, saying that I was tired. Edina seemed keen to come with me, and with a look of practised concern on her face, she whispered, 'Is it the war, dear? Or is it something else?'

'No, Edina, I'm simply tired.'

I was in my bedroom, had unpinned my hair, when I realised that I hadn't bid my brother, George, goodbye, and he'd be leaving within the hour. I went back downstairs to the dining room, stood for a moment outside the door, and then opened it.

'Issa! Are you going to join us for a glass?' Henry asked and then laughed, the port decanter raised in one hand, a cigar in the other.

I looked over at Tom, who'd moved to the opposite side of the table. He smiled at me, wearily.

'I wanted to say goodnight, and goodbye to George,' I said. 'I'm going to my bed.'

'Aha, beauty sleep, that's the secret, eh, Clarissa?' Charlie said, turning to me.

I moved over to George, who stood up and wrapped his arms around me.

'You're so brave, Issa, coming in here with all these obnoxious young men,' he said to me quietly, and then he kissed my forehead.

I looked up at him. 'When will you next be home?'

'I really don't know, but soon I hope.'

'If you *have* to go and fight—will you be able to come home first?'

'That I also don't know,' he said.

I put my head on his chest, held him tightly for a moment, then looked up at him and kissed him on both cheeks, 'I love you, Georgie.'

'I love you too, darling,' he replied, to an echo of, 'Aah!'

I moved towards the door.

'Do we each get a kiss?' Charlie asked. 'Have pity, Clarissa, it may be our last chance.'

I turned back to them, and—with a little affectation and perhaps rather dramatically—I blew them each a kiss. Tom smiled, and I allowed myself to look back at him for longer than the others.

'I say! That's not fair! That's cheating!' Jimmy shouted out.

'Yes, that doesn't count, doesn't count at all,' Charlie said.

And as I turned to close the door, I glanced over once more at Tom, but he'd already turned away and was deep in conversation with Henry and Archie.

Oddly enough, I fell asleep very quickly that night. But I had a most peculiar and muddled dream, which I later recorded in my journal. I was in an enormous building, walking down a long corridor with doors either side. I was searching for a particular door and when I found it, it had the letters 'VR' painted upon it in purple. I opened it, and immediately inside, in a lobby area, Mama was standing clutching a telegram. 'Clarissa, you shouldn't be here,' she said. 'Tom is performing an exam and he mustn't be disturbed.' Then I heard Venetia's voice and I pushed past Mama to see Venetia lying on a bed with Tom bending over her. He looked up at me. 'She's unattainable,' he said.

'You need to send for a doctor.'

I shouted, 'I know what you're doing, Tom!' And then Henry appeared and said, 'But it's only a game, Clarissa,' and when I looked back at Tom, he'd changed into Charlie Boyd and was dressed as a soldier.

I awoke early the following morning, stirred from my fretful dreams by the sounds of activity in the house: doors opening and closing; voices and footsteps in the hallway downstairs. I dressed hastily and went to find Mama. She was not in her room and so I rushed downstairs, where I found everyone sitting in the dining room, in a collective sombre silence. Mama looked up at me and I knew immediately.

'We're going to war?'

She reached out, took hold of my hand. 'We *are* at war, Clarissa,' she replied.

* * *

. . . I was resting in the hammock, contemplating all of this, & what lies ahead. It's all too worrying & depressing. Lord K is asking for another 100,000, & H is determined to sign up . . . my very dearest dear, I fear our 'plan' may have to wait. D

CHAPTER EIGHT

Over the next couple of days there was a flurry of activity at Deyning, but none of the activity any of us had hoped for or imagined that summer. My cousins and Aunt Maude left Deyning to return to their home in Devon, and Venetia, Jimmy and Charlie all returned to London. At the time I wondered why: why did they all have to cut short their stay with us? Surely it wasn't going to make any difference where *they* were. But almost immediately the fighting had begun; Kitchener was asking for volunteers; church was packed, special prayers said. It was upon us, and yet to me it all seemed to happen so quickly, so suddenly. By the end of the week Henry had been to Godalming to try for a commission in Kitchener's army and was waiting to hear. And Will was in a conundrum. He considered himself a pacifist and found the notion of war abhorrent, but he was also a patriotic Englishman.

I'd heard Mrs Cuthbert and others say that the war would be over by Christmas, and the vicar, too, seemed to hold that belief. But my parents were not so optimistic. In the middle of August, barely two weeks after George returned to Aldershot, my parents received word that he'd arrived safely in France with the British Expeditionary Force. The very same day, Henry received his commission.

In Guildford, with Mama, I'd seen the billboards and the posters calling for volunteers: 'There is still a place in the line for you . . .' they said, and I wondered which line, where? And on a trip to London, to visit Mama's dressmaker, we'd passed through Trafalgar Square and Piccadilly Circus and from the back of the taxicab I'd looked out at the smiling faces of pristine, uniformed young men. To me, their faces didn't appear to be troubled, worried or anxious; they looked excited, happy to be going off to war. Later, we'd intended on going to Lyons Corner House for tea, as we usually did before returning home, but the place was packed with soldiers, and with crowds outside on the pavement too. So we went straight to the station, where Mama held on to my hand tightly as we manoeuvred our way through a chaotic, heaving mass of khaki. And as we headed back through the sleepy meadows and pastures, I could hear the soldiers bound for France and singing, further down the train.

'How *can* they be so jolly?' I asked Mama.

'Because they're proud and patriotic,' she said. 'And now they know their purpose, and how noble it is.'

My mother, like my father, believed and lived by noble principles: duty, sacrifice, and honour, truth and fidelity. And the war, still new and fresh, bound up in flags and bunting and patriotic rhetoric, offered her and others—including my brothers and all those other young men—an opportunity to truly live by and test those principles. After all, was there anything nobler than self-sacrifice?

We were standing under the chestnut tree in lower meadow, sheltering from a shower, when Tom told me he was going to volunteer. I'd been expecting it, waiting for him to tell me. He didn't look at me as he spoke, but gazed ahead, across the field to the lake beyond, and there was an unfamiliar formality to his tone.

'Everyone should sign up,' he said. 'I'm going to go to Guildford tomorrow, and I intend to ask William to come with me.'

I couldn't bring myself to say anything. What was there to say? 'Don't go; stay here with me'? It would have been pointless. We'd already lost so many of the men on the estate and were left with only those who were too old or too frail to enlist. I'd heard Father repeating Kitchener's words, 'Every man should do his duty.' It was a mantra, spoken with a stern face. It was The Cause.

'I shall miss you,' I said.

He turned to me, reached out and pushed my damp hair back from my face. 'And I shall miss you, Clarissa.'

I wanted him to kiss me then but, like all those other moments before, he moved on and began speaking of something different, steering us away from that point. I didn't hear his words. All I could think was that he, too, was going to war; that he, too, was leaving Deyning, leaving my world. I'd only just found him, only just realised that the universe included someone named Tom Cuthbert and now he was about to disappear. It seemed already the war had found me. It had reached into my life, interrupting my summer and all those anticipated days of picnics, eating strawberries on the lawn, tennis and croquet tournaments. It had taken my brothers, and now it was taking him, Tom. And even then, in the slipping away, I sensed something more: an almost imperceptible queer tilting feeling. As though a magnet in the core of the earth was very gently, very slowly moving, and pulling me with it.

The rain stopped and we walked on in silence towards the lake. As we descended the bank I didn't bother to lift my skirt, and it clung about my ankles, wet and heavy. He offered me his hand, said my name, 'Clarissa.' I loved to hear him say my name, he said it so differently to anyone else: as though it was a question in itself. I took his hand, and as we walked on neither of us released our grip.

We stood by the water's edge, side by side, hand in hand. It didn't matter any more that anyone saw us; I no longer cared what the servants or anyone else thought. And I wanted to savour that moment, there, with him. A steam was rising from the water and the air already smelled of autumn. I had just turned seventeen.

From that day until the day he was called up we spent every possible moment we could together, as far away from the house and those prying eyes as we could. The night before he left I excused myself from the drawing room after dinner, saying I had a headache. I kissed my parents goodnight, climbed the stairs and went to my room. I arranged the pillows in my bed to look as best they could like a slumbering body, then I tiptoed back along the landing to the service lobby and down the stairs that led to the kitchen. I could hear Mrs Cuthbert's voice in the servants' hall, along with Mabel and Edna, discussing the day's news: the Germans had taken Brussels. I crept along the passageway, through the scullery and stillroom into the garden room, and then out to the yard. There was little light outside and I had to feel my way ahead, but once away from the house I knew the pathway and the light from the moon became brighter. And standing in the moonlight, next to the boathouse, smoking a cigarette, there he was: my Tom.

I smoked my first cigarette that night, there, with him. We sat on the wooden steps of the boathouse for almost an hour, talking about things we might do one day, places we'd like to see. 'I shall go to the desert one day and ride across it on a camel,' I said, and when he laughed I felt so stupid.

He must have sensed my embarrassment,

because he said to me, 'I'm sorry . . . we all have our dreams, and yours are no more amusing than mine.'

But he still made me feel like a child; he *and* my brothers. And then, as I looked down, wishing yet again that I'd thought before I'd spoken, he took my hand and said, 'Clarissa, you must surely know by now . . . how very fond I am of you.'

I looked up at him. 'Yes,' I answered. 'Yes, thank you, Tom.'

I wasn't sure what to say. What does one say? It was a compliment and I'd been taught to be gracious.

'You've made this summer so much more than I'd anticipated,' he added.

'But I so wish you didn't have to go,' I said, tearfully, unable to be like my mama, unable to hold back.

He turned to me. 'Perhaps it's for the best that I shan't be able to see you, at least for a while. You'll be coming out soon enough, and I've no doubt, no doubt at all, that it'll be just as Venetia predicts . . . you'll be inundated with admirers, Clarissa . . . and I'm not sure I'd like that.' He smiled. 'You see, I'm very much aware that I've had you to myself these past few weeks.' He lifted his hand to my face, ran his finger down my cheek. 'And I've known you in a way that no one else will ever again be able to. Because I've seen you before . . . before life's touched you.'

I smiled, even though I wasn't altogether sure what he meant.

'And please, Clarissa, promise me one thing. Promise me that you won't go and get married, not yet.'

I tried to laugh. 'Tom, I'm only *just* seventeen, of

course I'm not going to get married yet.'

'Promise me . . .'

'I promise.'

He'd never been overseas, never crossed the Channel, but if he was afraid of what lay ahead of him he never for one moment showed it. As we sat huddled together on the step, he played with my hands, threading them in and out of his own, turning them this way and that, holding them up to his lips, smelling the scent I'd dabbed on to my wrists before I'd left my room, laying my palm over his mouth. I longed for him to take me in his arms and kiss me. My entire body ached for him. I knew a clock was ticking, knew the moment had to be snatched.

'Tom . . .'

'Clarissa . . .'

'Why have you . . . why have you never kissed me?'

He looked down at my hand, held in his. 'Because . . .' and he sighed, closed his eyes for a moment. 'Because kissing *you*, Clarissa, would be dangerous.'

'Dangerous?'

He turned to me. 'You don't understand, do you?'

'Yes, I think I do, actually. You mean that you don't feel *that* way inclined. That you don't like kissing women.'

And he laughed, laughed so loudly that I pulled my hand away from his.

'Clarissa . . . Clarissa, what on earth goes on in that beautiful head of yours?' he said. Then he put his arms around me and pulled me to him. 'I've spent the last six weeks fighting with myself . . . six weeks trying to do the right thing, trying *not* to kiss you . . . and the reason kissing you, *you*, Clarissa, not anyone else, could be dangerous . . . is simply because I might not want to stop.' He looked into my eyes. 'Now do you understand?'

In the moonlight, and up close, his features had taken on the silver hue of a Greek god—chiselled from ancient stone. I looked from his eyes to his mouth, and then I placed my lips upon his. We kissed slowly, tenderly. He moved his face, pressed his nose against my mouth, ran his tongue across my lips, as though they were a flower whose scent he wished to taste and feel, and smell. He cupped my head in his hands, moved his lips back to mine, and I felt myself falling, sinking down into a place I'd only ever imagined. I wrapped my arms around him, pulling him closer and, as he moved his mouth down on to my neck, I heard him moan, say my name. Then, suddenly, he stopped and pulled away from me. He sat forward, his head in his hands, and I could hear his breathing, loud and fast.

'I'm not terribly good at kissing yet,' I suggested, wondering if perhaps I'd been a disappointment to him.

He shook his head. 'We can't, we mustn't . . .' he said, his voice strained, almost hoarse. And he didn't look up at me.

We sat there for a minute or two in complete silence, and I wondered if I should leave him, if he wanted me to go. But I couldn't leave him, not yet. I reached out, placed my hand upon his shoulder. And then I said, 'I love you, Tom.'

I hadn't planned to say it; I'd simply thought it out loud. But after I'd said it I realised it was what I'd gone to tell him that night. You see, I wanted him to know, wanted him to have something to hold on to, to come back for. And though I longed for him to say it back to me, he didn't. He said, 'No, I don't want you to say that, not yet. Love me when the war is over. Love me when I come back, Clarissa.'

I moved in front of him, crouching down, and when he raised his head and looked back at me his eyes were filled with tears. I took hold of his hand. 'Can I not love you now *and* when the war is over? Because I'm not altogether sure that my heart is able to postpone what it feels.'

He frowned, attempting a smile at the same time, and as we rose to our feet he wrapped his arms around me and held me, so tightly I could barely breathe. He released his grip a little, looked down at me. 'I shall hold you to your promise, Clarissa, because my heart has to know that you're mine.'

'I am yours. I'm yours.'

'Then may I be so bold as to request another promise? Promise me that your lips belong to me too.'

'My lips as well as my heart?'

'As well as your heart, and your mind . . . oh, and your body too,' he added, smiling.

I think we said goodbye at least twenty times before we finally released each other's hands. He made me walk back to the house ahead of him, but followed close enough that I could hear him, behind me. When I reached the stable-yard gate, I turned back to look for him, but he'd gone. I wanted to run back, find him, but as I stood there I heard Mr Broughton's voice, somewhere beyond Mrs Cuthbert's cottage, saying, 'All ready for tomorrow then, Tom?' And I swiftly moved through the gate and back towards the house.

I'd intended on rising early the following morning. I wanted to wave Tom off with the others. But when I awoke it was already seven o'clock. I hurriedly dressed and raced downstairs to the kitchen, colliding with Mabel and a bucket of coal at the baize door.

'Oh, Miss Clarissa, you're up early this morning.'

'Has Tom gone yet, Mabel?' I asked, breathlessly.

'You've missed him. He left for the station with Broughton about five minutes ago. He's going for the seven thirty-eight . . .'

I ran through the kitchen, through the servants' passage, out of the house, across the yard, and grabbed my bicycle. I can't remember the journey to the station that morning, but I remember arriving there, seeing the dogcart and dropping my bicycle to the ground. The train was just pulling up to the platform and at first I couldn't see him—didn't know which way to turn. Then I saw him, and I ran down the platform shouting out his name. He looked startled at first, quite panic-stricken, and then he smiled, walked towards me, and I literally fell into his arms. He held my face in his hands and kissed me.

And I have no idea what Broughton thought of the spectacle in front of him at that moment, how shocked he was or otherwise.

'I love you. I love you, Tom Cuthbert,' I whispered in his ear, and I realised I was crying.

He stood back from me, holding my face in his hands. 'Clarissa,' he said, and then he turned, picked up his bag and climbed on board the train. He leant out of the open window of the carriage door, reached for my hand and then the guard shouted something, blew his whistle and the train began to pull out of the station. I watched him go, never taking my eyes away from his, until he disappeared into a cloud of steam and out of sight.

I didn't hear Broughton at first; I'd quite forgotten he was there.

'Miss . . . Miss Clarissa? I think we should get you back home, don't you?'

Dazed, I followed Broughton out to the cart and climbed up at the front as he picked up my bicycle and placed it on the back. Then he climbed up, pulled on the reins, and we turned back towards Deyning. It was a beautiful morning, a morning which didn't go with war. The sky was pale and bright, completely cloudless, the countryside still asleep. And as we passed through the quiet lanes, I thought of Tom, on his train, bound for France, and of all the other young men heading out to the trenches. None of it made any sense to me. Life made no sense.

We said nothing, Broughton and I, on that journey home, until we reached the gate, and then he said, 'God bless them all. We have to keep faith . . . pray for their safe return. All of them.'

'Yes, we do,' I said. But even then I wasn't sure.

Faith . . . Somehow it seemed a flimsy, insubstantial thing set against a war, like walking out in winter in a fine silken shawl meant only for summer months. Was it enough? Would it be enough? I wondered. I would test God, I decided: I would keep faith in Him—if He kept faith in me; kept Tom safe, and returned him to me, unharmed.

I cleared my throat. 'Mr Broughton, I don't wish to compromise you, but I'd prefer it if you kept my visit to the station this morning quiet.'

'Of course, I understand,' he replied.

I glanced at him. 'Thank you.'

He turned to me and smiled. And I remember thinking how handsome he was, despite his age. He had the look of Romany about him, with his dark butterscotch skin and chocolate eyes; his hands—scorched by sun, stained by earth—so different to my father's pale unblemished hands. He'd been with us for so long I couldn't remember a time when he hadn't been in my life. He was as much a part of Deyning as the old sycamore tree, as rooted and as timeless. And yet I knew so little about him.

I think Broughton kept his promise, but of course I'd forgotten about Mabel, and word of my hasty early-morning departure had been passed on to my mother's loyal maid, Wilson. As soon as I entered the house Mama appeared in the hallway.

'I wish to speak with you, Clarissa. Please go up to your room, I shall be along presently.'

Minutes later, she appeared in my room and asked me to sit down. She picked my nightdress up from the floor, folded it and placed it under my pillow. Then she sat down on the chair by the fire.

'I understand that you cycled to the station this morning, Clarissa,' she said, looking out through the window.

There was no point lying. 'Yes, that's right. I did.'

'And this was all to say goodbye to Tom Cuthbert?' she asked, looking directly at me.

'Yes, Mama.'

'You do realise—you've made rather a fool of yourself, and very possibly tarnished your reputation?'

'I don't think so. I wanted to see him off and I'd

overslept. I don't think cycling to the station and bidding a friend adieu is a scandal. He's going off to war, Mama.'

'Yes, I know that, and I wish him, your brothers, and all the other young men Godspeed and a safe return home. But . . . it doesn't alter the fact that you were seen by the servants, dashing off and in quite a state, as I understand. It's not right, Clarissa, surely you can see that.'

I made no comment. I no longer cared what the servants thought: what did it matter? But I needed to hear all she had to say. And I knew there was more to come, I could tell by the tone of her voice. I watched her as she lifted her hand to a stray curl, twisting and tucking it back in place; each movement slow and measured.

'You need to tell me what has taken place between you and Tom Cuthbert. You need to tell me the truth, Clarissa.'

I hated the way she said his name: over-enunciating the vowels in that manner.

'I don't know what you mean. Nothing has taken place. We're simply friends, Mama, that's all. And I like him . . . enjoy his company. He's been one of us this summer.'

She smiled, closed her eyes for a moment. 'Clarissa . . . Clarissa, you're not a child, you're a young lady now. You know he's not one of us, nor can he ever be. I was happy for him to enjoy some tennis and croquet with you and the boys, but that's as far as it should have gone. I had no idea that you and he had . . . had forged a *friendship*,' and she looked at me, narrowing her eyes, and added, 'or become close.'

'We have not become close, Mama. I told you,

we're friends, nothing more.'

'Well, I do hope you're being truthful with me. You see, it would be very sad for you if it were otherwise, because nothing could ever come of it. Do you understand?'

'Of course,' I replied, looking away from her, my eyes stinging.

'It would be a truly *pointless* and impossible liaison, and only lead to heartache—for you, and for him.'

'I know this, Mama.'

'Good. I'm pleased that we've had this little chat. It's always good to clear the air.'

She rose to her feet, came towards me, where I sat on the edge of my bed. 'You know, you're infinitely precious to me, and to your father. You're our only daughter, our baby.' She stroked my hair. 'We want nothing but the very best for you, the very best,' she said, and then she bent down and kissed my head. 'Now, please tidy yourself up and come down to breakfast.'

And then she disappeared through the door, leaving her words behind her.

Nothing could ever come of it . . . a truly pointless and impossible liaison . . . only lead to heartache—for you and for him . . .

* * *

My Dear, no, I do not believe I have been 'hasty' in my judgement (of that situation), but there is a war now, and tender hearts—even yrs—are NOT always innocent . . . which is precisely why I intervened. Yrs D

CHAPTER NINE

In a matter of days my world changed. And though the sun continued to shine, and the bumblebees and butterflies went about their business, oblivious to world events, the peaches and nectarines in the walled garden went unpicked and began to rot.

Haymakers disappeared from the fields, and the place was eerily quiet, with the air of somewhere after a party has perhaps suddenly and unexpectedly ended. People had gone but an echo of their presence lingered; their voices held in the atmosphere, passed on in the whisper of trees. Croquet mallets lay abandoned by the summerhouse, where Henry and Will had left them after our last game; their tennis racquets out on the veranda, along with Henry's battered Panama hat and George's cricket bat. And there, in a jar upon the table, the wild flowers Tom had picked for me in the meadow now drooped forlornly, wilting in the late summer sun. Sometimes I fancied I saw one of them—Tom, Henry, George or Will—out of the corner of my eye, walking across the lawn, towards me. Once I even thought I heard one of them calling out my name, and I called back across the terrace towards the trees, 'Hello! I'm here! Where are you?'

I wandered in a daze, unable to comprehend the suddenness of so much departure. I walked along silent pathways, through lines of gigantic petal-less delphiniums and foxgloves, standing shoulder high, erect and perfectly still. They'll be back soon, I told myself; they'll all be back soon.

Perhaps they'd be back before the end of summer . . . perhaps everyone could come back and we could resume our summer. But I knew, even then, that this was unlikely to happen. Too many had gone for them all to be able to return before the season's close. It would be autumn, autumn at the earliest, I concluded. And meanwhile, I had an important task to complete.

For my birthday Henry had given me a painter's case: a small square mahogany box with a brass handle, containing tiny tubes of watercolour, a small bottle for water, a folding palette and three brushes. It was old, second-hand, and I liked that. I liked the thought that it had travelled, been carried about over fields, perhaps beyond England; and the case alone was beautiful, a treasure even without its usefulness. The day after my birthday, Tom had presented me with what at first appeared to be a small leather-bound notebook, a new journal I thought; but it was an artist's notebook, containing proper watercolour paper. The first thing I paint in it shall be for you, I told him. And it was. I set myself up down at the boathouse one day and, after roughly sketching out the vista immediately ahead of me, more shapes than detail, I christened my new paints. When I showed Papa my effort later that day, in the library, he'd held it upside down and said, 'Charming, my dear . . . what is it?'

I turned the book the correct way. 'It's the lake and the island . . . and that's the sky,' I said, pointing to the wash of pink and blue.

'Hmm, yes . . . now I see. But isn't it a little *too* blurred?'

I took the book from him. 'It's meant to be. It's impressionistic, Papa.'

I looked back at the painted paper. I'd planned on sending it out to Tom, but now I wondered what he'd see. Would he recognise what I'd tried so hard to capture? Or would he, too, hold it upside down and see only a blurred mess of pale colours?

'Perhaps you should work on it some more. Add a little more detail . . .' Papa suggested, smiling at me. And he was right. It needed more work.

'Yes, I think you're right . . . it's much too pale. I need to add darkness . . . give it more depth,' I said, but he was distracted and had turned back to his map of Europe.

He'd recently pinned the map on the wall above his desk and had it marked with pins and little bits of red and blue ribbon. I suppose he thought he was doing his bit: keeping track, following events. Around the house all anyone spoke of was the war, and now I too was keen to hear about it, to join in. When I left Papa in the library that day I went to the kitchen, where Mabel and Edna sat peeling vegetables at the long pine table. It seemed to me that between them they knew everything, every figure and statistic. And their conversation, so different to the other side of the green baize door, was an endless stream of fascinating detail.

Edna had been with us for years, since before I was born, and Mabel, for at least five years. They were both unmarried and, along with the other female servants, had rooms on the east side of the house, above the kitchen and servants' hall, looking out over the stable yard. They were both younger than they appeared, and I only knew this because Mama had told me. She'd mentioned that Mabel was, surprisingly, *considerably younger* than Edna. So, I'd estimated, Edna was probably nearer to

don't know . . .'

Monkswood Hall, the estate bordering ours, had twice or even three times as much land, a folly, its own chapel, and at least two farms. It also had three times as many servants. The Hamiltons, who owned it, had made their fortune building ships, and were rumoured to be descendants of Emma Hamilton. This rumour seemed to be confirmed by their choice of name for their eldest son, Horatio (known to everyone as Harry). And they were obviously fond of alliteration, for the four younger children's names also began with H: Howard, Helena, Harriett and Hugo. We'd seen quite a bit of the Hamilton children growing up, and I'd attended the last hunt ball at Monkswood with my parents. Like my brothers, all three Hamilton boys had gone off to fight, and I was distracted for a moment by the mention of Monkswood, the memory of that ball, and my dance with Hugo Hamilton.

'But how many have *we* lost?' Mabel asked. 'Got to be pushing a dozen now, countin' John and Frank, and them boys down at the farm. Mr Broughton says at this rate there'll just be him and his barra' left.'

'John and Frank . . . they've gone?' I repeated.

'Been gone since a week past Friday, and Frank's mother—beside herself,' Mabel replied, staring at me, wide eyed.

'But . . . but Frank's not old enough, surely. He's only a few months older than me . . .'

'That's as may be, miss. But them young 'uns always finds a way.'

I thought of Frank, immediately saw his sweet blushing face, and my heart sank. I hadn't said goodbye to him, or to John. And now they'd gone. I looked to Edna, who smiled back at me. 'Don't you fret,' she said, 'the Lord'll keep the good 'uns safe.'

'My cousin . . . she says we'll all have to do our bit . . . all have to do more,' I offered.

Mabel raised her eyebrows. 'Is that right, miss? Well, there ain't enough hours in the day to do what I have to do now—let alone *more*.'

Edna shook her head again. 'Things'll change, that's for sure.'

'And when you think of poor Lottie Baverstock,' Mabel said, looking up from her work for a moment and out through the window. 'Her only just married . . . and him *over there* now.'

'Well, at least she saw some action!' Edna said, and they both laughed, then glanced at me and back at each other.

Edna rose to her feet, the bowl of peeled potatoes tucked beneath her bosom. 'We'll have to settle for dancing with each other at the harvest festival dance, I reckon. What do you say, Mabel?' And she wiggled her broad hips as she moved through the scullery door.

Mabel sighed. 'And there was my Jack about to propose as well.'

'You're to be married?' I asked.

She stared at me. 'Well, yes, miss . . . eventually.'

Growing up at Deyning, the kitchen had always been a place of extraordinary mystery to me, as well as mouth-watering delights. It was an intoxicating muddle of comforting shapes and smells, manpower and secrets, and I'd longed to taste more. For so many years I'd wanted to be part of that camaraderie, wanted to know where Mabel and Edna and all the others had come from, what their stories were. I wanted to understand their jokes and repartee. But by being there, within the warmth of the old range and their banter, I'd caught a glimpse of something: something quite different to the formality of my parents' world. They laughed, and loudly, at things I knew they shouldn't laugh at; they slapped each other's backs and danced without music; and for a while, at least, they had allowed me to join in: to giggle and sing with them, to eat with my fingers and lick spoons. But latterly these interludes had ceased. And now, it seemed, I was no longer allowed that glimpse.

During those first days and weeks of the war I suppose we were all stunned, all in shock. We'd had no time to think, no time to prepare, and almost immediately, even as we grappled with the very notion of war, the carnage had begun. Each day the ironed print of the newspaper delivered us straight to France, to strange-sounding, unknown villages; places we'd never heard of, and perhaps would never have known of, but places whose names we'd be unable to forget for the rest of our lives. By the start of September it was estimated that fifteen thousand British troops had already been killed. Fifteen thousand. Wiped out within a month of summer. And I thought once more of those men I'd heard singing on board the train; singing their way to death.

* * *

. . . I cannot bear to leave this place, & the not knowing when or if we will return, whether it be months or years (as some now say) breaks my heart, & you know why . . . Today we had the Belgian soldiers (8 of them) here for tea at 3 &

afterwards took an excursion through the lanes in the Landau—for what I suspect will be the last time . . . I smiled the whole way, but inside I was screaming.

* * *

The first time I heard them I thought it was thunder: a storm, sweeping in from the sea, over the hills. I lay in my bed listening to it, waiting for it to move in—or fade away. But it didn't. It continued. A dull, distant rumbling, punctuated every so often by something louder, a boom. Those were the *big guns*, Papa told me.

One particularly windy morning my father arrived back from the farm in a state of excitement. He came rushing into the morning room, where I was sitting quietly with Mama—reading the newspaper.

'You should hear it out there,' he said, smoothing down his windswept hair. 'From the bottom of long field woods you'd think the fighting was just beyond those hills. Remarkable,' he added, shaking his head. 'Quite remarkable . . .'

I raced outside and jumped into the dogcart to return there with him, but Mama refused to come. She had no desire, she said, to hear the distant barrage of warfare, particularly not one in which her sons were fighting. We sat in the dogcart on a track at the southernmost point of the estate; and we sat in silence for ten minutes or more, listening to the intermittent juddering and booms, swept across the Channel and into our fields.

'It seems so near . . .'

'It is near,' my father replied. 'Only a narrow

channel of water separates us from that fighting, Clarissa.'

And as we turned and headed home it suddenly hit me: *a narrow channel of water*. If the enemy could push forward, break through our lines, reach the coast of France . . . they could cross that channel of water. I wanted to ask my father questions; wanted to ask him the likelihood of that happening, for if anybody would know, I thought, he would. But I didn't want him to have to think about that possibility. I didn't want him to have to consider that. So I remained quiet. But as we headed back towards the house I couldn't stop this train of thought. For already I could picture the German soldiers arriving at Deyning, marauding about the place, pulling it apart and laughing loudly. And what would we do? What would I do? And what if it happened at night? Of course, of course it would happen at night, was bound to happen at night—under the cover of darkness. I'd have to have a gun, I thought . . . have to be able to defend myself. And I saw myself in my room, my locked door being broken down by laughing German soldiers as I stood brandishing a pistol.

I took a deep breath. 'Papa, I think I should have a gun,' I said. 'I think we should all have a gun by our beds.'

He laughed. 'A gun? But you don't know how to use a gun, Clarissa. And why ever do you need one?'

I didn't want to worry him, didn't want to have to explain to him how things *could* unfold.

'For reasons of safety, of course,' I said. 'To defend myself and Deyning.'

He turned to me. 'You're quite safe here, my

dear. And you really don't need a gun. At least not yet.'

I didn't notice August's end, or September's start. I was hungry only for news: news of the war. I read the newspaper, often from cover to cover and sometimes out loud, repeating entire paragraphs in order to try to comprehend them. As I read of battles, battalions and bombs, my world expanded and took on a different hue. I looked at fatality lists: incredulous, aghast. For how could so many be killed? They had only just gone. And though I tried to accept that my three brothers, along with Tom, were unseen players in that macabre daily news bulletin, it still seemed unreal. Life, our routines, continued at Deyning, but it was different. Everyone was already in some infinitesimal way altered by the sudden cessation of that summer.

My mother, ever resourceful and fervently patriotic, threw herself wholeheartedly into the war effort. She attended the Appeal to Women meetings at the local village hall, and returned full of plans and ideas for a working party; informing my father that we should offer up all of our young and healthy horses, and asking him if the middle meadow could be used as a rifle range. She had endless meetings with Mr Broughton to discuss how best to utilise the kitchen gardens, and even toyed with the idea of digging up the parterre in order to increase Deyning's vegetable production. She briefed the servants on new rules concerning the running of the house, had the drawing room and ballroom shut up, and reassigned the usage of rooms in order to conserve coal. And she set about organising all of us women at home to make war garments: balaclavas, gloves, scarves and socks—

anything deemed useful for *our boys* at the front.

She had George's new gramphone relocated to the morning room and, each evening after dinner, with the air of a colonel organising his regiment, she rounded up her *knitting party*, which included Wilson, Mabel, Edna, Mrs Cuthbert, and myself, fulfilling the role of a private, and delegated the unravelling and rewinding of balls of wool, and the sewing up of mittens. As we sat in a circle, round the fire, serenaded by the crackling strains of Tchaikovsky or Beethoven, we seemed to knit and sew in time with the music. And I wondered who'd wear these things we'd made with so much fervour. Would they hear the music?

'I was thinking, Mama, wouldn't it be wonderful if these mittens were to end up on George or Henry or William's hands?' (Or on Tom's, I thought, glancing at Mrs C.)

'Really, Clarissa, I do so wish you'd think less and try to be a little more industrious,' she snapped back at me.

Her weekly trips to London had stopped, and without them she seemed to me to be unnecessarily short tempered. Could her incessant train journeys and interviews with parlourmaids and the like really be so important to her? One evening she'd burst into tears when I asked her if she'd one day take me to stay with her at the Empress Club. And I wondered then if she simply enjoyed the hurly-burly of travel and if there was not some neglected Romany spirit lurking beneath that immaculate, pale exterior.

I wrote to Tom almost every day. And cycling to the end of the lane—where the road forks and the postbox stands in the middle of a triangle of grass—I felt the thrill of subterfuge: for I was having an *illicit* affair. Yes, it was a love affair, the beginning of a Great Love Affair, and the thought of him holding my letter in his hands, casting his eyes over my words, was intoxicating, heady stuff. When the weather became inclement I coerced Broughton into posting my letters for me. After all, he knew my secret, he'd seen me; seen us. And I'd already told Tom to send his letters to me via Broughton, at his cottage. Broughton appeared quite untroubled by this arrangement and became used to me, I'm sure, appearing at his door or by his side somewhere in the garden. He'd pull the paper from the pocket of his apron and hand it to me with a curious, knowing smile. But quite often he'd be with Mama, and usually in the greenhouse or the hothouse, bent over some tiny specimen in a terracotta pot, examining its possibilities. And then I'd swiftly turn.

I sent Tom my watercolour of the lake, though I still wasn't at all happy with it. But it was home, I thought, something for him to remember and hold on to; and I'd painted it for him. I shall treasure it, always, he wrote to me, and I couldn't help but wonder if he knew what or where it was. But did it matter?

I told him of the magnificent white owl in the pine tree beyond my bedroom window; how I'd watched it fly off towards a huge silvery moon one night and imagined it was flying straight to him, carrying a tiny rolled-up note from me. But what would that tiny rolled-up note say? he'd asked. 'That my heart beats only for you,' I replied. I told him about the enormous spider recently taken up residence outside my windowpane, its shimmering fly-filled web growing day by day. I like to think of that spider, he replied; I like to imagine I'm that spider, looking back at you through your window, watching you. I told him of my solitary afternoon excursions, rowing across the lake to the island: the water murky, the air damp and filled with smoke from bonfires. I shall row you there one day . . . I shall take you there, and spend the whole day listening to your voice, studying your face, he wrote. Do you think of me? Do you think of me now? I asked, hungry for more. Always, he replied, *You're my vision, Clarissa, my beacon of hope.*

I found myself seeking out Mrs Cuthbert more and more; being with her made me feel closer to Tom, and I often had to stop myself from blurting out her son's news, having received a more up-to-date letter than she. I sat at the table in the kitchen, chatting to her, asking her questions, gathering whatever snippets I could: stories and anecdotes about his childhood, which I later recorded in my journal. There was never any mention of Mr Cuthbert, and I'd long since dismissed Henry's queer remark in the dining room that day. And Tom had told me anyway, told me what he knew: that his father had died shortly before he was born, that there'd only ever been him and his mother. But he must have been a tall man, I thought, a handsome man; and quite different to Tom's mother, who, sweet as she was, was a diminutive woman with no obvious beauty. They looked so different, and Tom had such an entirely different demeanour to that of his mother. Sometimes it was hard for me to imagine that Mrs Cuthbert had actually given birth to *my* Tom.

We were still counting the war in days then.

Sunday, November the first, was the ninetieth day, and in church we all prayed once again for a swift end to the fighting. Could it end by Christmas? Would my brothers and Tom be home by then? I imagined us all singing carols under the tree in the hallway, the war already in the past, already a memory.

In one of his letters to me Tom quoted some lines from Blake, I think: *To see the world in a grain of sand, And a heaven in a wild flower, To hold infinity in the palm of your hand, And eternity in an hour . . .*

But I could tell by the tone, by the words he chose not to write, that he was living through something too awful to speak of. He never mentioned love, never mentioned the future, but he told me that he thought of me upon waking and when he closed his eyes and tried to sleep. I prayed for him in church, and for my brothers too. I thought of him as I walked through the grounds, had conversations with him in my head; I pictured him smiling; imagined his hand in mine, his lips touching mine; and each night I dreamt of him.

I played games with myself, handing out questions for the universe to answer: if this pebble lands beyond the jetty, he'll come back to me; if *that* leaf blows down from the roof, it means he'll marry me; if the owl hoots once more it means I shall receive a letter from him in the morning post.

I had to be careful to rein in my ecstasy after receiving any letter from him. This was certainly not the time to be wandering about the place singing or whistling a jolly tune. And so I tutored myself in the art of solemnity, kept my euphoria private, and adopted a serious demeanour in keeping with everyone else and the general ambience of the house. I continued my solitary daily walks about the estate, carefully choreographing scenes and conversations yet to happen. I returned to those places of our clandestine moments together, replaying them in my head, languishing in his treasured words . . . and sometimes adding more. I stood under frosty sunsets, my warm breath mingling with the cold evening air as I watched the silent flight of birds across the sky. And even in those twilit autumnal days I felt a light shine down upon my path. For though he was no longer at Deyning, no longer in England, the fact that he lived and breathed had already altered my vision; and nothing, not even a war, could quell my faith in the inevitability of his presence in my life.

* * *

. . . I am close to our front line now, not far from Neuve Chapelle, & close enough to hear the fighting. It's been rather warm here of late, and the roads—all cobble-stoned—are hell to march on, particularly in the heat, but the Route Nationale is as straight as a die & one can see for miles & miles across the countryside. Did I tell you, we're not allowed to have white handkerchiefs? In case we're tempted to raise them up into the air and wave them about like a white flag. Those who knew absolutely no French now know 'Mouchoir rouge'! In fact, we seem to be inventing new French words by the day, Franglais. I'm compiling a list (of those suitable for your eyes) and will send them on to you soon . . . I know you'll be amused.

CHAPTER TEN

MDD, Yes, he knows . . . he knows that which I crave is the very thing he is quite unable to give me . . . but I fulfil my role, and this is what matters to him. It is futile . . . & yet to give up on the dream is like killing off a part of oneself. That part which was once everything, a guiding light, a promise, a hope. Life is NOT simple, but it is to be LIVED. Yr D

*   *   *

Christmas came, but it was not the same, and there was no end to the war. We read about the ceasefire, the Christmas truce on the Western Front, and then we heard about it from Henry, and from William too. In separate letters and in different words they told us how they'd sung carols and exchanged gifts with the Germans. They'd shaken hands with the enemy in no-man's-land and, Henry told us, played football with them. And I found it more than a little confusing to reconcile these images of bonhomie and fellowship with the subsequent and ongoing killing. How could they sing and be joyful, thankful, together, then kill each other? And why? I pondered on this and then asked my father, but he could offer me no satisfactory answers, nothing that made any sense.

Early the following year my parents and I decamped to our house in London: a tall, stucco-fronted Georgian building, overlooking Berkeley Square. The place had been shut up since the previous spring, for though Mrs Watson, our cook and housekeeper, and Mr Dunne, the elderly butler, remained in situ there, my parents preferred to use their respective clubs for short excursions up to town rather than open up the house. The added complication of the transference of servants from Deyning to London always caused my mother some consternation, and with Deyning running with less than its full complement of staff, this had become even more of a headache to her. Prior to our departure there had ensued a great deal of debate about who, exactly, was to come with us to London and who should remain at Deyning. In the end, only Wilson and Mabel came with us, and my mother yet again faced the prospect of trying to recruit servants.

Our London home was, I suppose, simply a smaller, more compact version of Deyning, with rooms situated in a less predictable order. Here, the servants were based below ground, in a warren of basement rooms, including the kitchen and servants' hall; at ground level, my father's study, with a connecting door to his billiard room, and a smoking room; on the first floor, the formal reception rooms—including the drawing room and dining room; immediately above, and taking up the whole of the second floor, Mama's suite of rooms, with its Chippendale Chinoiserie furniture and hand-painted Chinese silk walls. My father's bedroom and dressing room, as well as my brothers' bedrooms were situated on the third floor, whilst my room and three spacious guest rooms occupied the fourth floor; and, at the very top of the house, the servants' attic bedrooms.

The view from my bedroom window in London

was quite different to that at Deyning. Facing westwards, not south, it looked out upon the back of town houses like ours, across slate rooftops, stables and small courtyards. Unlike ours, few of the houses appeared to have any garden, and but for the occasional ornamental tree, rising up tantalisingly from a moss-covered brick wall, my view was devoid of Mother Nature's soft curves. But when the sun slipped down behind the rooftops, and the sky turned from a smoky grey haze to a brilliant pink, everything in my room took on that luminous blush: the dark brown wood of polished mahogany transformed to a fiery coral; the cream silk of my bedcover to a shimmering rose.

However, I was not to witness many sunsets that particular season, for despite the lack of eligible dance partners my mother was determined that I should still have some sort of coming out, and sooner rather than later. And so, after being fitted out with new gowns, we began the somewhat muted merry-go-round of tea dances, entertainments and *At Homes*. At that time, I had no idea that my mother's determination to get me up to London—away from Deyning—was in any way linked to Tom. Fate, I thought, seemed to be conspiring against us. For without Broughton, without anyone to attend to the actual postage and receipt of letters, it was impossible for me to correspond with him.

It was my father, still commuting between London and Deyning at that time, who informed us that Tom had been home, on leave, and that he'd seen him, spoken with him. I was bereft. He'd been home for two nights, Papa said, and the morning before my father left he'd saddled up his horse for him, and politely enquired after me.

'Decent chap, young Cuthbert,' my father said. 'He'll make his mother proud of him yet.'

I wanted to ask my father so many questions; I wanted to say, how did he look? What else did he say? Where is he now? When will he return? But Mama's eyes were already upon me and so I said nothing. But I wrote to him later that evening, determined to get a letter to him if only to explain my absence, and my silence.

The following morning I asked Mama if I could take Caesar for a walk across the square. It was frosty and cold, but the sun was shining. Yes, she said; yes, do that. And so I marched out across Berkeley Square, and then scuttled off in the direction of Bond Street, with Caesar, and the letter, hidden inside my coat, tucked into my dress, next to my heart. In that letter, I explained that I was stuck in London, that I'd had no choice in the matter, and that I was devastated to have missed him at Deyning. I told him that the parties and tea dances were all a crashing bore, littered with silly giggling girls and awkward boys with weak chins. I told him that none of it meant anything to me. I told him that I'd write to him whenever I could, and that he should continue to write to me via Mr Broughton, and I'd be able to collect his letters when I returned to Deyning:

. . . And I'll wait for you, my darling. Even if it means waiting until I'm old and grey, I'll wait for you. Because I love you with all my heart and everything I am. And nothing anyone can say shall ever alter that . . . So know that I am yours, and will only ever be yours: heart, mind, lips and body, yours, always,

Clarissa

I walked back to the house deliriously happy,

and even Caesar must have picked up on my mood because he yapped excitedly all the way home.

It was not impossible. It was my life, and he was My Love.

The following week Mama hosted a party for me: *Mrs Granville, At Home . . . Dancing 9.30.* But I had no interest in that party, or in any of the other rather sombre dances and parties we attended. When the band played the national anthem at the end of each event (each ordeal), I felt relief. I hated the endless introductions, the pointless conversations, and those stupid, fawning boys. All I could think about was Tom, and his letters—waiting for me with Broughton. And I longed to get back to Deyning. I wanted to tell the other girls, 'This is not really me. I'm only doing this to please my mother; I've already met the man I shall marry . . .' But of course I didn't. I danced with young officers and played the game, under my mother's watchful eye.

'So-and-so seemed awfully keen, Clarissa,' she would say, always encouraging, steering me towards a particular young man she'd spotted, taken a shine to. And I was always vague and non-committal in my response. 'You really do need to give a little more of yourself, dear,' she said to me after one particular ball. And I couldn't say to her, 'But Mama, I have nothing to give, my heart is taken,' so I pretended that I didn't understand what she meant and inadvertently allowed her the opportunity to coach me in the art of flirting.

'You need to smile more,' she said. 'Perhaps giggle at their jokes, *even* if you don't find them amusing . . . look at them when you speak . . . and accept their compliments graciously.'

thirty than forty, despite her matronly appearance, and Mabel—a good few years younger.

I showed them both my painting, asked them what they thought.

'Oh yes,' Edna said, squinting at it under the light. 'It's pretty . . . very pretty, miss. Is it the lake?'

And I think I yelled, 'Yes! It is, it's the lake, and look, that's the island . . . it's not finished, of course, still needs more work.'

'Very atmosphereful. Oh yes, you're artistic, Miss Clarissa. Always have been. Hasn't she, Mabel?'

Mabel wiped her hands, took hold of the book and studied it for a moment. She was always more reticent than Edna, and compliments were not easy for her.

'Yes . . .' she said, looking up at me with a tight smile. 'Very good.'

'Shall I . . . would you like me to paint something for you, Edna?' I asked, glancing over at her and smiling.

Her face lit up. 'Ooh, yes, I should say. Yes, I'd like that. I don't have any paintings, you know? Not one.'

'I'll do it then,' I said. 'I'll paint something for you next. But it might be . . . it might be more abstract.'

'Abstract? That sounds lovely, dear,' she said, as I took the book from Mabel and sat down at the table.

And as I pondered on my next 'commission', they resumed their conversation: the one I'd interrupted when I'd walked into the kitchen.

'And over twenty more gone last Friday—an' most of 'em from Monkswood too,' Edna said, shaking her head. 'How they'll cope there now I

It was all so tedious, so unnecessary. I watched the other girls and thought how ridiculous they seemed, for their mamas, too, had obviously coached them, and seeing them put into practice everything my own mother had tried to teach me made me determined not to fall in line. Somehow my defiance, my aloof demeanour, appeared to have the opposite effect, and I was inundated with dance partners and overtly keen suitors. And Mama, forgetting her previous advice, said, 'Of course, the other gels are much too keen and far too flirtatious. The reason you're so popular, my dear, is not simply because of your beauty, but because you hold back a little, and that's always quite intoxicating to a man.'

Tea, it seemed, was a much bigger, grander occasion in London than in the country. And everyone dressed for it. In gowns of sable-trimmed silk, satin brocade and velvet, and gathered around white linen-covered tables, piled high with sandwiches, scones, muffins, crumpets and cake, the latest gossip was passed on. But none of it, no matter how sensational or titillating, was of any real interest to me. You see, in my head I'd begun to write the story of my life: the story of my life with Tom, how it could be, how it *would* be. I was stranded between two worlds, lost in a twilight place of never-ending possibilities. Occasionally, and often in the clatter of real conversation, I'd find myself mouthing the words of an imaginary conversation, one yet to take place. And once or twice Mama had felt the need to surreptitiously tip me out of my reverie with a little kick or a sharp nudge. Then, usually en route home, she'd pour forth. 'Really, Clarissa, you seem to be growing more distracted by the month! Gels are supposed to grow out of daydreaming when they become young ladies, otherwise they appear . . . well, simple.' She'd sigh, turn and look out of the window. 'I'm tempted to take you to Doctor Riley . . . truly I am.'

Once, after Venetia had hosted a tea dance for me, I'd overheard a conversation between her and Mama. The two of them had removed themselves upstairs, to Venetia's boudoir, and I'd gone up to tell them that people were beginning to leave. I could hear Venetia's voice beyond the door, slightly ajar, and I stopped.

'I'm quite certain you've no cause to worry . . . she may be dreamy, but weren't we all once? And she's a sensible girl.'

'Sensible?' Mama repeated. 'It's not a word I would necessarily use to describe Clarissa . . .'

'But she's growing up, dear. Working her way through that filtering process. I remember it well, and it is somewhat daunting. Especially for a girl who has had such a sheltered life . . . perhaps you should have had her up to London more often.'

'Yes, you're right, and I realise that now. She's spent far too much time down at Deyning . . . on her own . . . traipsing about the fields, reading poetry . . . talking to the trees . . .'

Venetia laughed. 'Ah, but she's beautiful . . . and the boys do seem to fall at her feet, not that she notices—as you say—but then that in itself is *très charmant*. I'm sure she'll forget about him in time. Truly, I shouldn't fret; these sorts of crushes do fade, and if we're honest, haven't we all fallen foul of them—at some stage or another?'

I heard Mama sigh, then Venetia added, 'We need to steer her in the right direction, my dear, that's all. And perhaps the sooner we can have her engaged the better.'

I didn't want to hear any more. I coughed, opened the door.

'People are leaving,' I said flatly, staring at my mother.

'Oh gracious, and we were just about to come down, my dear,' Venetia replied quickly, moving forwards. She stopped, ran the back of her hand down my cheek. 'Such a beautiful goddaughter.'

I was furious: angry with my mother for talking about me in that way, and for discussing Tom with Venetia. Venetia who had been seducing Henry for goodness knows how long. But perhaps Mama knew, perhaps she condoned that sort of behaviour. Perhaps that sort of behaviour was acceptable within the confines of her tight circle of friends, for it seemed to me as though there were distinctly different rules for different people.

As we walked home from Venetia's that day I was quiet, mono-syllabic in my replies to her. I half wondered if she'd say something to me about her conversation with Venetia, if she'd realised that I might have overheard. But she was distracted; worried she was late for a meeting. Her latest rallying cry was for the Belgian refugees. She'd become involved with the Red Cross, attending endless meetings—trying to arrange housing for them. She had also recently been assigned a 'district' and visited the workhouse in Marylebone each week. But the plight of the Belgian refugees seemed to have come between her and her wits, and having already proposed that the parkland at Deyning be handed over to the army for training purposes, she'd suggested to Papa that we offer up the house to the homeless Belgians. She was a patriot, determined to do her bit, stalwart in her defence of her world.

When Mama and I returned to Deyning, briefly, and with Papa, I could barely contain myself. There would be at least twenty letters, I thought, waiting for me with Broughton, and all I had to do was get to him, to think of a pretext to get out of the house and meander towards his cottage. I felt dizzy and sick with excitement. And I was becoming cunning in my duplicity.

'Shall we go for a long walk, Mama? To deep dene perhaps, and then back by the lake?' I suggested, as our motor car passed through the white gate. I knew that the very last thing my mother would feel like was a long walk after the journey from London. And I was right.

'Oh, Clarissa, I think you'll have to take your walk alone, dear. I'm much too tired and I need to speak with Mrs Cuthbert and the servants . . .'

* * *

I couldn't understand it. There were no letters. None at all, he said.

'But are you quite sure? You see, it simply doesn't make sense, Mr Broughton.'

We were standing by the greenhouse in the walled garden, and he didn't look at me. As he spoke he kept his eyes down, looking into the wooden barrow in front of him, piled to a peak with darkest earth.

'Yes, I'm quite sure. There've been no letters . . . none at all.'

'I see.' I turned and walked away.

No letters, no letters . . .

I wasn't ready to go back inside the house, to face Mama, who'd immediately notice the change in my mood. I wandered down the pathway, towards the gate I'd skipped through only minutes earlier, and as I turned to close it I paused and looked back at Broughton. He was standing in the same spot, staring back at me, folding his hat in his hands. But then he looked away, put his hat back upon his head, picked up the long handles of the barrow and disappeared inside the greenhouse.

I walked through the stable yard, past Mrs Cuthbert's cottage. He'd been there, quite recently, I thought, glancing up at the small window poking out from the red tiled roof. He'd been back and I wasn't there. I stopped at the gate, ran my hand over the gnarled oak of the thick gatepost. His hand had touched that: had he thought of me? Then I lifted the iron latch and walked on into the field. The grass was long, heavy with dew and shimmering with gossamer. In my haste, I hadn't changed my shoes, hadn't supposed I'd be walking far.

No letters, no words . . .

When I reached the boathouse I sat down upon the damp steps and looked out across the lake. The day had a lifeless feel to it: the countryside silent and perfectly still, the water colourless and flat, and the air cooler than I'd anticipated. The sky hung low, so close to the earth it seemed to almost touch the water in front of me. I looked down at my feet, began to pick off the blades of wet grass clinging to the leather of my shoes. We'd made a pact, I thought; and I'd risked so much to get one letter to him. And I'd copied out a poem for him, by Emily Brontë.

In summer's mellow midnight
A cloudless moon shone through
The open parlour window
And rose trees wet with dew.

I sat in silent musing
The soft wind waved my hair
It told me heaven was glorious
And sleeping earth was fair . . .

* * *

. . . Yesterday we marched some 20 miles, stopping for tea and rum, & then on again, but the rum keeps us warm—& morale is quite high. Some of the men who joined us have gone for weeks without any real sleep or respite, & have not removed their boots in as long. They've had no proper meals, nothing hot, and the temperature has suddenly plummeted. When they fell out of line we tried to pick them up, but the CO came along with his stick. He had to. He couldn't leave them there—they'd have frozen to death . . .

CHAPTER ELEVEN

Dearest T, I do what I believe is best for ALL of us, which is not always easy, & my responsibilities—to everyone—weigh heavily on me. I too cannot bear this reality, but what choice do we have? We must nurture

brave hearts, & pray for peace & for all that is noble, and good and fine. I neither know nor understand what 'might lie ahead', but I do know that without US my life would be devoid of all hope and beauty. It makes me utterly and unbearably miserable to think of you lonely and sad, & to know also that it is beyond my power to ease your suffering, but I want to remind you how very close you are to my heart, now & always . . . and ever in my thoughts . . . in haste,
Yr D

* * *

We remained at Deyning for only three days before returning to London, and for me it was a thoroughly miserable time. The house had been requisitioned and my parents and Mrs Cuthbert were preoccupied with inventories, organising the removal of paintings and any items of value. Mrs Cuthbert, Mr Broughton and a few others were to remain at the house, as caretakers, but my father was upset and agitated at the prospect of army personnel trampling through his precious home. 'It'll be wrecked,' he said, shaking his head. Huts for soldiers were going up in the grounds, and the whole place had already taken on a somewhat gloomy, neglected look. Windows now stood bare, their views somehow altered and made ordinary by their lack of lavish frame. Stripped of its furniture and glorious interior colours, Deyning had become like a museum emptied of its exhibits. Certain rooms were to be used for storage and would remain locked, their ghostly contents shrouded in dust sheets. Other things were to be transported to London. The rooms I'd known since childhood now stood bare of family treasures and personal memorabilia. The curtains, carpets, rugs and tapestries, which had for so long cushioned our existence, lending the place softness and warmth, had been taken down to be put away for the duration of the war, and the whole place echoed with an unfamiliar sadness.

'But what if the war ends soon?' I asked my mother. 'What if we wish to come back here?'

'Sadly, I don't think that will happen, Clarissa. People are saying that this war may go on for years.'

I sat upon the staircase, watching Broughton and the few remaining men from the estate carrying endless tea chests and crates, furniture and carpets. Back and forth, and back and forth across the marble floor, directing each other as they manoeuvred larger pieces through doorways.

'Steady there . . . a little to the left . . . that's it. Careful now . . .'

I felt as though I was watching the dismantling of a stage set; theatre in itself. I watched as they carefully carried Mama's portrait—covered in a blanket—from the drawing room through the front door and out to a waiting wagon. It was moving to London along with us. I watched them carefully take down the chandelier in the hallway, for that, too, was moving up to London. I shuffled along the step as Wilson and Mrs Cuthbert trudged up and down the staircase carrying hatboxes, bags, and tied bundles of linen and towels.

I remembered all the Christmases we'd celebrated, always with a huge tree, situated next to the staircase where I now sat. As a child, I'd sat upon that same step, huddled up against the balusters, studying the tree, its shape and decorations; enthralled by the magical light and shadows upon the walls around me. Dancing. Over Christmas the only light in the hallway had come from the silver candelabra burning on the hallway table. But on Christmas Eve and Christmas Day night small candles were attached to the branches of the tree, their soft light reflected in the vast chandelier suspended high above and thrown back across the walls like stars across the universe. I remembered the smell, that mingling of pine and wax and burning logs: the smell of home, the smell of happiness. I'd sat there in my nightgown, listening to the chime of crystal; the laughter, music and voices emanating from another room, an adult world I could only imagine. And always hoping for a glimpse of Mama, as she whooshed across the marble floor, beautiful, resplendent . . . invincible.

It was nearly always Stephens, my nursemaid, who'd find me there and march me back up to the nursery floor. 'But I only wanted to see Mama,' I'd plead, as she secured the gate at the top of the stairs.

'Your mama is busy, Miss Clarissa; you know that. And she wouldn't be pleased to see you running about the place in your nightgown now, would she?'

I wasn't sure. Would she be so displeased? Mama loved me. She told me so. More than anything in the world, she said. Stephens didn't know this of course. Stephens didn't understand. How could she? She didn't have a mama like mine.

Quite often Stephens found me hiding behind the jardinière in the corner of the hallway, trying desperately to align myself with its narrow stand, trying to be invisible; but my usual hiding place had been inside the dumbwaiter, which carried Mama's breakfast tray and meals up to the nursery floor each day. Oh, how much fun my brothers and I had had playing in that! We'd sent each other up and down and up and down, with Henry inevitably in charge of the pulley, as the rest of us gathered intelligence, spying on Mama and the servants . . . and hiding from Stephens and the dreaded Miss Greaves. And only once did it get stuck: with poor Georgie inside it. The ropes had become tangled—from overuse, Stephens later said. We could hear his desperate cries for help echoing throughout the house, as though he were trapped down a very deep well. And then, when I became somewhat hysterical and began to cry, because I really did wonder if we'd ever get him back, Henry had shouted at me to shut up, which had only made me cry all the more.

Of course those childhood games and adventures had long since ceased, but they remained a part of Deyning, a part of the world I was leaving.

'You all right there, miss? Not too cold?' Wilson asked as she passed me on the stairs.

I was freezing. Without carpets and furniture the house was cold, and colder still from every door standing open to the elements, and the air had a dusty, acrid smell to it. But I continued to sit there, lost in the warmth of my memories. Occasionally Mama appeared, directing operations with a slight frown but a steady, calm voice. My father remained in his library, amongst his last remaining boxes of books. Later, in her boudoir, Mama told me how hard it was for him.

'This place is everything to him . . . everything,'

she said, tearfully. 'We must rally him, Clarissa. You mustn't allow him see you looking so miserable . . . otherwise he will feel even sadder.' But I realised at that moment that she was speaking of herself. Though my father was unsettled by the upheaval and chaos around him, he was essentially a pragmatic man. It seemed to me that it was Mama who was shaken and sad. And I was surprised, and wondered why, because she'd been the one who'd wanted to hand the place over to the army, and to the Belgian refugees; and because I was unused to seeing my mother upset or agitated by anything. And it still seemed so unnecessary. Why did our home have to be packed away? Why could Papa not have said 'no' to the army? It was *his* home after all.

My parents' grim acceptance of a long war shocked me. It seemed defeatist in itself; a blindly pessimistic acquiescence in something which had for me, up until that point, at least, been a temporary state; something which *could* be endured and lived through, and then, at its end, normality restored. But their quiet acknowledgement of a long struggle ahead and the sight of our home, our lives, being dismantled and packed away for an indefinite period shook me out of that dream. And it made me begin to realise that perhaps I hadn't fully come to terms with what was taking place across Europe.

*   *   *

. . . I don't understand why you haven't written, and now my heart is fit to burst & I feel even more desperate, because we are leaving here, leaving Deyning, & I shan't be here when you

return (there is no IF, only WHEN). Today I walked down through the meadow to the lake & I thought only of you, I thought of you all day, & all day yesterday, and the day before that . . . If this reaches you, please write to me . . . write to me in London. Everything here is truly awful, but nothing compared to what you're going through . . . Oh my darling, I love you, I do love you, & I don't care what you say about waiting until this thing is over . . . I know only what I FEEL.

* * *

On our last night at Deyning we retired to our beds early. With nothing of comfort to sit upon—and nothing much to look upon—it seemed the only thing to do. In my bedroom I stood for a while in my nightgown looking out of the window. But there was little to see or bid adieu to. The moon lay on its back, slumped in the distance beyond the trees: a bright white sliver of a crescent, rocking low in the blackness, like a deflated balloon, which had shrivelled and then slipped.

Perhaps not surprisingly, I slept badly that night, my dreams filled with Deyning, and angst-ridden conversations with a whole array of people about its future. And for the first time in years another dream came back to me.

When I was young I'd had a recurring dream about an invisible door, a kind of opening in the ceiling of the drawing room, through which all sorts of strange children were able to enter the house. Literally, dropped in from above. That night I dreamt I was standing in that place once again, and this time the sun shone down through the invisible hole in the ceiling. I felt its heat, and an utterly sublime sense of peace. Then, through the sunshine, it began to rain, and as I stood there, my arms outstretched under that heavenly shower, and looking up into the light, a tiny girl fell through the hole to my feet. She was a child, but so very, very small, with black hair and the brightest blue eyes. She smiled up at me with perfect white teeth. 'He's always here,' she said, pointing. I turned, and looked into darkness. And when I turned back to her—she'd gone.

Early the following morning, before setting off for London, I stood on the terrace with Papa watching armoured biplanes fly over the house. Like a swarm of tiny toy flying machines they buzzed high above us, moving in and out of mist and low cloud.

Will . . .

My brother William, by now attached to the Royal Flying Corps, had been taught to fly in a matter of weeks, and had only recently been deployed to the war zone, piloting one of those tiny wooden biplanes over the muddy fields of France and Flanders. I turned to my father, and when I saw his face he looked so different to the Papa of my childhood: anxious and, suddenly, old.

I took his hand in mine. 'Don't worry, Papa, God will keep William safe.'

He looked down, shook his head. 'I'm not so sure . . . no, I'm not so sure God can keep them safe.'

'Don't say that,' I said, gripping his hand. 'We have to keep faith . . . we have to. The war will end one day soon,' I went on determinedly, and despite knowing that no one, least of all my father, believed this. 'Then things will go back to normal. All will be as it was.'

I'd never heard my father talk like that, never seen him look so troubled.

He sighed, looked skywards again. 'Yes, yes, the war will end one day, Clarissa, it has to; but England will be a different place, the world will be a different place . . .' He turned to me. 'And you know, I rather liked things as they were. I've never wished for change . . . and I'm too old for it now,' he added, releasing my hand and walking away.

I took one last look across the ragged, uncut lawns. The air smelt of decay and rotting vegetation, and a chilled grey mist hung over the place, almost but not quite obliterating colour and shape, but blurring lines, rendering everything in front of me gloomy and drab: a ghost of what she once was, I thought.

Minutes later, as our motor car pulled away, I turned and looked back at the house. In front of it stood Mrs Cuthbert, Mr Broughton and the handful of servants who'd helped to pack the place up. And as we moved away, down the long avenue of beech trees, I watched them become smaller and smaller, and smaller still, until they disappeared into the stone façade of Deyning, and then, finally, it disappeared too. As we passed by the white gate and turned out on to the road I wondered if we'd ever again live at Deyning, if life would ever be the way it used to be. And I thought of *him*, somewhere in France. He'd return there, God willing, but I'd no longer be there. Deyning was not part of my life any more, and, it seemed, neither was he.

* * *

. . . When we finally arrived in the town we simply flooded the place, & then lay about in the streets waiting to find out where we were to be billeted. A few of the chaps here seem to think the worst is over, & we're all praying, hoping that this is the case, and that by the time our turn comes we'll have had some good news . . . but in truth I know this is unlikely. Anyway, I am in a small farm cottage with five others, and a fire! So for now, at least, I am warm, and able to think . . . think of you.

Part Two

CHAPTER TWELVE

We regret to inform you . . . the telegram began. *Seen to fall . . . shot down over enemy lines.*

I didn't and couldn't believe the words, though I saw them for myself. For how could my brother, William, be dead? He'd only just learnt to fly, only just gone. And the war would surely be over soon. It was a mistake, it had to be. There'd be another telegram, I told Mama; another one to tell us that they'd made a mistake. He was twenty years old, people didn't die at that age, didn't get killed. His face flashed before me, animated, laughing; alive. It was a mistake, it had to be; a dreadful mistake. But I saw the line in my mother's brow, an ever-deepening line. I saw my parents' grief. And the sight of them sobbing into each other's arms told me that the only mistake was my heart's inability to accept my brother's fate. William *had* been killed. And I kept saying it to myself: *William is dead . . . William is dead.*

Weeks after we'd learned of Will's death Papa took ill with pneumonia, and my mother's grief was postponed while she focused her attention and energy on him. The doctor came to the house each morning, and as I stood on the landing, straining to hear the hushed conversation below me, I heard him repeat one word: grief. I wondered then if Papa felt guilty, for he'd been the one who had persuaded William, eventually, to go and fight. I'd heard them arguing in the library, days before William signed up. 'No son of mine will be a shirker!' Papa had said, and in an unusually loud and angry voice.

Of course, there could be no funeral for Will: like so many others, his body, what—if anything—was left of him, could never be recovered. All that had been returned to us were a few items of uniform, two books and some letters. I pondered on that, and on those words, *seen to fall*. But I could not bear to think of my brother falling from the sky; hurtling towards the ground, on fire, knowing he was about to die. It was too much. And without a body, without evidence, how could they know for sure that he'd been killed? Could he have survived? Was it possible? Sometimes this train of thought offered me a glinting light of hope. I imagined Will arriving back at home, laughing at us for thinking him dead, and then explaining that he'd been on some secret mission: under cover, behind enemy lines. It *was* possible. It could happen. At other times it made sense to me that my brother, the theology student, the one closest to God, had been plucked from this life in the heavens. I'd close my eyes. Of course! William didn't spiral back down to earth; he simply cast off that reluctant soldier's body . . . his soul remains up there, in the sky. William: an angel.

I thought of Tom, wondered where he was. Did he think of me still? Did he remember me? I tried to recall our conversations, but fact and fiction had muddled themselves, and I couldn't now be sure if some of the lines I credited him with were mine and not his. I tried to picture his face, those dark solemn eyes, but already his image had begun to fade. Sometimes his face would come to me, in all its beauty, and then slip away again. And I'd struggle, struggle so hard to conjure it back, focusing on a specific moment . . . that evening by the ha-ha, when I'd watched him as he smoked his cigarette; and I could *almost* picture his profile. But like every other cherished memory of that last summer, it too had faded. I tried to remember his kiss, the feel of his lips upon mine, but it seemed as though that memory, too, was slipping away from me.

Don't leave me; never leave me.

My mother forgot all about parties and balls. She spent her days scouring the newspaper for names she knew, searching through the Roll of Honour, tracking the movement of regiments, battalions, and events *over there*. Henry was mentioned in despatches, and so too was Jimmy Cooper. But a son's fearlessness on a battlefield in another country only exacerbated the sense of fear and dread at home. And, rather than an end in sight, we appeared to be going further and further away from *the beginning*, from that point of faith and hope and optimism.

Long numbers, numbers with more noughts than I'd ever seen before, were printed each day: 500,000 men to Rumania; 300,000 more men needed; 70,000 more men despatched; 126,000 men taken prisoner, 258,000 casualties . . . endless numbers, printed in heavy black ink. We read of the German prisoners transported to Frimley, where crowds had gone to see them—only to discover they'd already been transported to the Isle of Man. We read of the German submarines off the coast, torpedoes and air raids; bombs dropped on familiar seaside resorts up and down the country. And we read of the continuing struggle at Ypres. We read about asphyxiating gases and pulled out the encyclopaedia; of the events in Basra, the Dardanelles and Gallipoli—and pulled out the atlas. We read of the sinking of the *Lusitania* and of more airship raids on the coast. And in the early hours of the morning of May the thirty-first the Zeppelin arrived, and we heard the bombs fall on London.

Together and separately we surveyed the endless daily images of war published in the *Illustrated London News:* double-page black and white photographs straight from the front; drawings of scenes of carnage, our troops and the fighting. I studied these pictures with a morbid fascination, for the churned-up, charred landscape they depicted was unlike any I had ever seen or could ever—even in my worst nightmares—have imagined. It was the landscape of Hell. And the notion that Tom or my brothers could be one of the murky figures in the foreground was too horrendous to contemplate.

Somehow, amidst all of this, life continued. Father slowly recovered and began to come downstairs in the evenings. He listened to me play my new pianola, and we played bridge and piquet. We read *The Gates of Doom*, and then *From China to Peru*, with my mother and I taking it in turn to read a chapter out loud. When Papa was stronger we went out to the pictures and to the theatre. London hadn't shut down. We saw *Flag Lieutenant* at the Haymarket and *A Girl Like Me* at His Majesty's. We joined in the fervour of patriotism, celebrating our troops' victories and sending parcels out to *our boys* taken prisoner in Germany. Each evening in London there was an atmosphere of camaraderie and defiance; we were stalwart, ready for anything, we thought. If our sons and brothers at the front could cope, so could we.

* * *

. . . Why have you not written? Why have you not replied to my letters? I know that you're out there, I know in my heart that you're alive, & I pray to God every single night to keep you safe. Please, please, if this reaches you, get word to me—somehow, let me know that you are still mine, for I am yours, & shall always be YOURS.

* * *

I'd known Charlie Boyd almost all of my life. He'd been at school and at Cambridge with Henry; was one of The Set, as Henry called it. In physical appearance he was the opposite of Tom: shorter, broader and fair, with freckles, blue eyes and strawberry-blond hair. He was without doubt the funniest of Henry's friends and took delight in sending himself up. I liked that about him more than anything else. I thought, underneath all that bluff and bravado there was something very decent and, perhaps, rather vulnerable too.

My parents knew the Boyds well, and Mama adored Charlie. He'd written to her about Will, assuring her that his death would have been instantaneous; that it was far better for him to have died a valiant hero's death than to have been left disfigured, traumatised or disabled for life. He succeeded in making Mama believe that Will's life had not been in vain, that she must be proud of her son's sacrifice and, though I remained unconvinced, I was grateful for the comfort his words gave my parents.

*   *   *

. . . We are all in shock & utterly bereft at our loss, and though I feel the aching void in his passing, a part of me feels equal to the country now in my suffering. And yet what strange justification—to offer up our sons & align ourselves in grief, as though our sacrifice were all the more noble by its magnitude. But I hold steadfast & will not succumb to self-pity, and I could not have lived through these past few weeks without your words, so wise, so considered, & so true. He was, as you say, a radiant force for good . . .

*   *   *

I can't remember when I began to write to Charlie, but I imagine it was shortly after Will died, after he'd written to me. I began to look forward to his letters, they were always upbeat, and there was always something reassuring in the words he chose to write. He'd been in our lives for so long, was a part of a continuum; part of our family, I suppose. At first our letters were the letters between dear friends, or brother and sister, but they quickly became something more. It was inevitable. The war heightened all emotion, every sentiment was amplified, every longing accompanied by a sense of urgency. There was no time to ponder, to reason or to speculate; each thought and feeling had to be recorded and passed on. It was our duty as women, we were told, to keep our boys' morale high: to let them know that they were missed, that they were loved; that someone was waiting for them back at home. And in a way I think I truly believed that my letters and thoughts would keep Charlie safe, keep him alive.

It had been almost a year since I'd last heard from Tom, and though I still thought of him, wondered where he was and included him in my prayers, I'd begun to wonder if I'd ever see him again. And the thought that I might not, the thought that we might never again know each other, had slowly begun to reduce me, eroding my hopes, and the potential of my life. I knew I could survive without him—yes, I would survive—but the thought of a lifetime without him made the path ahead narrower, dimmer.

Over the course of one year my life had irrevocably altered. I had changed and I knew he would be changed too. We would never again be the sweethearts who'd sat upon the steps of the boathouse looking up at the stars. And even if we did, if we could return to that place, if we could recapture that moment, would we see the same stars? Would he look at me that same way: tilting his head to one side, staring at me sideways through a wave of almost black hair, smiling? We could never again be who we were; and we would never be the people we'd once been destined to be. He would always have a special place in my heart, but he no longer held it, I reasoned. And I could not allow him to. I could not have that breadth and brightness back—only for it to disappear once more. For that, I knew, would surely kill me.

* * *

. . . He is raging about the newspapers & says it will be a bad thing for us if America declares war on Germany, but—after the Lusitania*—I'm not so sure. The feeling in America seems to be very strong, but at least the newspaper editors here are being restrained—for once . . . In the meantime, I am v busy with my district, the refugees have been moved and now we have POWs in their place, and all sorts of criminals! And London continues to stand tall.*

CHAPTER THIRTEEN

. . . I have no wish to describe this place to you . . . except to say it is Hell, a squalid, sickening & rancid Hell, inhabited by brave-hearted lunatics. I close my eyes & try to imagine you, so perfect, so beautiful. You remain my vision, my beacon of hope . . .

* * *

It was just after Christmas, the second Christmas of the war. Charlie had had one week's leave and was returning to the front. He'd come to stay with us overnight in London, and had already asked if I'd see him off the next day; and it was the thing to do. That evening, after dinner, my parents retired to bed unusually early, leaving Charlie and me alone in the drawing room. We'd been sitting side by side on the sofa when he took my hand in his and said, 'You must know, I think, how terribly fond I am of you, Clarissa.'

'Yes, yes, I think I do,' I replied, looking down at my hand in his and wondering what was to come.

He cleared his throat, turned towards me. 'I'd like to think that perhaps you felt the same way . . .'

'Oh yes, of course. I'm very fond of you too, Charlie.'

He smiled, his pale blue eyes suddenly quite misty. 'Thing is, Clarissa, I think I'm more than fond of you. Thing is, I . . . well, I love you.'

For a moment I thought he was going to cry. He looked down, squeezed my hand tightly. 'You see, I've always rather liked you, but it's grown into something more . . . and your letters, well, they've kept me going, you know. A letter from you, your name, it somehow makes me feel invincible.' He looked up at me. 'You mean the world to me, Clarissa, the world . . .'

I pulled my hand from his, lifted it to his face, and ran my finger down his cheek. 'Dear Charlie, you are adorable.'

And then he leant forward and kissed me.

His kiss was different to Tom's: tentative, gentler; less passionate, but perhaps kinder. He wrapped his arms around me and pulled me to him. And then, in a playful and overly effusive way, he began to cover my face in kisses, telling me, between each one, that he loved me. The way Papa used to do when I was a child. I began to laugh and then he did too. 'I'm so happy,' he said, looking at me and smiling. 'If I die, I shall die a happy man.'

'No! Don't say that. You're not going to die, Charlie Boyd, do you hear me? You are not going to be killed in this wretched war. Otherwise I shall be very, very cross with you.'

He laughed again. I loved to see him laughing like that. There'd been so little laughter in our home for so long and Charlie had brought it back.

We sat in silence for a moment, and he held my hand once more. Then he moved from the sofa down to the floor, and on to one knee. He took hold of my hand again, looked up at me with newly serious eyes.

'Clarissa . . .' he began, and I knew what was coming. 'This may be a little premature, may not be the perfect time, but I have to ask you . . . will you do me the honour . . . will you marry me?'

I wasn't prepared. I hadn't expected a proposal that evening. And what could I say? I couldn't say 'no'. I couldn't let him return to war burdened further by my rejection. I thought of Tom, and I heard my mother's words: *Nothing could ever come of it . . . a truly pointless and impossible liaison . . . only lead to heartache—for you and for him* . . . I stared back at Charlie, into those kind blue eyes.

'Yes, Charlie . . . yes, I will marry you.'

* * *

The foyer of Waterloo station that evening was chock-a-block: parents seeing off sons, wives clinging to husbands, children wrapped around the legs of their fathers.

'This is a bloody nightmare,' Charlie said. 'Let's get a cup of tea or something.'

We walked arm in arm across the heaving concourse to the station restaurant, and inside we managed to find a table tucked away in a corner. As Charlie summoned over a waiter and ordered a pot of tea for two, I removed my gloves and unbuttoned my coat. When I looked up, there he was: sitting a few tables away from us, with a girl.

I didn't quite know what to do. Charlie had his arm around me, was busy saying something about his train and without thinking I moved my chair away from his and looked in the opposite direction. I felt sick. I didn't want to see him with that girl; didn't want him to see me with Charlie.

A moment later he was standing in front of us.

'Oh, hello, Tom,' I said, as though we'd seen each other quite recently; as though I didn't really care. 'I think you may have met Charlie at Deyning. Charlie, you remember Tom, Tom Cuthbert . . .'

Within a minute the four of us were huddled round the small table: Tom, his girl, Gloria, Charlie and me; looking for all the world like reunited old friends.

'I'm so sorry about William,' he said. I nodded but said nothing. I still wasn't able to talk about Will in the past tense. In fact, I didn't like to speak about him at all.

'You know the trains are all cock-a-hoop, old boy? With a bit of luck we may find ourselves stuck here for sometime,' Charlie said, and then he turned to me and added, 'But poor Clarissa so hates these wretched goodbyes, don't you, darling?' And he pulled me to him in an overly tight embrace.

He and Charlie would be travelling on the same train to Dover and as they discussed the journey ahead of them, what time their crossing was likely to be, Gloria leant towards me. Wide eyed and smiling, she said, 'Tom's only had a few days. But we've made the most of it—if you know what I mean,' and I felt myself my face tingle. I glanced over to him, caught his eye.

'Yes,' I said. 'Yes, of course.' I didn't know what else to say to her, didn't want to talk to her.

'You haven't seen him in a while, have you?' she asked, quietly.

'No, it's been . . . been some time,' I said, pretending to look for something in my bag. It had been sixteen months.

'I could tell. He looked like he'd seen a ghost when you walked in here,' she whispered.

'So, what have you two lovebirds been up to?' Charlie asked, smiling at Gloria, who giggled. 'Making up for lost time, I'll bet!' he added.

I glanced at Tom again, who looked awkward and attempted to smile back at me. And then I stood up and excused myself. In the ladies room I lit a cigarette and smoked it slowly. I was in no hurry to return to our impromptu little tea party and Charlie was irritating me with his *bon vivant* manner. As I sat in front of the mirror, swaddled in my new fur-collared coat, smoking, I pondered on Tom and his girl: they'd quite obviously spent his entire leave *making up for lost time* as Charlie had so succinctly put it. What on earth did he see in her? She wasn't his type at all, I thought, and then, as I stubbed out my cigarette, she appeared.

'I do so like your coat, Clarissa,' she said. 'And I bet it cost a bob or two.'

'Thank you,' I said, rising to my feet, picking up my bag.

She was short, a good few inches shorter than me, and curvy in a way that was no longer fashionable. Perhaps he liked that shape. Perhaps I was not his type after all.

'Have you and Tom known each other long, Gloria?' I asked, glancing at the mirror and tucking an imaginary curl back in place.

'Oh no, not long at all. But you know how it is—when you feel as though you've known someone for ever? That's how it is with us.' And then she disappeared behind the lavatory door.

When I returned to the table, Charlie and Tom were drinking glasses of beer.

'You'd better not let anyone see you drinking,' I said as I sat down.

The King, along with various members of the government, had recently vowed to abstain from alcohol for the duration of the war, to set an example and encourage others to do the same.

'Ha! I hardly think one beer's going to lead to ruin. And apparently we've another hour, darling. I'm sorry, I know how much you hate these places,' he said.

'No, not at all,' I replied. And then I leant over and kissed him on his cheek.

He looked quite bashful for a moment, glanced at Tom, and said, 'Golly, what it is to be loved, eh, Tom?'

Tom said nothing, and I didn't look at him; I continued to stare at Charlie with what I imagined to be love-struck devotion. And even when Gloria sat back down at the table, I kept my gaze resolutely upon Charlie, who glanced back at me with a look I can only describe as muted excitement.

'Would either of you girls like a little something?' Charlie asked, beginning to seem agitated by my continued gazing. 'Clarissa? A cocktail, perhaps? I'm sure they'll be able rustle you up *something* . . .'

'Not for me, thanks, Charlie. I don't on Sundays,' Gloria said.

'Darling?' Charlie asked again.

'Yes, why not. A glass of champagne, please,' I replied.

Gloria giggled again.

'I'm not sure they'll have champagne here, sweetheart . . .' Charlie said, looking about for our waiter. 'But I shall go and enquire.'

I watched Charlie get up from the table, kept my eyes on him as he moved through the crowd towards the bar, as though mesmerised by some vision just beyond the khaki uniforms. I heard Tom say my name, 'Clarissa . . .' but I continued staring in Charlie's direction. I don't know why. But I couldn't bear to turn and look into his eyes.

Then she spoke. 'Clarissa . . .'

I turned to her, smiling.

'I think Tom was trying to talk to you, Clarissa.'

'Oh, I'm sorry. Yes, Tom?' I said, finally looking directly at him, into his solemn, unsmiling eyes. And for a moment, as he held me there, in silence, I knew that we both wished away our sweethearts. I knew that we were both in agony.

'How is your father? I heard he's been quite ill,' he said.

'He's much better now, thank you.'

'And your mother? Is she well?'

'She's quite well, thank you. And yours?'

'Yes, she's also well.'

He glanced down at my hand, resting on the table, moved his own towards it, and then looked up into my eyes. 'And you, Clarissa . . . how are you?'

I stared at him, unable to speak. From the corner of my eye I could see Gloria glancing from me to him then back to me.

'Sorry, darling, no champagne, I'm afraid, so I've

ordered you a sherry . . .'

I wrenched my gaze away from Tom to Charlie. 'That's perfectly fine,' I said. 'And perhaps more appropriate. After all, we have nothing to celebrate. Not yet.'

Charlie turned to me, smiling, took hold of my hand and said, 'Or perhaps we do . . .'

I shook my head, mouthed the word 'no'. We'd agreed to keep our engagement quiet, at least for the time being, and so no one apart from our respective parents knew. He squeezed my hand, nodded. I glanced over at Tom; he was watching us and I wondered what he'd seen, if he knew.

We sat there for what seemed to me an interminable time. I hardly uttered a word, but Charlie and Gloria chatted animatedly, and Tom managed the situation with a quiet calm. I was aware of him watching me as I sipped my drink, as I glanced about the place, as I smiled from time to time at Charlie and at Gloria, feigning interest in the conversation. I tried not to look at him. I tried but I couldn't. And when I did, when I finally allowed myself to look back into his eyes, I could barely breathe. My longing for him simply overwhelmed my senses, blocking out all other sight and sound.

'I imagine Clarissa's changed somewhat since you last saw her, eh, Tom?' Charlie said, and I realised he must have noticed Tom staring at me.

'Yes. Yes . . . she's quite grown up,' he replied, still looking at me.

Charlie picked up my hand, kissed it. 'And you know what? I think I'm the luckiest chap in all of England.'

Gloria laughed. 'Aah, isn't that lovely,' she said,

addressing me. 'You're a lucky duckie and a half. I wish someone would say that about me,' she added, winking at me, and then she glanced at Tom, who'd turned away and was looking across the restaurant.

I pulled my hand away from Charlie and said, 'I think we'd best get going now, dear.'

And as Charlie finished his drink and summoned the waiter for the bill, he said, 'Allow me to get this, Tom.' Then he turned to Gloria and said, 'It's been a rather pleasant surprise to have had this little seeing-off party to ourselves, has it not?' and she laughed again.

I glanced once more at Tom as Charlie settled the bill, but he didn't look at me. He stared out of a window behind me, frowning, his jaw set. I wondered what he was thinking, and I yearned to touch him: to reach out and take hold of his hand. When we stood up and moved outside to say goodbye, before those final, private adieus on the platform, he simply shook my gloved hand.

'Goodbye, Tom. And good luck,' I said, forcing a smile.

He stared at me, into my eyes. 'Goodbye, Clarissa.'

My heart lurched as he turned and walked away, his girl on his arm, and Charlie must have seen something in my expression, because he said, 'Is everything all right, darling? You've been acting a little peculiar all evening.'

'These goodbyes . . . they're just so wretched,' I said.

On the platform, as Charlie held me, I looked for Tom. But I couldn't see him, or his girl.

'You best go now, get yourself a seat,' I said.

'So long as you're sure you're fine.'

'I'm fine, Charlie, really I am. *Bon voyage*, sweetheart.' He held me, kissed me, but I was distracted—and I know he sensed it. And as he climbed on board the train, I felt my heart shiver. 'And Charlie . . . please, do look after yourself.'

I stood there for some moments, and then, as the guard passed by, I asked how long until the train departed. He pulled out his pocket watch: 'Three minutes, miss,' he replied. I moved down the platform, searching the packed carriages, excusing myself as I weaved my way through uniformed soldiers, embracing couples and bags. I know it sounds awful now, as though I didn't care about Charlie, and I did, I really did care, but I had to see Tom again. I knew I'd hear a whistle blow at any moment and that would be it. I knew that I might be making a fool of myself but I didn't care. I knew he had his girl with him but it didn't matter. Nothing mattered. I was almost at the end of the platform when I stopped and glanced through a window, and there he was.

As soon as he saw me we smiled at each other and in a way that would have been enough: enough for me to hold on to and perhaps enough for him too. But he leapt up, disappeared for a moment and then reappeared at the open window of the carriage door. And I was already there, of course. We had seconds.

He reached out and took hold of my hand as I climbed up on to the footboard. He pulled off my glove, held my palm over his mouth; his eyes closed. And I couldn't speak. I wanted to say so much but the words wouldn't come.

Then he looked at me. 'Clarissa,' he said. And that was all he said: my name. The whistle blew, he let go of my hand and I stepped down. As the carriage lurched and began to pull away I stood perfectly still, my eyes fixed on him: his eyes, his face, and then his outline; until the front of the train curved away, and he disappeared from view.

I stood there for some time watching the packed carriages as they moved along the platform, a blur of khaki and smoke, and unknown smiling faces. And even after the light at the end of the train had vanished I continued to stand there, staring down the empty track into the blackness. I can't recall anyone else on the platform, yet I know it was crowded, that I was surrounded by people. I thought: my heart is on board that train; my heart is bound for France. It wasn't over. It would never be over.

*   *   *

In the taxicab, heading home, I realised I was missing one glove.

CHAPTER FOURTEEN

My father died on September the seventh, 1916. He was fifty-eight years old and for me, at least, his death was sudden and premature. He'd never completely regained his former health or vitality after his bout of pneumonia the previous year, and when he became ill for a second time, my mother had feared the worst and tried to prepare me. He was laid to rest in the mausoleum he'd built at the churchyard close to Deyning.

Three weeks after my father's death, late one evening, we received a telegram. Mama read it out. And for an indeterminable time everything stopped, and I was there and not there.

Then I screamed.

A scream so loud it shattered and splintered into a dreadful chorus that rattled and shook my brain and bones and cells and soul. I grabbed the telegram from Mama's hand, threw it on the fire, ran out of the room into the hallway, and then outside, into the square; and I continued running, zigzagging down streets, through mews, on and on, as though I could escape from that moment; escape my brother's death and run back through time.

Eventually, I stopped running. I stood in the darkness on a street corner and looked up at the sky. It's a mistake, I whispered; it's mistaken identity. *Mistaken identity . . . identity mistaken . . . not George . . . would never let himself get killed . . . professional soldier . . . mistake.* Then, shivering, my head pounding, numb with shock and the cold night air, I turned and began to walk home.

When Mama led me upstairs, holding on to my hand, she said to me, 'We have to be strong . . . we have to be brave; we have to be heroic, like George and William.'

Oh yes, Mama, they're all heroes . . . they're dying by the thousand to be heroes.

She made me take a pill, told me it would help me sleep, calm me. But I didn't need a pill, for there was nothing left in me; no sound to make, nothing to say.

The telegram I'd destroyed had informed us that George had been badly wounded at Flers-Courcelette, and that he'd been taken to a casualty clearing station, where he'd died from his wounds, hours later, on September the seventeenth. George had died exactly ten days after Papa's death, and I wondered if he'd known, and I hoped he had not. Mama had of course written to both him and Henry, but she'd refused to send either of them a telegram and had delayed her letters to each of them until after Papa's funeral.

Still in the depths of a very private grief, my mother was plunged further. And though she'd spoken of bravery and strength, it was then, immediately after this unspeakably cruel coincidence, that I saw her character momentarily crumble. For days after we learned of George's death she remained within her room, in her bed, unable to speak, unable to eat, unable to cry. In the space of twenty-four months she'd lost two of her sons, her husband, and her home.

Unlike Will, George was returned to us. Mama arranged for his body to be collected from Waterloo station and taken to a nearby undertaker. On the evening of his return she finally rose from her bed. She asked me to accompany her to the chapel of rest, but I couldn't bear the thought of seeing George, dead, so I waited in the motor car while she went inside. When she finally emerged from the building and stepped back inside the car, she looked even more fragile, and unspeakably pale. I took hold of her hand, and she turned to me and smiled.

'He's at peace now,' she said. 'He's with William, and Papa.'

The following morning we returned to the chapel of rest, and I watched as my brother's coffin was carefully placed inside the hearse, our wreath of white lilies laid on top. Mama had been adamant that we should accompany him, that he should have every honour befitting a beloved son, a fallen hero. She'd shuddered when the undertaker had visited us and spoken about train times to Guildford and onward connections. 'I shall take him,' she'd said, as though she planned on driving him there herself.

We followed the hearse slowly and in silence through soot-blackened streets, through the wide leafy avenues of newly built suburbs, and then out on to the meandering country lanes. It had rained heavily overnight and the roads were awash with mud, fallen branches and debris from the fields and hedgerows. A few miles from the churchyard, where the road forks in two and the postbox stands on a grassy triangle, there had been a landslide, forcing us to take a different route: the road past the entrance to Deyning. And I remember thinking, it's meant to be, we have to take George this way. And as we came round the bend in the road, over the brow of the hill, I could see the chimneys, the rooftops in the distance.

I said, 'There it is, Mama, there's Deyning.' But she didn't look. And even as we passed by the white gate she didn't turn her head.

At the church there were a few of the staff from the house, including Mrs Cuthbert, Mr Broughton and some of the servants from London. Mabel and Edna—both now employed at a factory near Croydon—Stephens and Wilson, Venetia, Aunt Maude and a handful of Mama's friends made up the small gathering of mourners. Inside the tiny church, we prayed for George's soul. We prayed for peace. And we sang. We followed the coffin out of the church, down the muddy pathway towards the mausoleum. And there, I watched my brother's journey end. Weeks away from his twenty-first birthday, his life was over.

. . . ashes to ashes, dust to dust; in sure and certain hope of the Resurrection to eternal life, through our Lord Jesus Christ . . .

I felt my eyes sting, my lip begin to quiver. I turned to Mama, standing next to me. She held her gloved hands firmly in front of her, her heavy black veil concealing any private agony. I heard the iron door close. I glanced over at Maude, who looked to Mama and then moved towards her. I bit my lip, clutched on to my purse. And as I closed my eyes I heard myself whisper my brother's name: *Georgie*.

A few days later a brown paper parcel containing my brother's uniform arrived at our home in London. I unpacked it myself, in the hallway. It stank, was stiff with mud and blood: George's blood. I stood holding it, looking at it, unsure of what to do with it. It wasn't until Mrs Watson appeared and placed her arms around me that I realised I was crying.

'But what will you do with it?' I asked, as she tried to take it from me.

'It'll have to be burned, miss . . . you can't keep something like that, now can you? And if you ask me, it's not right it's been sent back here, not right at all.' She pulled the last remnants of George from my hands. 'Should never have been sent here,' she repeated. 'I'll get Mr Dunne to deal with it. Now don't you worry . . . you go upstairs and Mrs Watson'll bring you a nice cup of tea.'

I saw them do it. Saw them burn it, in the garden outside. I watched from my bedroom window. George's blood, posted back to us for old times' sake, rose up in a plume of dark grey smoke and disappeared into the London dusk. And Mama knew nothing about it.

In the weeks that followed, ever mindful of her own decorum, my mother struggled to regain her former equilibrium, but she appeared unsure of herself and, I suppose, of the events taking place around her—over which she had no control. She became needy of me, reluctant to leave the house, and she fretted endlessly about Henry, the last of her boys. Her boys: her three boys, now one. Looking back, I realise it was also around this time that she began to worry about money.

I comforted myself with the knowledge that George, a born soldier, had died as he would have wished: in battle, fighting for his country. Unlike Will, and a professional soldier, George had never had any doubt about his duty; never been tortured by any moral dilemma about the notion of war or, it seemed, of killing men. I remembered the debates my brothers had had in those tense days immediately before war was declared. George had been resolute, uncompromising in his views, whilst Will had prevaricated, and Henry been somewhat flippant.

Without Papa, and with Henry away, I had to be strong. I heard my father's voice in my head: 'You must be strong, Clarissa . . . stay strong for your mama.' And so for a number of weeks, perhaps even months, I ran my mother's home. I dealt with the servants, handled the accounts and tried to keep the place looking as it always had. I wrote to friends and family, and I wrote to Henry, informing him of George's death. I mourned my brother, cried in private, and I wondered not if, but when another telegram would arrive. What then would we do?

The intoxication of youth, snuffed out, extinguished in a matter of months, left in its place only a numbing sobriety. For too many young souls had already been sacrificed, too many lives shattered. And to those of us left standing, impotent, on the sideline, with splintered hearts and broken dreams, light had all but vanished from our lives. No matter what happened in the future, things could not be undone. George and William, and thousands upon thousands of other young men would never be coming home. None of us could return to that briefest of moments before the war, when the heady anticipation of a life unfulfilled lay before us. It had gone for ever.

Each day I had studied the casualty list published in the newspaper, running my finger down it, quietly saying the names out loud and all the time silently pleading with God for there not to be a Granville, a Boyd or a Cuthbert on the list. But after George's death I stopped looking. I no longer wished to see that ever-growing list of names. I even suggested to Mama that we cancel our daily newspaper delivery. But she was insistent upon following events. As long as Henry and others she knew were out there in the trenches, she could not abandon her vigil.

Like me, the newspaper editors appeared to be growing demoralised and losing their patriotic fervour. They were preoccupied by the country's grievances, and the outcry against the food shortage seemed to outweigh the outcry against the guns and munitions shortage. A 'Food Controller' was hastily appointed by the government, but with

German submarines increasing in number almost daily, there was little for him to control. There were complaints, too, that too many shirkers had evaded the 'call-up', that Mr Asquith and his government had not been forceful enough, and the whole country seemed to be in an angry, malevolent mood.

Night raids had become more frequent. The maroons sounded and I'd head down the four flights of stairs, from plain carpet to patterned carpet to marble and then, finally, to the linoleum of the cellar steps, along with Mama, Mrs Watson, Mr Dunne, and whomever else was in the house at that time. There, we'd all sit around an old pine table, trying to play cards by candlelight, once or twice to a juddering vibration, and the tinkling of the chandelier in the hallway above us. I'd watch Mama fix her gaze upon the ceiling, concentrating, willing the monstrous thing not to fall. But I can't recall any hysteria or melodramatic outburst. When the all-clear eventually sounded, there was never a rush, never an immediate departure back up the linoleum-covered steps. We'd all invariably sigh, sit in silence for a few minutes, then, slowly, collect ourselves and begin the move back upstairs by candlelight: Mama to her Chippendale Chinoiserie and hand-painted silk walls; me to my rosebuds.

Mama continued going to church and, though I usually accompanied her, I'd begun to feel ambivalent about a god who presided over so much death and destruction. I no longer wished to take Holy Communion, though I did, simply to keep Mama happy. The body and the blood of Christ: what did it mean any more? I mimed the words of hymns; *all things bright and beautiful* and England's *green and pleasant land* no longer resonated with the times. And I found myself questioning the words of our prayers. *He that believeth in me, though he were dead, yet shall he live: and whosoever liveth and believeth in me, shall never die*. But there could be no resurrection, I thought; no bugle would ever herald *their* return. The dead were dead and would never be coming home. They lay buried in the blood-red mud of another country for all eternity. How serene could peace be after this? How sweet would any victory be?

Even though I walk through the valley of the shadow of death, I will fear no evil . . .

The valley of the shadow of death . . . it seemed to me a fittingly concise description of our country. For though we weren't living in those squalid trenches, though we weren't facing that endless juddering barrage, we were living through a time of extraordinary darkness, when life seemed only to be about death.

*   *   *

I had heard nothing from Tom, nothing at all, but Mama had been kind enough to tell me that Mrs Cuthbert was well, and still at Deyning. Then, one evening, as we sat playing piquet, she said, 'I hear Tom Cuthbert's an officer now . . . a captain. He was mentioned in despatches . . .'

And there he was again.

I imagine she thought it safe to mention him, now that I was engaged to be married. Both she and Papa had been delighted by my engagement. She'd told me that I'd made my father very proud, and happy; that it was the one good piece of news in years.

'Oh really?' I replied, without looking up.

'I know you quite liked him, Clarissa. I know you and he had a . . . a friendship,' she continued, arranging the cards in her hand, 'but it could never have worked, never. You must realise that by now,' she added.

I glanced up from my cards. For a moment I contemplated saying something; telling her that I hadn't *liked* him, I'd loved him, and always would; that it wasn't a friendship, it was a love affair. But then I thought better of it. After all, she'd been through so much.

I looked back at my cards. 'Mrs Cuthbert must be very proud of him,' I said.

'I'm sure. He was a nice enough chap. Your father always said that, had a great deal of time for him.'

I looked up at her. 'Yes, I think he rather liked him.'

She smiled, closed her eyes for a moment. 'I'm sure he did, but he was a servant, dear. I don't suppose your father would have liked the idea of him as your suitor.'

'He was not a servant, Mama. He was studying, studying law . . . and he may yet end up practising it.'

'And good luck to him. I hope that he survives this wretched war and makes something of his life. But you, my dear . . . well, your life was always destined to be *quite* different to his. And still will be. Quite different.'

I stared at her. 'All our lives will be different after this war, Mama. Look at us: our lives have already changed.'

I felt irritated by the way my mother was talking. How was I so different now? How were we so different? Her sons had been as fallible as any others on the battlefield.

She looked down at her cards, sighed. 'Clarissa, Clarissa . . . your head's always so full of romantic notions. We must accept the life we're born into, my dear, no matter how irksome or dull we find it at times. The war will end . . . one day, hopefully soon, and then you shall resume your life. You'll marry; have a family, a home of your own. And Charlie will make a fine husband. A very fine husband.'

I said nothing more. Mama still had her dreams for me: an eligible husband, Charlie, a big society wedding, a town house and a country house, children. But I was already having doubts: doubts about marrying Charlie, doubts about everything. Nothing seemed certain, and I wasn't sure what, exactly, I wanted in my life any more; wasn't even entirely sure who *I* was any more. The girl I'd once been, the girl who'd been able to imagine the future—glistening with promise—had gone. I could no longer see ahead, no longer see the possibilities. And if Tom Cuthbert wasn't to be part of my future, what was there? For he had starred in every fantasy, each and every dream.

I still thought of him, dreamt of him, but so much had changed, and my life in London had propelled me down a path he was not on. I had no idea where he was, how he felt or what he was thinking. I knew nothing other than the fact he was alive, somewhere. For news of any death travelled quickly and my mother's continued obsession with the daily fatality list ensured an up-to-date, albeit grim, knowledge of our ever-diminishing circle of friends and acquaintances. He may have met someone, may be engaged; may even have married Gloria, I thought.

If I'd received one letter, a note, anything at all, I'd have stopped my progression down that path. But there was nothing. He'd never written to me after our meeting at the station that day, and though I'd hoped, even prayed, that our paths might cross again, somewhere, anywhere, they had not. I'd half expected to see him at some party or other, there were always so many army personnel and officers, and I'd gone to any number searching for him amongst the uniforms. I'd scan rooms looking for his face, and occasionally my eyes would pick out a tall, dark-haired man in the crowd and my heart skipped a beat. But it was never him. Why would it be? He was not part of the crowd I mixed with in London. His life wasn't there and never had been. And I was weary from longing, exhausted by my imaginings, and all those anticipated meetings and reconciliations. So I began to tell myself that Tom Cuthbert would never be part of my life again; that he was a memory.

When Henry came home on leave, he'd done his best to be like Papa. He'd sat in Papa's place, assured Mama and me that all would be well. But things were changing, and changing rapidly. Unbeknown to any of us, Deyning had been mortgaged. My father, ever the entrepreneur, had taken risks on the stock market and his losses, which he'd kept from almost everyone, had in all likelihood contributed towards his ailing health. Now death duties coupled with those losses meant that Deyning would probably have to be sold.

Henry had done the sums, with a lawyer, of course. It was simply too expensive to run, he said, and, with the servant problem, much too much of a headache. He'd sat down with Mama and me to try to explain this to us.

'No,' Mama said, quite emphatically, 'Deyning is your birthright, your inheritance, Henry. Things will get better once this wretched war ends . . . and then, then our lives will resume. Things will return to normal *and* we shall return to Deyning.'

'I agree with Mama,' I said. 'We can't possibly sell Deyning, Henry . . . it's our home.'

Henry sighed, shook his head. 'I don't believe things will be the same, and, as much as it saddens me, I don't in all honesty believe that we'll be able to keep Deyning.'

Mama laughed. 'Rubbish! This country has survived many a war. One doesn't start reinventing oneself simply because of a war, dear. We have to stand firm and together, and we have to hold on to all that we believe in, all that we are. Papa would turn in his grave to hear you speaking this way. Deyning was everything to him, you know that . . . and the costs, the servants, well, perhaps we shall have to do what they call *economise* . . . run with fewer servants, though for the life of me I can't imagine how. But . . . if it has to be so, then it has to be so.'

I saw Henry shake his head again, but he left it at that. There was no point in trying to convince Mama, certainly not at that time. Later, I wrote to Charlie: 'Everything is changing. Nothing is fixed or certain any more.'

* * *

. . . Can you believe they sent his uniform home to us? Mr D set fire to it outside in the garden, and I watched it as it burned . . . I still can't believe he is gone, that both of them are gone, & in so short a space of time. I keep expecting one of them—both of them—to appear here, on the doorstep, in the hallway, poking a head around my door, just as they always did, bright-eyed little boys smiling back at me. And this is what I dream of, night after night . . . I try to comfort myself with the knowledge that they were loved, and enjoyed a supremely happy childhood & youth, but yes, a part of me is angry. And, in my darkest and most private moments, & though I know it's hideous and selfish, and that others have suffered just as much, I find myself wishing that He could have taken another, another two, and spared mine. And I wonder, am I culpable? For I let them go . . . encouraged them, and despite knowing how cruel it would be. And now I keep thinking if W hadn't joined the RFC—hadn't gone up in one of those wretched machines—he might still be here, & if G hadn't been so very brave & hadn't gone back to get that boy—he'd still be here . . . but people tell me how noble their (& my) sacrifice, and speak so poetically of Heroism. And though at first I thought I might not live, & felt all my courage slip away, & so much so that I was unable to move or feel or speak or think, it has slowly returned, enough for me to continue living. And of course, I owe it to them, and to those still here. But life will never be the same, & I shall never be the same, for something in me is broken

and can never now be mended.

CHAPTER FIFTEEN

. . . They played a searchlight on us all through the night & then at dawn the bombardment started—the very worst I have experienced so far, with shells raining down all around us . . . it lasted an hour perhaps, no more, but so intense that my ears, head, hands and heart continued to ring & tremble & vibrate for hours afterwards. Three of our horses were killed, and later, we had to load the mutilated carcases on to a wagon and then bury them in a ready-made ditch close by. I hate this place. Hate all of it, & with every part of my being, and yet I know this hatred might very well help keep me alive . . .

*   *   *

I didn't particularly feel like going out to a party that night, but both Henry and Charlie were home on leave, and Henry was keen to be out and about 'on the circuit', as he called it. Food rationing had begun to affect everything, and though restaurants remained open, most had cut down to one or two courses, and—like the theatres—closed early. But behind shuttered windows the whoopla of a party and thumping of a piano could be heard most nights. Nightclubs had arrived in London and bands played on until the small hours; for those boys home on leave were determined to have a good time. We were all determined to have A Good Time.

I spent longer than usual getting ready that evening. I think I almost preferred the anticipation to any actual event. Those idle hours languishing in my bath, listening to music from the gramophone next door; then selecting a gown, and jewellery. Perhaps it was because the evening still lay ahead, uncharted and unknown. It could be anything I wished for it to be. And I loved my room. Mama had allowed me to select new wallpaper and furnishings when we'd moved up permanently from Deyning, and I'd created a rosebudded sanctuary, with matching wall coverings, curtains and bedspread. It was a girlish symphony of pink, and it reminded me of the old rose garden at Deyning.

That evening I chose to wear a navy blue satin gown, one I'd worn before, the previous week, but one Charlie hadn't yet seen and one I knew he'd like. It suited me well, and Henry had told me I'd be 'sure to capture any man's heart in that dress'. I'd borrowed Mama's diamond choker, again, and wore her blue fox stole over my shoulders. The three of us—Henry, Charlie and I—drove only two streets away, to drinks at the Millingtons' before heading on to Venetia's son Jimmy's party, on South Audley Street. Although Jimmy had been at school with Henry and Charlie, he had gone on to Oxford, not Cambridge, and he was the only one of Henry's friends, apart from Charlie, whom I genuinely liked. I wondered then if Henry's affair with Venetia had ended, or if it was still going on. I'd never mentioned it to anyone, and now it didn't seem important. I no longer cared whom my elder brother was sleeping with, just so long as he was alive.

We could hear the revelry as soon as we pulled

up outside Jimmy's. 'Sounds promising,' Henry said, rubbing his hands together. Inside, the place was heaving; the hallway jam-packed with people, noise and smoke; faces I knew and a few I didn't. Almost all of the men were in uniform and everyone seemed exuberant, over-animated. I think back now and realise there was an air of desperation at those parties; as though each one had to be better than the last; as though each one was the last.

We'd been there a little while when Charlie and Henry disappeared off together in search of a bottle and I found myself ensconced in a corner of the hallway with Rose Millington—whom I'd just seen at her parents' house—and a few others. I was laughing at Rose's impersonation of her mother—she was so funny, a brilliant mimic—and as I turned away, as I turned away from her, laughing, I glanced up and saw him: sitting on the staircase, watching me. And I looked away quickly, I'm not sure why, perhaps because it had happened before; because I'd been to any number of parties where I thought I'd spotted him, only to realise it wasn't him. I thought I'd imagined it. So, I turned again, slowly, and looked back.

I felt my stomach tighten, couldn't move; couldn't even smile. And I can't recall him moving down the staircase, but a moment later he was standing in front of me.

'Hello, Clarissa,' he said, so close we were almost touching.

'Tom . . . what are you doing here?'

I didn't mean it as it sounded. I was shocked, unprepared.

He raised one side of his mouth, half smiling in

that way I remembered. 'I bumped into Jimmy on the boat train yesterday,' he said. 'I saw you arrive, was on the stairs . . . thought you'd seen me.'

I shook my head. 'No . . . no, I didn't see you.'

His face had changed: older, thinner, and so very pale, as though he had not been out in the sun for years. Like most of the others he'd grown a moustache, and that wave of almost black hair, which had once hung down over his eyes, had gone. And those eyes—staring back into mine—seemed darker, with a new intensity, a new depth and vulnerability to them.

'I've three days' leave. I'm heading down to Deyning tomorrow,' he said, and then he frowned. 'I was so sorry to hear about your father . . .'

'And I imagine . . . I imagine you know about George,' I said.

He nodded. 'Yes, I heard. You've been through such an awful time, Clarissa . . . awful.'

'No different to anyone else really. Life's not exactly turned out the way we all expected, has it?'

He looked down, shook his head.

'But you're here,' I added, desperate to lighten the ambience, 'and that . . . that *is* good.'

He bit his lip, looked back at me, his head tilted to one side, and I placed my hand upon his arm. 'I can't begin to imagine what's it been like for you, Tom . . . what it must be like out there.'

And because he didn't speak, didn't reply, and because I thought I needed to fill that silence with words, I continued, 'And I've thought of you . . . I've wondered about you, how you are, where you are . . . and wondered if our paths would cross . . . and now . . . now they have.'

But he said nothing. And then, for what seemed

to me an interminable time, but may have only been seconds, we held each other's gaze; and in that time, in that look, we said everything. And without any sound, without any words spoken, I heard him think my name, over and over.

'Are you going to introduce us, Clarissa?'

I turned. Rose was standing at my side, her eyes fixed on Tom.

'Yes, of course . . . Rose, this is Tom . . . Tom Cuthbert, an old friend of mine, from Deyning.'

'How do you do,' she said, extending her hand, and no doubt expecting him to take it to his lips. But he didn't. He glanced at her, shook her hand and smiled politely, then looked back to me.

'You must forgive me, Rose. I haven't seen Clarissa for some time and I'm keen to hear her news . . .'

'Oh. Oh, I see. Yes, of course, don't mind me,' she replied, and turned back towards the others.

It was so crowded in that hallway, with people arriving all the time, calling out to friends they recognised and loudly pushing forward. And forced even closer by the crush of that revelry, I grabbed hold of his shoulder to steady myself, and he put his arm around me and held me to him. In that great swell of bodies no one could see the firmness of his hold, my arms around him, our bodies pressed together. Neither of us spoke, we simply stood there, looking at each other, dazed by our sudden reconciliation.

'Is Gloria here?'

'It was nothing, Clarissa. It meant nothing.'

'I rather think it did to her.'

'Perhaps, but it's the way of the war,' he said.

'You never wrote to me.'

He shook his head. 'I wrote. Please, can we go somewhere? I think we need to talk.'

'Yes, but I need to—' I began, but he took hold of my hand, and gripping it as though his life depended on it, he led me through that merry chaos and out of the front door.

Outside, people loitered on the steps, smoking, and leant against the railings in intense, intimate conversation. And it felt strange, almost illicit, to be out there, alone—with him.

'I can't stay out here,' I said, pulling my hand from his. 'Henry's here and he'll—'

'And he'll tell your mama? Let me have a moment with you, please? Just a moment, Clarissa.'

'But I'm cold,' I said, shivering, and he took off his regimental jacket, placed it around my shoulders, then lit us both a cigarette.

'I wrote to you . . .' he said, and then sighed. 'I wanted to tell you, wanted to tell you that day at the station. The reason you didn't receive my letters, Clarissa, is because your mother intercepted them. She found out—don't ask me how—about your arrangement with Broughton. And she spoke to my mother.' He paused. 'She asked my mother to inform me that I was, under no circumstances, to correspond with her daughter again,' he added, imitating Mama's voice, and pulling his jacket around me more tightly. 'I wanted to write to you,' he continued, 'I longed to write to you. I wanted to tell you all of this, but there was no way I could. I knew you were here, in London, but I knew that if I wrote to you here your mother would simply take my letters.'

I didn't say anything. I was piecing things together, running over what he'd told me in my mind. Mama had taken his letters; his letters to *me*.

'Clarissa . . .'

'Let's walk,' I said.

'But . . . Henry?'

'He'll not notice. Has he seen you? Does he know you're here?'

'No, I'm not sure . . . I don't think so.'

'Come along then,' I said, taking hold of his arm.

We walked down the street slowly, in silence. Then, a little faster, we crossed Park Lane and entered Hyde Park. It was black and it was cold, but all I wanted was some time alone with him. All I wanted was to feel his arms around me once more and know that he was mine.

We moved quickly across the grass, under the low branches, and then up against the damp bark, he pulled me to him. 'Clarissa . . .' he whispered, taking my head in his hands, and then his mouth was over mine, his tongue wrapping itself around my own. He moved his lips down my neck on to my shoulder, murmuring my name again. And as I lifted his head I traced the contours of his face with my fingers. I found his mouth with my own, pushed my tongue into it as his hands moved up through my hair, cradling my head as we kissed. And as I sank further into a state of bliss, I heard myself say his name and drew him closer, wrapping him into me, into his jacket, so that we were cocooned, melting into the ancient tree; invisible to the world, lost in the blackness.

And as his kisses became harder, more desperate, I felt his hands move over my breasts, down my gown to my hips; his breath quickening as he lifted folds of satin, his open mouth pressed on to my neck. I heard him moan as his fingers strayed above my stockings, caressing my bare flesh. And I was lost; I was nowhere. Nothing existed other than him, his touch. I moved my hands down his back, on to his buttocks, pulling him to me. All I knew was my own desire. He was there; he was real. I couldn't see him but I could hear him, taste him, smell him. And lost in that blindness—in the heart of a city at war—we had found each other again.

He moved, tugging at the belt of his trousers, and then I felt his fingers: pulling aside silk, probing; pushing gently. I heard myself say his name again, and I didn't care. I was conscious only of my need, his need, our hunger for each other; and then him, inside me; his hands easing me up to him, on to him; my legs wrapped around him, his mouth over mine. And all at once I was rising on a great swell; floating away from him, away from myself, up, up into the ether. I was the night, I was the darkness; I was the universe. I heard myself cry out as his body tensed, and then I heard my name, in one long, breathless shudder.

When I opened my eyes I could see. I could see the lights of the city glinting through the trees; hear the traffic in the distance.

'Please . . .' he whispered. 'Wait for me, Clarissa. Tell me you'll wait for me . . .'

'I'll wait for you, my darling. I promise I'll wait for you.'

We walked back across the park, hand in hand, stopping to kiss each other with every few steps. And then, as we neared the house, we pulled away. Once inside, I excused myself and went upstairs to the bathroom. I looked at myself in the mirror: I appeared quite different, I thought. I was pink cheeked, yes, and a little dishevelled. But there was something altogether changed about me. I smiled at my reflection, splashed cold water on to my face and then pressed it into the soft white hand towel. I checked my dress, pulled off my new silk camiknickers and pushed them into my evening bag. I took out my tiny hairbrush, tidied my hair; dabbed my nose with powder.

I loved Tom Cuthbert and after the war was over we would be married. I had no doubts. Even if we had to elope, it *would* happen.

Tom was waiting for me at the bottom of the stairs, and as I descended, sidestepping people and glasses, he watched me intently, smiling. We had a new secret now. As I reached his side he slipped his hand around mine and squeezed it tightly. And then he turned in towards me. 'You're *so* beautiful,' he whispered. 'I want you . . . again.'

I turned to look at him. He was the most handsome man there, I thought. And soon we'd have to part again; for how long, I wasn't sure. I wanted to give him something, wanted him to have something of mine, but what? I reached inside my bag, pulled out the tiny roll of flimsy silk and pushed it into his pocket.

'What's that?' he asked.

'Something for you. Something for you to remember me by,' I said, looking into his eyes, smiling.

'As long as I know you're mine—I don't need anything else.'

'I'm yours. You must know that by now.'

'Yes,' he said. 'Yes, I think I know that.'

'Ah! There you are! And look who you've found. I'll be damned . . . Tom Cuthbert!' It was Henry, worse the wear from drink, and unsteady on his feet. I let go of Tom's hand. 'Charlie's been looking for you, sis . . . Tom, my man! How the hell are you?'

'Really? We've been here all the time,' I said, without flinching, as Tom took hold of Henry's outstretched hand.

Henry swayed, his eyes half closed, and then turned and shouted over to Charlie, who wound his way over to us.

'Clarissa . . . I've been looking all over for you . . .'

'Then you need to get your eyes tested, Charlie Boyd. I've been here with Tom, catching up . . . remembering old times.'

I said goodbye to him that night without a kiss, or a handshake, without any sign at all. I walked away. I had to. What else could I do? At the door, as we said goodnight to Jimmy and a few others, I looked back for him but he wasn't there. He'd disappeared, as if he'd been part of a dream.

Later, in my bed, I closed my eyes and relived each second of our time together. I could still feel his hands; still taste him in my mouth. And beyond my window, somewhere in the city, I knew he was thinking of me, dreaming of me. I had no idea where, what street or under which roof, but it didn't matter. Out there in the ether our spirits remained entwined.

Despite everything, despite everything that happened afterwards, I've never for one moment regretted that night in the park. I wanted Tom to be my first. I wanted Tom. It was our moment and I knew it may never come again, and if it didn't, if we hadn't made love then and there, I'd have regretted it for the rest of my life. It had to be, was meant to be. Some things are.

CHAPTER SIXTEEN

. . . The landscape here is quite blown to pieces: farms, churches, villages and towns simply reduced to piles of stone & rubble, & the trees—entirely stripped, no more than charred stumps, protruding from the churned-up earth like ghosts. And the guns go on and on . . . But I think I have become immune to it all, the horror. Unimaginable sights, which not so very long ago would have made me ill, have little impact now. The dysentery is possibly the worst thing, truly awful, & robs the men of what little dignity they have left—before it kills them . . . The stench & the noise is enough to make a man insane. We are all desensitised, completely brutalised, but it seems to me the only way to survive . . .

* * *

Outside my window there was a tree. I watched its leaves turn from palest gold to burnished copper. I watched them fall, fluttering against my windowpane, tumbling through damp air to the sodden path beneath. I looked out through naked branches to an unknown, opaque sky, heard the sighs of time with each tick of the clock. And as my belly grew, daylight dwindled.

Emily Cuthbert Granville was born on Monday, November the twelfth 1917, with a mop of dark hair and brilliant blue eyes, at St Anne's, a convent and a type of nursing home, in Plymouth, Devon. She weighed almost eight pounds at birth and she was, the sisters told me, one of the healthiest and most robust babies they'd had in a long while. We weren't Catholic, but it was the place my mother had chosen for me to stay for the duration of my confinement. Aunt Maude lived in Taunton, and it was, Mama had said, perfectly feasible that I should have gone to stay there for a while, with family, and quite enough to tell people. There could be no further communication with Tom Cuthbert, she said, not now, not ever. And she would make sure that no one knew anything, for *no one* could know: not him, his mother, or even Henry . . . no one.

'I hardly know what to say to you, Clarissa,' she'd said to me, after Dr Riley left the house that day; the day he confirmed what I already knew and what Mama had undoubtedly suspected. I had just confessed, only just told her the name. And as I'd spoken his name, I'd seen her wince. There was a sharp intake of breath as she raised her hand to her chest and then closed her eyes, as though at that very same moment she'd experienced a sudden and acute pain. For some minutes she did not speak, and then she said, 'I never want to hear you speak his name again.' She opened her eyes. 'And I hope we never—either of us—set eyes on him again.'

She sat in the armchair by the window in my room, looking anywhere except at me, still lying upon my bed, fully clothed; for Dr Riley hadn't taken long to deliver his prognosis. He'd asked me a few simple questions, in his usual quiet and kindly way, and smiling at me all the while: could I recall when I had last menstruated? Did my breasts feel somewhat tender, larger? Had my waist thickened . . . were my clothes a little tighter? Then he'd asked me to lift my blouse and unbutton my skirt.

He pressed his hand down upon my distended abdomen. 'Hmm, yes,' he said, and then turned to Mama and nodded.

Mama did not visit me in Plymouth. It was much too complicated, she said, and anyway, she needed to be in London for Henry. Aunt Maude was my only visitor during my stay at St Anne's. She came each week, on Wednesday afternoon: the only day we were allowed visitors. Charlie continued to write to me, care of Maude, and she brought his letters, along with any from Mama, and took away my replies. I pretended to Charlie that I was having a splendid time in Taunton; that life was gay and all was well. I invented excursions, events, even conversations. And in his letters he told me how very sensible it was for Mama to have sent me there, and how much he longed to see me. He told me that he loved me and that when the war was over we would be married. And, if I still loved Devon, he'd buy a cottage for me there.

My mother's letters to me were measured, formal, and always without any reference to the circumstances. I could easily have been a friend, an acquaintance even, on holiday in Devon. She updated me on the weather in London, her visitors, and on Henry's movements and news. And she always included a précis of her recent correspondence: who was where, with whom and doing what. Each letter ended, 'You are ever in my prayers . . .'

But Mama and our house in Berkeley Square felt so far away, so long ago; for days in Devon lasted longer, much longer than days in London. And I inhabited a dimly lit world. A world, it seems to me now, without any dawn or sunset; a place adrift, almost outside of time. Minutes flattened, stretching into shapeless hours; days merged with nights, weeks with months. I used my voice little, and my eyes even less. I retreated to that place of warmth and light, breathed in the scents of lavender, jasmine and rose; I stood under a Sussex sky, the clouds high above, the cornfields in the distance, and Tom—watching me.

Kiss me . . . kiss me now . . .

I made only one friend at St Anne's: her name was Edith Collins. Edith was a year younger than me, though she could easily have passed for five years older. I can't recall where, exactly, she came from, but she'd been working as a kitchen maid in a large house somewhere in the West Country and had 'fallen'—as she put it—to the son of her employer. I don't think I saw her shed a tear once. Her approach was pragmatic, her attitude one of defiant optimism; she would put this behind her and move on, she said, although she wasn't entirely confident that it wouldn't happen again. 'What would I do with a baby?' she said. 'Far better for him to have a life with a proper family than be stuck with me.'

At first I didn't tell Edith too much about myself, or my circumstances, and she, still mindful of her place, didn't ask. Mama had made me swear never to tell a living soul of my predicament; had made me promise to never again mention the name *Tom Cuthbert*, to anyone. But after knowing Edith for a few weeks, and realising that I'd probably never again see her, I decided to tell her my story. Unlike her, I cried the whole way through my shameful confession.

'But what's the problem? You love him, he loves

you—you could get married . . .' she said, putting her arm around me.

'No, no,' I said, shaking my head, still crying. 'You don't understand. It's impossible . . . would never be allowed.'

'Says who, your mother? You could elope . . . you could, you know, plenty have.'

I tried to explain. I told her that Tom wasn't even aware I was having his child, and then, through my sobs, that he may not even be alive. 'It's hopeless, Edith . . .'

For nineteen days I nursed my baby. And each day, as I held her, I watched the dusk descend earlier and earlier: a damp, colourless blanket enshrouding that unfamiliar place. For nineteen days I watched her feed and sleep and grow. Her tiny pink fingers curled tightly around my own as she suckled at my breast, a silent drizzle weeping at my window. I sat by her crib, studying her features, memorising her perfect face, listening to the sound of her breathing. For nineteen days she belonged to me.

I told her all about her father, and about Deyning. I described the gardens, the house, each room, my bedroom, reminding myself of who I'd once been. I took her for walks through my memory; following all those familiar paths to secret places. I carried her through the fields, walked down through the lower meadow and stood with her by the lake. I showed her off and introduced her to people she'd never meet, a life she'd never know, and that place called home.

* * *

. . . Home, it has become an ideal, like heaven, inhabited by angels. A place we dream about & speak of & long for. And all those things we once complained about, found irritating & annoying, those people we disliked & avoided, those places so dull and dreary to our untired, untrained eyes, we now long for, & would surely welcome with joy & open arms. Out here, the next best thing to Home is Heaven, and so each day hundreds gallantly march across that threshold, like a doorway back to safety . . .

* * *

I wrote to Tom: *I wonder where you are now, if these words will ever be read . . . and if you will ever come back to me. We have a baby, my darling, a beautiful baby girl, but I can't keep her . . . I'm not allowed to keep her.*

And then I tore up my words.

The night before they came, Edith handed me a small green bottle. She instructed me to mix its contents with a little of the quinine, in a separate bottle. It would help me sleep and, she said, soothe my nerves. The sisters had told me that Emily would, eventually, go to a good home; to a childless couple who'd prayed for a perfect little baby girl just like mine. There was nothing for me to fret about, all would be well; and once I'd recovered I could make a new start. It would take time, they said, but my baby would be loved and cherished, and surely that was what mattered. I must pray, they said; pray to the Good Lord for his forgiveness and for his blessings upon my poor illegitimate daughter.

was living in London, working as a nurse at one of the general hospitals, and had recently become engaged to a doctor. Lucy remained at home with her parents. Maude had already lost both of her sons, my cousins. Archie had been dead for over a year, and Johnnie killed that June. And she spoke about the war: the war, the war, the bloody war. At that moment it was a background noise in my life. An irritation I didn't need; something I didn't want to think about or hear about. And then, when she finally said, 'It'll all come good, Clarissa. It's for the best,' I began to cry again, and so did she.

It was dusk when we arrived at Paddington, and as I stepped off the train on to the platform, I remembered the girl with the swollen belly who'd passed through that same station months before, and I stopped, and placed my hand upon my stomach. Maude took hold of my arm, but for a moment I could neither move nor speak. 'Come along, dear,' she said, 'your mother will be waiting.' And I contemplated running, where to I don't know; perhaps back on to the train, back to Plymouth.

'I don't want to go home,' I said.

'Oh now, don't be silly, dear. Your mama is longing to see you . . . longing to see you.'

As we passed through the streets of London, heading from the station towards my mother's home, I noticed the shop windows, ablaze with twinkling lights and tinsel, festooned Christmas trees and garlands. I hadn't thought of Christmas, hadn't realised it was upon us. I felt as though I was returning from a long exile in another country, as though I'd been away for years.

At the house, as the cab driver lifted our bags

out on to the pavement, my mother appeared at the door. She never opened her own front door and, looking back, I suppose that in itself was a gesture. But it meant nothing to me at the time. She took me in her arms and held me. I remember her perfume, so familiar; my lips touching the pearls of the choker she wore around her neck. She looked as she always did: immaculate and in control. And I felt nothing. Nothing at all.

Inside, the house looked exactly the same. And it struck me then how queer that whilst my life had been turned upside down, nothing in my mother's home was in any way altered. There were flowers, a winter arrangement, I think, of berried holly and white roses on the hallway table; a fire burned there and another in the drawing room, where a maid I'd never met before brought in the tea tray. As Mama and Maude discussed the journey and our timings, the maid served tea, offering me milk and sugar, as though I were a new caller. I watched my mother as she spoke with Maude; saw her glance across at me once or twice, then lift her hand, trying to find a curl she could twist and tuck back in place.

'We've already had so many heavy frosts,' she said to Maude, 'the pavements have been lethal, quite lethal. Only this morning I had to ask Dunne to put down more salt on the steps outside.'

I sat in silent numbness, felt myself disappearing, shrinking in front of them: a fallen woman, a disgraced daughter, indelibly stained. When, eventually, I rose to my feet and asked to excuse myself, to unpack I said, Mama looked at me anxiously and said, 'Yes, you do look a little pale, dear. Perhaps you need to rest after your journey.'

My journey, my journey . . . the one you sent me on.

That night I did not go down to dinner and I have no idea what Mama and her sister spoke of. Did they mention me? Did they talk about my baby, the baby I'd given away for Christmas? I don't know, and at the time I didn't care. I never wanted to leave my room again. I wanted to disappear, forever. Later, she came to my room, sat down upon my bed and took my hand in hers.

'My darling, what you need is a good night's sleep in your own bed. Everything will seem so much better once you're properly rested.'

I looked up into her eyes, those beautiful doleful eyes. She pushed my hair back from my brow. 'Perhaps you'd like me to get Antoine over to do your hair tomorrow, hmm?' she asked, referring to her hairdresser.

I stared at her, felt my eyes sting, but said nothing.

'Well, perhaps later in the week,' she said, rising to her feet. She stood still for a moment, her back to me, her hands clasped in front of her, as though she wasn't quite ready to leave the room; as though there was something more she wished to say to me.

'The gels are so looking forward to seeing you again. Rose in particular . . . she's missed you.'

Then she left the room.

I heard her footsteps descend the staircase, her door close as she disappeared into her suite of rooms on the lower floor. I rolled on to my side, took hold of a pillow, wrapped my arms around it and held it to me. I closed my eyes, felt the sun on my face, the grass against my legs, and I could see him, there, in the distance: waiting for me.

Maude stayed with us for three days, during which time neither she nor my mother ever mentioned the baby or my time at St Anne's. After Maude left I wondered if my mother would talk to me, ask me about Emily, her granddaughter, but she did not, and I quickly realised that it was not and never would be a subject for discussion between us.

*   *   *

. . . The fighting raged on for three days and nights, & yesterday young Norton was struck. I somehow managed to drag him through the mud and back to the trench, but he'd been hit in the stomach and for almost an hour he lay in my arms—crying for his mother. He'd told them he was eighteen, but I very much doubt he was even sixteen . . .

*   *   *

I remember a white moth amongst the pink rosebuds of my bedroom wall. A small white moth. The only one. It came one day and seemed reluctant to leave, even when I held open the window and tried to coax it out to freedom. Sometimes it moved to another rosebud, another wall, but it was never drawn to the open window. Then, perhaps two days after it first appeared, I could no longer find it amidst the buds upon my wall. I searched the pattern, searched the floor, and then, finally, I found it on the window sill. I picked it up, held it in the palm of my hand. And I wondered again why God created so many beautiful but infinitely fragile things.

I stretched my arm out through the open

window, willing it to live. *Fly . . . fly* . . . I watched it as the breeze swept it from my hand. Watched it fall through the air and land upon the roof below. And there it lay, completely still.

The next morning it had gone. I couldn't be sure if the wind hadn't picked up that tiny white moth, carrying it further across the rooftops of London. But I like to think it had flown.

Strange, the things we remember.

* * *

. . . Last night five of us went out on a listening patrol. We crawled on our bellies through a gap in the wire—through the mud into no-man's-land—and tried to get as close as we could. We couldn't hear anything, nothing at all, and no one speaks or even understands German anyway—so it was a hopeless, pointless exercise &—in my opinion—v badly thought through . . . but then so much is here. I suppose the COs are desperate, we're all desperate.

* * *

It was Henry who said it, and at the time I was grateful.

Tom.

Hearing his name spoken out loud broke a spell, made him real, and released me from a promise; a solemn but unsigned agreement that had become a burden to my conscience. He said he'd seen him with her at a party; that it was quite obvious they were 'at it'.

Rose and Tom . . .

'Jeepers, do you remember when you had such a crush on him, Issa?'

'No, not really,' I said. 'We were friends, Henry, that's all.'

We were friends . . . that's all.

'Rubbish. You had the hots for him—and in a big way, as I recall. And you know? I think he rather liked you too.'

. . . *He rather liked me.*

'So, did you speak to him?' I asked, without looking up from my book.

'Yes, of course I spoke to him. I quite like him actually. Doesn't seem to care too much what people think, which is . . . really rather refreshing.'

'And so . . . what was his chat?'

'Oh, this and that. Where he'd been . . . he's an officer now.'

. . . *Captain Tom Cuthbert.*

'Yes, I know. Did he ask after Mama?'

'He asked me about you. Said he'd heard of your engagement, asked when the wedding was,' he replied, removing his shoes, putting his feet up on the ottoman.

'And what did you say?'

'Said I didn't know, that it would all depend on when Charlie was next home and when you both deemed it necessary, ha!'

'And how long . . . how long has he been seeing Rose?' I asked, closing my book, looking up at him.

'Haven't the foggiest. But I can't imagine her parents know. If they did they'd be livid. Anyway, what is it with him? I mean, I know he's handsome and all, but he *has* nothing.'

. . . *He has nothing; he is no one; can never be one of us.*

'It's not his wealth then, is it?' I replied. 'But you know, people don't select who to fall in love with according to their wealth or lineage, Henry.'

He narrowed his eyes and looked at me quizzically for a moment; opened his mouth as if about to say something, then thought the better of it and said nothing.

'It may be the case with who they choose to marry, but not where love's concerned,' I added.

'Hark you, my wise sister. And where, pray tell, does this newfound knowledge come from? Or are you thinking back with regret and longing to dear old Cuthie?'

I managed a smile. 'Not at all. And I'm quite sure Rose Millington shan't marry Tom Cuthbert. She's much too ambitious. But she'll enjoy his attention. He's . . . quite intense, and women like that—for a while at least.'

I looked away, saw Tom staring into Rose's pale eyes, his lips moving towards hers.

'You're all the same: fickle,' Henry continued. 'You want everything . . .' he paused, sighed, 'the promise of eternal love and adoration, and then, when you think you have it, when you think you have it all, you no longer want it. Isn't that true?'

I didn't answer.

'Well? Isn't it?'

'Perhaps, but I don't believe men are any different. You all long for what you don't own and can't afford, and as soon as you own it, as soon as you're sure of it—it loses its appeal. So, perhaps it's a human trait and not specific to either sex.'

'Ha! Yes, but it's the unattainable that's always the most desirable.'

'The unattainable . . .' I repeated. And the

poignancy of that word hit me like another blow.

He stretched out in his chair and sighed. 'Have you noticed how old and cynical we sound now, dear?' he said.

'I suppose that's what the war has done to us,' I replied.

Later, I sat at my dressing table, staring at my reflection in the looking glass. I would soon be twenty-one; I would soon be married. I hadn't heard his name in so long, and Henry's blasé mention of him had thrown me more than I'd realised. One syllable, one syllable was all it took. He had been a moment in my life, a wonderful reckless moment, nothing more. Nothing more, I told myself out loud. I picked up my hairbrush, moved it slowly through my hair. An unsmiling face stared back at me, beseeching me. And when I closed my eyes it was still there. 'He used you,' Mama had said, but I knew he hadn't used me any more than I had used him. My heart ached for him and for our baby, the child whose existence he knew nothing of; the child I'd given away, handed over to a stranger like an unwanted parcel. I clutched my stomach, felt myself begin to shake, and somewhere—somewhere in the distance—I could hear someone crying: great convulsing, breathless sobs. I put my hands to my mouth; heard his name, muffled, desperate; and then a shout, followed by another, and then another. I saw a girl sitting on a pink carpet in my white nightgown, swaying to and fro, rocking empty arms. And the sadness I felt for her was overwhelming.

I don't remember Mama entering my room. In fact, I can't recall anything that happened in the subsequent days and weeks.

* * *

. . . Four men were shot for desertion this morning. They'd been here for 3 or 4 months, & without any break . . . Every few days the names are read out to us—as a warning, but some would rather face a firing squad than stay here another day. Last week another young boy in my battalion was shot. He'd become hysterical, lost his nerve and couldn't face going back into the line. He was tied to what was once a tree, in his civilian clothes, a piece of white cloth pinned over his heart. Now, rumour has it, his father and uncle are joining up to avenge his death on the Germans . . . What are we doing? Why are Englishmen shooting Englishmen? Best to suspend all thought & reason.

CHAPTER SEVENTEEN

Dearest T, I have delayed my response to your last simply because it was (to me) incomprehensible. There is no hypocrisy on my part, is there on yours? I endeavour to do what I believe is right for each of us, and this in itself is a burden to me, and yes, to my conscience, which I now realise is that part of me you neither understand nor have any desire to understand . . . and I am deeply sorry if I have failed you. Do not for one moment think I am untouched or untroubled by this, I have given it a great deal of thought, but it is the only way, & nothing to do with being part of any 'smart set'. Dearest, you speak of love as though it were a thing beyond morality—or what is decent—and yet didn't you also once tell me how inherently noble and good Love is? Can you not see how it would be otherwise? I'm afraid there was no alternative. Yrs, D

* * *

Was it some sort of nervous breakdown? I'm not sure. I'm not sure I'd heard that phrase then, or even if it had been invented. But weeks slipped by and I rarely left my room; I didn't want to, couldn't face anyone, couldn't face life. Dr Riley came to call once or twice, but he spoke to my mother and not to me. He prescribed tablets; to help me sleep, Mama said. But I didn't need tablets to help me sleep; I needed tablets to help me wake up, to help me wake up from my nightmare. The only person I saw, apart from Mama and the doctor, was Venetia, once, when she came up to my room to see me. She brought me a silk scarf from Liberty's and was as effervescent as ever.

'Your mama's told me you've been a little off colour, dear; not quite yourself since you returned from Devon . . .'

I tried to smile.

'Well, really, it was always a bad idea. I told your Mama that at the time . . . I said to her, "Edina, Devon is so terribly, terribly damp, and so very far away!"' She reached out, stroked my cheek. 'Poor child, I'm not surprised, not surprised in the least that you've returned here lacklustre and depressed. I should too, I'd imagine—had I been sent there!'

She went on to give me her summary of news, a catalogue of back-dated events I'd missed, and snippets of gossip, punctuated every so often by a roll of the eyes, a sigh or a shrug.

But I didn't hear any of it. I watched her as though I was watching someone on a stage, a character from a play; I even saw myself upon the same stage: the sickly girl in the bed. And I found myself wondering about Venetia and her life. Had she ever known heartache or loss? Perhaps she had. But it struck me that day how childlike she was, the extraordinary result of a life spent in a rarefied, cosseted world. The world I'd once been destined for. And suddenly I felt years older than my godmother, a woman who had only ever ventured beyond Mayfair to attend the theatre or the opera, or to stay in a grand country house. But I was different, I realised. And, though Venetia saw the same Clarissa, lying next to her, albeit pale and *lacklustre*, I was already changed, already altered by the path of my life. I would never be the person I'd once been destined to become.

I wondered who her latest lover was, which young officer was dedicating poetry to her from the trenches, and what she said to them. Did she speak to them of love? Is that what it was that drew them to her? Or was it something else? Yes, she was beautiful, and yes, she was voluptuous, but was that enough to sustain them? And then it dawned on me: perhaps it was. Perhaps Venetia, with her love of all things frivolous and gay, and her tactile maternal ways, offered them a backward glance; reminding them of that other time, what they had left behind; what we had all of us left behind.

Later, I heard them on the landing, talking.

'Well, you know Clarissa, she's always been a sensitive creature . . . always felt life a little *too* much. And this blasted war . . . our own losses have hit her hard,' Mama said, and I smiled, as much at her ingenuity as her disingenuousness.

When I remembered the time before the war, it was the light I remembered most of all. As though the killing fields of France and Flanders had released tiny particles into the atmosphere, filtering out the sun's rays, absorbing that brightness I remembered. And with each year the air had grown thicker and darker still. And with each year my memories of that time had intensified in their luminosity; cherished snapshots now phosphorescent beacons.

Can it really be three summers since we all sat about on the lawn, like children, drinking lemonade, the boys full of bravado and desperate to impress the girls? Has it only been three years?

At night I'd pull back the curtains of my bedroom window and stare out across the darkened city. I'd follow the searchlight's nervous beam up, up, up through the clouds into the inky black sky, staring into heaven, seeking out the enemy. Like a wound healing, there was a nerve in me slowly coming back to life. The ache for my baby had lessened; now only occasionally did I experience that gnawing agony, that wrench. And I'd learnt to live with it. I had to. I'd limited my thoughts of her to the abstract. She was a name, and though she was my baby, in my mind she had to become *a* baby. I could not bear to think of anything specific as to her situation or her whereabouts; whether she was lying in a cot of some far-flung orphanage, alone, or in someone else's arms, looking up into their eyes.

I simply couldn't follow her path, either in reality or in my imagination. I'd handed her over, I'd given her away, and in doing so I had no rights to any imagined smile or gurgle. But sometimes, alone in my room, I said her name out loud.

'Emily . . . Emily Cuthbert.'

'There'll be another. There'll be more babies for you. You'll see, when the time is right . . . when you're a little older, married,' one of the sisters had said to me, shortly before I left Plymouth, as though my grief was for a misplaced favourite hat.

I'm sure that Mama, and Charlie too, thought that planning our wedding would give me something to look forward to, something to help me recover from whatever it was I was suffering from. But I had no interest in any wedding, least of all my own. So, as Mama brought swatches of duchesse satin and silks to my room for me to hold and compare, I feigned preferences for this one or that. She sat patiently with her notebook in hand, listing guests we'd need to invite: a depressing task in itself, due to the names of those absent from that list or any future list. She made a point of being cheery, talking of the future, never the past. And she never mentioned Papa, or Will, or George. She never mentioned Deyning, or Tom Cuthbert, and of course she never mentioned my baby.

'When the war is over,' she said to me one day, 'I shall take you to Paris, darling. You never had your time there, I'm quite aware of that. I'll take an apartment . . . and we'll do all the things you always wished to do. We'll shop on the rue St Honore . . . visit Worth . . . go to the Louvre. Would you like that?'

'Yes, Mama. That would be nice.'

Sometimes she'd look into my eyes with such sadness in her own that I wondered what, exactly, she wanted to say; for I sensed her burden, the weight of words unspoken, still longing to be said. But my mother had never allowed herself such freedom. Truth was something one held tight, like honour and sacrifice, and all those other now tattered ideals she hung on to. And I wondered how many words she'd never uttered; how many tears she'd never shed; how many secrets she held in her heart, and all those words, all those words she'd never allowed herself to say.

But I knew three of them, at least. Three words she'd never utter, no matter what. Because speaking them would mean admitting a mistake; and Mama *never* made a mistake. And yet, already, I knew that I had: I'd made a mistake in agreeing to marry Charlie. I was fond of him, I loved him—loved him like a brother, but I could not marry him; I could not lie, say 'I do' and become his wife.

I decided not to speak to my mother about this. It was between me and Charlie, and no one else. For a while I contemplated writing to him, to try to explain. I composed a few different versions of a letter to him in my head. But it seemed so cruel, so uncaring, to put those words of rejection—no matter how dressed up—down on paper, and then post them out to him, with a 'love from Clarissa' at the end. I imagined him in some dark and muddy trench, leaning against a pile of filthy sandbags, reading my letter, his heart aching . . . his heart breaking. And I couldn't do it. It would have to wait. I'd tell him in person.

* * *

. . . I too am sorry. I do not speak about it because I do not wish to, and, I imagine, neither does she. She is fine, a little fragile, and—as ever—somewhat distracted, but she is moving on with her life, and this is good. I try so very hard to be brave, to keep faith, but I am severely tested. I am weary of writing letters of condolence, of trying to find words—which no longer seem to carry any meaning or weight. What can one say? We have all suffered, & too much for any words of sympathy . . . and the sight of more weeping mothers in the street—preceded by yet another Union Jack-covered coffin, cause me to question everything I once believed in, & all that I am.

CHAPTER EIGHTEEN

. . . I am not sure where to send this letter, or even if I will post it, but I want you to know that I forgive you. I forgive you for not writing to me, I forgive you for abandoning me, & I forgive you for not caring about what has become of me. Shall I tell you? Shall I let you in on the secret? Well, for a while I went quite doolally, oh yes, quite doolally-lally. In fact, I may even still be, in which case you can ignore everything I write here and resume normal duties. You see, I'm not altogether sure that I'm equipped to deal with this war, this bloody bloody bloody stupid bloody war, & this awful life. No one issued me with a tin hat, or a uniform, or any armour, and I shall

When they lifted her from my arms I was in a laudanum haze, scarcely stirring and conscious of nothing but the vaguest sense of being alive. And then, for some reason, the words of the twenty-third psalm: *Even though I walk through the valley of the shadow of death, I will fear no evil . . .*

Later, I did pray, but not for God's forgiveness: I prayed for my daughter's forgiveness. I prayed that one day she would find it in her heart to know and understand my actions. And I prayed that one day we'd find each other; that I'd be able to hold her and love her again. I don't remember much about that time now, and in the years that have since passed I've tried to understand why my mother did what she did. I tell myself, she did what she believed was right; she did what she thought was best. It was different then.

It was different then . . .

Two days after Emily left St Anne's, I did too. I said goodbye to Edith, whose own baby was due any day, and I returned to London on the train, accompanied by Aunt Maude. I stared up out of the carriage window at the bruised sky hanging over England: all black, blue, pale purple, grey and yellow. Beneath it, a dark patchwork of meadows and pastures, sewn together by hedgerow and thicket; then a farm, a cottage; and every so often the huddled stone and steeple of a village. I thought of the people inside those farms and houses and cottages, gathered around a fire, or perhaps in the kitchen by the range, and I wondered if Emily would soon be carried into one of those homes; if she'd be held and made warm.

Maude tried hard not to mention her. She spoke of trivial things, chit-chat, and gossip. Edina

'No, not Henry . . .' I said, sitting up in my bed, putting down my book.

'No, darling, not Henry,' she said, taking hold of my hand. 'I'm afraid it's Charlie . . .'

The telegram was from Henry: Charlie had been badly injured.

My mother telephoned the Boyds immediately. Charlie had been injured in an ambush on a night patrol. Nine of his men had been killed. He'd already been returned home and admitted to one of the London general hospitals.

The next day Mama and I went to visit him. He lay in a small bed curtained off from the rest of the ward—his torso and arms bandaged like an Egyptian mummy, his legs under some sort of cage, covered by a sheet—in an open-eyed state of coma, seemingly deaf and dumb. I looked on in silence, stood at the end of the bed and watched my mother as she spoke to him. But he couldn't see her, couldn't hear her. I glanced about the ward—at the other injured servicemen, but none of it was real, none of it touched me. That small green glass bottle had continued to be my comforter, nullifying my senses, and, like Charlie, I was locked in a dream. Only I could hear and move and speak, and sometimes even smile.

We visited Charlie almost daily for two months before he was transferred to Craiglockhart, a military hospital near Edinburgh—specialising in the treatment and care of shell-shocked servicemen. A friend of Mama's, a doctor, had told us that the rate of war neurosis was much higher among officers than among regular soldiers, simply because their positions required them to repress their emotions and set an example. These men were often ashamed of their fear, he said, and, in his opinion, it was no coincidence that the most severe cases occurred in officers who'd also made a name for themselves as heroes, performing daredevil acts to prove to their men that they were not afraid. It made sense. And at that moment I could imagine Charlie, my ever-cheerful ebullient fiancé, at the front. At Craiglockhart, we were told, Charlie would be able to have the new electric shock treatment, he would learn how to walk and speak properly again.

I watched him slowly begin to recover from his physical injuries, but he was not as he should have been. He walked badly, dragging one leg, and putting together even the simplest of sentences seemed to be a struggle. At first he'd been unable to control both the pronunciation of words and the loudness of his voice, often shouting out in such a way that I'd jump. And he looked different too: wide eyed and haunted, and so very tired. He told me that he was afraid to sleep, afraid of the nightmares that delivered him straight back to the trenches. But sometimes these nightmares came to him in the middle of a sentence; and then he'd shriek, cry out a name, or begin whimpering like a wounded dog. He suffered appalling headaches, heart palpitations, dizziness, and sweats; and once, in front of Mama and me, he had what appeared to be some sort of fit—his whole body jerking violently upon the bed, shaking its tiny frame. He'd burst into tears a few times when we were there, and I knew, I knew then that Charlie believed he, too, should have been killed; that he wished for death, not life.

Perhaps it was seeing Charlie in that state, or

perhaps it was watching the nurses who attended him, but I finally decided that I needed to do something, something useful. I'd heard that the hospitals were still desperate for volunteers, albeit for menial work, and so, the same day Charlie was transferred, I walked to the Russian Hospital for Officers on South Audley Street, and asked if they could use me.

The sister who interviewed me—a solid, fearsome woman, with tiny blue eyes and a Scottish accent—told me that I'd need to be there by seven each morning, 'bright eyed and bushy tailed. You'll be working down in the basement kitchens,' she said. 'It's by no means glamorous, so I suggest you come attired a little differently.'

I looked down at what I was wearing. 'Yes, of course.'

'From time to time you may be needed to help out on a ward . . . cleaning, stripping beds, that sort of thing. Is that acceptable to you, Miss Granville?'

'Yes, yes,' I replied eagerly.

'Good. But I should warn you, many of the men we have here are traumatised . . . incontinent of mind *and* body. It's not pleasant—not nice for any of us, or for them—but it has to be done, and we're all run ragged . . .' She paused, smiled at me. 'Unfortunately we don't have time for the manners and courtesies you're no doubt accustomed to, Miss Granville. You'll have to get used to that. You'll have to think on your toes and look sharp. But I'm sure if you can do that and keep your head, you'll be fine.'

'I am a pantry maid!' I declared to my mother when I returned home.

'But are you quite sure? Are you certain you're

able to cope?'

'Yes of course. And I have to do *something*, Mama.'

It was mindless work, and no one really spoke to me. When they did I was simply addressed as 'Granville'. But I was happy to be doing something, happy to be useful at last. And I had no time to think, no time to dwell on Tom Cuthbert, my baby, or Charlie. I worked in a small, windowless pantry in the hospital's basement, next to the kitchen. In a long white apron, thick hair net and white cap, it was my job to set the breakfast trays each morning, stack the trays on a trolley and wheel it through to the kitchen. There, I helped the kitchen maids—working from a list—to add food to the trays. Some were bestowed with nothing more than a plastic cup of yellowish milky liquid and a straw, a blue note placed next to it, with a name and a number; crockery and cutlery removed—for me to return to the pantry. Others, soft food—porridge, stoned prunes or scrambled eggs—served in a bowl, never on a plate, with a spoon and never a fork, and a pink note. And a few received something more substantial, with the full complement of cutlery, and no note. Then I took the trolley up to the wards with one of the kitchen maids, leaving her there to help the nurses hand them out, whilst I returned to the kitchen. By the time I'd finished clearing the kitchen, the trays had arrived back and I had to wash, dry and stack everything away for the next day. Sometimes I was asked to stay on for an hour, to do extra cleaning or mop out the kitchens, but I never saw inside the wards, never really saw the men, though I heard them, once or twice. The *blue notes*.

It was around this time, shortly after Charlie had been sent to Edinburgh, that Jimmy Cooper called on me. He was home on leave and took me to dinner at the Savoy. We drank champagne, ate caviar, foie gras, and lobster, and later, that same evening, we went to a party at the Millingtons'. I was apprehensive. I hadn't seen Rose in a while, and I wondered if Tom would be there, home on leave, and if they were still seeing each other. He wasn't there and I was pleased. I don't think I could have borne it if he'd been there, been with her.

'Darling!' Rose said, kissing the air to both sides of my head. 'I simply love the new you!'

Much to my mother's horror, I'd had my hair cut in the new 'short' style. I'd had Antoine cut it. It was, he told me, all the rage in Paris. Times, fashions, and everything else seemed to be changing, and I noted that Rose, like me, was wearing a new, rather daring, shorter gown.

Rose had always been a city girl: her vista happily confined to the angles of streets and pavements and rooftops. On her occasional visits to Deyning, I remembered, she'd always preferred to stay on the terrace or flagstoned pathways rather than walk on the grass or amongst the trees. She had a morbid fear of mud and didn't like the weather, any weather it seemed to me: summers made her sneeze and she found winters in the countryside *too, too depressing*. But in London, amongst the shops and cafés and theatres, she thrived. And though we were the same age she'd always seemed to me to be years older: more sophisticated, more knowing. Mama had once called her a flibbertigibbet sort, and perhaps she was.

'We never seem to cross paths these days . . . but

I'm so, so pleased that dear Jimmy's brought you along. Oh darling, we simply must have a good old catch-up. And . . . I've a little treat for us upstairs,' she added in a whisper.

In my ever-diminishing group of friends in London there was a new craze: injecting morphia. The drug not only worked on physical pain, its effects produced a pause long enough to obliterate reality, suspending thought and reason. It removed those light-absorbing particles and made things shine once more; made *us* shine once more. And life just seemed too short not to burn brightly.

At that time it wasn't fashionable, certainly not amongst those I knew, to drink. To appear in any way inebriated—by alcohol, at least—was considered quite vulgar and rather *louche*. And, under pressure from the temperance movement, and then the newspapers, the government had severely restricted the sale and consumption of alcohol anyhow. Shortly after the war began, hotels, restaurants, bars and public houses had had what was known as 'The Beauty Sleep Order' imposed on them, and sometime later, this lights-out rule had been brought forward, from ten thirty to nine thirty. I'd heard of a few places, certain dubious Soho nightclubs and bars, which somehow managed to stay open into the small hours, but most of the people I knew entertained at home. It was easier. And, I suppose, it allowed us to do whatever we wished in private.

My mother, like so many others, caught in the grip of a xenophobic obsession about spies and foreigners in the city, had once asked me if I'd come across drugs at any of the parties I went to. She'd read in the newspaper that itinerant immigrants and foreign soldiers were targeting young English women—to sell on into prostitution and white slavery. She mentioned opium and cocaine, and I was shocked. Shocked that she knew these words. Of course I'd lied to her, told her I knew nothing; said I hadn't seen anything.

But the craze for these things had been around for a few years by then, and the war, the never-ending news about it and about death, served only to accelerate the need for escape. All of us had friends working in one or other of the London hospitals, and with so many doctors, nurses and VADs about, the drugs were easy enough to obtain. Even our local Mayfair chemist, the place my mother liked to patronise, advertised their gelatine sheets impregnated with morphine and cocaine as *USEFUL PRESENTS FOR FRIENDS AT THE FRONT*. And a few very fashionable London girls I knew carried the most exquisite, beautifully enamelled silver bonbonnières of morphia grains or cocaine in their handbags.

Later that evening, as we sat side by side on her bed, Rose took my arm. 'Now don't worry, darling, it doesn't really hurt,' she said, examining my flesh, tapping at it. And it didn't. I felt nothing. For what's a pinprick? She disappeared to the bathroom, to sterilise the needle, she said, and when she returned I watched her inject herself. She pulled out the needle with a sigh, turned to me and smiled. And we sat there for a while, sharing a cigarette, chatting about who was seeing whom, and who'd died. Then, with a queer sort of drifting feeling, as though I wasn't completely there, I heard myself ask her about Tom: was she still seeing him, writing to him? And I heard my voice, slightly slurred and slow.

'Good grief, Clarissa, I was never *seeing* him as such. It was just a thing, you know? He's hardly one of us, is he?'

'But I thought . . . Henry said you were . . .'

'Well, strictly between you and me, I was with him . . .' She got up, walked over to the window. 'He is rather handsome . . . and quite compelling, but can you imagine what my parents would say? No, no, it was a momentary thing.'

'And . . .' I heard myself say, egging her on for the detail of their *thing*, '. . . tell me more.' And then I lay back against her pillows, a blissful mellowness creeping into my senses.

For a moment I thought she wasn't going to divulge anything further; then she came and sat down on the bed next to me.

'Come along, Rose,' I said, half closing my eyes, ready to test the pain. 'Tell me . . .'

'It was here,' she said, looking above me, above my head, remembering. 'He made love to me here. Oh, I know how preposterous it sounds, darling . . . but it was a moment of complete abandon.'

And in my blissful haze, through the morphia, I felt a twinge in the pit of my stomach.

'Yes,' I said, 'a moment of complete abandon . . . how wonderful.'

'I suppose if his circumstances were different I might fall in love with him,' she said, still staring at a patch of wall above my head. 'And truly, it was sublime. But I know—I know what you're thinking. You're thinking I'm a little tart to go with such a person, but he's altogether different to other men. There's something unusual . . . rather extraordinary about him . . . It's hard to explain, but I think you know what I mean, don't you?'

'Yes,' I said, 'I can imagine.'

'He's so passionate . . .'

'Really?'

'So desperate . . .'

'Yes . . .'

'And quite obviously experienced with women,' she said, looking at me with a wicked grin.

'Oh?'

She sighed. 'To be honest, I'd be more than happy to have him as a lover for the rest of my life.' She moved closer. 'The things he knows, Clarissa . . . seriously, darling, it would make your hair curl. I said to him, "I don't know where you've learnt about women, but surely it can't have been in the trenches."'

'And what did he say?'

'I can't quite recall now. I think he said it was Paris. You know they all go there, don't you?'

'No I didn't know. You mean they go there to pick up women?'

She laughed. 'Oh Clarissa, really. They don't need to pick them up, they pay for it, darling. And you know what they say about French prostitutes . . .'

'No,' I said, beginning to feel dizzy. 'What do they say?'

'Well, that they invented everything. Every debauchery known to man . . . or woman, ha! And they're everywhere at the front, brothels all over the place. Apparently there are more cases of syphilis and gonorrhoea there than anything else. Isn't that just so horrendously . . .' she glanced about the room, searching for the word, 'sad,' she said at last.

Suddenly I felt sick. 'Must be the morphia,' she said, and showed me to the bathroom.

I looked at myself in the mirror. He'd made love to her. He'd said her name and made love to her. I closed my eyes. *He made love to her as I had his baby.* I saw myself back in my room at St Anne's in Plymouth; saw them together on her bed. And then I vomited.

'Are you all right in there, darling?' Rose asked through the door.

'Yes . . . yes, I'm fine,' I said, staring back at the girl in the mirror. 'You go down. I'll see you there.'

'Are you sure? I can wait, dear.'

'No, Rose. You go back down. I'm fine . . . I'll be along in a jiffy.'

I heard the bedroom door close, and stood staring at my reflection. My eyes appeared unusually large and dark; my complexion a luminous ivory. I picked up the tablet of rouge on the marble washstand in front of me, and applied it to my cheeks. A touch of colour: *a mask; theatre; a beautiful sad creature from a Greek tragedy.* I lifted a tortoiseshell hairbrush, pushed it through my shorn hair, away from my face.

'You're not Clarissa,' I whispered. 'Clarissa doesn't look like that.'

I walked slowly down the staircase, moving my hand along the polished wood of the handrail, and then on, through a small sea of vaguely familiar faces.

'Clarissa!'

'Are you quite all right, dear? You look a little pale . . .'

'Clarissa?'

I smiled, kept moving, looking ahead of me

all the time, and then on into the Millingtons' ballroom, into the crowd. I closed my eyes, lifted my arms, swaying in time with the music: this is good; this is fine . . . I am good, I am fine.

I opened my eyes; saw Jimmy standing in front of me.

'Clarissa?' He sounded strange, quite far away.

'I think I need to go home now, Jimmy,' I said.

Later, in my room, I lay on my bed, staring at rosebuds, drifting. I smiled. I was home now. I was safe. He was gone. All I needed to do was bury him. I had to extinguish every sensation I associated with him. But how? How do you kill everything you've ever felt to be good without killing some of yourself?

I rose from my bed, walked across to my desk, opened the drawer and pulled out my journal and pen . . .

You may survive this war, but from today you are dead to me.

I climbed back into my bed and pulled the covers up. I wanted to be lost; I wanted to be found: found by him. I wanted him to feel my pain and beg for my forgiveness. I wanted to give myself to someone, anyone, and for him to know. For him to *feel* each touch, each and every kiss, like small shards of glass pressed into his flesh.

I would do it. I would.

I would make him feel the pain.

I stared at pink rosebuds between slow blinks, and I hated them. I'd never again be the girl on the gate, longing, and waiting for friends. I'd never again be the girl he'd made love to in the park. I'd never walk across a meadow and hear a lark or a cuckoo with that same sense of wonder. I'd never watch the sun set and feel at one with the universe or gaze up at the moon and stars and feel that same sense of awe. And I'd never again look at a baby and smile.

CHAPTER NINETEEN

Oddly enough, it was around this time I began to see more of Rose. I couldn't and didn't blame her for what had taken place between her and Tom. After all, she had no idea, knew nothing at all of my seemingly doomed relationship with Tom Cuthbert, or the child I'd given birth to months earlier. But then neither did he. And in reminding myself of that, in reminding myself of that pertinent fact, and knowing that he had been with Rose after he'd learnt of my engagement to Charlie, offered me a degree of comfort.

Rose was a socialite, a true Mayfair girl. The only child of indulgent parents, and with a healthy trust fund, she always seemed to carry notes, not coins. She was the one who arranged and hosted tea parties and soirees; the one who picked up the bills at the Ritz and other places, and then, afterwards, paid for the ridiculously short taxicab rides home for us all. She liked to visit fortune-tellers, and would quite often take a taxicab all the way to the outer suburbs, only to hear, yet again, that a tall dark stranger in uniform was on his way into her life.

But, and even aside from Tom, even before I learnt of their 'thing', I'd always been confused by my feelings for her. I admired her bravado, her *joie de vivre* and her generosity, and yet, in a way, those were the very same qualities I disliked about her, and viewed as shallow and insensitive. She seemed to me to be a girl without poetry in her blood, someone who'd never looked up and noticed the sky; someone who'd simply fail to see the full spectrum, or the differing hues and tones of any single colour. But that was Rose. And Rose was Rose.

For a short while our friendship was quite intense. We saw each other most evenings after work and sometimes, at her house, in her room, we took morphia; and then lay about trying to imagine the future, our future. *A future.* Perhaps that's the reason it became intense: the morphia, or 'morphy' as she called it.

She said to me, 'You know, dear, I keep thinking, and really . . . the thing is, soon there'll be no one left to marry . . . we'll all end up old maids . . . childless and unloved.' She turned to me. 'Doesn't it worry you, darling? I mean to say, I know you're engaged and all that, and poor Charlie's invalided, but what if he has to go back . . . what if something happens to him? It must cross your mind, dear . . . must cross your mind all the time.'

We were lying on her bed, side by side, and as I turned to her I noticed the flecks of red in her hair—Titian red—spread out over the pillow.

'I don't think about it.'

She turned towards me, on to her side. 'Really? Never?'

'No. What's the point? Whatever will be will be.'

'Clarissa! But you love him—don't you?'

I closed my eyes. 'I suppose so. Sort of.'

She lay back, and for a while we lay in silence,

the only noise the rumble of traffic going up and down the wet street outside. Then she said, 'But has he made love to you? You don't have to tell me, of course . . . but I was wondering, wondering if you're still a virgin.'

I didn't answer her immediately. The morphia made me drift, made my thoughts loose and shapeless; and it was a difficult question to answer.

'No,' I said, after a while, 'he hasn't made love to me, Rose.'

I didn't say any more, and neither did she.

And I have no idea who or what she was thinking of, where she was inside of herself, but I was with *him*.

For a while, I'm not altogether sure how long, but perhaps no more than a few weeks—and I know that it was spring, because I vividly recall the blossom on the trees as I walked home—we took *morphy* quite often; most days, I think. It made everything infinitely better, made the world . . . kinder, softer, warmer. And it took away all of my pain and heartache, all of my loneliness, and replaced it with the most sublime sense of peace.

Sometimes, its effects literally transported us to another place. And once, when Rose and I attended a private exhibition of paintings—and had taken only the smallest dose, hours earlier—we both fancied we'd seen the colours change and move about the canvases. Another time, when we read poetry out loud to each other, it was as though I was able go inside the poem, able to see and *feel* the vibration of every single word.

My mother never noticed a thing. Oh, she'd comment from time to time that I looked a tad pale or tired, but she'd always considered me dreamy, distracted and, I suppose, particularly at that time, fragile. If she thought something was amiss she never voiced it, but that was her character: she'd rather arrange flowers than deal with reality. But I was becoming needy, greedy for my share of grains, and I'd begun to pay Rose, because as she'd quite rightly said, she shouldn't have to pay for *everyone else's fun.*

* * *

It was Rose who asked me if I'd help out at the kiosk: a small buffet for soldiers arriving back from the trenches, situated on one of the platforms at Waterloo station. She and a few other girls from our neighbourhood ran it together, working on a rota so that it was open round the clock, day and night. We served tea, buns and cigarettes, all paid for by donations, but mainly by Lady Astley, a friend of Mama's, who'd set it up. So, I continued to work at the Russian Hospital each morning and cycled to Waterloo station each afternoon. There were always at least three of us working there, a few more if we knew it was going to be frantic, when the boat trains were due in. But the time of arrival of any trains was always a matter of conjecture. If they were late in the evening, as they quite often were, we'd all be there until the small hours, and then I'd leave my bicycle chained up at the station and share a taxicab home with the other girls.

Lady Astley came down to see us all at least twice each week, bringing supplies from Fortnum and Mason and often staying for a good few hours, helping to serve tea and chatting with the men. She liked us to look our best, said it mattered to *never be awarded anything. I shall receive no badge or medals, and no one is allowed to know . . . will ever know. Oh, but I forgot, it's different for me, isn't it? I don't need to 'win' anything. I must be content with loss, & losing . . .*

* * *

For me there was no beginning, no middle and no end, there was just one long and bloody war. I tried to imagine a time when there would be no war, but that great well of optimism, like my sense of patriotism, had almost run dry. I tried to remember that summer, the summer before the war, but it seemed to me a lifetime ago. And it was. It was hundreds of thousands of lifetimes ago. For how many had gone? Everyone I knew had lost brothers, cousins, lovers, fiancés, and friends. And yet we, the young still living, browbeaten by numbers and anaesthetised by grief, clung on to our stale dreams and shrivelled hopes, and that fine silver thread, the future.

Sometimes I smiled when I wanted to cry, and cried when I should have been laughing. We all did. I can recall so many occasions when repressed, muddled emotions resulted in someone inadvertently laughing at a piece of tragic news, or bursting into tears at a joke. We spoke of death the way one speaks of the weather: 'Did you hear so-and-so had been killed?' had become a standard point in any conversation, usually immediately after a 'How are you?'

When my mother walked into my room, clutching an envelope, I knew as soon as I saw her face that it was more bad news.

the men. 'They need to see smiles and pretty faces when they step off those trains,' she said. And we weren't just to serve them: we were to greet them, she said; to cheer them up, chat to them and listen to them. After all, they were heroes, each and every one of them, she told us. And so, with a smile on my face, I handed out tea to Tommies and to officers. I chatted to the walking wounded and to the seemingly fit and able, and I sat with those badly injured on stretchers, limbless bodies with boyish faces, holding a teacup to their parched lips, placing a cigarette to their mouths, and then lifting it away as they exhaled. In that miasma of putrid flesh and seeping wounds, blood, dirt, sweat and vomit, I held hands and stared into black-ringed eyes. I smiled at their generosity, their never-ending compliments and propositions of marriage, and sometimes I winked back at them. Yes, I flirted, we all did; even Lady Astley, I think.

And to them all, I was Clarissa.

''Ere, Clarissa, Arthur says he's in love with you, already!'

'Clarissa! Another cuppa over here, love, and bring them lips with you, ha!'

The station was always pandemonium when the trains came in, especially at night: filled with volunteers like us, Red Cross workers, nurses and ambulance men waiting to collect the injured. Depending on the time of day, there would sometimes be a crowd of fervently patriotic members of the public to welcome their returning troops with a song, as well as a few vividly painted ladies.

All of the men were exhausted and, not surprisingly, dazed; startled by their welcome, and perhaps the recognition of something near to normality, near to a memory. Many were suffering from the effects of mustard gas: half blind, skin blistered, eyes weeping, stuck together, or covered by a bandage; they moved along the platform in a long automated line, hands upon the shoulders of the man in front, zombie-like.

In the hut, for that's all it really was, we had an iron boiler, an enormous tea urn, three old jugs and a pail for washing up in. But somehow we managed. More than that, we did it all with gusto. Lady Astley's two daughters, Flavia and Lily, were there almost every day, and Rose too.

I don't think I'd ever felt as alive or, bizarrely, laughed as much. And this was perhaps what struck me more than anything else: that these men, men who'd been living on their wits, fighting for survival, and in such appalling conditions—for by then we all knew about life in the trenches—could still laugh, and sing; still flirt and smile. My vocabulary expanded, and I learnt a few new songs. None of them Mama would have liked, all of them I loved.

'You're a looker and a half mind, ain't ya? Gotta sweetheart, love?'

'Here! Bert! Come and meet me new fiancée, Clarissa . . .'

Of course I looked out for Tom, and for Henry too. And once, during my first few weeks, Jimmy Cooper appeared; astounded and delighted to find me there, thinking I'd somehow anticipated his arrival as I ran towards him shouting out his name. But I never saw Tom. Oh, occasionally there'd be a man down the platform, emerging through the steam, half lost in the sea of pale, thin faces and khaki uniforms, and yes, for a moment, I'd think, *it's him, it's him*. I'd catch my breath, forget what I was doing as I tried to follow that face. And then I'd lose it. *It wasn't him . . . it can't have been him.*

Then, one day, when I arrived to take over from Rose, she said, 'You'll never guess whom I've just been talking to, literally—just gone on the last train.'

'Who?' I asked, hanging up my coat on the inside of the door.

'Tom Cuthbert!'

I turned. 'Really? Just now?'

'Yes . . . minutes ago, dear,' she replied. 'He had a three-day pass, said he'd been down to Deyning.'

She must have seen something, sensed something, 'You all right, dear?' she asked, reaching out and touching my arm.

'Yes, fine,' I said, raising my hand to my head. 'Just a headache, that's all.'

'Do you want Flavia to stay? Do your turn, dear? She can, you know . . . she's already said that. She said she can stay until later.'

Flavia was hovering beside her, the two other girls standing further back.

'No, I'm fine. Truly, it's nothing.'

Rose lit a cigarette, picked up her handbag.

'Right-o then, see you tomorrow, dear. Don't expect it'll be too busy tonight, nothing much seems to be happening, but you never know.'

She turned to go.

'Rose!'

'Yes, darling?'

'Tom . . . Tom Cuthbert, how did he seem?'

'He looked exhausted, like the rest of them . . . said it was his first leave in ten months . . . said he'd slept for three whole days.'

'Did he . . . did he mention me?' I couldn't help it; I had to ask.

She looked at me, perplexed for a moment. 'No, darling, he didn't. And do you know I completely forgot to tell him that you were helping here too, completely forgot. How silly of me.'

'Oh well,' I replied, smiling back at her, 'not to worry. See you tomorrow then.'

I watched her go. Watched her and Flavia move off down the platform, their arms linked, their heads leaning inward, already deep in conversation. And I stood there completely still. Frozen on that spot. *He was here . . . moments ago he was here*. I closed my eyes, tried to imagine him standing where I now stood. I breathed in the dusty station air as though inhaling the echo of his energy, his breath. I took myself back through the preceding minutes. I'd been on my bicycle, cycling down the Strand . . . and then over Waterloo Bridge . . . and he'd been there. And I had that feeling once again: the queerest feeling of being out of kilter with the rest of the universe.

He was here.

We had missed each other by seconds.

I turned, went inside the hut, and began stacking the clean cups on to a shelf. Then I unstacked them, and put them into lines. I noticed one was chipped at its rim. A strange, perfectly formed chip, in the shape of a V. I stood there for some time, staring at that chipped cup, running my finger round and round its imperfect rim, until my flesh finally caught its sharp edge, and tore.

* * *

I was lying on my back, stretched out on the pale pink velvet chaise longue at the end of her bed, and she said, 'You know, dear, you'll ruin your hair, lying like that.'

We should have been at Flavia Astley's twenty-first birthday party, or at least on our way. But by now it was after nine.

'Do you really want to go, Rose? I'm not sure I can be bothered . . . think I'd rather stay here.'

'Hmm. I think we should . . . don't you? We'll have missed the dinner by now, of course, but if we don't turn up . . . and there's my parents, your mother . . . we did say we'd follow on.'

An hour earlier, as the front door slammed shut, and Rose's parents—along with my mother—headed off to the Astleys' party, two streets away, I'd once again taken a needle to my arm, after I'd injected Rose. She only wanted a light dose, she said. She'd taken a sixth of a grain. I had a quarter, I think, or perhaps a little more.

I said to her, 'Tell me about your thing with Tom again . . . Tom Cuthbert.'

I don't know why, but some dark, perverse part of me, my brain, wanted to hear her speak about it. It was a scrap, of something, sustenance, and—no matter how unappetising—I was famished, my heart desperate. And I thought just to say his name, hear another speak his name, might somehow satiate those splintered molecules of my being.

She lay on the bed next to me, her feet on the pillow, her head propped in her hands.

'Tom Cuthbert,' she said slowly, slurring the syllables, 'is really . . . *quite* . . . delicious.'

I turned on to my side, looked up into her eyes: tiny black pinprick pupils swimming in a watery grey.

'You know, Rose, your eyes are the colour of the sea.'

She looked down and smiled at me.

'I think I need to tell you something,' she said. She moved on the bed, pulled a pillow down and rested her chin upon it. 'In fact . . . I need to tell you two things, darling.'

'Hmm, and so,' I said, watching her.

'Well, that night with Tom, the time I said I was with him . . . I sort of lied.'

I stared at her. 'Sort of?'

'I didn't mean to . . . he did kiss me . . . but nothing more. I made up the rest.'

I didn't say anything. I wondered if I'd heard her correctly.

Did she just say she made it up?

After a minute or two I came up with one word to say to her: why?

'Oh . . . I don't know,' she said, sounding quite angry and burying her face in the pillow.

Then she lifted her head. 'You asked me, you egged me on, and I wanted to be able to tell you something . . . something more than the fact that he'd kissed me when he was drunk.' She paused, sighed, and then turned over, on to her back. 'You don't understand,' she said, staring up at the ceiling. 'Nothing exciting ever happens to me. No one's ever been in love with me . . . desired *me*.'

'But Henry said you were seeing him.'

'Yes, because that's what I told him. I wanted Henry to think that . . . I wanted to make him jealous. Oh really Clarissa, I've been in love with your brother for years . . . and I don't think he's even noticed me.'

‘That’s not true, he really does rather like you Rose, I know that.’ I sat up, slowly. There was a quivering sort of glow about the room and I could feel my heart palpitating, my whole body trembling, as though everything were caught in the same vibration. I said, ‘Tell me the truth Rose, what happened between you and Tom Cuthbert?’

She rolled on to her stomach, lifted her head and looked back at me. ‘Nothing, really, that’s just it. Oh, we kissed, but . . .’

‘Yes?’

She frowned, began to fiddle with the lace on the pillow. ‘He was drunk, and it was dark . . . and he seemed to think I was you, dear. You see, he said your name; he kept on calling me *Clarissa*.’

CHAPTER TWENTY

Charlie and I were married in October 1918, at the church round the corner from our home in Mayfair. He’d told me, and more than once, that it was all he was living for, to marry me. In the end, there seemed little point in waiting. Both Mama and the Boyds had said so. ‘The sooner you marry the better,’ Mama had said. ‘It will give poor Charlie the motivation he needs to pull through and make a full recovery.’

In the weeks leading up to my wedding Mama had repeatedly told me that I was a little too thin, a little *too* pale. But I had no appetite for food, and no appetite for marriage. On the day, an hour or so before the service, and sitting on my bed with Rose, I pushed a needle into my vein, and she said, ‘I’m really not sure it's a good thing for you to be doing this at this moment in time . . .' Minutes later, she stood with me, holding back my veil, as I'd retched over the lavatory, and then she held me as I cried silently on her shoulder. It was the last time I ever took morphia.

Henry had managed to secure two days' leave and came home to give me away, and after the wedding we had a small reception at Claridges. Our wedding photograph appeared in *The Times*, the *Tatler* and *Country Life* magazines: Charlie in his uniform, stern faced and minus his walking stick, and me, looking serene and wan in my gown of ivory duchesse satin and Mama's long lace veil, staring back—unsmiling—at the camera with peculiarly dark eyes. Of course, it was not the wedding my mother had once hoped for, not the wedding she'd planned for me for so many years. There were simply too many missing for it to be a fulfilment of that dream. And there could be no honeymoon. The war was not yet over, and Charlie had to return to Craiglockhart to continue his convalescence and treatment. So we had only one night together, our wedding night, in the honeymoon suite at Claridges.

We were both nervous, and the combination of champagne and pills had made Charlie even more emotional. When I emerged from the dressing room, wearing the long silk negligee I'd selected at Selfridges only the week before, he smiled. 'You're so beautiful,' he said, and then burst into tears. He was sitting on the edge of the bed in his pyjamas, and I immediately moved over to him, sat down next to him and held him in my arms. I wasn't sure if it was wedding-night nerves or something else.

But he told me then, through his tears, that I'd made him so happy; that our life together would be good. 'We're going to be so happy together, Clarissa,' he said, looking down at my hand, held in his.

We lay in each other's arms for quite some time, talking about the future, where we might buy a house, how we'd like it to be. And we talked about the war, the likelihood of it ending in the coming months.

'I don't want you to get better too soon . . . not if means you have to go back and fight. Not now,' I said, looking up at him.

He stared up at the ornate cornicing on the ceiling. 'And I don't want to go back there. Ever.'

I think I realised that night that he would never be the Charlie I'd known before. The witty quips, the jesting and teasing I'd always associated with him seemed to have gone from his character for ever. There was a new intensity to him, which frightened and excited me at the same time. And he seemed so much older than the other Charlie.

He said, 'I want you to know I'm not a virgin, Clarissa.'

I didn't say anything. I wasn't sure why he had told me this, what he expected me to say, but I didn't want to ask questions, and I didn't want him to ask me any. He reached over to his side, switched off the lamp, then he moved down the bed, alongside me, and took me in his arms. 'I shall be very gentle with you, darling.'

'Yes.'

We kissed slowly, and as his hands moved over my body, following its lines and curves, I could hear his breathing, becoming heavier, quicker. 'I love you . . . love you so much,' he murmured. He pulled up my nightgown, moved his hand up my leg to the inside of my thigh. I felt him against me, felt his hardness. He pushed my legs apart with his own, pulled my nightgown up further still. I was beginning a descent, slowly moving through the blackness to a memory. I wrapped my arms around his neck, placed my lips upon his shoulder. 'I'll be gentle,' he said again, in a whisper, and moving himself between my legs. I could hear the rumble of traffic in the distance, feel *his* lips upon my neck, *his* hands exploring . . . And then, as he entered me, and moaned loudly, I came back into the room.

'I'm sorry, darling, I don't think that was quite as pleasurable for you as it was for me,' he said, moments later. 'It'll get better though, I promise. First time's never very enjoyable for the lady.'

I felt a tear escape. 'Don't worry, it's been a long day . . . we're both tired.'

'I didn't hurt you, did I?'

'No, no,' I said, 'you were gentle, very gentle.'

We lay in each other's arms in silence, and as his breathing slowed I quietly moved away. I lay on my back, my eyes wide open to the darkness, and I pondered on that momentous day, my wedding day. None of it was as I'd once imagined. This is my new life, I thought, I am married: for I had said, *I do*.

I rewound the events of the preceding twelve hours: arriving at the church with my dashing elder brother; walking down the aisle on his arm, and seeing Charlie, standing there in his uniform, smiling nervously, leaning heavily on his stick; the small sea of ostentatious hats and plumage; the oversized arrangements of white roses, eucalyptus and ivy; Mama, turning to look at me with a queer, sad smile.

I do . . .

I whispered those words once more. I had married Charlie, for better, for worse, for richer, for poorer, in sickness and in health.

I do . . .

The following morning, after breakfast, Charlie delivered me back to my mother's house, and then went to catch his train. He'd been in a strange mood that morning, distracted and monosyllabic. When he bid me goodbye, kissing me on my cheek, his manner was brusque. But I put this down to the fact that he didn't wish to leave me, didn't wish to go back to hospital.

Venetia was already at the house that morning, and she and Mama both fussed over me. I was a new bride; I had just had my wedding night.

'Aha! Well, you look radiant, dear. And you were an absolute vision yesterday . . . stunning, wasn't she, Edina?'

'Yes, beautiful, very beautiful,' Mama said, looking up at me from where she sat and taking hold of my hand. 'Your father would have been so proud . . . so proud.'

My mother had never once asked me if I loved Charlie. And, to be honest, the idea of marrying for love, per se, seemed . . . indulgent, outdated, and unrealistic, like another pre-war luxury that didn't fit with the times; didn't fit with austerity. Marrying for love belonged to another era, an era when there had been enough time to dream. For now it was enough to be married; to have someone still alive and in one piece to claim as one's own. And I imagine that Mama was relieved. Relieved to have me married, respectable, and in safe hands.

In the weeks that followed, the weeks between my marriage and the end of the war, I tried to focus on my new life, on being healthy and happy. I told myself it was a new beginning, and when I began to tremble and shake, I repeated the phrase Mama had used—*a fresh start*—in my head, and sometimes out loud.

For a while I avoided seeing Rose. I continued my work, and I played bridge—with girls who liked playing bridge; I went to matinees at the Gaiety cinema and to the theatre with Mama and Venetia, and for dinner to Kettners, Scotts and the Carlton Grill. Of course it felt no different to be married. I was still living with Mama, still sleeping in my rosebudded sanctuary; only my name had changed. I was now Clarissa Boyd, and I practised my new signature endlessly. I found myself talking about 'my husband' and planning a future, our future. And soon, I'd have my own home. The plan was for us to live with Mama once Charlie had been discharged, or when the war was over, and from there, to look for something of our own.

There was an end and a beginning in sight, and I sensed it within every pore of my being. There was a future, a future without a war.

On November the eleventh, the day we'd all prayed for finally arrived. At 11 a.m. the maroons sounded across London—and this time for the armistice and not an air raid. The war was over. Within minutes celebrations erupted across the city, and I heard the shouting, the jubilant crowds making their way to Trafalgar Square and Piccadilly, but it was a bittersweet moment, tinged with the most profound sadness. For Mama and I, like so many others, could only think of those we'd lost, those unable to share in that victory and national euphoria.

Mama appeared quite calm, almost subdued as she poured us each a glass of sherry, and then, with a shaky hand and tears in her eyes, she made a toast: 'To our long-awaited victory . . . and to my brave, brave boys, William and George, and all the others who can't be here today.'

The war is over.

I held the tiny glass out, clinked it against Mama's, and as I raised it to my lips I thought of Tom. Was he on his way home? Or was he already back, and in London? I knew he had to be alive, had to have survived, otherwise I'd have heard; I'd have sensed something. I'd have known.

As Mama disappeared from the room, to go below stairs and tell the servants they could all have the day off, I walked over to the window and looked down on to the square. Already there were crowds of people, shouting, dancing, linking arms, and some even kissing. One young chap had managed to climb up one of the trees and waved a flag there; another, immediately below him, stood on a bench, his hat clutched to his chest, singing; and in the midst of this riotous frenzy were cars and taxicabs, spilling over with people, hooting loudly as they headed through the square.

And I began to laugh. 'The war is over,' I said out loud, and then I unlocked and opened the door on to the balcony.

'The war is over! The war is over!' I shouted out across Berkeley Square.

A uniformed man shouted back up to me, 'God save the King!'

'God save the King!'

'And to France!' another called up.

'Vive la France!' I called back, laughing.

And another voice: 'To victory!'

'To victory!'

Then Rose and Flavia and Lily Astley appeared below me.

'Come down! Come down! We're going to celebrate, come down now!' Rose shouted up.

Minutes later, I was on the top of a bus, crammed to capacity with girls and soldiers, everyone shouting and singing, and crowds cheering back at us as we passed by. We got off the bus at the Ritz and drank champagne with friends in the packed bar, and then we headed on—to the Carlton—to meet more friends. From there, and with an opened bottle of *free* champagne, we travelled on the roof of a taxicab to Trafalgar Square, where it seemed to me the entire country had gathered, and where we sang songs, made toasts, and vowed eternal loyalty and love to everyone we saw. And later still, we followed the throng to Buckingham Palace, and there, with aching throats and ragged voices, and linking arms with those around us, we cheered our King and Queen. That night and all through the night London continued to celebrate. Out on the streets people sang, laughed and wept; cars, buses and taxicabs hooted, and we all waved, blew kisses and shouted back. Each and every house opened its doors, welcoming strangers like long-lost relatives.

It seemed to me as though order had been restored and then rapidly magnified; the world was once again a place of peace and goodwill, and love. How could we *ever* have been at war? People like us, so reasonable, so just; so magnanimous? And walking home down Curzon Street, with my heart fit to burst, I noticed the moon, winking and blinking at me between clouds. That sweet heavenly face, still promising light and dawn. And I whispered to her once again.

You see, it was a moment; one of those moments you never, ever forget.

'The war is *over*,' I said, as I climbed into my bed, elated, exhausted.

The war is over . . .

Then, at the very edge of wakefulness, it hit me: the sheer magnitude and permanence of our loss. How could we forget them—those missing from the party? How could we dance and sing and celebrate? And as I lay there, I tried to count up all the boys I'd known who'd been killed in the war: my brothers, their schoolmates and friends, the brothers of my own friends, my cousins, all three of the Hamilton boys from Monkswood, so many of the men from the estate, and Frank and John.

'Frank and John,' I said out loud.

I hadn't thought of them in such a long time, and at that moment they came to me so clearly, so vividly—those two young under-gardeners—as though I'd seen them both only days before. But Frank had been killed in the very early days of the war, his nimble cricketer's feet stepping on a mine within days of arriving at the front. John had survived almost two years, been invalided home, only to return to the trenches to be killed. No garden would ever again know their toiling hands, no girls the colour of their hearts. No village green would ever again see Frank's white figure run forward, his arms encircling the air, spinning a ball towards the wickets.

Goodnight, sweet boys, goodnight.

The following morning Mama handed me the newspaper, saying, 'You may well see yourself in one of those photographs.' And as I glanced over the front page I noticed the date, November the twelfth. Emily's first birthday. Amidst the Forgotten, she'd been forgotten too.

*   *   *

A few days after the armistice we received a letter from Henry. He told us that there were no celebrations at the front. Many there believed that the armistice was temporary and that the war would soon resume. After so many months and years of living under intense strain, in mortal danger and thinking only in terms of war and the enemy, the abrupt release was physical and psychological agony. Some, he said, suffered total collapse, and some could only think of their dead friends, whilst others fell into an exhausted sleep. All of them were stunned by the sudden meaninglessness of their existence as soldiers; their minds numbed by the sudden silence, the shock of peace. Those of us back at home continued to read about death in the newspapers: the soldiers killed by stray bullets after the ceasefire; and those already in oblivion, unaware of peace, who'd later died from their wounds.

It would be weeks before Henry could return home. He had to see to it that arrangements for the transportation of his men and others were in place and then managed. It was 'chaos', he told us in another letter. The logistics of demobilising our troops—trying to get them all back home in time for Christmas—was nigh on impossible, and, as an officer, he would have to stay until all of the men under his command were on their way. He wasn't sure when he'd be back, but soon, he hoped.

Those days, the days immediately after the armistice, were strange for us too. For once the euphoria of victory slowly ebbed, I sensed a queer sort of atmosphere and awkwardness about the city, and with people I knew. How did we begin to pick up the pieces of our lives? And what were we left with? How could we look each other in the eye again, smile, and say, 'How do you do!' in that cheery, universally acknowledged British way? And how *did* we do? Those of us who had not been in the trenches, who'd not lived in squalor—with mud and rats, discarded limbs and rotting bodies, that deafening barrage and stench of death—could never pretend to know or understand. We had no visible injuries, no scars, no tattered uniform or medal, but we too were damaged: damaged by grief and loss, damaged through association; and associated through guilt.

The demobilisation of five million men was upon us, and as disorienated men in mud-caked uniforms began to appear on the streets—unsure of what to do or where to go—the mood in London changed, and we seemed to be grappling with a new dilemma. For suddenly the horror of the war was there, on display in front of us, as hundreds of thousands of men arrived back from the trenches. Delivered back into the bright lights of normality, they flooded the city's streets, stations and squares, and assembled in parks, where temporary camps had been set up as holding stations for them. They loitered by tube stations, and on the corners of Oxford Street, Regent Street, in Leicester Square and Piccadilly: traumatised, bewildered souls, often drunk, and sometimes begging. So very different to those pristine uniformed young men I'd seen there years before. And those wretched scraps of men, the ones who'd been disfigured, their bodies chewed up and spat out for their country, were there too: limbless, and in freakishly painted tin masks to hide their missing faces. There was no escape, we had to see what we had done, had to confront the consequence of our actions. And here they were: our valiant young heroes.

There could be no return. None of us, no matter our situation or circumstances, could pick up the pieces of life as it had once been, before the war. We had all been changed, and our lives as we'd known them had gone, and gone for ever.

* * *

. . . We will undoubtedly have to sell off the land, but I am praying we might somehow be able to save the house (and the garden), despite the rather desperate need for funds, and so I try to be optimistic for H's sake, for this is all such a dreadful worry to him, & he is in no fit state to deal with it. Everything seems adrift, unstable, and I feel as though with each passing day we are nearing another calamity—not another war, God forbid, but an exhausted collapse of our ragged economy. It is inevitable, I believe. And what a life for those who fought for their country! What meagre life their reward. Sometimes I can't help but wonder if it wouldn't have been better for the Germans to have arrived on these shores . . . for perhaps then the men would have work, a

sense of pride, & my boys still here . . .

CHAPTER TWENTY-ONE

I finally returned to Deyning late in the spring of 1919. Some weeks before, Henry had had a lawyer come to the house in London to explain things to Mama, and to me. It was impossible, financially impossible, for us to keep it. The entire estate—the house, the land and the farm—would have to be sold, he said. It would be divided up and auctioned as separate lots, allowing interested parties to buy some or all of the estate, and ensuring, he hoped, that we got the best price.

My mother had been stoical, nodding her head as she cast her eyes over the pages of numbers laid out upon the dining-room table. But I couldn't believe it. Those numbers meant nothing to me, and Deyning—everything.

Henry was already at the house when Mama and I arrived. He'd gone down a couple of weeks before, taking two friends with him for company, and was supposed to be working through the inventory, making a list of repairs to submit to the army. Mama and I were to oversee the packing up before the auction, which was to be held the following month. He had telephoned the week before, warning me, and telling me to prepare Mama about the state of the place. But nothing could have prepared us.

When we motored up the driveway that day we were stunned by what we saw. The gardens, only five years before so lovingly tended and well kept, were lost, hidden under giant thistles and waist-high weeds; cows roamed about, grazing on what had once been the tennis lawn, and the whole place was littered with debris: dilapidated huts, piles of wood, rolls of barbed wire, abandoned wheels and oil drums. 'Like a gypsy encampment,' Mama said, staring out of the car window as we approached the house. Tank tyre tracks had slewed up the earth where manicured lawns and neatly arranged flower beds had been; and great clumps of grass, dandelions and rampant ivy clung to every ornamental wall and flagstone pathway. Without Mama, without the gardeners, the wilderness had finally marched in on the place, exactly as I'd once imagined.

I wondered then if Tom Cuthbert might be about. I knew Mrs Cuthbert still lived at Deyning, in the same cottage, but I'd never once heard Tom's name mentioned. In fact, I had no idea where he was or what he was doing with his life. And though I still dreamt of him from time to time, I hadn't actually thought of him in a while. I'd been busy, looking after Charlie and seeing to our new home. We'd recently moved into a house not far from Mama's, and she and I had spent the preceding weeks selecting wallpapers, fabrics and new furnishings. The move had distracted me, and perhaps Mama too, from the impending loss of Deyning. And she seemed to have finally accepted that Deyning, like William and George and Papa, belonged to the past and not the future.

As our car came to a standstill I felt a sense of dread, and wondered what awaited us inside. But my father had been right: the house *had* been wrecked. Spindles—and even some of the balusters—had disappeared from the staircase; shelves and panelling—gone; a number of doors were missing, others, hung splintered from shattered hinges; and broken windowpanes, crudely boarded over, made the place appear even more dark and gloomy. My mother quietly wept, shaking her head in dismay as she walked about the place, moving slowly from room to room, unable to comprehend the decimation.

'I can't believe it,' I said. 'It's only been five years.'

'But a long five years,' Henry replied.

'Yes. A very, very long five years,' my mother whispered.

'Mrs Cuthbert's been wonderful, and Mabel's come back to help too. She's in the kitchen, I think. We've all worked jolly hard. You should've seen the place when we arrived here . . . it was bloody filthy,' Henry said and then laughed, but his laugh was forced and shrill.

My mother moved towards him, lifted her hand to his face, and stroked his cheek. She said, 'Henry, my darling boy, your father would be so proud of you. This is not what he would have wished for, not what he would have wished to see happening, but he would be proud of you, my dear.'

But the atmosphere was strange, and Henry's mood odd and unpredictable. He pulled away from her, began to rub the place she'd touched, as though wiping away something, as though in pain.

'It's all right, Henry,' she said, in a barely audible monotone. 'Everything is fine. All will be well.'

I suppose she knew the signs, even then; knew when Henry was about to have an attack.

'Clarissa, could you please ask Mabel to serve tea

now. Henry and I will be in the morning room.'

I walked away, down the passageway towards the kitchen, and at the door I stopped and turned back to look at them. Henry's head rested upon Mama's shoulder, and I thought he looked as though he was crying. She was stroking his hair, whispering to him. It was the first time I'd seen what my mother would later refer to as Henry's 'panic attacks'.

The following morning I rose early. I'd decided to have a final ride across what was still our land, on Father's old horse, Brandy. We'd always kept livestock at Deyning, always had horses. Before the War, before our younger horses went off to the front, I think we'd had over a dozen. But now there was only Brandy; and he, too, despite all my pleadings, was going to auction.

It was a bright morning, the stable yard filled with sunshine and the warm smell of manure. I saddled up Brandy myself, and as I stood in the shadows—on the mounting block—I was vaguely aware of someone out of the corner of my eye. I took no notice, thinking it to be one of the men from the village Henry had brought in to help clear the place up.

I mounted Brandy, gathered up the reins.

'Hello, Clarissa.'

It took me a moment to realise it was him. He looked so different: unshaven, shabby. And for a split second I thought I might be dreaming, that perhaps he wasn't real, was a vision. I'd heard that sometimes—even when we're least expecting it—we're able to conjure up absent loved ones, like ghosts. He must have sensed my shock, because he grimaced as he turned away from me.

'Tom . . . I didn't know . . . didn't know you were

here. No one said.'

He stood with his hands in his pockets, looking down at the ground. Then he raised his head and without turning to look at me, he said, 'I think my congratulations are a little late, Mrs Boyd.'

I didn't say anything because I didn't know what to say.

He moved across the cobblestones towards me, and I could feel my heart, pounding so violently I thought I might faint.

'I saw your wedding photograph, of course . . . in *some* magazine or other,' he said, standing in front of me, reaching out to stroke the horse's nose. 'And I wish you both well. Charlie's a decent chap . . . and a lucky man,' he added.

He leant forward, rubbing the side of his face against Brandy's jaw. And I wanted to reach down, touch him; run my hand through his hair.

I said, 'So, how are you? You look . . . a little different.'

He didn't look up, but kept his face pressed against the horse.

'I am different,' he said. 'And you are too, Clarissa.'

'Yes, we're all changed, Tom. Life's changed.'

He stepped back, raised his eyes to me. 'It is. And times move on.'

'Yes, times move on . . . they have to,' I said, feeling that tug: a pull in my solar plexus. 'And doesn't it seem like a lifetime ago,' I continued, trying to sound like an old friend, 'that we were all last here, all of us together?'

He stared at me. 'Yes, a lifetime. It's a different world.'

'A different world,' I repeated.

'But a lovely morning for a ride,' he added. Then he turned, walked across to the stable-yard gate and opened it for me. I pulled on the reins, moved across the cobblestoned courtyard, and as I passed through the gate I looked down at him and simply said, 'Thank you,' the way I would to anyone. As I entered the meadow, looking out upon that place which had once been ours, I shut my eyes. Then I heard the clunk of the gate behind me—like a latch dropping on my heart—and I turned back, but he'd already disappeared.

My ride was not the ride I'd anticipated. All I could think of was him. Each point along the way led me back to him: every tree and field, each fence and gate and stile. Every familiar point on the horizon, memorised and cherished for the moments I'd spent there with him, or thinking of him; each landmark and vista reminding me of him. A white veil of mist hung over the lake, and beyond it, a windless, serene landscape: dream-like and out of reach.

When I returned to the stables, an hour or so later, a young boy helped me to dismount and took Brandy from me. And I contemplated going to Mrs Cuthbert's cottage and knocking on the door. I wasn't sure what I'd say, or even if he'd be there, but I wanted to see him, wanted to say so much. But how could I? And what was there to say now? I was married. I was Mrs Boyd.

Over breakfast, and before Mama came down, I asked Henry what was to become of Mrs Cuthbert. He told me she'd be fine; she'd stay on in her cottage, he thought; probably continue as housekeeper at Deyning. It wasn't the right time to ask too many questions, and Henry didn't seem to cope well with questions—so I tried to leave it at that. I tried but I couldn't.

'I saw Tom Cuthbert this morning,' I said, as I buttered my toast.

'Oh yes,' Henry replied, from behind the newspaper.

'Has he been here for long?'

He lowered the paper, stared across the table at me. 'He's been here for years, Issa. You know that.'

'Yes, yes . . . I know he's lived here for some years, but he went away to war too,' I said, wondering if Henry had somehow momentarily forgotten about the War. 'What I meant was has he been back here long?'

'Oh, I've no idea. He's certainly been around for the last couple of weeks, but how long before that I'm really not sure.' He shuffled the newspaper, folding it and laying it down next to him, then added, 'Yes, now I come to think of it, he did ask after you.' He looked across at me and smiled. 'You know I always had a hunch that he . . . rather liked you. Even looked a tad despondent when I told him you *and* your husband would be coming down.'

'Charlie had to stay in London . . . he's still having treatment. And, anyway, he wouldn't have coped with the chaos and upheaval here.'

Mama had already informed me that our day was to be spent listing all of the items that were to be sent to London, and those that were to remain at the house to be auctioned. A full day's work, she'd said to me the previous evening. I couldn't disappear, and I knew that she would not be pleased to know Tom Cuthbert was about, back at Deyning. And, though I was worried about how she would react to that news, I decided I had to tell her

I'd seen him; explain to her, prepare her. But the thought of uttering his name to her made me shake so much that when I lifted a slice of toast to my mouth I noticed my hand already trembling.

In the end it was easier than I'd anticipated. We were sitting in what was once her boudoir, ticking off items on Henry's scrawled inventory.

'Yes, I knew he was here,' she said, without looking up at me. 'How is he?'

'He's . . . fine. Older, of course,' I said, surprised by her lack of reaction, her calmness.

'How was he with you?' she asked, moving papers about.

'Perfectly fine. It was brief, Mama. We said very little, but he wished me well on my marriage.'

'Good,' she said, and then she looked up at me. 'Do you still love him?'

I couldn't quite believe she'd asked me that question, so boldly, so openly. And even now, I find it hard to believe that she did. For in those five words she finally acknowledged something: that I had loved Tom Cuthbert.

'I don't know,' I answered, honestly.

'I do what I think is best for each of you . . . both of you,' she said, lowering her eyes again. 'It could never have come to anything. But I think you realise that now.' She peered at me, over her spectacles, and I could tell she wasn't quite finished. 'You've been through a great deal, Clarissa, but it's all in the past now. Leave it there. Don't be tempted to revisit those dark days.'

At first I wondered what she meant. Was she referring to my baby? Was she worried I'd tell Tom?

'I have no intention of revisiting them, Mama,' I

replied, looking away from her to the list in front of me.

It had been two years. Two years since I'd discovered I was pregnant with Tom's child, and yet it felt to me more like ten. So much had happened in that short space of time: I'd been sent away, given birth to my daughter and given her away; and now I was married. But of course only my mother knew all of this. A piece of my history, those *dark days*—that indelible part of my story—could never be acknowledged; never be spoken of. Some losses, it seemed to me, particularly in wartime, were noble sacrifices, but the loss of an unplanned, illegitimate child was beyond shameful; it was, quite simply, unmentionable. Later, upon relfection, I knew exactly why my mother was so concerned. She was worried that my seeing Tom Cuthbert again would reopen what had once appeared to her to be a gaping, messy wound. After all, it had tidied up nicely, left no visible scars.

That evening, having our before-dinner drinks in the dismantled drawing room, he appeared; dressed for dinner, shaven and dapper. I was shocked. I half expected my mother to ask him to leave, but instead she moved towards him, asked him how he was, spoke to him kindly, even tenderly, and he was nothing less than a gentleman in his demeanour and replies to her. Henry was in the mood for a party and played 'I Wonder Who's Kissing Her Now' on the gramophone.

'Come along, Issa . . .' he shouted, tugging at my hand, already half drunk. He sang the words of the song, pulling me across the bare floorboards, a cigarette hanging from his dry lips, as Mama looked on, smiling nervously, her head slightly lowered—

ready, expectant of anything. He would peak early and collapse, I thought, and I'm sure she thought that too.

Julian Carter and Michael Deighton had been in the same year at school with my brother. They were Henry's only two surviving friends—along with Charlie and Jimmy—from what he'd once called The Set. Almost their entire year had been killed in action. Michael had been a patient at the same hospital in Edinburgh as Charlie for a while and was a gentle, fragile soul, with a nervous smile and quiet manner. Julian had once been like Henry: handsome, loud, and full of fun; but all arrogance had been knocked out of him. He'd served in the Royal Flying Corps and had been badly burned and blinded when his aeroplane crashed returning from a night mission. No girls would ever again be rushing to kiss his mauled lips and badly grafted face.

As Henry pulled me across the drawing-room floor in an attempt to dance, these two damaged boys, for that's really all they were, sat together quietly like old men, watching—or in Julian's case, listening—to the young at play. And then the gong sounded, and we all marched into the dining room, overly gay, overly animated. I hadn't spoken to Tom in the drawing room, but at dinner we were seated opposite each other, and I felt a little too aware of his presence, especially in front of Mama. He and Henry, now seated in Father's place, smoked incessantly, and, I noticed, drank more than they ate. The conversation was mainly politics, with a few ridiculous and highly implausible stories from Henry, who was on dangerously sparkling form. I saw my mother watching Henry, and then saw her whisper something to Tom, seated on her right. And I suddenly realised why she'd wanted him there: to keep an eye on Henry, to look after him. She knew he would, you see.

After dinner, I noticed Mama whispering to Tom once again, in the hallway, before she excused herself and bid everyone goodnight. The rest of us, four war-torn damaged young men and me, returned to the drawing room. We'd been drinking champagne, the last of the good stuff from my father's cellar. 'Let's celebrate,' Henry said, returning from the kitchen with two of the young girls Mrs Cuthbert had hired from the village, *and* another bottle. 'Let's bloody well celebrate being alive, eh?' he said, smiling at Tom, and passing him the hand of one of the girls. And in a way it almost seemed like the old days. For there we were, celebrating, and dancing to Geroge's gramophone records. It was a party, a party at Deyning, and but for the missing furniture and carpets, and the absence of two of my brothers, it could have been . . . how it should have been.

'I say, Issa, Georgie would have loved this,' Henry called out to me as he whirled round the young blonde, and it was true: George always loved an impromptu party.

I stood on my own, sipping champagne, swaying in time to the music, watching Tom and his partner. I couldn't recall ever having seen him dance before, and he moved well, his feet keeping perfect time. I watched him guide her over to where Michael and Julian sat, and a beaming Michael rose to his feet and eagerly took her hand. Tom glanced over at me, then sat down and lit a cigarette. No, he won't dance with me, I thought; we can't dance together. Not now. I looked at Julian and my heart ached for him. I wasn't sure if he wanted to dance, or even if he was able, but I walked over to where he sat with Tom.

'Julian . . .' I said, putting down my glass and placing my hand upon his, 'will you dance with me?'

'Ah, Mrs Boyd, I thought you'd never ask,' he replied, rising unsteadily from his chair.

As I led him to the middle of the room, slowly, he said, 'Do you remember the last time we danced together, Clarissa?'

'No, I don't,' I said, taking his hand and placing it on my waist. 'When was it?'

'It was here, Henry's twenty-first birthday party, the year before . . . before the War broke out,' he said, trying to smile, stretching the tight skin of his new, colourless mouth.

'Yes, of course it was, of course. I remember now . . . you told me that you were waiting until I was eighteen, and then . . . then you were going to ask for Papa's permission to marry me. You really were such a flirt.'

He laughed. 'Those were the days. I don't suppose I'll be doing much flirting now, do you? More likely scare the girls off.'

'Don't say that.'

'Just as well I can't see myself really. But I want to know, do I . . . do I look particularly gruesome? Tell me, Clarissa; tell me the truth. Do you think anyone might see beyond this face . . . might love me?'

He'd stopped shuffling; we'd stopped moving.

'Well,' I began, looking back at him, almost wanting to cry, 'you're not quite as handsome as you were Julian, which at least means you give the others a chance now . . . and you're certainly not going to win any dancing competitions . . .' He laughed. 'And if all you'd ever wished for was someone to love you for your good looks, then you may well be disappointed. But if you let someone see inside your soul . . . see who you really are, then yes, you'll be loved, darling, and she'll be a very lucky lady too,' I added. And then, quite spontaneously, for I certainly hadn't planned on kissing Julian Carter that night, and I'm still not sure what came over me or why I did it, I took his head in my hands, placed my lips where his had once been and held them there for a moment. As I stepped back from him, I heard Henry clapping and then shout, 'Encore! Encore!'

I turned to Tom, and he stared back at me—his head lowered, as though he'd meant to look away.

Julian said, 'My God, Clarissa . . . I wasn't expecting that. You're the first person to kiss me since . . . in years.'

Minutes later, I led Julian back to his chair.

Tom stood up. 'I suppose if I ask you to dance *now*, it might seem like I want a kiss too,' he said. And Julian laughed.

I placed my hand upon his shoulder, felt the warmth of his flat against my back, and I let him guide me across the floor. I didn't, couldn't look into his eyes. I stared at his tie, his shirt collar, the line of his jaw, his mouth. Then, as Henry disappeared—twirling his dance partner through the open French doors—he pulled me closer, and I felt his breath on my face, his fingers spread out over my spine. A woman's voice sang out forlornly, 'I ain't got nobody,' and as he moved his hand in mine, interlinking our fingers, I looked up at him, into his eyes. He didn't smile, or speak, he simply held my gaze.

But I'd begun to feel light headed. I'd drunk far more than I was used to that night, and my physical proximity to him—his touch—seemed to have exacerbated the effects of the champagne. So, as the record finished, and with my head slightly spinning, I said, 'Please excuse me, I need some air.'

There was a full moon that night, a long shadow stretching across the driveway in front of the house. I don't know how far I walked, but I remember standing against a fence, trying to light a cigarette, when he appeared by my side. I knew he'd come. I knew he'd follow me. He took my cigarette, lit it and handed it back to me, and we stood there for a while, smoking, without saying a word.

'You hate me,' I said at last, without looking at him.

I heard him sigh. 'No, I don't hate you, Clarissa.'

'Did you ever love me?'

'Do you want me to have loved you? Is that what you want?'

'I want you to tell me the truth. I want you to be honest with me. I need to know.'

'But you belong to someone else now.'

I looked at him and I wished away the world; wished away Deyning, my mother, my brother, Charlie and everything else I knew.

He reached out, stroked my cheek. 'Beautiful Clarissa,' he said. But as I moved towards him he stepped back from me. 'You said you'd wait for me, you promised.'

'I did wait . . . I waited so long.'

'I can't stand the thought of you with him . . . with anyone else.'

'I don't want to be with anyone else. I've only ever wanted you.'

He stood holding on to the fence, staring out across the moonlit field.

'I think I should go away, leave here; leave England.'

'But you've only just come back . . . no, no, don't say that. Please . . .'

He turned to me. 'Clarissa, you're married. You have a life now . . . a life with Charlie. What do you suggest I do? Wait for you to one day fit me into your diary, so that we can meet for tea and reminisce about *old times*. Wait in the hope of one day being invited to your home for dinner—so that I can see you, so that I can watch him with you, watch him love you . . .' He turned away, ran his hands through his hair. 'We have to move on. I have to move on.'

'No. I won't let you,' I said, and I reached out but he pulled away again.

'What do you want from me, Clarissa? Do you want us to have an affair? Is that what you want?'

'No! Oh, I don't know . . . but I can't—'

'I could be your butler, eh? Or perhaps Charlie's valet . . . polish his shoes for him, service his wife when he's not about. Is that the idea? Am I getting a little warmer?'

'Tom!'

He closed his eyes, shook his head. 'We can't, Clarissa, we can't . . .' He turned to me. 'Look at me, I have nothing.' He shrugged. 'I'm nobody. How could I ever take care of you?'

'But I love you, Tom.'

'Forget about me; love your husband, Clarissa.'

And then he jumped over the fence, and walked off through the paddock towards the light of his mother's cottage.

CHAPTER TWENTY-TWO

I didn't want to go back to London, but I knew Mama would. She didn't want to stay and watch what was left of her home, dismantled, packed into crates. She'd said to me the previous day, 'I shouldn't have to do this . . . I shouldn't have to see this.' And she was right, I thought.

'I've been thinking, Mama, perhaps I should stay here with Henry,' I suggested over breakfast. 'It seems wrong for us to leave him, for him to be here on his own—sorting everything.'

'But what about Charlie?' she asked.

'He'll be fine. We have Sonia now,' I said, referring to our new maid. 'She'll look after him. I can stay here until the end of the week, and get Charlie to come down and fetch me then.'

She looked at me quizzically, and I saw the thought flash through her mind: Tom Cuthbert. Then she said, 'You're right, of course, I would feel better if one of us were to stay here with him. But are you quite certain that Charlie shan't mind?'

'Quite. I'll telephone him now.'

'Mama would prefer it if I were to stay here with Henry. Would you mind awfully if I did?'

'Yes, I jolly well would. Do you really have to? There's no doubt a bloody army of helpers there—*and* those two friends of his.'

'There's not an army of helpers here, Charlie. And Julian certainly can't do anything,' I added. 'I think Henry only brought him down for a break. And to be honest, Henry's not much use either. He's simply not able to cope with it all on his own.'

'Really, Clarissa, I need you here . . . I need you here with me.'

'But it'd only be for the week.'

'The week! You mean I shan't see you all week?'

'I'll call you. Every day. I promise. And on Friday, you can drive down here.'

He muttered something, then said, 'Well, it doesn't seem as though I have any choice in the matter. But it's really not on, you know. You're my wife . . . you're meant to be here for *me*.'

'You'll be fine, dear. And they do say absence makes the heart grow fonder . . .'

It wasn't as though I was planning anything sinister. I simply wanted to stay a little while longer at Deyning. And even if Tom Cuthbert hadn't been there, I'd have elected to stay and help Henry. But yes, I wanted to see Tom again too. I couldn't leave him. Not yet.

After waving off Mama, I spent the morning sorting china and crockery with Mabel in the dining room, listing each dinner and tea service, checking for chips and cracks before she wrapped them in newspaper and placed them into a crate. Henry had gone down to the farm, where there was to be an auction of livestock the following week, and I wasn't altogether sure where Michael and Julian were, or even if they were still at Deyning.

'I think we'll make that do for now, Mabel. I'd quite like to take a walk, have some fresh air. Perhaps we can finish off later this afternoon.'

I saw her roll her eyes. 'Right you are, miss. Well, I'll be helping Mrs C if you need me,' she said, and then she picked up another box and carried it from the room.

I wandered outside, on to the terrace. It was a warm day, already humid, and I wondered whether to walk to the lake, take a swim. I wondered where Tom was. He could be anywhere, I thought.

I walked back into the house and headed for the kitchen.

I poked my head around the baize door. 'Mrs Cuthbert?'

She appeared in the scullery doorway, wiping her hands on her apron. 'Oh, hello, Miss Clarissa. Can I get you something?'

'Actually, I need Tom. I wondered if he'd help me move some boxes.'

'Oh, Mabel and I can do that for you, dear.'

'No, these are very heavy boxes. Books.'

'Ah. Well, I imagine he's still at home, I'll go and fetch him for you.'

'No, no, it's quite all right, I'll go,' I said, and then I disappeared before she could say anything else.

I knocked on the cottage door, waited a moment and then turned the handle and stepped into the small hallway. 'Hello!'

I glanced into the room on my left: a tiny room with a low beamed ceiling and crammed with furniture. I stepped back over the hallway and opened another door: a kitchen, even smaller. Ahead of me, a steep, narrow staircase. I climbed it, quietly, not sure what I'd find, but wondering if Tom would be there, in his bed, asleep. At the top of the staircase I opened the door immediately on my right. Mrs Cuthbert's bedroom: immaculately tidy, with a pink bedspread on a small single bed. I stepped back out of the room, gently closing the door, turned to the other the door and lifted its latch. The room was in semi darkness, the curtains still closed. And there he was: lying face down, sleeping.

I could have left. I could have descended that narrow staircase and left the cottage, but I didn't. I entered the small sloping roofed room closing the door behind me, and then I slipped off my shoes, went over to his bed and knelt down on the floor next to him. I didn't touch him; I sat listening to his breathing, watching him. A faded blue curtain gently swayed by the open window next to me, and but for the sound of birds outside, the place was perfectly silent. I closed my eyes for a moment: *thank you for keeping him alive . . . thank you for keeping him safe*.

A white sheet wrapped tangled around his midriff; two legs, so perfectly formed, sprawled out across another; and an arm hung listlessly from the edge of the bed.

I studied that forearm, dangling in front of me, noting its shape, its dark hairs and scars; and then I lifted it, and pressed my lips to his flesh. He stirred, pulled his arm away, moved on to his side and opened his eyes, blinking at me.

'Am I dreaming?' he asked, in a thick, sleepy voice. A voice I'd never heard before.

'Yes,' I replied, rising to my feet, 'this is a dream, Tom . . . just a dream.'

I unfastened the buttons down the front of my dress, stepped out of it and laid it over a chair, on top of his clothes. I rolled down my stockings, one by one, and placed them carefully over the same chair. I untied my camisole, lifted it up over my head and placed that too upon the chair. And then I pulled the comb from my hair, and placed it upon a chest of drawers. I turned to him, watched his eyes pass over my body, saw him swallow, his mouth open slightly, and then I climbed into his bed, next to him, naked.

We made love without uttering any coherent word. And afterwards, I dressed in silence and left the cottage. I remember walking back to the house feeling the most sublime sense of peace. Had I no shame? No, not with him; never with him.

A little while later, I walked to the lake. I changed into my bathing costume at the boathouse and then swam across to the island. And as I sat on the jetty looking back at Deyning in the distance, I remembered all the summers and all the picnics I'd shared there—on that island—with my brothers. I saw them rowing over the water towards me, calling out my name, laughing. And then I saw a figure, standing by the boathouse, completely still, looking back across the lake at me. I watched him strip off his clothes, dive into the water and swim towards me. And I watched him emerge from the water.

'Miss Clarissa, will you be needin' anything . . . anything at all?' he asked standing in front of me, naked.

'Hmm. That depends what you had in mind, Cuthbert,' I replied, looking up at him, squinting into the sun.

'Can I be gettin' yer summit to drink, p'raps?'

'Yes . . . that would be rather nice. A glass of champagne, I think . . .'

'Very well, m'lady.'

And he turned, and dived back into the water.

'Tom! No! Come back!'

A few minutes later I saw him emerge at the other side of the lake. And I giggled out loud as I watched him pull on his clothes and then run up through the field, towards the house. *What on earth is he up to?*

I lay back against the warm timber and looked up at a never-ending blueness. How perfect some moments are: there was not a cloud between heaven and me. And as I languished there in the sunshine, I could hear the unabashed joy of young birds in the trees behind me, the rumbling of a distant motor. I closed my eyes, remembering our love-making of earlier that morning. And then I thought of Charlie. *Dear Charlie*. I didn't want to hurt him, didn't want to deceive him. But somehow it didn't feel wrong to be with Tom. You see, I'd given *him* my heart, promised it to him so many years before.

When I sat up, there he was, rowing towards me this time, fully clothed, a cigarette in his mouth. He climbed out of the boat, lifted out a large basket and a rug, and walked towards me.

'You were quick.'

'Time is of the essence, ma'am.'

'Oh God, I do hope you're not stuck in character for the whole afternoon.'

'Why? Do you not like it? I thought it might excite you . . . me playing that part.'

'I don't need you to play any part,' I said, as he spread the rug out next to me. 'Though I do rather like having you wait on me.'

'Aha! I knew it. Well then, m'lady, I'll be applyin' for yer position as lady's maid.'

'Gosh, that would be novel,' I replied, and giggled. 'And I can just see you in the uniform.'

'Yes, and it shall be my job to see to it that you're properly dressed . . . and undressed, each day, of course,' he continued, sitting down, and pulling a bottle of champagne from the basket. 'But there may be more undressing than dressing,' he added, glancing at me.

I rolled on to the rug and lay on my stomach.

'But you can't undress me more than once.'

'Yes, I can,' he said, glancing at me again with a wicked grin. 'I could spend all day dressing and undressing you.'

He popped the champagne, pulled a glass from the basket and poured it, licking the spillage from his hand and handing me the glass.

'Where did this come from? Papa's cellar?'

'Of course.'

'I thought we'd finished that.'

'Not the bottles I'd purloined.'

'You're shameless!'

'I know. But I happen to know this very gorgeous creature,' he said, lying down next to me, 'who rather likes champagne. It was an act of mercy, really.'

I laughed. 'You think champagne will keep her alive and gorgeous?'

'Absolutely. Champagne and me. Lots and lots of me.'

I rolled on to my side and looked up at him. 'You're right. Lots and lots of you will keep me alive.'

He turned to face me, his head propped in his hand. 'I think we should build a house here . . . and shoot anyone who comes across the water.'

'That's not very friendly,' I said, smiling at him, his humour.

'I don't feel like being friendly with anyone apart from you.'

I reached out, stroked his face. 'We'd have to have some friends . . . we'd get bored of each other, cooped up here on an island, day in, day out.'

'No we wouldn't. We could simply pretend to be other people when we got bored of our real selves.'

I laughed again. 'Ah, you mean you play lady's maid to Miss Clarissa.'

'Yes, that sort of thing. And I'm sure I can come up with a few more.'

'Such as?'

'Let me think . . . Groom to Miss Clarissa—or rather to her horse?'

'*Horses*, please. I'd have more than one.'

'Gardener to Miss Clarissa?'

'Broughton!'

He raised an eyebrow. 'And then we'd have to spend an awful lot of time in the hothouse . . .'

I smiled. 'You do seem bent on domestic service.'

He ran a finger down my nose. 'But of course. It's my family's line of business.'

'Perhaps I could be Issie, the extraordinarily well-endowed parlourmaid to Lord Cuthbert,' I suggested.

He looked up at the sky and shook his head. 'No. I'm afraid I can't see you being very convincing in that part.' He turned to me, 'You can only ever be Clarissa.'

We lay there for a while staring at each other, smiling. We'd already finished our glasses of champagne when he rose to his feet.

'Come,' he said, offering me his hand.

'But where?' I asked.

He placed the bottle and glasses back into the basket, threw the rug over his shoulder, and then led me away from the jetty, into the trees.

'But where are we going?' I asked again, carefully dodging nettles, ducking branches, but happy enough for him to lead me on.

'Away from eyes,' he replied.

When we emerged from the shadows, at the other side of the island, he stood on the bank looking about; surveying the landscape for *eyes* I presumed. Then he put down the basket and spread the rug out once more. I was cold, shivering.

'You really need to take that off . . . let it dry,' he said, sitting down. 'Here, take my shirt.' He pulled it off, over his head, and handed it to me, then turned away as I rolled down my bathing suit and put on his shirt. I hung the damp costume over a branch and sat down next to him on the rug. Ahead of us was nothing but water and empty cornfields, the hazy outline of hills in the distance. He took hold of my hand and for a while we sat in complete silence, staring out in front of us.

'I did wait, Tom,' I said at last.

'No, let's not speak of it, not now,' he said, and then he took hold of me, pulled me down on to the rug and kissed me.

We made love again, there, under that bright Sussex sky, and afterwards we swam in the lake; moving through the water separately then coming together once more, our bodies entwined under its dark wetness. When we emerged from the water, teeth chattering, he wrapped the rug around us both and held me in his arms. We spent the remainder of that afternoon lying on the bank, cocooned and naked inside the rug. We talked about his plans for the future. He said he simply wanted to get on with his life now and wouldn't be returning to Oxford.

'But what about the bar?' I asked.

'I don't want to go into law, not now. I couldn't go back to all that now.'

'What will you do?'

'I'm not entirely sure.' He turned to me. 'But I've been thinking about America . . .'

'America?'

'Yes. There are opportunities there. Opportunities to make a lot of money.' He paused, staring at me. 'You could come with me.'

'Come with you?'

'Yes, come with me. Come with me, Clarissa.'

'But what about Charlie, and Mama?'

'Leave Charlie and come with me.'

My head was swimming. 'Leave Charlie?' I repeated. 'But it would kill him. He loves me, I'm everything to him . . . all he has.'

He looked away, closed his eyes.

'I have to see you, Clarissa. I can't stand the thought of living in the same city, the same country, and not being able to see you . . . be with you.'

I pressed my lips against his neck. 'But you've lived without me for quite a while . . . and survived.'

'That was different. There was a war on. I wasn't free, wasn't able to see you.' He sighed. 'And now I've seen you,' he tightened his grip around me, 'held you, tasted you . . . I can't bear to let you go again.'

'And Charlie?' I asked, again.

'What about him? Were you thinking of him

when we made love this morning?'

'No! Of course not. But it's different here. You belong to me here . . . and I belong to you here.'

'Here,' he repeated, wistfully. 'And *here* is about to disappear. Deyning is about to be sold. So, after these few days, is that it?'

'Please, don't make it sound so brutal.'

'Well, it is, isn't it?'

'No, it's not. But I can't see any other way,' I said, sitting up, putting my head in my hands. 'America . . . it's just not possible.'

He grabbed hold of my wrist, pulled me back down to him, and wrapped his arms around me. 'I want to make love to you for the rest of my life,' he said, kissing my face. 'And when I breathe my last I want you there. I want the last word I utter to be your name, the last face I look upon to be yours . . .'

And I began to cry, for I too couldn't bear the thought of a future without him in it.

'Don't go to America, please Tom, don't go to America,' I said through tears. 'Stay here, in England, there are jobs here . . . opportunities here . . .'

'Clarissa . . .'

'Promise me, promise me you won't go.'

'I can't, I can't make that promise,' he said, lifting his hand to my face, wiping away the wetness. 'I can't make that promise,' he said again, kissing my forehead. 'But I shall try, for a while at least, not to go.'

We didn't leave the island until early evening. He rowed us across the water slowly and in silence, and then he sat on the jetty as I changed back into my clothes in the boathouse. We walked through the pink blush of the meadow and stopped by the tree—'Our tree,' he said—and looked back at the lake. It had been a perfect day. One etched on to my memory for ever.

Of course, I'd entirely forgotten about any arrangement with Mabel, or the fact that Henry had had no idea where I was. And as I walked across the hallway, towards the stairs, Henry's voice boomed at me from the doorway of the drawing room. 'Issa, thank God! Where the hell have you been?'

I stopped in my tracks. 'Oh, hello,' I said, calmly. 'Where've I been? I've been having a wander about the estate, and I rowed out to the island.'

He moved towards me, and I immediately saw from his face how frightened he'd been.

'You can't just disappear off like that, for hours on end and on your own; don't you realise? Don't you realise anything could happen to you?' He was shouting, in a state.

'I'm so sorry, Henry. I forgot the time,' I said, reaching out and touching his arm. 'But I'm here now, darling, and as you can see I'm perfectly safe and unharmed,' I added, looking up into his anxious eyes.

For a moment I thought he might cry. I could feel the tension in his body; see the strain in his face. And I felt immeasurably guilty to have caused him such distress.

'Bloody stupid . . . bloody stupid . . .' he muttered, as he turned and walked away.

Later that evening, before dinner, I telephoned Charlie.

'Yes, it's been a heavenly day here too, though I haven't seen much of it,' I lied. 'Mabel and I have been so busy packing up the place.'

CHAPTER TWENTY-THREE

I'd already decided that I wanted to spend all the available time I had that week with Tom. I knew that our time was limited, and I also knew that though it would be unbearable to say goodbye to him, I had no choice; I had to. Somehow, in my mind, there seemed to be a degree of absolution for my sins, my infidelity with Tom, if I returned to my husband. My unfaithfulness was finite. I would, ultimately, do the right thing, I thought.

I'd invited Tom to join us for dinner that evening. Henry was drinking heavily again, and he, Michael and Julian were reminiscing about the War—about the brothels at the front. Tom and I barely spoke. Instead, we conducted a conversation with our eyes, knowing the others would not notice. After dinner the five of us retired to the drawing room and played gramophone records once again. And I danced with him once more as the other three sat around smoking, watching us. I'm really not sure what they saw, but they must have seen, must have known. Whilst we were dancing, holding each other, I whispered to him to come back to the house later, through the servants hall and up the back staircase. I knew Henry would soon be out for the count. And, perhaps sadly, Michael and Julian didn't really matter.

'Goodnight, all,' I said, when I left the room, leaving all four men there, and blowing them each a kiss.

As I climbed into my bed I heard Henry and the other two singing their way up the staircase, followed by an attempt—by Henry, I presumed—to play The Last Post on his bugle. Tom, I thought, must have gone home but would be back shortly. Then my door opened, and there he was.

'Tom! Henry has only just gone to bed.'

'Clarissa, they barely know what day of the week it is let alone where I am or what *we* may be up to,' he replied, pulling off his tie.

'Are you absolutely sure? If he finds out he's bound to tell Mama.'

He didn't answer me. He took off his clothes, leaving them scattered across the floor and climbed into bed with me. Then he said, 'If we're going to have an affair, Clarissa, can you please stop mentioning your mama?'

'I'm sorry.'

'And that's another thing, you must stop apologising to me.'

He took hold of me, kissed me passionately.

'I've been longing to do that all evening,' he said, and then he reached over and turned out the lamp.

The next few days were blissful. We spent every afternoon together, usually on the island with a picnic. Once, when it rained, we rowed back across the lake and spent the remainder of the afternoon locked inside the boathouse. We scripted and acted out a play all about life at Deyning, with each of us playing a multitude of different parts. Tom, of course, proved to be the better mimic, adding something more—'a soupçon of wickedness,' he said—to each familiar figure: an unsurprising but ridiculously lascivious Mr Broughton, with a penchant for being naked whilst gardening; a lusty Edna, with a preference for women; and an acutely observed spoilsport called Mabel. And as I rolled about the wooden floor, half naked and crying with laughter, I didn't think about tomorrow or next week. I didn't think about the future, or the past.

But sometimes, in our quiet moments, I'd watched a frown creep into his brow. I'd felt him wince, his whole body tense, seen him shut his eyes. And I knew in those moments that he was remembering the War. Not inviting it back, but having it forced forward in his memory. And I didn't want to ask him about it, because I didn't want him to have to go back there, to remember. And the one time I had asked him, when I'd said, 'Tell me. What is it? You can tell me . . . I want you to know you can talk to me about it,' he'd turned to me and said, 'No. I don't want to talk about it. I'll never talk about it.' He'd looked at me with such intensity, such fear and pain in his eyes. 'I don't want you to know,' he said. 'I don't want you to know what I've seen . . . what I've done.'

Each evening, after dinner, we danced; and later, upstairs in my bed, we made love. On our last night he said to me, 'We will be together, one day; I know it. And if I thought for a moment it wasn't to be, I think . . . I think I might stop breathing.'

I wanted to tell him then about Emily. I wanted to but I didn't know how to. I hadn't uttered her name to a living soul, and I'd buried her so deep inside my own that it was almost impossible for me to think of her as being real. Had I actually had a child? Was there really a little girl somewhere looking out on to the world with those same serious dark eyes?

Emily.

She'd be two years of age: walking, speaking, part of another family. And that was my comfort, the one thing I'd held on to: that she *belonged* to someone, somewhere. For if I wasn't able to love her, the idea that she belonged, that she was held close, loved and cherished, offered a degree of assuagement.

But if I spoke her name—what would happen?

On our last night together I did speak her name. As we lay in bed, wrapped in each other's arms, I said her name out loud.

'Emily . . .'

He turned on to his side. 'Emily? And who, exactly, is Emily?'

I closed my eyes. *He said her name.*

'A little girl. She's a little girl,' I said.

He laughed. 'And *where*, pray tell, does Emily live?' he asked. 'Or is she one of your imaginary friends?'

'Yes, I suppose she is.'

I couldn't tell him. I couldn't tell him we had a child, one I'd misplaced, given away, and then, after telling him that, leave him myself. So I played a game with him; a game dictated by him.

'And what does she look like?'

'Oh, she's very small . . . with dark hair and very dark eyes. Serious eyes.'

'Hmm. And is she kind?'

'Oh yes, she's very kind, but quite shy.'

He reached out, stroked my hair. 'Is she here now?' he asked.

I stared up into the blackness. 'Yes and no . . . I like to think she's here.'

'Well, perhaps you can leave little Emily here with me tomorrow. And perhaps . . . perhaps occasionally I shall send her back to you with a message.'

I swallowed, closed my eyes again. 'Yes, I think she'd like that,' I said, beginning to cry. 'I think she'd like that very much.'

He took me in his arms and held me tightly. 'You'll know when I'm thinking of you now, because Emily will be there,' he said.

* * *

The following morning Charlie arrived. I hadn't expected him until later in the day, and, luckily, I was still at the house, attending to another list with Mabel.

'Charlie!'

He stood in the doorway for a moment, smiling, then came towards me. 'Hello, darling, I thought I might as well take the day off—come down here early and surprise you.'

'Thank you, Mabel,' I said, and then I whispered, 'Oh, and Mabel, would you be so kind and let Mr Cuthbert know that my husband has arrived, and I shan't be needing his help with the boxes.'

I'm not sure what Mabel thought. She must have known that Tom hadn't lifted a box all week. But she nodded at me and said, 'Yes, miss. I'll let him know.'

That evening Tom declined my invitation to join us for dinner and sent a message via his mother that he was 'otherwise engaged'. I sat in the dining room with the men, but I hardly spoke, and I couldn't eat a thing. I looked down at the food on my plate, glanced up at Henry and the others as they spoke; and I tried to smile back at Charlie. I stared at the bare walls, felt each and every minute as it slipped away; and I longed for him. I wanted to run to the cottage, find him and hold him once more. And when Charlie climbed into my bed later that evening and reached over to me, I finally felt the shame of infidelity. For I *was* being unfaithful: I was being unfaithful to my heart.

Early the next morning, as we said our goodbyes, Tom was nowhere to be seen. Looking back, it was probably better that way. I couldn't have coped with a farewell, or even a polite adieu, and I knew he didn't want to see me with Charlie.

As we drove away I felt physically sick. And I didn't look back. I didn't want to see my world disappearing from view. I wanted to stop the car, get out and run back up the driveway, home, and to him. I wanted to tell Charlie. I wanted to say to him, 'I'm sorry. I'm so very, very sorry, but I love someone else . . .' And then he spoke. He said, 'I know how hard this must be for you, Clarissa. I know you feel as though you're leaving behind everything you've ever loved. But you have a new life now, a life with me. And I know we're going to be happy.' He reached over, placed his hand upon mine. 'So happy.'

* * *

. . . Yes, the sale of the place is sad, very sad, it is a loss, the end of an era—as you say, but in truth that era ended for me when William and George died. It is all gone now, that life, & those halcyon days; it went with them, & belonged to them . . . and in my dreams I see them in the Elysian Fields . . . at Deyning.

Part Three

CHAPTER TWENTY-FOUR

. . . What worries me most is not the financial struggle, but H's increasing alcohol addiction and fragile state of mind. He was once so full of life & ambition—easily the most ambitious of the three—but that aspect of his character has completely gone, & now all he does is sit & stare, lost in a trance, and often quite unable to hear me. He continues to suffer from nightmares, & is prone to weeping, about what he cannot tell me.

* * *

Had I known, that morning in the spring of 1919, how my life was to unfold, had I known how infinitely precious love is, I would have told Charlie everything and run back to Tom. But the War had just ended and I was still young and craved some semblance of the life I'd been brought up to live. I was neither mature enough nor strong enough to cope with any estrangement from the remnants of my shattered family. My mother had suffered such loss, and Charlie, mentally as well as physically fragile, was dependent upon me. It seemed to be up to me to try to restore a sense of normality to our lives, to be the Granville who lived happily ever after. My marriage to Charlie—our future together—was the foundation of that, I thought.

When I left Deyning that day I hadn't allowed myself to dwell upon a future without Tom. At that time I still lived from day to day, week to week. I simply didn't think about the years ahead. And, apart from those few weeks we'd shared before the War, and that final week at Deyning, Tom and I had never spent any time together. Not really. He was not and had never been a part of my life. Oh, in my head, in my heart, he'd been everything, but that remained a secret, my secret. So, I followed a path through muted seasons, occasionally allowing myself to think of him, wonder about him, but I was resigned to the separateness of our lives; resigned to that sensation of *loss* as being part and parcel of life. Brothers, cousins and friends didn't grow old, but remained childhood memories; fathers passed on; homes changed, and babies, too, could be taken. Why would the man I'd fallen in love with not disappear from my life too? It was part of a pattern. It seemed to me that anything, everything, I loved and held dear, I would be estranged from.

One month slid into another, and then into another, and I moved on with my new life: my life in London as Charlie's wife. I'd already lived in the city for a number of years, already become acquainted with its many and various tones of grey, accustomed to—and even admired—its hard lines: the almost black shiny new roads and smooth slate rooftops; the murky shape of skeletal trees through smog, and those glinting, hot summer pavements. But now I felt only its weight, and that weight deep and heavy in my heart, as though I was holding in my breath, not fully exhaling. As though I was waiting. Waiting.

But waiting for what?

It had all gone, everything. There would be no dawns or sunsets like those I'd known at Deyning; no early-morning mists to watch rise up from a lake, and no moonlit-drenched trees to wish upon. And there was no Tom. No Tom. He and everything I'd cherished had gone and could never come back. Yes, I'd lost all I held dear. I'd lost everything. And so I began to go back there, quietly, in my mind. I began to measure time—days, weeks and months—against that place: against the past.

But all of us were burdened, none of us free. For we'd been the children destined for a *great war*. The ones who'd run at it, into it, singing, and shouting happy adieus; now tormented souls, haunted by our stolen youth and absent friends, and our memories of another time. And peace, peace of mind and heart, was not a God-given, not our birthright. Instead, it floated around us, teasingly. Peace. We all spoke of it, liked the sound of it, but it was a word already worn thin. And that other time, like a half-forgotten dream, came in flashes of colour, light and shade; vaguely familiar shapes and fragmented images. Silence took me back, and stillness too. The scents of summer, its sounds: the whisper of the giant beeches in the park, the distant hum of a mowing machine; the sight of children picnicking, or out in boats on the lake; a lone butterfly, dancing amidst the geraniums and lavender of a window box. Yes, all of these carried me back.

I had no idea then that grief is never entirely spent. No idea that it can be suspended, frozen, sometimes for years. War had anaesthetised us, numbed our senses, and even the warmth of summer could not thaw that chill around our hearts. Birthdays, Christmases, high days and holidays; family celebrations and simple pleasures, once so treasured for their languid, perfect moments were irrevocably altered by those missing:

those forever young, smiling faces. And so my life was not the life I'd once imagined for myself. How could it be? My cast of players had gone; Deyning had gone; and my heart had been displaced. My marriage to Charlie was not how it should have been, for I wasn't able to give myself fully, or to love him the way I knew I could. And we were both haunted. Haunted by the memory of how we'd once been, who we had once been, and that childish notion of unfettered happiness.

Charlie's love was of a different nature. Our relationship had not been founded on physical attraction, or chemistry, though—initially, at least—it had flickered. I had married him to do the right thing, and, perhaps, to be safe, secure: to be *married*. And he'd probably married me for the same reasons: to have a wife, someone he could call his own, look upon and feel proud of, the way one would anything one deemed valuable, and perhaps rare and pleasing to the eye. To Charlie, our marriage, I knew, was something of an achievement.

During those early days, I didn't allow myself to ponder on our relationship. I embraced my role as best I could and distracted myself perfecting the part. There were people to see and entertain, a husband to amuse and look after. And we tried, I think, in those early years, to be happy together, to be in love. We both wanted children, wanted that cushion around us, and it was my fault, I thought, my fault no children came. My body seemed unwilling to produce that seal of approval without my heart's agreement. And it seemed a fitting punishment.

I went to see doctors, specialists, and,

unbeknown to Charlie, tried any number of remedies and potions from women in far-flung parts of London promising me a baby. I'd lied, of course, when doctors had asked questions. I'd pleaded ignorance to the workings of my body and never said, 'But I know I can do it; I've done it before.' Perhaps it was that. Perhaps it was simply the tedium and disappointment of living with that longing for a child, but the complexion of our marriage changed. We stopped discussing possibilities, the future, and children. And then, three years into our marriage, we stopped sleeping together.

Of course I'd known from the start that my marriage to Charlie was a mistake. But I had *promised* to marry him, and I'd made him that promise when he was a fit and able-bodied man, fighting for his country, for all of us. I couldn't have abandoned him when he returned home, invalided; as though a war-damaged fiancé was somehow not quite up to scratch. And so, though I was lonely, hungry for love and physical intimacy, there was no way out. Happiness, I realised, was an ideal as elusive as peace.

I once tried to talk to Mama about my marriage, but she stopped me almost as soon as I began. 'Clarissa, Clarissa,' she said, her eyes fluttering closed, smiling, 'a successful marriage is not about physical love, or passion. That type of love—however intoxicating—simply doesn't endure. A successful marriage is founded upon a partnership; it is an *alliance*, an understanding. And it is about companionship and, sometimes, forgiveness and tolerance too . . .'

I didn't tell her how much I'd already tolerated,

how often I forgave Charlie. I'd never spoken to her about his black moods or his unreasonable and increasingly volatile behaviour: the rages about something being out of place or dinner not served at the correct time. I'd never mentioned the silences, the evenings when he refused to speak or even look at me, and then, later, disappeared off into the night.

'But I'm still young, Mama. I need to be loved.'

'You are loved, my dear. Charlie adores you.'

'I don't want that . . . adoration. I want *real* love.'

She sighed, looked at me, narrowing her eyes, as though trying to tune into my thoughts. 'Life is about compromise, Clarissa. We all have to make sacrifices; all of us . . . even me.'

I looked up at her. 'But you had a perfect marriage. You and Papa loved each other . . . had children and were together until . . . until he died.'

She smiled, closed her eyes again for a moment. 'Yes, I loved your father, not least because we shared four children. We shared a life. And it was a good marriage, but no marriage is perfect.' She sighed again. 'And my marriage was not *always* perfect.'

I stared at her. I'd never heard my mother speak of her marriage before, never known her admit to imperfection in any area of her life. All at once a door had opened, and I wanted to know more. I wanted to know who my mother was; what she'd known, how she'd felt. Had she, too, known grand passion? Had she ever been forced to question her life, her marriage to my father? Had someone come between her and Papa?

'Have you . . . have you ever loved anyone apart from Papa?' I asked.

There was a pause. She looked away from me, and I knew there was something.

'Yes . . . there was someone, once; many years ago now.' She raised her hand to her chest, searching for her pearls. 'But it was not to be.'

'Before you married Papa?' I asked, silently willing her to tell me, to say more.

She stared at me.

'After you married Papa?'

She closed her eyes, momentarily, and I knew that to be a *yes*.

I wanted to ask her more questions, but I wasn't sure how, *or* if she was prepared to tell me any more. Then she said, quite calmly, in a matter-of-fact voice, 'It was a long time ago, and it was impossible.' She smiled at me. 'I had you, your brothers—and, of course, there was Papa. And it was . . .' she twisted the long strand of pearls through her fingers, ' . . . could never have come to anything.'

'I had no idea.'

'Of course not. Why would you? You were still a child.'

'Did Papa know?'

'No, he did not. Oh, he may have had his suspicions, and we went through a few . . . a few difficult years. But I loved your father, Clarissa. And I have no regrets.'

This was all my mother was prepared to tell me at that time. It was another lesson in compromise and sacrifice.

*   *   *

My life in London was quite different to that

time during the War, and my circle of friends had changed too. Charlie was working in the city and we saw more of his friends and work colleagues than we did of my old crowd. A number of them had moved on anyhow, were married and living in the country. But occasionally, at a party, we crossed paths with one or other of them.

Jimmy Cooper had remained in the army after the War. He'd been out in India for two years and had only recently returned when we bumped into him at a charity dance at the Hyde Park Hotel. I knew Jimmy, like his mother, to be a diligent correspondent. He always seemed to keep track of everyone, knew who had married whom and where they were living. And as I stood chatting to him that night, he did indeed seem to know more—was more up to date on everyone's movements—than me, despite having been away for two years.

'I can't believe you've been away for two whole years, Jimmy Cooper, and yet *you* have all the gossip!' I said to him, and he laughed.

'I have to admit, most of it's passed on to me from Mama. You know how much she loves to know *everything*,' he said with a smile.

'Yes, and hand it on. I think that's the part she likes best, don't you? She'd have won a medal during the War—for reconnaissance!'

'Ha! You're right. She'd have been a superb spy . . . though perhaps a little too conspicuous behind enemy lines.'

I laughed. The thought of Venetia, trussed up in all her finery, crawling through no-man's-land, was a bizarre but highly amusing image. And whilst it was good to be laughing, to be able to make jokes about that time, I had a sudden stab of guilt: guilt that we were standing there, at a dance, laughing about the War. And I felt a twinge of guilt about Venetia too. I hadn't seen her in a while. In fact, if truth be told, I'd been avoiding her. The last time I'd called upon her she'd asked me too many questions: questions about my marriage and about Charlie. 'You and Charlie . . . you're happy?' she'd asked, staring at me with those piercing violet eyes.

'Yes,' I'd replied, 'Yes, of course.'

'It's just that . . . well, you sometimes seem a little distracted, dear, a little lost.'

I'd shrugged, shaken my head, unsure what to say. 'I'm fine, it's fine,' I said, looking away from her.

'*Fine?* Fine does not make my heart sing, Clarissa. Fine does not evoke that flutter of happiness I so wish to feel when I look at you. And you know, you can tell me . . . you can. I'm always here for you. You're the daughter I never had . . . as dear and as precious to me as my own.'

'Mama says that marriage is about compromise . . . and sacrifice. She says passion does not endure.'

She smiled. 'Ah, I see. And you . . . you've known passion?'

I hesitated, and then I said, 'Yes, yes I have.'

'But not with your husband, not with Charlie?'

I looked down, shook my head.

She sighed. 'You're still in love with him, aren't you? You're still in love with Tom Cuthbert.'

At that moment I was relieved to hear her say his name. She knew, and I was pleased she knew. I wanted someone to know the truth. When I began to cry she moved over to me and took me in her arms.

'Please, please promise me that you shan't say

anything to Mama.'

'Of course I shan't. I wouldn't dream of it . . . there are many things I don't tell your mama, Clarissa.' She took my head in her hands and looked at me. 'But you have to try and make your marriage work, my dear. Otherwise . . .' she stared at me, unsmiling, with tears in her eyes now too. 'Otherwise you have years of loneliness ahead of you, and I simply can't bear the thought of you lonely and unhappy.'

Even later that same day I'd regretted telling her. I wasn't convinced that she wouldn't report back to Mama or inadvertently say something. And so, for the next few weeks, I'd purposefully avoided her, hoping to put a distance between that sad outburst and myself. Hoping we'd both forget. But weeks had turned into months, and now I felt guilty.

'I must visit your mother,' I said to Jimmy. 'I've been a little lax in my calling of late.'

'Yes, you must. You know how much she adores seeing you . . . adores seeing you both.'

I glanced over at Charlie. He'd moved further away from us, was talking with a group of people I didn't recognise, and so, with practised nonchalance, I took the plunge.

'And do you ever hear anything of Tom Cuthbert?'

'Ha! Now there's a name that doesn't often crop up,' he said, stopping a waiter and grabbing us each another glass of champagne. 'But Cuthbert was never the best correspondent. Bloody unreliable, I'd say.'

'But now that you're back—will you be seeing him?'

'Good grief, didn't you know? He's in America.'

'America? No, no . . . I didn't know.'

'Yes, been there for almost two years now, I think,' he said, sipping his champagne. 'And doing quite well for himself too, from what I understand.'

'Really . . . I had no idea.'

And it struck me then, the separateness of our lives. For Tom had been living on the other side of the world, living on another continent, for almost as long as I'd been living my new married life in London.

'How strange,' I said, thinking out loud.

'Why's that?' Jimmy asked.

'Oh, nothing. I just thought . . . thought he would be living here in London . . . thought he would be in the city.'

He laughed. 'No, not Cuthbert. He was always restless, even at Oxford. Never quite . . . fitted in. And I suppose he's gone *to make his fortune*.' He laughed again, and for some reason I did too.

And then I said, 'But you know . . . he probably will, Jimmy.'

'Ha! Yes, you're right, he probably will. And he'll no doubt return here one day waving his crisp American dollars in all our faces!'

'No, he'd never do that. He'd never be arrogant or ostentatious in that way.'

He looked at me curiously. 'You rather liked him, didn't you?'

'Yes,' I said, smiling, 'yes I did.'

That same night, back at our home, Charlie had come to my room. I was tired, told him I wanted to sleep. He was drunk, and more unsteady on his feet than usual. He hated his walking stick, hated his disability and, perhaps, hated himself. He was in an angry, belligerent mood, and when he stumbled and

I climbed from my bed to help him, he turned and shouted, 'No! I don't need your help! I don't need a bloody nurse, I need a wife.'

'You have a wife, Charlie. I'm your wife.'

He moved over to me, his face inches from mine. 'Yes, you're my wife and you're *stuck* with me, Clarissa. And I'm *stuck* with you!'

'Is that what you think?' I asked quietly. 'Is that how you feel?'

'What do you care how I feel? What do you know? You know nothing . . . nothing at all about suffering and pain, real pain. Oh yes, yes, you lost your brothers—and you never let us forget that, but you've never had to give up anything, anything of yourself, never had to sacrifice anything. You don't know what it's like . . . you have no idea. And look at you . . . you can't even produce a baby.'

I closed my eyes, waited a moment before I spoke. 'I know it's difficult for you, and I try to understand . . . really I do.' I reached out, touched his arm. 'I'm sorry.'

He turned to me. 'But you're always bloody sorry!' he shouted. And then he pushed me back on to the bed. 'And if you're really sorry,' he continued, unbuckling his belt, 'you'll fulfil your obligations . . . as my *wife*.'

I didn't protest, didn't say anything. And I didn't push him away. I didn't move. I lay on the bed, exactly where I'd fallen. I looked away from his contorted face, closed my eyes and tried to shut out the pain; tried to imagine I was somewhere else: *. . . the lower meadow . . . the lower meadow; under the tree . . . look up, see the sky . . . see the clouds . . .*

When he'd finished, he struggled up from the bed, picked up his stick, and then left the room. He didn't say anything, didn't speak. What could he have said? What was there to say? I was his wife. He was my husband.

Minutes later, I heard him leave the house.

I'm not sure how long I lay there. All I remember is a burning pain, and the *tick-tock* . . . *tick-tock* . . . *tick-tock* . . . of the clock. I didn't want to cry. I didn't want to acknowledge what had just taken place in any sob or sound of anguish. Even then, I knew it had to be locked away. Forgotten.

'America,' I whispered. 'America . . .' I said again, louder. I wanted to hear myself speak, to shatter the silence, break through the hideous echo. And as I spoke the name of that faraway continent I imagined Tom, standing, looking out from one of those very tall buildings; so tall and so high he could see across the curve of the earth's surface to England, to London, to the light of my room, to me.

'Tom . . .'

Was that to be it? I wondered. Were my snatched moments with him to be the sum total of my experience of passion and real love in this life? Were they already spent? Had I already and unknowingly passed through my zenith: that moment of unutterable perfection, when everything is the very best it can be, will ever be?

Oh, but you had it, you had it, Clarissa, and you knew it . . .

And at that moment I thought of William, hurtling towards the ground in a burning aeroplane. I thought of him *and* George. They had both died so young; had either of them ever known *real* passion, passionate love? And I so hoped that they had. I hoped that each of them had known at least one moment, one splendid, unforgettable moment;

one that in the hour of their death they'd been able to return to; to know that they had lived, truly lived.

I felt a solitary tear slide down my temple into my hair.

No self-pity, Clarissa, no self-pity . . . think of them; think of all of them.

And I did.

I saw Frank's whitened cricket shoes, Hugo Hamilton's bow tie; Julian's pale lips, and Archie's smile; I saw hands waving back at me from a train carriage window, and boys in uniform—standing proud and tall. I saw my father, his map and his pins and his bits of ribbon, and the men at the station, tattered and frayed and caked in mud; and the men in red coats, and the posters and words; the words, and the gloves . . . the gloves, the balaclavas, the socks; the socks and the gloves, and the uniforms sent home . . . the mud and blood and the uniforms sent home. Home.

CHAPTER TWENTY-FIVE

. . . I am quite well, & continue to distract myself with the social merry-go-round here, and my friend V's (who's quite the Bohemian now) new interest in Spiritualism. She's rather keen for me to attend one of her séances, telling me that G or W may well 'come through', and though it's tempting, I'm not sure . . . Of course, there was a time when I would never have entertained such an idea, but V assures me that no HARM can be done, & that her Madam Zelda (apparently the very best & most fashionable in all of London)

never fails to bring Them through . . .

*　　*　　*

When I recall the winters of my childhood they're inevitably bathed in a pure white light, the reflection of a frozen landscape. I remember awakening to that brilliance, seeping into my room through the heavy winter drapes; the rush of chilled air as I threw back the eiderdown and climbed from my bed; the ice on the inside of the windowpanes; and the world beyond, a place of strange new shapes and alabaster stillness.

Once, when I was still quite young and my parents away in London, we awoke at Deyning to find the thickest blanket of snow I'd ever seen. It was over a foot deep. 'A right rare dumping,' Edna had called it. We were cut off, completely stranded for the best part of a week, the servants and me. And Mr Broughton had to walk five miles through the snow-covered fields to the village, to send a telegram to my parents. For the first few days normal routines and lessons were suspended, but conditions were so bad that Miss Greaves forbade me to venture outside. So I'd sat at the nursery window looking out upon that still, eerie landscape: the skeletal trees and frozen lake; the dark shapes of the deer moving slowly across the white parkland in the distance; and that low hanging sky, so full of snow it seemed to billow with the weight. Each evening I ate downstairs, in the kitchen, with Miss Greaves and the others. I was allowed to stay up late, and we sang songs and hymns—with Miss Greaves at the piano—in the servants' hall. And one night, terribly late, ready for bed and in my nightgown, Edna took my hand, led me through to the scullery, and then lifted me up on to the slate bench.

I stood there transfixed, watching tiny white crystals spiralling out of the blackness, sliding down the skylight above me. And when I turned to her, for her to lift me down, she wrapped her arms around me, kissed me and held me to her so tightly, and then she carried me all the way back to the servants' hall just as though I were a baby, her own baby. I used to tell her all the time that I loved her, and I did.

I didn't want the snow to melt, didn't want things to return to normal. But as soon as my parents returned home, and despite more snow, everything changed. Evenings of song beyond the green baize door stopped, routines and order resumed, and even Miss Greaves appeared less than enthusiastic at the resumption of lessons on the nursery floor.

I can't recall another winter as severe as that, and I certainly never again experienced the warmth of that *snowed-in* camaraderie, but for a few weeks during January 1925 snow fell steadily over London. Frozen days gave way to nights of glistening, moonlit frosts. No number of blazing fires could keep us warm, and no number of clothes could stop us from shivering. And it was then, in the depths of that particularly hostile month, that my brother Henry slipped further from us. It had been a gradual sink into the abyss, a slow dance into oblivion. The hedonistic mix of parties, pills and whisky, which had once alleviated his anguish, had become increasingly ineffective. And that keyhole in his memory, that small glinting light of who he'd once been, finally faded.

Unlike Charlie, who, despite his disability, had managed to pick up the pieces of his life, and had gained employment working at a city-based firm of solicitors, Henry was still without a job, and without any wife. He lived in a rented flat in Marylebone, spent his nights at bars and parties, and gambling, and his days sleeping. I don't think he'd ever expected to have to work and, after the War ended, though he'd toyed with idea of staying in the army, and at one stage had even talked of going out to India, he'd slowly drifted into a malaise.

Henry had always been extravagant; it was part of him, his character. He'd been indulged, brought up to have certain standards, expectations, and he enjoyed life too much to embrace or understand any need for financial planning or frugality. He'd inherited some money, of course, after the sale of Deyning, but our home had been sold at the worst time, and for a ridiculous sum. And my father's debts—coupled with taxes and death duties—had eroded my brother's inheritance to no more than enough to live on adequately for a few years, not a lifetime. By that winter he'd run out of money and, it seemed, energy.

Mama was of independent means, with an income derived from a trust set up by her father for her and her siblings. But in the years immediately after the War that income had fallen, and fallen dramatically. And, though entitled to some of the proceeds from the sale of Deyning, she'd forfeited her share in favour of Henry. She'd felt guilty about Henry's *shabby inheritance*, and she said it would, at the very least, give him a start. But whatever monies Henry had received from the sale of our home had long gone and, more latterly, Mama had had to bail him out: paying off the arrears on his rent and clearing his gambling debts. She'd tried talking to him, told him that it couldn't go on, that she couldn't afford to fund his precarious lifestyle any longer. And I'd talked to him too, or I'd tried; but he'd stopped making sense, and appeared neither willing nor able to listen.

'It's not fair on Mama, Henry,' I said. 'She can't be expected to support you now, at this stage . . . it's simply not fair on her.'

We were sitting in my drawing room. He'd called on me unexpectedly, wanting money, telling me he'd be able to repay me in a few days. But he looked dreadful: pale, dishevelled and exhausted, his hair uncut and unwashed, his coat threadbare.

'That's why I've come to you,' he said, running his hands through his hair. 'And I hate myself for doing this to you, Issa, really I do . . .'

It was snowing outside, already dark. I noticed he was shivering, and I rose to my feet and placed another log upon the fire.

'But I have no money, Henry. Nothing apart from the pin money Charlie gives me,' I said, standing in front of the fire, my back to him.

'I'll pay you back in a few days, I promise. Anything . . . anything's a help. I've just got myself rather stuck, you see.'

I turned to him. 'But you're always rather stuck, dear. And it can't go on . . . you know that. You know Mama has limited funds now.'

He stared at the fire. 'Yes,' he said, 'I know that. And I intend to find myself a job, but I just need to sort a few things first.'

I walked out to the hallway table and picked up my purse.

'I can only give you two pounds, I'm afraid. It's all I have,' I said, returning to the room. He was standing by the fireplace, his back to me, and when he turned to face me he looked so wretched.

'I'm sorry, Henry, but it's all I have,' I said again.

He turned away, leant his head upon the mantelshelf. 'You know, Issa, I sometimes wish I'd not come back . . . wish I'd joined the others.'

'No, don't say that. You must never think that.'

I moved over to where he stood, placed my hand upon his shoulder. 'You just need to pick yourself up, dear, get a job . . . sort yourself out. Look at Charlie, and Jimmy too. If they can do it—you can.'

He sighed, and then turned to face me. 'Yes, you're right, of course. I need to sort myself out . . . I'm a bit of a mess at the moment, I know that.' He smiled down at me, wearily.

I put my arms around him. 'Don't worry, Henry,' I said, 'it'll be fine. It'll all be fine.'

When I walked him to the door, he said to me again, 'I'll pay you back, I promise.'

'Don't worry about the money, Henry. Just promise me, please promise me you'll get yourself sorted.'

I watched him walk off down the deserted snow-covered street, holding his collar up around his face, and my heart ached for him.

About a week later, early one evening, Mama telephoned. Henry's landlord had called on her, only minutes before, demanding money, she said, and telling her that Henry had not been at his flat in over a week. My mother wanted Charlie to try to find him. She thought Charlie might know where he was. Yes, Charlie said, he'd see what he could do; he'd go out immediately and make enquiries.

So, as Charlie disappeared in a taxicab, in search of Henry, I headed on foot to my mother's house.

Had he made a decision? I wondered. Had he finally decided to join *the others*? Would his body be washed up on the muddy banks of the Thames? And I prayed that he hadn't taken his own life. That he was somewhere, drunk and perhaps lost, but not dead.

Charlie was unable to find out anything that evening. He'd been to his club, asked the doorman, and others there, when they'd last seen Henry: not for some time, weeks at least, they'd told him. He'd been to a few bars and to the public house near Charlie's flat; yes, they knew who Henry Granville was, but no one could recall having seen him of late. Charlie did his best to reassure Mama. He said it wasn't unheard of for men . . . those who had survived the trenches, to do this sort of thing. He'd heard of such cases before, and usually these men turned up again, safe and unharmed. He would resume his search the next day, and he'd make a few calls, put a few people on to it.

'But he can't just disappear,' I said to Charlie, as we walked home from Mama's later that evening.

'Yes, he can,' he replied, lighting a cigarette. 'And to be honest, Clarissa, I'm not entirely surprised.'

'What do you mean? Do you think he's taken his own life?'

'Well, that can't be ruled out, but no, I don't think so. Your brother may be many things, but he's not a coward. No, I think he's gone. I think he's fled London, for the time being at least.'

I stopped. 'Fled? Fled London? But to where? And with what? He has no money, Charlie.'

'Yes, he's certainly left a trail of debts behind him, and I didn't want to say in front of your mother, but a lot of rather angry people too.' He took my arm and led me on. 'His debts are more substantial than we'd supposed. Only last week he cashed a rather sizeable cheque with the landlord at his local public house.'

'But how? Mama says he has no money . . . nothing in his bank account. Nothing at all.'

'He doesn't. The cheque was not honoured by the bank.'

'So he owes this man money as well?'

'He did, and a considerable amount too. Tonight has been a rather costly evening in more ways than one . . .'

I stopped again. 'You mean to say you've had to clear all these debts? You've had to give people money?'

He laughed. 'I do indeed, and I did. And I'm rather keen to catch up with your errant brother myself now.'

We continued walking, and then I asked Charlie, 'And do you really think he's gone, gone away somewhere?'

'It would make sense, wouldn't it? Leave all his troubles behind. And I went to his flat, went through his things . . . his passport's nowhere to be found.'

'You went through *his things*?' I said, slightly aghast, and knowing how Henry would feel.

'Yes, of course I did. I was trying to find out *where* he might be. Oh really, I don't know, Clarissa. Perhaps he'll appear tomorrow . . . or next week, or next month, but I've a feeling we shan't be seeing him for some time.'

Over the next few weeks Charlie and I played a rather duplicitous game with my mother. We had no choice. At first, when it became apparent that Charlie wasn't able to locate my brother, she'd wanted to go to the police, even though the last thing she wished for was a scandal, or any publicity. But Charlie very swiftly advised her against taking this course of action. He told her that it would only expose Henry's sad situation, the circumstances surrounding his disappearance. He said as soon as Henry's name appeared in the newspapers, which undoubtedly it would, all sorts of unscrupulous people would come forward to sell their tawdry tales.

At that time, the newspapers, and certain magazines, were filled with stories of society figures embroiled in scandal—having affairs, or lost to drug addiction or alcohol. In the absence of war they'd had to find something else, I suppose, to secure their readership. But it seemed to me unnecessarily cruel that those viewed in any way privileged, no matter their circumstances, or how browbeaten, damaged or lost, had been so viciously exposed and held up as examples. And it had made people paranoid: paranoid that even the most off-the-cuff remark—let alone a conversation—would be sold and appear in the next day's news.

No, Mama said, there must be no publicity. So more weeks passed, and then Mama spoke of hiring a private detective. She'd seen advertisements in the newspaper, had even cut some out, and she showed them to Charlie and me. It appeared not altogether unusual, she said, sounding reassured and quite motivated, for people to disappear. She was right, of course, and, in a way, hiring a private detective made perfect sense. But it would be costly, and though my mother was by no means poor, she no longer had the income she'd once enjoyed. Charlie suggested that we wait a while. And so we did. We waited for my brother to contact us, to write or telephone, but months passed by and no letter or telephone call came.

I never told my mother the extent of Henry's debts, or of the sad state of his tiny flat, which I'd had to clear; nor did I tell her of his missing passport. But I eventually explained the likelihood of him no longer being in London, that he may well have fled the country.

'But why? Why on earth would he do such a thing? Really, it simply doesn't make any sense . . . none whatsoever.'

'But if he wasn't happy, had no money, felt his life here was . . . worthless, going nowhere, then perhaps it does make sense.'

She shook her head. 'No, I'm sorry, I still don't understand why he'd choose to disappear . . . after *everything* we've gone through, Clarissa.'

'Maybe he thought it would be easier this way, Mama. Perhaps he couldn't face telling us how he really felt . . . couldn't tell us the truth. And by disappearing, going some place where no one knows who he is, where no one knows anything about him at all, he can be whoever he wants to be.'

She stared at me, wide eyed. '*Whoever he wants to be?* You mean change his identity . . . his name?'

I said nothing.

'Thank the Lord your father's not alive to witness this.'

'I'm sure he'll turn up, Mama, sooner or later. He has to. He'll get in touch with us eventually.

Charlie's quite certain of that.'

This, too, was a lie. And it was to be years before we found out what had happened to my brother Henry.

CHAPTER TWENTY-SIX

No one other than the very rich lived the way we once had at Deyning. The lack of an heir, extortionate death duties and the absence of anyone willing to go into domestic service made it nigh on impossible to run such places. Large country houses had been abandoned, left to wrack and ruin, or razed to the ground in order to avoid paying taxes, and almost inevitable bankruptcy.

I knew that Deyning had been standing empty for a couple of years. The American family we'd sold it on to had lost a fortune and been unable to sell it, and I'd recently seen it advertised across a whole page in *Country Life*. I'd gasped at the upset price, and at the state of the gardens. It looked like a relic of a bygone era, a ghostly place. I'd peered through a magnifying glass at the hazy photographs, and there it was, that place I knew so well. Where each pathway, tree and rotting stump had meant so much; where every hollow and incline, each fence and stile and gate had once been so eagerly anticipated. But how different it now looked.

It had been photographed in winter, the trees, stark and black against a gloomy sky; the house, bereft, and suitably grey; the terrace, empty of its detail, and statues and urns; the lawns, overgrown, shrunken by rampant rhododendron and shapeless shrubs. And those broad herbaceous borders, once exuberant drifts of vibrant colour, gone, lost in the tangled undergrowth. There, too, was the view: the lake, a dark expanse in the foreground, the fields beyond, strangely colourless, and the South Downs, reduced to a murky smudge.

'Looks no different to the last time I saw it,' Charlie said, dismissively, when I showed him the photographs.

'No, it looks worse . . . much worse,' I said, looking once more at the photograph of the house's southern façade, and my old bedroom window. I could almost see myself there, peering out at that forlorn landscape, waiting for someone to come and rescue the place and, perhaps, me.

'Someone will buy it . . . bound to. It's going for a song,' Charlie said. 'You wait and see. It'll go to one of these new property developer types.'

And it was through Charlie that the news came to me. He'd been sitting alone in a quiet corner of the bar at his club when he heard the name, Deyning. He didn't recognise the voice with a hint of an American accent, he said, and remained where he was, his back to the gentleman, listening. The man was busy explaining to another that he'd purchased the place at a severely knocked-down price. 'Yes, yes, it's been on the market for some time, and in a dreadful state too. The army were there through the War, absolutely trashed the place, and the people who took it on never lived there . . . did nothing with it.'

'And what will you do with it?' the other gentleman asked.

'Return it to its former glory, I hope.'

'And then what?'

'And then . . . I'm not entirely sure.'

As Charlie relayed the story to me, relishing its tiny details, I listened, unaware of what was to come but knowing there was something, something that had to be told. He'd stood up, he said, turned, and looked across the room. He didn't recognise either of the men at first, supposed them both to be new members, and so he focused his attention once more on the voice he'd listened to, the one who'd spoken about Deyning, the one who had just bought Deyning. Tall and dark, and dressed in a well-cut suit, he looked *almost* like any other gentleman in the club that evening, 'but perhaps a little too suave . . . a little too handsome,' Charlie added, and then laughed. Yet there was something, something about him so familiar, he continued. He'd moved towards him, and as he neared, as he approached the two men, he suddenly recognised him. He looked so different out of uniform, Charlie said.

Tom Cuthbert.

I could no longer hear Charlie. He continued to speak but the definition of his words was lost, distant and muffled, as though an invisible wall had sprung up between us. I looked away from him, tried to focus on something, anything, but my head felt heavy, too large for my body, and awash with his image. *Tom.* I focused on my breathing, trying to slow my heart. Charlie moved towards me, handed me a drink, and as I took the glass from his hand I smiled up at him, or at least I think I did. You see, I was drowning, drowning in the moment, in the mention of his name.

I quietly sipped my drink, looking down into the glass, holding on to it tightly with both hands; and as my heart slowed and the room began to stop spinning, I heard my husband's voice once more.

They had spoken at some length, he said, had had a drink together. Neither one could recall the last time they'd seen each other, but they thought it had been at Jimmy Cooper's, at a party there during the War. Yes, I thought, yes, it was then, it was that night, for they'd never come face to face during that last week at Deyning. Tom had only recently returned from America, Charlie said, had been away over six years. And then he told me, told me I'd be able to speak to Tom myself, for he and his fiancée would also be at a party at our American friends', the Blanchs', the following evening.

I could barely breathe. Not only was Tom back, and in London, but also I was to see him the very next day. Charlie sat down, lit a cigarette, and continued to muse aloud on Tom Cuthbert, his good looks *and* his new fortune.

I wasn't able to ask Charlie the pertinent questions I'd have liked to ask. I'd been blasé, told him, yes, of course I remembered Tom Cuthbert. And I could tell already that Charlie was intrigued, almost captivated by Tom's charm and obvious success. He sat opposite me, clutching his glass upon the arm of his chair, staring at the floor through half-closed bleary eyes, smiling to himself. And every so often I'd see another flash of their conversation ricochet through his memory, and he'd lift his head, smiling to himself; half laughing.

'And he asked after you, dear,' he said. 'He said, "And how is your *wife*, Charlie, how is Clarissa?"'

'Oh, really . . . and what did you say?'

He turned to me with a queer, sad sort of smile. 'That you were well, of course.'

For a few minutes we sat in silence. Charlie lost in his impressions, me in my memories.

'I do wonder where all his money's come from,' I said, at last, rising to my feet.

'Haven't the foggiest. Done very well for himself though . . . made a pile and bought a pile, ha!'

'He was always destined to go far,' I said, as I left the room.

Of course I wasn't really surprised to hear how well Tom had done for himself. Even before the War, when he was still studying, he had been determined to succeed, driven by something neither my brothers nor most other young men I knew possessed: ambition. I'd heard mention of him only once of late, from Jimmy Cooper once more. He'd recently attended a college reunion dinner at Oxford and had heard from a mutual acquaintance that Tom was *doing very well* in New York, and making 'a packet'. The mention of his name at that time had rocked me, and for a while I'd had vivid dreams about him. In those dreams I was always searching for him, always in a crowd trying to find him. I'd wake up and feel that same desperate longing, as though I'd only just left him. Eventually, but for the odd occasion, I'd stopped dreaming of him, and I concluded that it was probably for the best that an ocean separated us.

But now the circle was closing: Tom Cuthbert was in my orbit once more.

That night, after Charlie had come home and told me about Tom buying Deyning, I couldn't sleep. And when I did, when I finally fell into an exhausted, nervous sleep, just before dawn, I dreamt of him once more: him and me back at Deyning—together. The following morning I awoke long after Charlie had left the house and gone to work, and I lay in my bed for quite some time pondering on the evening ahead. I contemplated falling ill: feigning a headache or the symptoms of a mysterious virus. I hadn't seen him since our last night together at Deyning, just after the War, and I wasn't sure what to expect, or even if I'd cope. Would he be the same? Would we be the same?

Later, over coffee with my mother, I wondered whether to tell her the news. The names Deyning and Tom Cuthbert had for so long been synonymous in my mind but, I knew, were mutually exclusive in hers. Occasionally she'd mention Deyning, referring back to that time when all of us were together, but such memories only brought pain. Our lives had changed, and Tom's name—no longer uttered by either one of us.

That day, as she spoke, I imagined her reaction, the look upon her face: first, the horror at the mention of the name, Tom Cuthbert; that I could still utter these three syllables after so many years; and then, as the news sank in, the realisation of a new order. For where did that leave us? And where did that place her judgement? Tom Cuthbert, who had not been good enough for her daughter to look at, let alone marry, now presided over all that had once been hers, all that she'd once held dear. Like a stain burnished on our souls, his name was in our lives for ever.

I decided not to tell her. She'd know soon enough.

CHAPTER TWENTY-SEVEN

. . . No one is able to tell us anything, or give us any answers. We have tried, interviewed everyone we can think of, but it really is as though he's evaporated into the ether. C assures me that he will turn up—eventually, she tells me that he may well have taken on 'another name', a new identity, & that this might actually be something good (for him, at least). What perilous & decidedly queer times we live in.

* * *

After much deliberation I chose to wear a new silver-blue silk chiffon dress, one I'd had made that season. It was short, daringly short, and sleeveless too, with an asymmetrical hem just below the knee, a broad sash at the hips and a deep V neckline.

The fashion continued for a boyish shape and I had taken to wearing one of the new-style brassieres, which laced up at the sides to flatten one's chest. It was a look quite the opposite of my mother's and Venetia's day, when curves had been accentuated, even worshipped, when women had been held in by whalebone, heavily upholstered like an item of furniture. Now it was all the rage to look shapeless, and *bare*, with uncovered arms, and legs revealed in flesh-coloured silk stockings. It was a bold modern look for a bold modern world. But it was a step too far for Mama, who loathed the new fashions, and considered them hideously unfeminine and quite immoral. She blamed alcohol, cocktails, the new jazz music, the craze for dancing—particularly the Charleston—and even the suffragettes, for what she perceived to be an unstoppable moral decline. The day she'd spotted a lady *wearing trousers* outside her home in Berkeley Square, she'd used the telephone—which she insisted should only ever be used in emergencies—to call me up and tell me. 'I don't know what the world's coming to,' she said. 'And where will it all end? With gentlemen in tea gowns?'

That evening, Charlie and I arrived at the Blanchs' late. After handing our coats to the butler we made our way up the staircase to the first-floor drawing room. I was nervous, more nervous than I could remember ever having been, and it was my fault we were late. I'd had something of a panic attack before we'd left home, and had locked myself in the bathroom with a large brandy, telling Charlie—through the door—that I had what I thought was the onset of a migraine. Even in his ignorance he'd not made my ordeal any easier, and had simply lectured me on punctuality and the importance of timekeeping—in what I now thought of as his *army voice*. I'd sat perched on the edge of my bathtub, listening to him as he paced about the room, waiting for me to emerge, giving minute-by-minute time checks as though we had an appointment with the King. When, eventually, I opened the door, ready for him to continue his diatribe about my hideously sloppy timekeeping, he'd simply stared at me and smiled, as though he'd suddenly recognised a long-lost friend; as though he hadn't seen me in years.

'Good God, Clarissa . . .' he said, 'are you out to break hearts tonight?'

As we entered the Blanchs' drawing room I was determined not to look about the room for him, but when I walked in, there he was: unmissable, unmistakable; a dark, smouldering presence that caught in my throat, took my breath away.

He stood by the fireplace, directly in my line of vision, and we saw each other—eyes locked—instantaneously. I turned away, moved towards our hosts, Davina and Marcus. I took a glass of champagne from a maid holding a tray, stood with my back to him and tried to make conversation, my heart pounding so violently I thought the whole room might feel its rhythm. Then I heard Charlie call out, 'Clarissa! Clarissa! Do come over and say hello to Tom . . . here he is, my dear.'

As I crossed the room he watched me, but he didn't smile.

I held out my hand, 'Tom . . . how lovely to see you.'

His flesh was warm and smooth.

'Clarissa . . . small world.'

Charlie laughed, slightly nervously, I thought, and then said, 'By Jove, you're right, Tom, it is a small world too. Uncanny really.'

He looked the same, and yet different: a little older, more . . . polished, I suppose, and impeccably groomed. His dark hair was slicked back, and I'd forgotten, perhaps intentionally, how handsome he was, how penetrating his gaze, and that in itself threw me. He was smoking, a crystal tumbler in his hand, and when he smiled, lowered his eyes and looked down into his glass for a moment, I realised that he, too, was nervous. But when he raised his eyes and stared back into mine, it was my turn to look away. For there was something about him—his face—that dazzled me, quite literally dazzled me: as though he were a light much too bright to gaze upon directly. And *in* that light I was naked; every sensation amplified; each thought audible.

'You don't look a day older,' he said, and I turned to Charlie and smiled, rather than look back into his eyes.

I noticed the girl standing to his side, looking rather uncomfortable, staring at me. 'Oh, and this is Penny . . . Penelope Grey, my fiancée. Penny, this is Clarissa Granville, I'm sorry . . . Clarissa *Boyd*. Clarissa grew up at Deyning.'

'It's a stunning place,' she said, taking my hand, glancing at the diamonds on my neck. 'You must have had a heavenly childhood, growing up there.'

'Yes, it was . . . idyllic really.'

'And Tom lived there too,' she added, as though I needed reminding.

I smiled at her. 'Yes, yes, he did.'

'We were only out on the lake last Sunday,' she went on, and I glanced at Tom: *how could you? How could you take someone else out on the lake?* 'And Tom said it's simply sublime there on a hot summer's day. Oh, but I imagine you have some wonderful memories!'

'Yes, wonderful memories . . .'

'Well, once Tom's restored the place, once the renovations are complete, you and your husband must come down and visit, mustn't they, Tom?'

I turned to him. He'd been watching me, watching me intently, but as I turned he looked away. And for a moment I thought he was ignoring her, pretending he hadn't heard her. Then he looked at me and said, 'Yes, yes . . . you must come down. Both of you.'

'So, is there a great deal of work to be done?' I asked.

'Good Lord, yes. I don't suppose I'll be in until next year—at the earliest.'

'Oh, so you're planning on living there?'

'As opposed to?'

'Well, an investment. I hear you got the place for a song.'

'You're right. I bought it at a ridiculous price. The days of those big places are over, I'm afraid.'

'Apparently not for some,' I said, smiling.

He pulled out his lighter, lit another cigarette, glancing up at me through thick dark lashes.

'No, well, I intend to use it as somewhere to entertain clients. It doesn't need a full-time staff that way, so the costs of running the place will be kept to a minimum. And yes, to be honest, it's an investment as well.'

'And I hear you've a place here in London now too.'

He smiled. 'Yes, I've been fortunate, Clarissa; it's been a good time to be in my line of business.'

I still wasn't altogether sure what his *line of business* was, exactly. He'd made money in America, on the stock market, Charlie said, and he seemed to have quickly invested in property in London.

I watched him glance across the room; lift his glass to his mouth. And, already, I wanted to reach out and touch his face. Just to know he was there; that he was real.

'He has a beautiful place down the road, Clarissa,' Penny said.

'Oh, really. Where, exactly?'

She replied quickly, 'Hyde Park Gate.'

'Gosh, not far then,' I said, looking back at Tom. 'Strange that our paths have never crossed . . . but I suppose you haven't been back here long.'

'No, not long,' he replied.

'And London's like that, isn't it? You could be living next door to your own family and not even know it,' Penny said, taking hold of his hand. She had a slight Irish accent and I wondered where they'd met, how long they had known each other.

'And so . . . are you back for good?'

'I'm not altogether sure,' he said, enigmatically. 'What I mean is . . . I'm sure I'll be going back to America—at some stage—but I'm not sure when, or for how long.'

I glanced at Penny, wondering how she felt about a transatlantic engagement; she blinked and smiled back at me.

I'd already had a drink before leaving home, and now I felt quite giddy. But it wasn't the alcohol. I'd just discovered that not only did Tom Cuthbert own Deyning, the place that would forever be home to me, but that he was also, for the time being at least, living quite close to me in London. And right at that moment it was too much. I looked for Charlie, who'd moved away and was speaking with Marcus Blanch and another couple, and I wished he'd come and talk to Penny, talk to Tom, rescue me.

'So, you two have already met . . . known each other before,' Davina said, appearing at my side, putting her arm around me as though she sensed my discomfort.

'Yes, but quite a few years ago, Davina,' I replied.

'How fabulous. I do so love it when paths cross over once again, particularly if there are *old secrets* to be told,' she said. And I felt her pinch me.

'No secrets, I'm afraid,' Tom said, and then, glancing at me, he added, 'Unfortunately Clarissa was always out of my league.'

'Aha! But not now,' she replied, and then, smiling at Penny, she quickly added, 'I mean if you were both single and all that.'

I tried to laugh, and so did he.

Later, as we moved through to the dining room, Davina took my arm and whispered, 'I've put you next to Mr Cuthbert, darling. You can reminisce together.'

'Oh God, no.'

'Why ever not?' she whispered. 'He's absolutely divine, darling. Take no notice of the fiancée, she's a little limpet. It won't last.'

Davina was right. Penelope Grey was a limpet. All through dinner she watched us, Tom and me, as we spoke. It was tricky. We sat side by side and spoke mainly of Deyning and what he planned to do with it, without ever looking at each other. Marcus Blanch, sitting to my left, at the head of the table, asked Tom if he and Penny would live there once they were married. 'Grand house for a big family, eh?' he said, with a wink at Tom.

'We'll have to see,' Tom replied.

'When is the wedding?' I asked.

'I'm not sure . . . perhaps . . . next year,' he replied. And I thought, yes, Davina's right: there'll be no wedding.

It wasn't that I didn't want him to be happy. Of course I wanted him to be happy. But it was obvious to me that he wasn't in love. Why he'd become engaged, I don't know. Perhaps because he thought he should, thought it was the right thing to do. But he could do so much better than Penelope Grey. Was I jealous that night? No, because he still didn't belong to anyone. Yes, he was there with someone, but she didn't own his heart. And though I was no longer sure if I ever had, I knew I'd had more, much more of him than Penelope Grey.

Towards the end of dinner, as Charlie, Marcus and a few others stepped out on to the balcony for a cigar, Tom moved a little closer and asked me, quietly, if I was happy.

'Yes . . . yes, I suppose so,' I lied. 'And you?'

'I've been too busy to know about happiness,' he said.

'I can't believe that you're going to be living at Deyning. It's all so strange . . .' I shook my head. 'So strange.'

'To be honest, Clarissa, I'm taking a punt, a bit of a gamble—in more ways than one,' he added, glancing at me. 'The place is a mess, a *big* mess.' Suddenly he sounded so American. 'It needs a tremendous amount of work—*and* a pile of money, that's why it went for so little. The Fosters, the people who had it after you, they never lived there, didn't do anything to it. And you know the state it was in.' He turned to me and smiled. 'I don't imagine your mother would recognise her beautiful interior now.'

Tom. There he was, once more staring back into my eyes, a smile playing at one side of his mouth. I wanted to say so much. I wanted to say how wonderful it was to see him again; how much I'd missed him; how often I'd thought of him, dreamt of him. I watched him turn away, lift his cigarette to his lips, and I found myself once again studying that profile: those cherished features etched on to my heart; that line of forehead, nose, mouth and chin. I wanted to raise my hand to his face, trace its outline and memorise it so that I'd never, ever forget.

He turned to me, opened his mouth as though about to say something, then stopped and held my gaze for a moment, an impossible moment, where time unravelled and placed us far beyond that room of strangers. I saw him look to my lips, saw his eyes move over my face, taking in all of me; knowing all of me.

'Clarissa . . . Clarissa Granville . . .' he said.

I could hear his thoughts; feel the rhythm of his heart in time with my own, the warmth of his skin against mine. I stared back into his eyes, into the darkness of the lake, and I saw us once more under the sweeping boughs of the chestnut tree in the lower meadow. I saw us walking through the fields, hand in hand, the honey-hued stone of my home glistening in the distance, following a path, dreaming of a future. Together.

I saw him look to my hand, resting on the table, and I immediately thought of that day, so long ago, at the station restaurant. We'd shaken hands then, shaken hands this night. I'll say goodbye and shake his hand, I thought. And I felt a tear, brimming at the very edge of my eyelid, and I knew that if I blinked it would fall, and he would see. Everyone would see. So I struggled to keep my eyes wide open, trying desperately to summon other things, conjuring random images: my engagements for the coming week . . . my diary, lying open on the desk at home . . . the striped wallpaper . . . the old brass lamp that needed fixing . . . and then, out of nowhere, Emily.

Emily.

But I didn't want her to be there, not now, not at that moment; so I tried to blot her out. I picked up a spoon lying on the table in front of me and studied it as though I wasn't entirely sure what it was, as though I'd never seen one before. But I was aware of him watching me, so I turned to him and attempted a smile. 'Isn't this all rather queer?' I said, my throat tightening, the room becoming smaller. 'You and me . . . here together . . .'

'Queer and wonderful . . . wonderfully queer.'

He moved round in his chair, placing his arm along the back of mine.

I felt his hand graze my dress . . . then a finger—a stroke, a single stroke—at the base of my neck, and a frisson, like a small electric shock: reawakening, reigniting. Then the doors opened in a clatter, and Charlie and Marcus stepped back into the room. Davina called down the table, asking everyone—all of her *darlings*—to please go through to the drawing room. 'So much more comfortable,' she said, rising to her feet—with a shimmy and a twirl. I felt his hand move away, his warmth dissipate.

In the drawing room Marcus put on a record, a medley of piano music: George Gershwin, I think. I sat down on the sofa, and for a moment Tom stood about, looking awkward, one hand in his pocket. Then Charlie appeared and sat down next to me. Tom moved to the other side of the room, sat down in an armchair directly opposite us. And as the others filed through—an overly noisy, overly happy tribe—I avoided his gaze. I looked about the room as though it was an Aladdin's cave of treasure.

And it was. For Davina, like my godmother, Venetia, had an eye for the exotic and unusual, and the room, littered as it was with *souvenirs*—a foible of its owner's character—appeared a veritable mish-mash of styles: a cornucopia of the places she had visited, or perhaps longed to. Strangely hypnotic tribal masks and primitive art jostled with English pastoral scenes, and Italian marble, Chinese lacquer and French Empire furniture—as well as what my mother would describe as *bric-a-brac*—all vied for the eye.

When Davina finally danced her way into the room and perched herself upon the arm of Tom's chair, I felt a sharp twinge. And I could tell she'd taken something. She waved her hands about over animatedly, kept sniffing and touching her nose. I watched her as she laid her head upon his shoulder, then lifted it and whispered something in his ear. And when she smiled over at me, I turned and looked away.

Strange though it may seem, I wasn't remotely jealous of Penny that night, but Davina's flirtatious behaviour, her physical proximity to Tom, rankled. She was able to reach out and touch him in a way I could not, for I could never play that game with him. We could never pretend. So I tried to smile, join in the peripheral conversation. I laughed when others laughed, lit a cigarette, and glanced from person to person; I nodded, tapped my hand in time to the music, and all the time the only thing I could *feel* was him: his presence.

And all the while I could hear his voice, hear him talking; talking to Davina about America, and American music; telling her how much he loved it, how exciting the jazz scene, how exciting the whole country. And though I longed to be able to go and sit with him, to hear about his time there, I was jealous of that country too: jealous of America.

A place I didn't know, a place that had taken him and kept him for six years. Suddenly, that loud, brash big continent, with all her money and modern music, was more of a threat than Davina or Penny, or any other woman in England. I hate America, I thought. And how could he *love* it? How could he love it if it was nothing to do with us?

I think everyone in the room heard Davina say, 'So, Tom, do tell—what was Clarissa like when she was a girl? Were you *in love* with her?' I looked away, closed my eyes for a moment. She was teasing, playing, I knew, but it was so inappropriate. When I turned back, he was looking straight at me.

'Of course . . . of course I was, still am,' he said, without flinching.

I laughed, and so did Charlie. And then Marcus appeared, handing me another glass of champagne, and said, 'You do realise, we're *all* in love with you, Clarissa,' and pulled me up on to my feet to dance. I was embarrassed, no one else was dancing, and as he led me across the floor he held on to me a little too tightly.

'Really, darling, we need something with a bit more life to it!' Davina called out, and then she rose to her feet and disappeared from the room. I looked over at Tom, watching me—in contemplative pose, his index finger tapping upon his lips. I raised my eyebrows, smiled at him.

Take me away from here . . .

He stood up, took hold of Penny's hand, and led her across to where Marcus and I were dancing. And for few minutes he danced with Penny as I moved with Marcus. Then he turned to Marcus. 'All change!' He passed Penny's hand to Marcus, took mine, and pulled me to him. I remember the warmth of his hand in mine, the smell of him—his cologne. But then the music changed: louder, faster. Davina had found what she was looking for. As everyone rose to their feet—to *Charleston*—we continued our slow dance, out of time with the music, estranged from the room. He whispered something in my ear. I looked back at him, shook my head. He leant forward, spoke again, but still I couldn't hear his words. And then Charlie appeared at my side. He smiled at Tom, looked at me and pointed to his wristwatch. It was time to leave. Unable to dance, Charlie couldn't stand to watch others do the things he once enjoyed. So I shrugged at Tom, attempted a smile, released his hand and moved away.

And after bidding our hosts goodnight, I picked up my bag and followed Charlie across the room. I paused at the doorway and turned. He was dancing with Davina, looking back at me.

Thank you. Thank you for reminding me.

CHAPTER TWENTY-EIGHT

That night, after Davina's dinner party, Charlie had been in a foul mood. En route home he'd accused me of dancing only to upset and annoy him. He said I was without compassion, had no sensitivity, and that even Tom Cuthbert must have felt sorry for him: having a wife who rubbed her husband's nose in his disability. I didn't say much at all. I apologised, told him that I hadn't meant to upset him, hadn't thought.

'But that's just it. You never think!'

When we reached the house, he went straight to his study, and I to my room. I locked the door and sat down upon the bed. I never quite knew what to expect, how he would be, especially late in the evening. His mood swings had become increasingly erratic, and his anger—always there, just beneath the surface—exacerbated by alcohol.

And that night, coming home, I'd recognised the signs: the tugging at his collar, the fidgeting and overly bright look in his eyes. I could hear him below me, shouting to himself, slamming doors; and I was frightened. We'd never spoken about that night, the night of the charity dance at the Park Lane Hotel, never acknowledged what had happened. But a few weeks later it had happened again. That time, the second time, I'd put up a fight, or had tried. He didn't strike me, but he was rougher, angrier, more violent, and had held me down by my wrists, which I'd had to keep covered up for days afterwards. The third time, as I'd tried to escape from him, out of my room, he'd struck me across my back with his stick. Not as hard as he perhaps could have done, but hard enough. After that, I'd had the broken lock on my bedroom door mended. And now I spent most of my evenings there, behind a locked door.

As I sat on the bed listening to his movements downstairs, I wondered what he'd do if he came up to my room and discovered that locked door. Would he break it down? Was he capable? I thought of our cook and maid, both asleep at the top of the house . . . they'd hear, surely they'd hear. Then, at last, I heard the front door slam shut. And I lay back on my bed and cried.

The following morning I realised I'd left my

shawl at Davina's, and I telephoned her to ask if I could call in and collect it later that day. Yes, she said, do come over; she had a monstrous headache but would love *a bit of a chat*. I knew immediately that she'd probably want to quiz me about Tom and, sure enough, minutes after I'd arrived there, she said to me, 'So . . . come along, darling, do tell.'

'About what?'

'Ha! You know! About him, about Tom Cuthbert!'

'Nothing to tell,' I replied.

'Oh, come on, I wasn't born yesterday. It's perfectly obvious that you and Tom Cuthbert have had—or even *are* having—an affair . . .'

'We are not having an affair, Davina,' I said, and laughed. 'I can assure you of that. We had a . . . a friendship . . . a childish infatuation, but it was years ago.'

'Well, you could've fooled me,' she replied. 'It's quite clear to me the man's besotted with you. And you . . . well, really, darling—how could you not be?'

I didn't want to be drawn and I wasn't about to tell Davina Blanch anything. She was a notorious gossip; someone one only ever told those things one wished to have published without incurring any cost.

'I wonder if he'll get in touch with you . . .' she said, thinking aloud, excited by the possibility of another affair for her to disclose. 'Or has he *already* been in touch with you?'

'No, he hasn't. He doesn't have my telephone number, *or* my address. And, to be honest, I doubt he will. I'm married, Davina, and he's engaged . . . engaged to be married.'

She leant back in her chair, rolling her eyes heavenwards. 'You really think that stops men when they see something they want? Men like him? The only thing that makes men think is their wallet, darling. How much it will cost them. And let's face it, Tom Cuthbert might be new money, but he's big new money. He doesn't need to think about his goddamn wallet. But you know, it's a mystery to everyone where, exactly, his money's come from. There's talk of speakeasies, bootlegging . . . that sort of thing. Anyway, you know me, I'm not one for gossip, and who cares . . . he's delicious material for an affair,' she added, winking at me.

I laughed. 'Really, I don't know *where* his money's come from, and to be honest, I'm not interested.'

'I don't believe you. I simply don't believe you. No, not for one minute.'

'Davina, it won't happen.'

'I bet poor little Pen's distraught,' she continued. 'She must have seen the way he looked at you last night. Poor little limpet. But, darling, what'll I do if he calls me for your number?'

'You can give him my telephone number by all means, and I've no doubt that I'll see him again, at some stage, somewhere. We seem to be moving in the same circle these days. But please, Davina, don't discuss me with him.' And as I said that I realised immediately that I'd made a fundamental error: by asking Davina *not* to talk to Tom about me I'd only fired her curiosity more. Now, she wouldn't be able to help herself, she'd have to discuss me with him; in fact, she'd probably think of some pretext to call him up the very next day.

'Of course not. I wouldn't dream of it, darling,'

she said, as we made our way back downstairs, 'but seeing as it was me who brought you back together, you must keep me posted.'

'Yes, I'll keep you posted,' I said, 'but don't hold your breath.'

Driving home, I wondered if I'd hear from Tom. Would he get in touch? Would he telephone? I crossed Oxford Street, heading towards home, but I didn't want to go back. I didn't want to return to that empty house, my home; and so I turned right instead of left, towards Hyde Park. And then I parked the car, walked down the street, across Park Lane, and into the park. It was a beautiful summer's evening, not late, perhaps around six, and I walked in a southerly direction.

I'm not altogether sure why, but I wanted to go back to that place, to try to find the tree: the tree where Tom and I had made love that night, so many years before. I walked quite briskly at first, smiling and nodding at people as I passed them. I imagine they thought I was running late for an engagement, or perhaps a mother rushing home to her children. And for a while I imagined that too. I imagined that I was heading home to a family, a husband and children: Emily and Tom. A house in Belgravia perhaps, with a glossy black-painted front door and an ornate polished brass knocker; three children . . . or even four . . . yes, four: two girls, Emily the eldest, and two boys. They'd be waiting for me in the nursery, bathed and smelling divine; creamy skinned and pink cheeked; dark eyes peering out of a high window, waiting for their mama. He'd anticipate my return too; greet me with outstretched arms, smiling. We'd climb the staircase together, hand in hand, feeling whole once more, feeling complete.

And there she is, Emily, almost ten, the eldest of our offspring . . . standing at the top of the stairs. 'Where have you been?' she says. 'I've been waiting.'

'I'm here now,' I reply, wrapping my arms around her. 'I'm here now.'

As I reached the southernmost point of the park, I stopped.

Somewhere here . . . somewhere here.

But there were so many trees: some huge, old and established; others younger, possibly planted in the intervening years. *Ten years.* I stepped away from the pathway on to the grass, looked back towards Park Lane and tried to remember that night: it had been dark . . . we'd crossed over, entered the park . . . walked upon grit and then grass . . . But where had we crossed? Which path had we taken? A military band played on in the distance, its vaguely familiar melody distracting me, muddling me further, and I sat down upon a bench under the beech trees of Rotten Row.

Once, before I knew about war and death and loss, the earth had drawn me to it, pulling me into its shapes and colours, curling up around me and enveloping me in its warmth. Sometimes, I'd even fancied I could see it trembling, hear it breathing, but not any more. The earth had no heartbeat, it had stopped, perhaps with mine; for all I could see was what I could see, and nothing more.

I closed my eyes, half listening to the strains of a waltz drifting across the park. *I am a memory, unspoken, unseen. I am but a whisper, a glance. The echo of that other time . . . the rhythm, the dance* . . . Then, through the shuffle and hubbub, through the din of traffic, I recognised the music: 'The Blue

Danube', my father's favourite.

When, eventually, I returned home, as I stood in the hallway pulling off my gloves, Sonia appeared. She told me that a gentleman had telephoned, twice: a Mr Cuthbert, she said.

'Was there a message?'

'No, ma'am, but he said he'd try again later.'

It was around 8.30 p.m. when the telephone rang out, and though I'd been sitting staring at it, waiting for it to ring, I jumped. I was on my own, had no idea when Charlie would be home and had no wish to see him. 'I'll get it!' I called out into the empty hallway, and then I closed the drawing-room door and picked up the receiver. And as soon as I heard him, as soon as I heard his voice, I wanted to cry.

There were many pauses, achingly long silences in that conversation, for at times I simply couldn't speak. Words wouldn't come. And so he spoke, and I listened.

'It was wonderful . . . wonderful to see you again, Clarissa. And I'm pleased, pleased if you're happy.'

I closed my eyes.

'But I wanted to call you . . .' he continued. 'I want you to know that I'm not getting married.'

'Oh, I see . . .'

'It's not the reason for my call, of course, but I want you to know that anyway.'

'Yes,' I said.

'It's over between Penny and me; in fact, it was over before yesterday evening.'

Through the crackle on the line I could hear him light a cigarette.

'And the other thing I need to tell you . . . is that I'm going back to America.'

I didn't say anything. I could feel myself begin to

shake. That wobbling feeling that starts deep inside and then, quite quickly, moves outside—to one's head and hands, and legs and knees. A tremor.

'Clarissa?'

I nodded.

'I really hadn't expected to have to return—at least not yet, not now—but something's cropped up . . . it's difficult. It's not . . . it's not work, it's a personal matter . . . but I wanted you to know, and I . . .'

I heard him suck on his cigarette.

'I don't want you to think I've just disappeared, you see. I don't want you to . . .'

'I understand,' I said.

I heard him sigh. 'No, you don't understand. I know that. You can't understand. And I wish I could tell you more . . . but I can't.'

There was a silence, a long silence. And then I said, 'When will you be back?'

'I'm not altogether sure, but hopefully in a few months.'

A few months . . . a few months . . .

'I'd like to see you again before I leave.' He sighed again, and I could see him running his hand through his hair. 'I'm sailing from Southampton next Tuesday . . . and I'll be staying there—at the South Western—the night before.'

Another silence.

'Clarissa?'

'Yes. The South Western.'

'Next Monday . . . I'll be there on Monday . . . Monday evening. From around six.'

I nodded. 'Yes, next Monday.'

'From around six,' he said again.

'Yes, around six,' I repeated, smiling.

I can't remember now what we said, if anything, after that.

CHAPTER TWENTY-NINE

It was Davina who found me: Davina who unlocked my bedroom door. I'm not sure what I'd intended. But I don't think—no, I can't think—that I'd wished for death. Or had I? I knew he'd sailed that morning, knew that he'd have waited for me the night before. But it had all been so poorly planned; by me, at least.

Charlie said, 'I don't think so.'

'But it's almost a day trip, Charlie . . . after all, I shall only be staying for one night. I'll be back tomorrow . . . I'll be back tomorrow morning, and Edina,' I went on, referring to my cousin, who now lived at Sevenoaks, 'is so looking forward to seeing me. I haven't seen her since she had little Archie. I've never met him.'

He lowered his newspaper. 'I forbid it,' he said, without looking at me. And then he refilled his teacup.

I think that's when I stood up. And as I moved away from the breakfast table, towards the door, and towards him, I said, 'I don't care what you say . . . I'm going.'

And then, as I passed him, he must have reached out and grabbed hold of my wrist; because I remember him holding on to it and saying, 'You will not be going anywhere overnight, and you're certainly not gallivanting off to Kent on your own, Clarissa.'

I tried to pull my arm free. I remember that, and his grip, so tight, burning my flesh.

The rest is all a muddle. There was a fight. I picked up his cup of tea, threw it at him. He hit me. I screamed, and then . . . and then I think I screamed again. And I said, 'I'm going, Charlie, and I'm never coming back!'

It was he who locked me in my room as I packed. I know that.

And I remember panicking, throwing everything movable, anything throwable—pillows, cushions, ornaments, silver and china—at the door, and shouting for him; shouting for him—or anyone—to let me out.

Mess, mess, mess . . . Everything broken. Me broken.

I remember the tick-tock of minutes and the chime of each hour; and lying on the carpet surrounded by tiny white feathers and slivers of porcelain. I remember daylight fading, darkness descending; barely breathing.

And then the bottle of sleeping pills in my bedside cabinet.

Kiss me; kiss me now . . .

A few days later, my doctor called on me. He spoke to me about something called *neurasthenia*, and prescribed more pills. Of course, he didn't know what I'd done, didn't understand. He told me that these new pills would *help my nerves.* And they did. In the weeks and months that followed I glided through life, moving effortlessly through doorways and rooms, along flagstoned pavements in a dreamy mellow state, smiling. I sat in Hyde Park, lost in the cacophony of the city's traffic: the sound of horns and whistles and motors, and the clippety-clap of hoofs. I watched open taxicabs and horse-drawn delivery wagons, men with barrows and street sellers; the organ grinder, surrounded by hordes of children; the ubiquitous war veteran, balanced upon his crutch, a harmonica pressed to his mouth; and the ever-present military band, playing on in the distance. I watched people scurrying, people dawdling; courting couples and windswept picnics. I watched the world pass by, watched people for hours and hours.

At home, I quietly arranged flowers and stared at menus. I tried to read, attempted a few books, but couldn't quite absorb the words or sentences on those pages. I preferred to look at the pictures inside magazines and newspapers, and imagine the stories that went with them. I dined alone most evenings, waited on by the servants; the table set for one, with the very best bone china and crystal. And Charlie didn't bother me. In fact, I hardly saw him. On the few occasions I did, he rarely looked me in the eye, and preferred to speak of mundane matters. If he felt any remorse, he neither showed nor expressed it.

Davina called on me, and quite regularly, but I never told her anything. Luckily, there'd been only enough pills in the bottle for me to knock myself out for a few hours, no more, nothing more sinister. By the time she'd found me I was—to all intents and purposes—lying asleep on my bed. The debris in my room—the result of a huge argument with Charlie, I'd said. Yes, I'd been hysterical. And yes, yes, I'd packed; I'd planned on returning to my mother's, for that night at least, I'd told her.

'Men! They can be such beasts . . . and they're all the same,' she said, looking at me, holding on to my hand. 'You know, I sometimes feel like running away too . . . but where could I go?' She shrugged. 'Where could either of us go? Other than back to our mothers,' she added, rolling her eyes. 'All marriages are hard work, *bloody* hard work, darling . . . all of them. Don't let anyone tell you otherwise. But the sad truth of the matter is,' she went on, 'women like you and me . . . we're not meant to be . . . independent, on our own. We'd be no good, no good at all . . .' She looked down into her lap. 'Sometimes I think we've simply been bred to be sold on, to be *breeding machines* . . . to be owned.' She looked up at me with a queer smile. 'We'll never be free.'

After she left that day, I pondered on her words, for there was more, much more than a grain of truth in them. Had I ever been free? I'd never, not once, had any say in my life, my destiny. It had all been decided long ago, by my parents, and then by Mama, and then, after my marriage, by my husband. I'd always been owned—but never by me.

I think most of that year passed in a blur, for I have no recollection of anything of note, only the solitude and quietness of my life. But I know that it was almost exactly a year—exactly a year after Davina's party—when the by-word-of-mouth invitation came.

He'd contacted Charlie regarding some legal issue to do with his ever-increasing property empire, or that's how Charlie saw it.

'He's very kindly invited us down to Deyning. I think he's having quite a crowd . . . house-warming sort of thing. I said I'd have to check with you, of course, but he said he thought you'd be interested to see what he's done with the place. You quite liked him—when you met him at Davina's—didn't you? Thing is, he's potentially a *very* good client for us . . . and he's looking to break away from Chester and Goring.'

I didn't look up at him; didn't say anything.

'Clarissa?'

'I'm not sure,' I said.

'You know I had a sneaky feeling you didn't like him; could tell . . . could tell at that party. I saw him trying to win you over, flirting with you.'

'He didn't flirt, Charlie. He doesn't flirt.'

'Hmm. I think he was a tad star-struck. Understandable, I suppose . . . when one bears in mind his background and yours.'

His comment irked me. I looked up at him. 'Actually, yes . . . yes, let's go. I rather would like to see the old place again.'

'Bravo!' he said, clapping his hands together. 'You won't necessarily have to see much of him, you know . . . there'll be quite a houseful. Anyway, I shall let him know.'

'Who's the latest girlfriend?' I asked, flicking through the pages of a magazine; knowing there'd be another.

'Oh, someone called Nancy, I think.'

He still hadn't married and I wondered if he ever would; if he would ever commit to someone and live a domesticated life. I'd heard he was back in London, and, according to Davina, and others, he seemed to have the Midas touch. He'd recently acquired a number of central London properties, all at upset prices, and, apparently, planned on converting them into smaller dwellings, flats and new modern offices. Davina predicted that one day Tom Cuthbert would own *great swathes of central London*. She'd told me he didn't attend too many parties, that he spent all of his time working, seemingly in the pursuit of money. But she'd seen him a few of times of late, each time with a different girl on his arm. He'd asked after me, she said, but that was all. 'Do tell her I asked after her.' And to me it sounded perfunctory, cold.

And hearing his name was wonderful and awful at the same time. For each time I heard it, there he was: Tom. And yet how I longed to be the one to say it, to own it, but now, now it belonged to everyone. *Tom Cuthbert*. That shining light, the hope, the proof, surely, that someone could emerge from the darkness intact, erect, head high, sane, undamaged, still beautiful, whole. And so each time I heard his name I said nothing.

* * *

. . . But haven't you heard, dear? Oh my, good gracious, the man's the toast of the city! . . . and such humble origins . . . but of course it's a changed world now . . . an unfathomably queer character . . . doesn't wear his fortune comfortably . . . new money must be such a tremendous burden . . . one gets the distinct impression it's rather something of an ordeal for him . . .

* * *

It was a beautiful midsummer's afternoon when Charlie and I drove through the old white gates of Deyning. As our car motored up the driveway, I asked Charlie to slow down. I wanted to take it all in, I said. I felt as though I was in a dream, as though I might wake up at any moment. But then what would my reality be? To wake up and discover that I was married to Tom, and not Charlie? To awake and find myself young again, back at Deyning with my family . . . and that Tom had only ever been the figment of a dream? How things had changed. And I suddenly wondered what my father would have made of it all, had he been alive.

My mother, of course, had heard, eventually, through a friend, that a businessman named Tom Cuthbert had bought Deyning. It took her six months to mention it to me, believing, as she did, that she was the initial bearer of this astonishing piece of news.

'Yes, Mama, I know,' I'd said to her. 'I heard some time ago.'

'Really? And you never told me . . .'

'I wasn't sure you'd want to know.'

'And do you see him, cross paths with him? He certainly seems to have elevated himself . . . seems to be mixing in rarefied circles these days.'

'Yes, I've seen him,' I replied.

She stared at me but said nothing.

'He's done very well, Mama.'

'Obviously.'

It was too much for her. She couldn't bring herself to talk to me about him. It would mean undoing so much, which had, in her mind, been done. After that terse exchange I couldn't bring myself to tell her that Charlie and I were going down to Deyning as Tom's guests. It was easier to lie. We were off to Charlie's sister's place in West Sussex, I'd said.

Tom and his new American fiancée, Nancy, had

invited about twenty or so of us to their Saturday to Monday house party, but the only other people I knew who'd be there were the Blanchs. I was curious to meet Nancy. Davina had told me she was as rich as she was beautiful—'In that American way'.

When we pulled up outside the house there were quite a few cars, more than I'd ever seen at the place, but I didn't want to go inside. Not yet.

'I think I'll take a stroll,' I said to Charlie.

'Is that not rather rude? I think we should announce our arrival, say hello first, don't you?'

'You go and say hello. I need some fresh air,' I said. 'I shan't be long.'

I walked slowly, following the path around the house to the south terrace. I noticed the rose garden, completely replanted. It looked just as it had back in our day. And the parterre too, restored and put back as it was before the army had trampled across it. Then, as I neared the terrace, I could hear voices and laughter, and I turned and headed back towards the stables. I crossed the yard, went quickly through the gate, and as I walked down through the meadow I realised I was walking into a memory, and I felt a great swell of unharnessed emotion rise up in me. Everything looked just as I remembered, just as it had always been, only more beautiful, so much more beautiful. Perhaps it was this, or perhaps it was the sound of my brothers' voices in the distance, but by the time I reached the chestnut tree I was crying. I sat down on a wrought-iron bench, and the certain knowledge that Tom had put it there only brought on more tears.

When I heard my name, I didn't look up. The

last person I'd expected to appear was him. I'd imagined he'd be busy entertaining his newly arrived house guests, but of course he knew where to find me. And I felt embarrassed to be sitting there, alone and crying. He crouched down in front of me.

'Clarissa . . .'

For a moment I couldn't speak. I simply nodded, and tried to smile.

He took hold of my hand. 'I knew it would be hard for you—coming back here, but I wanted you to see the place, see what I've done. It's all as it used to be, isn't it?'

I nodded again.

He pulled a handkerchief from his pocket and passed it to me.

I don't know how long we were like that, me sitting on the bench, him crouched in front of me, staring at each other. But words were superfluous, and everything that passed between us in those few silent minutes swept us back, and opened us to each other once more.

'We should go back,' I said, eventually. 'You're our host, Tom. You've all these people to amuse and entertain.'

'But there's only one person I want to be with, and she's right here.'

I shook my head. 'No, don't say that. You can't say that. I'm here with Charlie. And you . . . you have Nancy now, and a house full of guests. Please,' I said, standing up. 'We need to go back. Charlie will be looking for me.'

'Yes, there's always someone looking for you, Clarissa.'

I said nothing, and we walked through the

meadow in silence, then, as we reached the track back to the gate, he stopped. 'It's all for you.'

I looked at him. I didn't know what to say, wasn't entirely sure what he meant. Then I heard my name and saw Charlie standing at the gate.

'Come along, I want you to show us round the house.'

'I wish no one else was here but us. Shall I ask everyone to leave now? Tell them I only invited them all to get you here?'

'Please, Tom. Charlie's watching us.' I glanced back at the gate and waved. 'Please . . .'

Minutes later, he was guiding Charlie and me through the house; my old home, now his. And he was as attentive to Charlie as he was to me. As we entered each room, I was aware of him watching me, searching my face, waiting for my reaction. And each time I turned to him—to smile—a look of anxiety would melt from his features, and he'd smile back at me. He took time to explain the work carried out in each room, pointing out the detail and craftsmanship. Charlie was impressed. And Tom had done a magnificent job, particularly in the library. There, he'd improved on my father's design. Rather than the former dark wood panelling and shelves, there were now modern pale oak shelves and panelling; unadorned windows, allowing daylight to flood the room; and in the middle, two sofas and an ottoman. As he explained to Charlie what he'd done with the room, the room he now used as his study, I wandered over to his desk in front of the window. I looked out towards the South Downs. This was his view. *This is what he looks out upon; this is what he sees*. I wished Charlie wasn't there, and when I turned and looked back at Tom

I knew he was thinking the same: wishing we could be as we once were.

Finally, he showed us to our room: my old room.

'I know this was once Clarissa's room . . . and I thought you might like to stay here again,' he said, glancing at me as he opened the door.

I stared at the twin beds, a panic rising up inside me. I hadn't actually thought about the fact that Charlie and I would have to share a room.

'Still pink,' I said, referring to the décor, and moving across the room to the window.

'Yes. I don't suppose it's altered too much since you were last here,' he said, sounding awkward for a moment.

'Fit for a princess!' Charlie said, and all three of us laughed.

I stared out through the window, beyond the ha-ha, still dividing the formal gardens from the parkland and fields, to the purple hills in the distance, suffused in midsummer sun. Nothing had changed; nothing had altered. The landscape ahead, windless and still, just as it had been that last summer.

Yes, all the same . . . all the same.

'Well, the view's certainly not changed, but for the electricity cables,' I said, and then I turned and looked about the room.

Our bags had already been unpacked, our clothes put away. I noted the crystal vases of roses on almost every surface, and then, on the table next to one of the beds, a book. I walked over, picked it up: a volume of Emily Brontë's poems. He'd remembered. All those years and he'd remembered. And I wanted to run over to him, wrap my arms around him.

I looked up at him. 'Thank you, Tom.'

He smiled. 'I'd better get back now. But I look forward to seeing you both in a little while,' he said and disappeared out of the door.

'Nice chap, eh?' Charlie said, testing one of the twin beds.

'Yes, charming,' I replied, returning to the window.

I looked down to the terrace below. I could see Davina, in full flow, and a crowd of people I didn't know. I wondered which one of them was Nancy, but I saw no female who particularly caught my eye, and I heard myself sigh. I saw him emerge. I watched him stride over to a group sitting at a table; watched him run his hands through his hair as he listened to one of them speak, then throw back his head and laugh.

Tom.

He looked so at ease, so confident, and so casual too: dressed in pale trousers, a white open-necked shirt with a dark blue paisley silk cravat. I watched him speaking, wondered what it was he was saying. I lifted my fingers to the pane, ran them down over his shape.

'Right-o then, I think we should go down and be sociable now, don't you?' Charlie said.

'You go. I'll freshen up and follow you down.'

He came over to where I stood, and I felt myself freeze. 'I do realise that this must be very, very difficult for you. To be back here, I mean; very strange . . . can't imagine.' He tried to put his arm around me.

'I'm fine, really I am,' I said, moving away from him and looking about the room for my vanity case.

'You don't mind then . . . if I go down?'

'No, Charlie, you go down,' I said, placing the small case upon a bed, and wishing he'd leave the room.

'So, how long will you be?' he asked.

'Not long,' I said, without looking up at him.

As soon as he left the room I sat down upon the bed. I was going to have to share a room with my husband—for two nights. Oh, he was fine now, perfectly civil, but what about later? I closed my eyes. What was I doing here? Why had I come back?

I rose from the bed, walked over to the window and looked down again. I saw Charlie on the terrace now, leaning on his stick, standing with Tom; and I could almost hear him telling Tom that I was *taking a moment* to myself. Then I saw Tom look up to the window and I quickly moved away.

When I eventually left the room and went downstairs, outside on to the terrace, Tom was nowhere in sight.

'He had to make an important telephone call,' Charlie said, by way of explanation, and I immediately felt the light grow dimmer.

I helped myself to a cup of tea and sat down next to Charlie, who was talking to an Austrian couple. He introduced me to them, but I was distracted and uncomfortable, more uncomfortable than I'd anticipated. I looked about for Davina, who was standing by the steps talking to a man. She saw me, raised her hand, but made no attempt to move, and so I sat in silence sipping my tea, smiling from time to time at a stranger, and wishing I were back at home. I wished Tom would reappear and take me off to the lake; wished he'd row us across to the island where we could be alone. And I lost myself in a daydream, remembering that time at the end of the War, when we'd spent so many afternoons there on our own.

It was Davina who interrupted my reverie, standing in front of me with another woman.

I stood up. 'Clarissa, this is Nancy, Tom's fiancée,' she said.

She was not at all as I'd imagined: handsome rather than pretty, with a strong masculine jaw, and tall and dark, like me. She told me she'd heard a lot about me, but it later transpired that this was from Davina, and not Tom. 'How very odd *Tam* never mentioned to me that you once lived here too,' she said in her New York drawl.

I shrugged. 'Well, perhaps he forgot,' I suggested, smiling.

'It's not like him to forget anything,' she said, and laughed. 'Anyway, I better go see where he's gotten to.' She leant towards me. 'He's hopeless,' she whispered. 'No good at small talk, you know.'

I smiled. *Yes, I know, and neither am I.*

CHAPTER THIRTY

Tom never reappeared on the terrace that afternoon and it wasn't until a few hours later, over cocktails in the ballroom, that he emerged, looking more handsome than I'd ever seen him, and with an altogether different demeanour. He was in an irreverent mood, playful and witty. As I watched him with his assembled guests, I tried to remember the shy young man I'd been introduced to in that very same room, so many years earlier. But there was no trace of him, he'd gone, and in his place was someone quite sure of himself, and of his position in the world. Handsome, rich and charming, in control of everything, he enthralled us: each and every one of us.

I was standing by the open casement doors, listening to an unfeasibly tall, good-looking American with one of those ridiculous names: Hudson D. Weiner Junior. He asked me to call him Hud, which struck me as a little familiar at the time, but Americans were very friendly in that way, still are. We were all drinking champagne cocktails and a gramophone was playing some new American jazz music. It was Hud who told me it was American, I really wouldn't have known. When he asked me to dance, I laughed.

'As a rule, Hud, we don't normally dance before dinner,' I said. 'But perhaps later.'

'I bet you say that to all the guys,' he replied, leaning over me, his arm against the wall.

'Only the Americans,' I said, smiling.

I saw Tom looking over, watching us, and I smiled back at him, but he turned away.

I could hear Charlie on the other side of the room, his voice already a little too loud. And I could see Davina, a cigarette dangling from her painted lips, gesticulating wildly in over-animated enthusiasm. Hud was regaling me with a long and overly detailed story about a bear he'd once shot, and moving closer all the time. I could see Marcus, Davina's husband, sitting at the grand piano with a petite, dizzy-looking blonde—flirting, threatening to play. I glanced back at Tom, leaning against the mantelpiece, smoking, talking to a couple I couldn't recall having seen earlier. He saw me look at him, threw his cigarette down into the fireplace, said something to the couple and walked towards me.

'Weiner!' he called out, stemming the flow. 'I hope you're not boring the beautiful Clarissa . . . and not another of your bear stories, eh?'

'Ha! Cuthbert, you old rogue. I thought I was doing rather well there.'

Tom looked at me. 'I'm afraid I have to steal her away from you now, Weiner.' And before the American could say anything, Tom took hold of my hand and led me out through the open doors behind us.

Outside, on the terrace, a few people sat about smoking, and I wondered if he was going to introduce me to one of them.

Someone called out, 'Aha! Tom!'

'Back in a jiffy,' he replied, without pausing to look at them. So I smiled at them, shrugged as he led me past them. I wasn't sure where he was taking me or why, and I wasn't sure who was watching us. But he must have sensed my apprehension because he said, 'Don't panic, Clarissa. I shall return you to your rightful owner in due course.'

We descended the stone steps and proceeded across the lawn, then through the parterre. He kept hold of my hand, marching so quickly that I had to run with every few steps. Then I saw something, at the end of the pathway, and I stopped, pulling my hand from his.

I turned towards him, my hands over my mouth, incredulous.

'A tent . . . an Arabian tent . . .'

I looked back at the tent, began to walk towards it, slowly. The sides of the canvas were pinned back, a dozen or so flickering lanterns encircling it upon the grass. Standing to one side was the solemn-looking older man I'd seen earlier; Tom's *man*, I presumed, his valet. I noted the bottle of champagne in an ice bucket on a stand to his side.

'Good evening, sir . . . ma'am,' the man said, nodding at Tom and then at me.

'Good evening Walter,' Tom replied, and then the man picked up the bottle and released the cork.

I turned to Tom.

'Go on . . .' he said, smiling back at me, 'take a look.'

I stepped inside the tent, running my hand down the richly coloured tapestries draping its interior walls. A vividly coloured rug and large cushions lay about the floor, and in the centre a brass-topped table with a lantern and two champagne glasses set upon it. I sat down on a cushion and looked up. Above me were hundreds of minuscule, glinting gold stars, sewn into the richest, deepest blue.

I shook my head. 'It's beautiful, Tom,' I said, staring up at the stars as he stepped inside the tent, holding the bottle. 'But what's it for?'

He laughed. 'It's for you, of course. I told you, it's all for you.'

I turned to him. 'Tom . . .'

I was speechless, didn't know what to say. And really, it was all too much.

'But it's perfect . . . perfect, and so beautiful,' I said again. 'And exactly like the one . . . the one I'd imagined.'

He said nothing but glanced over at me as he poured champagne into a glass, smiling. I lay back against a pile of cushions, propped myself on one arm and watched him. How could I not love him? His ingenuity, the romance of him. I took a sip of champagne and stared back at him, unable to stop smiling.

'I can't believe you did this for me . . . can't believe you remembered.'

'Of course I remembered. You never did get your Arabian tent, did you? Anyway, it's for you, it's yours.'

I laughed. 'But, Tom, I have *nowhere* to put a tent. I live in a town house—with a garden not much bigger than this,' I said, gesturing. 'It would be pointless . . . impossible. But I love it. I love it and I want to sleep here, under these stars.' I put down my glass, lay back once again to look up at the stars glistening in the fabric above our heads, and for a few minutes neither one of us spoke.

Then he said, 'You didn't come.'

And I knew what it was he referred to.

I closed my eyes. 'I couldn't . . . I couldn't come, it was impossible,' I said.

'I waited for you. I waited all night.'

I turned my head, looked up at him. 'It wasn't meant to be, Tom.'

He shook his head. 'It could have been.'

And then I saw myself: saw my deranged self, hurling china figurines, scent bottles, silver-framed photographs and brocade cushions at my locked bedroom door. He has no idea, I thought, no idea. 'I wanted to come, I wanted to . . .'

'Then please, come here later . . . later tonight,' he said.

I'd been no more than a foolish girl when I'd told him I wanted to sleep in an Arabian tent on the lawn, and here we were, so many summers later. He was sitting cross-legged, close to me, staring down at me, and without thinking I reached out to him.

He took my hand to his mouth, kissed it. 'Tell me you'll come here later . . . please.'

'I'll try,' I said, my eyes fixed on his. 'I'll try.'

He kissed my hand again, ran his nose over my wrist. 'You smell of my dreams, Clarissa Granville.'

Tom.

I had left my moorings, was already adrift, floating out across a lake with him, and nothing else mattered, no one else mattered, to either of us. They were the reeds beneath the water, hampering our crossing to that place where we could be together, and alone.

When we walked back up the steps on to the terrace everyone had disappeared and all was silent.

'Oh dear,' he said, with affected solemnity, and we walked on, quickly, through the ballroom, into the lobby and towards the dining room, where people were filing through the doorway in a noisy huddle of smoke and laughter.

'I say! Here they are!' Davina called out. 'Darlings! We did rather wonder where you'd disappeared to . . . were about to send out a search party.'

Davina, as unsubtle as ever.

'Ha! I was showing Clarissa the new tennis court. Do you play, Davina?' Tom said, moving swiftly ahead of us, with smiles and nods. 'We should have a game, tomorrow . . .' he called back to her.

Nancy, standing at the doorway to the dining room, smiled at me as I passed her, but it was a queer sort of smile, and it made me feel guilty. More than guilty, it made me feel wicked.

I was placed next to him, on his right, with Davina directly opposite me, on his left. The meal was an ordeal for me, and I suspect for him too. We'd begun our subterfuge and each time I caught his eye I felt a mix of guilt and longing. I took another glass of champagne rather than wine, and I could feel its effects. Any resolve I'd had was melting fast, and in its place was a yearning; a yearning I'd not known since I was sixteen years old. I watched him as he spoke with Davina, smiling and laughing; I watched him as he stood up and made a toast, and then sat back down and looked immediately to me. Yes, yes, I was proud of him, and yes, I loved him and wanted him. I knew I'd risk my marriage for him. I knew I'd risk everything for him.

Thankfully, Davina was as verbose as ever, but I was aware of her scrutiny, not of one of us, but of us both. And each time Tom turned and spoke to me, no matter how mundane the words, he looked at me in such a way that though I couldn't take my eyes away from his, and though I couldn't see Davina's expression, I could feel her watching us and I knew she'd see that something had passed between us. From time to time I caught Charlie's eye, sitting at the opposite end of the table, a few places away from Nancy, and I tried to smile back at him. He looked happy enough, I thought; he was enjoying himself. And Nancy? I'm not sure what she saw, or what she thought. In his toast Tom had thanked her for her help and complimented her on her 'exceptional' organisational skills, but he could have been speaking of an employee, I thought, not the woman he was about to marry.

After dinner, the men adjourned to the smoking room for brandy and cigars, and we ladies removed ourselves to the drawing room for coffee. There,

Nancy came and sat down next to me. She asked me about my childhood, and then quizzed me on Tom: if I'd seen much of him growing up at Deyning, and when I'd last seen him. I was vague about the old Deyning days, and very specific on when I'd seen him last. 'Oh, golly . . . not for almost a year. In fact, it was at Davina's we last saw each other,' I said, and then added, 'But we hadn't seen each other for many years before that.'

She told me of their wedding plans. It was to take place towards the end of the summer, at the church down the road, and afterwards a 'small' reception—here, at the house. 'Perfect,' I said. 'And any honeymoon plans?'

'Oh, I don't suppose so. Tom may be marrying me but he's already married—to his work!' she replied.

'And so . . . will you live here?' I asked.

'Between here and the place in London,' she said, and then added, 'and as and when we have children, Tom wishes them to be brought up here, in the country.'

I remember thinking, so they've discussed it; they've made plans. They shall have a family and live here at Deyning. And I could suddenly picture it all, it was so easy. I saw them in years to come: Tom, surrounded by a large brood of dark-haired children, playing with them out on the lawn; up a ladder, decorating a Christmas tree; and Nancy, the matriarch, chatelaine of Deyning Park, Mrs Tom Cuthbert; reliable and efficient, organising their lives.

'Do you have children, Clarissa?' she asked.

'No, sadly, I don't,' I replied, and for some reason I smiled as I said it.

A few minutes later I excused myself. It was after midnight, and the conversation had turned to babies and children, which I always found difficult. For years I'd practised smiling inanely as other women spoke of their children. I'd feigned empathy and interest, nodding attentively, and sympathising with them in their tribulations: oh, the ordeals of raising a family! I'd laughed at their funny stories of little Johnny's antics, sat in silence as they'd discussed schools, and the neatly planned paths for their offspring. But sometimes, sometimes it became too much. And as I climbed the stairs at Deyning that night I struggled to hold back my tears, for I could never join in those conversations. I was a mother, yet I was no one's 'Mummy'. And I knew, knew the moment I left the room, that Davina would take it upon herself to explain my sad predicament; explain to those straining ears how there were no babies—no children for the Boyds. Not now, and, perhaps, not ever. And in my head I could hear their momentary sighs of sadness.

No, no babies for Clarissa.

It must have been after one when Charlie came to bed. But I pretended to be asleep, and within seconds he was snoring. I lay there for almost an hour wondering what to do. I knew I had a choice: I could remain in my room, or I could go to Tom. But would he be there? And what if someone saw me, saw us? But it was late and everyone had had so much to drink . . . surely they'd all be asleep.

The room was dark but for a strip of light under the door. I reached for my robe, hanging on the back of the door, then opened it and stepped out on to the landing. I stood perfectly still for a moment, struck by a sense of déjà vu. The last time I'd done this was the night before Tom left for war, when my parents had been downstairs and I'd used the back stairway. I could feel my heart pounding, hear Charlie's snoring beyond the closed door, or was it snoring from another room? And somewhere, giggling, and muffled voices. If I met anyone, I'd say I couldn't sleep; that I was going to find a book in the library. I moved quickly down the carpeted staircase, across the marble hallway—tiptoeing on bare feet—and then on, along the polished wood floor to the ballroom. There was a lamp on, and a casement door stood open. I hurried through the door, across the flagstones and down the steps. It was a glorious clear, starry night, and I was seventeen again.

In the distance I could see the lanterns, still flickering around the outside of the tent, a glow inside. He's there, I thought, he's there. I ran along the path through the parterre and across the velvet pile of the lawn, and then, breathless, I pulled back the canvas. A lantern on the table still burned and the smoke of a cigarette lingered. He'd been and gone. Whilst I'd dithered, he'd been waiting for me and now he'd gone. My heart lurched. I stepped back out of the tent unsure of what to do, and then I looked up into the night sky, closed my eyes and made a wish: *make him come back to me, make him come back . . .*

I felt a hand upon my shoulder—and there he was.

'I thought you'd gone,' I said, turning to him, almost in tears. 'I thought you'd gone,' I said again, wrapping my arms around him.

'Never,' he said, lifting my face up to his. 'Never,' he repeated, leading me back inside the tent.

CHAPTER THIRTY-ONE

It was light by the time I walked back through the garden towards the house. The air was warm and a cloudless sky stretched out high above me: a transparent wash of pink, pale blue and yellow. I stood on the terrace for a moment, looking back at the tent, and the bucolic vision beyond. Patches of mist hung over the sleepy hollows of the fields and the lake in the distance, and not a leaf stirred. I'm not sure I'd ever looked out upon that cherished landscape at such an early hour before. And it struck me how timeless and ethereal it was in its stillness.

Tom had made me return to the house first, and I tiptoed up the staircase and back to my room, closing the door behind me as quietly as I could. Charlie lay on his back, his mouth open, snoring. And as I climbed into my bed, I heard another door close, and wondered if it was Tom returning to his room. I longed to go back to him, to lie with him and wake up in his arms. Our night together had been so short, and ahead of us—another day of pretence.

I didn't wake until almost midday, stirred by voices—including Charlie's—outside on the terrace beneath the open window. The pink and white floral curtains remained drawn across each of the four tall windows but a very particular light, a bright Sussex morning light, so familiar to my senses, flooded through them and into the room, and I stretched out like a cat, savouring its warmth and energy. And still echoing in my head—my name: a deep, desperate whispering in my ear; against my skin; on my neck, my shoulder. And I stretched out once more, smiling.

I decided to take my time getting ready. I ran a bath and lay in it until the water was almost cold, reliving the events of hours earlier: his words, his touch, his love. When I finally dressed and went downstairs—the book of Emily Brontë's poems clutched in my hand—it was a somewhat depleted group sitting outside under the awning on the terrace. I'd missed breakfast but Nancy kindly organised some coffee for me. Tom was nowhere to be seen, and I chose not to ask where he was. Davina said, 'We've all been looking at the Arab tent, Clarissa. Have you seen it? You must go and take a peek, darling . . . it's quite magical. Apparently Tom's only just had it put up—in time for this weekend, so we're quite honoured. I think I might even sleep in it tonight!'

'Oh, yes I shall, I'll go and take a look later,' I said.

'Sleep well, dear?' Charlie asked, as he sat down next to me.

'Yes, perfect, thank you. And you?'

'Now what do you think? I don't even remember coming to bed! Though I must say, I'm quite astonished that my head doesn't hurt more this morning. Champagne, wine *and* brandy—not a very clever mix . . . but you, you've slept almost twelve hours,' and he looked at me, almost tenderly, and patted my hand.

'Yes, I must have been more tired than I realised.'

'It's called beauty sleep, Charlie boy. Not that Clarissa needs it—or perhaps that's her secret . . .'

Weiner said, from behind sunglasses.

He was sitting next to Davina, in polka dots, and I could tell immediately they had a thing going. Their deckchairs were pushed up together and they spoke in whispers, punctuated by giggles. I looked around for Davina's husband, Marcus, but he was nowhere to be seen. Perhaps he was with Tom, I thought.

It was a perfect day, with a bright blue cloudless sky. I moved away from the table, where Charlie sat reading the newspaper, walked along the terrace and down the steps to a swing-chair set out upon the lawn. I sat back in it, gently rocking myself, and closed my eyes, listening to the conversations behind me. I could hear Nancy, who'd appeared back on the terrace, announcing that we were to have a picnic on the island in the middle of the lake. There were three rowing boats and if we organised ourselves into groups of no more than four we should, she said, be able to do it with each of the three boats making two trips. Those playing tennis would be back soon and we'd set off then, she said. That's where he is, I thought: playing tennis.

A little while later, as people began to assemble, ready to set off to the lake, I heard his voice and looked up from my book. In tennis whites, and looking unbearably handsome, I listened as he told people to go on ahead, he'd catch up. He glanced across to me, turned as if to go inside the house, then turned back again and moved quickly across the terrace, and down the steps towards me.

'Let them all go on ahead,' he whispered, standing in front of me, shining with sweat, still breathless from his game.

'But I can't . . . what can I say?'

'I don't know,' he replied, smiling at me. 'Think of something.'

Then he ran back across the lawn, leapt up the steps and disappeared into the house.

'Clarissa!' Charlie shouted. 'Do come along, darling, we're off to the lake.'

I walked up to the terrace. 'I need to put my book away—and fetch my hat . . . you go on,' I said to Charlie.

'I'll get it for you, dear,' he replied, taking the book from my hand. Minutes later, he was back with my hat. But as we moved along the terrace, a straggling parasol-laden group, I spotted Mrs Cuthbert, coming through the archway of the walled garden.

'Oh, but there's Mrs C. I must go and say hello to her,' I said to Charlie. 'I'll catch up with you.' And before he could say anything, I ran down the bank, my hat flying. 'Mrs Cuthbert! Mrs Cuthbert! It's me . . . Clarissa,' I shouted, and I realised I sounded like a child again. She turned to me with a broad smile, put down her trug and stretched out her hands.

'I'm so pleased to see you,' I said, taking her hands in mine.

'Miss Clarissa,' she said, looking me up and down, smiling and nodding her head. 'Tom only told me yesterday that you'd be here. How lovely . . . how lovely to see you again, dear. And my, he's right, you're more beautiful than ever.'

'Oh, I don't know about that—a little older, like all of us,' I said.

I wanted to put my arms around her, hug her, but it would have been inappropriate, so I purposefully kept hold of her hands as we spoke.

'It's wonderful that you're still here . . . that Deyning's now Tom's. You must be so proud of him,' I said.

'Oh yes. Yes, very proud of him, but I was always proud of him, you know that,' she said. 'And he's so happy that you came, that you came back.'

'Yes, I'm pleased that I did. He's done a wonderful job with the place. And it's just perfect, perfect you can continue living here.'

'Thirteen years now . . . and over five when the old Earl lived here too.'

'Gosh, yes, I'd forgotten about that. But that was before Tom was born, wasn't it?'

'Oh yes, before Tom came along. And it feels like a few lifetimes ago to me now, miss.'

'I think I know that feeling,' I said.

'And so, you're all off for a picnic, are you?'

'We are indeed, and I'd better go and catch up. But I hope I might see you later,' I added.

'Well then, why don't you come and have tea with me? You know I'm in Broughton's cottage now, don't you?'

'Yes, Tom mentioned that you didn't want to move into the main house.'

'No. I like the old cottage, it suits me fine. And he had it all redone for me, you know? New roof, electricity, mains water, a new range . . . even a bathroom.' She laughed, and went on, 'And all redecorated as well. He wanted to buy me new furnishings too, but I told him there's no need. I like my old things . . . I'm attached to them. Oh yes, it suits me fine. But come and see it, come and have a cup of tea and tell me all your news, and about your mother too. I'd like to hear how she is.'

'I'll do that,' I said, releasing her hands. 'I'll

come when we get back from the lake.' And then I turned, picked up my hat, and walked on up the pathway towards the stable yard.

I stood at the gate for a moment, watching them all in the distance: a meandering trail of pale linen and straw hats, following the coterie of servants carrying picnic paraphernalia: umbrellas, rugs and hampers. I contemplated going back inside the house, up to his room, but I wasn't sure where Mrs Cuthbert had gone, or who else was still about at the house. So I opened the gate and walked on into the field, following the path the others had cut through the long grass. It felt indescribably good to be back there, looking out across that landscape, and I stopped, put my arms up into the air, and then wrapped them around myself with joy.

'You're a vision,' he said, appearing by my side, 'my perfect vision.'

'Are you happy?'

'Happily tormented,' he replied, looking into the distance, frowning.

We began to walk, and I reached out, brushed his hand with my fingers. I could already see the three boats, slowly moving across the water towards the island.

'Oh God, Clarissa . . . what are we going to do?'

'Enjoy today . . . look forward to tomorrow.'

'Hmm. It's not enough, I'm afraid. I need more than that.'

'But I don't think there is more.'

'Yes, there is: there's you.'

'I'm having tea with your mother later,' I said, trying to lighten the conversation.

He turned to me. 'Yes, so she said.'

'Ah! Here they are!' I heard Charlie say to

Nancy, as we approached them.

'Charlie, my man . . . you take Davina and Nancy in this one,' Tom said, nodding over at a boat sitting in the sunshine at the end of the jetty. 'I'll wait here with Clarissa and Walter for the next one to come back.' And he spoke with such authority that no one, least of all Charlie, would have dared suggest an alternative plan. Nancy shot him a glance, and either he didn't notice or he chose to ignore it. A few minutes later, with Charlie at the oars, they were off. Davina's wave and broad smile seemed teasing, but I really didn't care any more. We stood side by side watching them move away across the water, then he grabbed my hand and led me up the steps, into the boathouse.

'But they'll see us, and Walter's there . . . he's right there.'

'Clarissa, you more than anyone should know a loyal servant sees and hears nothing,' he said, pressing me against the timber wall. 'Let's not go . . . let's go back to the house.'

'No, we can't . . .' I said, closing my eyes, moving my head as he kissed my neck. 'We have to go . . .'

But I didn't want to go to the island either, not with all of them. It was *our* place; meant only for us. And so we remained there, in the boathouse, for some time, kissing, holding on to each other, staring back into each other's eyes, unable not to smile. And each long second postponed the agony of letting go, again.

When we finally emerged, Walter was sitting in a boat at the end of the jetty, waiting; the boy who'd helped carry things over to the island and had rowed the boat back—long since disappeared. And so, with his back to Walter and facing me, Tom rowed us across the water. Neither of us uttered a word, and I'm not sure what Walter thought. He'd seen us at the tent the previous evening, been standing guard presumably on Tom's instruction; and now he'd sat and waited for us to come out of the boathouse. But he was elderly, and I imagine he'd seen it all before a thousand times.

Huddled together on that small island there was no escape, no opportunity to disappear and nowhere to disappear *to*, other than by boat. So, we sat about in deckchairs and on rugs, and ate and drank, and whiled away a couple of hours. A few, including Davina and Nancy, strolled off beyond the trees. Charlie fell asleep in his deckchair; and lying close to me, on a rug under the shade of a tree, Tom nodded off too. It was peaceful, heavenly really, if there'd only been Tom and me there. But I began to feel slightly claustrophobic, uncomfortable and hot; and I wanted to go back to the house and freshen up before I had tea with Mrs Cuthbert. So I quietly asked Walter to row me back across the lake.

I hadn't intended on looking in on his room, I'd already seen it anyway, when he'd shown Charlie and me around the place the previous day. But the door was ajar and it was just too tempting. I walked in, and immediately noticed that his bed was unmade. Shabby, I thought; he needs to have a word with the servants. Then I remembered it was Sunday: most of the servants would have had the day off. I walked over to one of the windows, facing due south, looking out over the terrace and gardens. This had once been Mama's room, and I smiled at that thought: the thought of Tom Cuthbert inhabiting my mother's former bedroom.

Out of the window, to the left, was the walled garden, and I wondered if he'd seen me talking to his mother.

I moved away from the window, walked about the room, taking it all in once again and noticing the changes he'd made, and then I wandered through to his dressing room, once Mama's. I opened the doors of his wardrobes, ran my fingers over the rows of shirts and suits on hangers, and then moved on, to his bathroom. His tennis shorts and shirt lay on the floor, his shaving brush and razor by the basin, a damp towel next to them. And I picked it up and held it to my face for a moment. Then I walked back into the bedroom and sat down upon the bed.

A pile of books lay on a bedside table next to a wireless: *The Seven Pillars of Wisdom*, by T.E. Lawrence; *Love Among the Artists*, by George Bernard Shaw; *Heart of Darkness*, by Joseph Conrad. The latter, at the top of the pile, had what I took to be a bookmark poking out from it, and for some reason I picked it up and opened it. A small, rather badly executed but nonetheless lovely watercolour lay on the page in front of me, and I heard myself gasp. *My painting . . . my painting; all these years he's kept it with him . . .*

The paper, once stiff, was now soft and worn like fabric. And it had quite obviously spent a good few years folded and flattened. Now heavily creased, frayed at the edges and torn in the middle, it could have been an antique; an ancient scrap of something perhaps once much larger. But as I sat holding it, looking at it, I remembered each stroke of my brush; and each thought that had accompanied each stroke: Tom.

I placed the paper carefully back inside the book, and the book back on top of the pile. And then I lay back, turned my head, and buried my face in white linen.

CHAPTER THIRTY-TWO

Mrs Cuthbert opened the door of her cottage looking quite different and altogether prettier than I'd ever seen her, without any apron, and in a navy-blue jersey dress and triple-strand pearl necklace. 'Miss Clarissa,' she said, smiling at me, 'this is such a treat for me.' I handed her the flowers I'd picked from the garden and entered the cottage, the place that had once been Broughton's. It was exactly as I'd imagined, and not dissimilar from her previous cottage, but for the freshness of new fitted carpets and wall coverings. She showed me into her parlour, a cosy, immaculately tidy room, with chairs covered in a familiar floral chintz, and a large dark wood display cabinet filled with glass and china.

She'd already laid out the tea tray, and as she busied herself in the kitchen, boiling the kettle and filling the pot, I glanced about the room. There were two framed photographs sitting side by side upon the mantelshelf, next to a clock, a bible and a palm cross; both of Tom. One of him aged perhaps eleven or twelve, and the other, taken around the time when I'd first met him, in his uniform. I picked up the photograph of him in uniform and moved over to the window.

'Ah, that's how you'll remember him, I expect,' Mrs Cuthbert said, entering the room and putting down the teapot.

'Yes, exactly like this. He was so handsome . . . still is.'

She came over to where I stood, looked at the photograph with me for a moment, then took it from me and placed it back upon the mantelshelf.

I sat down as she poured out our tea, and then offered me some of her homemade Madeira cake, saying, 'Now, I hope you're not watching your figure, you certainly don't need to and you always liked that particular one, as I recall. I baked it *specially* for you.'

We chatted about the old days and she brought me up to speed on the circumstances of those who'd once been a part of Deyning. She kept in touch with almost all of the old staff: told me where they were living, who'd married whom, and who'd had babies. Mr Broughton still hadn't married, but had returned to his *roots*, she said, and I smiled. He was living somewhere in Devon, she thought, but not gardening.

'Not gardening?' I repeated.

'No, teaching, I think. But you know he was from rather a well-to-do family, don't you?'

I shook my head; I'd had no idea.

'Oh yes,' she said emphatically, 'he was a very educated man . . . but a bit of a *black sheep*,' she added. And I was tempted to tell her that, according to Edna, he'd been more of a *dark horse*. She went on, told me Edna was still in service, working as cook for the new owners of Monkswood, people who owned a London department store, she thought, but she couldn't recall which one. But that place had all changed, she said, because the estate had been divided up after old Mr Hamilton died.

And Mabel? Married, mother to *three boys*, and living in South London.

'And you, no little ones yet?' she asked, her head tilted to one side and smiling.

'No, no little ones, I'm afraid.'

She said nothing, but I sensed she was waiting for me to say something more. *Yes, I had a child, your grandchild. But I gave her away one Christmas, many years ago.*

'One sometimes thinks life could be better, that the grass is perhaps greener somewhere, but I'm not altogether sure that it is, Mrs Cuthbert. And really, I consider myself to be lucky, very lucky, with or without children,' I added, looking away and taking a sip of tea.

She asked after Mama, spoke sweetly of my father; said he was 'a good man . . . one of the best'.

'But you've known such grief,' she said. 'To lose two of your brothers . . . and so young,' she shook her head, 'so young.'

'We all did,' I said. 'They were all too young to die.' I glanced at the bible on her mantelshelf. 'But God spared Tom.'

'Yes, he did. He heard my prayers, and there's never a day goes by that I don't feel gratitude and thank Him for that.'

Yes, I thought, He kept His side of the bargain; He kept Tom safe.

'And he's done so terribly well, Mrs Cuthbert.'

'He was always going to. He's very bright, you know . . . like his father.'

'Oh?' I said, looking back at her, expectantly.

'Yes, like his father . . .' she repeated, glancing away. Then she turned to face me and added, 'And now—at last—he's to be *married*!'

'Yes indeed—' I said, trying to smile. 'It's lovely news. You must be pleased, excited.'

'Oh yes, I am. It's not right for him to be on his own . . . not now, not after all these years. He needs to . . .' she looked away and shook her head. 'He needs to move on with his life . . . have a wife, a family . . . a proper home.'

'Of course.'

She began fiddling with the brocade trim on the arm of her chair. 'I want to see him settled. I won't be here for ever . . . and I'd like to see him happy. We can't always have what we want in life . . . no matter how much money we have. And money isn't everything. It doesn't buy happiness, as he's discovered.' She looked across at me. 'And I'm sure you'd like to see him settled and happy too . . .'

I heard a latch drop and he appeared, standing in the doorway, smiling.

'Well, this is rather nice,' he said.

He moved towards his mother, bent down and kissed her cheek. He towered over her, over us both, his head grazing the ceiling. And it was queer to think he'd once inhabited such a small space, for Mrs Cuthbert's previous cottage had certainly been no bigger, and very possibly smaller. He picked up a slice of cake, pushed it into his mouth whole. 'Mm, that's good,' he said, and sat down upon the arm of my chair. Then, in front of his mother—as she looked on, smiling at us—he lifted his hand and stroked my hair. I looked down at the floor, astonished, embarrassed; unsure what to do.

'I'll go and make a fresh pot,' Mrs Cuthbert said, rising to her feet.

'Why on earth did you do that?' I whispered, as the door closed.

He smiled at me. 'Do what?'

'Touch me like that . . . in front of your mother?'

'Why not? She knows. She knows everything . . . well, almost everything,' he replied, standing up and pulling out his packet of cigarettes.

'No, please, please don't say that. She can't—she mustn't . . .'

'Oh, for God's sake, she's not going to say anything, tell anyone. She's known for years.'

'Known *what* for years?'

He lit his cigarette and sat down on the floor by my feet. He felt so comfortable there, in that cottage, I could tell. He reached up, took hold of my hand.

'You mustn't fret. She's my *mother*, not some stranger. She loves me . . . wants for me whatever I want, whatever makes me happy.'

I whispered, 'She wants you *settled* and married, Tom.'

He squeezed my hand, turned to look up at me.

'I can't . . . I can't . . .' I said.

'Can't what, Clarissa? Can't allow me to touch you in front of her? Can't bear me to love you in front of anyone? Is that it?'

'No . . . no,' I said, but I knew how it sounded; how he was making it sound. 'You don't understand, we've just been talking about—'

'If she was Lady Cuthbert would that make it any easier for you?'

'No! That's not fair, Tom . . . that's not the point at all, and you know it.'

'Then prove it to me. Prove to me that you can at least allow me this sanctuary . . . that I can be myself with you here.'

When the door opened and his mother walked

back into the room, we may as well have been making love; we *were* making love. I pulled my hand away swiftly. It was an automatic response, spontaneous, and without thought. I'd have done the same regardless of where I was, whoever I was with, but I knew and felt Tom's reaction. His intake of breath, his sudden pulling away from me was all part of a chain reaction and no matter what I did or what I said, I couldn't undo that.

We sat there, in Tom's mother's parlour, for a full five minutes without speaking, like a couple who'd had a row—which we were, and had had—as she poured fresh tea, cut Tom another slice of cake and then returned to the kitchen for another plate. I wanted to say something; I wanted to prove to Tom that it wasn't the way he thought. I wanted to say, 'Mrs Cuthbert, I love your son as much as I love life itself.' But I didn't. I sat there, frozen, sipping tea, with Tom on the floor, sprawled out like a child at my feet. I wanted to reach out and touch him, but I couldn't do it. Everything I was, everything my upbringing had taught me came together in those few minutes: I was Clarissa Granville once more; taking tea with our former housekeeper. I couldn't let it go, you see. I couldn't reinvent myself in minutes.

And so, eventually, I put down my cup and saucer and rose to my feet. 'I must go now. But it's been lovely, thank you so much, Mrs Cuthbert.'

I didn't look at Tom and he didn't move, didn't even stand up when I left the room. Mrs Cuthbert saw me to her door.

'Thank you, Clarissa,' she said, and I realised immediately that she'd called me Clarissa and not *Miss Clarissa*. I leant forward and kissed her cheek.

'I love him,' I whispered, tears stinging my eyes. 'I need you to know, need you to understand.'

She frowned, took hold of my hand. 'Yes, I understand. I understand more than you know, dear. But you have to let him go. You have to let him move on. Otherwise . . . otherwise he's going to waste his life waiting for something he can never have. And he deserves some happiness.'

I nodded. 'Yes, yes he does.'

Later that evening, at dinner, he was in a peculiar mood, and barely looked at me. Instead, he focused his attention on the petite American blonde, sitting where Davina had been sitting the previous evening. He flirted with her in the most obvious way, and I suspected he simply wanted to annoy me, make me jealous.

'You know, I think I prefer American women,' he said, leaning towards her. 'I find you all . . . so much less uppity than English *ladies*.'

I said nothing.

'I don't suppose all English ladies are uppity, Tom,' the blonde replied, glancing at me. 'Clarissa's certainly not.'

'Ah, Clarissa . . . but you see, I know *Miss Clarissa* slightly better than you, and . . .' He leant towards her and whispered something in her ear. She looked at me, raised her eyebrows and then giggled.

'Don't you know it's rude to whisper, Tom,' I said without looking at him.

'There you go! They're all obsessed with bloody manners!'

'Tom . . .'

He turned to me. 'Yes, my love?'

I shook my head.

'No? Is that a no, or a no thank you?'

The blonde laughed again. He refilled her glass, and his own, and then turned to me, straight-backed in his chair, the bottle poised over my glass. 'More wine, ma'am?'

I didn't speak.

'Will that be all, ma'am?' He leant forward, raised an eyebrow. 'Or will ye be requirin' me services later?'

I looked across the table, tried to smile.

There were others who'd joined us for dinner that night, neighbours I presumed, and, thankfully, with something in the region of perhaps thirty sitting down to dinner, the room was unbelievably noisy. My mother's dinner parties had been sedate affairs by comparison, I thought, never this riotous. I could hear Hud's booming voice somewhere further down the table, and, from time to time, Davina's shrieks and laughter, but I couldn't make out any conversation, other than Tom's.

'Miss Clarissa . . .' he began, lighting a cigarette, and pulling at his tie, 'Miss Clarissa likes the *old ways*, don't you, darling?'

'Please, Tom . . .'

He lifted his cigarette to his lips, staring down the table. 'Please, Tom . . . please, Tom,' he repeated quietly, imitating my voice, my accent. 'Please, Tom . . . I'll wait for you, my darling. I'll wait, I promise,' he went on, mimicking a young breathless girl: me.

I leant towards him and whispered, 'You're being unfair . . . and you're being uncouth.'

He didn't look at me, but sighed, loudly. 'Ah! What it is to be rich and uncouth. Of course, that's why the English don't particularly like Americans, you know?' he continued, turning to the blonde again. She looked nervous, and I wanted to tell him then to stop, but I knew we'd say things, I knew there'd be a scene. 'Because you're all so damned rich and uncouth!' He leant forward, smiling at her now, and her eyes darted from him to me and back to him.

'Oh dear, I do hope not,' she said. And as she reached for her wine, she knocked over Tom's glass.

I placed my linen napkin over the wet tablecloth. 'Don't worry,' I said.

'No, don't worry,' he repeated, refilling his glass. 'It's only ten pounds a bottle.'

'Tom! Please . . .'

He turned to me. 'Please what?' And then he moved closer. 'Can we leave now? I don't want to be here . . . I want to be with you.'

I glanced across the table, tried to laugh, and then looked back at him. 'I think you've had enough to drink,' I said in a whisper.

He sat back in his chair, surveying the table, his guests; his eyes half closed. And I wondered how much he'd had to drink. It was so unlike him, I thought, to be this angry, this rude.

'I think our host is a tad weary,' a voice on my left suddenly said, and I turned to a man I'd barely spoken to all evening, but one who Tom had introduced me to earlier. His name was Oliver Goddard and he was some sort of business adviser to Tom, though I couldn't for the life of me work out what exactly he advised him on.

'Yes . . . perhaps,' I replied, knowing that *our host* had had little to no sleep the previous night.

At that moment Tom rose to his feet and

excused himself from the table. The blonde looked relieved, and I turned my attention to Mr Goddard.

'Please, do call me Oliver. Mr Goddard sometimes sounds to me like the name of an undertaker.'

Oliver was unmarried, lived in London, but came down to Deyning quite often. He'd heard from Tom that I'd grown up there and wanted to know more. He seemed particularly impressed by the library, and so I told him of my father's collection of books, how vast it had been, and how many volumes we'd sold at auction for pennies. And we spoke about books—poetry in particular. I failed to notice Tom's return to the table, possibly because Oliver was in the midst of reciting 'The Green Eye of the Little Yellow God' to me.

'I love that poem,' I said, when he'd finished, 'but I'm afraid I don't have the brain to memorise verse like that.'

'And I have the brain to memorise, but not analyse,' he replied.

'I think women analyse more than men. We like to cogitate and ponder on all things—particularly the human condition . . . and the soul.'

Oliver laughed, lifted a match to my cigarette. And perhaps it was that, or perhaps he thought we were flirting, but Tom suddenly interrupted our quiet, civilised conversation and said, in a voice loud enough to silence some of the table, at least, 'For God's sake, Goddard, don't try and impress her ladyship with your fucking poetry and intellectual mutterings. If she's out of my league, dear boy, she's sure as hell out of yours!'

I was mortified. And he must have seen something in my face, because all at once he adopted the demeanour of a chastened child, without any word uttered from me—or anyone else. I glanced at Charlie, who gave me a nod, as if to say, it's all right, he's drunk. He was drunk; he didn't know what he was saying. And of course I was the only one there privy to his *torment*.

Davina appeared at my side. She suggested we go through to the drawing room for coffee and, as I rose to my feet, Oliver stood up. I smiled at him, glanced at Tom—who stared down the table with a look of sulky defiance. I wasn't angry for me, I was angry at the way he'd spoken to Oliver, who seemed so pleasant, so harmless.

'I need some fresh air, Davina . . . do you mind?'

'Shall I come with you?'

'You are kind, but can you give me five minutes on my own?'

'Yes . . . yes, of course,' she said. 'But, Clarissa, you know you can tell me—if there's something you need to share, if you need a confidante.'

'Thank you, Davina. But I don't need a confidante, just a breath of fresh air. I'll be back in a moment,' I said, and walked off towards the front door.

Outside, a yellow light shone out across the driveway, upon the trees and parkland, creating eerie shadows where there should have been none. Everything has changed, I thought: Deyning—all shiny and bright, with its dazzling electric lights in every room—and me and Tom. We couldn't turn back time; we couldn't go back to how we'd once been. And neither could Deyning.

As I walked down the driveway, I thought of him. I knew he'd feel wretched and my heart ached for him. And though I'd seen it all before—the mood swings, the rage—I wondered how often his anger boiled over, how often he lost control. Everything in his life appeared immaculate and ordered, even the woman he'd chosen to marry. But I'd seen the bottle of pills in his bathroom, prescribed 'as and when necessary'.

He deserves some happiness . . .

The glow emanating from the house faded, ahead of me blackness; so I stopped and stood for a while, next to the fence where Tom had first told me he was going to leave England. I thought back to that night, remembering my dance with Julian Carter: how I'd grabbed his head in my hands and kissed him. *Oh, stupid, stupid girl . . .* The following year, shortly after Christmas, in his room at a home for disabled servicemen and war veterans, Julian had placed a gun against his temple and put a bullet in his brain. Now I wondered if with that kiss I'd inadvertently reminded him of something; something he'd never again know.

I walked on a little further, distancing myself from that thought with small steps into the darkness, and then I stopped again, and stared up at the heavens, trying to see the stars. But even the night sky appeared peculiarly illuminated. It was not quite a full moon, and high above me silver-edged clouds moved quickly across her misshapen face, for I'd never seen the man in the moon, only ever *She*: an infinitely patient, nurturing and maternal force. And with such power too: the power to control tides and seasons, fertility and farming, and, perhaps, even sanity. 'Oh!' She seemed to be saying to me now, open mouthed, aghast.

Slowly, stars began to appear, and if I kept my

eyes fixed, concentrated, more and more became visible, until the sky was literally filled with them. And then I heard a boyish voice say, 'They're all there, you know, if you look hard enough.'

'But what shall I do, *Georgie?* What do I do?'

Let him go . . . let him move on . . .

I heard an owl call out from the top of a tree beside me, and I turned and looked back at Deyning, shining into the darkness like a rampant beacon. Yes, everything has changed, I thought; and I began to walk back towards the house.

Inside, as I crossed the hallway, I could hear the men in the dining room, and Tom's voice: light, back in control, charming. But I didn't want to go and join the women for coffee. I was embarrassed by Tom's outburst, unsure who had heard, and I had no wish to hear about weddings and babies, or flowers and gowns. So I went up to my room, undressed, and lay down upon the bed.

It's impossible, Impossible. Soon he'll be married; have a family of his own . . . he deserves some happiness.

I could hear someone clapping; voices and laughter downstairs. My mother had always said that the marble floors—'those blasted floors'—made the house too noisy, and she was right, everything echoed. There would be no rendezvous that night: we'd had our night together. And I reached over and turned off the lamp.

I don't think we exchanged any words the following morning, and his mood was noticeably sombre.

'Thank you so much, Tom,' I said, shaking his hand as we stood outside the house on the driveway. 'It's been splendid . . . really quite splendid.'

He stood with Nancy and watched us go, but I didn't wave, and as our car pulled away I didn't look back.

As we headed down the driveway, Charlie said, 'Queer sort of outburst last night. What do you suppose brought that on?'

'I've no idea,' I replied, turning away, staring out of the car window.

'Hmm. Well, just so you know, he apologised to me after breakfast this morning. Said he hoped he hadn't offended you.' And as we pulled out of the driveway, on to the road, he must have seen my face, because he added, 'Oh dear, he did upset you.'

He reached over and patted my hand. 'He'd had a lot to drink, dear . . . and you know, he's a decent enough chap. He'd be mortified if he thought he'd upset you, or any of his guests.'

I pulled a handkerchief out from my bag. 'He didn't upset me, Charlie, really,' I said. 'I'm simply sad to be leaving Deyning, again . . . that's all.'

* * *

I read of his marriage in *The Times* two months later. Charlie had been surprised, even a little piqued that we hadn't been invited. 'It wasn't a big affair,' I said. 'Davina told me that they were only having about a hundred.'

'Still, seems jolly rude to have had a wedding there, at Deyning, and not to have invited *you*.'

'I wouldn't have gone anyway.'

'Really? Why ever not? You love weddings.'

'Sometimes,' I replied.

* * *

There's a one-eyed yellow idol to the north of
Kathmandu,
There's a little marble cross below the town;
There a broken-hearted woman tends the grave
of Mad Carew,
And the Yellow God forever gazes down.

Part Four

CHAPTER THIRTY-THREE

. . . I never said I 'would not', I simply said I wasn't sure, but it really was the most extraordinary and uplifting experience, not at all as I'd imagined, & a tremendous (and unexpected) comfort to me—just to know that they are at peace on the other side, & together. Did I tell you that she was v emphatic that H is alive & well? Across the water, she said, but she couldn't say which water. And I'm still mystified about 'the child' . . .

* * *

When Charlie told me about the invitation to a drinks reception at the new Cuthbert-Deyning offices in Park Lane, I told him immediately that I didn't wish to go. The thought of seeing him again, and with Nancy, was too much.

Tom had recently appointed Charlie's firm as his corporate lawyers, and though Charlie saw him occasionally, in business meetings or at his club, I had not seen him since our weekend at Deyning. Almost another year had passed. During that time there had been a number of events, dinners and such like, occasions where I could have seen him, but I'd managed to wriggle out of them and sent Charlie on his own.

'I don't know for the life of me why you're so reluctant,' Charlie said. 'He's really a jolly nice chap. Very down-to-earth and quite unlike a lot of these new-moneyed sorts.'

'Yes, yes, I know he's very nice. It's not so much him . . . it's his wife,' I said, clutching at straws, desperate to find a reason why I might not wish to go.

'Ah yes, the American,' he said. 'Well, she may not be there. She wasn't with him at the Blanchs' last time, and she certainly wasn't with him at the Hyde Park Hotel last week.'

'But it's a business thing, Charlie,' I said. 'Is it really so important that I go along with you?'

'He's invited us both. Look at the invitation,' he replied, pointing to our mantelshelf.

'Oh, he'd have had his secretary write that for him,' I said, knowing full well it was Tom's handwriting.

'No, darling, that's his hand. I know it.'

On the day, Charlie said he'd meet me there; come straight from his office in the city. And all day I felt sick. I toyed with the idea of telephoning Charlie to tell him I was ill, and I tortured myself with the possibilities, how the evening *could* unfold. Would Nancy be there? I wondered. Would they be holding hands as they circumnavigated the room, nodding and smiling at all of Tom's minions and business associates? Would I be standing in line waiting to shake his hand too?

And yet, I wanted to see him; longed to see him again.

I ran a bath, and took a drink with me, even though it wasn't yet six. And as I lay in the bath, looking down at my body, I realised that physically, at least, I hadn't changed much over the preceding decade. My body had produced only one child, when my shape was still young enough to recover quickly. Like Mama, and blessed with her looks,

I was naturally slim, and her insistence on good posture and lessons in deportment had paid off. I held myself tall, carried an invisible book upon my head. But I'd recently celebrated my thirtieth birthday and become acutely aware of my age, and of the passing of time. Perhaps that had something to do with Tom. Being displaced, estranged from one's heart served only to make the years more desolate. And I had nothing, nothing at all to show for my life: no children I could talk about; no work or vocation I could speak of.

Clarissa: beautiful, unfulfilled, useless, and childless.

It was a glorious spring evening, and I walked for quite a way before hailing a taxicab. I was no longer nervous. In fact, I felt rather calm and mellow as the cab headed towards Park Lane. I thought of the gardens at Deyning; the rhododendrons would be coming into bloom, the old wisteria too. And then I thought of him. Every unguarded thought led me back to him.

When I arrived at the building, I took the lift to the top floor, as Charlie had instructed me. It was eight o'clock, half an hour later than the time on the invitation. Charlie was bound to be there, I thought. He would be looking out for me, see me emerge from the lift.

The room was full of men in suits and, I noticed, a few very glamorous women. I took a glass of champagne from the waiter who greeted me, and then walked on into the crowd, looking for Charlie.

'Clarissa! Over here!'

It was Davina, in crimson satin with matching lips (and teeth).

'But darling, I'm rather surprised to see you

here,' she said. 'You normally avoid these sorts of things.'

'Yes, well . . . *normally* I let Charlie attend these affairs on his own. He receives so many invitations. And you know what he's like. Can't say no.'

'But I'm sure Tom'll be pleased you're here,' she said, looking at me with a curious smile.

'And where is he?' I asked.

She leant towards me. 'Right behind you,' she whispered.

I turned. He'd seen me, was watching me. I smiled at him as he spoke with a huddle of eager people, and then I turned back to Davina. I tried to make small talk, the way one does at those types of gatherings, but I was distracted and Davina was smiling a little too broadly, too obviously for my liking, and so, after a few minutes, I moved away, saying I must look for Charlie. I walked through the room, smiling and excusing myself through strangers, looking for my husband, and for once hoping he was there. But I was aware of someone following in my pathway. I could hear him behind me: 'Good to see you . . . thank you for coming.' And as I reached the other side of the room, I stepped out on to a balcony, overlooking Park Lane.

'Are you trying to escape from me?'

I looked straight ahead, over Hyde Park. The sun was just beginning to set, slipping down behind the trees, and I didn't turn; I kept my gaze on that pink ball of fire.

'No, not at all, I was looking for Charlie, actually,' I replied, still unable and unready to meet his eyes.

'He telephoned earlier. I'm afraid he's going to

be stuck at the office until late . . . at least ten,' he said. And I thought, *as flies to wanton boys* . . .

'That's a shame, he was looking forward to being here.'

He moved alongside me, placing his hands upon the painted wrought-iron rail, inches from my own. Beautiful hands: hands that had touched me, loved me.

'I suppose you'll just have to make do with me,' he said.

I turned to face him. 'Yes, it would seem that way,' I replied.

'Will you have dinner with me later?'

'And Nancy?'

'She's not here. She's in New York.'

I looked away; felt that knot in my stomach, hard and tight from years of longing, years of wanting. Was it always going to be like this? Was I always going to give in to one man?

'Yes. Yes, I'll have dinner with you,' I said.

'I'm pleased you came. It's been a while . . .'

'It's always been a while.'

'It doesn't have to be, you know that.'

I said nothing.

'I have to mingle now, say a few words . . . wait for me,' he added, and then he stepped back inside the room.

I stood in the doorway, watching him as he moved through the room: smiling, greeting people, shaking hands. I watched him as he stepped away from the huddle and began his speech. And I looked away as I listened to his voice: so cultured, so assured. I clapped with everyone else, moved further into the room and spoke to a few people. Had I known him long? Had I been at the wedding?

Was I a friend of Nancy's? Yes, he was charming—and yes, rather humble with it too. No, I hadn't been at the wedding; I didn't really know Nancy. Yes, it was such a shame she wasn't there.

I could see him on the other side of the room, head bowed, listening intently as someone spoke to him. And he shone. For there was a light that emanated from him, his soul, his substance. I hadn't seen it when I was young, or perhaps I had but had failed to recognise it. But now I saw it, saw it quite clearly, and even at a distance I felt its heat. *Tom*. He looked up, straight at me, as though he'd heard me think his name. Then he turned, said something to the gentlemen he was standing with, and moved over to me. He stood alongside me without uttering a word, and as the fabric of his jacket brushed my arm I felt that current once more: a bolt of electricity travelling through my veins, straight to my heart.

'Right, I'm done. Let's go,' he said, taking my arm, and leading me through the room, towards the lift. As we stepped into it, he sighed, lit a cigarette—the first I'd seen him smoke all evening—then he looked at me and said, 'And now, Clarissa . . . now to business.'

He was being funny, of course, and I laughed. I was as relieved as he to be away from that ordeal. When we stepped out of the building on to the street, a cream-coloured Bentley was waiting—pulled up by the kerb. He opened the door, saw me inside, closed it, and said something to the uniformed driver.

'Where are we going?' I asked, as he climbed inside the car.

'Home, of course,' he replied.

There was a bottle of already corked champagne standing in an ice bucket in the back of the car. He lifted the top of the walnut compartment between our seats, pulled out two glasses and poured the champagne.

When he said *home*, I'd presumed he meant *his* home; that he was taking me back to his place in London, though I wasn't entirely sure where that was, and I knew he owned a number of properties in the city. I was nervous and couldn't help but wonder if he kept a place specifically for taking women back to. I wasn't convinced he'd be a faithful husband to Nancy, in fact, I imagined he'd have more than one glamorous girlfriend. After all, he was rich and handsome—what was to stop him? But had he assumed I'd be the same? Was I simply another conquest? As we headed over the river, and then through the streets of Battersea, I began to feel irritated, and mildly alarmed. I pictured some seedy flat in the outer suburbs, and I turned to him and said, 'Tom . . . *where*, exactly, are you taking me?'

'Don't worry,' he said, turning to me and smiling. 'Everything's been sorted.'

'No really, I need to know. Charlie will be worried.'

'Charlie knows. I have your husband's permission.'

'Knows what, exactly? Have his permission for what?'

'Permission to take you out for dinner.'

I laughed. 'But *where*?'

'Deyning.'

'Deyning! And you arranged this with Charlie?'

'Yes, I did. He's working on a rather big deal for

me tonight, so I said—I said the least I could do was take you out to dinner.'

'But did you tell him *where* you were taking me to dinner?'

He ran a hand through his hair. 'No, I'm not sure that I did.' He turned to me. 'But to be honest, Clarissa, at that point I hadn't decided where I was going to take you.'

I'd been kidnapped, albeit politely, and with my husband's approval. How convenient, I thought, that Charlie should be stuck at the office working on Cuthbert-Deyning business. Tom's company was his biggest client, there'd have been no way he could have said anything other than 'yes' to whatever Tom Cuthbert suggested. I could hear their telephone conversation in my head, hear Tom telling Charlie not to worry about me; he'd see to it that I was looked after. And of course my husband—oblivious to my feelings, insensitive to any chemistry—no doubt thought it an ideal time for me to get to know what a 'jolly nice chap' his rich client, Tom Cuthbert, was.

At that time I hadn't worked out the exact level of Tom's duplicity, but I later realised he'd set the whole thing up so that I'd be on my own. He'd learned from Charlie that we would both be attending his drinks reception, and on the day, late in the afternoon, he'd specifically requested Charlie to handle an *urgent* piece of business. 'Work through the night if you have to,' he'd said to him. And I suppose Charlie saw the enormous fee he'd be able to invoice Cuthbert-Deyning. It was all too strange, too wonderful for words. There I was, going back to Deyning, with Tom, alone.

CHAPTER THIRTY-FOUR

From the moment we arrived at Deyning I didn't think of Charlie. Not once. Deyning was nothing to do with him and everything to do with Tom and me. In my mind it was sacred, like our love for each other; like all the snatched moments of the preceding years. Stacked together they amounted to so little, and yet I had lived more, felt more alive during those moments than any time in between.

I remember breathing in that soft smoky night air, the scents of pine and cedarwood so familiar to my senses. And for a split second, as I stepped through the open doorway, time reversed and I was back to that summer: I saw Mama's roses standing in a crystal vase on the hallway table; Caesar, clip-clapping across the marble floor towards me; George, disappearing down the passageway towards the library. Then I saw myself, hat in hand, coming down the staircase, en route to meet Tom.

He stood behind me, in the doorway, leaning against its frame, smoking, watching me. 'Home,' I said, turning to him, and he smiled.

I walked on, into the lamp-lit drawing room, glanced about, and then went back into the hallway, down the passageway to my father's library, now his study. I walked along the shelves of books and stood by his desk at the window. But for the light from the hallway the room was dark. I could see the lake in the distance, a shimmering mirror, reflecting the vast night sky. Yes, I was home, I was where my heart lived, and I turned and wrapped my arms around him.

There was no dinner, nothing at all prepared and no one about. And I realised that he'd been truthful in the car: he'd decided at the very last minute to take me back to Deyning. In the kitchen, as I looked about, noting all the modern new conveniences, he disappeared down to the cellar, and returned with a bottle of wine, saying, 'I've been saving this for a special occasion.' And so we ate there, at the table, pulling at a carcass of a cold chicken with our bare hands, and giggling like children at the mess in front of us, and on our faces. Then he picked up the bottle and our glasses and said to me, 'Let's go down to the lake.'

'But I can't, look at me.'

I was in heels, still dressed for a formal night out in London. He scratched his head, then pulled a 'eureka' face. 'Come with me.'

He led me upstairs to the small room opposite his own bedroom, which I recalled—much to his amusement—as once having been known as 'the sewing room'. It was Nancy's dressing room.

'No, I don't want to wear her clothes,' I said. 'I can't wear her clothes.'

'Then I'm afraid you'll have to improvise, Miss Clarissa.'

'Don't call me that. I hate it.'

He took me through his bedroom, turned on the light of his dressing room, stepped back and sat down upon the bed as I moved hangers—looking through his wardrobe for something, anything. As I pulled down my dress, I glanced up through the open door and caught his eye. I pulled on a pair of his trousers, made a point of showing him the rather roomy waist.

'There's a belt in the top drawer, the one on the

left,' he said.

I chose a pale pink cashmere sweater, and as I pulled it over my head, I breathed him in, wanted to wrap my face in its softness; languish in the feel of it against my skin.

When I emerged through the doorway, he smiled: 'You could be seventeen.'

'Really, is *this* what I looked like then?' I asked, looking down at myself in mock horror.

We took the back stairs down to the kitchen, grabbing at the cold chicken as we passed by the table, and then we headed through to the garden room. He was still in his dinner suit, minus his tie, and as he bent down to help me into a pair of Wellington boots, he said, 'I always said I'd be a rather good lady's maid to you.' And I giggled.

We walked down through the meadow hand in hand, and as we passed the chestnut tree he glanced over at it. 'You know, I often see you there.'

'You mean like a ghost?'

'Yes, I suppose so . . .'

At the lake, he brought out two deckchairs from the boathouse, and we sat in silence, side by side, looking across the water—opalescent and vast, and stretching all the way up to the stars. Even if I'd wanted to, I couldn't speak; I was in some blissful state beyond words, beyond a here and now. And being there, back there with him, all my years of pain and loneliness evaporated. You see, he was my world, my life: he was my universe.

When he rose from his chair and began to strip off his clothes, I laughed. I watched him run naked along the jetty and dive into the water, and for a few minutes I remained where I was, seated. Then I stood up, pulled off my ridiculous ensemble, all of it, and walked to the end of the jetty.

He called out from the water. 'It's perfect. Not cold at all.'

I remember the coolness of the water as I dived into it, under it. And I remember emerging, looking up at the stars, and shrieking. As we swam, never too close, we laughed at the memory of that day, after the War, when he'd swum over to me on the island. But there was an almost embarrassed self-consciousness to us both, an invisible barrier, and one that seemed hard to cross. As though we'd both become more aware of the passing of time, the distance between then and now; as if those days which had bound us had slipped further, creating a space, a void.

He climbed out of the water, walked along the jetty to the boathouse, then reappeared, wrapped in a towel, holding another out to me.

'Gosh, such luxury,' I said, as I climbed out of the water and grabbed the towel from his hand. 'We never kept towels down here in *our* day.'

I went to the boathouse, dried myself and put on my clothes, or rather *his* clothes. 'Wasn't that glorious?' I said, when I emerged. But he didn't speak, and suddenly I felt apprehensive. Perhaps he'd regretted bringing me back. I moved over to him, placed my hand upon his bare shoulder. 'Don't feel guilty,' I said.

'I don't feel guilty, Clarissa . . . I feel sad.'

He took my hand, pulled me to him, on to his lap, and I laid my head against his cheek, closed my eyes, and once more wished away the life I'd been born into. For even then, it seemed, so many years had passed us by, swallowing up our lives; gulping up our love. I wrapped my arms around his neck, pressed my lips against his skin. I was lost, I was found; I was with him once more.

'I think I owe you an apology,' he began, 'about my behaviour . . . that last night you were here, with Charlie. I was angry, and, I think, quite vile to you.' He moved his head closer. 'Forgive me.'

I ran a finger down the side of his face. 'Forgive you? I forgave you that very night.'

He took hold of my hand. 'And I need to tell you something,' he said, closing his eyes, turning away. 'Nancy . . .' he paused: 'We're having a baby, Clarissa.'

We're having a baby . . .

'A baby . . . But how wonderful. Congratulations.'

I felt my head begin to spin; the carousel begin to move once more.

A baby . . .

He turned to me, frowning. 'I'm sorry.'

'Good gracious, don't be sorry,' I said, rising to my feet. 'It's happy news . . . lovely news.'

He shook his head. 'You know what I wish? Shall I tell you what I wish?'

'No. Don't tell me,' I said quickly.

I moved towards the water, stood with my back to him as I heard him go inside the boathouse to dress. It's good news . . . happy news, I whispered. Be happy for him. I closed my eyes. *He deserves some happiness.*

We walked back through the meadow—past our tree—in silence. And as we passed his mother's cottage, I saw him look up at a light still shining from an upstairs window. Inside the house, he took hold of my hand and led me up the stairs, and I said, 'I'm tired . . . so tired.' In his bedroom, he undressed me, pulled back the covers and helped me into his bed. He got down on to his knees, kissed my forehead and said, 'I never, ever want to let you go.'

'No, don't let me go. Never let me go.'

I'm not sure what woke me, but the room was still quite dark, the house deathly quiet. And for a moment I thought I was at home, in London; thought it was Charlie in my bed, lying next to me with his arms around me. And I was confused. I turned over, and as I did so I remembered where I was: I was with him; I was at Deyning. I reached out, ran my hand over his bare flesh. He sighed, turned on to his back, and I moved with him, wrapping myself into him. I held on to him, listening to his breathing. And I lay there, wide awake, until dawn.

And then I fell asleep.

When I opened my eyes, he was there, watching me; his head propped on one hand. 'You've been talking in your sleep.'

I reached up to his face. 'Oh really, and what was I saying?'

'You were speaking of your *little friend* . . .'

'My little friend?' I had no idea what he meant.

'Emily . . . your imaginary friend.'

'Ah . . . yes, Emily.'

'She's still with you, isn't she?'

'Yes . . . I suppose she must be. What was I saying?'

He ran a finger along my brow. 'I'm not sure . . . couldn't make it out. But you were calling for her.' He smiled, shook his head, then lifted my hair, moved his lips slowly down my neck, on to my shoulder. I closed my eyes. I wanted to cry. I wanted to tell him not to take me back to London, to Charlie, to that house, to let me stay there with him. Forever. I pushed my hands through his hair, pulled him to me.

By the time we had breakfast it was almost ten o'clock. And still I didn't think of Charlie: what I would say, what I would tell him. I wanted to walk through the grounds, see the gardens before I left. So we strolled to the bench by the ha-ha, looking out towards the lake, the South Downs in the distance.

'Do you remember when we first sat together here?' he asked, looking straight ahead. 'It's when I fell in love with you. You were so beautiful, so innocent.'

'*Were*?' I repeated.

'Well, you're certainly no longer innocent . . .' he said, glancing at me with that half-smile. 'You were a child then. You believed that everything and everyone was good. Your world was perfect, and I longed to be part of it. Part of the Granville world . . . Clarissa's world.'

He leant forward and lowered his eyes, smiling at a memory.

'What?' I asked, watching him, smiling too.

He shook his head. 'I was so consumed by you, so intoxicated . . .' He paused for a moment. 'But I've learnt to live without you, had to live without you, and yet . . . it never feels *right* . . . nothing ever feels right. Bit like wearing clothes that don't fit, I'd imagine,' he added, looking sideways at me.

I reached out, took hold of his hand.

'Do you ever wish we could go back?' I asked.

'No,' he replied quickly. 'No, I don't. I was no one then . . . I was the housekeeper's son, always looking from the outside in, never quite part of things. Look at me now: the owner of Deyning Park. I've achieved everything I ever wanted, bar one thing . . .' And I closed my eyes, for I knew what was to come. 'I don't have you.'

'It's impossible . . .'

'Yes, it would seem so,' he said, nodding. Then he laughed, but it was a hollow, hard laugh. 'Here I am, trapped in the place that belongs to you . . . without you.' He looked up into the sky. 'Such a waste,' he added.

Walter drove us back to London, and I felt as though I was going to a funeral, perhaps my own funeral. That hard knot had returned to my stomach, accompanied by a feeling of dread. We sat in the back of the car holding hands, and from time to time he lifted my hand to his lips, and held it there, pressed to them. But he seemed distant now, preoccupied. As we headed into the sprawl of London I turned to him, but he didn't look at me. He kept his eyes straight ahead, as though concentrating on the road, our journey. And so we passed through the streets of Battersea and Chelsea in silence. And when the car finally came to a standstill outside my home, he turned to me and said, 'I need you to understand . . . try to understand—there's a child now.' He closed his eyes. 'I can't leave her, Clarissa. I can't abandon my child.'

I nodded.

He climbed out of the car and moved swiftly to my door, but I'd already stepped out. 'Thank you,' I said, and I reached up to his face, placed my hand upon his cheek. 'I wish only for your happiness, Tom.'

I didn't look back; couldn't bear to watch him go.

But as I closed my front door I heard another slam shut, then the rumble of an engine, slowly fading as it moved away down the street. I put down my bag, walked through to the drawing room and poured myself something—I'm not sure what—from a decanter, and sat down upon the sofa. It was Sonia who later came into the room and asked me if everything was quite all right; if there was a reason why I'd locked and double-bolted the front door.

That evening, Charlie returned home from work earlier than usual, muttering about the traffic and some ghastly man he'd had to sit next to on the tube. I sat in silence with a book in my hand as he poured us each a drink. And I wondered why he'd come home early: was it to interrogate me, accuse me? I had no plan, no idea what I was going to say, but I wasn't going to say anything until he'd laid the ground, as it were. *Innocent until proven guilty*.

'So, did you have fun last night?' he asked, his back to me, as he replaced the glass stopper in the decanter. 'Tom tells me he took a few of you back to Deyning for dinner,' he continued. 'Must have been a blast.'

'Yes, yes, it was. It was fun.'

He sat down opposite me. 'So . . . who went down there?'

'Oh golly, I really don't know . . . some of his and Nancy's friends. Such a shame you couldn't make it. Did you manage to get your work finished?'

He sniffed, looked away. 'Yes, eventually. We finished at three . . . that's why I didn't come home . . . made sense for me to sleep at the office. But what time did you get back?'

I shrugged. 'Oh, probably around that same time.'

He nodded. 'You're not cross then?'

'No, of course not. Not at all.'

'It was unfortunate timing, but he's putting so much business our way now . . . well, you know.'

'Yes, yes, of course. I understand.'

'And he promised me, promised me that he'd make sure you weren't left on your own, and that he'd take you to dinner. You see, I told him, told him how much you hate those sorts of things, how you usually avoid them, and how wretched I felt at having talked you into attending—only to abandon you. Although, I have to say I had no idea he was going to take you back to Deyning . . . and when he told me today, well, I did rather wonder.'

'Wonder?'

'Yes, you know, wonder if you'd got caught up in some jamboree you didn't feel part of, and then been forced to go back there with them all. I said to him, "Oh dear, I do hope my wife isn't going to be cross with me—otherwise I may have to increase your fee, ha!"'

I laughed. 'Really, Charlie, it was perfectly fine, I was fine.'

'Good. He's a decent enough sort, isn't he?'

'Yes, he is. He's charming.'

Later, over dinner, Charlie asked me more about the evening, my trip down to Deyning, and I heard myself lie. We'd eaten in the dining room, I said, had beef—cooked to perfection, and then a wonderful chocolate pudding. Yes, the house had looked the same, and yes, it was his usual driver who'd brought me home. I was vague once more about who'd been there, but as I tried to recall names and describe non-existent people, he'd helped me out, offering me a few to grab on to. Then I said, 'Ask Tom, he knows who they all were.'

'I can't ask him that,' he replied.

'Why ever not?'

'I'm his lawyer not his bloody mother, Clarissa.'

I knew I wouldn't hear from Tom again after that day. He had a proper family now, or the start of one. And anyway, what could we have done from there? We couldn't have had an affair. Secret rendezvous and snatched afternoons in London hotels were not an option for us. We wanted *all* of each other, everything. We both knew it had to be all or nothing; we couldn't share, you see. We couldn't have a part-time stake in each other's lives. To embark upon an affair would have been tantamount to my leaving Charlie, and him abandoning his wife and soon-to-be child. I knew the scandal would ruin him, and kill my mother. And so, my life continued. Ahead of me, years and years of emptiness, stretching as far as the eye can see, like the Sahara Desert.

CHAPTER THIRTY-FIVE

. . . M Zelda almost came up with yr name yesterday. Of course, I feigned confusion, but she would keep on at it, in that way of hers, & insisted that there was something 'more'. She said she saw a curtain over my life, and behind it a man, & V suggested it was my father. 'NO!' said MZ, 'this is not a father . . . this is a love, a lover.' I nearly fell off my chair.

* * *

It's always been something of a mystery to me what exactly motivated her to get in touch with me when she did, but a few weeks—perhaps a month—after I'd seen Tom I received a letter from his mother. My address would have been easy enough for her to find, Charlie and I were listed. She said that she was coming to stay in London with a cousin and would very much like it if I could meet with her, perhaps for tea. Of course, I replied, I'd love to catch up with her over tea. I suggested a time and venue, to which she replied—by way of a postcard—and confirmed our arrangement.

We met in the tearoom at Swan and Edgar, and after ordering afternoon tea for two we settled into predictable, cosy reminiscences of life at Deyning before the War. I wondered if perhaps she was simply lonely, had wanted to see me to go back to a time in her life when she'd been needed. Then she mentioned him, telling me 'in the strictest confidence' that his marriage was 'not what it ought to be'. She said she suspected her son was not a faithful husband; that he was unhappy and that he should never have married 'an American'.

'Well, Mrs Cuthbert, I'm certainly no expert on marriage. And, it has to be said, Tom's a grown man now, a man of the world.'

'I don't know why he married her, I really don't.' She shook her head. 'I wanted him to be settled.' I nodded. 'I wanted him to have a family. I thought that's what he needed, you see—to make him happy. But it hasn't turned out like that. And perhaps I was being selfish, because I knew . . . I knew at the time he didn't love her, not the way he should've done. And there was me thinking of grandchildren and oh, I don't know what . . .'

'All marriages, it seems to me, are rather hard work,' I said.

She shrugged, sighed. 'I wouldn't know, and that's part of the problem. You see, I want him to have someone to share his life with . . . not end up like me. But really, what can I do now?'

'Nothing,' I replied, refilling her teacup. 'You simply can't blame yourself, Mrs Cuthbert. I know, I know as his mother you only wish for his well-being and happiness, but . . . there's a baby to think of now.'

She looked perplexed for a moment. 'Oh, you'd heard?'

'Yes, I'd heard . . . I can't recall through whom,' I said, quickly, and I wondered if that was why she'd wanted to meet me: to tell me about Tom's baby. 'Who knows, perhaps this baby is what he needs, what the marriage needs.'

She shook her head again. 'I'm not so sure. It's not as straightforward as that with him.'

No, I thought, nothing ever is with Tom. 'Oh, really?'

'He's like me. Once he's given his heart, he can never give it to another.'

I remained silent. She looked so small and vulnerable, and for a moment I thought she was about to cry.

'You see, he fell in love so many years ago, and he's never got over that.'

I picked up my cup and saucer. I wasn't sure what to say. What could I say?

'Life's not turned out the way I expected either,' I said, looking down into my teacup. 'Sometimes it's not easy . . . not for any of us.'

'But I think you know . . . I think you know, Miss Clarissa. There's never been another . . .'

I looked up at her and smiled.

'You're *everything* to him. You always have been.' She looked down at her lap, twisting a white handkerchief in her hands.

It was awkward. More awkward than I can begin to explain: for there I was, taking tea with Mrs Cuthbert, hovering on the brink of talking to her intimately about her son. I wasn't sure what, exactly, she knew, what Tom had told her, and I was flummoxed to know what to say to her. And all at once, I felt my mother's presence. I could see her wide-eyed stare; feel her bemusement.

I reached out, placed my hand over hers. 'Mrs Cuthbert, you told me I had to let him go; you said I had to let him move on . . . and I did. And now . . . now . . .' I stopped; I don't really know why, don't know what it was I was going to say from there, but I suddenly thought of Emily, my child, her granddaughter. I stared at her, into her pale grey eyes, and I saw the years of sadness behind them.

'The thing is, Miss Clarissa,' she began again, and at that moment I wished she'd stop calling me *Miss Clarissa*. It sounded so . . . subservient, so wrong.

'Please, please—no *Miss*, just Clarissa,' I said.

She smiled. 'Clarissa, the thing is, I need to explain . . . I want to tell someone . . .' She paused again.

'Yes?

'About Tom's father.'

'Mr Cuthbert?'

'That's just it. You see, there never was a Mr Cuthbert.'

'Oh. Yes, I see,' I replied, realising what my mother had always suspected.

She took a deep breath, looked into my eyes, and then announced, in an unequivocal, clear voice, 'Tom's father was the Earl Deyning.'

I was silent for a moment. Stunned, and a little shocked by the thought (and concurrent image) of Mrs C and the old Earl *at it*. But I remember thinking how utterly perfect. And I almost wanted to rush to the public telephone to inform Mama. It had never made an iota of difference to me whether Tom's father was an earl or a pauper, but I'd have liked to have broadcast that particular piece of news to quite a few people, some dead, others still living.

I lit a cigarette. 'Does Tom know this?' I asked.

'No, he does not. Oh, I've wanted to tell him, and so many times, but it's so hard . . .'

'But why . . . why did you want to tell me this?'

'Because someone should know. I'm old. My days are running out and I want someone to know the truth. He loves you . . . and I think he believes in his heart that one day . . . one day you'll be with him.'

She looked tearful again, and I felt for her. I wanted to tell her that of course I loved her son. I'd always loved him, always would. But I couldn't.

'Don't worry. Your secret is safe with me. I promise you that.'

She wiped her nose. 'Thing is . . . if anything were to happen to me, if I'd never told him, would you?'

'Do you really wish me to?'

'Yes. I want him to know, and I want him to understand why . . . why I never told him, why I couldn't tell him.'

'Then of course I shall. Of course.' I put my hand over hers once again. 'You have my word, Mrs Cuthbert.'

She smiled. 'Please, call me Evelyn. It's my name . . . and no one ever uses it. No one calls me Evelyn any more. Not for years.'

'Evelyn,' I said, gripping her hand.

'You said to me that day—when you came back to Deyning—that you loved him. Do you still love him?' she asked, looking at me beseechingly.

'Perhaps I'm like you and Tom. Once I've given my heart I can never give it to another.'

When we emerged from the department store into the London throng that day she looked out of place, quite lost; and I wanted to put my arms around her. I wanted to take her home with me. This was Tom's mother; this was Emily's grandmother. We were connected in love and in blood. As we said goodbye, I held on to her hand, and when I kissed her cheek I was struck by its softness, and the faint fragrance of lily of the valley. But as I walked away up Regent Street, I felt wretched, and all at once sad beyond words, and I turned and began to walk in the opposite direction, towards Piccadilly. I'm not sure why I needed to go back to her, to find her, or what I wanted to say to her, but at that moment my whole life seemed to depend upon it.

I found her, eventually, in the bus queue for Acton, and I wrapped myself around her as though she were my own long-lost mother. What people in the queue must have thought, I really don't know. She said to me, 'You're very special, Clarissa, so very special.' And I stood there with her, holding on to her hand, until the bus came, and when she climbed on board, I shouted after her, 'Evelyn! Evelyn! I'll come and visit you, I'll come down and visit you soon.'

I moved along the bus looking in at her through the window and watched her take her seat. She raised her hand, waved at me, and I blew her a kiss. Then the bell rang, and as the bus pulled away I felt the most profound love for her: Tom's mother. I stood and watched it disappear down Piccadilly.

I'm pleased I went back to her that day.

*   *   *

Charlie and I didn't travel, mainly because of his disability. Our life was firmly London based, and so, but for the occasional Saturday to Monday at a familiar house in the country, we rarely ventured far. He did not cope well with unknown, uncharted terrain; could no longer ride or dance, or pursue so many of the activities being a house guest in the country seemed to entail. I suspect he'd always liked predictability and order in his life. But his time in the army, coupled with the limitations incurred through his injuries, had made him a zealous adherent of routine, and fearful of any spontaneity or disruption to that routine.

We didn't often visit Charlie's sister, but it was a house he knew and could cope with. And the following spring, perhaps six months or so after I'd met Mrs Cuthbert, we went down to Sussex to stay with Flora and her husband David. They lived about fifteen miles from Deyning at that time, in a sixteenth-century timber-framed cottage: a hotchpotch, rambling place, and, like so many others, still without electricity or running hot water. Their two sons, my nephews, were both away at school, and they lived a somewhat eccentric, Spartan existence, tucked away there, without any luxuries and with only candlelight at night.

I hadn't planned to drive over to Deyning, but on the Sunday, the day after we'd arrived, there was a pause in the day and it seemed the perfect afternoon for a drive. It wasn't long after Easter and the countryside was just beginning to take on the soft, luminous hue of springtime. And of course, being so close to Deyning, I couldn't *not* think of the place; couldn't *not* think of him. The previous evening, over dinner, Flora had mentioned him to me, and I'd immediately felt that momentary sense of loss, a feeling I had each time I heard his name. It was different with my brothers, I'd often thought, because two of them were dead; they had gone and could never return. And Henry? Henry may have disappeared but he was alive somewhere, I knew that, and I also felt sure he would return to us some day. But Tom, Tom had not died, nor had he disappeared. He lived and breathed on the periphery, somewhere on the edge of my life. Flitting in and out of conversation, lurking in the shadows.

Flora told me that she and David had been to a charity fund-raising dinner at Deyning a month or so earlier. 'Golly, he is a dish,' she said, leaning towards me, as David and Charlie talked business. 'But he's not at all at ease with himself. And for all his money, he doesn't strike one as . . . particularly happy.'

I smiled but said nothing. I did and didn't want to talk about him. I wanted to ask questions, but didn't altogether wish to hear the answers. Then she said, quietly, 'Of course, there's talk that the marriage has been in trouble from the word go.'

'Oh?'

'Mm,' she said, taking a sip of wine and glancing at David. 'Apparently he's in love with someone else.'

I looked at her. 'Perhaps he just works hard,' I replied.

She smiled, knowingly. 'I think there's a little more to it than that, dear.' She'd hooked me. I was intrigued.

'And . . .'

'Well, you'll recall Mrs Wade, who cooks for us?'

'Yes,' I said, although I didn't really.

'She sometimes helps out over at Deyning, when they have big dinners there and so forth, and she's been there rather a lot of late.' She paused, lit a cigarette from the candle on the table. 'She told me it's common knowledge *he's* in love with someone else, someone in London, I think, and that the marriage is in trouble.'

'And how does Mrs Wade know this?'

She laughed. 'Clarissa, really, you more than anyone should understand that servants know *everything*.'

'Yes, but they're not meant to tell, Flora,' I said.

'I think those days are well and truly gone, darling. We're all exposed now. Anyway, Mrs Wade says there've been quite a few big arguments and rather a lot of door-slamming going on at Deyning, not that *he's* there much. But when he is . . .'

'But I thought . . . I'd heard that she was . . . that a baby was due?'

She shook her head, shrugged. 'No . . . no babies. We saw them only a month ago, and she certainly isn't expecting anything . . . other than perhaps a letter from *his* lawyers,' she added, raising her eyebrows. 'I think divorce is imminent, dear. And he'll no doubt have his pick for Mrs Cuthbert number two . . . all that money and those looks, really.'

So, as we sat outside after lunch, replete, and enjoying one of those blissful lazy Sundays, rustling newspapers and watching clouds roll across the sky, I said, 'I think I might take a drive.'

'Oh really? Where to? I might come with you,' Flora said.

'I don't know . . . perhaps to Midhurst.'

'Darling, there'll be absolutely no one about, nothing at all happening . . . you know it's really terribly dull there.'

I managed to get away on my own and took the road back towards Deyning. I had no intention of motoring up the main driveway, but I knew the road that led to the farm, and the track from there towards the woods by the lake. There'd be no one about; no one would see me. I turned off the London road and drove down the narrow lane towards the farm. I drove past two children, waving to them as I crossed in front of the red-brick farmhouse, and then I picked up the track towards the lake, and stopped the car at the gate before the woods.

I stepped out of the car, on to the track where Papa and I had sat and listened to the sounds of guns so many years earlier, and, for a second or two, I thought I could hear them once more. I moved on, opened the gate, and walked into the dappled light of overhanging branches, lifting them up out of my path. The track had narrowed, was overgrown with weeds and thistles, and I caught my skirt on them more than once. I hoisted it up, tucking it into my belt, and walked on again until I came to a clearing and another gate, beyond which was the lower path around the lake; the one Papa had taken me to when I was a child. I wondered if the bench was still there. It was a warm spring day, not hot, and not entirely sunny, but clear and bright. I took off my shoes and my stockings, left them by the gate and headed down towards the lake.

I found the bench, collapsed and rotting; no more than an ancient piece of timber lying on the edge of an overgrown pathway, and I walked on slowly as the house came into view. I couldn't be sure if anyone was there, but there were no obvious signs of life, and it was too tempting not to continue. I kept to the pathway, my head down, picking my way through sharp twigs and the shells of acorns beneath my feet. Then I glanced up and saw the chestnut tree in the lower meadow, the empty bench beneath its branches. When I reached the boathouse I looked up again, towards the house. A number of trees had disappeared, cut down to make the view from the windows on the south-east side of the house more picturesque, I assumed. I could clearly see the gate to the stable yard, but there was no one about, not a sound, so I moved on, along the jetty, and sat down. I dangled my legs over the side, my toes skimming the water, and then leant back; lifting my face up to a blink of sun between shadows. *Home*.

Was he there? I wondered. Was he sitting yards away, at his desk, staring out towards the water my feet now touched? I remembered Flora's words of the previous evening . . . *no babies . . . an affair . . . a separate life*. I closed my eyes, and for a moment I fancied I could hear his voice in the distance; a memory held and carried back amidst the rustling of trees.

'Have you not read the signs, miss? This is private property . . . trespassers *will* be prosecuted.'

I turned. A man I'd never seen before was standing at the other end of the jetty.

'I'm terribly sorry,' I said, quickly rising to my feet, rearranging my skirt. 'I used to live here . . . I grew up here.'

He said nothing, didn't move.

'Actually, I happen to know the present owner, Tom Cuthbert, Mr Cuthbert . . . and I'm quite sure, quite sure that he wouldn't be in the least bothered by my being here . . .'

'That may be, miss, but I have my job to do. And Mr Cuthbert'll no doubt already have been informed we have an intruder. You came through the farmyard, didn't you?'

'Yes, that's right, I did. But, as I'm sure you can see, I'm not a poacher . . . not an intruder. I simply wanted to take a walk . . .' I said, moving back along the jetty. 'I can go now.'

'I'm sure you mean no harm, miss, but I have my job to do,' he repeated, as I scurried past him. And as I quickened my pace, back along the path, I could hear voices somewhere. And they were not the voices of ghosts from my past: these voices were male and very much alive. Oh God, I didn't want to be caught looking like a snoop, a spy, and I picked up my skirt and ran.

I ran along the path in agony as my feet crunched on acorn shells, pebbles and holly; my hair tugged and pulled at by newly hostile branches. I stopped by Papa's rotting bench, breathless, and glanced back; I could see three figures, all of them looking in my direction, and I took off again, up the pathway towards the woods, and the gate where I'd left my shoes. When I reached the gate, my shoes and stockings had gone and I yelled out, because I couldn't possibly drive in bare feet. But there was nothing for it, I'd have to try. I passed through the gate, breaking a nail *and* ripping my blouse on its latch, and shouting out again, 'No!' I continued back along the track towards the car, in tears, in physical as well as mental anguish. And then I stopped. Why was I running? I'd done nothing wrong . . . I'd simply gone to look at my old home. *My home*. I stood still for a moment, collecting my thoughts, calming my breath. I needed my shoes; I couldn't drive without them. And so I turned and walked back towards the gate I'd just passed through and left ajar. I saw the man from the jetty walking up the bank towards me, carrying something, and I stopped by the gate and waited for him.

'Mi-iss! Miss Larissa!' he called out. And I thought, oh God, he may have my name wrong but he knows who I am, and that meant only one thing: one of the men by the boathouse had been Tom.

'Yes, hello . . . hello again,' I answered, closing my eyes as he came towards me, carrying my shoes and stockings.

'I'm sorry, Miss Larissa,' he said, huffing and puffing, 'but you know how it is . . . we get all sorts here . . . can't be too careful. And being as Mr Cuthbert has some very valuable antiquities up at the house . . .'

'Oh really,' I said, snatching my shoes and stockings from his arms. 'It's *Clarissa*, by the way.'

He looked confused.

'My name, it's Clarissa—not *Larissa*.'

He smiled at me. 'A very pretty name too, miss,' he said. 'And Mr Cuthbert would like you to know that you're very welcome to . . . to have a paddle in the lake.'

I laughed. 'I was not paddling, I simply dipped my feet into the water,' I replied and then I realised how I sounded, and added, 'and I know, you're just doing your job.'

I glanced towards the boathouse, but could see no one, and so I looked back at him and said, 'And do thank Mr Cuthbert for his very kind offer of a paddle, but I must get back to . . . to London.' And I turned and began to walk back towards the car, knowing full well how I must have looked to the old gamekeeper, with my torn blouse, bare feet and dishevelled hair.

Oh God, how I wished I hadn't gone there. To be caught *trespassing*, and then to have run off like that! I pictured him, Tom, standing with his gamekeeper, as the old man explained that he'd chased off a rogue *paddler*. And I could see him, see his smile. I leant against the bonnet, rolled up my stockings, one by one, and put on my shoes. I got into the car, slammed the door shut and as I started the engine, put the car into reverse, I saw him, Tom, in front of me, hurriedly marching through the grass towards the gate. I saw him raise his hand, shout something, but I pushed my foot down on the accelerator and turned away; and I kept my head turned away until I reached the entrance to the farm, and then I quickly turned the car back towards the main road and my sister-in-law's house.

Why did I rush away from him that day? I suppose because I was embarrassed to have been caught there, trespassing; trespassing on his life. And it only made me feel more desperate, because I wasn't altogether sure whether I'd returned to Deyning to look at the place, or whether I'd gone there in search of him. And so I drove back to Flora's at a ridiculous speed, chastising myself all the way, and crying. When I arrived back at the cottage I went straight to my room, cleaned myself up and changed. Then I went outside into the garden. Charlie and David were both asleep in their deckchairs. Flora glanced up at me. 'Nice drive, dear?'

'Yes, heavenly,' I said, and I picked up a magazine and sat down.

CHAPTER THIRTY-SIX

Mama moved from her house in Berkeley Square to a flat in Kensington in the summer of 1928. Still proud, she told people that the house was much *too large* for her now, on her own, but in truth it was simply too costly for her to run. She'd grown weary of struggling on with too few servants, was tired of meetings with sympathetic, overly keen young bankers and their talk of *economies*. What did they know? she'd said to me: they had no idea, no idea at all of how things were, before the War. 'It was a different world.'

And my mother belonged to that different world; Berkeley Square belonged to that different world: a world slowly fading. Like the Chinese painted silk upon Mama's walls, now discoloured and watermarked by damp; like the chipped paintwork on the doors and staircase, and the unseen cobwebs, floating listlessly, clinging to the ornate cornicing of once busy rooms. The house exuded an ennui reflected in Mama's own lassitude, and even Wilson's devotion to my mother seemed to have taken on a lazy, apathetic air. For Mama herself looked not quite right, as though she *and* her maid had forgotten all about Edina Granville, the woman who'd once presided over so much, and with such innate confidence. Her glossy chestnut hair had faded to a dull, flat grey, its texture altered with its colour, and the once delicate fine curls carefully arranged about her face now replaced by an unruly frizz. Without her garden, without access to that fresh country air, her pallor, too, had lost its bloom: that luminosity I recalled from my youth. And, perhaps in a bid to restore that vibrancy, she'd taken to wearing make-up. But her powder was a little too pale, her rouge a tad too vivid, and the whole effect, somehow, altogether wrong.

There was a strange shrinking down of my mother at that time. Not just a shrinking down of her material world, but of her, her substance. Her life, once commanded on such a grand scale, distilled itself once more, and she seemed to fold herself into that small place; a place of dusty treasures, no longer fashionable antiques, and sun-bleached silk brocades.

And something happened to me too around this time. I began to change, or perhaps I didn't change so much as begin to know at last who I was, what I wanted and didn't want in my life. For a while I'd contemplated finding a job. I'd looked at advertisements in the newspaper, wondering what, if anything, I could do. I'd gone to an employment bureau on Oxford Street, where I spent ten minutes in a poky upstairs office, in front of a bespectacled middle-aged man, who'd glanced at my wedding ring and asked me if my husband knew where I was. He sat behind a desk, his hands clasped in front of him, smiling at me, and then told me that it really was advisable for me to have my husband's permission before embarking upon *a career*. He'd recently had quite a few young ladies like me through his door, he said, and laughed. 'Emboldened by the times, I suppose,' he added. But really, why would someone like me want to work? What about charity work? he asked. I told him I already helped my mother with her *district* and various charitable causes, but that I wanted something more. He suggested I take up a new hobby, so I thanked him for his time and left.

At home, I continued to play a part, for I wasn't a wife, not in the real sense, nor had I been for many years. And I was lonely, desperately so. My house was immaculate, my life a tidy, ordered affair. But I was bored of arranging flowers that only I looked upon; bored of agreeing menus for what I knew would be a solitary supper; bored of shop windows, parks and teas; bored of afternoon card games and matinees, and bored of climbing into my bed each night alone. I'd contemplated an affair, and more than once, but of course there was only ever one man in my dreams: only one man and one fantasy.

And I continued to hear about him . . .

I was in Liberty's, looking at material for a new

dress, when Rose tapped me on the shoulder. We tried to remember when we'd last seen each other; had it been at Venetia's New Year's party five years ago? No, I told her, it had been longer than that. And it had. I hadn't seen Rose in almost ten years, not since shortly after the end of the War. I realise now that it was probably a conscious decision on both our parts—to move on, to try to leave those we'd shared a kind of darkness with behind, to be happy. I'd heard that she'd married a major in the army and had moved to Oxfordshire, and she confirmed this that day, telling me she'd been living in the country, raising her own brood.

'I simply can't believe it!' she said, as we sat down together in the tearoom.

She looked more or less the same, a little fuller of face, rounder of figure, and had dyed her short bobbed hair to the Titian red it always promised to be. She talked me through her wedding—'A very quiet affair in the country,' she said, looking at me sheepishly—and the births of her children; and she told me how blissfully happy she was. Then she produced a photograph of her three girls from her purse.

'They're beautiful, Rose,' I said.

'And you? No babies?'

'No,' I replied, with an impeccably rehearsed smile. 'I'm afraid not.'

'Such a shame. But I suppose we can't have it all, can we? And let's face it, darling, you were blessed with *more* than your fair share of good looks. I remember all those boys, so besotted by you, so in love . . .'

I laughed.

'Strange to think of that time now,' she said

wistfully, picking up her cup and staring at it. Then, perhaps inevitably, we began the grim roll call of those missing.

'But what about Henry? I heard, of course, through my parents. Still no word?'

I shook my head. 'No, nothing.'

She stared at me, as though perhaps I knew something more. Then she sighed in an exaggerated fashion. 'Well, it's a strange thing, that's for certain, to just disappear—into thin air.'

'I don't suppose for one minute that Henry has actually disappeared into *thin air*, Rose,' I said, perhaps a little tartly. 'He's somewhere, I know that, and I've no doubt we'll hear from him, eventually.'

'Yes, yes of course you will, dear. But it must be simply horrendous for you and your poor mama, simply horrendous.' She sighed again, shook her head. 'And when I remember poor dear William and George . . . and all the others—seems like only yesterday they were all here.'

'Do you really think so? Seems like a lifetime ago to me.'

She reached out and placed her gloved hand over mine. 'Yes, darling, I imagine it does. You and your family have certainly suffered.'

At that moment I didn't want Rose's sympathy. And I didn't want to think about my family. I looked at my wristwatch. 'Gracious, I hadn't realised the time, Rose. I'm afraid I'll have to be off in a minute. I have to call in on Mama on the way home.'

'And how is she? How is you mama?'

'Oh, she's fine,' I said. 'Yes, really quite fine.'

But I wasn't convinced.

The previous week, I'd called on my mother unexpectedly. It was the middle of the afternoon and I'd found her sitting at her dining-room table, surrounded by papers, her travelling jewellery case directly in front of her. She seemed unusually flustered, and had quickly gathered up the papers lying about the table.

'I'm sorry if I'm interrupting you,' I said.

'Not at all, I was sorting through old paperwork—to do with Deyning, that's all,' she replied, looking up at me, smiling. But I knew this to be a lie; I could see perfectly well that they were letters and postcards: handwritten, personal. And I could tell she'd been crying. I stepped back from her, walked about the room as she finished collecting up the cards and papers, folding pages with trembling hands, placing them back inside the jewellery case.

'There!' she said, closing the lid of the case.

I sat down next to her at the table. She asked me about my day, where I'd been, and I thought her words seemed a little slurred. She's upset, I thought, quite obviously upset. In her hands, resting on the table, she fiddled with the small tasselled key to the case, and I immediately noticed the ring on her wedding finger. It was a ring I vaguely remembered having seen once before, a gentleman's signet ring: gold, and rather heavy looking, but unlike the signet rings of my father and brothers, this one had no crest. It had, instead, initials engraved upon it, overlapping and entwined. Was that an S and an E, or was it a B, and perhaps a D? I couldn't make it out. But she must have seen me staring at it because she swiftly covered it with her other hand. And at that very same moment, as

I glanced up and caught her eye, I heard Georgie whisper in my ear. Of course: it was the King's ring, the one *not for playing with*.

Rose frowned. 'Oh, but what a shame. I could sit and talk with you for hours and hours. We have so much to catch up on, dear. And I haven't even asked you—how is dear Charlie? And what about the Astley girls? Do you ever see them?'

I opened my mouth, about to tell her that yes, Charlie was well, and that I hadn't seen either Flavia or Lily Astley in some time when she began again. 'And what about Tom Cuthbert then?'

I hesitated, wondering what on earth she meant. 'What about him?'

'Oh my God, Clarissa, don't you know? You must know . . . he's worth a fortune, darling. In fact, he now owns your family's old place in the country, *and* half of London!'

'Yes, sorry, of course, I do know that. I'm very much aware of how successful he's been, Rose.'

'I should say! And to think we *all* turned our noses up at him, ha! How times have changed. But I must tell you, dear, although I'm not sure when you last saw him . . .' she stopped, looked at me, and I shrugged. She narrowed her eyes for a moment, as though performing some complex internal calculation, and then continued. 'Well, anyway, we crossed paths with him at a house party, oh, a few months ago now . . . the Langbournes? Blandford Forum?'

I shook my head.

'He was there with his wife, an *American*.' She arched an eyebrow. 'Not entirely sure . . . quite haughty and aloof, I thought. Anyway, and more to the point, Mr Cuthbert is, I can tell you, still as divine as ever. Do you remember how handsome he was?'

'Yes, I do.'

'Well, I can tell you he's even *more* handsome now, darling. Money and impending middle age certainly suit him. Oh, it's too depressing! Handsome men just become better looking as they age, whilst we ladies simply fade.' She laughed, raised her eyes heavenward, then turned to me again. 'But I must say, you haven't faded at all, Clarissa. But that's probably because you haven't had children. You know they really *do* take such a huge toll on one's body . . . and one's energy.'

I blinked, smiled.

She leant towards me, conspiratorially. 'On our second night at the Langbournes' I was placed next to him at dinner . . .' She clasped at her string of pearls. 'And he remembered me.'

'Ah!'

'Well, I think he did. He didn't mention our little *thing* as such, but he certainly remembered that time . . . the madness, all of us on that dizzy circuit.' She paused again, lost in her memory of that time, and perhaps of him. 'Anyway,' she continued, 'I had only recently discovered that he'd bought Deyning Park, and so of course I reminded him that you and I had been dear, dear friends . . . and that I knew the house from way back when. "Oh really?" he said. "I never knew that." And then he said, "Do you ever see Clarissa?"' She stared at me, waiting for something—I wasn't sure what, perhaps a gasp.

'So I told him,' she went on, 'that I hadn't seen you for years, which was a shame, because you were on my shortlist as a potential god-mama to Sophia . . . and that I was determined to look you up again soon. It's been too, too long, dear.'

I was distracted, doing my own internal calculation. I realised that Rose must have seen him not long after my unfortunate encounter—trespassing.

Rose continued. 'And so he said, "Should you see her, Rose, would you be so kind as to pass on a message?" Of course, I told him, because—really—I was determined to catch up with you, darling. "Would you tell her that I still have her *tent* . . ."' she paused, looking at me, wide eyed, '"and that . . ."' she looked away again, struggling to remember the remainder of the message.

'Yes?' I leant towards her. 'And that . . .'

'And that . . .' she repeated, now transfixed by the linen tablecloth. 'And that . . . Oh dear, Clarissa, I'm so sorry, I can't remember. Anyway, he has your tent, dear, and I shan't ask any questions. You know me, I *abhor* indiscretion and gossip.'

She sat in silence for a moment, waiting for me to elucidate, but I chose not to say anything. Five minutes later, as I rose to my feet, she said, 'But how simply lovely . . . and how fortuitous our meeting like this.'

'Yes, it's been so nice, Rose,' I said, bending down to kiss her, and then, as I began to walk away, she shouted after me, 'An island! He has *your* tent on some island, dear.'

I turned and smiled at her. And I continued to smile as I walked down the wooden staircase and out of the shop. I travelled home by bus that day, but I didn't see any street, person, or vehicle. I saw my Arabian tent, on the island at home. And I saw Tom, lying inside it, gazing up at those tiny stars, thinking of me; remembering us.

* * *

Trust, Mama once told me, is the cornerstone of a marriage. Without trust, she said, there is nothing: for what can be achieved without it?

But Charlie and I led increasingly separate lives. We occasionally attended dinners, parties and the theatre together, smiling, but in private, at home, we avoided each other as best we could, and rarely ate together. When we did, we spoke of mundane matters, trivia. He returned home from the city late most evenings, and often went out again, later still. I asked no questions. I didn't want to know. And I only discovered his affair because he told me. He had to tell me.

Of course it wasn't the first. There had been other liaisons before that, I knew, and I'd chosen to turn a blind eye to them. But this one was different. Madge Parsons had lived with us for over a year, employed as our parlourmaid. And Madge had succeeded where I'd failed: she was pregnant with my husband's baby. I went to stay with my mother, leaving him to deal with the debris. I was not heartbroken, but I was humiliated, defeated. And I wasn't sure what to do. I did not love my husband and our marriage was a sham, but it had taken two people, I thought, to create that sham. I was not blameless. And which was better, the sham of respectability or the shame of divorce? Although I'd never told my mother, or anyone else, of the way Charlie *loved* me in private, I knew her thoughts on divorce. It was anathema to her.

Charlie swiftly removed Madge from our home.

He begged me to give our marriage another chance. He promised me that he would be different; that he would be a better, more faithful husband. And my mother sat me down and told me once again, 'Marriages involve sacrifice and compromise; they're not something one simply abandons at the first hurdle.' She took it upon herself to explain to me that men have different needs to women; they require . . . *other things*, she said. And I'd immediately imagined a garment of some type: a hat, a scarf or a pair of mittens. Charlie wrapped up for winter. Then I imagined how she'd react if I told her about the *other things* my husband required. I thought of Mademoiselle, and momentarily wondered where she was; was she still alive, somewhere? Was she explaining to some young housebound girl that men had never evolved properly? And perhaps she was correct; perhaps some men hadn't, but it seemed to me then that Mama and Mademoiselle had more in common than I'd realised.

But I didn't want to resume my unhappy life with Charlie. I could no longer breathe around him, or in that house. I didn't love my husband. We barely spoke. And I yearned to be free, to be able to make my own decisions, to live my own life. Charlie and I were two different people to the idealistic young officer and naive dreamy girl who'd become engaged during the War. At that time I'd wanted to please my mother; I'd wanted to make her happy again, proud of me. I'd yearned for normality, for some sort of order to be restored to our broken lives, and I'd thought that marriage would deliver that, as well as a sense of security and, perhaps, even happiness. But my marriage to Charlie had not brought me what I'd craved. I could never love him the way he wanted me to, or the way I knew I could love. Despite everything, I still cared about him and would continue to, but not as a husband and certainly not as a lover. I knew the time had come: I had an opportunity to change my life. I owed no explanation to my husband, but I knew my mother would be aghast at my desire for independence. And so, 'Trust, Mama, is the cornerstone of a marriage. Without trust, there is nothing. Without trust what can be achieved?'

* * *

. . . I'm delighted. It is the only photograph I had of the two of you together, and quite right that you should have it. As you say, in the blink of an eye. I too have thought of those times, & oh how often! And yes, I remember the boathouse . . . I remember it all. But I do believe everything has turned out as it was meant. Time, rightly or wrongly, is a great leveller of emotion, & of ambition also, and certainly we have ALL mellowed . . . Yes, my life is different, but it is fine and I am happy, and though this place is small, I must admit—it is rather cosy, & very manageable. In fact, I can say I feel rather liberated to be relieved of the accumulated paraphernalia. But how peculiar to have spent a lifetime collecting it—only to dispose of it!

CHAPTER THIRTY-SEVEN

When spring finally comes she never ceases to surprise me with the lightness and warmth of her touch, her early dawns and frenzied revelry. She is a symphony of rapturous colour and vibrant luminosity; she is memory restored, senses reawakened—brought back to life; and I fall in love once more. For is there another season that inspires so many unabashed romantic notions? Is there any other time of the year when we can truly luxuriate in the feeling of being at one with our universe?

I remember this season at Deyning. I remember the cuckoo, the woodpecker and the lark. I remember the blackbird that nested in the tree beyond my bedroom window, and the song thrush upon the roof above my room. I remember looking out on to a never-ending green world. And for a moment I am back there. I feel that soft, breathless air upon my face, hear their song once more.

From the day I moved into my small flat in Kensington, I felt free. I could at last be whoever I wanted to be. I could breathe. For the very first time in my life I was living on my own, making my own decisions and in charge of my destiny. I'd finally taken that leap into the great unknown: independence. Within the space of twenty-four hours my world condensed itself into five rooms, and could easily have fitted into what had once been my bedroom and dressing room at Deyning. But I felt no sense of confinement, or that sense of claustrophobia I had lived with for so many years. I looked out on to a bustling street, where buses passed by my window and people once again looked back at me and smiled. London, it suddenly seemed to me, was filled with friendly faces and limitless possibilities.

It was during those first heady days of my late-found independence that I began to make plans: plans for me and about me. I received money each month from Charlie, enough to live on and pay my rent, and I had some savings in a bank account, money left to me by my grandfather. But I still longed to do something with my life, to be fully independent, earn my own money. The man at the employment bureau had succeeded in making me feel something of a joke, unemployable, so I began to think about other avenues, a business, a shop: a flower shop . . . a hat shop . . . a dress shop. Then, for a while, I contemplated a bookshop: an antiquarian bookshop.

What I hadn't anticipated when I embarked upon my new singular life was my own ineptitude. I had never shopped for food, or cooked a meal, either for myself or anyone else; never done any laundry, or sewn or mended clothes; and I had never truly managed a penny, let alone a pound. I'd never uncorked a bottle of wine; never cleaned, or polished or dusted; never disposed of household rubbish; and I'd never used an iron. I could have employed someone, a cleaner, a cook, but it seemed a ridiculous extravagance for one person. So, I purchased a book and set about teaching myself the rudiments of cookery, starting with the basics, such as boiling an egg. I confess I did, however, employ a local service to do my laundry, and, eventually, once the novelty of cleaning and washing up burnt pans had worn off, I employed a woman to come in two mornings a week. It was all a new experience, all of it, and I loved it.

Sometimes I shopped for food in Fortnum and Mason or Harrods, mesmerised by the colourful displays and choice, and, perhaps inevitably, returning home with enough food for an army. But usually I patronised the local bakeries, greengrocers and butchers. I became familiar with another world, a place I'd glimpsed once before, beyond the green baize door; the place Edna, Mabel, Stephens and Wilson had come from. At last the world had opened up to me, and it welcomed me with more warmth than I could ever have imagined. And it struck me how queer it was that the smaller, more confined my material world, the more freedom and space I sensed around me; as though God, nature, the universe or whatever it is, is somehow able to balance one's experience—one's lot in life—upon a scales. At Deyning I'd had everything and nothing; now I had nothing—and everything.

I enrolled in an art class and began to paint once more; I met new people, was invited out to new places. I was wooed by a French diplomat, and very nearly fell in love with my art teacher. I realised that I could survive alone, and I enjoyed life in a way I hadn't for years. Then, at a dinner party, I met Antonio Capparelli. Antonio owned a gallery in Mayfair, and he was impressed by my knowledge and love of art, surprised that I'd done nothing with it, with my life. I'd explained to him that I'd had no real education, that girls like me were simply expected to marry and produce children. Something I'd clearly failed at. He suggested I work for him, at his gallery, two or three days a week perhaps, whatever I wanted, and it was tempting, but not enough. And then it came to me: a gallery, I'd set up my *own* gallery.

I used my savings as the down payment on premises just around the corner from where I lived, on the Fulham Road, and, initially at least, I considered the whole enterprise a type of experiment. If it failed, at least I'd tried. My mother, of course, was mortified; and not just because I'd plundered what little money I had into what she considered to be a reckless business venture. To have a daughter who'd elected to be a *divorcee* was bad enough, but to have a daughter who wanted to work as well was quite beyond her.

And so, 'It's a different world, Mama.'

I'd been reassured, encouraged, and advised by my new friend, Antonio. It had been his idea that I should only exhibit work by new, undiscovered British artists; that I should focus my attention there, and visit art schools in London and any local exhibitions. And so for those first few months I spent my time getting to know some of the new up-and-coming artists on the scene, visiting Chelsea Art College, the Slade and various other more far-flung institutions. I'd decided early on that any profits from the gallery—once I'd paid myself enough to live on—should go to charities supporting war veterans and families of those killed in the War, in memory of my brothers. I had no need of money, and my motivation to set up a business was never about making money for myself.

I named my gallery, the Deyning Gallery. I couldn't think of a better name at the time, and it never occurred to me that there might be any conflict of interest with Tom Cuthbert's burgeoning business empire. Although there were a few people who enquired as to whether the gallery was a '*part of Cuthbert-Deyning*'.

The gallery did well, very well. And I had a number of loyal patrons who seemed keen to invest and purchase new paintings. One collector, who remained nameless, and whom I never actually met, always knew exactly what I was exhibiting. I'd receive a telephone call from a Mr Pritchard who'd later arrive by taxicab, to pay for and remove the painting, or paintings, his employer had heard of or noticed.

'Does he live locally then, your employer?' I asked, as I wrapped yet another framed canvas for Mr P.

'No, madam, he does not.'

'Are you able to disclose his name to me?'

'No, madam, unfortunately I'm not at liberty to do that.'

Of course, he wasn't the only one. There were a few collectors who simply didn't want to be seen to be spending money on something as frivolous as art, particularly modern art. And Antonio had told me it was the norm, even before the War.

I hadn't planned on having an affair with Antonio. He was sixteen years my senior, and I'd always considered his flirting to be something synonymous with his Italian character. We met regularly for lunch and often attended exhibitions, auctions and private views together. And then one night after dinner, he came home with me.

Passionate, handsome, educated, and amusing, Antonio made me feel like a girl of sixteen again. He called me *Clereeza*, and liked me to say certain words so that he could repeat them, mimicking my accent.

'Haughty . . .'

'*Hor-tee*,' he repeated.

'Peculiar . . .'

'*Pick-u-lee-ar*.'

'Gorgeous . . .'

'*Gor-juz*.'

Life with Antonio was anything but dull. And, after Charlie, I was once again in the maelstrom of life. We invariably ate out each evening and attended the theatre two or three times a week; and I laughed in a way I hadn't for years. I was more than content: I was happy. But things have a habit of creeping up on us when we're least expecting them, or need them.

I'd kept track of Tom, through a grapevine of sorts. I'd heard that he and Nancy had separated and that Deyning stood empty once more. Davina saw him, and reasonably often, and she'd informed me that he'd recently purchased another prime site in central London. 'He's unstoppable!' she'd exclaimed, her eyes flashing with excitement. And then she told me of his penchant for beautiful women.

'Oh well, he has the lifestyle, and the money—why not?' I replied. 'But it sounds as though he's become everything I wish to escape from,' I said, somewhat disingenuously. For of course I had thought of him, and thought of him often.

When I saw him with Venetia in the bar of the Theatre Royal that evening—and I saw them before they saw me—I was shocked. And I thought twice about going over to speak to them.

Venetia and Tom.

I panicked, and Antonio must have seen something in my face.

'Whatever's the matter, my darling? Why the frown and look of alarm?' he asked. And so I told him.

'There's an old friend of mine . . . over at the bar, with . . . with my godmother.'

He turned to look. 'Ah, yes, I see . . . I see. But Venetia, she very much likes the handsome young men.'

'Actually, he's not *that* young,' I said. 'He's rather rapidly approaching forty.'

But the irony wasn't lost on me: there I was, with a man almost old enough to be my father, and there was he, with a woman *definitely* old enough to be his mother.

'Shall we say hello?' Antonio asked.

'Let me take a moment, please, Antonio,' I said, still not entirely sure whether I wished to step forward and speak to them.

As I deliberated, I watched him. I noticed his skin was tanned, and he had that unmistakable air of success about him. He wore an impeccably cut dark suit, a white shirt and a dark blue tie. And as he moved a bronzed hand through the air, the glinting gold of his wristwatch caught my eye. He looked like a rich playboy, I thought, freshly arrived back from the Riviera. And Venetia appeared spellbound.

He stood with his back half towards me, and I could easily have slipped away; they need never have known I'd been there, standing feet away from them in the crowded bar that night. But I couldn't do it. I had to go and speak to them. I wanted to know more. And that night, like most other nights, it was impossible to miss Venetia. She wore a long red kimono, and a vividly coloured scarf wrapped around her head and fastened in place by an enormous diamond butterfly brooch. The Japanese look, I thought, watching her. She seemed to move quite swiftly from continent to continent, in terms of fashion, and was always caught under the spell of some opera. Her husband, Hughie, had not long been dead, but she abhorred black, said it added ten years at least to a woman's face, and she hated the rituals of mourning. The very worst of Englishness, she said: *so passé, and so horribly Victorian!*

'Venetia!' I called out as I approached, sounding a warning shot.

Not surprisingly she looked startled. 'Clarissa! *Darling!*'

I saw him turn, but I ignored him and moved towards my godmother, kissing her on both cheeks. 'What a surprise,' I said, flatly, without any smile.

'Yes . . . well, Tom called on me unexpectedly, and . . . and here we are!'

I turned to him, forced a smile. 'Hello, Tom.'

His tanned features froze, and for a few seconds he seemed unable to speak.

Then he said, 'My God, Clarissa . . . and looking as *divine* as ever.' And I thought, no, that's not you; that's not the way you speak. But I continued to smile, and then I introduced Antonio.

He glanced at Antonio, looked to me, then back at Antonio. 'Antonio,' he said, shaking his hand and elongating the syllables in an unnecessary way. Making a point, I thought. I could tell he was taken aback: he seemed unsure of what to do or say, or even where to look. But as Antonio greeted Venetia, he turned away from them, towards me.

'Fate, eh?' he said, staring at me.

'Coincidence,' I replied.

'There's no such thing as coincidence. You of all people should know that.'

I couldn't fathom what he meant, but it certainly wasn't the time to embark on any deeper analysis. Trying to keep the conversation light hearted, the way one would if one had bumped into any old friend, I resorted to the obvious questions: how was he? He looked very well: had he been away? Did he still own Deyning? Still spend time there?

Yes, he was well, very well; life was good. He'd just returned from Monte Carlo, been back only a day. He was thinking of selling Deyning; it cost too much to run, was too big for one person, he said, searching my face.

'Oh . . . I hope not. I hope you don't sell it.'

'No . . . no, well, perhaps I shan't,' he replied.

And I thought, how easy, what luxury to be able to change one's mind at whim.

He asked after my mother, and then, when I asked—somewhat perfunctorily—after his own, he told me: told me of her death only three months earlier. And I immediately saw her, sitting on board that bus, waving back at me. I'd known then, I think, that I wouldn't see her again, and right at that moment I wondered if she'd come to me knowing that too.

'I'm so sorry,' I said, swamped by sadness, the memory of that soft, powdered cheek. *Lily of the valley.* 'I only wish I'd gone to see her,' I added, looking down at the glass in my hands.

'Well, you saw her; you saw her at Deyning—when you had tea with her, and she very much enjoyed that.'

'But I should have gone to visit her,' I said,

tearfully. 'And I told her I would . . . I said to her, as I saw her on to the bus, I'll come and visit you, Evelyn . . . and I never did.'

He stared at me, wide eyed. *'Evelyn?'*

I bit my lip, looked away.

'She came to see you . . . my mother came to see you—here in London?'

I glanced back at him, nodded.

'I think we need to talk.'

'Yes, I think we do. But not now, not here.'

'No, not now.'

'And what are you two whispering about?' Venetia asked, stepping towards us.

'Catching up,' Tom replied, looking at me.

He sucked hard on his cigarette, staring at me in that way, which always made me feel uneasy, embarrassed. I suppose he knew me so well, knew my secrets. But it was more than that, of course: I felt exposed and vulnerable under his scrutiny; as though he were able to read my mind, see and *feel* my thoughts.

I saw him watching Antonio, looking him up and down out of the corner of his eye, and I wondered what he was thinking. Was he shocked? Jealous? I couldn't tell. But when the bell rang for us to take our seats and Antonio moved over, slipping his arm around my waist and kissing me gently upon my head, I saw him close his eyes and turn away.

'I must say, you're looking quite sensational, darling,' Venetia said, smiling at me. 'And *so* much happier too . . .'

'Yes, well . . . I am. I am happier,' I replied, not looking at any of them.

'And *I* have dedicated my life—my life's purpose—to the happiness of Clarissa,' Antonio said, with a newly operatic tone to his voice.

Venetia laughed. 'To happiness!' she said, raising her glass of water, and as we all clinked glasses I met Tom's eyes, and immediately looked away.

'Let's have dinner together, later, the four of us, eh?' Antonio suggested, and I so wished that he hadn't.

'What an exceedingly good idea! You know, I haven't seen my goddaughter in an absolute age, Antonio. I think you rather like to keep her to yourself, hmm?'

Antonio laughed. 'You're right, of course, I have no wish to share her with anyone.' He lifted my hand, kissed it. 'But perhaps tonight, for a little while, I'll share her with you both,' he added, winking at Venetia, who suddenly seemed to find everything hilarious.

I glanced at Tom, forcing a smile. But he didn't smile back. So I said, 'Is that agreeable with you, Tom?'

He didn't answer, and Venetia laughed again, and then said, 'But of course it's agreeable . . . utterly agreeable.'

'Tom?' I repeated. I wanted him to answer me.

'Yes . . . *spiffing*,' he said, and then turned away to stub out his cigarette.

When we returned to our seats I was distracted: unhearing, unseeing. Thankfully, we were seated in the dress circle, and they in the stalls, and I was relieved; relieved they weren't anywhere near us; relieved I couldn't see him with her. But as the lights dimmed, an image flashed before me: I saw him making love to a turbaned Venetia, saw him draped across her mountainous breast, nuzzling feathers and lace. It had to be an affair, I thought, had to be. Venetia had always preferred younger men as lovers, and there was always someone. Always had been. I wondered how long it had been going on; possibly years, I thought, and closed my eyes. Suddenly it all fitted together, all made sense: how Jimmy always knew about Tom's movements; why Venetia had been so interested in my marriage, and my *friendship* with Tom . . .

I shuffled in my seat, and sighed—surprisingly loudly. Antonio reached over, taking hold of my hand and anchoring it just as though I were a fidgeting child. But each time I thought of them a surge of anger rose up in me. *Venetia and Tom* . . . The sense of betrayal—or possible betrayal—was, quite literally, breathtaking. And as the play progressed I wondered if I could somehow fall ill, have an emergency at home . . . How I wished I had a dog, at least, to have to rush back to. I picked up my theatre binoculars, leant forward and peered down into the stalls, scanning along each row. And then I saw them, towards the front, the lights from the stage picking up the brilliant scarlet of Venetia's kimono: the scarlet lady indeed, I thought. How aptly attired.

Later, as I stood in the kerfuffle of the lobby, waiting for Antonio to fetch my coat, they appeared together by my side, Venetia beaming broadly, looking rather pleased with herself, I thought. He mentioned a French restaurant, just round the corner, barely looking at me, and said to follow on—in a somewhat dismissive tone.

'Fine. See you there,' I said flatly, and Venetia frowned and shook her head.

It was a strange, uncomfortable meal: strange to be sitting opposite him, looking at him once again.

And I don't remember anyone other than Antonio actually eating. At first Tom seemed inclined to ignore me and talked mainly to Antonio, about art. He knew Antonio's gallery, knew all of the central London galleries, but so many of them sold rubbish, he said. So I pretended to listen to Venetia, and, as she talked, I heard him tell Antonio that he'd recently purchased a painting by Matisse, and was planning on adding another to his collection. I heard Antonio extend an invitation to him, to a private view of a new Italian artist he was particularly excited about.

'And of course Clarissa has a discerning eye, Tom. You may also know her gallery: the Deyning?'

I glanced quickly at Tom, caught his eye, and he smiled at me.

'Really? No, I had no idea.'

I knew at that moment he was lying. Perhaps it was his smile, or, and more likely, his rudeness and lack of interest, but he suddenly changed the subject. He picked up the wine bottle in front of him and began to speak—once more to Antonio—about wine: Italian wine. Antonio looked at me, conscious of the snub, and shrugged.

As the evening wore on he became increasingly provocative.

'So, Antonio,' he said, looking at me and *not* at Antonio, 'how long have you two known each other?'

'I feel as though I've known Clarissa all of my entire life,' Antonio replied, effusively, and then placed his hand over mine. 'We're soulmates, Clarissa and me.'

'Really,' he said, still staring at me. 'Is that true, *Clereeza*? Have you found your soulmate in

Antonio?'

I laughed, looked away.

'And so . . . whereabouts in London do you live, Tom?' Antonio asked.

'Knightsbridge,' he replied, slurring the word.

'Oh, Antonio lives in Knightsbridge too,' I said.

'Well, what a coincidence,' he replied. 'My driver can run us all home then. That is, if we're *all* heading that way . . .'

Antonio intervened. 'Thank you, Tom, but we'll make our own way. We're going back to Clarissa's,' he said.

'Ah, Clarissa's . . . yes, yes of course.'

I wanted to leave. I recognised the mood he was in, could tell by the look in his eyes.

'Back to Clarissa's . . .' he repeated, staring into his glass, then lifting it to his lips.

'Shall we get the bill?' I asked, turning to Antonio.

'Please, allow me,' Tom interrupted. 'I insist.'

When we all stood up, to say goodbye, he reached into his wallet, pulled out a card and scribbled a number on to it.

'I hope you might find time to call me one day, *Clereeza*,' he said, handing me the card.

'Thank you, Tom. Yes. I shall. I'll do that.'

We didn't kiss, we didn't shake hands, we simply said goodnight. And then Antonio and I went out on to the street in search of a taxicab.

'I think you broke his heart,' Antonio said to me on the way home.

'Why, what makes you say that?'

'He's a wretched man, a tortured soul. He has everything and he has nothing. And I could see . . . I could see.'

'But he's with Venetia now.'

Antonio laughed. 'You are adorable. He may have escorted your god-mama to the theatre tonight, but I have a feeling that's as far as it goes.'

Later, as we made love, I thought of him. I tried not to, but it was as though he was there, in the room, watching us.

At that time his name was everywhere, the newspapers filled with advertisements for Cuthbert-Deyning new offices and property developments, and the business papers often quoted their most recent acquisition. Over the next few days I pulled his business card out from my purse any number of times. I looked at it, stared at the number he'd scrawled on to it, and I thought about picking up the telephone and calling him. But what would I say? What would *it* say? No, it was for him to call me, I decided. If he really wanted to see me he could easily find my number.

But of course, eventually, my resolve would waver.

CHAPTER THIRTY-EIGHT

I'd been out to a private view, alone. And I'd been drinking champagne. Someone had mentioned his name, said he was *the* collector, the one to watch out for, the one buying up new modern art. I didn't say anything at the time, didn't let on that I knew him. And yet the mention of his name always capsized me into that well of loneliness, reminding me of my loss.

Later, as I'd lain in bed, unable to sleep and

thinking of him, I wondered, as I'd done before, if he was in fact one of my anonymous patrons. And then I wondered if he was with Venetia. Was he lying next to her? Had he made love to her that evening? Was he making love to her *now*? I rose quickly from my bed, agitated and angry with myself for allowing *him* to keep me awake yet again. I went into the kitchen, lit the stove and placed the kettle on top of it.

It had been some weeks since we'd bumped into each other at the theatre and I'd recently ended my affair with Antonio, though we remained firm friends. Seeing Tom again had made me realise that there could only ever be one man for me, and, if I couldn't be with *him*, then . . . then I may as well be single. What was the point in pretending? I didn't want a fiancé, or another husband. And they all seemed to want ownership of some kind. No, I'd reasoned, it was probably my destiny to be on my own.

But I wanted to see him. And I needed to see him.

I didn't want to know—didn't want to hear—about him and Venetia, but I had to tell him about his father. After all, I'd promised Evelyn.

'Business,' I said, out loud, as I watched the kettle upon the stove. 'It's like business, that's all.'

But of course it wasn't, because my heart was involved, and because there was more.

I'd recently decided that I had to try to find my daughter. Not to interrupt her life or to try to reclaim her, but to know where she was, what had become of her. I had to know, you see. I had to know that she was cared for and happy. And I wanted Tom to help me find her.

I walked back into the sitting room, pulled my purse from my handbag and pulled out his card. I sat holding the card in my hand for some time; looking from it to the telephone and back at it. Then I picked up the receiver. Minutes away, I thought; he's only minutes away.

'Hello . . .'

It was him: awake and alert. 'Hello,' he said again.

'Are you busy?' I asked. I'm not sure why I said that. It was half past one in the morning, but I suppose I thought he might have been in the midst of passion with Venetia, or another.

'Clarissa.'

'Yes, it's me.'

'Let me take this somewhere else,' he said, and there was a click.

I immediately felt stupid. Wanted to hang up. I knew the only reason he'd be moving to another room, another telephone, was for reasons of privacy. He was with someone: in bed with someone. Was it Venetia? And already I could see her, lying back in a feathered turban, reciting poetry as he made love to her.

'Hello,' he said again, and I wasn't sure what to say. I didn't speak, couldn't speak.

'Don't go silent on me . . . Clarissa? Is everything all right?'

'Yes . . . yes,' I said, half laughing, trying to sound blasé. As though I'd called him up simply to compare notes on the weather. 'Everything's fine, perfectly fine. I was just wondering . . .' I began, not sure what I was going to say, not sure what I'd been wondering. And I felt myself panic. What on earth was I doing? How could I begin to talk to him about Emily or his father over the telephone?

'I was just wondering . . .' I said again.

'Yes?' he said, and I could hear the smile in his voice.

'I was just wondering how one makes a Singapore Sling,' I said quickly.

He laughed. 'I don't know. How does one make a Singapore Sling?'

'No, seriously, it's not a joke. I need the list of ingredients . . .'

I could hear him, lighting a cigarette, inhaling.

'You're making cocktails? Really? Now, at . . . one thirty a.m.?'

'No, not at this moment, but later . . . tomorrow.'

I closed my eyes, wanted to scream; wanted the ground to swallow me up.

'Please, tell me the truth: you haven't called me up in the middle of the night for a list of cocktail ingredients—have you?'

'No,' I replied.

'Shall I come over?'

'No!'

'Old lover-boy still there then?'

'Oh God, look, I'm sorry. I don't know why I called. I couldn't sleep and . . . and for some reason I thought of you.'

'Clarissa . . .'

'Is Venetia there?' I asked, and then winced.

I could hear him sigh; almost see him shake his head. 'I could meet you somewhere . . . at a hotel . . .'

'Tom! Good grief, do you think I've called you up because . . . because . . .' I faltered, rising to my feet, searching for the cigarette box.

He laughed. 'Clarissa, I'm teasing you.'

'I'd better go,' I said, feeling like a total fool. 'I'm not sure why I called you. I'm sorry.'

I heard him sigh again. 'Don't be sorry . . . never be sorry. Look, I'm leaving for Paris in the morning, but let's meet up when I get back. I'll telephone you.'

'Yes, fine. Have a lovely time. And do give my best to Venetia.'

He laughed again. 'I'm pleased you telephoned. I was wondering when you would.'

'When?' I repeated, irritated by his presumption.

'You said you would, remember?'

'Yes, I did. I mean, I do remember.'

'And Clarissa . . .'

'Yes?'

'Try and be good for me.'

'Goodnight, Tom,' I said, and hung up the receiver.

I didn't really expect him to call me upon his return from Paris, whenever that might be. And I didn't want to wait for disappointment. After all, he'd made no mention of how long he was to be away for, or when he'd be back. It could be a week, a month or longer. I began to regret my ridiculous middle-of-the-night telephone call to him. Upon reflection, his tone had been quite dismissive, I concluded. *I'll call you* . . . What had I been thinking? And did I really want to meet up with him—*alone*? Being newly single, the thought of seeing him again—on my own—filled me with more than a little trepidation. Would I succumb to him, yet again? Or would I feel spurned by his lack of interest? No, I reasoned, it was probably for the best that we didn't see each other again. We could leave it to fate, and perhaps cross paths once every few years.

Then, late one evening, only a few days after my call to him, the telephone rang, and as soon as I heard the voice I smiled. 'Hello, Tom.'

'Clarissa,' he said, again, slightly slurring my name.

'How are you?' I asked.

'I'm very, very well, my darling, and how are you?'

He's drunk, I thought, and immediately stopped smiling. 'Yes, I'm well, Tom. About to go to my bed, actually. Do you realise what time it is?'

'It's half past Clarissa o'clock,' he replied, and laughed. 'And I was wondering . . . I was wondering are you're up for cocktails tonight? We could share ingredients . . .'

'Tom, you're drunk. You need to go to bed. And anyway, where are you?'

'Where am I? Where do you want me to be? I can be anywhere you want me to be.' There was a clunk at that point and I realised he'd dropped the receiver.

'Hello . . . Clarissa?'

'Yes, I'm here.'

'But where is here?'

'Tom, you're not making any sense. I'm going to hang up now.'

'No, don't go. I need you. I need to hear your voice.'

'And why do you need to hear my voice? Have you no one to keep you company tonight? Is Venetia tired?'

'Clarissa, Clarissa—don't be like that.'

'Oh Tom, really, I think you need to drink some water.'

Then the line went dead, and I, too, put down the telephone.

The following morning he called again, apologising for his late-night call to me. It had been a long day, he said. 'Stuck in a bloody meeting.'

'I see,' I replied, waiting for him to say something.

'I'll be back in London tomorrow—and I wondered, can I take you out to dinner?'

CHAPTER THIRTY-NINE

We met for dinner two days later, at the Savoy. He was at the restaurant when I arrived, sitting smoking at the table, and looking rather anxious. As I walked towards him he turned, saw me, and immediately stood up. 'Hello, Tom,' I said and smiled. He stepped forward as though about to kiss me, then looked down and took my hand. And for a split second he was once again that shy, nervous boy in the ballroom at Deyning, unable to look me in the eye, or smile back at me. He hovered on his feet as the waiter pulled out my chair and I sat down. And then he, too, sat down, and immediately lit another cigarette.

'How's Venetia?' I asked. I couldn't help it. I was still angry.

He closed his eyes, shook his head. 'Please, can we not talk about Venetia tonight?'

'Oh yes, if it's private, of course . . .' I replied, looking down at the menu.

He sighed. Loudly. Sounding exasperated already.

We sat at a table tucked away in a corner, next to the window. And I was pleased. I could pretend to be distracted by anything beyond the glass, I thought, turning away from him and catching my own reflection. He didn't ask me what I'd like to drink, but summoned over the sommelier, ordered a glass of champagne and a whisky, and then a bottle of Château Lafite. But there was a particular year he wanted, which he couldn't seem to find on the list. He pulled out a pair of spectacles, perched them on his nose. And as the sommelier, the maître d' and another fluttered about him, I smiled. For they all knew his name, knew exactly who he was: Mr Cuthbert . . . Mr Cuthbert, they repeated, seemingly as many times as they could fit into a sentence without completely eliminating all other words. And I could tell he was used to it; long used to it.

When they finally dispersed, having identified and ascertained *Mr Cuthbert's* choice of wine for that evening, he removed his spectacles, looked over at me, sighed heavily, and smiled. 'So, Clarissa,' he began, 'do you realise how significant this day is?'

I shrugged; wondering if I'd forgotten some feast day or national holiday, then shook my head.

'This is our very first date.'

A *date*, I thought: so American. 'Oh, really. Is this a date then?'

'You know what I mean,' he said, turning his head away in mock exasperation. 'It's taken me . . .' he paused, staring at me. 'It's taken me sixteen years to get to this point . . . to take you out to dinner.'

'Yes, here we are, after all these years.'

The waiter appeared, placed our drinks upon the table. We raised our glasses. 'So, here's to us: Clarissa and Tom,' he said, smiling back at me. And it struck me then, he was in an unusual mood. One I didn't know, couldn't recall ever having seen before.

'Are we celebrating something?' I asked.

'Yes, we are. We're celebrating us. We're going to be very selfish this evening, because no one's going to claim either one of us; no one's waiting for you, or for me. And we're here. We're here together . . . after all these years.'

It was true enough. Every moment we'd been together, every single moment we'd managed to snatch in the preceding sixteen years, there'd always been someone somewhere, waiting for me, or for him.

I smiled. 'Like all our rendezvous,' I said.

'Down by the lake . . .'

'In the meadow . . .'

'At the boathouse . . .'

'Under the chestnut tree . . .'

'On the lawn . . .'

'By the ha-ha . . .'

'In the walled garden?'

'No! We never met there,' I said. 'That was always Mama's territory.'

He stubbed out his cigarette, shook his head. 'I remember the first time I set eyes on you. Just as though it was yesterday.'

'And so do I,' I replied quickly. 'It was in the ballroom at Deyning.'

He looked up at me. 'Wrong. *That's* when we were introduced. No, the first time I saw you, the very first time I set eyes on you, you were running through the garden, in the rain.' He looked away, remembering. 'You were shrieking, laughing, and you looked so completely free . . . a vision.' He paused, his eyes half closed, concentrating. 'You didn't see me, didn't notice me, but I saw you. I watched you, and I'd never seen anything or anyone as beautiful.'

'Yes, well, that was a long time ago . . .'

He shook his head. 'Feels like a moment ago.'

'You're right, sometimes it does. But then I remember . . . I remember all those who are no longer here. My brothers, my cousins, so many friends . . . and it all seems so long ago. Lifetimes ago.'

He stared back at me, into my eyes, and I began to feel that yearning once more: a yearning for another time and place, for him. He looked down at my hand resting on the table. 'But when I look at you I go back to that time, and I see you as you were that day.'

'Good!' I said, pulling my hand away. 'I think I'd far rather you saw me forever sixteen.'

He looked up at me. 'I see you as you are, Clarissa,' he said. 'I've always seen *who* you are.'

I'd taken a taxicab to the Savoy that evening, quietly practising my lines, what I wanted to tell him, all the way there; trying to anticipate his reaction and what I would say.

'Yes, Tom, that's right . . . we had a baby. Emily. She'll be almost twelve years old by now, and I need to find her . . . I need you to help me find her . . .'

But after one glass of champagne those rehearsed lines had already muddled themselves. And after another, I felt my edges begin to blur, my anger melt away into something else. Something far removed from the anger I'd carried with me into the Savoy earlier that evening. Each time I looked back into his eyes, that same desperate yearning returned, flooding my senses, drowning me. For he was still the boy I'd stood with by the lake. And I felt overwhelmed by sadness. Sadness at all the days and months and years that had been spent and were gone forever: sadness at the waste.

I noticed his hair, now greying at the temples of his brow; the lines around his eyes, upon his forehead; and as the waiter refilled our glasses, I excused myself and went to the powder room. I sat there for some time trying to remember the order of the words, what it was I had to say. What it was I wanted to tell him.

When I returned to the table his mood was noticeably lighter. He teased me, telling me he'd thought for a moment I'd gone, already bored of his company. But I knew, knew by the slight frown and the look in his eyes that he'd seen my sadness.

'So, how's business? How's the gallery doing?' he asked.

'Doing very well,' I replied. 'I'm extending it—into the shop next door.'

'That's wonderful, Clarissa,' he said, and I could tell he was being sincere.

'Tom,' I began, emboldened by alcohol, 'have you ever *seen* my gallery?'

He hesitated, pondered on that question for a moment. 'Yes,' he replied, 'yes, I think I do know it.'

'And have you purchased anything from me? And by that, I also mean through a third party.'

He laughed. 'Aha! What a question. What makes you ask that?'

'Because I have a few—or I seem to have a few—anonymous patrons,' I replied.

He glanced down at the table. 'I might have done.'

'Please, Tom, tell me the truth . . .'

'Yes. Yes, I have bought some paintings from you.'

'How many?' I asked.

'A few,' he replied, holding my gaze. 'Does it really matter how many?'

'No . . . no, I suppose not,' I said. But in a way it did. Was he one or all of the men who came in taxicabs and private cars to collect paintings?

We moved on. He asked me about Charlie. I spoke of my impending divorce and he talked about his. He said he felt no sadness, no bitterness, and that it had been wrong from the start. Said he'd known the day he was married that it wouldn't last.

'Why did you do it then?'

'Good question. I suppose at the time it seemed the obvious thing to do . . . everyone else was married. You were married.'

'But *you* didn't have to marry.'

'No, perhaps not, but I was lonely. I wanted to share my life with . . .' he paused, staring at me. 'What I wanted I couldn't have, so I compromised. And I've never been much good at compromise.'

'I thought you wanted children?'

'Yes, I suppose I did for a while, or there was a time when I thought I did. But after I married Nancy, I quickly realised I didn't, or perhaps not with her. And then . . . then we lost a baby. Anyway, it didn't happen, wasn't meant to be.' He lifted his glass to his lips and said, 'But what about you? You didn't have children either.'

And it stung.

'No, it didn't happen for me either,' I said looking down at my plate, pushing at a slice of carrot.

'Shame. I've always thought you'd make a wonderful mother.'

I looked up at him and smiled, and I pondered for a second or two, wondering what I should say. 'Yes, well, we can't have it all,' I said, repeating Rose's tidying-up phrase. I could have told him then, perhaps. And perhaps I had an opportunity, but it still didn't *feel* like the right moment. You see, I'd practised this for so long and in so many different locations, but we'd never been sitting there, in the Savoy—having dinner together. It had never been like that.

'And so . . . what about Venetia?' I asked. I had to. And you know, I really didn't want to. I didn't want to hear.

He leant back in his chair, smiling.

'Yes?' I said, staring back at him, waiting; blinking.

'You know, I think you ought to speak to Venetia yourself,' he said.

I shook my head. 'I don't. Quite frankly, Tom, I think it's rather pathetic.'

His smile broadened, and I could feel a simmering rising up inside of me again. I stared back at him, resolute, I thought; defiant. 'Yes, really rather pathetic,' I repeated.

He leant forward, his arms on the table. 'And what, exactly, is *rather pathetic*?'

I realised we were dangerously close to having a row, and on this, our first proper date, it seemed unfortunate to say the least. But I had to keep going; I had to persevere. After all, he'd stepped over a line, not me.

'That you and Venetia have been . . .'

'Yes?'

I shook my head, sighed. 'That you're carrying on with someone old enough to be your mother, Tom.'

He laughed, and continued to laugh for quite a while. 'Clarissa,' he said at last, reaching over for my hand, but I pulled it away.

'No! Don't. Please don't. I saw you together, I know, Tom.'

He sat back in his chair and sighed loudly. 'You know, you're head's always so *bloody* muddled, Clarissa.' And I was really rather astounded, because he suddenly sounded quite angry. 'It's not something I wish to talk about with you here, tonight,' he continued, 'I think *you* need to speak to your godmother; you need to talk to Venetia. And then . . . then perhaps we'll resume this conversation.'

I felt more than a little chastened. He had spoken to me like one of his employees, I thought—one who'd perhaps stepped out of line.

'Fine,' I said. 'And yes, I shall. I shall do that.'

We sat in silence for a while, drinking our wine, each of us staring across the room. *It's a disaster . . . it's a disaster*, I thought. *We have nothing in common any more. He's turned into a monster; one of those rich playboys Mama loves to hate*. I glanced at him, saw him close his eyes. *He's hating this: he'd rather be with her, Venetia*. Then I caught his eye, and he smiled, but I looked away, across the restaurant floor.

'Please, Clarissa, can we . . . shall we be friends?'

I turned to him. 'Yes, of course.'

He smiled again, but I could sense something more in his smile: amusement, I thought.

He ordered a brandy, and I wondered how Venetia coped with his drinking. She hardly touched a drop herself. And I saw them again, in her dressing room, upon the daybed: Tom, tie undone; his head to her bosom.

No!

He must have seen me wince, must have seen something in my expression, because he leant forward at that moment and said, 'Please . . . trust me, believe me. There is nothing between Venetia and me . . . other than a mutual interest.'

Later, when we left the restaurant, he suggested that we go dancing, but I didn't want to.

'I think I should get home, Tom,' I said.

'Then please, at least allow me to see you home.'

I wasn't sure. I was still irked by the thought of him and Venetia, and whatever it was going on between them. But I had to tell him about Emily, and I knew it was a conversation we had to have alone, in private.

CHAPTER FORTY

We took a taxicab back to my flat, sitting in silence, side by side, and as we turned into my street, I said, 'Would you like to come in for a nightcap . . . a coffee?'

I realised how it sounded, and I was nervous, so much so that I couldn't get my key into the lock, and eventually had to admit defeat and hand it to him. And it felt strange opening the door on to my small, singular world, walking into my home with him. I saw him look about the hallway, taking it all in. In the sitting room, as I took off my coat and shoes, he wandered about the place, glancing up at the paintings on the wall; bending down to view a photograph, picking one up.

'Rather different to Deyning,' I said.

'But you've made it beautiful . . . as only you could,' he replied, loosening his tie. I turned away from him, walked into the kitchen to fill the kettle, and as I lifted it I heard him collapse into an armchair with a loud sigh. When I returned to the room he'd closed his eyes, and I thought perhaps he was about to leave me, drift off into an alcohol-induced slumber.

No, please, don't fall asleep . . . not now . . .

I sat down on the rug by his feet. Was it the right moment? Would it be a huge shock? Would he be angry, walk out?

'I need to talk to you, Tom,' I said, quietly, wondering if he could still hear my words. 'I need to tell you something . . .'

And with his eyes still closed, he said, 'Yes, I know, and I'm longing to hear.'

I was confused. Had he some idea of what it was I was about to tell him? No, it was impossible, surely: the only two people who knew were Mama and myself. But my mind raced on into a freefall of possibilities. Had Mama told Venetia and she in turn told Tom? *A mutual interest*, he'd said.

At that moment the kettle began to whistle, and I jumped to my feet and returned to the kitchen.

That night . . . that night in the park . . . well, we had a baby, Tom . . . yes, that's right, we had a baby.

'We had a baby,' I whispered, stirring the coffee.

I walked back into the room, handed him his cup and saucer and sat down on the floor once more. He moved in his chair and I turned to look up at him. He stared back at me, raised his eyebrows expectantly. 'So . . . are you going to tell me why my mother came to see you—or not?'

I gasped: a strange mix of surprise, frustration and relief. I'd entirely forgotten about Tom's mother's meeting with me, or the fact that I'd inadvertently mentioned it to him in the theatre that evening. And here I was, my heart racing, my mind entirely focused on telling him about his daughter; now forced to tell him of his unknown father.

'Well, that was what you were about to tell me, wasn't it?' he asked, looking a little bemused by my hesitation.

I turned away. 'Yes, of course . . . that's what I was about to tell you.'

I closed my eyes for a moment, steadying myself; realising Emily would have to wait a little longer.

But I wasn't altogether sure how or where to begin about that day, the day his mother came to see me.

Begin at the beginning . . .

'She wanted to talk to me about you,' I said, shuffling nearer to his chair, allowing myself to lean against it, against him.

'And?'

Just tell him. Be honest . . .

'She told me you loved me, and that . . .' I paused, unsure how to navigate from there.

'That what?'

'That you'd always loved me.'

I was half expecting a shrug, a joke, a witty quip,

but he said nothing.

I reached up, took hold of his hand. 'And she told me about your father, Tom.'

'Ah, my father . . . I see. So she came to see you to tidy up a few loose ends then.'

'I suppose she did in a way, yes. She wanted someone to know the truth; someone who cared, cared about you.'

I paused, waiting for him to say something, but he said nothing.

'Your father, Tom . . . your father was the Earl, Earl Deyning.'

I turned and looked up at him. He stared at me.

'So, I'm the bastard son of the old Earl . . .'

'Tom!'

'Well, really, what a lot of codswallop.'

'No, it's not . . . it's the truth. Why do you say that?'

'Why do I say it? Because, my darling, what does it matter now?' He shrugged. 'I am who I am. I wasn't good enough to marry you . . . wasn't good enough to be part of the Granville family. I think it's rather funny, don't you? I mean funny in an ironic way, of course.'

He was right. We'd lost so many years. And really, what did it matter?

'Truly, it means nothing to me, not now,' he continued. 'Perhaps if someone had told me ten years ago . . . or even before the War, when I needed to know *who* I was, what I was . . . where I fitted in, it would have meant something, but no, not now. And anyway, I realised a long, long time ago that I'd probably been born out of wedlock. My mother was never able to furnish me with any information about my father—other than the fact

I looked like him—so I assumed they'd been . . .' he shrugged, 'ships in the night, so to speak. And then there was the small matter of who'd paid for my education, where the money had come from to get me through university.' He paused, shook head. 'And other monies . . . quite sizeable amounts, which my dear mother could never explain. I had my suspicions, of course, and I imagine so did quite a few others.' He paused again. 'I suppose the greatest irony of it all is that I ended up purchasing my birthright, Deyning. Although that was only ever because of you, and nothing to do with any notions of grandeur on my part.'

'Because of me?'

He looked down at me. 'Yes. I thought if I could buy back Deyning, if I could present you with what you'd lost, what you loved most in the world, I might just win you back. It was a simple enough plan. All I had to do was make money.' He paused, smiling at me, and then added, 'And let's face it, I've been rather good at that.'

'Yes, you have been rather good at that.'

'I didn't—perhaps couldn't—foresee the complications . . . your mother, your marriage, your life with Charlie . . . my inability to be on my own. I thought I'd be able wriggle out of any liaison as soon as I had a sign from you. And then, when you didn't come to Southampton, when you didn't appear—well, I thought that was a pretty clear sign.'

'Oh Tom . . .' I looked away. I didn't want to think of that day, that time; my agony, his agony.

'Strange how life turns out, isn't it?' he continued. 'And here I am . . . Tom *Deyning*. How very apt that I decided to call my company

Cuthbert-Deyning . . . maybe I do have foresight, after all.'

For some minutes he remained silent, staring just beyond me with narrowed eyes. As though, despite what he said, despite his somewhat flippant, cynical reaction, he needed a moment's reflection: a moment to cogitate upon the details of his birth, his mother and now, suddenly, his father. He moved his head back, looked up at the ceiling and sighed. 'So my mother and the Earl, eh? The lord and his servant . . . rather a cliché, don't you agree?'

'She loved him, I think . . . truly loved him.'

He moved his head, stared down at me. 'True love, it knows no boundaries, does it?'

'No. It knows no boundaries,' I repeated. I wasn't sure what he meant, whether he was referring to his parents, or to us, but I could sense his sadness. And as I lifted his hand, still held in mine, I could hear the drift of his thoughts, the word *cliché* echoing.

'Perhaps all love is a cliché, Tom,' I said. 'Every love . . . apart from ours.'

He looked down at me and smiled, and right at that moment my heart sang out for that smile.

'So . . . tell me, did you buy *all* of my paintings?' I said, longing to see him smile again. And he laughed.

'No! I have not bought *all* of your bloody paintings. Though, as you're being so persistent, I can tell you I happen to have a fair few.'

'And is Pritchard one of your employees?'

'Really, you're impossible,' he said, turning away from me for a moment.

'Well?'

'Well what?'

'Is he?'

'Yes, yes he is. Happy now?'

I released his hand, placed my head against his knee, and we sat like that for some time, without either of us uttering a word.

'It's late. I should let you get to your bed,' he said at last, and as he rose to his feet, he added, 'So . . . dinner, tomorrow night?'

I stood up. 'Yes,' I said, 'sounds lovely.'

He put his arms around me, pulled me to him. 'Where would you like to go?'

'Oh, I don't know . . . you choose.'

We didn't kiss. We walked through to the hallway holding hands, and at the door, he said, 'I'll pick you up at seven thirty.' He lifted each of my hands to his lips in turn and kissed them. 'Sweet dreams, Clarissa.'

As he moved through the doorway, he stopped, looked back at me:

'A bientôt.'

CHAPTER FORTY-ONE

I had to know what had taken place between Venetia and Tom. Had they been lovers, or was there something else between them? Was it possible, I wondered, for a passionate yet platonic love to exist between a man and woman; one that needed no expression in physical adoration; one free from all sensual desire? All I'd known was passionate love: a single overwhelming force directing me to one person, one man. And it could never be platonic, never be a friendship. It had shaped my world, consumed my senses.

As I drove to Venetia's house that morning I pondered upon this; and as I passed along the edge of Hyde Park, I realised that my love for Tom was and always had been reflected in everything around me. For every place I knew continued to reverberate and echo with it. As though an imprint—something of *it*—had been left in the atmosphere. And that verdant expanse of central London, the place I'd returned to so often, and for so many years my unlikely refuge, had once again changed its form: the trees had pulled back their shadows, and the road around them—as broad as my vision.

I parked directly outside Venetia's house, walked up the steps and rang the doorbell. I had no recollection of the young maid who answered the door, so I said, 'Good morning, I'm Mrs Cooper's goddaughter, Clarissa Boyd. Is Mrs Cooper at home?' Of course I knew she would be.

'Is she expecting you, ma'am?'

I smiled. 'No, she isn't, but I'm sure she'll be quite happy to receive me.'

The maid led me up to the salon on the first floor. Venetia—always fatigued by the commonplace and with a lifelong hankering after the exotic—disliked English words, particularly at home. She could never have tolerated anything so unimaginative as a drawing room in her house. Everything had to be French; the salon, the chambre, the hall d'entrée, la cave, and, of course, *never* the lavatory—always the toilette.

As I waited for her to come down, for it wasn't quite eleven and I knew she didn't normally rise until around that hour, I perused the invitations propped up around the oversized ormolu clock on the mantelshelf. The room itself was testament to my godmother's character and style, a European style: a large Louis XV settee, and French Empire chairs upholstered in jewel-coloured velvets; an Italian specimen marble table, and an Empire centre table adorned with framed miniatures and photographs; against the wall, between the three tall windows, two marble-topped bombe commodes with matching gilt-framed mirrors above each; and opposite, Venetia's escritoire, where she penned her many and various letters, notes, and RSVPs. And an eclectic collection of oil paintings, watercolours and sketches of all sizes hung from picture rails against the dark gold wallpaper.

'Clarissa!'

She was wearing what appeared to be an Arabian costume: a kaftan—of sorts, full length, with a pearl-encrusted headband around her hair, and armfuls of silver bracelets.

I moved over to her, kissing each powdered cheek. 'I've been meaning to call on you for so long,' I said. 'Too long.'

'Yes, too long . . . and it's a delight to see you, my dear,' she said, as she sat down, 'but isn't it rather early for you to be out and about making calls?'

There was no point beating around the bush. I had come on a mission.

I sat down opposite her, cleared my throat. 'Yes, it is a little early and I apologise, but I need to speak with you about something . . . something perhaps a little delicate.'

She looked worried for a moment. 'I see.'

'It's about Tom . . . Tom Cuthbert.'

'Ah, yes of course. Tom.' She smiled, seemed quite relieved as she relaxed back into her chair.

'I know he's been calling on you, Venetia.' I looked down, away from her eyes. 'I know that you and he have a . . . a friendship, you see, and I need to know . . .' I hesitated, and she immediately spoke.

'You wish to know why he's been to see me?' she said, in a perfectly matter-of-fact manner.

I looked up at her, nodded. 'Yes, yes that's right, I do.'

She stood up, walked over to the table in the centre of the room and opened a silver cigarette box. 'And, of course, you have every right to know, dear . . .' She placed a cigarette into a long black holder, lifted it to her lips. 'Every right,' she said again, tilting her head and blowing a plume of smoke towards the chandelier above her. Then she sat back down, turned to me, and asked, 'But first, would you like something . . . tea, coffee?'

'No, no thank you. I have to be at Mama's by twelve,' I said. I had promised to call in on my mother to help her select yet another painting to put into auction.

'Tom . . . Tom Cuthbert,' she said, staring at me, 'came to me for advice, Clarissa.'

'Oh really. And advice on what, exactly?'

She smiled. 'Well, advice on *you* of course, dear.'

'Me?'

She laughed. 'Yes, why on earth else would Tom Cuthbert call on me? And I have to say, I knew the moment he appeared why he'd come!'

'And . . .'

'He wants you!' she said, dramatically. 'Wants to win you back *and* have your Mama's blessing.'

'But what did he tell you, what did he say?'

'Oh, he told me he'd heard about you and

Charlie, but he said he'd always known that you didn't love Charlie because . . . because you love him.' She paused, smiling at me rather coquettishly, her eyes twinkling. 'He told me that he, too, was getting divorced, and that he had plenty enough money to look after you . . . but one thing, *one thing*,' she repeated with emphasis, 'still stood in his way.'

'Mama.'

She nodded. 'He wished me to speak with your mother, talk to her, persuade her . . .' She stared at me, her violet eyes brighter than ever, and then she reached out for my hand. 'He loves you very much, Clarissa.' And as she gripped my hand, I felt a tear make its way slowly down my cheek, into my mouth. 'You see, he understands, he knows that you won't—can't—do anything without your mama's approval or blessing. That's why he came to me.'

'And . . . and have you . . .'

'Yes, I have. I've spoken with your mother. Oh, she knows nothing of Tom's visit to me, nor can she ever. But I have spoken with her, and at some length, and I think . . . I think she sees things a little differently now. We've all changed, life has changed, and you . . . well, my darling, you deserve to be happy. More than anything else, you deserve to be happy.'

I looked down into my lap. 'But I wonder if Mama thinks that.'

'Of course your mother wants you to be happy! My dear, she loves you . . . you're her daughter, her precious, precious daughter. But she was always so protective of you, so very protective, she *and* your father. They only ever wanted the best for you.'

I moved forward in my chair, sat up, straight-backed. 'So tell me, what do I do from here?'

'You must speak to your mother. You must have a conversation with her, a difficult conversation perhaps, but one that's long overdue. I can do no more.'

'He's a good man, Venetia, but I think you know that.'

'Oh yes, I do know that. I most *certainly* know that,' she replied, with great emphasis once again. Then she glanced across at me with a new expression, half frowning, quizzical.

'What? What is it?' I asked.

She looked away, her eyes scanning the room, searching for words. 'Has he . . . has Tom mentioned anything to you regarding Henry?' she asked, her eyes focused back upon me.

'Henry?' I shook my head. 'No, why would he?'

She sighed. 'Oh dear.' She closed her eyes for a moment. 'I do so loathe all this skulking about and subterfuge,' she said, shaking her head.

'What subterfuge . . . what is it about Henry? Does Tom know something? Does Tom know where Henry is?'

She stared at me, wide eyed. 'My dear, Tom Cuthbert has been *keeping* your brother these past two years.'

'Keeping . . . I don't understand. What do you mean?'

'Henry is in New York, Clarissa, and has been for some time,' she said quickly, and then stopped.

'New York?'

'Yes, but I must add—have to add—that I only discovered this myself quite recently. And Tom doesn't wish you to know, or not yet, it would seem. He said he'd tell you all in *good time* . . . once Henry was quite recovered and back on his feet.' She paused again, pursing her lips, then continued, 'It was Henry who found Tom, not the other way round, of course. At that time Tom had no idea, absolutely no idea that Henry had left England . . . vanished!' She threw her hands in the air with a jangling, tinkling sound. 'He simply turned up there one day, at Cuthbert-Deyning's Manhattan office . . . and looking like a hobo, from all accounts.'

'I see. And what is it he's recovering from?' I asked. 'Obviously not amnesia.'

'Oh my dear, you must try not to be angry, nor must you breathe a word of this to your poor mama. It seems he'd become embroiled in some sort of . . . illegal importation scam. I don't know the details—nor do I wish to—but I do know he was in a mess, a rather frightful mess, but as far as I understand, he's much better now. And he's working, my dear, working for Tom—in his New York office,' she added, smiling at me brightly.

I looked down at the floor, closed my eyes.

Henry.

Yes, he'd have known, known immediately he saw the name Cuthbert-Deyning; known it was Tom, known he'd lend him money . . . *just till I'm sorted, old chap.*

'I knew he'd turn up sooner or later, but I never imagined . . .'

'No.'

I explained to Venetia that I'd have to tell Mama something; I had to let her know Henry was alive, and well. She made me promise that I wouldn't mention her name, and that I shouldn't say anything to Tom, but should wait for him to tell me.

I rose from my chair, moved over to her and kissed her. 'Thank you . . . thank you, Venetia.'

She began to laugh, tearfully. 'Oh my dear, you have nothing to thank me for, truly. Whatever I've done—whatever I have said—should have been said years ago. But some of us acquire wisdom later than others,' she added. 'I only wish I could go back upon my life with what I now know.' She looked up at me. 'Wouldn't that be a marvellous thing?'

CHAPTER FORTY-TWO

I wasn't sure how to begin that conversation with Mama; that so long overdue conversation. And yet I felt no fear, no sense of dread, for I had already determined what I would do, with or without my mother's approval.

We selected not one but two paintings for auction, which Mama then asked Wilson and another maid to remove from the wall and wrap, and we discussed which pictures could be moved, hung in their place. She seemed strangely happy to be relieved of yet more 'paraphernalia'—as she'd taken to calling all of her furniture and possessions now. And I suggested to her that she shouldn't sell anything else; not for a while, at least, I said. But the place remained over-furnished. For Mama, Deyning Park and Berkeley Square had all converged there, into a cramped emporium of cluttered surfaces, and antiques much too large and ostentatious for their modest abode.

As we sat down, she said, 'And so, are you staying to lunch?'

She didn't speak, but kept her hand to her brow, covering her eyes as though dazzled by a very bright light somewhere close to where I sat.

'Mama . . .'

She lowered her hand. 'I did what I thought was best, Clarissa,' she said, opening her eyes and staring down into her lap. 'I did what I thought was right. It was not the way . . . not possible . . .'

I rose from my chair, moved across the room and sat down upon the velvet ottoman in front of her. 'I know, I know you did what you thought was right . . . but perhaps, perhaps in hindsight you're able to see that it wasn't right.' I reached out, took hold of her hand. 'Look at me, look at my life. I've one failed, childless and unhappy marriage behind me. I have nothing, nothing to lose . . . and everything to gain. My heart has been constant, and so has his. And the world . . . the world *is* changed.'

She nodded. Then she said, 'And does he know? Does he know about . . .'

'Emily. Her name was Emily, Mama,' I said. 'No, no he doesn't, not yet. But I intend to tell him. He has to know. He has a right to know.'

'And then what?'

'*Then* . . . I'm not entirely sure. But I shan't leave him. Not for you, or anyone else.'

She didn't look at me and, though I waited for her to speak, she said nothing.

'You once told me that you'd loved someone, someone other than Papa . . .'

She sighed. 'That was a long time ago,' she replied. 'And it was . . . it was impossible . . .'

'Impossible—like Tom and me?'

She looked up at me at last, and my heart ached for her. You see, I no longer felt any anger towards her, none at all, only sadness and regret at all the years we'd lied to each other. Always pretending, hanging on bravely to the idea of what we should be, how we should be, each of us burdened by the knowledge of our hearts.

Then she spoke. 'His name was Edward,' she said, glancing away from me once more.

'Edward,' I repeated.

And I don't know why or how, but at that moment a montage of images suddenly surfaced in my memory: I saw them emerging through the gateway of the walled garden, Mama smiling, turning to look up at him, reluctant to leave his side; I saw them standing together in the hothouse, discussing exhibits for a flower show, looking into each other's eyes as though their lives depended upon some silly rosette; and I saw them once more as they disappeared down the driveway, Mama waving back at me, more animated than ever. Edina and Edward.

Edward Broughton . . .

And in the instant of unravelling, it all fell into place. I remembered the day we left Deyning, when Mama had wept. Her tears had never been about leaving Deyning. I thought of my arrangement with him, regarding Tom's letters: Broughton had been my accomplice, my partner in crime. Had he been the one who'd told Mama? Had he felt duty bound to tell her? Or had he simply seen a pattern of events, a mirroring of situation and circumstance? Something he couldn't have; something she couldn't have.

By the end of the War he'd disappeared from our lives for ever, and I couldn't recall my mother ever having mentioned him. But Mrs Cuthbert had;

she'd told me he'd gone back to the West Country, where he had family, and she'd spoken of that family too . . . *rather well-to-do* . . . he'd been the black sheep, she'd said. Now I remembered. But at the time I'd not listened, for my head had been so full of Tom, Tom and me.

'Edward,' I said again.

And I saw once more the King's ring upon her finger, her wedding finger, and the initials—quite clearly now: EB. It was his ring, his signet ring. He'd given it to her, a symbol of his identity, just as surely as he'd given her his heart.

She turned to me. 'It wasn't sordid, Clarissa. There was nothing tawdry about it.'

'No. No, I'm sure.'

But at that moment I thought of Papa, and felt a ripple of guilt at my mother's duplicity. Had he known? I wondered. Had he suspected?

'He was different . . .' she continued, wistfully. 'And he cared about me, cared about me deeply . . . I was lonely, you see. Your father was away so much, and I . . . well, I enjoyed his company,' she added, glancing at me. 'He was an educated man . . . without any arrogance at all.'

I closed my eyes for a moment. Of course, I thought, of course she'd been lonely. And I had seen it, known it, and then forgotten it. That ineffable, unspeakable sadness about her had been pushed away, denied, and replaced by an enigmatic beauty, unfathomable, unreachable, and simply called *Mama*.

I wanted to say the name Broughton, wanted to say it out loud and see what would happen, but I knew it had to come from her. It would have been somehow altogether wrong and inappropriate for me to speak that name, at that moment, and it seemed to belong to her now. Oh, I could have challenged her, spoken of hypocrisy and double standards, but what was the point? Nothing could alter the past, and I'd made up my mind, she knew that. I imagine that's why she finally allowed herself to say the name. It was her way of holding out the proverbial olive branch. And though she wasn't prepared to give up that secret entirely, she'd finally shared something of herself with me.

She altered tempo and moved on, telling me once again that she had no regrets, that she'd loved my father first and foremost; that life was about compromise, and that we can't always have everything we wish for. 'And anyway,' she concluded, with a heavy sigh, 'I had you to think of. And my children . . . have been my life.'

I wanted to tell her about Henry, but I wasn't sure how she'd receive the news. And yet it had to be, I had to tell her. And in that atmosphere of openness and honesty, it seemed the perfect time. So I took a deep breath, and told her that Henry was alive, and well, living in New York, and working for Tom; that Tom had been looking after him these past two years. Not surprisingly, she was startled by the news at first, and then somewhat confused. She asked me questions: how had Henry found Tom? But *where*, exactly, was he living? Why had he not written? When was he coming home? What did Tom say? I couldn't tell her that it was Venetia, and not Tom, who had told me all of this. And so I said that I really didn't know any more, but I would, of course, speak to Tom and find out Henry's address.

Before I left my mother that day, as I was putting

on my coat and hat, she asked me to wait a moment and then left the room. When she reappeared, clutching a small tapestry bag—one with curved faux bamboo handles, which I remembered from when I was young as having been her petit point bag—she simply handed it to me without any words.

'What's this?' I asked, smiling. 'You know I don't sew—or embroider . . .'

She didn't reply, but pointed, gesturing for me to open it.

I unclipped the bag, peered inside, then reached into it and lifted out a handful of unopened letters. There must have been twenty or more, each one addressed to Miss C. Granville, c/o E. Broughton, 2 Stable Cottages, Deyning Park; all in Tom's unmistakable hand. And I burst into tears at the sight of my name. For how many days and weeks and months had I waited, longing to see those words: my name and a letter from him?

She came forward, her arms outstretched. 'I'm sorry,' she said, falteringly. 'Forgive me.'

* * *

We didn't go out to dine that evening. By the time Tom arrived to collect me, I'd read all of the letters, once, twice, some three times. I'd gone back to those dark days, been with him in the trenches, and at Gallipoli, and Passchendaele. And so, that night, when I opened the door to him, saw him standing there, I fell into his arms—weeping.

He held me, asking me over and over what had happened, then led me back to the sitting room, and sat down with me on the sofa, and I told him about my conversation with Mama, about Broughton, and about his letters—still strewn across the floor. He rose to his feet, took off his jacket and tie, gathered up a few of the letters, and sat back down with me. And with my body curled up to him, my arms wrapped around him, my face pressed against his chest, he glanced through them, and then read some in silence, and some out loud to me: 'Last week, another young boy in my battalion was shot. He'd become hysterical, lost his nerve and couldn't face going back into the line. He was tied to what was once a tree . . . a piece of white cloth pinned over his heart . . .'

And though exhausted from that journey back in time, and from weeping, I couldn't seem to stop crying. So he said things like, 'Better late than never, eh?' and, 'At least you know now that I wrote,' and commented upon his spelling and grammar—in a bid to make me smile. But I could see, I could see as he pondered on his own long-forgotten words, that it was difficult for him too; that he was being strong only for me.

'I somehow managed to drag him through the mud and back to the trench, but he'd been hit in the stomach and for almost an hour he lay in my arms—crying for his mother. He'd told them . . . told them he was eighteen, but I very much doubt he was even sixteen . . . *Norton*.'

Eventually, he picked me up and carried me through to the bedroom. He lay down next to me on the bed, his head propped in one hand, watching me.

'Don't look at me, I look hideous,' I said, for I'd been crying for hours and was exhausted by the emotion of that day, and the previous night.

He shook his head. 'You could never look hideous, never,' he replied, smiling at me, stroking my cheek. His touch was balm to my senses: more blissful and calming than any morphia or pills. And for a moment I contemplated telling him then and there about the morphia, about that time, when I'd stood alone at the very edge of the abyss. I wanted him to know, and he had to know—had to know everything, all of me. But not now; I couldn't go back there at that moment. It could wait.

'Please . . . read some more,' I said.

And so we lay there, together, and he read out more of his words from that time. I listened to his voice. 'Home, it has become an ideal, like heaven, inhabited by angels. A place we dream about . . . and speak of and long for . . .'

I closed my eyes, felt his hand move over my hair . . . felt myself drifting . . .

I looked up at the ceiling. The little dark-haired girl appeared. She said, 'I'm not coming down, Clarissa. I have to stay here now.'

I opened my eyes, glanced up at him, still reading out loud, quietly.

'Are you going to tell him? Are you going to tell him about me?'

'Yes, yes . . . of course, but not now. A little later.'

'You say that all the time . . .'

'But I'm tired . . . so tired. I'll tell him later, I promise.'

I felt cold, opened my eyes. 'Tom?'

He was on his feet, next to me, undressing me.

'You need to sleep,' he said.

'Don't go . . . don't leave me.'

He got down on to his knees, his face level with mine, took my head in his hands. 'I'm not leaving . . .

I'll never leave you.'

'No,' I said. 'Don't ever leave me.'

I felt a warmth come up over me, then the tucking in; the sound of water—a tap; a click, darkness; and then his body next to me, his arms around me.

'Tell him about me, Clarissa; you have to tell him about me.'

'Come down . . . come down and I'll tell him.'

'I can't come down. Not now. I have to stay here now.'

And then she moved away, disappeared from view.

Hours later, as daylight crept into the room, I was stirred by the warmth of kisses, along my shoulder, the back of my neck, my spine. I turned, and in the dim light I saw his face and knew it hadn't been a dream. He was there, in my bed; he was with me. And when we kissed, I felt myself pulled back: I was at the boathouse by the lake; I was in the darkness of night in Hyde Park; I was in an Arabian tent, and I was his once more.

'Promise me you'll never leave me . . .'

'I promise. I promise I'll never leave you.'

CHAPTER FORTY-THREE

We'd been to the theatre, and afterwards dined at the Criterion. And it was he who brought up that night in the park, the night we'd first made love. He was in a provocative mood, playful, trying to embarrass me, I think. But he couldn't, of course. That's one of the few benefits of ageing; it becomes almost impossible to be embarrassed by one's misspent youth, simply because we later revel in those early misdemeanours.

'You know, you really were rather wicked,' he said, leaning forward, smiling.

'Wicked? No, I don't think so.'

'Do you remember what you pushed into my pocket—that night at Jimmy's party?'

I smiled. 'Yes . . . yes, I do.'

He raised his eyebrows. 'I shan't tell you what happened to the garment in question.'

'Ha! So you want me to know . . .'

He leant back in his chair, studying me. Then he lit a cigarette and watched it as it burned in the ashtray.

'Well?' I said. 'Are you going to tell me?'

He glanced up at me, his head tilted to one side. Then he bit on his lip, pondering, wondering. 'I must have relived that night a thousand times and more in my head.'

'Yes, and so have I.'

'You know, I still have your glove as well,' he said, breaking into a smile.

But all I could think about was her, our daughter; the child conceived that night, in the middle of a war. And I knew I had to tell him. I wanted to tell him. I longed to be able to talk to someone about Emily, to speak her name out loud, at last; for her to be acknowledged by someone; and who better than her own father? But there was no way I could raise this subject in a restaurant, surrounded by people, strangers. So, when we returned to my flat, as we sat together with our nightcaps, I took that leap.

'I need to tell you something, Tom; something about that night.'

'Mm, what's that, my darling?' he replied, without turning to look at me.

'After that night, that night in the park . . .'

'Yes . . .'

Here it was at last, my moment. I knew I had to say the words clearly, precisely, slowly, calmly:

'I had a baby.'

There, that was it. I'd said it. I'd finally said it. *I had a baby*.

Those four words, locked up for so long, were finally uttered. And I think he thought he'd misheard me.

'What? Who had a baby?'

'I did.'

'*You* had a baby?'

'Yes, yes, I did. I had a baby,' I said, eagerly, as though I'd been waiting a lifetime to confirm this fact. 'We had a baby, Tom.'

I was sitting on the very edge of my armchair and he'd been lounging on the floor, his back pressed against it. He sat up, turned on to his knees and faced me, and his confusion, his shock, was palpable and seemed to fill the room.

He looked at me: astonished, dumbstruck. '*We* had a baby?'

'I had a baby,' I repeated half laughing, and beginning to cry at the same time.

Perhaps I'd thought I could tell him, talk about it all in a perfunctory way. It had all happened so very long ago. Perhaps I'd thought I'd be able to recite dates, facts, as though I was clearing up something almost akin to a business matter.

'I had a baby,' I said again, like a record stuck. And as I said those four words they tore open my heart, and I heard myself say them again. 'I had a baby.'

'Clarissa . . . what are you telling me? We had a child? We have a child?'

'Yes. We had a child, Tom. I named her Emily . . . after Emily Brontë,' I added, remembering. 'She was born on November the twelfth, nineteen seventeen . . . in Plymouth. She was born in Devon,' I said, trying to remember how I'd planned it; how I'd planned to tell him.

I looked directly at him as I spoke, but as his image blurred, my head began to shake, as though I was telling him something and saying 'no' at the same time.

'A *daughter*? You had a *baby*, Clarissa?' he said, repeating words, checking facts, staring at me.

'I had a baby,' I said again, his face barely visible. And then I heard myself say it again, and again: *I had a baby . . . I had a baby . . .*

He stood up, moved to the fireplace, his back to me, and I saw him grip the marble mantelshelf. Then, suddenly, he was in front of me, and once more on his knees.

'You had a baby,' he said, looking at me, into my eyes. '*We* have a child . . .'

I nodded my head, and I couldn't stop nodding my head. 'Yes, yes, we did . . . we do,' I said.

He stared at me, searching my face as though he'd find every answer hidden there. Then he took my head in his hands and said, 'But why . . . why did I not know? Why did you not tell me this?'

I can't remember now what, exactly, I told him about the events of that year, but I told him everything there was to tell. Everything I could remember. I told him about my mother, Aunt Maude, Edith Collins, St Anne's—and the moment

I'd handed over Emily. And by the time I'd finished he'd covered his face with his hands. And so I lowered myself down on to the floor and held him.

'I'm so sorry,' I said. 'I'm so very sorry.'

He looked up at me, his face contorted. 'No . . . No,' he shook his head. 'I'm sorry . . . I'm sorry that you went through all of this alone, without me. I'm sorry that I was not there for you—for her. I'm sorry that you've carried this with you for so long. That I . . .' and he began to pull at his hair. 'That I quizzed you on why you'd never had children.' He stared at me, his face crumpled; defeated. 'And that's who *Emily* was . . .' he said. 'There was no imaginary friend . . . Emily's our child.'

I nodded.

That night we lay awake, frozen in each other's arms; each of us searching for that inaccessible moment in our past; the point to which we could return and then perhaps somehow change our now. The point to which we could return, reclaim our child, and from there rewrite our story, her story. How it *could* have been . . . how it should have been. Unlike me, Tom had lived his life without ever knowing he had a child. By withholding that information I'd spared him from the slow and steady stream of loss, a meandering trickle of dates and reminders, only to submerge him in the deluge of one almighty torrent.

The next morning, each of us weakened and spent by grief, he told me that he was going to find her. And it became his consuming passion for the next few weeks. But it proved more difficult than he'd anticipated.

'Perhaps she doesn't want us to find her,' I said to him one evening.

'No, we'll find her,' he said, turning to me and smiling. 'I've already put Goddard on to it.'

'But we might not find her, Tom. We might not . . .'

He stared at me, ran a finger across my forehead, down my cheek. 'I'll find her, my darling,' he repeated. 'I'll find her,' he said again.

* * *

. . . Yesterday I sat alone and reread all of your notes & letters to me. I put them all in chronological order, & then jumbled them up again . . . so that one day, they might be a treasure trail of clues—should anyone be interested! We did have such a perfect, heavenly time, didn't we, that last summer?

CHAPTER FORTY-FOUR

There's an old white gate at the end of the avenue of my dreams. It's where I sit and watch the world pass by. From there I see my brothers go off to war. From there I see my daughter, playing in a distant field. And from there I see my love, walking back to me.

Unbeknown to me, Tom hadn't just *put Goddard on to it*: he'd put quite a few people on to the task of tracing our daughter. But it was Oliver Goddard who later told me the pieces of the story Tom couldn't bring himself to tell me. It was Oliver who told me that he and Tom had driven down to Plymouth, to speak with the sisters at St Anne's.

And it was Oliver who'd tell me so many parts of the story Tom would never speak of.

They'd been gone overnight. Tom had told me he had business in Bristol, but he'd telephoned me late in the evening. I'd missed him, and told him so. And he said, 'But it's only one night, darling. I think we can cope with one night apart . . .'

It's strange to me, even now, the thought of him retracing my steps; moving through the silent passageways of St Anne's; glancing out of those narrow windows, so many years after I'd been there. For that time seems more than a lifetime ago, and my recollection of it—and the place itself—is hazy. Like the remembrance of a dream, there are gaps I know I shall never be able to fill. Oh, I can still see a girl, the girl I once was, sitting in a room, staring out through a window, but somehow it's not me, for I was never *really* there. I was always with him.

Oliver told me that St Anne's had kept records on everyone who'd passed through their doors: the date of arrival, due date of baby, and room assigned. There were no medical notes of course, only the most basic of information. And apparently the place was quite empty of *fallen women*. Different to during the War, one of the sisters had said, by way of explanation. Tom had asked to see my room, and then asked if he could have a moment there on his own. So Oliver and the young sister had waited outside the closed door, in the hallway, in silence. By the time they left St Anne's they had the name and address of an adoption agency. Mission accomplished, Oliver said. They'd returned to London without stopping, and when Tom came into the flat that evening he'd rushed over to me, to where I was standing in the kitchen, taken me into his arms and said, 'I'm never going to leave you again, not even for one night.' He pulled me tighter. 'I want to see your face each night before I fall asleep, and every morning when I awake. And one day, one day when I take my last breath,' he whispered, 'I want to be looking into your eyes.'

We received a reply from the adoption agency almost one month after Tom's letter to them. They told him that yes, Emily Cuthbert Granville had been adopted, five months after she'd left me, and by a couple from London. At that stage it seemed as though they couldn't or wouldn't give any further information. And all I could think of was those five months . . . those five months she'd been on her own; those five months I'd been tucked up in Berkeley Square, unravelling and in agony. Five months.

And I realised that's when it started, the lie that became my life, for I hadn't been whole, hadn't been complete, since that time. Something of me—a piece of my soul, a sliver of light—had quietly been extinguished at Plymouth in 1917, without any ceremony, mourning, or fuss. And I'd kept it a secret for so long that I'd become *the secret*: unspoken, unsaid, denied. Not-quite-but-almost Clarissa: haunted by nothing more sinister than the truth.

For so many years I'd tried not to think of her. I'd purposefully blurred and blotted out those early years, when she was still a baby, still a small child; when I'd been married to Charlie. I'd celebrated her precious birthdays in oblivion, and when no babies came, I'd accepted it as my punishment. It made sense. And I'd felt relief. The thought of

'No, Mama, I'm afraid I can't today. I've been out all morning . . . at Venetia's.'

'Oh, I see,' she said, brushing down her skirt and turning to look at me. 'I didn't know you'd—'

'And I'm seeing Tom later,' I interrupted.

She stared at me. 'Tom?'

'Yes, Tom,' I replied. 'We're going out to dinner.'

She looked away, towards the window, and then down into her lap. She lifted a hand to her hair, trying to find a stray curl to twist and tuck back in place. She turned her head to the table next to her, and then up to the wall: a square of bright colour where a picture had hung.

'Well,' she began, her head still turned away from me, 'I hardly know what to say, Clarissa.'

'You don't have to say anything Mama,' I replied, my voice steady, kind.

She turned to me, fluttering her eyes shut for a moment. 'So, you . . . you and Tom Cuthbert . . . you're friends once again?'

'Yes, we are. In fact, we've always been friends . . . more than friends.' I paused. 'We've been lovers, off and on, for years, almost sixteen years, Mama.'

She closed her eyes once more, shook her head.

I continued. 'And I'm sorry, I'm sorry if it pains you to hear this, to hear me speak about him, but I want you to know. I want to be able to be honest with you, for you to know the truth. I love him, Mama, but you know that. You know I've always loved him.'

She raised a hand to her brow.

'I'd like to have your blessing, we'd both like your blessing.'

another chance, another child, terrified me. For how could I, a mother already, a mother who had given away a beautiful healthy baby, be expected to love and look after another? I was not worthy of motherhood. And through my self-hatred I'd almost destroyed myself. And for a while I'd hated my own mother too: the person who'd made me give up my right to motherhood.

Of course no amount of drugs or alcohol had been able to assuage my guilt, or extinguish my love for my child, Tom's child. I'd thought of her each and every day of my life since the day we'd parted. I'd tried to imagine her, what she looked like, how she spoke, where she lived: who she'd become. Twelve years had passed since I'd handed her into the outstretched arms of a nameless woman in a brown coat at St Anne's. Did she even know I existed? And if she did, if her adoptive parents had told her the pathetic details of her birth, had she ever thought about me, her mother?

Despite the passing of years, in my dreams she remained a baby. The memory of her soft, clean skin, her tiny fingernails, her bright blue eyes, her smell; all of her, preserved and held there. But occasionally, every so often, she'd come to me as a child: a miniature version of Tom. She'd speak my name, 'Clarissa'; a sweet voice, so familiar to me. She'd reach out to me, smiling, and I'd take her into my arms. *Emily*. 'But where have you been? I've been waiting,' she'd say.

'I'm here . . . I'm here now.'

So many years had passed, but I needed to know. And not to absolve myself: for there could be no absolution. All I needed to know was that my daughter was alive and well, and happy; yes, happy.

My heart wobbled as he stood in front of me. And I watched him as he pulled the pages from a large brown envelope. He knew what was coming, of course; he'd already read every word in that envelope, but he had to tell me, had to deliver the news. He dismissed the flimsy covering note, and then looked at me with a strange serious face. And I for some reason laughed. 'Yes . . .' I said, extending my hand, 'Come along then.'

He said nothing, handed me the sheet of paper: *a certified copy of an entry of death*.

'Oh, well, this isn't right,' I said. 'No, no, this isn't right . . .'

I looked at the name: *Elizabeth Rachel Healey . . . Date of death, December the twenty-first, 1919 . . . Cause of death, Influenza* . . .

'No, this is wrong . . . this is definitely wrong. That's not her. That's not her name,' I said. 'They've obviously made a mistake.'

I didn't want to look at any more. I put down the sheet of paper and walked about the room. It was a mistake, I said again. *Bloody useless people*. I lit a cigarette, looked out of the window. 'It's not her,' I said. 'It's not her, Tom. They've made a mistake . . . it's the wrong person. That's not her . . . it's not her.'

There was no mistake. The people named Healey had adopted our daughter. They'd given her a new name, a life and an identity we could never give her. And for almost eighteen months she'd lived with them, as their child. And then, one night before Christmas, not long after her second birthday, and in the middle of the Spanish flu epidemic, Emily had died.

She had never celebrated a third, fifth, sixth, or

even a tenth birthday; and there would never be any meeting between us. I would never know what she had become, because she had not *become*. I would never hear her voice or know what she looked like, because she had never grown up. My remembrance of her would only ever be as a three-week-old baby.

Grief can be held off for a lifetime, and mine, for the baby I'd given away, took over twelve years to arrive. When it came, it came with the same force of any held-back torrent. It flooded my senses, drowned my perspective. And, though submerged, I occasionally caught my breath long enough to see the debris and driftwood of my life float past me, all pinned with one word: *waste*; the waste of time; the unnecessary waste of love. And the only thing I could hold on to was him, Tom.

Later, he called the number Oliver Goddard had given him, and asked for more information, and someone eventually called him back. Because the child was dead, they said, they were prepared to give a little more information than was usual. They told him that Albert Healey had been a greengrocer, and the family—his wife, and our daughter, Emily—had lived above the shop, in Battersea, London.

And he found her eventually too: in a cemetery at Wandsworth. We drove there together, late one afternoon. The day after he told me of his discovery.

That day, at the cemetery, he seemed to know exactly where to go. And he was remarkably calm, surprisingly in control. He held on to my hand tightly as he led me through row upon row of tombstones, down a pathway to a dank corner, and the name we now knew, chiselled into a lopsided stone: Elizabeth Rachel Healey, 1917–1919.

Emily Cuthbert.

We stood there together in silence, staring at that name. Then I stepped forward and placed the arrangement of white roses I'd had a Sloane Street florist prepare next to the stone. It looked extravagant, expensive, and incongruous: too big for a baby, too pathetic for the circumstances. She'd lain there for over a decade, serenaded only by the rumble of London traffic. Had anyone visited her? I wondered. Had anyone mourned her? Did others come to that place bestowed with memories I would never have? There were no signs of anyone having been, certainly not recently. No fresh or dying flowers; no plants in pots; nothing. And here we were, her parents, standing side by side under an umbrella as a smoky drizzle descended: too late to hold her, too late to know her, too late to explain.

He didn't weep, didn't shed a tear. And even then, through my own tears, I noticed this. How strong and in control he was. But he had been through a war, seen so much, and he was a businessman, I thought. It wasn't until later, much later, that I learned Tom had been on his own to visit Emily's grave before he ever took me.

As I stood in the rain that day, all I could think of was the tiny baby I'd held and nursed; the baby I'd given away: my baby. And I didn't want to leave. Even when the rain became heavier and he pulled on my arm, I didn't want to leave. I didn't want to leave her again, you see.

Eventually, he led me back through the tombstones, up the wet path towards the gate, and I could feel my chest tightening: that wrench, still there. He helped me into our waiting car, carefully tucking in my coat, closing the door, and then he moved to the other side of the vehicle and climbed in himself. And as we pulled away he turned to me, took hold of my hand and said something. Numb, and immersed in my grief, I couldn't hear his words. But as we headed out through the sprawling southern suburbs I realised what he'd said: *I'm taking you home now.*

I turned to him. 'Home?'

'Yes, home . . . we're going home, Clarissa.'

And as we passed through the old white gate I looked up out of the car window. A pale grey-blue sky stretched out above us, stretched further and illuminated by elongated wavy pink clouds: evensong clouds. And in a split second of déjà vu I finally grasped something: that there is no such thing as the passing of time, only the arc of seasons: a circle and not a line.

Moments can and do come back to us.

EPILOGUE

London, May the fifth 1930

Dearest Ted,

I hope this letter finds you well and that Devonshire is basking in the same blissful sunshine we have been fortunate enough to enjoy here in London these past few weeks. There really is no better time of year, is there? The light, which for some reason I always forget, is altogether different and truly quite heavenly, and the air fresh, & fragrant with new blossom.

I must apologise to you for the tardiness of this letter, but we have had a busy & eventful time of late. C and T were married three weeks ago, on April the fourteenth (six days after her divorce was made final) at the Register Office here in Kensington. It was a very simple, quiet affair, with Venetia Cooper and a business associate of T's—a Mr Goddard—acting as 'witnesses', and afterwards, a small luncheon party—including V & the aforementioned Mr G, Jimmy C (V's son), H and myself—at a favourite restaurant of C & T's on the Fulham Road, all terribly informal—and MODERN.

Unfortunately I was forced to miss the nuptials in order to meet H from the boat train. T had arranged his passage (as a surprise for C) and I had anticipated him being home the day before, but the crossing was delayed due to storms in the mid-Atlantic. As I'm sure you can imagine, it was rather a shock to dear C when I walked in to the restaurant with H on my arm, but the perfect surprise for her on her wedding day. All of us, including me, shed a tear when she rushed into his arms. It was such a happy day, one of the happiest of my life, and I think you would have been very proud.

They are expecting a baby, due early October I think, and so, though T had had all sorts of wonderful ideas & exotic sounding locations planned for their honeymoon, the doctor quite rightly advised against any foreign travel.

She is so happy, Teddy, radiantly happy, and they're quite inseparable, like a couple of children, & utterly content to spend all of their time at Deyning—with T now running & managing the farm, & C the house and gardens. Edna is with them, back as housekeeper and cook, but I have no idea how they manage without servants—& just the one gardener! However, C assures me that this is how they want it.

And I too am to move back there, into the place that was once yours, & ours, at the end of the summer. Oh I can see you smiling now, and yes, it will be queer to be back there—living in THAT cottage. Do you remember, all those years ago, when that was our dream? They are knocking the two cottages (yrs & what was, in yr time, Mrs C's) into one, so it will be plenty big enough for me now.

I enclose a photograph for you—taken on the day, on the steps of the Register Office. She does look beautiful, and so happy—doesn't she? I know it will make your heart sing to see that face once more. And they make such a handsome couple, don't they? I have no doubt they'll produce rather dashing offspring, and I'm simply longing to be 'Grandma'.

Do write to me soon and send me your news. In the meantime, & as always, I remain . . .

Yours,

Dina

ACKNOWLEDGEMENTS

Thanks to my supportive early readers: Venetia Welby, Sandie Dent and Kim Curran. Thanks to Ali Gunn, for her passion and faith in me; and to Jo Lloyd, for her editorial input and advice. Thanks to everyone at Headline: to Kate Byrne, who read the manuscript so many times and whose comments were invaluable to me; to my copyeditor, Jane Heller; to Helena Towers, and to Frankie Gray. Special thanks to my editor, Imogen Taylor. Extra special thanks to Max and Arabella, and to my mother—for never doubting.

PLAYS BY RENAISSANCE AND RESTORATION DRAMATISTS

General Editor: Graham Storey

WYCHERLEY

VOLUMES IN THIS SERIES

PUBLISHED

The plays of Cyril Tourneur, edited by George Parfitt: *The Revenger's Tragedy; The Atheist's Tragedy*

The selected plays of Philip Massinger, edited by Colin Gibson: *The Duke of Milan; The Roman Actor; A New Way to Pay Old Debts; The City Madam*

The selected plays of Thomas Middleton, edited by David L. Frost: *A Mad World, My Masters; A Chaste Maid in Cheapside; Women Beware Women; The Changeling* (with William Rowley)

FORTHCOMING

The selected plays of John Webster, edited by Inga-Stina Ewbank and Jonathan Dollimore: *The White Devil; The Devil's Law Case; The Duchess of Malfi*

The plays of George Etherege, edited by Michael Cordner: *The Man of Mode; She Would if She Could; The Comical Revenge*

The selected plays of Ben Jonson, edited by Johanna Procter: *Sejanus; Epicoene*, or *The Silent Woman; Volpone; The Alchemist; Bartholomew Fair*

The selected plays of John Marston, edited by M.D. Jackson and Michael Neil: *Antonio and Mellida; Antonio's Revenge; The Malcontent; The Dutch Courtezan; Sophonisba*

The selected plays of John Ford, edited by Colin Gibson: *'Tis Pity She's a Whore; The Broken Heart; Perkin Warbeck*

THE PLAYS OF WILLIAM WYCHERLEY

Love in a Wood

The Gentleman Dancing-Master

The Country Wife

The Plain-Dealer

EDITED BY
PETER HOLLAND
University Assistant Lecturer in English, and Fellow of Trinity Hall, Cambridge

CAMBRIDGE UNIVERSITY PRESS
CAMBRIDGE
LONDON NEW YORK NEW ROCHELLE
MELBOURNE SYDNEY

Published by the Press Syndicate of the University of Cambridge
The Pitt Building, Trumpington Street, Cambridge CB2 1RP
32 East 57th Street, New York, NY 10022, USA
296 Beaconsfield Parade, Middle Park, Melbourne 3206, Australia

First published 1981

Printed in Great Britain at the University Press, Cambridge

British Library Cataloguing in Publication Data

Wycherley, William
The plays of William Wycherley. – (Plays by Renaissance and Restoration dramatists).
I. Title II. Holland, Peter III. Series
822′.4 PR 3770 80-41199
ISBN 0 521 23250 3 hard covers
ISBN 0 521 29880 6 paperback

PREFACE TO THE SERIES

This series provides the best plays (in some cases, the complete plays) of the major English Renaissance and Restoration dramatists, in fully-annotated, modern-spelling texts, soundly edited by scholars in the field.

The introductory matter in each volume is factual and historical rather than critical: it includes, where appropriate, a brief biography of the playwright, a list of his works with dates of plays' first performances, the reasons for the volume editor's choice of plays, a short critical biography and a note on the texts used. An introductory note to each play then gives the source material, a short stage-history, and details of the individual editions of that play. Facsimiles of the original or early title-pages are given.

Annotation is of three types. Short notes at the foot of the page are designed to gloss the text or enlarge on its literary, historical or social allusions. At the end of the volume, in two separate appendices, editors have added more substantial explanatory notes and have commented on textual variants.

The volumes are intended for anyone interested in English drama in two of its richest periods, but they will prove especially useful to students at all levels who want to enjoy and explore the best work of these dramatists.

Graham Storey

CONTENTS

INTRODUCTION

Life

William Wycherley was born in March 1641. He was the eldest son of Daniel Wycherley, a fairly wealthy but obsessively litigious man, adept at making money and keeping it; at this time Daniel was steward to the Marquess of Winchester. William was brought up at Clive Hall, Shropshire, the Wycherley family home for two centuries, and educated at home by his father. When Wycherley was about fifteen, his father sent him to France, where he became part of the circle at Angoulême surrounding the brilliant Julie-Lucine d'Angennes, Madame de Montausier, head of one of the greatest of the *salons*. Intriguingly, her husband has traditionally been held as the source for Alceste, the central character in Molière's *Le Misanthrope*, the source of Wycherley's last play, *The Plain-Dealer*. At this time, as Madame de Montausier's protégé, Wycherley was converted to Catholicism.

Wycherley returned to England in 1659 and entered the Inner Temple in October. His father had done so a year earlier in pursuit of a new career as a barrister and it is more probable that Wycherley was being groomed for a similar career than that he was using the Inns of Court as the usual end of a fashionable gentleman's education. In July 1660, Wycherley entered Queen's College, Oxford as a fellow-commoner. He did not stay in Oxford long and did not matriculate, though he was reconverted to Protestantism by the Provost of Queen's. For the next few years our knowledge of Wycherley is fragmentary. He was in Ireland with the Earl of Arran's regiment of guards in 1662 and he may have been the Wycherley who accompanied Sir Richard Fanshawe, ambassador to the Spanish court, in 1664, reaching Madrid in June and returning to London in February 1665. In a poem Wycherley claimed to have fought in a sea-fight and he probably served in the second Dutch War in 1665, including the defeat of the Dutch fleet at the Battle of Harwich.

In 1669, Wycherley published anonymously his first work, a burlesque parody of the story of Hero and Leander. Two years later, in 1671, with the production of his first play, *Love in a Wood*, Wycherley acquired both a literary reputation and a famous mistress, the Duchess of Cleveland (see additional note, p. 490). He also gained the friendship of another of his mistress's suitors, the Duke of Buckingham. *The Gentleman Dancing-Master*, Wycherley's next play, appeared early in 1672.

By this time he was one of Buckingham's equerries and, in June, was made Captain-Lieutenant in the Duke's own company; he was probably on active service in the winter of 1673 and in February 1674 was appointed Captain, a commission he resigned after one week. In a less military vein, a traditional anecdote recounts how Wycherley tried to use his friendship with Buckingham to help Samuel Butler, who was desperately impoverished; the attempt failed when Buckingham left in pursuit of some passing prostitutes. In 1677, when Buckingham was imprisoned in the Tower, Wycherley, with some courage, wrote a verse-letter of support.

With *The Country Wife* and *The Plain-Dealer*, Wycherley established his position as the foremost satirical playwright of his time, praised by Dryden and others for his power and wit. But the success of *The Plain-Dealer* (1676), a success that he owed to his friends' support for the play, is the highpoint of Wycherley's career. From then on, his life is marked by a succession of illnesses and disastrous mistakes. He did not write another play.

In 1677 Wycherley was seriously ill with a fever which left his health ruined and his memory permanently impaired. He was visited in his lodgings by the King – so highly was he esteemed – and Charles gave him £500 to pay for a recuperative holiday abroad. In addition, in 1679, Charles made Wycherley tutor to one of his bastards, the Duke of Richmond, at a salary of £1500 a year. But, though John Dennis placed the incident a year later, it appears that in the spring of 1678 Wycherley met by chance the Countess of Drogheda while in Tunbridge Wells. They fell in love at once and, when Wycherley left for Montpellier in the summer, the Countess sent her servant after him with a gold ring. In June 1679 the Earl of Drogheda died and by October Wycherley had married his countess. The King was furious at the news of the secret marriage and Wycherley lost all favour at court.

The traditional anecdotal picture, supported by more reliable evidence, shows Wycherley's wife as a passionate and frequently hysterical woman, jealous in the extreme. As John Dennis relates, 'their lodgings were in Bow Street, Covent Garden, over against the Cock, whither if he at any time went with his friends, he was obliged to leave the windows open, that the lady might see there was no woman in company, or she would be immediately in a downright raving condition'. Even more disastrous for the always indebted writer was the revelation that his aristocratic wife was not wealthy: the Earl of Drogheda's will was contested by his family and she was already in debt to a number of people, including her maid. When she died, probably in 1685, her will was contested by her relations, and Wycherley found himself involved in another long and expensive lawsuit and surrounded by ever-increasing debts. Though it was said that Wycherley was in prison for seven years, he seems to have managed to evade arrest until October 1685, when he was committed to the Fleet Prison for non-payment of debts amounting to over £1500. Wycherley wrote for help to his friend, the Earl of Mulgrave, and it was probably at Mulgrave's instigation that *The Plain-Dealer* was performed at court before the new king, James II, on 14 December 1685. James's interest in the author's whereabouts led eventually to Wycherley's release from the Fleet in April 1686 with a present of £500 and an annual pension of £200. But Wycherley failed to declare the full extent of his debts, which were eventually settled by his father.

When James fled in 1688 Wycherley lost his pension and, from then on, spent much of his time at Clive Hall. In 1697 Daniel Wycherley died, leaving his estate tied up in such a way that his son could not ruin it; frightened of Wycherley's careless way with money, Daniel took the normal course of action and limited his son's tenure of the estate to a life tenancy, thereby making it impossible for Wycherley to raise money on the estate.

Eight years after it had been announced for publication, Wycherley's *Miscellany Poems* was published in 1704; a massive folio volume, it was prefaced by a bitter attack on the prejudice of his critics, but the poems themselves are largely mediocre, weak verse, rarely showing his earlier satiric bite. The melancholy frontispiece to the book is an engraving taken from Lely's painting of Wycherley at 28, with a sad Vergilian motto underneath, 'quantum mutatus ab illo' – 'how changed from that'. At about this time Wycherley became friends with the young Alexander Pope. Pope cultivated the friendship with the old man as a means of access to the 'literary scene' of which Wycherley was still part, presiding over the group of wits at Will's coffeehouse. Pope helped Wycherley revise his poems. When Wycherley's *Posthumous Works* were published in 1728, edited by Theobald, Pope instantly produced a rival volume, disguised as volume two, correcting Theobald's errors and publishing for the first time his correspondence with Wycherley.

On 20 December 1715 Wycherley married for the second time and died, eleven days later, on New Year's Eve. If his first marriage had been a faintly comic matter of fortune-hunting thwarted, his second was a black and tragic farce. Ill, feeble, with a weak mind, Wycherley was bullied and victimised, terrorised with the prospect of a pauper's burial, by his cousin, Thomas Shrimpton; eventually he gave in and married a supposed heiress, Elizabeth Jackson, who was in fact Shrimpton's mistress. Wycherley barely knew what was happening to him in the bizarre marriage service. He was buried at St Paul's Church, Covent Garden.

Works

All dates are those of first publication

Hero and Leander in Burlesque	1669
Love in a Wood	1672
The Gentleman Dancing-Master	1673
The Country Wife	1675
The Plain-Dealer	1677
Epistles to the King and Duke	1682
Prologue to Catherine Trotter's *Agnes de Castro*	1696
'The Answer' (verse letter to Shadwell), in *Poems on Affairs of State*, vol. 3	1698
Miscellany Poems	1704
On His Grace the Duke of Marlborough	1707
'To My Friend Mr Pope on his Pastorals', in *Poetical Miscellanies*, part 6	1709
Posthumous Works, vol. 1 (edited by Theobald)	1728
Posthumous Works, 'vol. 2' (edited by Pope)	1729

The text of this edition

The text of Wycherley's plays does not present many problems. In each case the first edition is the only textually significant one and I have relied on it as copy-text for each play. Professor Friedman argues that Q2 of *The Plain-Dealer* contains corrections by Wycherley but I remain unconvinced. I have recorded the very few substantive emendations to the copy-text in the notes; I have not recorded subsequent variations since, given that the later editions have no authority, such details are best left to full-scale old-spelling editions. I must here record my very substantial debt to all previous editors of Wycherley; I have pillaged their work unashamedly and, rather than giving specific attributions in each and every note, I have opted to indicate my gratitude here in the hope that none will feel offended.

In modernising Wycherley, the only significant problem, apart from Monsieur's French (discussed in the Textual Note to *The Gentleman Dancing-Master*), is punctuation. Wycherley writes, and the compositors reflect, enormous free-flowing paragraphs in which the syntax is often vague. It is always easy to speak Wycherley's lines in the theatre but often difficult to read them off the page. In repunctuating I have tried to keep such punctuation as may reflect stage pauses but to convert semi-colons to full stops where the pressures of modern practice seemed to demand it. I do not think I have distorted the meaning of the text by adopting this method. The stage directions are Wycherley's unless enclosed by square brackets.

A select bibliography

Editions

The only complete modern edition of Wycherley is edited by Montague Summers in four volumes (London: Nonesuch Press, 1924). This is less eccentric than some of Summers's other work on Restoration drama but the text is far from reliable. In any case, this is a comparatively rare limited edition. W.C. Ward edited a modernised text of the plays for the Mermaid series in 1888, with a few notes and a clutch of errors. Much more important are the two recent old-spelling editions: Gerald Weales's (New York: Doubleday Anchor, 1966) is a delightful mine of useful and witty annotation; Arthur Friedman's (Oxford: Clarendon Press, 1979) will undoubtedly become the standard text of Wycherley. There is a fine thesis-edition of *Love in a Wood* and *The Gentleman Dancing-Master*, edited by D.S. Rodes (Stanford University, 1968). G.B. Churchill's edition of *The Country Wife* and *The Plain-Dealer* (Boston: D.C. Heath, Belles Lettres Series, 1924) is still useful.

Biography

There is no good modern biography of Wycherley. Willard Connely's attempt, *Brawny Wycherley* (New York: Scribner's, 1930) is flowery and over-extended. In addition to the material in Summers's and Friedman's editions and in K.M. Rogers's book (see below), the following articles explore odd parts of

Wycherley's life: W.G. Hargest and E. Boswell revealed the truth about 'Wycherley and the Countess of Drogheda' (*T.L.S.*, 21 November 1929, p. 960; 28 November 1929, pp. 1001–2); W.R. Chadwick showed how long Wycherley had been in the Fleet Prison in 'Wycherley: the seven lean years' (*Notes and Queries*, 216 (1971), 30–4); H.P. Vincent found the lawsuit that revealed Shrimpton's machinations in 'The death of William Wycherley' (*Harvard Studies and Notes in Philology and Literature*, 15 (1933), 219–42). Since so much of Wycherley's biography is dependent on early anecdotes, it is well worth reading Charles Gildon's *Memoirs of the Life of Wycherley* (1718) and John Dennis's letter containing 'Some Remarkable Passages of Mr Wycherley's Life' (1720, reprinted in J. Dennis, *The Critical Works*, ed. E.N. Hooker (Baltimore: Johns Hopkins Press, 1939–43)).

Criticism

Books

There have been three full-length modern studies of Wycherley's work. K.M. Rogers's *William Wycherley* (New York: Twayne, 1972) tried to cover the biography and all the works in a small space and is plagued by the conviction that *The Plain-Dealer* is a failure. R. Zimbardo's *Wycherley's Drama* (New Haven: Yale University Press, 1965) pushes too hard at the argument that each play derives from formal verse satire and runs into problems in trying to maintain that *Love in a Wood* is an extended commentary on Fletcher's *The Faithful Shepherdess* and *The Country Wife* derived from Juvenal's Sixth Satire. Nonetheless its sustained emphasis on Wycherley's satire is admirable. The best of the three is W.R. Chadwick's *The Four Plays of William Wycherley* (The Hague: Mouton, 1975), closely argued, perceptive and well-written.

Articles

The best introduction to Wycherley's plays is Anne Righter's 'William Wycherley', in *Restoration Theatre* (London: Edward Arnold, Stratford-upon-Avon Studies 6, ed. J.R. Brown and B. Harris, 1965), which sets Wycherley firmly in his context. Norman Holland, in *The First Modern Comedies* (Cambridge, Mass.: Harvard University Press, 1959) concentrates on Wycherley's use of language and imagery in the plays, with excellent results. P.F. Vernon has produced a useful brief survey in *William Wycherley* (London: Longman, British Writers and Their Work, 1965). C.S. Matlack has shown how Wycherley used contemporary casting for one particular end in 'Parody and burlesque of heroic ideals in Wycherley's comedies' (*Papers on Language and Literature*, 8 (1972), 273–86). T.W. Craik studied 'Some aspects of satire in Wycherley's plays' (*English Studies*, 41 (1960), 168–79).

Other studies are most conveniently explored play by play. The two earlier plays have received comparatively little attention, though there is a good study of 'Theme and structure in Wycherley's *Love in a Wood*' by E.S. Rump (*English Studies*, 54 (1973), 326–33) and P.F. Vernon has examined the link to Calderón, first identified by J.U. Rundle, in 'Wycherley's first comedy and its Spanish source' (*Comparative Literature*, 18 (1966), 132–44).

The list of articles on *The Country Wife* is long and rapidly increasing. Ronald Berman has studied 'The ethic of *The Country Wife*' (*Texas Studies in Literature and Language*, 9 (1967), 47–55). Thematic studies are represented by D.M. Vieth's 'Wycherley's *The Country Wife*: an anatomy of masculinity' (*Papers on Language and Literature*, 2 (1966), 335–50) and Vieth's line of approach was taken further by W. Freedman who found 'Impotence and self-destruction in *The Country Wife*' (*English Studies*, 53 (1972), 421–31). There have been the inevitable attempts to find one external model which will somehow provide an instant explanation of the play: A. Kaufman has tried 'Wycherley's *The Country Wife* and the Don Juan character' (*Eighteenth Century Studies*, 9 (1975), 216–31); C.A. Hallett has tried to find 'The Hobbesian substructure of *The Country Wife*' (*Papers on Language and Literature*, 9 (1973), 380–95); G. Beauchamp turned to Machiavelli in 'The amorous Machiavellism of *The Country Wife*' (*Comparative Drama*, 11 (1977), 316–30). More sensibly, P. Malekin started from Wycherley's theatrical technique in 'Wycherley's dramatic skills and the interpretation of *The Country Wife*' (*Durham University Journal*, n.s. 31 (1969), 32–40).

Many of the attempts to cope with *The Plain-Dealer* have tried to place Manly: A.H. Chorney identified him as a humours character in 'Wycherley's Manly reinterpreted' (in *Essays Critical and Historical Dedicated to Lily B. Campbell* (Berkeley: University of California Press, 1950); A.M. Friedson underplays his importance by comparison with Alceste in 'Wycherley and Molière: satirical point of view in *The Plain-Dealer*' (*Modern Philology*, 64 (1967), 189–97); Ian Donaldson has a brilliant approach to the audience's differing responses to Manly as satirist in *The World Upside Down* (Oxford: Clarendon Press, 1970). B.E. McCarthy has pursued Wycherley's changing attitude towards wit, culminating in this play, in 'Wycherley's *The Plain-Dealer* and the limits of wit' (*English Miscellany*, 22 (1971), 47–92). I have approached the disorienting effects of the play by starting from the original production in *The Ornament of Action* (Cambridge University Press, 1979). P.G. Adams has amusingly shown that critics cannot make up their minds about 'What happened in Olivia's bedroom' (in T.A. Kirby ed., *Essays in Honor of Esmond Linworth Marilla* (Baton Rouge: Louisiana State University Press, 1970)).

Last, but by no means least, E.L. Avery has charted the stage history of Wycherley's plays up to the end of the eighteenth century in three articles in *Research Studies*: '*The Country Wife* in the eighteenth century' (10 (1942), 141–72), '*The Plain-Dealer* in the eighteenth century' (11 (1943), 234–56), and 'The reputation of Wycherley's comedies as stage plays in the eighteenth century' (12 (1944), 131–54).

After this introduction was completed, B.E. McCarthy's *William Wycherley: A Biography* (Athens, Ohio: Ohio University Press, 1979) appeared. This is a useful, if solemn, account of the facts of Wycherley's life and I have made two small corrections in the light of its new information. Its only major error is in misdating Wycherley's birth to May 1641; he was baptised at Whitchurch, Hampshire, on 8 April 1641.

Love in a Wood,

OR,

S[t] James's Park.

A

COMEDY,

As it is Acted at the Theatre Royal, by his Majesties Servants.

Written by M[r] *WYCHERLEY.*

——Excludit ſanos helicone poetas Democritus;—— Horat.

LONDON,

Printed by *J. M.* for *H. Herringman*, at the Sign of the *Blew Anchor*, in the Lower-Walk of the New Exchange. 1672.

Title-page of the 1672 Quarto of *Love in a Wood*, reproduced by permission of the University Library, Cambridge.

Motto
Horace, *Ars Poetica*, 296–7:
'Democritus excludes sane poets from Helicon'

Title
'in a wood' means 'confused, perplexed'

INTRODUCTORY NOTE

Wycherley may have adapted his title for his first play from James Shirley's *The Changes or Love in a Maze* (1632), which was frequently performed after the Restoration; 'maze' and 'wood' are similar puns. But the major source is Etherege's *The Comical Revenge or Love in a Tub* (1664), the first great success of the Restoration stage. Wycherley takes from Etherege the form of his play with its multiple plots only loosely interrelated, ranging from a 'love and honour' world of duels to a low world of trickery and cunning. Only the high plot has a direct source; its London setting lightly disguises its Spanish origin in Calderón's *Mañanas de abril y mayo* (1632). Wycherley appears to have used the *tercera parte* of Calderón's comedies, published in 1664.

The reference in Wycherley's dedication to performances in Lent (l. 26) is the only guide to the exact date of the first performance, which is usually placed around March 1671 at the Theatre Royal, Bridges Street, by the King's Company. When it was revived at Drury Lane in August 1718, the bill announced that it had been 'acted but once these thirty years' and, except for a performance of an altered version in 1782, that revival seems to have marked the end of the play's career on the professional stage.

Love in a Wood was first published in 1672. There were further quartos in 1693, 1694 and 1711, and since then the play has only been reprinted as part of complete editions of Wycherley's plays.

TO HER GRACE THE DUCHESS OF CLEVELAND

MADAM,

All authors whatever in their dedications are poets but I am now to write to a lady who stands as little in need of flattery as her beauty of art; otherwise I should prove as ill a poet to her in my dedication as to my reader in my play. I can do your Grace no honour nor make you more admirers than you have already; yet I can do myself the honour to let the world know I am the greatest you have. You will pardon me, madam, for you know 'tis very hard for a new author, and poet too, to govern his ambition, for poets, let them pass in the world never so much for modest, honest men, but begin praise to others, which concludes in themselves and are like rooks who lend people money but to win it back again and so leave them in debt to 'em for nothing; they offer laurel and incense to their heroes but wear it themselves and perfume themselves. This is true, madam, upon the honest word of an author who never yet writ dedication; yet, though I cannot lie like them, I am as vain as they and cannot but publicly give your Grace my humble acknowledgements for the favours I have received from you. This, I say, is the poet's gratitude, which in plain English is only pride and ambition, and that the world might know your Grace did me the honour to see my play twice together; yet perhaps my enviers of your favour will suggest 'twas in Lent and therefore for your mortification. Then, as a jealous author, I am concerned not to have your Grace's favours lessened, or rather my reputation, and to let them know you were pleased, after that, to command a copy from me of this play – the way without beauty and wit to win a poor poet's heart. 'Tis a sign your Grace understands nothing better than obliging all the world after the best and most proper manner. But, madam, to be obliging to that excess as you are (pardon me if I tell you, out of my extreme concern and service for your Grace) is a

---

The Duchess of Cleveland: Barbara Villiers, made Duchess of Cleveland in 1670, was one of Charles II's mistresses and also, after the success of this play, Wycherley's. See Additional Note. The dedication is written in the conventional language of flattery but adds double meanings to words like 'favour' to hint at the real relation between poet and patroness.

13 *rooks*: cheats, con-men.

dangerous quality and may be very incommode to you, for civility makes poets as troublesome as charity makes beggars and your Grace will be hereafter as much pestered with such scurvy offerings as this – poems, panegyrics and the like – as you are now with petitions and, madam, take it from me, no man with papers in's hand is more dreadful than a poet – no, not a lawyer with his declarations. Your Grace, sure, did not well consider what you did in sending for my play; you little thought I would have had the confidence to send you a dedication too. But, madam, you find I am as unreasonable and have as little conscience as if I had driven the poetic trade longer than I have and ne'er consider you had enough of the play. But, having suffered now so severely, I beseech your Grace, have a care for the future, take my counsel and be (if you can possible) as proud and ill-natured as other people of quality, since your quiet is so much concerned and since you have more reason than any to value yourself, for you have that perfection of beauty, without thinking it so, which others of your sex but think they have, that generosity in your actions which others of your quality have only in their promises, that spirit, wit and judgement and all other qualifications which fit heroes to command and would make any but your Grace proud. I begin now, elevated by my subject, to write with the emotion and fury of a poet, yet the integrity of an historian, and I could never be weary – nay, sure, this were my only way to make my readers never weary too, though they were a more impatient generation of people than they are. In fine, speaking thus of your Grace, I should please all the world but you; therefore, I must once observe and obey you against my will and say no more than that I am,

Madam,

Your Grace's

Most obliged and most humble servant,

WILLIAM WYCHERLEY

65–6 *In fine*: in short, to conclude.

PROLOGUE

Custom, which bids the thief from cart harangue
All those that come to make and see him hang,
Wills the damned poet (though he knows he's gone)
To greet you ere his execution.
Not having fear of critic 'fore his eyes
But still rejecting wholesome, good advice,
He e'en is come to suffer here today
For counterfeiting (as you judge) a play,
Which is against dread Phoebus highest treason,
Damned damning judges, therefore you have reason –
You he does mean who for the selfsame fault
That damning privilege of yours have bought
(So the huge bankers when they needs must fail
Send the small brothers of their trade to gaol,
Whilst they by breaking gentlemen are made,
Then more than any scorn, poor men o'th'trade),
You hardened renegado poets, who
Treat rhyming brother worse than Turk would do,
But vent your heathenish rage, hang, draw and quarter,
His muse will die today a fleering martyr;
Since for bald jest, dull libel or lampoon
There are who suffer persecution
With the undaunted briskness of buffoon
And strict professors live of raillery,
Defying Porter's Lodge or pillory.
For those who yet write on our poet's fate
Should as co-sufferers commiserate;
But he in vain their pity now would crave
Who for themselves, alas, no pity have
And their own gasping credit will not save;
And those, much less, our criminal would spare

---

9 *Phoebus*: Apollo, patron of the Muses.
10 *have reason*: are right (Fr. *avez raison*).
11–12 Playwrights were granted free admission to the theatre.
15–16 *Whilst they . . . o'th'trade*: the small-scale bankers are made poor members of their profession by gentlemen who break their bonds rather than by the scorn they receive. Q2 places a comma between *any* and *scorn* making the lines mean 'the big bankers are made rich by ruining gentlemen and scorn the small brothers more than any'.
20 *fleering*: 'smiling flatteringly' and 'mocking'.
21 *lampoon*: scurrilous satire.
25 *Porter's Lodge*: prison in Whitehall Palace.

Who ne'er in rhyme transgress, if such there are.
Well then, who nothing hopes needs nothing fear
And he, before your cruel votes shall do it,
By his despair declares himself no poet.

THE PERSONS

Character	Actor
MR RANGER, MR VINCENT, MR VALENTINE — Young gentlemen of the town	*Mr Hart*, *Mr Bell*, *Mr Kynaston*
ALDERMAN GRIPE, seemingly precise but a covetous, lecherous, old usurer of the City	*Mr Lacy*
SIR SIMON ADDLEPLOT, a coxcomb, always in pursuit of women of great fortunes	*Mr Wintersell*
MR DAPPERWIT, a brisk, conceited, half-witted fellow of the town	*Mr Mohun*
CHRISTINA, Valentine's mistress	*Mrs Boutell*
LYDIA, Ranger's mistress	*Mrs Betty Cox*
MY LADY FLIPPANT, Gripe's sister, an affected widow, in distress for a husband though still declaiming against marriage	*Mrs Knep*
MRS MARTHA, Gripe's daughter	*Mrs Farlow*
MRS JOYNER, a match-maker or precise City bawd	*Mrs Corey*
MRS CROSSBITE, an old, cheating jilt and bawd to her daughter	*Mrs Rutter*
MISS LUCY, her daughter	*Mrs Betty Slade*
ISABEL, Christina's woman	*Mrs James*
LEONORE, servant to Lydia	*Mrs Cartwright*

Crossbite's LANDLORD and his PRENTICES; servants, waiters and other attendants

The Scene: *London*

---

5 *precise*: puritanical.
21 *Crossbite*: deceive, outwit.
22 *jilt*: cheating woman.

LOVE IN A WOOD

ACT I

SCENE I

Gripe's house in the evening.

Enter MY LADY FLIPPANT, MRS JOYNER.

FLIPPANT. Not a husband to be had for money. Come, come, I might have been a better housewife for myself, as the world goes now, if I had dealt for an heir with his guardian, uncle or mother-in-law; and you are no better than a chouse, a cheat.

JOYNER. I a cheat, madam!

FLIPPANT. I am out of my money and my patience too.

JOYNER. Do not run out of your patience whatever you do; 'tis a necessary virtue for a widow without a jointure, in truly.

FLIPPANT. Vile woman, though my fortune be something wasted, my person's in good repair. If I had not depended on you, I had had a husband before this time. When I gave you the last five pound did not you promise I should be married by Christmas?

JOYNER. And had kept my promise if you had co-operated.

FLIPPANT. Co-operated! What should I have done? 'Tis well known no woman breathing could use more industry to get her a husband than I have. Has not my husband's scutcheon walked as much ground as the citizens' signs since the fire, that no quarter of the town might be ignorant of the widow Flippant?

JOYNER. 'Tis well known, madam, indeed.

FLIPPANT. Have I not owned myself (against my stomach) the relict of a citizen, to credit my fortune?

4 *mother-in-law*: stepmother.
5 *chouse*: cheat.
10 *jointure*: estate settled on wife or widow for the remainder of her life.
21 *scutcheon*: coat of arms.
21–2 After the Great Fire of London many tradesmen moved their shops further westward into the more fashionable areas.
26 *relict*: widow.

JOYNER. 'Tis confessed, madam.

FLIPPANT. Have I not constantly kept Covent Garden Church, St Martin's, the playhouses, Hyde Park, Mulberry Garden and all other the public marts where widows and maids are exposed?

JOYNER. Far be it from me to think you have an aversion to a husband, but why, madam, have you refused so many good offers?

FLIPPANT. Good offers, Mrs Joyner! I'll be sworn I never had an offer since my late husband's. If I had had an offer, Mrs Joyner – there's the thing, Mrs Joyner.

JOYNER. Then your frequent and public detestation of marriage is thought real and if you have had no offer – there's the thing, madam.

FLIPPANT. I cannot deny but I always rail against marriage, which is the widow's way to it, certainly.

JOYNER. 'Tis the desperate way of the desperate widows, in truly.

FLIPPANT. Would you have us as tractable as the wenches that eat oatmeal, and fooled like them too?

JOYNER. If nobody were wiser than I, I should think, since the widow wants the natural allurement which the virgin has, you ought to give men all other encouragements, in truly.

FLIPPANT. Therefore, on the contrary, because the widow's fortune (whether supposed or real) is her chiefest bait, the more chary she seems of it and the more she withdraws it, the more eagerly the busy gaping fry will bite. With us widows husbands are got like bishoprics, by saying no, and, I tell you, a young heir is as shy of a widow as of a rook, to my knowledge.

JOYNER. I can allege nothing against your practice but your ill success and indeed you must use another method with Sir Simon Addleplot.

28–9 *Covent . . . Martin's*: St Paul's, Covent Garden, and St Martin-in-the-Fields (to the north of what is now Trafalgar Square) were the two most fashionable churches in London.

29–30 *Mulberry Garden*: a park on the site of Buckingham Palace, the setting for the last scene of *Love in a Wood*.

30 *marts*: markets.

47 *wenches that eat oatmeal*: women pining for a lover.

57 *bishoprics . . . no*: the conventional refusal when elected a bishop, 'nolo episcopari'.

FLIPPANT. Will he be at your house at the hour?

JOYNER. He'll be there by ten; 'tis now nine. I warrant you he will not fail.

FLIPPANT. I'll warrant you then I will not fail, for 'tis more than time I were sped.

JOYNER. Mr Dapperwit has not been too busy with you; I hope your experience has taught you to prevent a mischance.

FLIPPANT. No, no, my mischance (as you call it) is greater than that. I have but three months to reckon ere I lie down with my port and equipage and must be delivered of a woman, a footman and a coachman, for my coach must down unless I can get Sir Simon to draw with me.

JOYNER. (*aside*) He will pair with you exactly if you knew all.

FLIPPANT. Ah, Mrs Joyner, nothing grieves me like putting down my coach. For the fine clothes, the fine lodgings, let 'em go, for a lodging is as unnecessary a thing to a widow that has a coach as a hat to a man that has a good peruke, for, as you see about town, she is most properly at home in her coach; she eats and drinks and sleeps in her coach and, for her visits, she receives them in the playhouse.

JOYNER. Ay, ay, let the men keep lodgings (as you say, madam) if they will.

[*Enter*] GRIPE *and* SIR SIMON ADDLEPLOT *following him as his man, in the habit of a clerk, at one door, and* MRS MARTHA *at the other.*

FLIPPANT. Do you think, if things had been with me as they have been, I would ever have housed with this counter-fashion brother of mine (who hates a vest as

---

69–70 As Lady Flippant's reply indicates, Mrs Joyner is hinting at the risk of pregnancy.

72 *port*: retinue.

90 *vest*: this garment was introduced to the court by Charles himself in October 1666 and, not surprisingly, rapidly became *à la mode*. Pepys describes it as 'a long cassock close to the body, of black cloth and pinked with white silk under it' (15 October 1666). Gripe is opposed to court (vest) and church (surplice).

much as a surplice) to have my patches assaulted every day, at dinner my freedom censured, and my visitants shut out of doors? Poor Mr Dapperwit cannot be admitted.

JOYNER. He knows him too well to keep his acquaintance.

FLIPPANT. He is a censorious, rigid fop and knows nothing.

GRIPE. (*behind*) So, so –

JOYNER. (*aside*) Is he here? (*To* MY LADY FLIPPANT) Nay, with your pardon, madam, I must contradict you there. He is a prying Commonwealth's man, an implacable magistrate, a sturdy pillar of his cause and – (*To* GRIPE) But, oh me, is your worship so near then? If I had thought you had heard me –

GRIPE. Why, why, Mrs Joyner, I have said as much of myself ere now and without vanity, I profess.

JOYNER. I know your virtue is proof against vainglory but the truth to your face looks like flattery in your worship's servant.

GRIPE. No, no, say what you will of me in that kind; far be it from me to suspect you of flattery.

JOYNER. In truly, your worship knows yourself and knows me, for I am none of those –

FLIPPANT. (*aside*) Now they are in. – Mrs Joyner, I'll go before to your house; you'll be sure to come after me. *Exit* FLIPPANT.

JOYNER. Immediately. But, as I was saying, I am none of those –

GRIPE. No, Mrs Joyner, you cannot sew pillows under folks' elbows; you cannot hold a candle to the devil; you cannot tickle a trout to take him; you –

JOYNER. Lord, how well you do know me indeed and you shall see I know your worship as well: you cannot backslide from your principles; you cannot be terrified by the laws nor bribed to allegiance by office or preferment; you –

GRIPE. Hold, hold, my praise must not interrupt yours.

---

91 *patches*: small pieces of black silk stuck to the face to add beauty and cover blemishes.

97 *fop*: here *fool*, usually an affected and fashionable one.

102 *prying*: (*a*) diligently inquiring (*b*) snooping.

120–2 All these proverbs describe flattery.

JOYNER. With your worship's pardon, in truly, I must on.

GRIPE. I am full of your praise and it will run over.

JOYNER. Nay, sweet sir, you are –

GRIPE. Nay, sweet Mrs Joyner, you are –

JOYNER. Nay, good your worship, you are –

Stops her mouth with his handkerchief.

GRIPE. I say you are –

JOYNER. I must not be rude with your worship.

GRIPE. You are a nursing-mother to the saints: through you they gather together; through you they fructify and increase and through you the child cries from out of the hand-basket.

JOYNER. Through you virgins are married or provided for as well; through you the reprobate's wife is made a saint and through you the widow is not disconsolate nor misses her husband.

GRIPE. Through you –

JOYNER. Indeed, you will put me to the blush.

GRIPE. Blushes are badges of imperfection; saints have no shame. You are the flower of matrons, Mrs Joyner.

JOYNER. You are the pink of courteous aldermen.

GRIPE. You are the muffler of secrecy.

JOYNER. You are the headband of justice.

GRIPE. Thank you, sweet Mrs Joyner. Do you think so indeed? You are – you are the bonfire of devotion.

JOYNER. You are the bellows of zeal.

GRIPE. You are the cupboard of charity.

JOYNER. You are the fob of liberality.

GRIPE. You are the rivet of sanctified love or wedlock.

JOYNER. You are the picklock and dark lanthorn of policy and, in a word, the conventicle of virtues.

GRIPE. Your servant, your servant, sweet Mrs Joyner; you have stopped my mouth.

JOYNER. Your servant, your servant, sweet alderman; I have nothing to say.

SIR SIMON. The half pullet will be cold, sir.

GRIPE. Mrs Joyner, you shall sup with me.

JOYNER. Indeed, I am engaged to supper with some of your man's friends and I came on purpose to get leave for him too.

---

155 *fob*: (*a*) small pocket (*b*) trick, cheat.

157 *lanthorn*: lantern.

158 *conventicle*: meeting-place, particularly of Puritans.

GRIPE. I cannot deny you anything. But I have forgot to tell you what a kind of fellow my sister's Dapperwit is: before a full table of the coffeehouse sages he had the impudence to hold an argument against me in the defence of vests and protections and therefore I forbid him my house; besides, when he came, I was forced to lock up my daughter for fear of him – nay, I think the poor child herself was afraid of him. Come hither, child. Were you not afraid of Dapperwit?

MARTHA. Yes indeed, sir, he is a terrible man. – (*Aside*) yet I durst meet with him in the Piazzo at midnight.

GRIPE. He shall never come into my doors again.

MARTHA. Shall Mr Dapperwit never come hither again then?

GRIPE. No, child.

MARTHA. I am afraid he will.

GRIPE. I warrant thee.

MARTHA. (*aside*) I warrant you then I'll go to him. – I am glad of that, for I hate him as much as a bishop.

GRIPE. Thou art no child of mine if thou dost not hate bishops and wits. Well, Mrs Joyner, I'll keep you no longer. Jonas, wait on Mrs Joyner.

JOYNER. Goodnight to your worship.

GRIPE. But stay, stay, Mrs Joyner. Have you spoken with the Widow Crossbite about her little daughter, as I desired?

JOYNER. I will tomorrow early. It shall be the first thing I'll do after my prayers.

GRIPE. If Dapperwit should contaminate her – I cannot rest till I have redeemed her from the jaws of that lion. Goodnight.

JOYNER. Good gentleman.

Exeunt GRIPE *and* MARTHA.
Manent SIR SIMON ADDLEPLOT *and* JOYNER.

SIR SIMON. Hah, hah, ha, Mrs Joyner.

JOYNER. What's the matter, Sir Simon?

SIR SIMON. Hah, hah, ha! Let us make haste to your

---

172 *protections*: documents issued by the court guaranteeing immunity from arrest.

178 *Piazzo*: the Piazza was an open arcade on two sides of Covent Garden; Act V Scene iii of *The Country Wife* takes place there.

house or I shall burst. Faith and troth, to see what fools you and I make of these people!

JOYNER. I will not rob you of any of the credit. I am but a feeble instrument; you are the engineer.

SIR SIMON. Remember what you say now when things succeed and do not tell me then I must thank your wit for all.

JOYNER. No, in truly, Sir Simon.

SIR SIMON. Nay, I'm sure Dapperwit and I have been partners in many an intrigue and he uses to serve me so.

JOYNER. He is an ill man to intrigue with, as you call it.

SIR SIMON. Ay, so are all your wits. A pox, if a man's understanding be not so public as theirs he cannot do a wise action but they go away with the honour of it, if he be of their acquaintance.

JOYNER. Why do you keep such acquaintance, then?

SIR SIMON. There is a proverb, Mrs Joyner: you may know him by his company.

JOYNER. No, no, to be thought a man of parts you should always keep company with a man of less wit than yourself.

SIR SIMON. That's the hardest thing in the world for me to do, faith and troth.

JOYNER. What, to find a man of less wit than yourself? Pardon my raillery, Sir Simon.

SIR SIMON. No, no, I cannot keep company with a fool. I wonder how men of parts can do't – there's something in't.

JOYNER. If you could, all your wise actions would be your own and your money would be your own too.

SIR SIMON. Nay, faith and troth, that's true, for your wits are plaguily given to borrow; they'll borrow of their wench, coachman or linkboy their hire. Mrs Joyner, Dapperwit has that trick with a vengeance.

JOYNER. Why will you keep company with him then, I say? For, to be plain with you, you have followed him so long that you are thought but his cully, for every wit has his cully, as every squire his led-captain.

---

227 *raillery*: witty banter.
239 *cully*: dupe, often a cuckold.
240 *led-captain*: parasite, hanger-on.

SIR SIMON. I his cully? I his cully, Mrs Joyner! Lord, that I should be thought a cully to any wit breathing!

JOYNER. Nay, do not take it so to heart, for the best wits of the town are but cullies themselves.

SIR SIMON. To whom, to whom, to whom, Mrs Joyner?

JOYNER. To sem'steresses and bawds.

SIR SIMON. To your knowledge, Mrs Joyner. – [*Aside*] There I was with her.

JOYNER. To tailors and vintners, but especially to the French houses.

SIR SIMON. But Dapperwit is a cully to none of them, for he ticks.

JOYNER. I care not; but I wish you were a cully to none but me – that's all the hurt I wish you.

SIR SIMON. Thank you, Mrs Joyner. Well, I will throw off Dapperwit's acquaintance, when I am married, and will only be a cully to my wife – and that's no more than the wisest husband of 'em all is.

JOYNER. Then you think you shall carry Mrs Martha?

SIR SIMON. Your hundred guineas are as good as in your lap.

JOYNER. But I am afraid this double plot of yours should fail. You would sooner succeed if you only designed upon Mrs Martha or only upon my Lady Flippant.

SIR SIMON. Nay, then you are no woman of intrigue; faith and troth, 'tis good to have two strings to one bow. If Mrs Martha be coy, I tell the widow I put on my disguise for her; but if Mrs Martha be kind to Jonas, Sir Simon Addleplot will be false to the widow – which is no more than widows are used to, for a promise to a widow is as seldom kept as a vow made at sea, as Dapperwit says.

JOYNER. I am afraid they should discover you.

SIR SIMON. You have nothing to fear. You have your twenty guineas in your pocket for helping me into my service and if I get into Mrs Martha's quarters you have a hundred more, if into the widow's, fifty, happy-go-lucky. Will her ladyship be at your house at the hour?

---

250 *French houses*: fashionable eating-houses.
252 *ticks*: runs up bills without paying.

JOYNER. Yes.

SIR SIMON. Then you shall see, when I am Sir Simon Addleplot and myself, I'll look like myself; now I am Jonas I look like an ass. You never thought Sir Simon Addleplot could have looked so like an ass by his ingenuity.

JOYNER. Pardon me, Sir Simon.

SIR SIMON. Nay, do not flatter, faith and troth.

JOYNER. Come, let us go; 'tis time.

SIR SIMON. I will carry the widow to the French house.

JOYNER. If she will go.

SIR SIMON. If she will go! Why, did you ever know a widow refuse a treat? No more than a lawyer a fee, faith and troth; yet I know too.
No treat, sweet words, good mien but sly intrigue,
That must at length the jilting widow feague.

Exeunt.

SCENE II

The scene changes to the French house. A table, wine and candles.

Enter VINCENT, RANGER, DAPPERWIT.

DAPPERWIT. Pray, Mr Ranger, let's have no drinking tonight.

VINCENT. Pray, Mr Ranger, let's have no Dapperwit tonight.

RANGER. Nay, nay, Vincent.

VINCENT. A pox, I hate his impertinent chat more than he does the honest Burgundy.

DAPPERWIT. But why should you force wine upon us? We are not all of your gusto.

VINCENT. But why should you force your chawed jests, your damned ends of your mouldy lampoons and last year's sonnets upon us? We are not all of your gusto.

DAPPERWIT. The wine makes me sick, let me perish.

VINCENT. Thy rhymes make me spew.

---

295 *feague*: get the better of.
9 *gusto*: taste (Fr. *goût*).
10 *chawed*: chewed.

RANGER. At repartee already! Come, Vincent, I know you would rather have him pledge you. Here, Dapperwit. (*Gives him the glass*) But why are you so eager to have him drink always?

VINCENT. Because he is so eager to talk always and there is no other way to silence him.

[*Enter*] WAITER *to them.*

WAITER. Here is a gentleman desires to speak with Mr Vincent.

VINCENT. I come.

[*Exeunt* WAITER *and*] VINCENT.

DAPPERWIT. He may drink because he is obliged to the bottle, for all the wit and courage he has – 'tis not free and natural like yours.

RANGER. He has more courage than wit but wants neither.

DAPPERWIT. As a pump gone dry; if you pour no water down you will get none out, so –

RANGER. Nay, I bar similes too, tonight.

DAPPERWIT. Why, is not the thought new? Don't you apprehend it?

RANGER. Yes, yes, but –

DAPPERWIT. Well, well, will you comply with his sottishness too and hate brisk things in complaisance to the ignorant dull age? I believe shortly 'twill be as hard to find a patient friend to communicate one's wit to as a faithful friend to communicate one's secret to. Wit has as few true judges as painting, I see.

RANGER. All people pretend to be judges of both.

DAPPERWIT. Ay, they pretend – but, set you aside and two more –

RANGER. But why has Vincent neither courage nor wit?

DAPPERWIT. He has no courage because he beat his wench for giving me *les douces yeux* once and no wit because he does not comprehend my thoughts and he is a son of a whore for his ignorance. I take ignorance worse from any man than the lie because it is as much as to say I am no wit.

15–16 *you. Here, Dapperwit*: you here Dapperwit Q1.
40 *as few*: a few Q1.

VINCENT *returns.*

You need not take any notice, though, to him of what I say.

VINCENT. Ranger, there is a woman below in a coach would speak with you.

RANGER. With me? *Exit* RANGER.

DAPPERWIT. This Ranger, Mr Vincent, is as false to his friend as his wench.

VINCENT. You have no reason to say so but because he is absent.

DAPPERWIT. 'Tis disobliging to tell a man of his faults to his face. If he had but your grave parts and manly wit I should adore him but, a pox, he is a mere buffoon, a Jack-pudding, let me perish.

VINCENT. You are an ungrateful fellow. I have heard him maintain you had wit – which was more than e'er you could do for yourself. I thought you had owned him your Maecenas.

DAPPERWIT. A pox, he cannot but esteem me; 'tis for his honour. But I cannot but be just for all that, without favour or affection; yet I confess I love him so well that I wish he had but the hundredth part of your courage.

VINCENT. He has had the courage to save you from many a beating, to my knowledge.

DAPPERWIT. Come, come, I wish the man well and, next to you, better than any man; and I am sorry to say it, he has not courage to snuff a candle with his fingers. When he is drunk indeed, he dares get a clap or so – and swear at a constable.

VINCENT. Detracting fop, when did you see him desert his friend?

DAPPERWIT. You have a rough kind of raillery, Mr Vincent, but since you will have it (though I love the man heartily, I say), he deserted me once in breaking of windows, for fear of the constable.

---

63 *Jack-pudding*: buffoon, clown, fool.
67 *Maecenas*: rich patron.
77 *courage*: a courage Q1.
78 *clap*: dose of syphilis.
84–5 *breaking of windows*: a common night-time activity of rakes.

RANGER *returns.*

But you need not take notice to him of what I tell you; I hate to put a man to the blush.

RANGER. I have had just now a visit from my mistress, who is as jealous of me as a wife of her husband when she lies in – my cousin Lydia, you have heard me speak of her.

VINCENT. But she is more troublesome than a wife that lies in because she follows you to your haunts. Why do you allow her that privilege before her time?

RANGER. Faith, I may allow her any privilege and be too hard for her yet. How do you think I have cheated her tonight? Women are poor credulous creatures, easily deceived.

VINCENT. We are poor credulous creatures when we think 'em so.

RANGER. Intending a ramble to St James's Park tonight, upon some probable hopes of some fresh game I have in chase, I appointed her to stay at home, with a promise to come to her within this hour, that she might not foil the scent and prevent my sport.

VINCENT. She'll be even with you when you are married, I warrant you. In the meantime, here's her health, Dapperwit.

RANGER. Now had he rather be at the window, writing her anagram in the glass with his diamond, or biting his nails in the corner for a fine thought to come and divert us with at the table.

DAPPERWIT. No, a pox, I have no wit tonight; I am as barren and hide-bound as one of your damned scribbling poets, who are sots in company for all their wit, as a miser poor for all his money. How do you like the thought?

VINCENT. Drink, drink.

DAPPERWIT. Well, I can drink this because I shall be reprieved presently.

VINCENT. Who will be so civil to us?

DAPPERWIT. Sir Simon Addleplot. I have bespoke him a supper here, for he treats tonight a new rich mistress.

RANGER. That spark who has his fruitless designs upon

---

93 *lies in*: in the last weeks of pregnancy.

the bedridden rich widow down to the sucking heiresses in her pissing clout. He was once the sport but now the public grievance of all the fortunes in town, for he watches them like a younger brother that is afraid to be mumped of his snip and they cannot steal a marriage nor stay their stomachs but he must know it.

DAPPERWIT. He has now pitched his nets for Gripe's daughter, the rich scrivener, and serves him as a clerk, to get admission to her, which the watchful fop, her father, denies to all others.

RANGER. I thought you had been nibbling at her once, under pretence of love to her aunt.

DAPPERWIT. I confess I have the same design yet and Addleplot is but my agent whilst he thinks me his. He brings me letters constantly from her and carries mine back.

VINCENT. Still betraying your best friends.

DAPPERWIT. I cannot in honour but betray him, let me perish; the poor young wench is taken with my person and would scratch through four walls to come to me.

VINCENT. 'Tis a sign she is kept up close indeed.

DAPPERWIT. Betray him! I'll not be a traitor to love for any man.

[*Enter*] SIR SIMON ADDLEPLOT *to them with the* WAITER.

SIR SIMON. Know 'em! You are a saucy Jack-straw to question me, faith and troth. I know everybody and everybody knows me.

ALL. Sir Simon, Sir Simon, Sir Simon.

RANGER. And you are a welcome man to everybody.

SIR SIMON. Now, son of a whore, do I know the gentlemen? A dog, he would have had a shilling of me before he would let me come to you.

RANGER. The rogue has been bred at court, sure. Get you out, sirrah.

[*Exit* WAITER.]

SIR SIMON. He has been bred at a French house where they are more unreasonable.

---

126 *pissing clout*: nappy.
129 *mumped of his snip*: cheated of his share.
148 *Jack-straw*: worthless man.

VINCENT. Here's to you, Sir Simon.

SIR SIMON. I cannot drink for I have a mistress within, though I would not have the people of the house to know it.

RANGER. You need not be ashamed of your mistresses, for they are commonly rich.

SIR SIMON. And because she is rich I would conceal her, for I never had a rich mistress yet but one or other got her from me presently, faith and troth.

RANGER. But this is an ill place to conceal a mistress in; every waiter is an intelligencer to your rivals.

SIR SIMON. I have trick for that; I let no waiters come into the room – I'll lay the cloth myself rather.

RANGER. But who is your mistress?

SIR SIMON. Your servant, your servant, Mr Ranger.

VINCENT. Come, will you pledge me?

SIR SIMON. No, I'll spare your wine if you will spare me Dapperwit's company; I came for that.

VINCENT. You do us a double favour to take him and leave the wine.

SIR SIMON. Come, come, Dapperwit.

RANGER. (*aside*) Do not go unless he will suffer us to see his mistress too.

SIR SIMON. Come, come, man.

DAPPERWIT. Would you have me so incivil as to leave my company? They'll take it ill.

SIR SIMON. I cannot find her talk without thee. Pray, gentlemen, persuade Mr Dapperwit to go with me.

RANGER. We will not hinder him of better company.

DAPPERWIT. Yours is too good to be left rudely.

SIR SIMON. Nay, gentlemen, I would desire your company too, if you knew the lady.

DAPPERWIT. They know her as well as I; you say I know her not.

SIR SIMON. (*aside*) You are not everybody.

RANGER. Perhaps we do know the lady, Sir Simon.

SIR SIMON. You do not, you do not; none of you ever saw her in your lives. But if you could be secret and civil –

RANGER. We have drunk yet but our bottle apiece.

---

170 *intelligencer*: spy.
199 *bottle*: bottles Q1.

SIR SIMON. But will you be civil, Mr Vincent?

RANGER. He dares not look a woman in the face under three bottles.

SIR SIMON. Come along, then. But can you be civil gentlemen? Will you be civil gentlemen? Pray, be civil if you can and you shall see her.

Exit SIR SIMON.

Returns with MY LADY FLIPPANT *and* MRS JOYNER.

DAPPERWIT. (*aside*) How, has he got his jilt here?

RANGER. (*aside*) The widow Flippant!

VINCENT. (*aside*) Is this the woman we never saw?

FLIPPANT. (*aside*) Does he bring us into company, and Dapperwit one? Though I had married the fool, I thought to have reserved the wit as well as other ladies.

SIR SIMON. Nay, look as long as you will, madam, you will find them civil gentlemen and good company.

FLIPPANT. I am not in doubt of their civility but yours.

JOYNER. (*behind*) You'll never leave snubbing your servants. Did you not promise to use him kindly?

FLIPPANT. (*aside*) 'Tis true. – We wanted no good company, Sir Simon, as long as we had yours.

SIR SIMON. But they wanted good company, therefore I forced them to accept of yours.

FLIPPANT. They will not think the company good they were forced into, certainly.

SIR SIMON. [*aside*] A pox, I must be using the words in fashion, though I never have any luck with 'em. – Mrs Joyner, help me off.

JOYNER. I suppose, madam, he means the gentlemen wanted not inclination to your company but confidence to desire so great an honour, therefore he forced 'em.

DAPPERWIT. What makes this bawd here? Sure, mistress, you bawds should be like the small cards: though at first you make up the pack, yet when the play begins you should be put out as useless.

JOYNER. Well, well, jibing companion, you would have the pimps kept in only? You would so?

VINCENT. What, they are quarrelling?

231–3 Many card games, including picquet and ombre, were played without the low cards in the pack.

234 *jibing*: sneering.

RANGER. Pimp and bawd agree nowadays like doctor and apothecary.

SIR SIMON. Try, madam, if they are not civil gentlemen; talk with 'em while I go lay the cloth – no waiter comes here. (*Aside*) My mother used to tell me I should avoid all occasions of talking before my mistress because silence is a sign of love as well as prudence. (SIR SIMON *laying the cloth*)

FLIPPANT. Methinks you look a little yellow on't, Mr Dapperwit. I hope you do not censure me because you find me passing away a night with this fool; he is not a man to be jealous of, sure.

DAPPERWIT. You are not a lady to be jealous of, sure.

FLIPPANT. No, certainly. But why do you look as if you were jealous then?

DAPPERWIT. If I had met you in Whetstone's Park with a drunken footsoldier I should not have been jealous of you.

FLIPPANT. Fie, fie, now you are jealous certainly, for people always, when they grow jealous, grow rude. But I can pardon it since it proceeds from love, certainly.

DAPPERWIT. (*aside*) I am out of all hopes to be rid of this eternal old acquaintance. When I jeer her, she thinks herself praised; now I call her whore in plain English, she thinks I am jealous.

FLIPPANT. Sweet Mr Dapperwit, be not so censorious. I speak for your sake, not my own, for jealousy is a great torment, but my honour cannot suffer, certainly.

DAPPERWIT. No, certainly, but the greatest torment I have is your love.

FLIPPANT. Alas, sweet Mr Dapperwit, indeed love is a torment but 'tis a sweet torment; but jealousy is a bitter torment. I do not go about to cure you of the torment of my love.

DAPPERWIT. 'Tis a sign so.

FLIPPANT. Come, come, look up, man. Is that a rival to contest with you?

---

236 *and*: an Q1.
244 *yellow*: jealous.
251 *Whetstone's Park*: an area north of Lincoln's Inn Fields and south of Holborn, notorious for its prostitutes.

DAPPERWIT. I will contest with no rival, not with my old rival, your coachman, but they have heartily my resignation; and to do you a favour, but myself a greater, I will help tie the knot you are fumbling for now, betwixt your cully here and you.

FLIPPANT. Go, go, I take that kind of jealousy worst of all, to suspect I would be debauched to beastly matrimony. But who are those gentlemen, pray? – Are they men of fortunes, Mrs Joyner?

JOYNER. I believe so.

FLIPPANT. Do you believe so, indeed? Gentlemen – (*Advancing towards* RANGER *and* VINCENT)

RANGER. If the civility we owe to ladies had not controlled our envy to Mr Dapperwit we had interrupted ere this your private conversation.

FLIPPANT. Your interruption, sir, had been most civil and obliging, for our discourse was of marriage.

RANGER. That is a subject, madam, as grateful as common.

FLIPPANT. O fie, fie, are you of that opinion too? I cannot suffer any to talk of it in my company.

RANGER. Are you married then, madam?

FLIPPANT. No, certainly.

RANGER. I am sure so much beauty cannot despair of it.

FLIPPANT. Despair of it!

RANGER. Only those that are married or cannot be married hate to hear of marriage.

FLIPPANT. Yet you must know, sir, my aversion to marriage is such that you nor no man breathing shall ever persuade me to it.

RANGER. Cursed be the man should do so rude a thing as to persuade you to anything against your inclination. I would not do it for the world, madam.

FLIPPANT. Come, come, though you seem to be a civil gentleman, I think you no better than your neighbours. I do not know a man of you all that will not thrust a woman up into a corner and then talk an hour to her impertinently of marriage.

RANGER. You would find me another man in a corner, I assure you, madam, for you should not have a word of marriage from me, whatsoever you might find in my actions of it. I hate talking as much as you.

FLIPPANT. I hate it extremely.

RANGER. I am your man then, madam, for I find just the

same fault with your sex as you do with ours; I ne'er could have to do with a woman in my life but still she would be impertinently talking of marriage to me.

FLIPPANT. (*aside*) Observe that, Mrs Joyner.

DAPPERWIT. Pray, Mr Ranger, let's go. I had rather drink with Mr Vincent than stay here with you; besides, 'tis Park-time.

RANGER. (*to* DAPPERWIT) I come. – Since you are a lady that hate marriage, I'll do you the service to withdraw the company, for those that hate marriage hate loss of time.

FLIPPANT. Will you go then, sir? But, before you go, sir, pray tell me, is your aversion to marriage real?

RANGER. As real as yours.

FLIPPANT. (*aside*) If it were no more real than mine.

RANGER. Your servant, madam.

FLIPPANT. (*plucks him back*) But do you hate marriage certainly?

RANGER. Certainly.

FLIPPANT. Come, I cannot believe it. You dissemble it only because I pretend it.

RANGER. Do you but pretend it then, madam?

FLIPPANT. (*aside*) I shall discover myself. – I mean, because I hold against it, you do the same in complaisance, for, I have heard say, cunning men think to bring the coy and untractable women to tameness as they do some mad people, by humouring their frenzies.

RANGER. I am none of those cunning men, yet have too much wit to entertain the presumption of designing upon you.

FLIPPANT. 'Twere no such presumption, neither.

DAPPERWIT. Come, away, 'sdeath, don't you see your danger?

RANGER. Those aims are for Sir Simon. Goodnight, madam.

FLIPPANT. Will you needs go then? The gentlemen are a-going, Sir Simon. Will you let 'em?

SIR SIMON. Nay, madam, if you cannot keep 'em, how should I?

FLIPPANT. Stay, sir. Because you hate marriage, I'll sing you a new song against it. (*She sings*)

---

357 s.d. *She sings*: the music by Pelham Humphrey is most

A spouse I do hate,
For either she's false or she's jealous;
But give us a mate
Who nothing will ask us or tell us.

She stands on no terms,
Nor chaffers by way of indenture
Her love for your farms
But takes her kind man at a venture.

If all prove not right,
Without an act, process or warning,
From wife for a night
You may be divorced in the morning.

When parents are slaves
Their brats cannot be any other;
Great wits and great braves
Have always a punk to their mother.

Though it be the fashion for women of quality to sing any song whatever, because the words are not distinguished, yet I should have blushed to have done it now, but for you, sir.

RANGER. The song is edifying, the voice admirable, and once more, I am your servant, madam.

FLIPPANT. What, will you go too, Mr Dapperwit?

SIR SIMON. Pray, Mr Dapperwit, do not you go too.

DAPPERWIT. I am engaged.

SIR SIMON. Well, if we cannot have their company we will not have their room. Ours is a private back room; they have paid their reckoning. Let's go thither again.

FLIPPANT. But, pray, sweet Mr Dapperwit, do not go. Keep him, Sir Simon!

SIR SIMON. I cannot keep him.

Exeunt VINCENT, RANGER, DAPPERWIT.

It is impossible (the world is so):
One cannot keep one's friend and mistress too.

Exeunt omnes.

---

conveniently available in Weales's edition, p. 29. It appeared, with slightly different words, in John Playford's *Choice Airs and Songs* (Book 5, 1684).

363 *chaffers*: barters.

365 *at a venture*: as a commercial speculation, takes a chance.

ACT II

SCENE I

St James's Park at night.

Enter RANGER, VINCENT, DAPPERWIT.

RANGER. Hang me if I am not pleased extremely with the new-fashioned caterwauling, this midnight coursing in the Park.

VINCENT. A man may come after supper with his three bottles in his head, reel himself sober without reproof from his mother, aunt or grave relation.

RANGER. May bring his bashful wench and not have her put out of countenance by the impudent honest women of the town.

DAPPERWIT. And a man of wit may have the better of the dumb show of well-trimmed vest or fair peruke – no man's now is whitest.

RANGER. And now no woman's modest or proud, for her blushes are hid and the rubies on her lips are died and all sleepy and glimmering eyes have lost their attraction.

VINCENT. And now a man may carry a bottle under his arm, instead of his hat, and no observing spruce fop will miss the cravat that lies on one's shoulder or count the pimples on one's face.

DAPPERWIT. And now the brisk repartee ruins the complaisant cringe or wise grimace. Something 'twas, we men of virtue always loved the night.

RANGER. O blessed season.

VINCENT. For good-fellows.

RANGER. For lovers.

DAPPERWIT. And for the muses.

RANGER. When I was a boy I loved the night so well I had a strong vocation to be a bellman's apprentice.

VINCENT. I a drawer.

29 *bellman*: night watchman.
30 *drawer*: barman.

DAPPERWIT. And I to attend the waits of Westminster, let me perish.

RANGER. But why do we not do the duty of this and such other places, walk, censure and speak ill of all we meet?

DAPPERWIT. 'Tis no fault of mine, let me perish.

VINCENT. Fie, fie, satirical gentlemen, this is not your time; you cannot distinguish a friend from a fop.

DAPPERWIT. No matter, no matter. They will deserve amongst 'em the worst we can say.

RANGER. Who comes here, Dapperwit?

People walking slowly over the stage.

DAPPERWIT. By the toss of his head, training of his feet and his elbows playing at bo-peep behind his back, it should be my Lord Easy.

RANGER. And who the woman?

DAPPERWIT. My Lord What-d'ye-call's daughter that had a child by –

VINCENT. Dapperwit, hold your tongue!

RANGER. How are you concerned?

VINCENT. Her brother's an honest fellow and will drink his glass.

RANGER. Prithee, Vincent, Dapperwit did not hinder drinking tonight, though he speak against it; why then should you interrupt his sport? Now let him talk of anybody.

VINCENT. So he will, till you cut his throat.

RANGER. Why should you in all occasions thwart him, contemn him and maliciously look grave at his jests only?

VINCENT. Why does he always rail against my friends then and my best friend, a beer-glass?

RANGER. Dapperwit, be your own advocate; my game, I think, is before me there. *Exit* RANGER.

DAPPERWIT. This Ranger, I think, has all the ill qualities of all your town fops, leaving his company for a spruce lord or a wench.

VINCENT. Nay, if you must rail at your own best friends I may forgive you railing at mine.

---

31 *waits*: wind bands maintained by the city; they often played in the streets at night.

LYDIA *and* MY LADY FLIPPANT *walking across the stage.*

LYDIA. (*aside*) False Ranger, shall I find thee here?

VINCENT. (*to* DAPPERWIT) Those are women, are they not?

DAPPERWIT. (*aside*) The least seems to be my Lucy, sure.

VINCENT. Faith, I think I dare speak to a woman in the dark; let's try.

DAPPERWIT. They are persons of quality of my acquaintance. Hold.

VINCENT. Nay, if they are persons of quality of your acquaintance I may be the bolder with 'em.

The ladies go off; they follow them.

LYDIA *and* FLIPPANT *re-enter.*

LYDIA. I come hither to make a discovery tonight.

FLIPPANT. Of my love to you certainly, for nobody but you could have debauched me to the park, certainly; I would not return another night, if it were to redeem my dear husband from his grave.

LYDIA. I believe you, but to get another, widow.

FLIPPANT. Another husband, another husband, foh!

LYDIA. There does not pass a night here but many a match is made.

FLIPPANT. That a woman of honour should have the word 'match' in her mouth! But I hope, madam, the fellows do not make honourable love here, do they? I abominate honourable love, on my honour.

LYDIA. If they should make honourable love here, I know you would prevent 'em.

VINCENT *and* DAPPERWIT *re-enter and walk slowly towards them.*

But here come two men will inform you what they do.

FLIPPANT. Do they come? Are they men certainly?

LYDIA. Prepare for an assault; they'll put you to't.

FLIPPANT. Will they put us to't certainly? I was never put to't yet. If they should put us to't I should drop down, down certainly.

---

72 *least*: shortest.

LYDIA. I believe, truly, you would not have power to run away.

FLIPPANT. Therefore I will not stay the push. They come, they come, oh, the fellows come!

FLIPPANT *runs away,* LYDIA *follows and* VINCENT *and* DAPPERWIT *after them.* FLIPPANT *re-enters at t'other door alone.*

FLIPPANT. So I am got off clear. I did not run from the men but my companion. For all their brags, men have hardly courage to set upon us when our number is equal. Now they shall see I defy 'em, for we women have always most courage when we are alone. But a pox! The lazy rogues come not or they are drunk and cannot run. Oh drink, abominable drink! Instead of inflaming love, it quenches it and for one lover it encourages it makes a thousand impotent. Curse on all wine, even Rhenish wine and sugar –

Enter ADDLEPLOT *muffled in a cloak.*

But Fortune will not see me want; here comes a single bully – I wish he may stand,
For now anights the jostling nymph is bolder
Than modern satyr with his cloak o'er shoulder.
(*She puts on her mask*) Well met, sir.

SIR SIMON. How shall I know that, forsooth? Who are you? Do you know me?

FLIPPANT. Who are you? Don't you know me?

SIR SIMON. Not I, faith and troth.

FLIPPANT. I am glad on't, for no man e'er liked a woman the better for having known her before.

SIR SIMON. Ay, but then one can't be so free with a new acquaintance as with an old one; she may deny the civility.

FLIPPANT. Not till you ask her.

SIR SIMON. But I am afraid to be denied.

FLIPPANT. Let me tell you, sir, you cannot disoblige us women more than in distrusting us.

---

114 *Rhenish wine and sugar*: often a drink for invalids.
116 *bully*: rake.
118 *satyr*: half-man, half-goat in Greek mythology, drunken, lecherous companion of Bacchus.

SIR SIMON. Pish, what should one ask for when you know one's meaning? But shall I deal freely with you?

FLIPPANT. I love, of my life, men should deal freely with me; there are so few men will deal freely with one –

SIR SIMON. Are you not a fireship, a punk, madam?

FLIPPANT. Well, sir, I love raillery.

SIR SIMON. Faith and troth, I do not rally; I deal freely.

FLIPPANT. This is the time and place for freedom, sir.

SIR SIMON. Are you handsome?

FLIPPANT. Joan's as good as my lady in the dark, certainly. But men that deal freely never ask questions, certainly.

SIR SIMON. How then! I thought to deal freely and put a woman to the question had been all one.

FLIPPANT. But let me tell you, those that deal freely indeed take a woman by –

SIR SIMON. What, what, what, what?

FLIPPANT. By the hand and lead her aside.

SIR SIMON. Now I understand you. Come along then.

Enter torches and music at a distance.

FLIPPANT. What unmannerly rascals are those that bring light into the park? 'Twill not be taken well from 'em by the women certainly. (*Aside*) Still disappointed –

SIR SIMON. Oh the fiddles, the fiddles! I sent for them hither to oblige the women, not offend 'em, for I intend to serenade the whole park tonight. But my frolic is not without an intrigue, faith and troth, for I know the fiddles will call the whole herd of vizard masks together and then shall I discover if a strayed mistress of mine be not amongst 'em, whom I treated tonight at the French house, but as soon as the jilt had eat up my meat and drank her two bottles, she run away from me and left me alone.

FLIPPANT. (*aside*) Is it he? Addleplot! That I could not know him by his 'faith and troth'!

---

138 *fireship, punk*: both are slang words for prostitutes.
152 s.d. *torches*: linkboys carrying torches.
161–2 *vizard masks*: fashionable masks, later the sign of a prostitute.

SIR SIMON. Now I would understand her tricks because I intend to marry her and should be glad to know what I must trust to.

FLIPPANT. (*aside*) So thou shalt, but not yet.

SIR SIMON. Though I can give a great guess already, for, if I have any intrigue or sense in me, she is as arrant a jilt as ever pulled pillow from under husband's head, faith and troth; moreover she is bow-legged, hopper-hipped and, betwixt pomatum and Spanish red, has a complexion like a Holland cheese and no more teeth left than such as give a haust-goust to her breath – but she is rich, faith and troth.

FLIPPANT. (*aside*) Oh rascal! He has heard somebody else say all this of me. But I must not discover myself, lest I should be disappointed of my revenge, for I will marry him.

The torches and music approaching. Exit FLIPPANT.

SIR SIMON. What, gone? Come then, strike up, my lads.

Enter men and women in vizards and dance. ADDLEPLOT *for the most part standing still in a cloak and vizard but sometimes going about, peeping and examining the women's clothes. The dance ended, exeunt dancers, torches, music and* ADDLEPLOT. *Enter* FLIPPANT, LYDIA, *after them* VINCENT, DAPPERWIT.

FLIPPANT. (*to* LYDIA) Nay, if you stay any longer, I must leave you again.

VINCENT. We have overtaken them at last again; these are they.

FLIPPANT *going off.*

They separate too and that's but a challenge to us.

DAPPERWIT. Let me perish, ladies –

LYDIA. Nay, good madam, let's unite, now here's the common enemy upon us.

VINCENT. Damn me, ladies –

DAPPERWIT. Hold; a pox, you are too rough. Let me perish, ladies.

---

174 *or*: on Q1.
176–7 *hopper-hipped*: steatopygous, big-bottomed.
177 *pomatum*: face cream.
177 *Spanish red*: rouge.
178 *Holland cheese*: probably Texel, a green, sheep's milk cheese.
179 *haust-goust*: bad smell (Fr. *haut goût*: highly seasoned).

LYDIA. Not for want of breath, gentlemen; we'll stay rather.

DAPPERWIT. For want of your favour, rather, sweet ladies.

FLIPPANT. [*aside*] That's Dapperwit, false villain, but he must not know I am here. If he should I should lose his thrice agreeable company and he would run from me as fast as from the bailiffs. – What, you will not talk with 'em, I hope?

LYDIA. Yes, but I will.

FLIPPANT. Then you are a park-woman certainly and you will take it kindly if I leave you.

LYDIA. (*apart*) No, you must not leave me.

FLIPPANT. Then you must leave them.

LYDIA. I'll see if they are worse company than you first.

FLIPPANT. Monstrous impudence, will you not come? (*Pulls* LYDIA)

VINCENT. Nay, madam, I never suffer any violence to be used to a woman but what I do myself. She must stay and you must not go.

FLIPPANT. Unhand me, you rude fellow.

VINCENT. Nay, now I am sure you will stay and be kind, for coyness in a woman is as little sign of true modesty as huffing in a man is of true courage.

DAPPERWIT. Use her gently and speak soft things to her.

LYDIA. (*aside*) Now do I guess I know my coxcomb. – Sir, I am extremely glad I am fallen into the hands of a gentleman that can speak soft things and this is so fine a night to hear soft things in – morning, I should have said.

DAPPERWIT. It will not be morning, dear madam, till you pull off your mask. (*Aside*) That I think was brisk!

LYDIA. Indeed, dear sir, my face would frighten back the sun.

DAPPERWIT. With glories more radiant than his own. (*Aside*) I keep up with her, I think.

LYDIA. But why would you put me to the trouble of lighting the world, when I thought to have gone to sleep?

DAPPERWIT. You only can do it, dear madam, let me perish.

---

220 *huffing*: swaggering.

LYDIA. But why would you (of all men) practise treason against your friend Phoebus and depose him for a mere stranger?

DAPPERWIT. (*aside*) I think she knows me.

LYDIA. But he does not do you justice, I believe, and you are so positively cocksure of your wit, you would refer to a mere stranger your plea to the bay-tree.

DAPPERWIT. (*aside*) She jeers me, let me perish.

VINCENT. Dapperwit, a little of your aid, for my lady's invincibly dumb.

DAPPERWIT. (*aside*) Would mine had been so too.

VINCENT. I have used as many arguments to make her speak as are requisite to make other women hold their tongues.

DAPPERWIT. Well, I am ready to change sides. Yet before I go, madam, since the moon consents now I should see your face, let me desire you to pull off your mask, which to a handsome lady is a favour, I'm sure.

LYDIA. Truly, sir, I must not be long in debt to you the obligation. Pray, let me hear you recite some of your verses, which to a wit is a favour, I'm sure.

DAPPERWIT. Madam, it belongs to your sex to be obliged first. Pull off your mask and I'll pull out my paper. (*Aside*) Brisk again of my side.

LYDIA. 'Twould be in vain, for you would want a candle now.

DAPPERWIT. (*aside*) I dare not make use again of the lustre of her face. – I'll wait upon you home then, madam.

LYDIA. Faith no, I believe it will not be much to our advantage to bring my face or your poetry to light, for, I hope, you have yet a pretty good opinion of my face, and so have I of your wit. But if you are for proving your wit, why do not you write a play?

DAPPERWIT. Because 'tis now no more reputation to write a play than it is honour to be a knight; your true wit despises the title of poet as much as your true gentleman the title of knight, for as a man may be a knight and no gentleman, so a man may be a poet and no wit, let me perish.

---

244 *plea to the bay-tree*: claim to poetic laurels.

LYDIA. Pray, sir, how are you dignified or distinguished amongst the rates of wits? And how many rates are there?

DAPPERWIT. There are as many degrees of wits as of lawyers: as there is first your solicitor, then your attorney, then your pleading-counsel, then your chamber-counsel and then your judge; so there is first your court-wit, your coffee-wit, your poll-wit or politic-wit, your chamber-wit or scribble-wit and, last of all, your judge-wit or critic.

LYDIA. But are there as many wits as lawyers? Lord, what will become of us? What employment can they have? How are they known?

DAPPERWIT. First, your court-wit is a fashionable, insinuating, flattering, cringing, grimacing fellow and has wit enough to solicit a suit of love and, if he fail, he has malice enough to ruin the woman with a dull lampoon. But he rails still at the man that is absent, for, you must know, all wits rail, and his wit properly lies in combing perukes, matching ribbons and being severe, as they call it, upon other people's clothes.

LYDIA. Now, what is the coffee-wit?

DAPPERWIT. He is a lying, censorious, gossiping, quibbling wretch and sets people together by the ears over that sober drink, coffee. He is a wit as he is a commentator upon the Gazette and he rails at the pirates of Algiere, the Grand Signior of Constantinople and the Christian Grand Signior.

LYDIA. What kind of man is your poll-wit?

DAPPERWIT. He is a fidgeting, busy, dogmatical, hot-headed fop that speaks always in sentences and proverbs (as others in similitudes) and he rails perpetually against the present government. His wit lies in projects and monopolies and penning speeches for young parliament-men.

LYDIA. But what is your chamber-wit or scribble-wit?

DAPPERWIT. He is a poring, melancholy, modest sot, ashamed of the world. He searches all the records of

---

304 *Gazette*: *The London Gazette*, a semi-official newspaper, mostly with foreign news.

305 *Grand Signior of Constantinople*: the Sultan of Turkey.

306 *Christian Grand Signior*: Louis XIV of France.

wit to compile a breviate of them for the use of players, printers, book-sellers and sometimes cooks and tabacca-men. He employs his railing against the ignorance of the age and all that have more money than he.

LYDIA. Now your last.

DAPPERWIT. Your judge-wit or critic is all these together and yet has the wit to be none of them; he can think, speak, write as well as all the rest but scorns (himself a judge) to be judged by posterity. He rails at all the other classes of wits and his wit lies in damning all but himself; he is your true wit.

LYDIA. Then I suspect you are of his firm.

DAPPERWIT. I cannot deny it, madam.

VINCENT. Dapperwit, you have been all this time on the wrong side, for you love to talk all and here's a lady would not have hindered you.

DAPPERWIT. (*aside*) A pox, I have been talking too long indeed here, for wit is lost upon a silly, weak woman as well as courage.

VINCENT. I have used all common means to move a woman's tongue and mask; I called her ugly, old and old acquaintance and yet she would not disprove me. But here comes Ranger; let him try what he can do, for, since my mistress is dogged, I'll go sleep alone. *Exit.*

RANGER *enters.*

LYDIA. (*aside*) Ranger! 'Tis he indeed. I am sorry he is here but glad I discovered him before I went. Yet he must not discover me, lest I should be prevented hereafter in finding him out. False Ranger! – Nay, if they bring fresh force upon us, madam, 'tis time to quit the field.

Exeunt LYDIA, FLIPPANT.

RANGER. What, play with your quarry till it fly from you?

DAPPERWIT. You frightened it away.

RANGER. Ha! Is not one of those ladies in mourning?

DAPPERWIT. All woman are so by this light.

---

341 *dogged*: stubborn.

RANGER. But you might easily discern it. Don't you know her?

DAPPERWIT. No.

RANGER. Did you talk with her?

DAPPERWIT. Yes, she's one of your brisk, silly baggages.

RANGER. 'Tis she, 'tis she. I was afraid I saw her before. Let us follow 'em. Prithee make haste. (*Aside*) 'Tis Lydia.

Exeunt.

LYDIA, MY LADY FLIPPANT *return at the other door,* RANGER, DAPPERWIT *following them at a distance.*

LYDIA. They follow us yet, I fear.

FLIPPANT. You do not fear it certainly, otherwise you would not have encouraged them.

LYDIA. For heaven's sake, madam, waive your quarrel a little and let us pass by your coach and so on foot to your acquaintance in the Old Pell Mell, for I would not be discovered by the man that came up last to us.

Exeunt.

SCENE II

The scene changes to Christina's lodging.

Enter CHRISTINA, ISABEL.

ISABEL. For heaven's sake, undress yourself, madam; they'll not return tonight – all people have left the park an hour ago.

CHRISTINA. What is't a clock?

ISABEL. 'Tis past one.

CHRISTINA. It cannot be.

ISABEL. I thought that time had only stolen from happy lovers; the disconsolate have nothing to do but to tell the clock.

---

366 *Old Pell Mell*: now Pall Mall, running from St James's Street to the Haymarket, named after the game played there; Act IV Scene ii takes place there.

CHRISTINA. I can only keep account with my misfortunes.

ISABEL. I am glad they are not innumerable.

CHRISTINA. And truly, my undergoing so often your impertinency is not the least of them.

ISABEL. I am then more glad, madam, for then they cannot be great and it is in my power, it seems, to make you in part happy, if I could but hold this villainous tongue of mine. But then let the people of the town hold their tongues if they will, for I cannot but tell you what they say.

CHRISTINA. What do they say?

ISABEL. Faith, madam, I am afraid to tell you, now I think on't.

CHRISTINA. Is it so ill?

ISABEL. Oh, such base unworthy things.

CHRISTINA. Do they say I was really Clerimont's wench as he boasted and that the ground of the quarrel betwixt Valentine and him was not Valentine's vindication of my honour but Clerimont's jealousy of him?

ISABEL. Worse, worse a thousand times. Such villainous things to the utter ruin of your reputation!

CHRISTINA. What are they?

ISABEL. Faith, madam, you'll be angry; 'tis the old trick of lovers to hate their informers after they have made 'em such.

CHRISTINA. I will not be angry.

ISABEL. They say then, since Mr Valentine's flying into France, you are grown mad, have put yourself into mourning, live in a dark room where you'll see nobody nor take any rest day or night but rave and talk to yourself perpetually.

CHRISTINA. Now what else?

ISABEL. But the surest sign of your madness is, they say, because you are desperately resolved (in case my Lord Clerimont should die of his wounds) to transport yourself and fortune into France, to Mr Valentine, a man that has not a groat to return you in exchange.

CHRISTINA. All this hitherto is true; now to the rest.

ISABEL. Indeed, madam, I have no more to tell you. I was sorry, I'm sure, to hear so much of any lady of mine.

CHRISTINA. Insupportable insolence.

ISABEL. (*aside*) This is some revenge for my want of sleep tonight. (*Knocking at the door*) So, I hope my old second is come; 'tis seasonable relief.

Exit ISABEL.

CHRISTINA. Unhappy Valentine, couldst thou but see how soon thy absence and misfortunes have disbanded all thy friends and turned thy slaves all renegades, thou sure wouldst prize my only faithful heart.

Enter MY LADY FLIPPANT, LYDIA, ISABEL *to her.*

FLIPPANT. Hail, faithful shepherdess! But, truly, I had not kept my word with you in coming back tonight, if it had not been for this lady who has her intrigues too with the fellows, as well as you.

LYDIA. Madam, under my Lady Flippant's protection, I am confident to beg yours, being just now pursued out of the park by a relation of mine by whom it imports me extremely not to be discovered. But I fear he is now at the door. (*Knocking at the door. To* ISABEL *going out*) Let me desire you to deny me to him courageously, for he will hardly believe he can be mistaken in me.

CHRISTINA. In such an occasion where impudence is requisite she will serve you as faithfully as you can wish, madam.

FLIPPANT. Come, come, madam, do not upbraid her with her assurance, a qualification that only fits her for a lady's service. A fine woman of the town can be no more without a woman that can make an excuse with an assurance than she can be without a glass, certainly.

CHRISTINA. She needs no advocate.

FLIPPANT. How can anyone alone manage an amorous intrigue? Though the birds are tame, somebody must help draw the net. If 'twere not for a woman that could make an excuse with assurance, how could we

---

55 s.d. *Isabel*: Isabella Q1.

61 *Hail, faithful shepherdess*: a reference to Fletcher's *The Faithful Shepherdess* (1610), a delicate pastoral inquiry into the nature of love, performed as recently as 26 February 1669.

wheedle, jilt, trace, discover, countermine, undermine and blow up the stinking fellows, which is all the pleasure I receive or design by them, for I never admitted a man to my conversation but for his punishment certainly.

CHRISTINA. Nobody will doubt that, certainly.

ISABEL *returns.*

ISABEL. Madam, the gentleman will not be mistaken; he says you are here, he saw you come in, he is your relation, his name's Ranger and is come to wait upon you home. I had much ado to keep him from coming up.

LYDIA. (*to* CHRISTINA) Madam, for heaven's sake, help me; 'tis yet in your power, if but while I retire into your dining room you will please to personate me and own yourself for her he pursued out of the park. You are in mourning too and your stature so much mine it will not contradict you.

CHRISTINA. I am sorry, madam, I must dispute any command of yours. I have made a resolution to see the face of no man till an unfortunate friend of mine, now out of the kingdom, return.

LYDIA. By that friend and by the hopes you have to see him, let me conjure you to keep me from the sight of mine now. Dear madam, let your charity prevail over your superstition.

ISABEL. He comes, he comes, madam.

RANGER *enters.* LYDIA *withdraws and stands unseen at the door.*

RANGER. [*aside*] Ha! This is no Lydia.

CHRISTINA. What unworthy defamer has encouraged you to offer me this insolence?

RANGER. (*aside*) She is liker Lydia in her style than her face. I see I am mistaken but to tell her I followed her for another were an affront rather than an excuse. She's a glorious creature.

---

86 *wheedle*: cheat.

86 *trace*: track, pursue.

CHRISTINA. Tell me sir, whence had you reason for this your rude pursuit of me into my lodging, my chamber? Why should you follow me?

RANGER. Faith, madam, because you run away from me.

CHRISTINA. That was no sign of an acquaintance.

RANGER. You'll pardon me, madam.

CHRISTINA. Then it seems you mistook me for another and the night is your excuse, which blots out all distinctions. But now you are satisfied in your mistake, I hope you will go seek out your woman in another place.

RANGER. Madam, I allow not the excuse you make for me; if I have offended I will rather be condemned for my love than pardoned for my insensibility.

LYDIA. (*behind*) How's that?

CHRISTINA. What do you say?

RANGER. Though the night had been darker my heart would not have suffered me to follow anyone but you; he has been too long acquainted with you to mistake you.

LYDIA. (*behind*) What means this tenderness? He mistook me for her, sure?

CHRISTINA. What says the gentleman? Did you know me then, sir?

RANGER. (*aside*) Not I, the devil take me, but I must on now. – Could you imagine, madam, by the innumerable crowd of your admirers, you had left any man free in the town or ignorant of the power of your beauty?

CHRISTINA. I never saw your face before, that I remember.

RANGER. Ah madam! You would never regard your humblest slave; I was till now a modest lover.

LYDIA. (*behind*) Falsest of men.

CHRISTINA. My woman said you came to seek a relation here, not a mistress.

RANGER. I must confess, madam, I thought you would sooner disprove my dissembled error than admit my visit and I was resolved to see you.

LYDIA. (*behind*) 'Tis clear.

RANGER. Indeed, when I followed you first out of the park, I was afraid you might have been a certain relation of mine, for your statures and habits are the same, but when you entered here I was with joy convinced. Besides, I would not for the world have given her troublesome love so much encouragement to have disturbed my future addresses to you, for the foolish woman does perpetually torment me to make our relation nearer – but never more in vain than since I have seen you, madam.

LYDIA. (*behind*) How shall I suffer this? 'Tis clear he disappointed me tonight for her and made me stay at home that I might not disappoint him of her company in the park.

CHRISTINA. I am amazed! But let me tell you, sir, if the lady were here, I would satisfy her the sight of me should never frustrate her ambitious designs upon her cruel kinsman.

LYDIA. (*behind*) I wish you could satisfy me.

RANGER. If she were here she would satisfy you she were not capable of the honour to be taken for you (though in the dark). Faith, my cousin is but a tolerable woman to a man that had not seen you.

CHRISTINA. Sure, to my plague, this is the first time you ever saw me!

RANGER. Sure, to the plague of my poor heart, 'tis not the hundredth time I have seen you, for since the time I saw you first you have not been at the park, playhouse, Exchange or other public place but I saw you, for it was my business to watch and follow you.

CHRISTINA. Pray, when did you see me last at the park, playhouse or Exchange?

RANGER. Some two, three days or a week ago.

CHRISTINA. I have not been this month out of this chamber.

LYDIA. (*behind*) That is to delude me.

CHRISTINA. I knew you were mistaken.

RANGER. You'll pardon a lover's memory, madam. (*Aside*) A pox, I have hanged myself in my own line. One would think my perpetual ill luck in lying should break me of the quality but, like a losing gamester, I am still for pushing on till none will trust me.

CHRISTINA. Come, sir, you run out of one error into a greater; you would excuse the rudeness of your mis-

---

187 *Exchange*: the New Exchange, an arcade of shops in the Strand.

take and intrusion at this hour into my lodgings with your gallantry to me, more unseasonable and offensive.

RANGER. Nay, I am in love, I see, for I blush and have not a word to say for myself.

CHRISTINA. But, sir, if you will needs play the gallant, pray leave my house before morning, lest you should be seen to go hence, to the scandal of my honour. [. . .] Rather than that should be I'll call up the house and neighbours to bear witness I bid you begone.

RANGER. Since you take a night-visit so ill, madam, I will never wait upon you again but by day. I go that I may hope to return and, for once, I will wish you a good night without me.

CHRISTINA. Goodnight for as long as I live.

Exit RANGER.

LYDIA. (*behind*) And goodnight to my love, I'm sure.

CHRISTINA. Though I have done you an inconsiderable service, I assure, madam, you are not a little obliged to me. (*Aside*) Pardon me, dear Valentine.

LYDIA. I know not yet whether I am more obliged than injured; when I do, I assure you, madam, I shall not be insensible of either.

CHRISTINA. I fear, madam, you are as liable to mistakes as your kinsman.

LYDIA. I fear I am more subject to 'em; it may be for want of sleep, therefore I'll go home.

CHRISTINA. My Lady Flippant, goodnight.

FLIPPANT. Goodnight – or rather good morrow, faithful shepherdess.

CHRISTINA. I'll wait of you down.

LYDIA. Your coach stays yet, I hope.

FLIPPANT. Certainly.

Exeunt omnes.

209–10 *honour. [. . .] Rather*: Q1 repeats the speech-prefix *Christina* before *Rather* and a response from Ranger has probably disappeared.

SCENE III

The scene, the street.

Enter RANGER, DAPPERWIT.

DAPPERWIT. I was a faithful sentinel; nobody came out, let me perish.

RANGER. No no, I hunted upon a wrong scent; I thought I had followed a woman but found her an angel.

DAPPERWIT. What is her name?

RANGER. That you must tell me: what very fine woman is there lies hereabouts?

DAPPERWIT. Faith, I know not any. She is, I warrant you, some fine woman of a term's standing or so in the town, such as seldom appear in public but in their balconies where they stand so constantly one would think they had hired no other part of the house.

RANGER. And look like the pictures which painters expose to draw in customers. But I must know who she is. Vincent's lodging is hard by; I'll go and inquire of him and lie with him tonight. But if he will not let me I'll lie with you, for my lodging is too far off –

DAPPERWIT. Then I will go before and expect you at mine.

Exeunt.

SCENE IV

The scene, Vincent's lodging.

Enter VINCENT, VALENTINE *in a riding habit, as newly from a journey.*

VINCENT. Your mistress, dear Valentine, will not be more glad to see you. But my wonder is no less than my joy that you would return ere you were informed Clerimont were out of danger; his surgeons themselves have not been assured of his recovery till within these two days.

---

9 *term's standing*: one of the four terms of the law-year, hence recently arrived.

VALENTINE. I feared my mistress, not my life; my life I could trust again with my old enemy, Fortune, but not longer my mistress in the hands of my greater enemies, her relations.

VINCENT. Your fear was in the wrong place then, for though my Lord Clerimont live, he and his relations may put you in more danger of your life than your mistress's relations can of losing her.

VALENTINE. Would any could secure me her I would myself secure my life, for I should value it then.

VINCENT. Come, come, her relations can do you no hurt; I dare swear, if her mother should but say your hat did not cock handsomely she would never ask her blessing again.

VALENTINE. Prithee, leave thy fooling and tell me if, since my departure, she has given evidences of her love, to clear those doubts I went away with, for, as absence is the bane of common and bastard love, 'tis the vindication of that which is true and generous.

VINCENT. Nay, if you could ever doubt her love you deserve to doubt on, for there is no punishment great enough for jealousy but jealousy.

VALENTINE. You may remember I told you, before my flight, I had quarrelled with the defamer of my mistress but thought I had killed my rival.

VINCENT. But pray, give me now the answer which the suddenness of your flight denied me: how could Clerimont hope to subdue her heart by the assault of her honour?

VALENTINE. Pish, it might be the stratagem of a rival, to make me desist.

VINCENT. For shame; if 'twere not rather to vindicate her than satisfy you, I would not tell you how like a Penelope she has behaved herself in your absence.

VALENTINE. Let me know.

VINCENT. Then know, the next day you went, she put herself into mourning and –

VALENTINE. That might be for Clerimont, thinking him dead, as all the world besides thought.

VINCENT. Still turning the dagger's point on yourself.

---

13 *than your*: than you Q1.
40 *Penelope*: Odysseus' long-waiting wife.

Hear me out. I say she put herself into mourning for you, locked up herself in her chamber this month for you, shut out her barking relations for you, has not seen the sun or face of man since she saw you, thinks and talks of nothing but you, sends to me daily to hear of you and, in short, I think, is mad for you – all this I can swear, for I am to her so near a neighbour and so inquisitive a friend for you –

[*Enter*] SERVANT *to them.*

SERVANT. Mr Ranger, sir, is coming up.

[*Exit* SERVANT]

VINCENT. What brings him now? He comes to lie with me.

VALENTINE. Who? Ranger?

VINCENT. Yes, pray retire a little till I send him off, unless you have a mind to have your arrival published tomorrow in the coffeehouses.

[*Enter* RANGER.] VALENTINE *retires to the door behind.*

RANGER. What, not yet a-bed? Your man is laying you to sleep with usquebaugh or brandy, is he not so?

VINCENT. What, punk will not be troubled with you tonight, therefore I am – is it not so?

RANGER. I have been turned out of doors indeed just now by a woman – but such a woman, Vincent –

VINCENT. Yes, yes, your women are always such women –

RANGER. A neighbour of yours and, I'm sure, the finest you have.

VINCENT. Prithee, do not asperse my neighbourhood with your acquaintance; 'twould bring a scandal upon an alley.

RANGER. Nay, I do not know her, therefore I come to you.

VINCENT. 'Twas no wonder she turned you out of doors then and, if she had known you, 'twould have been a wonder she had let you stay. But where does she live?

---

63 *usquebaugh*: whisky.

RANGER. Five doors off on the right hand.

VINCENT. Pish, pish –

RANGER. What's the matter?

VINCENT. Does she live there, do you say?

RANGER. Yes, I observed them exactly, that my account from you might be as exact. Do you know who lives there?

VINCENT. Yes, so well that I know you are mistaken.

RANGER. Is she not a young lady of scarce eighteen, of extraordinary beauty, her stature next to low, and in mourning?

VALENTINE. (*behind*) What is this?

VINCENT. She is. But if you saw her you broke in at window.

RANGER. I chased her home from the park, indeed, taking her for another lady who had some claim to my heart, till she show'd a better title to't.

VINCENT. Hah, hah, hah.

VALENTINE. (*behind*) Was she at park then? And have I a new rival?

VINCENT. From the park did you follow her, do you say? I knew you were mistaken.

RANGER. I tell you I am not.

VINCENT. If you are sure it was that house, it might be perhaps her woman stolen to the park unknown to her lady.

RANGER. My acquaintance does usually begin with the maid first but now 'twas with the mistress, I assure you.

VINCENT. The mistress! I tell you she has not been out of her doors since Valentine's flight. She is his mistress, the great heiress Christina.

RANGER. I tell you then again, I followed that Christina from the park home where I talked with her half an hour and intend to see her tomorrow again.

VALENTINE. (*behind*) Would she talk with him too?

VINCENT. It cannot be.

RANGER. Christina, do you call her? Faith, I am sorry she is an heiress, lest it should bring the scandal of interest and design of lucre upon my love.

---

80 *Five . . . hand*: the line comes from Q1's list of errata; the text reads *He whispers.*

VINCENT. No, no, her face and virtues will free you from that censure. But, however, 'tis not fairly done to rival your friend Valentine in his absence and, when he is present, you know 'twill be dangerous, by my Lord Clerimont's example. Faith, if you have seen her, I would not advise you to attempt it again.

RANGER. You may be merry, sir; you are not in love. Your advice I came not for, nor will I for your assistance. Goodnight. *Exit* RANGER.

VALENTINE. Here's your Penelope, the woman that had not seen the sun nor face of man since my departure, for it seems she goes out in the night, when the sun is absent and faces are not distinguished.

VINCENT. Why, do you believe him?

VALENTINE. Should I believe you?

VINCENT. 'Twere more for your interest and you would be less deceived. If you believe him you must doubt the chastity of all the fine women in town and five miles about.

VALENTINE. His reports of them will little invalidate his testimony with me.

VINCENT. He spares not the innocents in bibs and aprons, I'll secure you. He has made, at best, some gross mistake concerning Christina, which tomorrow will discover. In the meantime, let us go sleep.

VALENTINE. I will not hinder you because I cannot enjoy it myself.
Hunger, revenge to sleep are petty foes
But only death the jealous eyes can close.

Exeunt.

ACT III

SCENE I

Crossbite's house.

Enter MRS JOYNER, MRS CROSSBITE.

JOYNER. Good morrow, gossip.

CROSSBITE. Good morrow. But why up so early, good gossip?

JOYNER. My care and passionate concern for you and yours would not let me rest, in truly.

CROSSBITE. For me and mine?

JOYNER. You know we have known one another long. I think it be some nine and thirty years since you were married.

CROSSBITE. Nine and thirty years old, mistress? I'd have you to know I am no far-born child and if the register had not been burned in the last great fire, alas! But my face needs no register, sure. Nine and thirty years old said you, mistress?

JOYNER. I said you had been so long married. But, indeed, you bear your years as well as any she in Pepper Alley.

CROSSBITE. Nine and thirty, mistress.

JOYNER. This it is: a woman nowadays had rather you should find her faulty with a man, I warrant you, than discover her age, I warrant you.

CROSSBITE. Marry, and 'tis the greater secret far. Tell a miser he is rich and a woman she is old, you will get no money of him nor kindness of her. To tell me I was nine and thirty (I say no more), 'twas unneighbourly done of you, mistress.

JOYNER. My memory confesses my age, it seems, as much as my face, for I thought –

CROSSBITE. Pray talk nor think no more of anyone's age. But say, what brought you hither so early?

JOYNER. How does my sweet god-daughter? Poor wretch.

CROSSBITE. Well, very well.

JOYNER. Ah, sweet creature! Alas, alas, I am sorry for her.

CROSSBITE. Why, what has she done to deserve your sorrow or my reprehension?

LUCY *comes to the door.*

LUCY. (*behind*) What, are they talking of me?

---

11 *far-born*: born long ago.

17 *Pepper Alley*: in the notorious suburb of Southwark, across the river from the city.

JOYNER. In short, she was seen going into the meeting-house of the wicked, otherwise called the playhouse, hand-in-hand with that vile fellow Dapperwit.

CROSSBITE. Mr Dapperwit! Let me tell you, if 'twere not for Master Dapperwit we might have lived all this vacation upon green cheese, tripe and ox cheek. If he had it we should not want it. But poor gentleman, it often goes hard with him, for he's a wit.

JOYNER. So then, you are the dog to be fed, while the house is broken up. I say beware, the sweet bits you swallow will make your daughter's belly swell, mistress, and, after all your junkets, there will be a bone for you to pick, mistress.

CROSSBITE. Sure, Master Dapperwit is no such manner of man?

JOYNER. He is a wit, you say, and what are wits but contemners of matrons, seducers or defamers of married women and deflowerers of helpless virgins, even in the streets, upon the very bulks; affronters of midnight magistracy and breakers of windows, in a word.

CROSSBITE. But he is a little-wit, a modest-wit and they do no such outrageous things as your great wits do.

JOYNER. Nay, I dare say he will not say himself he is a little-wit, if you ask him.

LUCY. (*aside*) Nay, I cannot hear this with patience. – With your pardon, mother, you are as much mistaken as my godmother in Mr Dapperwit, for he is as great a wit as any and, in what he speaks or writes, as happy as any. I can assure you he contemns all your tearing wits in comparison of himself.

JOYNER. Alas, poor young wretch, I cannot blame thee so much as thy mother, for thou art not thyself; his bewitching madrigals have charmed thee into some heathenish imp with a hard name.

LUCY. Nymph, you mean, godmother.

JOYNER. But you, gossip, know what's what. Yesterday, as I told you, a fine old alderman of the city, seeing

---

50 *junkets*: treats, pleasure-trips.
57 *bulks*: stalls outside shops.
69 *tearing*: grand, splendid.

your daughter in so ill hands as Dapperwit's, was zealously, and in pure charity, bent upon her redemption and has sent me to tell you he will take her into his care and relieve your necessities, if you think good.

CROSSBITE. Will he relieve all our necessities?

JOYNER. All.

CROSSBITE. Mine as well as my daughter's?

JOYNER. Yes.

CROSSBITE. Well fare his heart. D'ye hear, daughter, Mrs Joyner has satisfied me clearly. Dapperwit is a vile fellow and, in short, you must put an end to that scandalous familiarity between you.

LUCY. Leave sweet Mr Dapperwit! Oh furious ingratitude! Was not he the man that gave me my first farrenden gown, put me out of worsted stockings and plain handkerchiefs, taught me to dress, talk and move well?

CROSSBITE. He has taught you to talk indeed! But, huswife, I will not have my pleasure disputed.

JOYNER. Nay, indeed, you are too tart with her, poor sweet soul.

LUCY. He taught me to rehearse too, would have brought me into the playhouse, where I might have had as good luck as others; I might have had good clothes, plate, jewels and things so well about me that my neighbours, the little gentlemen's wives of fifteen hundred or two thousand pound a year, should have retired into the country, sick with envy of my prosperity and greatness.

JOYNER. If you follow your mother's counsel you are like to enjoy all you talk of sooner than by Dapperwit's assistance, a poor wretch that goes on tick for the paper he writes his lampoons on and the very ale and coffee that inspires him, as they say.

CROSSBITE. I am credibly informed so, indeed, Madam Joyner.

JOYNER. Well, I have discharged my conscience. Good morrow to you both.

Exeunt.

---

92 *farrenden*: farandine, a cloth made out of silk and wool or hair, much more genteel than worsted stockings.

100 *into the playhouse*: as an actress.

SCENE II

Crossbite's dining-room.

Enter DAPPERWIT, RANGER.

DAPPERWIT. This is the cabinet in which I hide my jewel, a small house in an obscure, little, retired street too.

RANGER. Vulgarly an alley.

DAPPERWIT. Nay, I hid my mistress with as much care as a spark of the town does his money from his dun after a good hand at play, and nothing but you could have wrought upon me for a sight of her, let me perish.

RANGER. My obligation to you is great; do not lessen it by delays of the favour you promised.

DAPPERWIT. But do not censure my honour, for if you had not been in a desperate condition – for as one nail must beat out another, one poison expel another, one fire draw out another, one fit of drinking cure the sickness of another, so the surfeit you took last night of Christina's eyes shall be cured by Lucy's this morning, or as –

RANGER. Nay, I bar more similitudes.

DAPPERWIT. What, in my mistress's lodging? That were as hard as to bar a young parson in the pulpit, the fifth of November, railing at the Church of Rome or as hard to put you to bed to Lucy and defend you touching her or as –

RANGER. Or as hard as to make you hold your tongue! I shall not see your mistress, I see!

DAPPERWIT. Miss Lucy, Miss Lucy. (*Knocks at the door and returns*) The devil take me if good men (I say no more) have not been upon their knees to me to see her and you at last must obtain it.

RANGER. I do not believe you.

DAPPERWIT. 'Tis such a she; she is beautiful without affectation, amorous without impertinency, airy and brisk without impudence, frolic without rudeness

---

6 *dun*: creditor.

21 *fifth of November*: anniversary of the Catholic Gunpowder Plot, an unsuccessful attempt to blow up King, Lords and Commons in Parliament.

and, in a word, the justest creature breathing to her assignation.

RANGER. You praise her as if you had a mind to part with her and yet you resolve, I see, to keep her to yourself.

DAPPERWIT. Keep her! Poor creature, she cannot leave me and, rather than leave her, I would leave writing lampoons or sonnets almost.

RANGER. Well, I'll leave you with her then.

DAPPERWIT. What, will you go without seeing her?

RANGER. Rather than stay without seeing her.

DAPPERWIT. Yes, yes, you shall see her. But let me perish if I have not been offered a hundred guineas for a sight of her by – I say no more.

RANGER. (*aside*) I understand you now. – If the favour be to be purchased then I'll bid all I have about me for't.

DAPPERWIT. Fie, fie, Mr Ranger, you are pleasant, i'faith. Do you think I would sell the sight of my rarity? Like those gentlemen who hang out flags at Charing Cross or like –

RANGER. Nay, then I'm gone again.

DAPPERWIT. What, you take it ill I refuse your money? Rather than that should be, give us it. But take notice I will borrow it – now I think on't, Lucy wants a gown and some knacks.

RANGER. Here.

DAPPERWIT. But I must pay it you again; I will not take it unless you engage your honour I shall pay it you again.

RANGER. You must pardon me; I will not engage my honour for such a trifle. Go fetch her out.

DAPPERWIT. Well, she's a ravishing creature; such eyes and lips, Mr Ranger.

RANGER. Prithee go.

DAPPERWIT. Such neck and breasts, Mr Ranger.

RANGER. Again, prithee go.

DAPPERWIT. Such feet, legs and thighs, Mr Ranger.

---

34 *justest*: both 'most suitable, exact' and, ironically, 'most faithful'.

53 *hang out flags*: advertisements for freak shows and other similar entertainments; hardly complimentary.

59 *knacks*: trinkets.

RANGER. Prithee, let me see 'em.

DAPPERWIT. And a mouth no bigger than your ring. I need say no more.

RANGER. Would thou wert never to speak again.

DAPPERWIT. And then so neat, so sweet a creature in bed that to my knowledge she does not change her sheets in half a year.

RANGER. I thank you for that allay to my impatience.

DAPPERWIT. (*knocking at the door*) Miss Lucy, Miss Lucy, Miss.

RANGER. Will she not open?

DAPPERWIT. I am afraid my pretty miss is not stirring and therefore will not admit us. [. . .] Fie, fie, a quibble next your stomach in a morning! What if she should hear us? Would you lose a mistress for a quibble? That's more than I could do, let me perish.

RANGER. Is she not gone her walk to Lamb's Conduit?

DAPPERWIT. She is within; I hear her.

RANGER. But she will not hear you; she's as deaf as if you were a dun or a constable.

DAPPERWIT. Pish, give her but leave to gape, rub her eyes and put on her day-pinner, the long patch under the left eye, awaken the roses on her cheeks with some Spanish wool and warrant her breath with some lemon peel, the door flies off of the hinges and she into my arms. She knows there is as much artifice to keep a victory as to gain it and 'tis a sign she values the conquest of my heart.

RANGER. I thought her beauty had not stood in need of art.

DAPPERWIT. Beauty's a coward still without the help of art and may have the fortune of a conquest but cannot keep it. Beauty and art can no more be asunder than love and honour.

RANGER. Or to speak more like yourself, wit and judgement.

---

84 *admit us. [. . .] Fie*: Q1 repeats the speech-prefix *Dapperwit*, indicating that a speech of Ranger has dropped out.

88 *Lamb's Conduit*: Lamb's Conduit Fields, built in 1577, a popular area to the north of the city.

92 *gape*: yawn.

93 *day-pinner*: a cap with two long flaps fastened at the breast.

95 *Spanish wool*: rouge.

DAPPERWIT. Don't you hear the door wag yet?

RANGER. Not a whit.

DAPPERWIT. Miss, Miss, 'tis your slave that calls. Come, all this tricking for him! Lend me your comb, Mr Ranger.

RANGER. No, I am to be preferred today; you are to set me off. You are in possession; I will not lend you arms to keep me out –

DAPPERWIT. A pox, don't let me be ungrateful; if she has smugged herself up for me, let me prune and flounce my peruke a little for her. There's ne'er a young fellow in the town but will do as much for a mere stranger in the playhouse.

RANGER. A wit's wig has the privilege of being uncombed in the very playhouse or in the presence –

DAPPERWIT. But not in the presence of his mistress; 'tis a greater neglect of her than himself. Pray lend me your comb.

RANGER. I would not have men of wit and courage make use of every fop's mean arts to keep or gain a mistress.

DAPPERWIT. But don't you see every day, though a man have ne'er so much wit and courage, his mistress will revolt to those fops that wear and comb perukes well. I'll break off the bargain and will not receive you my partner.

RANGER. (*combs his peruke*) Therefore, you see, I am setting up for myself.

DAPPERWIT. She comes, she comes; pray, your comb. (*Snatches* RANGER*'s comb*)

Enter MRS CROSSBITE *to them.*

CROSSBITE. Bargain! What are you offering us to sale?

DAPPERWIT. A pox, is't she? Here, take your comb again then. (*Returns the comb*)

CROSSBITE. Would you sell us? 'Tis like you, y'fads.

DAPPERWIT. Sell thee? Where should we find a chapman? Go, prithee, mother, call out my dear Miss Lucy.

---

117 *smugged*: smartened up.
122 *in the presence*: of the King.
140 *y'fads*: in faith.
141–2 *chapman*: trader.

CROSSBITE. Your Miss Lucy! I do not wonder you have the conscience to bargain for us behind our backs, since you have the impudence to claim a propriety in us to my face.

RANGER. How's this, Dapperwit?

DAPPERWIT. Come, come, this gentleman will not think the worse of a woman for my acquaintance with her. He has seen me bring your daughter to the lure with a Chiney orange, from one side of the playhouse to the other.

CROSSBITE. I would have the gentleman and you to know, my daughter is a girl of reputation, though she has been seen in your company, but is now so sensible of her past danger that she is resolved never more to venture her pitcher to the well, as they say.

DAPPERWIT. How's that, widow? I wonder at your new confidence.

CROSSBITE. I wonder at your old impudence, that where you have had so frequent repulses you should provoke another and bring your friend here to witness your disgrace.

DAPPERWIT. Hark you, widow, a little.

CROSSBITE. What, you have mortgaged my daughter to that gentleman and now would offer me a snip to join in the security!

DAPPERWIT. (*aside*) She overheard me talk of a bargain; 'twas unlucky. – Your wrath is grounded upon a mistake; Miss Lucy herself shall be judge. Call her out, pray.

CROSSBITE. She shall not, she will not come to you.

DAPPERWIT. Till I hear it from her own mouth I cannot believe it.

CROSSBITE. You shall hear her say't through the door.

DAPPERWIT. I shall doubt it unless she say it to my face.

CROSSBITE. Shall we be troubled with you no more then?

DAPPERWIT. If she command my death I cannot disobey her.

CROSSBITE. Come out, child.

---

150 *bring . . . the lure*: a hawking term for recalling the bird.
151 *Chiney orange*: the sweet orange (*citrus sinensis*), a delicacy at this time, sold in the theatre.

[*Enter*] LUCY, *holding down her head, to them.*

DAPPERWIT. Your servant, dearest miss, can you have –

CROSSBITE. Let me ask her.

DAPPERWIT. No, I'll ask her.

RANGER. I'll throw up cross or pile who shall ask her.

DAPPERWIT. Can you have the heart to say you will never more break a cheesecake with me at New Spring Garden, the Neat House or Chelsea, never more sit in my lap at a new play, never more wear a suit of knots of my choice and, last of all, never more pass away an afternoon with me again in the green garret? In – Do not forget the green garret.

LUCY. I wish I had never seen the green garret. Dem the green garret!

DAPPERWIT. Dem the green garret! you are strangely altered.

LUCY. 'Tis you are altered.

DAPPERWIT. You have refused Colby's Mulberry Garden and the French houses for the green garret and a little something in the green garret pleased you more than the best treat the other places could yield. And can you of a sudden quit the green garret?

LUCY. Since you have a design to pawn me for the rent, 'tis time to remove my goods.

DAPPERWIT. Thou art extremely mistaken.

LUCY. Besides, I have heard such strange things of you this morning –

DAPPERWIT. What things?

LUCY. I blush to speak 'em.

DAPPERWIT. I know my innocence, therefore take my charge as a favour. What have I done?

LUCY. Then know, vile wit, my mother has confessed

---

185 *cross or pile*: heads or tails.

187–8 *New . . . Chelsea*: New Spring Garden at Vauxhall, gardens for entertainment and refreshment; the Neat Houses at Chelsea were market gardens (Pepys took some friends there in August 1667); Chelsea is probably the Chelsea Bun Shop, another popular place with Londoners.

189 *suit of knots*: bow of ribbons.

193 *Dem*: damn.

198 *Colby*: probably the man who ran the restaurant at Mulberry Garden; see the last scene of *Love in a Wood.*

just now thou wert false to me, to her too certain knowledge, and hast forced even her to be false to me too.

DAPPERWIT. Faults in drink, Lucy, when we are not ourselves, should not condemn us.

LUCY. And now to let me out to hire like hackney. I tell you my own dear mother shall bargain for me no more; there are as little as I can bargain for themselves nowadays, as well as properer women.

CROSSBITE. Whispering all this while! Beware of his snares again. Come away, child.

DAPPERWIT. Sweet, dear Miss.

LUCY. Bargain for me! You have reckoned without your hostess, as they say. Bargain for me, bargain for me! *Exit* LUCY.

DAPPERWIT. I must return then to treat with you.

CROSSBITE. Treat me no treatings but take a word for all: you shall no more dishonour my daughter nor molest my lodgings, as you have done at all hours.

DAPPERWIT. Do you intend to change 'em, then, to Bridewell or Long's powdering-tub?

CROSSBITE. No, to a bailiff's house – and then you'll be so civil, I presume, as not to trouble us.

RANGER. Here, will you have my comb again, Dapperwit?

DAPPERWIT. A pox, I think women take inconstancy from me worse than from any man breathing.

CROSSBITE. Pray, sir, forget me before you write your next lampoon. *Exit* CROSSBITE.

[*Enter*] SIR SIMON ADDLEPLOT *in the dress of a clerk, to* RANGER *and* DAPPERWIT.

SIR SIMON. Have I found you? Have I found you in your by-walks, faith and troth? I am almost out of breath in following you. Gentlemen when they get into an alley walk so fast, as if they had more earnest business there than in the broad streets.

---

218 *hackney*: a hackney coach.

232 *Bridewell*: a house of correction, for prostitutes in particular, just off Fleet Street.

232 *Long's powdering-tub*: Long is unknown but the powdering-tub is the sweating-tub used in the treatment of venereal diseases.

DAPPERWIT. (*aside*) How came this sot hither? Fortune has sent him to ease my choler. – You impudent rascal, who are you that dares intrude thus on us? (*Strikes him*)

SIR SIMON. (*softly*) Don't you know me, Dapperwit? Sure, you know me.

DAPPERWIT. Wilt thou dishonour me with thy acquaintance too? Thou rascally, insolent pen-and-ink man! (*Strikes him again*)

SIR SIMON. (*speak softly*) Oh, oh, sure you know me, pray know me.

DAPPERWIT. By thy saucy familiarity thou shouldst be a marker at a tennis-court, a barber or a slave that fills coffee.

SIR SIMON. Oh, oh.

DAPPERWIT. What art thou? (*Kicks him*)

SIR SIMON. [*aside*] Nay, I must not discover myself to Ranger for a kick or two. – Oh, pray hold, sir; (*delivers him a letter*) by that you will know me.

DAPPERWIT. How, Sir Simon!

SIR SIMON. Mum, mum, make no excuses, man; I would not Ranger should have known me for five hundred – kicks.

DAPPERWIT. Your disguise is so natural, I protest, it will excuse me.

SIR SIMON. I know that; prithee make no excuses, I say, no ceremony between thee and I, man. Read the letter.

DAPPERWIT. What, you have not opened it?

SIR SIMON. Prithee don't be angry; the seal is a little cracked, for I could not help kissing Mrs Martha's letter. The word is 'now or never'; her father she finds will be abroad all this day and she longs to see your friend, Sir Simon Addleplot – faith, 'tis a pretty jest – while I am with her and praising myself to her at no ordinary rate. Let thee and I alone at an intrigue!

DAPPERWIT. Tell her I will not fail to meet her at the place and time. Have a care of your charge and manage your business like yourself for yourself.

SIR SIMON. I warrant you.

DAPPERWIT. (*aside*) The gaining Gripe's daughter will

---

256 *marker*: scorer.

make me support the loss of this young jilt here.

RANGER. What fellow's that?

DAPPERWIT. A servant to a friend of mine.

RANGER. Methinks he something resembles our acquaintance Sir Simon but it is no compliment to tell him so, for that knight is the most egregious coxcomb that ever played with lady's fan.

SIR SIMON. (*aside*) So; thanks to my disguise, I know my enemies.

RANGER. The most incorrigible ass, beyond the reproof of a kicking rival or a frowning mistress. But, if it be possible, thou dost use him worse than his mistress or rival can: thou dost make such a cully of him.

SIR SIMON. (*aside*) Does he think so too?

DAPPERWIT. Go, friend, about your business.

Exit SIR SIMON.

A pox, you would spoil all, just in the critical time of projection; he brings me here a summons from his mistress to meet her in the evening. Will you come to my wedding?

RANGER. Don't speak so loud – you'll break poor Lucy's heart. Poor creature, she cannot leave you and, rather than leave her, you should leave writing of lampoons or sonnets – almost.

DAPPERWIT. Come, let her go, ungrateful baggage. But, now you talk of sonnets, I am no living wit if her love has not cost me two thousand couplets at least.

RANGER. But what would you give now for a new satire against women ready made; 'twould be as convenient to buy satires against women ready made as to buy cravats ready tied.

DAPPERWIT. Or as –

RANGER. Hey, come away, come away, Mr Or-as –

Exeunt.

Enter MRS JOYNER, GRIPE.

GRIPE. Peace, plenty and pastime be within these walls.

---

301 *projection*: in alchemy, the stage of transmutation of base-metal into gold or silver.

317 Gripe distorts *Luke* 10.5: 'And into whatsoever house ye enter, first say "Peace be to this house" ', adding 'pastime', his special interest.

JOYNER. 'Tis a small house, you see, and mean furniture, for no gallants are suffered to come hither. She might have had ere now as good lodgings as any in town, her Moreclack hangings, great glasses, cabinets, China embroidered beds, Persian carpets, gold plate and the like, if she would have put herself forward but your worship may please to make 'em remove to a place fit to receive one of your worship's quality, for this is a little scandalous, in truly.

GRIPE. No, no, I like it well enough; I am not dainty. Besides, privacy, privacy, Mrs Joyner, I love privacy, in opposition to the wicked who hate it. (*Looks about*)

JOYNER. What do you look for, sir?

GRIPE. Walls have ears, walls have ears, but, besides, I look for a private place to retire to, in time of need. Oh, here's one convenient. (*Turns up a hanging and discovers the slender provisions of the family*)

JOYNER. But you see, poor innocent souls, to what use they put it, not to hide gallants.

GRIPE. Temperance is the nurse of chastity.

JOYNER. But your worship may please to mend their fare and, when you come, may make them entertain you better than, you see, they do themselves.

GRIPE. No, I am not dainty, as I told you. I abominate entertainments; no entertainments, pray, Mrs Joyner.

JOYNER. (*aside*) No.

GRIPE. There can be no entertainment to me more luscious and savoury than the communion with that little gentlewoman. Will you call her out? I fast till I see her.

JOYNER. But, in truly, your worship, we should have brought a bottle or two of Rhenish and some Naples biscuit to have entertained the young gentlewoman; 'tis the mode for lovers to treat their mistresses.

GRIPE. Modes! I tell you, Mrs Joyner, I hate modes and forms.

JOYNER. You must send for something to entertain her with.

---

321 *Moreclack hangings*: tapestries made at the famous works at Mortlake.

348–9 *Naples biscuit*: a crisp biscuit.

GRIPE. Again entertaining! We will be to each other a feast.

JOYNER. I shall be ashamed, in truly, your worship; besides, the young gentlewoman will despise you.

GRIPE. I shall content her, I warrant you; leave it to me.

JOYNER. (*aside*) I am sure you will not content me if you will not content her; 'tis as impossible for a man to love and be a miser as to love and be wise, as they say.

GRIPE. While you talk of treats you starve my eyes; I long to see the fair one. Fetch her hither.

JOYNER. I am so ashamed she should find me so abominable a liar. I have praised you to her and, above all your virtues, your liberality, which is so great a virtue that it often excuses youth, beauty, courage, wit or anything.

GRIPE. Pish, pish, 'tis the virtue of fools; every fool can have it.

JOYNER. And will your worship want it then? I told her –

GRIPE. Why would you tell her anything of me? You know I am a modest man. But come, if you will have me as extravagant as the wicked, take that and fetch us a treat, as you call it.

JOYNER. Upon my life, a groat! What will this purchase?

GRIPE. Two black pots of ale and a cake, at the next cellar. Come, the wine has arsenic in't.

JOYNER. (*aside*) Well, I am mistaken and my hopes are abused. I never knew any man so mortified a miser that he would deny his lechery anything. I must be even with thee then another way. *Goes out.*

GRIPE. These useful old women are more exorbitant and craving in their desires than the young ones in theirs. These prodigals in white perukes spoil 'em both and that's the reason, when the squires come under my clutches, I made 'em pay for their folly and mine – and 'tis but conscience. Oh, here comes the fair one at last.

Enter JOYNER *leading in* LUCY, *who hangs backward as she enters.*

---

380 *black pots*: beer mugs.
388 *white perukes*: powdered in the fashionable mode.

LUCY. Oh Lord, there's a man, godmother!

JOYNER. Come in, child. Thou art so bashful!

LUCY. My mother is from home too; I dare not.

JOYNER. If she were here she'd teach you better manners.

LUCY. I'm afraid she'd be angry.

JOYNER. To see you so much an ass. Come along, I say.

GRIPE. Nay, speak to her gently; if you won't, I will.

LUCY. Thank you, sir.

GRIPE. Pretty innocent, there is, I see, one left yet of her age. What hap have I! Sweet little gentlewoman, come and sit down by me.

LUCY. I am better bred, I hope, sir.

GRIPE. You must sit down by me.

LUCY. I'd rather stand, if you please.

GRIPE. To please me you must sit, sweetest.

LUCY. Not before my godmother, sure.

GRIPE. Wonderment of innocence!

JOYNER. A poor bashful girl, sir. I'm sorry she is not better taught.

GRIPE. I am glad she is not taught – I'll teach her myself.

LUCY. Are you a dancing-master then, sir? But if I should be dull and not move as you would have me, you would not beat me, sir, I hope?

GRIPE. Beat thee, honeysuckle! I'll use thee thus and thus and thus. (*Kisses her*) Ah, Mrs Joyner, prithee go fetch our treat now.

JOYNER. A treat of a groat! I will not wag.

GRIPE. Why don't you go? Here, take more money and fetch what you will. Take here, half a crown.

JOYNER. What will half a crown do?

GRIPE. Take a crown then, an angel, a piece. Be gone.

JOYNER. A treat only will not serve my turn. I must buy the poor wretch there some toys.

GRIPE. What toys? What? Speak quickly.

JOYNER. Pendants, necklaces, fans, ribbons, points, laces, stockings, gloves –

---

421 *wag*: stir.
425 *an angel, a piece*: ten shillings and twenty-two shillings respectively.
429 *points*: lace embroidery.

GRIPE. Hold, hold, before it comes to a gown.

JOYNER. Well remembered, sir! Indeed, she wants a gown, for she has but that one to her back. For your own sake you should give her a new gown, for variety of dresses rouses desire and makes an old mistress seem every day a new one.

GRIPE. For that reason she shall have no new gown, for I am naturally constant and, as I am still the same, I love she should be still the same. But here, take half a piece for the other things.

JOYNER. Half a piece!

GRIPE. Prithee be gone; take t'other piece then, two pieces, three pieces, five – here, 'tis all I have.

JOYNER. I must have the broad-seal ring too or I stir not.

GRIPE. Insatiable woman, will you have that too? Prithee spare me that; 'twas my grandfather's.

JOYNER. (*aside*) That's false; he had ne'er a coat. So now I go. This is but a violent fit and will not hold.

LUCY. Oh, whither do you go, godmother? Will you leave me alone?

JOYNER. The gentleman will not hurt you; you may venture yourself with him alone.

LUCY. I think I may, godmother.

Exit JOYNER.

What, will you lock me in, sir? Don't lock me in, sir!

GRIPE. (*fumbling at the door, locks it*) 'Tis a private lesson I must teach you, fair.

LUCY. I don't see your fiddle, sir. Where is your little kit?

GRIPE. I'll show it thee presently, sweetest. (GRIPE *setting a chair against the door*) Necessity, mother of invention. (*Takes her in his arms*) Come, my dearest.

LUCY. What do you mean, sir? Don't hurt me, sir, will you! (*Cries out*) Oh, oh, you will kill me! Murder, murder, oh, oh! Help, help, oh!

The door broke open, enter CROSSBITE *and two men in aprons, her* LANDLORD *and his* PRENTICE.

---

444 *broad-seal ring*: ring with a coat-of-arms on it for sealing documents.

447 *coat*: of arms, as well as a coat to his back.

458 *kit*: (*a*) dancing-master's small violin (*b*) equipment.

CROSSBITE. What, murder my daughter, villain?

LUCY. I wish he had murdered me, oh, oh!

CROSSBITE. What has he done?

LUCY. Why would you go out and leave me alone? Unfortunate woman that I am.

GRIPE. (*aside*) How now! What will this end in?

CROSSBITE. Who brought him in?

LUCY. That witch, that treacherous false woman, my godmother, who has betrayed me, sold me to his lust. Oh oh!

CROSSBITE. Have you ravished my daughter then, you old goat? Ravished my daughter, ravished my daughter? Speak, villain.

GRIPE. By yea and by nay, no such matter.

CROSSBITE. A canting rogue too. Take notice, landlord, he has ravished my daughter; you see her all in tears and distraction and see there the wicked engine of the filthy execution (*pointing to the chair*). Jeremy, call up my neighbours and the constable. False villain, thou shalt die for't.

GRIPE. Hold, hold. (*Aside*) Nay, I am caught.

CROSSBITE. Go, go, make haste –

LUCY. Oh, oh!

CROSSBITE. Poor wretch. Go quickly.

GRIPE. Hold, hold. Thou young spawn of the old serpent, wicked as I thought thee innocent, wilt thou say I would have ravished thee?

LUCY. I will swear you did ravish me.

GRIPE. (*aside*) I thought so, treacherous Eve. Then I am gone; I must shift as well as I can.

LUCY. Oh, oh!

CROSSBITE. Will none of you call up the neighbours and the authority of the alley?

[*Exit* PRENTICE.]

GRIPE. Hold, I'll give thee twenty mark among you to let me go.

CROSSBITE. Villain, nothing shall buy thy life.

---

478 *By yea and by nay*: Puritans were not allowed to swear but could declare 'by yea and nay'; it was a popular pejorative term for Puritans since it fitted their reputation for equivocation.

479 *canting*: hypocritically pious.

498 *mark*: thirteen shillings and fourpence.

LANDLORD. But, stay, Mrs Crossbite, let me talk with you.

LUCY. Oh, oh!

LANDLORD. Come, sir, I am your friend; in a word, I have appeased her and she shall be contented with a little sum.

GRIPE. What is it? What is it?

LANDLORD. But five hundred pound.

GRIPE. But five hundred pound! Hang me then, hang me rather!

LANDLORD. You will say I have been your friend.

[*Re-enter* PRENTICE.]

PRENTICE. The constable and neighbours are coming.

GRIPE. How, how! (*Kneels to* CROSSBITE) Will you not take a hundred? Pray use conscience in your ways.

CROSSBITE. I scorn your money; I will not take a thousand.

GRIPE. (*aside*) My enemies are many and I shall be a scandal to the faithful as a laughing-stock to the wicked. – Go, prepare your engines for my persecution. I'll give you the best security I can.

LANDLORD. The instruments are drawing in the other room, if you please to go thither.

CROSSBITE. Indeed, now I consider, a portion will do my daughter more good than his death – that would but publish her shame; money will cover it. *Probatum est*, as they say. Let me tell you, sir, 'tis a charitable thing to give a young maid a portion.

Exeunt omnes.

SCENE III

The scene changes to Lydia's lodging.

Enter LYDIA, MY LADY FLIPPANT, [LEONORE].

LYDIA. 'Tis as hard for a woman to conceal her indignation from her apostate lover as to conceal her love from her faithful servant.

525–6 *Probatum est*: It is proved; tried and tested.

FLIPPANT. Or almost as hard as it is for the prating fellows nowadays to conceal the favours of obliging ladies.

LYDIA. If Ranger should come up (I saw him just now in the street), the discovery of my anger to him now would be as mean as the discovery of my love to him before.

FLIPPANT. Though I did so mean a thing as to love a fellow, I would not do so mean a thing as to confess it, certainly, by my trouble to part with him. If I confessed love it should be before they left me.

LYDIA. So you would deserve to be left before you were. But could you ever do so mean a thing as to confess love to any?

FLIPPANT. Yes – but I never did so mean a thing as really to love any.

LYDIA. You had once a husband.

FLIPPANT. Fie, madam, do you think me so ill-bred as to love a husband?

LYDIA. You had a widow's heart before you were a widow, I see.

FLIPPANT. I should rather make an adventure of my honour with a gallant for a gown, a new coach, a necklace, than clap my husband's cheeks for them or sit in his lap. I should be as ashamed to be caught in such a posture with a husband as a brisk, well-bred spark of the town would be to be caught on his knees at prayers, unless to a mistress.

[*Enter*] *to them*, RANGER, DAPPERWIT.

LYDIA. Mr Ranger, 'twas obligingly done of you.

RANGER. Indeed, cousin, I had kept my promise with you last night but this gentleman knows –

LYDIA. You mistake me but you shall not lessen any favour you do me. You are going to excuse your not coming to me last night when I take it as a particular obligation that, though you threatened me with a visit, upon consideration you were so civil as not to trouble me.

DAPPERWIT. (*aside*) This is an unlucky morning with me: here's my eternal persecution, the widow Flippant.

29–30 *well-bred spark*: well-bred Q1 (Q2 supplies the missing word).

FLIPPANT. What, Mr Dapperwit!

RANGER. Indeed, cousin, besides my business, another cause I did not wait on you was my apprehension you were gone to the park, notwithstanding your promise to the contrary.

LYDIA. Therefore you went to the park to visit me there, notwithstanding your promise to the contrary.

RANGER. Who, I at the park, when I had promised to wait upon you at your lodging? But were you at the park, madam?

LYDIA. Who, I at the park, when I had promised to wait for you at home? I was no more at the park than you were. Were you at the park?

RANGER. The park had been a dismal desert to me, notwithstanding all the good company in't, if I had wanted yours.

LYDIA. (*aside*) Because it has been the constant endeavour of men to keep women ignorant, they think us so; but 'tis that increases our inquisitiveness and makes us know them ignorant as false. He is as impudent a dissembler as the widow Flippant who is making her importunate addresses in vain, for ought I see.

FLIPPANT *driving* DAPPERWIT *from one side of the stage to the other.*

FLIPPANT. Dear Mr Dapperwit, merciful Mr Dapperwit.

DAPPERWIT. Unmerciful Lady Flippant.

FLIPPANT. Will you be satisfied?

DAPPERWIT. Won't you be satisfied?

FLIPPANT. (*aside to* DAPPERWIT) That a wit should be jealous! That a wit should be jealous! There's never a brisk young fellow in the town, though no wit, heaven knows, but thinks too well of himself to think ill of his wife or mistress. Now that a wit should lessen his opinion of himself, for shame!

DAPPERWIT. (*softly apart to* RANGER) I promised to bring you off but I find it enough to shift for myself!

LYDIA. What, out of breath, madam?

FLIPPANT. I have been defending our cause, madam. I have beat him out of the pit. I do so mumble these

---

80 *beat him out of the pit*: victory in cock-fighting and in a wit-combat in the pit of the theatre.

80 *mumble*: handle roughly.

prating, censorious fellows they call wits when I meet with them.

DAPPERWIT. Her Ladyship indeed is the only thing in petticoats I dread; 'twas well for me there was company in the room, for I dare no more venture myself with her alone than a cully that has been bit dares venture himself in a tavern with an old rook.

FLIPPANT. I am the revenger of our sex, certainly.

DAPPERWIT. And the most insatiable one I ever knew, madam; I dare not stay your fury longer. Mr Ranger, I will go before and make a new appointment with your friends that expect you at dinner at the French house. 'Tis fit business; still wait on love.

RANGER. Do so – but now I think on't, Sir Thomas goes out of town this afternoon and I shall not see him here again these three months.

LYDIA. Nay, pray take him with you, sir.

FLIPPANT. No, sir, you shall not take the gentleman from his mistress. (*Aside*) Do not go yet, sweet Mr Dapperwit.

LYDIA. Take him with you, sir. I suppose his business may be there to borrow or win money and I ought not to be his hindrance, for when he has none he has his desperate designs upon that little I have, for want of money makes as devout lovers as christians.

DAPPERWIT. I hope, madam, he offers you no less security than his liberty.

LYDIA. His liberty! As poor a pawn to take up money on as honour! He is like the desperate bankrouts of this age, who, if they can get people's fortunes into their hands, care not though they spend them in gaol all their lives.

FLIPPANT. And the poor crediting ladies, when they have parted with their money, must be contented with a pitiful composition or starve for all them.

RANGER. But widows are commonly so wise as to be sure their men are solvable before they trust 'em.

FLIPPANT. Can you blame 'em? I declare I will trust no man; pray do not take it ill, gentlemen. Quacks in

---

109 *bankrouts*: bankrupts.
117 *solvable*: solvent.

their bills and poets in the titles of their plays do not more disappoint us than gallants with their promises. But I trust none.

DAPPERWIT. Nay, she's a very jew in that particular; to my knowledge, she'll know her man over and over again before she trust him.

RANGER. Well, my dearest cousin, good morrow. When I stay from you so long again blame me to purpose and be extremely angry, for nothing can make me amends for the loss of your company but your reprehension of my absence. I'll take such a chiding as kindly as Russian wives do beating.

LYDIA. If you were my husband I could not take your absence more kindly than I do.

RANGER. And if you were my wife I would trust you as much out of my sight as I could, to show my opinion of your virtue.

FLIPPANT. A well-bred gentleman, I warrant. Will you go then, cruel Mr Dapperwit?

Exeunt RANGER *and* DAPPERWIT.

LYDIA. (*apart*) Have I not dissembled well, Leonore?

LEONORE. But, madam, to what purpose? Why do you not put him to his trial and see what he can say for himself?

LYDIA. I am afraid lest my proofs and his guilt should make him desperate and so contemn that pardon which he could not hope for.

LEONORE. 'Tis unjust to condemn him before you hear him.

LYDIA. I will reprieve him till I have more evidence.

LEONORE. How will you get it?

LYDIA. I will write him a letter in Christina's name, desiring to meet him, when I shall soon discover if his love to her be of a longer standing than since last night and, if it be not, I will not longer trust him with the vanity to think she gave him the occasion to follow her home from the park, so will at once disabuse him and myself.

LEONORE. What care the jealous take in making sure of ills which they, but in imagination, cannot undergo.

---

131 *as Russian . . . beating*: a popular belief at the time.

LYDIA. Misfortunes are least dreadful when most near.
'Tis less to undergo the ill than fear.

Exeunt.

ACT IV

SCENE I

Gripe's house.

Enter MRS JOYNER *and* GRIPE *in a blue gown and night-cap.*

JOYNER. What, not well, your worship? This it is, you will be laying out yourself beyond your strength; you have taken a surfeit of the little gentlewoman, I find. Indeed, you should not have been so immoderate in your embraces – your worship is something in years, in truly.

GRIPE. Graceless, perfidious woman, what mak'st thou here? Art thou not afraid to be used like an informer since thou hast made me pay thee for betraying me?

JOYNER. Betray your worship! What do you mean? I an informer! I scorn your words.

GRIPE. Woman, I say again, thou art as treacherous as an informer and more unreasonable, for he lets us have something for our money before he disturbs us.

JOYNER. Your money, I'm sure, was laid out faithfully and I went away because I would not disturb you.

GRIPE. I had not grudged you the money I gave you but the five hundred pound! The five hundred pound, inconscionable, false woman! The five hundred pound! You cheated, trapanned, robbed me of the five hundred pound!

JOYNER. I cheat you, I rob you! Well, remember what you say; you shall answer it before Mr Double-cap, and the best of –

GRIPE. Oh impudent woman, speak softly!

---

20 *trapanned*: ensnared, beguiled.

JOYNER. I will not speak softly, for innocence is loud as well as bare-faced. Is this your return after you have made me a mere drudge to your filthy lusts?

GRIPE. Speak softly; my sister, daughter and servants will hear.

JOYNER. I would have witnesses to take notice that you blast my good name, which was as white as a tulip and as sweet as the head of your cane before you wrought me to the carrying-on the work of your fleshly carnal seekings.

GRIPE. Softly, softly – they are coming in.

Enter FLIPPANT *and* MARTHA.

FLIPPANT. What's the matter, brother?

GRIPE. Nothing, nothing, sister, only the godly woman is fallen into a fit of zeal against the enormous transgressions of the age. Go, go, you do not love to hear vanity reproved; pray be gone.

JOYNER. Pray stay, madam, that you may know –

GRIPE. (*aside to* JOYNER) Hold, hold, here are five guineas for thee; pray say nothing. – Sister, pray be gone, I say.

Exeunt FLIPPANT *and* MARTHA.

Would you prejudice your own reputation to injure mine?

JOYNER. Would you prejudice your own soul to wrong my repute, in truly? (*She seems to weep*)

GRIPE. Pray, have me in excuse. Indeed, I thought you had a share of the five hundred pound because you took away my seal-ring, which they made me send together with a note to my cash-keeper for five hundred pound. Besides, I thought none but you knew it was my wonted token to send for money by.

JOYNER. 'Twas unlucky I should forget it and leave it on the table. But oh, the harlotry! Did she make that use of it then? 'Twas no wonder you did not stay till I came back.

GRIPE. I stayed till the money released me.

JOYNER. Have they the money then? Five hundred pound!

GRIPE. Too certain.

JOYNER. They told me not a word of it. And have you no way to retrieve it?

GRIPE. Not any.

JOYNER. (*aside*) I am glad of it. – Is there no law but against the saints?

GRIPE. I will not for five hundred pound publish my transgression myself lest I should be thought to glory in't – though, I must confess, 'twould tempt a man to conform to public praying and sinning, since 'tis so chargeable to pray and sin in private.

JOYNER. But are you resolved to give off, a loser?

GRIPE. How shall I help it?

JOYNER. Nay, I'll see you shall have what the young jade has. For your money I'll make 'um use some conscience however. Take a man's money for nothing?

GRIPE. Thou say'st honestly indeed. And shall I have my pennyworths out of the little gentlewoman for all this?

JOYNER. I'll be engaged body for body for her and you shall take the forfeiture on me else.

GRIPE. No, no, I'll rather take your word, Mrs Joyner.

JOYNER. Go in and dress yourself smug and leave the rest to me.

GRIPE. No man breathing would give off a loser, as she says.

Exeunt.

Enter SIR SIMON ADDLEPLOT, *sitting at a desk writing as a clerk,* MY LADY FLIPPANT *jogging him.*

SIR SIMON. 'Tis a lord's mortgage and therefore requires the more haste. Pray do not jog me, madam.

FLIPPANT. (*aside*) Dull rascal.

SIR SIMON. They cannot stay for money as other folks. If you will not let me make an end on't I shall lose my expedition fee.

FLIPPANT. (*aside*) There are some clerks would have understood me before this.

SIR SIMON. Nay, pray be quiet, madam. If you squeeze me so to the wall I cannot write.

FLIPPANT. (*aside*) 'Tis much for the honour of the gentlemen of this age that we persons of quality are forced to descend to the importuning of a clerk, a butler, coachman or footman, while the rogues are as

68 *saints*: the Puritans' term for themselves.

dull of apprehension too as an unfledged country squire amongst his mother's maids. (*Jogs him again*)

SIR SIMON. Again! Let me tell you, madam, familiarity breeds contempt. You'll never leave till you have made me saucy.

FLIPPANT. I would I could see that.

SIR SIMON. I vow and swear then, get you gone, or I'll add a black patch or two to those on your face. (*Aside*) I shall have no time to get Mrs Martha out, for her.

FLIPPANT. (*jogs him again*) Will you, sir? Will you?

SIR SIMON. (*aside*) I must have a plot for her; she is a coy woman. – I vow and swear, if you pass this crevice I'll kiss you, in plain English.

FLIPPANT. I would I could see that. Do you defy me?

Steps to him. He kisses her.

SIR SIMON. (*aside*) How's this? I vow and swear, she kisses as tamely as Mrs Ticklish, and with her mouth open too.

FLIPPANT. I thought you would have been ashamed to have done so to your master's own sister.

SIR SIMON. I hope you'll be quiet now, madam!

FLIPPANT. Nay, I'll be revenged of you, sure.

SIR SIMON. If you come again I shall do more to you than that. (*Aside*) I'll pursue my plot and try if she be honest.

FLIPPANT. You do more to me than that! Nay, if you'll do more to me than that –

She throws down his ink and runs out; he follows her.

Enter JOYNER.

JOYNER. I must visit my young clients in the meantime.

SIR SIMON *returns, holding up his hands.*

What's the matter, Sir Simon?

SIR SIMON. Lord, who would have thought it?

JOYNER. What ails you, Sir Simon?

SIR SIMON. I have made such a discovery, Mrs Joyner.

114–15 Ward suggested that this comes from *Les Cents Nouvelles Nouvelles* (tale 23) and Bandello, *Le Novelle*. I do not think the stage business warrants such esoteric references.

132 *ails*: aile Q1.

JOYNER. What is't?

SIR SIMON. Such an one that makes me at once glad and sorry: I am sorry my Lady Flippant is naught but I'm glad I know it, thanks still to my disguise.

JOYNER. Fie, fie.

SIR SIMON. Nay, this hand can tell!

JOYNER. But how?

SIR SIMON. She threw down my ink-glass and ran away into the next room; I followed her and, in revenge, threw her down upon the bed but, in short, all that I could do to her would not make her squeak.

JOYNER. She was out of breath, man, she was out of breath.

SIR SIMON. Ah, Mrs Joyner, say no more, say no more of that.

Enter FLIPPANT.

FLIPPANT. You rude, unmannerly rascal.

JOYNER. You see she complains now.

SIR SIMON. (*apart*) I know why, Mrs Joyner, I know why.

FLIPPANT. I'll have you turned out of the house; you are not fit for my brother's service.

SIR SIMON. (*aside*) Not for yours, you mean, madam.

FLIPPANT. I'll go and acquaint my brother –

JOYNER. [*aside to* FLIPPANT] Hold, hold, madam, speak not so loud. 'Tis Sir Simon Addleplot, your lover, who has taken this disguise on purpose to be near you, and to watch and supplant his rivals.

FLIPPANT. (*aside to* JOYNER) What a beast was I, I could not discover it! You have undone me. Why would you not tell me sooner of it?

JOYNER. [*aside to* FLIPPANT] I thought he had been discernible enough.

FLIPPANT. [*aside to* JOYNER] I protest I knew him not, for I must confess to you my eyes are none of the best, since I have used the last new wash of Mercury water. What will he think of me?

JOYNER. [*aside to* FLIPPANT] Let me alone with him. – Come, come, did you think you could disguise

169 *Mercury water*: a mixture of aqua regia and corrosive sublimate used as a skin-wash – *very* harmful to the eyes.

yourself from my Lady's knowledge? She knew you, man, or else you had ne'er had those liberties. Alas, poor lady, she cannot resist you.

FLIPPANT. 'Tis my weakness.

SIR SIMON. How's this? But here comes my master.

Enter GRIPE *and* MARTHA.

GRIPE. Come, Mrs Joyner, are you ready to go?

JOYNER. I am ever ready when your worship commands.

FLIPPANT. Brother, if you go to t'other end of the town, you'll set me down near the playhouse.

GRIPE. The playhouse! Do you think I will be seen near the playhouse?

FLIPPANT. You shall set me down in Lincoln's Inn Fields then, for I have earnest business there. (*Apart*) When I come home again I'll laugh at you soundly, Sir Simon.

SIR SIMON. (*aside*) Has Joyner betrayed me then? 'Tis time to look to my hits.

GRIPE. Martha, be sure you stay within now. If you go out you shall never come into my doors again.

MARTHA. No, I will not, sir; I'll ne'er come into your doors if once I should go out.

GRIPE. 'Tis well said, girl.

Exeunt GRIPE, JOYNER, FLIPPANT.

SIR SIMON. 'Twas prettily said. I understand you; they are dull and have no intrigue in 'em. But, dear, sweet Mrs Martha, 'tis time we were gone. You have stole away your scarves and hood from your maid, I hope.

MARTHA. Nay, I am ready, but –

SIR SIMON. Come, come, Sir Simon Addleplot, poor gentleman, is an impatient man, to my knowledge.

MARTHA. Well, my venture is great, I'm sure, for a man I know not. But pray, Jonas, do not deceive me. Is he so fine a gentleman as you say he is?

SIR SIMON. Pish, pish, he is the – gentleman of the town, faith and troth.

MARTHA. But may I take your word, Jonas?

183–4 *Lincoln's Inn Fields*: site of the theatre used by the Duke's Company.

188 *to look to my hits*: to have an eye to the main chance.

SIR SIMON. 'Tis not my word; 'tis the word of all the town.

MARTHA. Excuse me, Jonas, for that; I never heard any speak well of him but Mr Dapperwit and you.

SIR SIMON. That's because he has been a rival to all men and a gallant to all ladies; rivals and deserted mistresses never speak well of a man.

MARTHA. Has he been so general in his amours his kindness is not to be valued then?

SIR SIMON. The more by you because 'tis for you he deserts all the rest, faith and troth.

MARTHA. You plead better for him than he could for himself, I believe, for indeed they say he is no better than an idiot.

SIR SIMON. Then believe me, madam, for nobody knows him better than I; he has as much wit, courage and as good a mien to the full as I have. He an idiot?

MARTHA. The common gull, so perspicuous a fop the women find him out, for none of 'em will marry him.

SIR SIMON. You may see now how he and you are abused, for that he is not married is a sign of his wit and, for being perspicuous, 'tis false – he is as mysterious as a new parliament-man or a young statesman, newly taken from a coffeehouse or tennis-court.

MARTHA. But is it a sign of his wit because he is not married?

SIR SIMON. Yes, yes, your women of the town ravish your fops; there's not one about the town unmarried that has anything.

MARTHA. It may be then he has spent his estate.

SIR SIMON. (*aside*) How unluckily guessed! – If he had, he has a head can retrieve it again.

MARTHA. Besides, they say, he has had the modish distemper.

SIR SIMON. He can cure it with the best French chirurgeon in town.

MARTHA. Has his practice on himself been so much?

SIR SIMON. Come, come.

240–1 *modish distemper*: syphilis.
242–3 *French chirurgeon*: surgeon specialising in venereal diseases.

Fame, like deserted jilt, does still belie men.
Who doubts her man must be advised by Hymen,
For he knows best of any how to try men.

Exeunt.

SCENE II

The scene, the Old Pell Mell.

Enter RANGER *and* DAPPERWIT.

RANGER. Now the Lucies have renounced us, hey for the Christinas. She cannot use me worse than your honourable mistress did you.

DAPPERWIT. A pox, some heir or another has promised her marriage. There are so many fools in the world, 'tis impossible for a man of wit to keep his wench from being a lady, let me perish.

RANGER. But have you no other acquaintance that sticks to her vocation in spite of temptations of honour or filthy lucre? I declare, I make honourable love merely out of necessity, as your rooks play on the square rather than not play at all.

[Enter,] to them, LEONORE, LYDIA*'s woman, masked, with a letter in her hand.*

DAPPERWIT. Come, the devil will not lose a gamester. Here's ready money for you; push freely.

RANGER. (*to her*) Thou'rt as well met as if by assignation.

LEONORE. And you are as well met as if you were the man I looked for.

RANGER. Kind rogue!

LEONORE. Sweet sir.

RANGER. Come, I am thy prisoner. Without more words, show but thy warrant. (*Goes to pull off her mask*)

LEONORE. You mistake, sir; here is my pass. (*Gives him the letter*)

RANGER. A letter, and directed to me. (*Reads*) 'I cannot put up the injuries and affronts you did me last

---

247 *Hymen*: god of marriage.
11–12 *on the square*: by the rules, without cheating.

night' – a challenge, upon my life, and by such a messenger! – 'therefore conjure you, by your honour, at eight a'clock precisely this evening to send your man to St James's Gate to wait for me with a chair, to conduct me to what place you shall think most fit for the giving of satisfaction to the injured Christina.' Christina! I am amazed! What is't a'clock, Dapperwit?

DAPPERWIT. It wants not half an hour of eight.

RANGER. (*to the maid*) Go then back, my pretty herald, and tell my fair enemy, the service she designs my man is only fit for my friend here, of whose faith and honour she may be secure of. He shall, immediately, go wait for her at St James's Gate, whilst I go to prepare a place for our rancounter and myself to die at her feet.

Exit LEONORE.

Dapperwit, dear Dapperwit.

DAPPERWIT. What lucky surprisal's this?

RANGER. Prithee ask no questions till I have more leisure and less astonishment. I know you will not deny to be an instrument in my happiness.

DAPPERWIT. No, let me perish, I take as much pleasure to bring lovers together as an old woman that, as a bankrupt gamester loves to look on though he has no advantage by the play, or as a bully that fights not himself yet takes pleasure to set people together by the ears or as –

RANGER. 'Sdeath, is this a time for similitudes?

DAPPERWIT. You have made miscarry of a good thought now, let me perish.

RANGER. Go presently to St James's Gate, where you are to expect the coming of a lady ('tis Christina), accompanied by that woman you saw ev'n now. She will permit you to put her into a chair and then conduct her to my lodging, while I go before to remove some spies and prepare it for her reception.

DAPPERWIT. Your lodging! Had you not better carry her to Vincent's? 'Tis hard by and there a vizard mask has as free egress and regress as at the playhouse.

RANGER. Faith, though it be not very prudent, yet she

---

38 *St James's Gate*: by St James's Palace, close to Pall Mall.

shall come thither in my vindication, for he would not believe I had seen her last night.

DAPPERWIT. To have a fine woman and not tell on't, as you say, Mr Ranger, –

RANGER. Go and bring her to Vincent's lodging; there I'll expect you.

Exeunt severally.

Enter CHRISTINA, ISABEL, *her woman.*

ISABEL. This is the door, madam; here Mr Vincent lodges.

CHRISTINA. 'Tis no matter; we will pass it by lest the people of our lodging should watch us. But if he should not be here now!

ISABEL. Who, Mr Valentine, madam? I warrant you, my intelligencer dares not fail me.

CHRISTINA. Did he come last night, said he?

ISABEL. Last night late.

CHRISTINA. And not see me yet, nay, not send to me! 'Tis false, he is not come. I wish he were not; I know not which I should take more unkindly from him, exposing his life to his revengeful enemies or being almost four and twenty hours so near me and not let me know't.

ISABEL. A lover's dangers are the only secrets kept from his mistress; he came not to you because he would not purchase his happiness with your fear and apprehensions.

CHRISTINA. Nay, he is come, I see, since you are come about again of his side.

ISABEL. Will you go in, madam, and disprove me if you can; 'tis better than standing in the street.

CHRISTINA. We'll go a little farther first and return.

Exeunt.

SCENE III

Vincent's lodging.

Enter VINCENT *and* VALENTINE.

VINCENT. I told you I had sent my man to Christina's this morning to inquire of her maid (who seldom denies him a secret) if her lady had been at the park last night, which she peremptorily answered to the contrary and assured him she had not stirred out since your departure.

VALENTINE. Will not chambermaids lie, Vincent?

VINCENT. Will not Ranger lie, Valentine?

VALENTINE. The circumstances of his story proved it true.

VINCENT. Do you think so old a master in the faculty as he will want the varnish of probability for his lies?

VALENTINE. Do you think a woman, having the advantage of her sex and education, under such a mistress, will want impudence to disavow a truth that might be prejudicial to that mistress?

VINCENT. But if both testimonies are fallible, why will you needs believe his? We are apter to believe the things we would have than those we would not.

VALENTINE. My ill luck has taught me to credit my misfortune and doubt my happiness.

VINCENT. But Fortune we know inconstant.

VALENTINE. And all of her sex.

VINCENT. Will you judge of Fortune by your experience and not do your mistress the same justice? Go see her and satisfy yourself and her, for, if she be innocent, consider how culpable you are, not only in your censures of her but in not seeing her since your coming.

VALENTINE. If she be innocent I should be afraid to surprise her, for her sake; if false, I should be afraid to surprise her for my own.

VINCENT. To be jealous and not inquisitive is as hard as to love extremely and not be something jealous.

VALENTINE. Inquisitiveness as seldom cures jealousy as drinking in a fever quenches the thirst.

VINCENT. If she were at the park last night 'tis probable she'll not miss this. Go watch her house, see who goes out, who in, while I in the meantime search out Ranger, who, I'll pawn my life, upon more discourse, shall avow his mistake. Here he is; go in. How luckily is he come!

Enter RANGER. VALENTINE *retires to the door behind, overhearing them.*

Ranger, you have prevented me. I was going to look

you out between the scenes at the playhouses, the coffeehouses, tennis-court or Gifford's.

RANGER. Do you want a pretence to go to a bawdy-house? But I have other visits to make.

VINCENT. I forget I should rather have sought you in Christina's lodgings, ha, ha, ha.

RANGER. Well, well, I am just come to tell you that Christina –

VINCENT. Proves not by daylight the kind lady you followed last night out of the park.

RANGER. I have better news for you, to my thinking.

VINCENT. What is't?

RANGER. Not that I have been in Christina's lodging this morning but that she'll be presently here in your lodging with me.

VALENTINE. (*behind*) How!

VINCENT. (*drawing back to the door where* VALENTINE *stood and speaking softly to him*) You see now his report was a jest, a mere jest. (*To* RANGER) Well, must my lodging be your vaulting school still. Thou hast appointed a wench to come hither, I find.

RANGER. A wench! You seemed to have more reverence for Christina last night.

VINCENT. Now you talk of Christina, prithee tell me what was the meaning of thy last night's romance of Christina?

RANGER. You shall know the meaning of all when Christina comes. She'll be here presently.

VINCENT. Who will? Christina?

RANGER. Yes, Christina.

VINCENT. Ha, ha, ha.

RANGER. Incredulous envy! Thou art as envious as an impotent lecher at a wedding.

VINCENT. Thou art either mad or as vain as a Frenchman newly returned home from a campaign or obliging England.

---

45 *Gifford's*: Mother Gifford's famous brothel.

62–3 *vaulting school*: brothel.

79 *obliging England*: either the Frenchman has obliged England (by fulfilling a task) or he has found England, particularly its women, obligingly complaisant and accommodating.

RANGER. Thou art as envious as a rival. But if thou art mine, there's that will make you desist (*gives him the letter*) and if you are not my rival, entrusting you with such a secret will, I know, oblige you to keep it and assist me against all other interests.

VINCENT. Do you think I take your secret as an obligation? Don't I know lovers, travellers and poets will give money to be heard? But what's the paper? A lampoon upon Christina hatched last night betwixt Squire Dapperwit and you, because her maid used you scurvily.

RANGER. No, 'tis only a letter from her to show my company was not disgustful to her last night but that she desires it again today.

VALENTINE. (*behind*) A letter from her.

VINCENT. A letter from Christina. (*Reads*) Ha, ha, ha.

RANGER. Nay, 'tis pleasant.

VINCENT. You mistake; I laugh at you, not the letter.

RANGER. I am like the winning gamester, so pleased with my luck I will not quarrel with any who calls me a fool for't.

VINCENT. Is this the style of a woman of honour?

RANGER. It may be, for ought you know. I'm sure 'tis well if your female correspondents can read.

VINCENT. I must confess I have none of the little letters, half name or title, like your Spanish epistles dedicatory. But that a man so frequent in honourable intrigues as you are should not know the summons of an impudent common woman from that of a person of honour!

RANGER. Christina is so much a person of honour she'll own what she has writ when she comes.

VINCENT. But will she come hither indeed?

RANGER. Immediately. You'll excuse my liberty with you; I could not conceal such a happiness from such a friend as you, lest you should have taken it unkindly.

VINCENT. Faith, you have obliged me indeed, for you and others would often have made me believe your honourable intrigues but never did me the honour to convince me of 'em before.

RANGER. You are merry, I find, yet.

VINCENT. When you are happy, I cannot be otherwise.

RANGER. (*aside*) But I lose time. I should lay a little

person in ambush, that lives hard by, in case Christina should be impatient to be revenged of her friends, as it often happens with a discontented heiress. Women, like old soldiers, more nimbly execute than they resolve. (*Going out*)

VINCENT. What now, you will not disappoint a woman of Christina's quality?

RANGER. I'll be here before she comes, I warrant you.

Exit RANGER.

VINCENT. I do believe you truly. What think you, Valentine?

VALENTINE. I think, since she has the courage to challenge him, she'll have the honour of being first in the field.

VINCENT. Fie, your opinion of her must be as bad as Ranger's of himself is good, to think she would write to him. I long till his *bona roba* comes that you may be both disabused.

VALENTINE. And I have not patience to stay her coming, lest you should be disabused.

Enter CHRISTINA *and* ISABEL.

VINCENT. Here she is, i'faith. I'm glad she's come.

VALENTINE. And I'm sorry. But I will to my post again, lest she should say she came to me.

CHRISTINA *pulls off her mask.*

VINCENT. (*aside*) By heavens, Christina herself, 'tis she!

VALENTINE. (*behind*) 'Tis she. Cursed be these eyes, more cursed than when they first betrayed me to that false bewitching face!

CHRISTINA. You may wonder, sir, to see me here –

VINCENT. I must confess I do.

CHRISTINA. But the confidence your friend has in you is the cause of mine – and yet some blushes it does cost to come to seek a man.

VALENTINE. (*behind*) Modest creature.

VINCENT. (*aside*) How am I deceived!

CHRISTINA. Where is he, sir? Why does he not appear to keep me in countenance? Pray call him, sir; 'tis something hard if he should know I'm here.

---

124 *person*: Ward emends to *parson*, which is what Ranger means.
139 *bona roba*: loose woman.

VINCENT. I hardly can, myself, believe you are here, madam.

CHRISTINA. If my visit be troublesome or unseasonable, 'tis your friend's fault; I designed it not to you, sir. Pray call him out that he may excuse it and take it on himself together with my shame.

VINCENT. (*aside*) How impatient she is!

CHRISTINA. Or do you delay the happiness I ask to make it more welcome? I have stayed too long for it already and cannot more desire it. Dear sir, call him out. Where is he? Above or here within? I'll snatch the favour which you will not give. (*Goes to the door and discovers* VALENTINE) What, do you hide yourself for shame?

VALENTINE. I must confess I do.

CHRISTINA. To see me come hither –

VALENTINE. I acknowledge it.

VALENTINE *offers to go out.*

CHRISTINA. Before you came to me. But whither do you go? Come, I can forgive you.

VALENTINE. But I cannot forgive you.

CHRISTINA. Whither do you go? You need not forge a quarrel to prevent mine to you, nor need you try if I would follow you. You know I will; I have, you see.

VALENTINE. (*aside*) That impudence should look so like innocence.

CHRISTINA. Whither would you go? Why would you go?

VALENTINE. To call your servant to you.

CHRISTINA. She is here. What would you with her?

VALENTINE. I mean your lover, the man you came to meet.

CHRISTINA. Oh heavens! What lover? What man? I came to seek no man but you, whom I had too long lost.

VALENTINE. You could not know that I was here.

CHRISTINA. (*points to* ISABEL) Ask her; 'twas she that told me.

VALENTINE. How could she know?

CHRISTINA. That you shall know hereafter.

VALENTINE. No, you thought me too far out of the way to disturb your assignation and I assure you, madam, 'twas my ill fortune, not my design; and, that it may appear so, I do withdraw (as in all good breeding and civility I am obliged) for, sure, your wished-for lover's coming.

CHRISTINA. What do you mean? Are you aweary of that title?

VALENTINE. I am ashamed of it since it grows common. (*Going out*)

CHRISTINA. Nay, you will not, shall not go.

VALENTINE. My stay might give him jealousy and so do you injury and him the greatest in the world. Heavens forbid! I would not make a man jealous, for though you call a thousand vows and oaths and tears to witness (as you safely may) that you have not the least of love for me, yet, if he ever knew how I have loved you, sure, he would not, could not believe you.

CHRISTINA. I do confess your riddle is too hard for me to solve; therefore you are obliged to do't yourself.

VALENTINE. I wish it were capable of any other interpretation than what you know already.

CHRISTINA. Is this that generous good Valentine who has disguised him so? (*She weeps*)

VINCENT. Nay, I must withhold you then. (*Stops* VALENTINE *going out*) Methinks she should be innocent; her tongue and eyes, together with that flood that swells 'em, do vindicate her heart.

VALENTINE. (*going out*) They show but their long practice of dissimulation.

VINCENT. Come back. I hear Ranger coming up. Stay but till he comes.

VALENTINE. Do you think I have the patience of an alderman?

VINCENT. You may go out this way when you will, by the back-stairs. But stay a little till – oh, here he comes.

RANGER *enters.*

VALENTINE. My revenge will now detain me.

VALENTINE *retires again. Upon* RANGER*'s entrance* CHRISTINA *puts on her mask.*

RANGER. (*aside*) What, come already? Where is Dapper-wit? – The blessing's double that comes quickly. I

230–1 the patience of aldermen was proverbial.

did not yet expect you here, otherwise I had not done myself the injury to be absent but I hope, madam, I have not made you stay long for me.

CHRISTINA. I have not stayed at all for you.

RANGER. I am glad of it, madam.

CHRISTINA. (*to* ISABEL *aside; removing from him to t'other side*) Is not this that troublesome stranger who last night followed the lady into my lodgings? 'Tis he.

RANGER. (*aside*) Why does she remove so disdainfully from me? – I find you take it ill I was not at your coming here, madam.

CHRISTINA. Indeed I do not; you are mistaken, sir.

RANGER. Confirm me by a smile then, madam; remove that cloud which makes me apprehend foul weather. (*Goes to take off her mask*) Mr Vincent, pray retire; 'tis you keep on the lady's mask and no displeasure which she has for me – yet, madam, you need not distrust his honour or his faith. But do not keep the lady under constraint; pray leave us a little, Master Vincent.

CHRISTINA. You must not leave us, sir. Would you leave me with a stranger?

VALENTINE. (*behind*) How's that!

RANGER. (*aside*) I've done amiss, I find, to bring her hither. (*Apart to* CHRISTINA) Madam, I understand you –

CHRISTINA. Sir, I do not understand you.

RANGER. You would not be known to Mr Vincent.

CHRISTINA. 'Tis your acquaintance I would avoid.

RANGER. (*aside*) Dull brute that I was to bring her hither! – (*Softly to her*) I have found my error, madam. Give me but a new appointment where I may meet you by and by and straight I will withdraw as if I knew you not.

CHRISTINA. Why, do you know me?

RANGER. (*aside*) I must not own it. (*Offers to whisper*) No, madam, but –

CHRISTINA. Whispering, sir, argues an old acquaintance but I have not the vanity to be thought of yours and resolve you shall never have the disparagement of mine. Mr Vincent, pray let us go in here.

RANGER. [*aside*] How's this! I am undone, I see, but if

I let her go thus I shall be an eternal laughing-stock to Vincent.

VINCENT. Do you not know him, madam? I thought you had come hither on purpose to meet him.

CHRISTINA. To meet him!

VINCENT. By your own appointment.

CHRISTINA. What strange infatuation does delude you all? You know he said he did not know me.

VINCENT. You writ him; he has your letter.

CHRISTINA. Then you know my name sure! Yet you confessed but now you knew me not.

RANGER. I must confess your anger has disguised you more than your mask, for I thought to have met a kinder Christina here.

CHRISTINA. Heavens! How could he know me in this place? He watched me hither, sure, or is there any other of my name? That you may no longer mistake me for your Christina, I'll pull off that which soothes your error. (*Pulls off her mask*)

RANGER. Take but t'other vizard off too, I mean your anger, and I'll swear you are the same and only Christina which I wished and thought to meet here.

CHRISTINA. How could you think to meet me here?

RANGER. By virtue of this your commission (*gives her the letter*) which now, I see, was meant a real challenge, for you look as if you would fight with me.

CHRISTINA. The paper is a stranger to me; I never writ it. You are abused.

VINCENT. Christina is a person of honour and will own what she has written, Ranger.

RANGER. (*aside*) So, the comedy begins. I shall be laughed at sufficiently if I do not justify myself; I must set my impudence to hers. She is resolved to deny all, I see, and I have lost all hope of her.

VINCENT. Come, faith, Ranger –

RANGER. You will deny too, madam, that I followed you last night from the park to your lodging where I stayed with you till morning? You never saw me before, I warrant.

---

297 *soothes*: proves true.

CHRISTINA. That you rudely intruded last night into my lodging I cannot deny but I wonder you have the confidence to brag of it. Sure, you will not of your reception?

RANGER. I never was so ill-bred as to brag of my reception in a lady's chamber, not a word of that, madam.

VALENTINE. [*behind*] How! If he lies I revenge her; if it be true I revenge myself.

VALENTINE draws his sword which VINCENT seeing thrusts him back and shuts the door upon him before he was discovered by RANGER.

Enter LYDIA and her woman, stopping at the door.

LYDIA. [*aside*] What do I see! Christina with him! A counterplot to mine to make me and it ridiculous. 'Tis true, I find, they have been long acquainted and I long abused. But, since she intends a triumph, in spite as well as shame (not emulation) I retire. She deserves no envy who will be shortly in my condition; his natural inconstancy will prove my best revenge on her – on both.

Exeunt LYDIA with her woman.

[*Enter*] *DAPPERWIT to them.*

DAPPERWIT. Christina's going away again. What's the matter?

RANGER. What do you mean?

DAPPERWIT. I scarce had paid the chairmen and was coming up after her but I met her on the stairs in as much haste as if she had been frightened.

RANGER. Who do you talk of?

DAPPERWIT. Christina, whom I took up in a chair just now at St James's Gate.

RANGER. Thou art mad. Here she is; this is Christina.

DAPPERWIT. I must confess I did not see her face but I am sure the lady is gone that I brought just now.

RANGER. I tell you again, this is she. Did you bring two?

CHRISTINA. I came in no chair, had no guide but my woman there.

VINCENT. When did you bring your lady, Dapperwit?

DAPPERWIT. Ev'n now, just now.

VINCENT. This lady has been here half an hour.

RANGER. He knows not what he says. He is mad, you are all so, I am so too.

VINCENT. 'Tis the best excuse you can make for yourself and, by owning your mistake, you'll show you are come to yourself. I myself saw your woman at the door, who but looked in and then immediately went down again, as your friend Dapperwit too affirms.

CHRISTINA. You had best follow her that looked for you and I'll go seek out him I came to see, Mr Vincent, pray let me in here.

RANGER. 'Tis very fine, wondrous fine!

CHRISTINA *goes out a little and returns.*

CHRISTINA. Oh, he is gone! Mr Vincent, follow him. He were yet more severe to me in endangering his life than in his censures of me. You know the power of his enemies is great as their malice; just heaven preserve him from them, and me from this ill or unlucky man.

Exeunt CHRISTINA, *her woman and* VINCENT.

RANGER. 'Tis well. Nay, certainly, I shall never be master of my senses more. But why dost thou help to distract me too?

DAPPERWIT. My astonishment was as great as yours, to see her go away again. I would have stayed her if I could.

RANGER. Yet again talking of a woman you met going out, when I talk of Christina.

DAPPERWIT. I talk of Christina too.

RANGER. She went out just now; the woman you found me with was she.

DAPPERWIT. That was not the Christina I brought just now.

RANGER. You brought her almost half an hour ago. 'Sdeath, will you give me the lie?

DAPPERWIT. A lady disappointed by her gallant the night before her journey could not be more touchy with her maid or husband than you are with me now after your disappointment. But if you thank me so I'll go serve myself hereafter. For ought I know I have disappointed Mrs Martha for you and may lose thirty thousand pound by the bargain. Farewell, a raving lover is fit for solitude. *Exit* DAPPERWIT.

RANGER. Lydia, triumph; I now am thine again. Of intrigue, honourable or dishonourable, and all sorts of rambling I take my leave. When we are giddy 'tis time to stand still. Why should we be so fond of the by-paths of love, where we are still waylaid with surprises, trapans, dangers and murdering disappointments?

Just as at Blind-Man's Buff, we run at all,
Whilst those that lead us laugh to see us fall,
And when we think we hold the lady fast
We find it but her scarf or veil at last. *Exit.*

ACT V

SCENE I

St James's Park.

Enter SIR SIMON ADDLEPLOT *leading* MRS MARTHA, DAPPERWIT.

SIR SIMON. At length, you see, I have freed the captive lady for her longing knight. Mr Dapperwit, who brings off a plot cleverly now?

DAPPERWIT. I wish our poets were half so good at it. Mrs Martha, a thousand welcomes – (DAPPERWIT *kisses and embraces* MRS MARTHA)

SIR SIMON. Hold, hold, sir. Your joy is a little too familiar, faith and troth.

DAPPERWIT. Will you not let me salute Mrs Martha?

MARTHA. What, Jonas, do you think I do not know good breeding? Must I be taught by you?

SIR SIMON. I would have kept the maidenhead of your lips for your sweet knight, Mrs Martha, that's all. I dare swear, you never kissed any man before but your father.

MARTHA. My sweet knight, if he will be a knight of mine, must be contented with what he finds as well as other knights.

SIR SIMON. So smart already, faith and troth!

404 s.d. *Exit*: Exeunt Q1.

MARTHA. Dear Mr Dapperwit, I am overjoyed to see you – but I thank honest Jonas for't.

SIR SIMON. (*aside*) How she hugs him!

MARTHA. (*she hugs* DAPPERWIT) Poor Mr Dapperwit, I thought I should never have seen you again – but I thank honest Jonas there.

SIR SIMON. Do not thank me, Mrs Martha, any more than I thank you.

MARTHA. I would not be ungrateful, Jonas.

SIR SIMON. Then reserve your kindness only for your worthy, noble, brave, heroic knight who loves you only and only deserves your kindness.

MARTHA. I will show my kindness to my worthy, brave, heroic knight in being kind to his friend, his dear friend, who helped him to me. (*Hugs* DAPPERWIT *again*)

SIR SIMON. But, Mistress Martha, he is not to help him always; though he helps him to be married, he is not to help him when he is married.

MARTHA. What, Mr Dapperwit, will you love my worthy knight less after marriage than before? That were against the custom, for marriage gets a man friends, instead of losing those he has.

DAPPERWIT. I will ever be his servant and yours; dear madam, do not doubt me.

MARTHA. (*she kisses* DAPPERWIT) I do not, sweet, dear Mr Dapperwit, but I should not have seen you these two days, if it had not been for honest Jonas there.

SIR SIMON. (*apart to* DAPPERWIT) For shame, though she be young and foolish, do not you wrong me to my face.

DAPPERWIT. Would you have me so ill-bred as to repulse her innocent kindness? (*Aside*) What a thing it is to want wit!

SIR SIMON. (*aside*) A pox, I must make haste to discover myself or I shall discover what I would not discover. But if I should discover myself in this habit 'twould not be to my advantage. But I'll go, put on my own clothes and look like a knight. (*To her*) Well, Mrs Martha, I'll go seek out your knight. Are you not impatient to see him?

MARTHA. Wives must be obedient; let him take his own time.

SIR SIMON. Can you trust yourself a turn or two with Master Dapperwit?

MARTHA. Yes, yes, Jonas, as long as you will.

SIR SIMON. (*aside*) But I would not trust you with him if I could help it.
So married wight sees what he dares not blame
And cannot budge for fear, nor stay for shame.

Exit SIR SIMON.

DAPPERWIT. I am glad he is gone that I may laugh. 'Tis such a miracle of fops, that his conversation should be pleasant to me even when it hindered me of yours.

MARTHA. Indeed, I am glad he is gone too, as pleasant as he is.

DAPPERWIT. I know why, I know why, sweet Mrs Martha. I warrant you, you had rather have the parson's company than his! Now you are out of your father's house 'tis time to leave being a hypocrite.

MARTHA. Well, for the jest's sake, to disappoint my knight, I would not care if I disappointed myself of a ladyship.

DAPPERWIT. Come, I will not keep you on the tenters; I know you have a mind to make sure of me. I have a little chaplain – I wish he were a bishop or one of the friars to perfect our revenge upon that zealous jew, your father!

MARTHA. Do not speak ill of my father. He has been your friend, I'm sure.

DAPPERWIT. My friend!

MARTHA. His hard usage of me conspired with your good mien and wit and, to avoid slavery under him, I stoop to your yoke.

DAPPERWIT. I will be obliged to your father for nothing but a portion, nor to you for your love – 'twas due to my merit.

MARTHA. You show yourself Sir Simon's original. If 'twere not for that vanity –

DAPPERWIT. I should be no wit; 'tis the badge of my calling, for you can no more find a man of wit without

---

82 *on the tenters*: on tenterhooks, in suspense.
85 *jew*: usurer.

vanity than a fine woman without affectation. But let us go before the knight comes again.

MARTHA. Let us go before my father comes; he soon will have the intelligence.

DAPPERWIT. (*pauses*) Stay, let me think a little.

MARTHA. What are you thinking of? You should have thought before this time or I should have thought rather.

DAPPERWIT. Peace, peace.

MARTHA. What are you thinking of?

DAPPERWIT. I am thinking what a wit without vanity is like. He is like –

MARTHA. You do not think we are in a public place and may be surprised and prevented by my father's scouts.

DAPPERWIT. What, would you have me lose my thought?

MARTHA. You would rather lose your mistress, it seems.

DAPPERWIT. He is like – I think I'm a sot tonight, let me perish.

MARTHA. (*offers to go*) Nay, if you are so in love with your thought.

DAPPERWIT. Are you so impatient to be my wife? He is like – he is like – a picture without shadows or, or – a face without patches – or a diamond without a foil; these are new thoughts now, these are new.

MARTHA. You are wedded already to your thoughts, I see. Goodnight.

DAPPERWIT. Madam, do not take it ill.
For loss of happy thought there's no amends;
For his new jest true wit will lose old friends.
That's new again, the thought's new.

Exeunt.

Enter GRIPE, *leading* MRS LUCY; JOYNER, CROSSBITE *following.*

GRIPE. Mrs Joyner, I can conform to this mode of public walking by moonlight because one is not known.

LUCY. Why, are you ashamed of your company?

GRIPE. No, pretty one; because in the dark, or as it were in the dark, there is no envy nor scandal. I would neither lose you nor my reputation.

JOYNER. Your reputation! Indeed, your worship, 'tis

well known there are as grave men as your worship – nay, men in office too – that adjourn their cares and businesses to come and unbend themselves at night here with a little vizard mask.

GRIPE. I do believe it, I do believe it, Mrs Joyner.

LUCY. Ay, godmother, and carries and treats her at Mulberry Garden.

CROSSBITE. Nay, does not only treat her but gives her his whole gleanings of that day.

GRIPE. They may, they may, Mrs Crossbite; they take above six in the hundred.

CROSSBITE. Nay, there are those of so much worth and honour and love that they'll take it from their wives and children to give it to their misses. Now your worship has no wife and but one child.

GRIPE. (*aside*) Still for my edification.

JOYNER. That's true indeed, for I know a great lady that cannot follow her husband abroad to his haunts because her farrendine is so ragged and greasy, whilst his mistress is as fine as fippence in her embroidered satins.

GRIPE. Politicly done of him indeed. If the truth were known, he is a statesman by that, umph!

CROSSBITE. Truly, your women of quality are very troublesome to their husbands. I have heard 'em complain they will allow them no separate maintenance, though the honourable jilts themselves will not marry without it.

JOYNER. Come, come, mistress, sometimes 'tis the craft of those gentlemen to complain of their wives' expenses to excuse their own narrowness to their misses – but your daughter has a gallant can make no excuse.

GRIPE. [*aside*] So, Mrs Joyner! My friend, Mrs Joyner!

CROSSBITE. I hope, indeed, he'll give my daughter no cause to dun him, for, poor wretch, she is as modest as her mother.

GRIPE. I profess, I believe it.

LUCY. But I have the boldness to ask him for a treat.

---

149 *six in the hundred*: 6%, the highest legal rate of interest.
158 *as fine as fippence*: finely dressed, with a hint of pride.

Come, gallant, we must walk towards the Mulberry Garden.

GRIPE. [*aside*] So! – I am afraid, little mistress, the rooms are all taken up by this time.

JOYNER. (*aside to* GRIPE) Will you shame yourself again?

LUCY. If the rooms be full we'll have an arbour.

GRIPE. At this time of night! Besides, the waiters will ne'er come near you.

LUCY. They will be observant of good customers, as we shall be. Come along.

GRIPE. Indeed and verily, little mistress, I would go but that I should be forsworn if I did.

JOYNER. That's so pitiful an excuse –

GRIPE. In truth, I have forsworn the place ever since I was pawned there for a reckoning.

LUCY. You have broken many an oath for the Good Old Cause – and will you boggle at one for your poor little Miss? Come along.

[*Enter*] LADY FLIPPANT *behind.*

FLIPPANT. Unfortunate lady that I am! I have left the herd on purpose to be chased and have wandered this hour here but the park affords not so much as a satyr for me (and that's strange); no Burgundy man or drunken scourer will reel my way. The rag-women and cinder-women have better luck than I – but who are these? If this mongrel light does not deceive me, 'tis my brother. 'Tis he! There's Joyner too and two other women. I'll follow 'em. It must be he, for this world hath nothing like him – I know not what the devil may be in the other.

Exeunt omnes.

Enter SIR SIMON ADDLEPLOT *in fine clothes;* DAPPERWIT *and* MRS MARTHA *unseen by him at the door.*

---

193 *pawned there for a reckoning*: left to pay the bill.
194–5 *Good Old Cause*: the Puritan rebellion.
200 *Burgundy man*: drunk.
201 *scourer*: rowdy rakes who roistered in the streets at night.
202 *cinder-women*: women whose job was to rake the ashes and carry out the cinders.

SIR SIMON. Well, after all my seeking, I can find those I would not find. I'm sure 'twas old Gripe and Joyner with him and the widow followed. He would not have been here but to have sought his daughter, sure; but vigilant Dapperwit has spied him too and has, no doubt, secured her from him.

DAPPERWIT. (*behind*) And you.

SIR SIMON. The rogue is as good at hiding as I am at stealing a mistress. 'Tis a vain, conceited fellow yet I think 'tis an honest fellow. But again, he is a damnable, whoring fellow and what opportunity this air and darkness may incline 'em to, heaven knows! For I have heard the rogue say himself a lady will no more show her modesty in the dark than a Spaniard his courage.

DAPPERWIT. Ha, ha, ha!

SIR SIMON. Nay, if you are there, my true friend, I'll forgive your hearkening, if you'll forgive my censures! I speak to you, dear Madam Martha, dear, dear! Behold your worthy knight –

MARTHA. That's far from neighbours.

SIR SIMON. Is come to reap the fruit of all his labours.

MARTHA. I cannot see the knight; well, but I'm sure I hear Jonas.

SIR SIMON. I am no Jonas, Mrs Martha.

MARTHA. The night is not so dark nor the peruke so big but I can discern Jonas.

SIR SIMON. Faith and troth, I am the very Sir Simon Addleplot that is to marry you, the same Dapperwit solicited you for – ask him else. My name is not Jonas.

MARTHA. You think my youth and simplicity capable of this cheat. But let me tell you, Jonas, 'tis not your borrowed clothes and title shall make me marry my father's man.

SIR SIMON. Borrowed title! I'll be sworn I bought it of my laundress, who was a court laundress, but, indeed, my clothes I have not paid for, therefore in that sense they are borrowed.

MARTHA. Prithee, Jonas, let the jest end or I shall be presently in earnest.

---

228 *far from neighbours*: praise of oneself.
229 *Is*: I's Q1.

SIR SIMON. Pray be in earnest and let us go. The parson and supper stay for us and I am a knight in earnest.

MARTHA. You a knight, insolent, saucy fool?

SIR SIMON. The devil take me, Mrs Martha, if I am not a knight now – a knight baronet too. A man ought, I see, to carry his patent in his pocket when he goes to be married; 'tis more necessary than a licence. I am a knight indeed and indeed now, Mrs Martha.

MARTHA. Indeed and indeed, the trick will not pass, Jonas.

SIR SIMON. Poor wretch, she's afraid she shall not be a Lady. Come, come, discover the intrigue, Dapperwit –

MARTHA. You need not discover the intrigue – 'tis apparent already. Unworthy Mr Dapperwit, after my confidence reposed in you, could you be so little generous as to betray me to my father's man? But I'll be even with you.

SIR SIMON. Do not accuse him, poor man, before you hear him. Tell her the intrigue, man.

DAPPERWIT. A pox, she will not believe us.

SIR SIMON. Will you not excuse yourself? But I must not let it rest so. Know then, Mrs Martha –

MARTHA. Come, I forgive thee before thy confession, Jonas. You never had had the confidence to have designed this cheat upon me but from Mr Dapperwit's encouragement – 'twas his plot.

SIR SIMON. Nay, do not do me that wrong, madam.

MARTHA. But since he has trapanned me out of my father's house he is like to keep me as long as I live – and so goodnight, Jonas.

SIR SIMON. Hold, hold, what d'y'mean both? Prithee tell her that I am Sir Simon and no Jonas.

DAPPERWIT. A pox, she will not believe us, I tell you.

SIR SIMON. I have provided a parson and supper at Mulberry Garden and invited all my friends I could meet in the park.

DAPPERWIT. Nay, rather than they shall be disappointed, there shall be a bride and bridegroom to entertain 'em; Mrs Martha and I'll go thither presently.

SIR SIMON. Why, shall she be your bride?

---

248 *in earnest*: (*a*) serious (*b*) money paid as security.
253 *patent*: the document conferring the title.

DAPPERWIT. You see she will have it so.

SIR SIMON. Will you make Dapperwit your husband?

MARTHA. Rather than my father's man.

SIR SIMON. Oh, the devil –

MARTHA. Nay, come along, Jonas, you shall make one at the wedding since you helped contrive it.

SIR SIMON. Will you cheat yourself for fear of being cheated?

MARTHA. I am desperate now.

SIR SIMON. Wilt thou let her do so ill a thing, Dapperwit, as to marry thee? Open her eyes, prithee, and tell her I am a true knight.

DAPPERWIT. 'Twould be in vain, by my life; you have carried yourself so like a natural clerk – and so adieu, good Jonas.

Exeunt MARTHA *and* DAPPERWIT.

SIR SIMON. What, ruined by my own plot like an old Cavalier; yet like him too, I will plot on still, a plot of prevention. So, I have it – her father was here ev'n now, I'm sure. Well – I'll go tell her father of her, that I will,
And punish so her folly and his treachery.
Revenge is sweet and makes amends for lechery. *Exit.*

Enter LYDIA *and her woman,* LEONORE.

LYDIA. I wish I had not come hither tonight, Leonore.

LEONORE. Why did you, madam, if the place be so disagreeable to you?

LYDIA. We cannot help visiting the place often where we have lost anything we value. I lost Ranger here last night.

LEONORE. You thought you had lost him before, a great while ago, and therefore you ought to be the less troubled.

LYDIA. But 'twas here I missed him first, I'm sure.

LEONORE. Come, madam, let not the loss vex you; he is not worth the looking after.

LYDIA. It cannot but vex me yet, if I lost him by my own fault.

LEONORE. You had but too much care to keep him.

LYDIA. It often happens, indeed, that too much care is

---

301 *natural*: (*a*) genuine (*b*) foolish.

as bad as negligence. But I had rather be robbed than lose what I have carelessly.

LEONORE. But, I believe, you would hang the thief if you could.

LYDIA. Not if I could have my own again.

LEONORE. I see, you would be too merciful.

LYDIA. I wish I were tried.

LEONORE. But, madam, if you please, we will waive the discourse, for people seldom, I suppose, talk with pleasure of their real losses.

LYDIA. 'Tis better than to ruminate on them; mine, I'm sure, will not out of my head nor heart.

LEONORE. Grief is so far from retrieving a loss that it makes it greater; but the way to lessen it is by a comparison with others' losses. Here are ladies in the park of your acquaintance, I doubt not, can compare with you; pray, madam, let us walk and find 'em out.

LYDIA. 'Tis the resentment, you say, makes the loss great or little and then, I'm sure, there is none like mine. However, go on.

Exeunt.

Enter VINCENT *and* VALENTINE.

VINCENT. I am glad I have found you, for now I am prepared to lead you out of the dark and all your trouble; I have good news.

VALENTINE. You are as unmerciful as the physician who with new arts keeps his miserable patient alive and in hopes, when he knows the disease is incurable.

VINCENT. And you, like the melancholy patient, mistrust and hate your physician because he will not comply with your despair. But I'll cure your jealousy now.

VALENTINE. You know all diseases grow worse by relapses.

VINCENT. Trust me once more.

VALENTINE. Well, you may try your experiments upon me.

VINCENT. Just as I shut the door upon you, the woman Ranger expected came upstairs but, finding another woman in discourse with him, went down again – I suppose as jealous of him as you of Christina.

VALENTINE. How does it appear she came to Ranger?

VINCENT. Thus: Dapperwit came up after, who had brought her, just then, in a chair from St James's by Ranger's appointment, and it is certain your Christina came to you.

VALENTINE. How can that be, for she knew not I was in the kingdom?

VINCENT. My man confesses, when I sent him to inquire of her woman about her lady's being here in the park last night, he told her you were come and she, it seems, told her mistress.

VALENTINE. (*aside*) That might be. – But did not Christina confess Ranger was in her lodging last night?

VINCENT. By intrusion, which she had more particularly informed me of, if her apprehensions of your danger had not posted me after you, she not having yet (as I suppose) heard of Clerimont's recovery. I left her, poor creature, at home, distracted with a thousand fears for your life and love.

VALENTINE. Her love, I'm sure, has cost me more fears than my life; yet that little danger is not past, as you think, till the great one be over.

VINCENT. Open but your eyes and the fantastic goblin's vanished and all your idle fears will turn to shame, for jealousy is the basest cowardice.

VALENTINE. I had rather, indeed, blush for myself than her.

VINCENT. I'm sure you will have more reason – But is not that Ranger there?

RANGER *enters, followed by* CHRISTINA *and her woman; after them,* LYDIA *and her woman.*

VALENTINE. I think it is.

VINCENT. I suppose his friend Dapperwit is not far off. I will examine them both before you and not leave you so much as the shadow of a doubt; Ranger's astonishment at my lodging confessed his mistake.

VALENTINE. His astonishment might proceed from Christina's unexpected strangeness to him.

VINCENT. He shall satisfy you now himself to the contrary, I warrant you. Have but patience.

VALENTINE. I had rather, indeed, he should satisfy my doubts than my revenge; therefore I can have patience.

VINCENT. But what women are those that follow him?

VALENTINE. Stay a little –

RANGER. Lydia, Lydia! Poor Lydia.

LYDIA. (*to her maid*) If she be my rival 'tis some comfort yet to see her follow him, rather than he her.

LEONORE. But if you follow them a little longer for your comfort you shall see them go hand in hand.

CHRISTINA. (*to* RANGER) Sir, sir!

LEONORE. She calls to him already.

LYDIA. But he does not hear, you see. Let us go a little nearer.

VINCENT. Sure, it is Ranger?

VALENTINE. As sure as the woman that follows him closest is Christina.

VINCENT. For shame, talk not of Christina. I left her just now at home, surrounded with so many fears and griefs she could not stir.

VALENTINE. She is come, it may be, to divert them here in the park. I'm sure 'tis she.

VINCENT. When the moon, at this instant, scarce affords light enough to distinguish a man from a tree, how can you know her?

VALENTINE. How can you know Ranger then?

VINCENT. I heard him speak.

VALENTINE. So you may her too. I'll secure you if you will draw but a little nearer. She came, doubtless, to no other end but to speak with him; observe.

CHRISTINA. (*to* RANGER) Sir, I have followed you hitherto but now I must desire you to follow me out of the company, for I would not be overheard nor disturbed.

RANGER. [*aside*] Ha! Is not this Christina's voice? It is, I am sure; I cannot be deceived now. – Dear Madam –

VINCENT. (*apart to* VALENTINE) It is she indeed.

VALENTINE. Is it so?

CHRISTINA. (*to* RANGER) Come, sir –

VALENTINE. (*aside*) Nay, I'll follow you too, though not invited.

LYDIA. (*aside*) I must not, cannot stay behind.

They all go off together in a huddle hastily. CHRISTINA, *her woman and* VALENTINE *return on the other side.*

CHRISTINA. Come along, sir.

VALENTINE. (*aside*) So I must stick to her when all is done. Her new servant has lost her in the crowd; she has gone too fast for him – so much my revenge is swifter than his love. Now shall I not only have the deserted lover's revenge of disappointing her of her new man but an opportunity infallibly at once to discover her falseness and confront her impudence.

CHRISTINA. Pray come along, sir; I am in haste.

VALENTINE. (*aside*) So eager, indeed! I wish that cloud may yet withhold the moon, that this false woman may not discover me before I do her.

CHRISTINA. Here no one can hear us and I'm sure we cannot see one another.

VALENTINE. (*aside*) 'Sdeath, what have I giddily run myself upon? 'Tis rather a trial of myself than her; I cannot undergo it.

CHRISTINA. Come nearer, sir.

VALENTINE. (*aside*) Hell and vengeance, I cannot suffer it, I cannot.

CHRISTINA. Come, come, yet nearer, pray come nearer.

VALENTINE. [*aside*] It is impossible; I cannot hold. I must discover myself rather than her infamy.

CHRISTINA. (*speaks, walking slowly*) You are conscious, it seems, of the wrong you have done me and are ashamed, though in the dark.

VALENTINE. (*aside*) How's this!

CHRISTINA. I'm glad to find it so, for all my business with you is to show you your late mistakes and force a confession from you of those unmannerly injuries you have done me.

VALENTINE. (*aside*) What! I think she's honest – or does she know me? Sure, she cannot.

CHRISTINA. First, your intrusion last night into my lodging, which, I suppose, has begot your other gross mistakes.

VALENTINE. (*aside*) No, she takes me for Ranger, I see again.

CHRISTINA. You are to know then, since needs you must, it was not me you followed last night to my lodging from the park but some kinswoman of yours, it seems, whose fear of being discovered by you prevailed with me to personate her, while she withdrew – our habits and our statures being much alike – which I did with as much difficulty as she used importunity to make me – and all this my Lady Flippant can witness, who was then with your cousin.

VALENTINE. (*aside*) I am glad to hear this!

CHRISTINA. Now, what your claim to me at Mr Vincent's lodging meant. The letter and promises you unworthily or erroneously laid to my charge you must explain to me and others or –

VALENTINE. (*aside*) How's this! I hope I shall discover no guilt but my own. She would not speak in threats to a lover!

CHRISTINA. Was it because you found me in Mr Vincent's lodgings you took a liberty to use me like one of your common visitants? But know, I came no more to Mr Vincent than to you; yet I confess my visit was intended to a man – a brave man till you made him use a woman ill, worthy the love of a princess till you made him censure mine, good as angels till you made him unjust. Why, in the name of honour, would you do't?

VALENTINE. (*aside*) How happily am I disappointed! Poor injured Christina!

CHRISTINA. He would have sought me out first if you had not made him fly from me. Our mutual love, confirmed by a contract, made our hearts inseparable till you rudely, if not maliciously, thrust in upon us and broke the close and happy knot. I had lost him before for a month, now for ever. (*She weeps*)

VALENTINE. (*aside*) My joy, and pity, makes me as mute as my shame. Yet I must discover myself.

CHRISTINA. Your silence is a confession of your guilt.

VALENTINE. (*aside*) I own it.

CHRISTINA. But that will not serve my turn, for straight you must go clear yourself, and me, to him you have injured in me – if he has not made too much haste from me as to be found again. You must, I say, for he is a man that will have satisfaction and in satisfying him you do me.

VALENTINE. Then he is satisfied.

CHRISTINA. How! Is it you? Then I am not satisfied.

VALENTINE. Will you be worse than your word?

CHRISTINA. I gave it not to you.

VALENTINE. Come, dear Christina, the jealous, like the drunkard, has his punishment with his offence.

[*Enter*] *to them* VINCENT.

VINCENT. Valentine, Mr Valentine.

VALENTINE. Vincent!

VINCENT. Where have you been all this while?

VALENTINE holds CHRISTINA by the hand, who seems to struggle to get from him.

VALENTINE. Here, with my injured Christina.

VINCENT. She's behind with Ranger who is forced to speak all the tender things himself, for she affords him not a word.

VALENTINE. Pish, pish, Vincent, who is blind now? Who deceived now?

VINCENT. You are, for I'm sure Christina is with him. Come back and see.

They go out at one door and return at the other.

[*Enter* RANGER *and* LYDIA]

RANGER. (*to* LYDIA) Still mocked, still abused! Did you not bid me follow you where we might not be disturbed nor overheard? And now not allow me a word?

VINCENT. (*apart to* VALENTINE) Did you hear him?

VALENTINE. (*apart to* VINCENT) Yes, yes, peace –

RANGER. Disowning your letter and me at Vincent's lodging, declaring you came to meet another there and not me, with a great deal of such affronting unkindness might be reasonable enough, because you would not entrust Vincent with our love. But now, when nobody sees us nor hears us, why this unseasonable shyness? –

LYDIA. (*aside*) It seems she did not expect him there but had appointed to meet another. I wish it were so.

RANGER. I have not patience. Do you design thus to revenge my intrusion into your lodging last night? Sure, if you had then been displeased with my company, you would not have invited yourself to't again by a letter. Or is this a punishment for bringing you to a house so near your own, where, it seems, you were known too? I do confess it was a fault but make me suffer any penance but your silence, because it is the certain mark of a mistress's lasting displeasure –

LYDIA. (*aside*) My cue is not yet come.

---

567 *cue*: the word has dropped out of some copies of Q1.

RANGER. Not yet a word? You did not use me so unkindly last night when you chid me out of your house and with indignation bid me begone. Now, you bid me follow you and yet will have nothing to say to me – and I am more deceived this day and night than I was last night, when, I must confess, I followed you for another. –

LYDIA. (*aside*) I'm glad to hear that.

RANGER. One that would have used me better, whose love I have ungratefully abused for yours, yet from no other reason but my natural inconstancy. (*Aside*) Poor Lydia, Lydia –

LYDIA. (*aside*) He muttered my name, sure, and with a sigh.

RANGER. But as last night by following (as I thought) her, I found you, so this night by following you in vain I do resolve, if I can find her again, to keep her for ever.

LYDIA. (*aside*) Now I am obliged and brought in debt to his inconstancy. Faith, now cannot I hold out any longer; I must discover myself.

RANGER. But, madam, because I intend to see you no more, I'll take my leave of you for good and all. Since you will not speak, I'll try if you will squeak!

Goes to throw her down. She squeaks.

LYDIA. Mr Ranger, Mr Ranger!

VINCENT. Fie, fie, you need not ravish Christina, sure, that loves you so.

RANGER. [*aside*] Is it she? Lydia all this while? How am I gulled! And Vincent in the plot too?

LYDIA. Now, false Ranger.

RANGER. Now, false Christina too. You thought I did not know you now, because I offered you such an unusual civility.

LYDIA. You knew me! I warrant you knew too that I was the Christina you followed out of the park last night, that I was the Christina that writ the letter too.

RANGER. Certainly, therefore I would have taken my revenge, you see, for your tricks.

VALENTINE. (*to* CHRISTINA) Is not this the same woman that took refuge in your house last night, madam?

CHRISTINA. The very same.

VALENTINE. What, Mr Ranger, we have chopped and changed and hid our Christinas so long and often that at last we have drawn each of us our own!

RANGER. Mr Valentine in England! The truth on't is you have juggled together and drawn without my knowledge. But since she will have it so, she shall wear me for good and all now. (*Goes to take her by the hand*)

LYDIA. Come not near me.

RANGER. Nay, you need not be afraid I would ravish you, now I know you.

LYDIA. (*apart to* LEONORE; RANGER *listens*) And yet, Leonore, I think 'tis but justice to pardon the fault I made him commit?

RANGER. You consider it right, cousin, for indeed you are but merciful to yourself in it.

LYDIA. Yet, if I would be rigorous, though I made the blot, your oversight has lost the game.

RANGER. But 'twas rash woman's play, cousin, and ought not to be played again, let me tell you.

[*Enter*] DAPPERWIT *to them.*

DAPPERWIT. Who's there? Who's there?

RANGER. Dapperwit.

DAPPERWIT. Mr Ranger, I am glad I have met with you, for I have left my bride just now, in the house at Mulberry Garden, to come and pick up some of my friends in the park here to sup with us.

RANGER. Your bride! Are you married then? Where is your bride?

DAPPERWIT. Here at Mulberry Garden, I say, where you, these ladies and gentlemen shall all be welcome, if you will afford me the honour of your company.

RANGER. With all our hearts. But who have you married? Lucy?

DAPPERWIT. What, do you think I would marry a wench? I have married an heiress worth thirty thousand pound, let me perish.

VINCENT. An heiress worth thirty thousand pound!

DAPPERWIT. Mr Vincent, your servant, you here too?

---

627 *blot*: in backgammon, a piece liable to be taken or forfeit.

RANGER. Nay, we are more of your acquaintance here, I think. Go, we'll follow you, for, if you have not dismissed your parson, perhaps we may make him more work.

Exeunt.

SCENE II

The scene changes to the dining-room in Mulberry Garden House.

Enter SIR SIMON ADDLEPLOT, GRIPE, MRS MARTHA, JOYNER, CROSSBITE, LUCY, [FLIPPANT]

SIR SIMON. 'Tis as I told you, sir, you see.

GRIPE. Oh graceless babe, married to a wit! An idle, loitering, slandering, foul-mouthed, beggarly wit! Oh that my child should ever live to marry a wit!

JOYNER. Indeed, your worship had better seen her fairly buried, as they say.

CROSSBITE. If my daughter there should have done so I would not have gi'n her a groat.

GRIPE. Marry a wit!

SIR SIMON. (*to* JOYNER *aside*) Mrs Joyner, do not let me lose the widow too, for if you do, betwixt friends, I and my small annuity are both blown up; it will follow my estate.

JOYNER. (*aside*) I warrant you.

FLIPPANT. (*to* JOYNER *aside*) Let us make sure of Sir Simon tonight or –

JOYNER. [*to* FLIPPANT *aside*] You need not fear it. (*Aside*) Like the lawyers, while my clients endeavour to cheat one another, I in justice cheat 'em both.

GRIPE. Marry a wit!

Enter DAPPERWIT, RANGER *and* LYDIA, VALENTINE, CHRISTINA *and* VINCENT. DAPPERWIT *stops 'em and they stand all behind.*

DAPPERWIT. (*aside*) What, is he here? Lucy and her mother?

GRIPE. Tell me how thou cam'st to marry a wit.

MARTHA. Pray be not angry, sir, and I'll give you a good reason.

GRIPE. Reason for marrying a wit!

MARTHA. Indeed, I found myself six months gone with child and saw no hopes of your getting me a husband, or else I had not married a wit, sir.

JOYNER. (*aside*) Then you were the wit.

GRIPE. Had you that reason? Nay then – (*Holding up his hands*)

DAPPERWIT. (*aside*) How's that!

RANGER. (*aside*) Who would have thought, Dapperwit, you would have married a wench?

DAPPERWIT. (*to* RANGER) Well, thirty thousand pound will make me amends; I have known my betters wink and fall on for five or six. (*To* GRIPE *and the rest*) What, you are come, sir, to give me joy? You, Mrs Lucy, you and you? Well, unbid guests are doubly welcome. (*To* SIR SIMON) Sir Simon, I made bold to invite these ladies and gentlemen – for you must know, Mr Ranger, this worthy Sir Simon does not only give me my wedding-supper but my mistress too and is, as it were, my father.

SIR SIMON. Then I am, as it were, a grandfather to your new wife's *hans en kelder*, to which you are but as it were a father – there's for you again, sir, ha, ha!

RANGER. (*to* VINCENT) Ha, ha, ha!

DAPPERWIT. Fools sometimes say unhappy things, if we would mind 'em, but – what, melancholy at your daughter's wedding, sir?

GRIPE. (*aside*) How deplorable is my condition!

DAPPERWIT. Nay, if you will rob me of my wench, sir, can you blame me for robbing you of your daughter? I cannot be without a woman.

GRIPE. (*aside*) My daughter, my reputation and my money gone – but the last is dearest to me. Yet at once I may retrieve that and be revenged for the loss of the other and all this by marrying Lucy here. I shall get my five hundred pound again and get heirs to exclude my daughter and frustrate Dapperwit.

30–1 *Holding up his bands*: in horror.
46 *hans en kelder*: Jack in the cellar (Dutch), the unborn child.

Besides, 'tis agreed on all hands, 'tis cheaper keeping a wife than a wench.

DAPPERWIT. If you are so melancholy, sir, we will have the fiddles and a dance to divert you. Come.

A dance.

GRIPE. Indeed, you have put me so upon a merry pin that I resolve to marry too.

FLIPPANT. Nay, if my brother come to marrying once, I may too. I swore I would when he did, little thinking –

SIR SIMON. I take you at your word, madam.

FLIPPANT. Well, but if I had thought you would have been so quick with me –

GRIPE. Where is your parson?

DAPPERWIT. What, you would not revenge yourself upon the parson?

GRIPE. No, I would have the parson revenge upon you; he should marry me.

DAPPERWIT. I am glad you are so frolic sir. But who would you marry?

GRIPE. (*pointing to* LUCY) This innocent lady.

DAPPERWIT. That innocent lady?

GRIPE. Nay, I am impatient. Mrs Joyner, pray fetch him up if he be yet in the house.

DAPPERWIT. We were not married here. But you cannot be in earnest.

GRIPE. You'll find it so. Since you have robbed me of my housekeeper I must get another.

DAPPERWIT. Why? She was my wench.

GRIPE. I'll make her honest then.

CROSSBITE. Upon my repute he never saw her before. But will your worship marry my daughter then?

GRIPE. I promise her, and you, before all this good company, tomorrow I will make her my wife.

DAPPERWIT. How!

RANGER. (*to* VALENTINE) Our ladies, sir, I suppose, expect the same promise from us.

VALENTINE. They may be sure of us without a promise but let us, if we can, obtain theirs, to be sure of them.

DAPPERWIT. (*to* GRIPE) But will you marry her tomorrow?

GRIPE. I will verily.

DAPPERWIT. I am undone then, ruined, let me perish.

SIR SIMON. No, you may hire a little room in Covent Garden and set up a coffeehouse; you and your wife will be sure of the wits' custom.

DAPPERWIT. Abused by him I have abused!
Fortune our foe we cannot over-wit;
By none but thee our projects are cross-bit.

VALENTINE. Come, dear madam. What, yet angry? Jealousy, sure, is much more pardonable before marriage than after it. But tomorrow, by the help of the parson, you will put me out of all my fears.

CHRISTINA. I am afraid then you would give me my revenge and make me jealous of you and I had rather suspect your faith than you should mine.

RANGER. Cousin Lydia, I had rather suspect your faith too, than you should mine. Therefore, let us e'en marry tomorrow, that I may have my turn of watching, dogging, standing under the window, at the door, behind the hanging or –

LYDIA. But if I could be desperate now and give you up my liberty, could you find in your heart to quit all other engagements and voluntarily turn yourself over to one woman and she a wife too? Could you away with the insupportable bondage of matrimony?

RANGER. You talk of matrimony as irreverently as my Lady Flippant. The bondage of matrimony! No –
The end of marriage now is liberty
And two are bound – to set each other free.

EPILOGUE, *spoken by* DAPPERWIT

Now my brisk brothers of the pit, you'll say
I'm come to speak a good word for the play;
But, gallants, let me perish if I do,
For I have wit and judgement, just like you,
Wit never partial, judgement free and bold,
For fear or friendship never bought or sold,
Nor by good nature e'er to be cajoled.
Good nature in a critic were a crime,
Like mercy in a judge, and renders him
Guilty of all those faults he does forgive;

Besides, if thief from gallows you reprieve,
He'll cut your throat – so poet saved from shame
In damned lampoon will murder your good name.
  Yet in true spite to him and to his play,
Good faith, you should not rail at 'em today
But, to be more his foe, seem most his friend
And so maliciously the play commend
That he may be betrayed to writing on
And poet let him be, to be undone.

THE

GENTLEMAN Dancing-Maſter.

A

COMEDY,

Acted at the

DUKE'S THEATRE.

By Mr. *Wycherley*.

Horat.—— *Non ſatis eſt riſu diducere rictum*
Auditoris : & eſt quædam tamen hic quoq; virtus.

LONDON,

Printed by *J. M.* for *Henry Herringman* and *Thomas Dring* at the Sign of the *Blew Anchor* in the Lower Walk of the *New Exchange*, and at the Sign of the *White Lyon* in *Fleetſtreet* near *Chancery-lane* end. 1673.

Title-page of the 1673 Quarto of *The Gentleman Dancing-Master*, reproduced by permission of the British Library.

Motto

Horace, *Satires*, I x 7–8:

'It is not enough to draw forth a laugh from the spectators; however, there is a certain value even in that'

INTRODUCTORY NOTE

Wycherley owes the device of the lover disguised as a dancing-master to Calderón's *El Maestro de Danzar* but he took little more than the basic idea from this source. More intriguing for source-hunters are the parallels with *Romeo and Juliet*: like Juliet, Wycherley's Hippolita is fourteen, refuses to marry her strict father's choice of a man named Paris and has a nurse-governess; like Romeo, Gerrard finds himself making an entrance through a window, the balcony metamorphosed into a scramble across from the roof of a neighbouring inn. As in Wycherley's later use of Shakespeare in *The Plain-Dealer*, it is the differences as much as the similarities that Wycherley seems to be pointing up. Hippolita's trick to make Gerrard come and rescue her from the imminent marriage, by making Monsieur tell Gerrard not to do so and thus implanting the idea in his mind, is so conventional as to have two equally probable sources: in Jonson's *The Devil is an Ass*, Mrs Fitzdottrell tells Wittipol not to appear at 'the gentleman's chamber-window . . . That opens to my gallery' (II ii 53–4), in order to make sure that he does; in Molière's *L'École des maris*, Isabelle makes Sganarelle reproach Valère for trying to carry her off by force, again with a similar result. The Frenchified fop had appeared in James Howard's *The English Monsieur* (first performed in 1663) and Wycherley may have derived some hints from Howard's Frenchlove. But, since French fops on stage must have derived from French fops in the audience, Wycherley's Monsieur almost certainly owes more to life than to any dramatic predecessor.

The Gentleman Dancing-Master was first performed by the Duke's Company at their new theatre, Dorset Garden; a performance listed for 6 February 1672 may well have been the first. This is Wycherley's only play for the Duke's Company and the reasons for the move are not clear. The traditional explanation is the disastrous fire that destroyed the Bridges Street Theatre on 25 January 1672 but it is most unlikely that the rival company would perform a play less than a fortnight later. It is more probable that Wycherley wanted to capitalise on the talents of Edward Angel and James Nokes who played Don Diego and Monsieur in the first production. In any case, a more farcical play would suit the city audience at Dorset Garden better. As John Downes records, *The Gentleman Dancing-Master* was 'the third new play acted' at Dorset Garden but 'being liked but indifferently, it was laid by to make room for other new ones' after an initial run of six performances (*Roscius Anglicanus* (1708), p. 32). It may have been revived when the play was reprinted but there are no records for performance after 1672 until this century. It was performed at the Maddermarket Theatre, Norwich, in December 1924 and by the Phoenix Society, as part of their programme of revivals of Restoration drama, at the Regent Theatre in December 1925. In May 1930 Tyrone Guthrie directed the play at the Cambridge Festival Theatre, with Robert Donat as Gerrard (and Flora Robson as Flounce). It was seen at the Vanbrugh Theatre, London, in 1960.

The play was first published in 1673 and reprinted in 1693 and 1702; thereafter it has appeared only in collections of Wycherley's plays.

PROLOGUE TO THE CITY,

Newly after the removal of the Duke's Company from Lincoln Inn Fields to their new theatre, near Salisbury Court.

Our author, like us, finding 'twould scarce do
At t'other end o'th'town, is come to you
And, since 'tis his last trial, has that wit
To throw himself on a substantial pit,
Where needy wit or critic dare not come,
Lest neighbour i'the cloak, with looks so grum,
Should prove a dun;
Where punk in vizor dare not rant and tear
To put us out, since Bridewell is so near.
In short, we shall be heard, he understood,
If not, shall be admired – and that's as good,
For you to senseless plays have still been kind,
Nay, where no sense was you a jest would find
And never was it heard of that the city
Did ever take occasion to be witty
Upon dull poet or stiff player's action
But still with claps opposed the hissing faction.
But if you hissed, 'twas at the pit, not stage,
So, with the poet, damned the damning age
And still, we know, are ready to engage
Against the flouting, ticking gentry who
Citizen, player, poet would undo.
The poet – no, unless by commendation,
For on the Change wits have no reputation
And, rather than be branded for a wit,
He with you, able men, would credit get.

---

new theatre: Dorset Garden, which opened on 9 November 1671.

2 *is come to you*: a reference both to Wycherley's switch from the King's Company to the Duke's and to his shift in subject matter to a more mercantile one.

3 *last*: latest.

6 *grum*: sullen.

7 *dun*: creditor.

8 *punk in vizor*: prostitute wearing a mask.

9 *Bridewell*: a house of correction, for prostitutes in particular, just off Fleet Street.

21 *ticking*: running up bills.

24 *Change*: the Royal Exchange, the business centre for merchants and bankers.

THE PERSONS

MR GERRARD MR MARTIN	Young gentlemen of the town, and friends.
MR PARRIS or MONSIEUR DE PARIS	A vain coxcomb and rich city-heir, newly returned from France and mightily affected with the French language and fashions.
MR JAMES FORMAL or DON DIEGO	An old, rich, Spanish merchant, newly returned home, as much affected with the habit and customs of Spain and uncle to De Paris.
MRS HIPPOLITA	Formal's daughter.
MRS CAUTION	Formal's sister, an impertinent, precise old woman.
PRUE	Hippolita's maid.
MRS FLIRT MRS FLOUNCE	Two common women of the town.
A little BLACKAMOOR	Lacquey to Formal.

A PARSON, a FRENCH SCULLION, servants, WAITER and attendants.

The Scene: *London*

15 *precise*: puritanical.

THE GENTLEMAN DANCING-MASTER

ACT I

SCENE I

Don Diego's house in the evening.

Enter HIPPOLITA *and* PRUE, *her maid.*

HIPPOLITA. To confine a woman just in her rambling age! Take away her liberty at the very time she should use it! O barbarous aunt! O unnatural father! To shut up a poor girl at fourteen and hinder her budding; all things are ripened by the sun! To shut up a poor girl at fourteen!

PRUE. 'Tis true, miss, two poor young creatures as we are.

HIPPOLITA. Not suffered to see a play in a twelvemonth –

PRUE. Nor to go to Ponchinello nor Paradise –

HIPPOLITA. Nor to take a ramble to the Park nor Mulberry Gar'n –

PRUE. Nor to Tatnam Court nor Islington –

HIPPOLITA. Nor to eat a sillybub in New Spring Gar'n with a cousin –

---

11 *Ponchinello*: the Italian puppet-show run by Anthony Devolto at Charing Cross.

11 *Paradise*: 'we went to see Paradise, a room in Hatton Garden furnished with the representations of all sorts of animals, handsomely painted on boards or cloth and so cut out and made to stand and move, fly, crawl, roar and make their several cries as was not unpretty' (John Evelyn in his *Diary*, 23 September 1673).

12 *Park*: Hyde Park or St James's Park.

12–13 *Mulberry Gar'n*: a garden of mulberry-trees on the site of Buckingham Palace, a very popular London park.

14 *Tatnam Court . . . Islington*: popular places to ramble to; Tottenham Court Road and Islington were both then firmly in the country.

15 *sillybub*: syllabub, made from milk or cream, curdled, usually with wine, and sweetened.

15 *New Spring Gar'n*: pleasure gardens at Vauxhall.

PRUE. Nor to drink a pint of wine with a friend at the Prince in the Sun –

HIPPOLITA. Nor to hear a fiddle in good company –

PRUE. Nor to hear the organs and tongs at the Gun in Moorfields –

HIPPOLITA. Nay, nor suffered to go to church because the men are sometimes there! Little did I think I should ever have longed to go to church!

PRUE. Or I either but between two maids.

HIPPOLITA. Not see a man –

PRUE. Nor come near a man –

HIPPOLITA. Nor hear of a man –

PRUE. No, miss, but to be denied a man and to have no use at all of a man!

HIPPOLITA. Hold, hold. Your resentment is as much greater than mine, as your experience has been greater. But all this while, what do we make of my cousin, my husband-elect (as my aunt says)? We have had his company these three days. Is he no man?

PRUE. No, faith, he's but a Monsieur. But you'll resolve yourself that question within these three days, for by that time he'll be your husband, if your father come tonight –

HIPPOLITA. Or if I provide not myself with another in the meantime! For fathers seldom choose well and I will no more take my father's choice in a husband than I would in a gown or a suit of knots, so that if that cousin of mine were not an ill-contrived, ugly, freakish fool, in being my father's choice I should hate him. Besides, he has almost made me out of love with mirth and good humour, for he debases it as much as a Jack-pudding and civility and good breeding more than a city dancing-master.

PRUE. What, won't you marry him then, madam?

HIPPOLITA. Wouldst thou have me marry a fool? An idiot?

---

18 *Prince in the Sun*: a tavern, probably the one in Shadwell.

20 *organs and tongs*: organs are pipes, not portable organs: ordinary fire-tongs were used to provide a rhythm in rustic music.

25 *two maids*: bridesmaids at her wedding.

43 *suit of knots*: bow of ribbons.

48 *Jack-pudding*: clown, buffoon.

PRUE. Lord, 'tis a sign you have been kept up indeed and know little of the world, to refuse a man for a husband only because he's a fool. Methinks he's a pretty apish kind of gentleman, like other gentlemen, and handsome enough to lie with in the dark, when husbands take their privileges, and, for the daytimes, you may take the privilege of a wife.

HIPPOLITA. Excellent governess, you do understand the world, I see.

PRUE. Then you should be guided by me.

HIPPOLITA. Art thou in earnest then, damned jade? Wouldst thou have me marry him? Well, there are more poor young women undone and married to filthy fellows by the treachery and evil counsel of chambermaids than by the obstinacy and covetousness of parents.

PRUE. Does not your father come on purpose out of Spain to marry you to him? Can you release yourself from your aunt or father any other way? Have you a mind to be shut up as long as you live? For my part, though you can hold out upon the lime from the walls here, salt, old shoes and oatmeal, I cannot live so. I must confess my patience is worn out.

HIPPOLITA. Alas! Alas! Poor Prue! Your stomach lies another way. I will take pity of you and get me a husband very suddenly, who may have a servant at your service. But, rather than marry my cousin, I will be a nun in the new Protestant nunnery they talk of, where, they say, there will be no hopes of coming near a man.

PRUE. But you can marry nobody but your cousin, Miss. Your father you expect tonight and be certain his Spanish policy and wariness which has kept you up so close ever since you came from Hackney School will make sure of you within a day or two at farthest.

---

56 *apish*: affected, foolish.

73–4 *though you . . . oatmeal*: the diet for a woman pining away for a lover – any lover.

80 *the new Protestant nunnery*: much discussed at this time; one was proposed by Edward Chamberlayne in his pamphlet *An Academy or College* (1671).

86 *Hackney School*: Hackney was famous for its fashionable boarding-schools.

HIPPOLITA. Then 'tis time to think how to prevent him. Stay –

PRUE. In vain, vain miss.

HIPPOLITA. If we knew but any man, any man, though he were but a little handsomer than the devil, so that he were a gentleman.

PRUE. What if you did know any man, if you had an opportunity, could you have the confidence to speak to a man first? But if you could, how could you come to him or he to you? Nay, how could you send to him? For, though you could write, which your father in his Spanish prudence would never permit you to learn, who should carry the letter? But we need not be concerned for that, since we know not to whom to send it.

HIPPOLITA. Stay, it must be so. I'll try however.

Enter MONSIEUR DE PARIS.

MONSIEUR. Serviteur, serviteur, la cousine, I come to give the bon soir, as the French say.

HIPPOLITA. O cousin, you know him, the fine gentleman they talk of so much in town.

PRUE. What, will you talk to him of any man else?

MONSIEUR. I know all the beaux monde, cousine.

HIPPOLITA. Mister –

MONSIEUR. Monsieur Taileur, Monsieur Esmit, Monsieur –

HIPPOLITA. These are Frenchmen.

MONSIEUR. Non, non, would you have me say Mr Taylor, Mr Smith? Fie, fie, tête, non!

HIPPOLITA. But don't you know the brave gentleman they talk of so much in town?

MONSIEUR. Who, Monsieur Gerrard?

HIPPOLITA. What kind of man is that Mr Gerrard? And then I'll tell you.

MONSIEUR. Why – he is truly a pretty man, a pretty man, a pretty so-so kind of man – for an Englishman.

HIPPOLITA. How, a pretty man?

MONSIEUR. Why, he is conveniently tall but –

---

115 *tête*: one of Monsieur's favourite expletives, formed by eliminating the name of God, like English *'sdeath* or *'swounds*; so, 'by God's head'.

HIPPOLITA. But what?

MONSIEUR. And not ill-shaped but –

HIPPOLITA. But what?

MONSIEUR. And handsome, as 'tis thought, but –

HIPPOLITA. But what are your exceptions to him?

MONSIEUR. I can't tell you, because they are innumerable, innumerable, mon foy.

HIPPOLITA. Has he wit?

MONSIEUR. Ay, ay, they say he's witty, brave and de bel humeur and well-bred with all that – but –

HIPPOLITA. But what? He wants judgement?

MONSIEUR. Non, non, they say he has good sense and judgement but it is according to the account Englis', for –

HIPPOLITA. For what?

MONSIEUR. For, jarnie – if I think it –

HIPPOLITA. Why?

MONSIEUR. Why? Why, his tailor lives within Ludgate; his valet de chambre is no Frenchman and he has been seen at noonday to go into an English eating-house.

HIPPOLITA. Say you so, cousin?

MONSIEUR. Then, for being well-bred you shall judge. First, he can't dance a step nor sing a French song nor swear a French oate nor use the polite French word in his conversation and, in fine, can't play at hombré but speaks base good Englis' with the commune home-bred pronunciation and, in fine, to say no more, he ne'er carries a snuffbox about with him.

HIPPOLITA. Indeed!

MONSIEUR. And yet this man has been abroad as much as any man and does not make the least show of it, but a little in his mien, not at all in his discour, jernie. He never talks so much as of St Peter's church and Rome, the Escurial or Madrid, nay, not so much as of

---

140 *jarnie*: a corruption of *je renie dieu*, 'I swear'.
150 *in fine*: to conclude.
150 *hombré*: ombre, a card game.
153 *snuffbox*: much more popular in France than England at this time.

Henry IV of Pont Neuf, Paris and the new Louvre, nor of the Grand Roy.

HIPPOLITA. 'Tis for his commendation if he does not talk of his travels.

MONSIEUR. Auh, auh, cousine, he is conscious himself of his wants, because he is very envious, for he cannot endure me –

HIPPOLITA. (*aside*) He shall be my man then for that. – Ay, ay, 'tis the same, Prue. No, I know he can't endure you, cousin.

MONSIEUR. How do you know it, who never stir out? Tête non!

HIPPOLITA. Well, dear cousin, if you will promise me never to tell my aunt, I'll tell you.

MONSIEUR. I won't, I won't, jarnie.

HIPPOLITA. Nor to be concerned yourself so as to make a quarrel of it.

MONSIEUR. Non, non.

HIPPOLITA. Upon the word of a gentleman.

MONSIEUR. Foy de chevalier, I will not quarrel.

PRUE. Lord, Miss, I wonder you won't believe him without more ado.

HIPPOLITA. Then, he has the hatred of a rival for you.

MONSIEUR. Mal à peste.

HIPPOLITA. You know my chamber is backward and has a door into the gallery which looks into the backyard of a tavern, whence Mr Gerrard, once spying me at the window, has often since attempted to come in at that window by the help of the leads of a low building adjoining and indeed 'twas as much as my maid and I could do to keep him out.

MONSIEUR. Au, le coquin!

HIPPOLITA. But nothing is stronger than aversion, for I hate him perfectly, even as much as I love you.

---

160 *Henry IV of Pont Neuf*: the statue of Henri IV on the new bridge over the Seine was a present from the King of Denmark.

160 *new Louvre*: the colonnade on the east façade was added between 1666 and 1670.

161 *Grand Roy*: Louis XIV.

183 *Mal à peste*: a plague on him.

188 *leads*: used for roofing.

191 *coquin*: rogue, rascal.

PRUE. (*aside*) I believe so, faith. But what design have we now on foot?

HIPPOLITA. This discovery is an argument, sure, of my love to you.

MONSIEUR. Ay, ay, say no more, cousin, I doubt not your amoure for me, because I doubt not your judgement. But what's to be done with this fanfaron? I know where he eats tonight; I'll go find him out, ventre bleu.

HIPPOLITA. Oh my dear cousin, you will not make a quarrel of it? I thought what your promise would come to!

MONSIEUR. Would you have a man of honour –

HIPPOLITA. Keep his promise?

MONSIEUR. And lose his mistress. That were not for my honour, ma foy.

HIPPOLITA. Cousin, though you do me the injury to think I could be false, do not do yourself the injury to think anyone could be false to you. Will you be afraid of losing your mistress? To show such a fear to your rival were for his honour and not for yours, sure.

MONSIEUR. Nay, cousin, I'd have you know I was never afraid of losing my mistress in earnest. Let me see the man can get my mistress from me, jarnie; but he that loves must seem a little jealous.

HIPPOLITA. Not to his rival. Those that have jealousy hide it from their rivals.

MONSIEUR. But there are some who say jealousy is no more to be hid than a cough. But it should never be discovered in me, if I had it, because it is not French, it is not French at all, ventre bleu.

HIPPOLITA. No, you should rally your rival and rather make a jest of your quarrel to him, and that, I suppose, is French too.

MONSIEUR. 'Tis so, 'tis so, cousin, 'tis the veritable French method, for your Englis', for want of wit, drive everything to a serious, grum quarrel and then would make a jest on't, when 'tis too late, when they can't laugh, jarnie!

---

200 *fanfaron*: swaggerer, rake.
202 *ventre bleu*: *bleu* is a euphemism for *Dieu*; 'by God's belly'.
225 *rally*: banter wittily.

HIPPOLITA. Yes, yes, I would have you rally him soundly. Do not spare him a jot. But shall you see him tonight?

MONSIEUR. Ay, ay.

HIPPOLITA. Yes, pray be sure to see him for the jest's sake.

MONSIEUR. I will, for I love a jeste as well as any bel esprit of 'em all, da.

HIPPOLITA. Ay, and rally him soundly, be sure you rally him soundly and tell him just thus: that the Lady he has so long courted from the great window of the Ship tavern is to be your wife tomorrow unless he come at his wonted hour of six in the morning to her window to forbid the banns, for 'tis the first and last time of asking, and, if he come not, let him for ever hereafter stay away and hold his tongue.

MONSIEUR. Ha, ha, ha, a ver good jeste, tête bleu.

HIPPOLITA. And if the fool should come again I would tell him his own, I warrant you, cousin. My gentleman should be satisfied for good and all, I'd secure him.

MONSIEUR. Bon, bon.

PRUE. (*aside*) Well, well, young mistress, you were not at Hackney School for nothing, I see, nor taken away for nothing. A woman may soon be too old but is never too young to shift for herself!

MONSIEUR. Hah, ah, ah, cousin, dou art a merry grig, ma foy. I long to be with Gerrard and I am the best at improving a jeste. I shall have such divertissement tonight, tête bleu.

HIPPOLITA. He'll deny, 'may be, at first that he never courted any such lady.

MONSIEUR. Nay, I am sure he'll be ashamed of it. I shall make him look so sillily, tête non. I long to find him out. Adieu, adieu, la cousine.

HIPPOLITA. Shall you be sure to find him?

MONSIEUR. Indubitablement. I'll search the town over but I'll find, hah, ha, ha. (*Exit* MONSIEUR *and returns*) But I'm afrait, cousine, if I should tell him you are to be my wife tomorrow he would not come;

---

244 *Ship tavern*: since it is in 'What-d'ee-call't' street (I ii 24), no particular tavern seems to be intended.

258 *merry grig*: madcap girl.

now I am for having him come, for the jest's sake, ventre.

HIPPOLITA. So am I, cousin, for having him come too, for the jest's sake.

MONSIEUR. Well, well, leave it to me! Ha, ha, ha.

Enter MRS CAUTION.

CAUTION. What's all this giggling here?

MONSIEUR. Hay, do you tinke we'll tell you? No, fait, I warrant you, tête non. Ha, ha, ha –

HIPPOLITA. My cousin is overjoyed, I suppose, that my father is to come tonight.

CAUTION. I am afraid he will not come tonight – but you'll stay and see, nephew.

MONSIEUR. Non, non, I am to sup at t'other end of the town tonight. La, la, la, la – ra, ra, ra –

Exit MONSIEUR *singing.*

CAUTION. I wish the French levity of this young man may agree with your father's Spanish gravity.

HIPPOLITA. Just as your crabbed old age and my youth agree.

CAUTION. Well, malapert! I know you hate me because I have been the guardian of your reputation. But your husband may thank me one day.

HIPPOLITA. If he be not a fool, he would rather be obliged to me for my virtue than to you since, at long run, he must whether he will or no.

CAUTION. So, so!

HIPPOLITA. Nay, now I think on't, I'd have you to know the poor man, whosoe'er he is, will have little cause to thank you.

CAUTION. No?

HIPPOLITA. No. For I never lived so wicked a life as I have done this twelvemonth since I have not seen a man.

CAUTION. How! How! If you have not seen a man how could you be wicked? How could you do any ill?

HIPPOLITA. No, I have done no ill but I have paid it with thinking.

CAUTION. O, that's no hurt; to think is no hurt. The ancient, grave and godly cannot help thoughts.

---

290 *malapert*: saucy.

HIPPOLITA. I warrant you have had 'em yourself, aunt.

CAUTION. Yes, yes! When I cannot sleep.

HIPPOLITA. Ha, ha, I believe it. But know I have had those thoughts sleeping and waking, for I have dreamt of a man.

CAUTION. No matter, no matter, so that it was but a dream. I have dreamt myself, for you must know widows are mightily given to dream, insomuch that a dream is waggishly called 'the widow's comfort'.

HIPPOLITA. But I did not only dream. Ih! (*Sighs*)

CAUTION. How, how! Did you more than dream? Speak, young harlotry, confess, did you more than dream? How could you do more than dream in this house? Speak, confess!

HIPPOLITA. Well, I will then. Indeed, aunt, I did not only dream but I was pleased with my dream when I waked.

CAUTION. Oh, is that all? Nay, if a dream only will please you you are a modest young woman still. But have a care of a vision.

HIPPOLITA. Ay. But to be delighted when we wake with a naughty dream is a sin, aunt, and I am so very scrupulous that I would as soon consent to a naughty man as to a naughty dream.

CAUTION. I do believe you.

HIPPOLITA. I am for going into the throng of temptations.

CAUTION. There I believe you again.

HIPPOLITA. And making myself so familiar with them that I would not be concerned for 'em a whit.

CAUTION. There I do not believe you.

HIPPOLITA. And would take all the innocent liberty of the town to tattle to your men under a vizard in the playhouses and meet 'em at night in masquerade.

CAUTION. There I do believe you again. I know you would be masquerading. But worse would come on't, as it has done to others who have been in a masquerade and are now virgins but in masquerade and will not be their own women again as long as they live. The children of this age must be wise children indeed

---

342 *tattle*: gossip.

if they know their fathers, since their mothers themselves cannot inform 'em! O, the fatal liberty of this masquerading age! When I was a young woman –

HIPPOLITA. Come, come, do not blaspheme this masquerading age like an ill-bred city dame whose husband is half broke by living in Covent Garden or who has been turned out of the Temple or Lincoln's Inn upon a masquerading night. By what I've heard 'tis a pleasant, well-bred, complacent, free, frolic, good-natured, pretty age and if you do not like it, leave it to us that do.

CAUTION. Lord, how impudently you talk, niece. I'm sure I remember when I was a maid –

HIPPOLITA. Can you remember it, reverend aunt?

CAUTION. Yes, modest niece – that a raw young thing though almost at woman's estate, that was then at thirty or thirty-five years of age, would not so much as have looked upon a man.

HIPPOLITA. Above her father's butler or coachman.

CAUTION. Still taking me up! Well, thou art a mad girl and so goodnight. We may go to bed for I suppose now your father will not come tonight.

HIPPOLITA. I am sorry for it, for I long to see him.

Exit CAUTION.

But I lie. I had rather see Gerrard here and yet I know not how I shall like him. If he has wit he will come and if he has none he would not be welcome.

Exeunt HIPPOLITA *and* PRUE.

SCENE II

Scene changes to the French house. A table, bottles and candles.

Enter MR GERRARD, MARTIN *and* MONSIEUR DE PARIS.

MONSIEUR. 'Tis ver veritable, jarnie, what the French

356 *Temple or Lincoln's Inn*: the Inns of Court, places for the study of law.

372 s.d. *Exit CAUTION*: after line 371 Q1.

s.d. *French house*: French restaurant.

say of you English; you use the debauch so much it cannot have with you the French operation – you are never enjoyé. But come, let us for once be enfinement galliard and sing a French sonnet. (*Sings*) La boutelle, la boutelle, glou, glou.

MARTIN. (*to* GERRARD) What a melodious fop it is!

MONSIEUR. Auh, you have no complaisance.

GERRARD. No, we can't sing but we'll drink to you the lady's health whom, you say, I have so long courted at her window.

MONSIEUR. Ay, there is your complaisance; all your English complaisance is pledging complaisance, ventre. But if I do you reason here (*takes the glass*) will you do me reason to a little French chanson à boire? I shall begin to you. (*Sings*) La boutelle, la boutelle –

MARTIN. (*to* GERRARD) I had rather keep company with a set of wide-mouthed, drunken cathedral choristers.

GERRARD. Come, sir, drink and he shall do you reason to your French song since you stand upon't. [*To* MARTIN] Sing him 'Arthur of Bradley' or 'I am the Duke of Norfolk'.

MONSIEUR. Auh, tête bleu, an English catch! Fie, fie, ventre.

GERRARD. He can sing no damned French song.

MONSIEUR. Nor can I drink the damned Englis' wine. (*Sets down the glass*)

GERRARD. Yes, to that lady's health who has commanded me to wait upon her tomorrow at her window which looks, you say, into the inward yard of the Ship tavern near the end of what-d'ee-call't street.

MONSIEUR. Ay, ay, do you not know her? Not you, vert et bleu.

---

5 *galliard*: the galliard is a quick French dance but Monsieur seems only to mean 'gay' ('gaillard').

5 (*Sings*): set as part of speech Q1.

14 *do you reason*: do you justice.

15 *chanson à boire*: drinking-song.

16 *shall*: shall shall Q1.

22–3 *'Arthur of Bradley' . . . 'I am the Duke of Norfolk'*: both were popular, traditional and very English ballads; the former is about a rural wedding; the latter's alternative title is 'Paul's Steeple' but its subject is unknown.

33 *vert et bleu*: corruption of *vertu Dieu.*

GERRARD. But, pray repeat again what she said.

MONSIEUR. Why, she said she is to be married tomorrow to a person of honour, a brave gentleman, that shall be nameless, and so and so forth. (*Aside*) Little does he think who 'tis.

GERRARD. And what else?

MONSIEUR. That if you make not your appearance before her window tomorrow at your wonted hour of six in the morning to forbid the banns, you must for ever hereafter stay away and hold your tongue, for 'tis the first and last time of asking, ha, ha, ha.

GERRARD. (*aside*) 'Tis all a riddle to me. I should be unwilling to be fooled by this coxcomb.

MONSIEUR. (*aside*) I won't tell him all she said, lest he should not go. I would fain have him go for the jest's sake. Ha, ha, ha.

GERRARD. Her name is, you say, Hippolita, daughter to a rich Spanish merchant.

MONSIEUR. Ay, ay. You don't know her – not you; à d'autre, à d'autre, ma foy. Ha, ha, ha.

GERRARD. Well, I will be an easy fool for once.

MARTIN. By all means go.

MONSIEUR. Ay, ay, by all means go. Hah, ha, ha.

GERRARD. (*aside*) To be caught in a fool's trap. – I'll venture it. (*Drinks to him*) Come, 'tis her health.

MONSIEUR. And to your good reception, tête bleu, ha, ha, ha.

GERRARD. Well, Monsieur, I'll say this for thee, thou hast made the best use of three months at Paris as ever English squire did.

MONSIEUR. Considering I was in a dam' Englis' pension too.

MARTIN. Yet you have conversed with some French, I see – footmen, I suppose, at the fencing-school. I judge it by your oaths.

MONSIEUR. French footmen! Well, well, I had rather have the conversation of a French footman than of an English squire. There's for you, da.

MARTIN. I beg your pardon, Monsieur, I did not think the French footmen had been so much your friends.

GERRARD. Yes, yes, I warrant they have obliged him at Paris much more than any of their masters did. Well, there shall be no more said against the French footmen.

MONSIEUR. Non, de grâce. You are always turning the nation françez into ridicule, dat nation so accompli, dat nation which you imitate so dat, in the conclusion, you butte turn yourself into redicule, ma foy. If you are for de raillery, abuse the Duch. Why not abuse the Duch, les grosse villains, pandars, insolents? But here in your England, ma foy, you have more honneur, respecte and estimation for de Dushe swabber who come to cheat your nation den for de Franch footman who come to oblige your nation.

MARTIN. Our nation! Then you disown it for yours, it seems.

MONSIEUR. Well, wat of dat? Are you the disobligé by date?

GERRARD. No, Monsieur, far from it. You could not oblige us nor your country any other way than by disowning it.

MONSIEUR. It is de brutale country which abuse de France an' reverence de Dushe. I vill maintain, sustain and justify dat one little Franch footman have more honneur, courage and generosity, more good blood in his veine an' mush more good manners an' civility den al de State General togeder, jarnie. Dey are only wise and valiant wen dey are drunke.

GERRARD. That is always.

MONSIEUR. But dey are never honeste wen dey are drunke. Dey are de only rogue in de varlde who are not honeste wen dey are drunk, ma foy.

GERRARD. I find you are well acquainted with them, Monsieur.

MONSIEUR. Ay, ay, I have made the toure of Holland but it was en poste – dere was no staying for me, tête non, for de gentleman can no more live dere den de toad in Irland, ma foy, for I did not see on' chevalier in de whole cuntré. Alway, you know, de rebel hate

---

81 With the Dutch War imminent, anti-Dutch jokes were only too easy to make, even to a city audience that might have more pro-Dutch than pro-French sentiments.

84 *swabber*: boorish fool.

99 *State General*: Holland; in line 115 it indicates the ruling representative assembly.

110 *toad in Irland*: toads had all been expelled by St Patrick, according to tradition.

de gens de quality. Besides, I had make sufficient observation of the canaille barbare de first nighte of my arrival at Amsterdame. I did visit, you must know, one of de principal of de Stat General, to whom I had recommendation from England and did find his excellence weighing soap, jarnie. Ha, ha, ha.

GERRARD. Weighing soap!

MONSIEUR. Weighing soape, ma foy, for he was a wholesale chandleer, and his lady was taking the tale of chandels wid her own witer hands, ma foy, and de young lady, his excellence' daughter, stringing harring. Stringing harring, jarnie!

GERRARD. So-h. And what were his sons doing?

MONSIEUR. Auh, his son, for he had but one, was making de tour of France, Espagne, Italy an' Germany in a coach and six – or rader, now I think on't, gone of an embassy hider to dere Master Cromwell whom dey did love and fear because he was sometinge de greater rebel. Bute, now I talk of de rebele, none but de rebel can love de rebele and so mush for you and your friend the Dush. I'll say no more and pray do you say no more of my friend de Franch, not so mush as of my friend the Franch footman, da.

GERRARD. No, no. But, Monsieur, now give me leave to admire thee, that in three months at Paris you could renounce your language, drinking and your country (for which we are not angry with you, as I said) and come home so perfect a Frenchman that the draymen of your father's own brewhouse would be ready to knock thee in the head.

MONSIEUR. Vell, vell, my father was a merchant of his own beer as the noblesse of France of their own wine. But I can forgive you that raillery, that bob, since you say I have the aire françez. But have I the aire françez?

GERRARD. As much as any French footman of 'em all.

MONSIEUR. And do I speak agreeable ill Englis' enough?

---

122 *daughter*: daughters Q1.

128 *Master Cromwell*: Monsieur is associating the rebels together in their Puritan beliefs.

144 *bob*: jest.

GERRARD. Very ill.

MONSIEUR. Veritablement?

GERRARD. Veritablement.

MONSIEUR. For you must know, 'tis as ill-breeding now to speak good Englis' as to write good Englis', good sense or a good hand.

GERRARD. But indeed, methinks, you are not slovenly enough for a Frenchman.

MONSIEUR. Slovenly! You mean negligent?

GERRARD. No, I mean slovenly.

MONSIEUR. Then I will be more slovenly.

GERRARD. You know, to be a perfect Frenchman you must never be silent, never sit still and never be clean.

MARTIN. But you have forgot one main qualification of a true Frenchman: he should never be sound, that is, be very pocky too.

MONSIEUR. Oh, if dat be all, I am very pocky, pocky enough, jarnie. That is the only French qualification may be had without going to Paris, mon foy.

Enter a WAITER.

WAITER. Here are a couple of ladies coming up to you, sir.

GERRARD. To us! Did you appoint any to come hither, Martin?

MARTIN. Not I.

GERRARD. Nor you, Monsieur?

MONSIEUR. Nor I.

GERRARD. Sirrah, tell your master, if he cannot protect us from the constable and these midnight coursers 'tis not a house for us.

MARTIN. Tell 'em you have nobody in the house and shut the doors.

WAITER. They'll not be satisfied with that; they'll break open the door. They searched last night all over the house for my Lord Fiske and Sir Jeffrey Janté who were fain to hide themselves in the bar under my mistress's chair and petticoats.

MONSIEUR. Wat, do the women hunt out the men so now?

---

165 *pocky*: having the pox, suffering from syphilis.
183 *Janté*: from French *gentil.*

MARTIN. Ay, ay, things are altered since you went to Paris. There's hardly a young man in town dares be known of his lodging for 'em.

GERRARD. Bailiffs, pursevants or a city constable are modest people in comparison of them.

MARTIN. And we are not so much afraid to be taken up by the watch as by the tearing midnight ramblers or houza women.

MONSIEUR. Jarnie, ha, ha, ha.

GERRARD. Where are they? I hope they are gone again.

WAITER. No, sir, they are below at the stair-foot, only swearing at their coachman.

GERRARD. Come, you rogue, they are in fee with you waiters and no gentleman can come hither but they have the intelligence straight.

WAITER. Intelligence from us, sir? They should never come here if we could help it. I am sure we wish 'em choked when we see them come in, for they bring such good stomachs from St James's Park or rambling about in the streets that we poor waiters have not a bit left. 'Tis well if we can keep our money in our pockets for 'em. I am sure I have paid seventeen and six in half-crowns for coach hire at several times for a little, damned, tearing lady and when I asked her for it again one morning in her chamber she bid me pay myself for she had no money – but I wanted the courage of a gentleman. Besides, the lord that kept her was a good customer to our house and my friend and I made a conscience of wronging him.

GERRARD. A man of honour!

MONSIEUR. Vert et bleu, pleasant, pleasant, mon foy.

GERRARD. Go, go, sirrah, shut the door. I hear 'em coming up.

WAITER. Indeed I dare not; they'll kick me downstairs if I should.

GERRARD. Go, you rascal, I say.

---

191 *pursevants*: deliverers of court summons.
194 *tearing*: roistering.
195 *houza women*: prostitutes; *houza* was used of rakes, especially noisy ones.

The WAITER *shuts the door. 'Tis thrust open again. Enter* FLOUNCE *and* FLIRT *in vizards, striking the* WAITER, *and come up to the table.*

GERRARD. (*aside*) Flounce and Flirt, upon my life. – Ladies, I am sorry you have no volunteers in your service. This is mere pressing and argues a great necessity you have for men.

FLOUNCE. You need not be afraid, sir. We will use no violence to you – you are not fit for our service, we know you.

FLIRT. The hot service you have been in formerly makes you unfit for ours now. Besides, you begin to be something too old for us; we are for the brisk houzas of seventeen or eighteen.

GERRARD. Nay, faith, I am not too old yet. But an old acquaintance will make any man old. Besides, to tell you the truth, you are come a little too early for me, for I am not drunk yet – but there are your brisk young men who are always drunk and perhaps have the happiness not to know you.

FLOUNCE. The happiness not to know us!

FLIRT. The happiness not to know us!

GERRARD. Be not angry, ladies; 'tis rather happiness to have pleasure to come than to have it past and therefore these gentlemen are happy in not knowing you.

MARTIN. I'd have you to know I do know the ladies too and I will not lose the honour of the ladies' acquaintance for anything.

FLOUNCE. Not for the pleasure of beginning the acquaintance with us, as Mr Gerrard says. But it is the general vanity of you town-fops to lay claim to all good acquaintance and persons of honour; you cannot let a woman pass in the Mall at midnight but, damn you, you know her straight, you know her. But you would be damned before you would say so much for one in a mercer's shop.

GERRARD. He has spoken it in a French house, where

---

226 *pressing*: being conscripted by a press-gang.
253 *Mall*: the new Mall was a walk in St James's Park, built for the game pell-mell.
256 *mercer*: seller, particularly of expensive fabrics.

he has very good credit, and I dare swear you may make him eat his words.

MONSIEUR. (*peeping under her scarf*) She does want a gown indeet. She is in her dishabilié. This dishabilié is a great mode in England; the women love the dishabilié as well as the men, ma foy.

FLIRT. Well, if we should stay and sup with you, I warrant you would be bragging of it tomorrow amongst your comrades that you had the company of two women of quality at the French house and name us.

MARTIN. (*aside*) Pleasant jilts.

GERRARD. No, upon our honours, we would not brag of your company.

FLOUNCE. Upon your honours?

MARTIN. No, faith.

FLOUNCE. Come, we will venture to sit down then. Yet I know the vanity of you men; you could not contain yourselves from bragging.

GERRARD. No, no. You women nowadays have found out the pleasure of bragging and will allow it the men no longer.

MARTIN. Therefore, indeed, we dare not stay to sup with you, for you would be sure to tell on't.

GERRARD. And we are young men who stand upon our reputations.

FLOUNCE. You are very pleasant, gentlemen.

MARTIN. For my part, I am to be married shortly and know 'twould quickly come to my mistress's ear.

GERRARD. And for my part, I must go visit tomorrow morning by times a new city mistress, and you know they are as inquisitive as precise in the city.

FLIRT. Come, come, pray leave this fooling. Sit down again and let us bespeak supper.

GERRARD. No, faith, I dare not.

MARTIN. Besides, we have supped.

FLOUNCE. No matter, we only desire you should look on while we eat and put the glass about or so.

GERRARD *and* MARTIN *offer to go out.*

---

288 *by times*: betimes, early.

295 s.d. *offer*: attempt.

FLIRT. Pray stay.

GERRARD. Upon my life I dare not.

FLOUNCE. Upon our honours we will not tell, if you are in earnest.

GERRARD. Pshaw, pshaw, I know the vanity of you women; you could not contain yourselves from bragging.

MONSIEUR. Ma foy, is it certain? Ha, ha, ha. Hark you, madam, can't you fare well but you must cry roast-meat?
You'll spoil your trade by bragging of your gains;
The silent sow, madam, does eat most grains.
Da.

FLIRT. Your servant, Monsieur Fop.

FLOUNCE. Nay, faith, do not go, we will no more tell –

MONSIEUR. Than you would of a clape, if you had it – dat's the only secret you can keep, jarnie.

MARTIN. I am glad we are rid of these jilts.

GERRARD. And we have taken a very ridiculous occasion.

MONSIEUR. Wat, must we leave the lady then? Dis is dam civility Englis', mon foy.

FLIRT. (*pulling him back*) Nay, sir, you have too much of the French air to have so little honour and good breeding.

MONSIEUR. Dé, you tinke so then, sweet madam, I have mush of de French air?

FLIRT. More than any Frenchman breathing.

MONSIEUR. Auh, you are the curtoise dame, mort bleu. I shall stay then, if you think so. Monsieur Gerrard, you will be certain to see the lady tomorrow – pray not forget. Ha, ha, ha.

GERRARD. No, no, sir.

MARTIN. You will go then?

GERRARD. I will go on a fool's errand for once.

Exeunt GERRARD *and* MARTIN.

FLOUNCE. What will you eat, sir?

MONSIEUR. Wat you please, madame.

FLOUNCE. D'ee hear, waiter, then some young partridge.

WAITER. What else, madam?

---

321 *Dé*: Monsieur's stab at pronouncing *Dieu*.

FLIRT. Some ruffs.
WAITER. What else, madam?
FLOUNCE. Some young pheasants.
WAITER. What else, madam?
FLIRT. Some young rabbits. I love rabbits.
WAITER. What else, madam?
FLOUNCE. Stay –
MONSIEUR. (*aside*) Dis Englis' waiter wit his 'Wat else, madam?' will ruin me, tête non.
WAITER. What else, madam?
MONSIEUR. 'Wat else, madam' again! Call up the French waiter.
WAITER. What else, madam?
MONSIEUR. Again! Call up the French waiter or quesinier, mort-tête-ventre. Vite, vite. Auh, madam, the stupidity of the Englis' waiter! I hate the Englis' waiter, mon foy.

Exit WAITER.

FLIRT. Be not in passion, dear Monsieur.
MONSIEUR. I kiss your hand obligeant, madam.

Enter a FRENCH SCULLION.

Chere Pierrot, serviteur, serviteur, or ça à manger. (*Kisses the* SCULLION)
SCULLION. En voulez vous de cram schiquin?
FLOUNCE. Yes.
SCULLION. De partrish, de faisan, de quailles?
MONSIEUR. [*aside*] This bougre vel ruine me too but he speak wit dat bel aire and grâce. I cannot bid him hold his tongue, ventre. – C'est assez, Pierrot, va-t-en.

Exit SCULLION *and returns.*

SCULLION. And de litel plate de –
MONSIEUR. Jarnie, va-t-en.

Exit SCULLION *and returns.*

SCULLION. And de litel plate de –

---

335 *ruffs*: male sandpipers.
349 *quesinier*: *cuisinier*, cook.
354 *Pierrot*: the diminutive of Pierre but also, perhaps, a reference to the character in the Harlequinade. Monsieur studied under Signior Scaramouche, see III i 48–51.
355 *cram schiquin*: crammed chicken, chickens fattened on a diet of raisins and breadcrumbs.
357 *faisan*: pheasant.

MONSIEUR. De grâce, go dy way.

Exit SCULLION *and returns.*

SCULLION. And de litel de –

MONSIEUR. De fourmage, de brie! Va-t-en, go, go.

FLOUNCE. What's that cheese that stinks?

MONSIEUR. Ay, ay, be sure it stinke extremente, Pierrot. Va-t-en – but stay till I drink dy health. Here's to dat pretty fellow's health, madam.

FLIRT. Must we drink the scullion's health?

MONSIEUR. Auh, you will not be disobligeant, madam. He is the cuisinier for a king, nay for a cardinal or French abbot. (*Drinks*)

[*Exit* SCULLION.]

FLOUNCE. But how shall we divertise ourselves till supper be ready?

FLIRT. Can we have better divertisement than this gentleman?

FLOUNCE. But I think we had better carry the gentleman home with us and, because it is already late, sup at home and divertise the gentleman at cards till it be ready. D'ee hear, waiter, let it be brought when 'tis ready to my lodging hard by in Mustard Alley at the sign of the Crooked Billet.

MONSIEUR. At the Crook Billet!

FLIRT. Come, sir, come.

MONSIEUR. Mort bleu, I have take the vow (since my last clap) never to go again to the bourdel.

FLOUNCE. What is the bourdel?

MONSIEUR. How call you the name of your house?

FLIRT. The Crooked Billet.

MONSIEUR. No, no, the – the bawdy-house, vert et bleu.

FLOUNCE. How, our lodging! We'd have you to know –

MONSIEUR. Auh, mort bleu, I would not know it. De Crooke Billet, hah, ha.

FLIRT. Come, sir.

MONSIEUR. Besides, if I go wit you to the bourdel, you will tell, mort bleu.

---

383 *Mustard Alley*: the road referred to remains unidentified but Partridge's listing of a later use of *mustard-pot* to mean *female sex* probably gives the clue to the name's significance here. The innuendo behind *Crooked Billet* is probably phallic.

388 *bourdel*: bordel, brothel.

FLOUNCE. Fie, fie, come along.

MONSIEUR. Beside, I am to be married within these two days. If you should tell now –

FLIRT. Come, come along. We will not tell.

MONSIEUR. But will you promise then to have the care of my honour? Pray, good madam, have de care of my honneur, pray have de care of my honneur. Will you have care of my honneur? Pray have de care of my honneur and do not tell if you can help it. Pray, dear madam, do not tell. (*Kneels to 'em*)

FLIRT. I would not tell for fear of losing you. My love for you will make me secret.

MONSIEUR. Why, do you love me?

FLIRT. Indeed, I cannot help telling you now what my modesty ought to conceal but my eyes would disclose it too. I have a passion for you, sir.

MONSIEUR. A passion for me!

FLIRT. An extreme passion, dear sir. You are so French, so mightily French, so agreeable French – but I'll tell you more of my heart at home. Come along.

MONSIEUR. But is your passion sincere?

FLIRT. The truest in the world.

MONSIEUR. Well then, I'll venture my body wit thee for one night.

FLIRT. For one night! Don't you believe that, and so you would leave me tomorrow. But I love you so I cannot part with you; you must keep me for good and all if you will have me. I can't leave you for my heart.

MONSIEUR. How, keep! Jarnie, de whore Englis' have notinge but 'keepe, keepe' in dere mouths nowadays, tête non. Formerly 'twas enough to keep de shild, ma foy.

FLIRT. Nay, I will be kept, else – but come, we'll talk on't at home.

MONSIEUR. Umh. So, so, ver vel. De amoure of de whore does alway end in 'keep'. Ha, keep, ma foy, keep, ha –

The punk that entertains you wit' her passion
Is like kind host who makes the invitation,
At your own cost, to his fort bon collation.

Exeunt.

ACT II

SCENE I

Don Diego's house in the morning.

Enter DON DIEGO *in the Spanish habit,* MRS CAUTION, *his sister.*

DON DIEGO. Have you had a Spanish care of the honour of my family, that is to say, have you kept up my daughter close in my absence, as I directed?

CAUTION. I have, sir. But it was as much as I could do.

DON DIEGO. I knew that, for 'twas as much as I could do to keep up her mother – I that have been in Spain, look you.

CAUTION. Nay, 'tis a hard task to keep up an English woman.

DON DIEGO. As hard as it is for those who are not kept up to be honest, look you, con licentia, sister.

CAUTION. How now, brother! I am sure my husband never kept me up.

DON DIEGO. I knew that, therefore I cried 'con licentia', sister, as the Spaniards have it.

CAUTION. But you Spaniards are too censorious, brother.

DON DIEGO. You English women, sister, give us too much cause, look you. But you are sure my daughter has not seen a man since my departure?

CAUTION. No, not so much as a churchman.

DON DIEGO. As a churchman, voto! I thank you for that. Not a churchman, not a churchman!

CAUTION. No, not so much as a churchman. But, of any, one would think one might trust a churchman.

DON DIEGO. No, we are bold enough in trusting them with our souls. I'll never trust 'em with the body of my daughter, look you. Guarda, you see what comes

---

s.d. *in the Spanish habit*: see Additional Note.
11 *con licentia*: 'con licencia', with permission.
22 *voto*: I swear.
28 *Guarda*: look out, beware.

of trusting churchmen here in England – and 'tis because the women govern the families that chaplains are so much in fashion. Trust a churchman! Trust a coward with your honour, a fool with your secret, a gamester with your purse as soon as a priest with your wife or daughter, look you, guarda. I am no fool, look you.

CAUTION. Nay, I know you are a wise man, brother.

DON DIEGO. Why, sister, I have been fifteen years in Spain for it, at several times, look you. Now in Spain he is wise enough that is grave, politic enough that says little and honourable enough that is jealous, and, though I say it that should not say it, I am as grave, grum and jealous as any Spaniard breathing.

CAUTION. I know you are, brother.

DON DIEGO. And I will be a Spaniard in everything still and will not conform, not I, to their ill-favoured English customs, for I will wear my Spanish habit still, I will stroke my Spanish whiskers still and I will eat my Spanish olio still and my daughter shall go a maid to her husband's bed, let the English custom be what 'twill. I would fain see any finical, cunning, insinuating monsieur of the age debauch or steal away my daughter. But well, has she seen my cousin? How long has he been in England?

CAUTION. These three days.

DON DIEGO. And she has seen him, has she? I was contented he should see her, intending him for her husband. But she has seen nobody else upon your certain knowledge?

CAUTION. No, no, alas, how should she? 'Tis impossible she should.

DON DIEGO. Where is her chamber? Pray let me see her.

CAUTION. You'll find her, poor creature, asleep, I warrant you, or if awake, thinking no hurt nor of your coming this morning.

---

47 *Spanish whiskers*: English gentlemen at this time preferred to be clean-shaven.

48 *Spanish olio*: the traditional Spanish stew containing meat, poultry and all sorts of vegetables.

50 *finical*: affectedly fastidious.

DON DIEGO. Let us go to her. I long to see her, poor innocent wretch.

Exeunt.

Enter HIPPOLITA, GERRARD, *and* PRUE *at a distance.*

GERRARD. Am I not come upon your own summons, madam? And yet receive me so?

HIPPOLITA. My summons, sir? No, I assure you, and, if you do not like your reception, I cannot help it, for I am not used to receive men, I'd have you to know.

GERRARD. (*aside*) She is beautiful beyond all things I ever saw.

HIPPOLITA. (*aside*) I like him extremely.

GERRARD. Come, fairest, why do you frown?

HIPPOLITA. Because I am angry.

GERRARD. I am come on purpose to please you then; do not receive me so unkindly.

HIPPOLITA. I tell you, I do not use to receive men. There has not been a man in the house before, but my cousin, this twelvemonth, I'd have you to know.

GERRARD. Then you ought to bid me the more welcome, I'd have you to know.

HIPPOLITA. What, do you mock me too? I know I am but a home-bred, simple girl but I thought you gallants of the town had been better bred than to mock a poor girl in her father's own house. I have heard indeed 'tis a part of good breeding to mock people behind their backs, but not to their faces.

GERRARD. (*aside*) Pretty creature! She has not only the beauty but the innocency of an angel. – Mock you, dear miss! No, I only repeated the words because they were yours, sweet miss. What we like we imitate.

HIPPOLITA. Dear miss! Sweet miss! How came you and I so well acquainted? This is one of your confident tricks too, as I have been told; you'll be acquainted with a woman in the time you can help her over a bench in the playhouse or to her coach. But I need not wonder at your confidence since you could come in at the great gallery-window just now. But pray, who shall pay for the glass you have broken?

---

98 *bench*: the only seating in the theatre.

GERRARD. Pretty creature! Your father might have made the window bigger then, since he has so fine a daughter and will not allow people to come in at the door to her.

HIPPOLITA. (*aside*) A pleasant man! Well, 'tis harder playing the hypocrite with him, I see, than with my aunt or father, and, if dissimulation were not very natural to a woman, I'm sure I could not use it at this time. But the mask of simplicity and innocency is as useful to an intriguing woman as the mask of religion to a statesman, they say.

GERRARD. Why do you look away, dearest miss?

HIPPOLITA. Because you quarrelled with me just now for frowning upon you and I cannot help it, if I look upon you.

GERRARD. O, let me see that face at any rate.

HIPPOLITA. Would you have me frown upon you? For I shall be sure to do't.

GERRARD. Come, I'll stand fair; you have done your worst to my heart already.

HIPPOLITA. (*aside*) Now I dare not look upon him lest I should not be able to keep my word.

GERRARD. Come, I am ready – (*Aside*) and yet I am afraid of her frowns. – Come, look. I – h – am ready, I – h – am ready.

HIPPOLITA. (*aside*) But I am not ready.

GERRARD. Turn, dear miss, come, I – h – am ready.

HIPPOLITA. Are you ready then? I'll look. (*Turns upon him. Aside*) No, faith, I can't frown upon him if I should be hanged.

GERRARD. Dear miss, I thank you. That look has no terror in't.

HIPPOLITA. No, I cannot frown for my heart; for, blushing, I don't use to look upon men, you must know.

GERRARD. (*aside*) If it were possible anything could, those blushes would add to her beauty. Well, bashfulness is the only out-of-fashion thing that is agreeable.

HIPPOLITA. (*aside*) I – h – h like this man strangely – I was going to say 'loved him'. Courage then, Hippolita; make use of the only opportunity thou canst have to enfranchise thyself. Women formerly, they say, never knew how to make use of their time till it was past but let it not be said so of a young woman of this age. My damned aunt will be stirring presently. Well, then, courage, I say, Hippolita, thou art full fourteen years old – shift for thyself.

GERRARD. (*aside*) So, I have looked upon her so long till I am grown bashful too. Love and modesty come together like money and covetousness and the more we have the less we can show it. I dare not look her in the face now nor speak a word.

HIPPOLITA. What, sir, methinks you look away now.

GERRARD. Because you would not look upon me, miss.

HIPPOLITA. Nay, I hope you can't look me in the face since you have done so rude a thing as to come in at the window upon me. Come, come, when once we women find the men bashful, then we take heart. Now I can look upon you as long as you will. Let's see if you can frown upon me now!

GERRARD. Lovely innocency! No, you may swear I can't frown upon you, miss.

HIPPOLITA. So, I knew you were ashamed of what you have done. Well, since you are ashamed and because you did not come of your own head but were sent by my cousin, you say –

GERRARD. (*aside*) Which I wonder at.

HIPPOLITA. For all these reasons, I do forgive you.

GERRARD. In token of your forgiveness then, dearest miss, let me have the honour to kiss your hand.

HIPPOLITA. Nay, there 'tis you men are like our little shock-dogs; if we don't keep you off from us but use you a little kindly, you grow so fiddling and so troublesome there is no enduring you.

GERRARD. O dear miss, if I am like your shock-dog, let it be in his privileges.

HIPPOLITA. Why, I'd have you know he does not lie with me.

GERRARD. 'Twas well guessed, miss, for one so innocent.

HIPPOLITA. No, I always kick him off from the bed and never will let him come near it, for of late indeed (I do

177 *shock-dogs*: lap-dogs, often poodles.

not know what's the reason), I don't much care for my shock-dog nor my babies.

GERRARD. O then, miss, I may have hopes, for after the shock-dog and the babies 'tis the man's turn to be beloved.

HIPPOLITA. Why, could you be so good-natured as to come after my shock-dog in my love? It may be indeed, rather than after one of your brother men.

GERRARD. Hah, ha, ha. – [*Aside*] Poor creature, a wonder of innocency.

HIPPOLITA. But I see you are humble because you would kiss my hand.

GERRARD. No, I am ambitious therefore.

HIPPOLITA. (*aside*) Well, all this fooling but loses time; I must make better use of it. – I could let you kiss my hand but then I'm afraid you would take hold of me and carry me away.

GERRARD. Indeed I would not.

HIPPOLITA. Come, I know you would.

GERRARD. Truly I would not.

HIPPOLITA. You would, you would, I know you would.

GERRARD. I'll swear I wo'not. By –

HIPPOLITA. Nay, don't swear, for you'll be the apter to do it then. (*Aside*) I would not have him forswear it neither. He does not like me, sure, well enough to carry me away.

GERRARD. Dear miss, let me kiss your hand.

HIPPOLITA. I am sure you would carry me away if I should.

GERRARD. Be not afraid of it.

HIPPOLITA. (*aside*) Nay, I am afraid of the contrary. Either he dislikes me and therefore will not be troubled with me or, what is as bad, he loves me and is dull or fearful to displease me.

GERRARD. Trust me, sweetest; I can use no violence to you.

HIPPOLITA. Nay, I am sure you would carry me away. What should you come in at the window for, if you did not mean to steal me?

---

185 *babies*: dolls.

GERRARD. If I should endeavour it you might cry out and I should be prevented.

HIPPOLITA. (*aside*) Dull, dull man of the town, are all like thee? He is as dull as a country squire at questions and commands. – No, if I should cry out never so loud; this is quite at the further end of the house and there nobody could hear me.

GERRARD. I will not give you occasion, dearest.

HIPPOLITA. (*aside*) Well, I will quicken thy sense, if it be possible. – Nay, I know you come to steal me away, because I am an heiress and have twelve hundred pound a year, lately left me by my mother's brother, which my father cannot meddle with and which is the chiefest reason, I suppose, why he keeps me up so close.

GERRARD. (*aside*) Ha!

HIPPOLITA. [*aside*] So, this has made him consider. O money, powerful money! How the ugly, old, crooked, straight, handsome young women are beholding to thee!

GERRARD. [*aside*] Twelve hundred pound a year!

HIPPOLITA. Besides, I have been told my fortune and the woman said I should be stolen away because, she says, 'tis the fate of heiresses to be stolen away.

GERRARD. (*aside*) Twelve hundred pound a year!

HIPPOLITA. Nay more, she described the man to me that was to do it and he was as like you as could be! Have you any brothers?

GERRARD. Not any! 'Twas I, I warrant you, sweetest.

HIPPOLITA. So, he understands himself now.

GERRARD. Well, madam, since 'twas foretold you, what do you think on't? 'Tis in vain, you know, to resist fate.

HIPPOLITA. I do know indeed they say 'tis to no purpose. Besides, the woman that told my fortune or you have bewitched me. (*Sighs*) I – h – think.

GERRARD. My soul, my life, 'tis you have charms powerful as numberless, especially those of your

---

226–7 *questions and commands*: an old-fashioned country game involving foolish questions and tasks and often involving kissing.

247 *pound a*: pound Q1.

innocency irresistible, and do surprise the wariest heart. Such mine was while I could call it mine but now 'tis yours for ever.

HIPPOLITA. Well, well, get you gone then. I'll keep it safe for your sake.

GERRARD. Nay, you must go with me, sweetest.

HIPPOLITA. Well, I see you will part with the jewel but you'll have the keeping of the cabinet to which you commit it.

GERRARD. Come, come, my dearest, let us be gone. Fortune as well as women must be taken in the humour.

Enter PRUE *running hastily to stop 'em,* DON DIEGO *and* MRS CAUTION *immediately after.*

PRUE. O miss, miss, your father, it seems, is just now arrived and here is coming in upon you.

HIPPOLITA. My father!

DON DIEGO. My daughter! And a man!

CAUTION. A man! A man in the house!

GERRARD. Ha! What mean these? A Spaniard!

HIPPOLITA. [*aside*] What shall I do? – Stay. Nay, pray stir not from me but lead me about as if you lead me a corant.

[GERRARD] *leads her about.*

DON DIEGO. Is this your government, sister, and this your innocent charge that has not seen the face of a man this twelvemonth? En hora mala!

CAUTION. O, sure, it is not a man, it cannot be a man! (*Puts on her spectacles*)

DON DIEGO. It cannot be a man! If he be not a man he's a devil. He has her lovingly by the hand too. Valga me el cielo.

HIPPOLITA. Do not seem to mind them but dance on or lead me about still.

---

272 s.d. *Enter PRUE . . . stop 'em*: Prue has not been offstage but she has been keeping watch at a distance. She now runs forward to stop them leaving, entering the action for the first time in the scene.

281 *corant*: the courante or coranto was, in spite of the quick music and the running steps, a stately dance.

284 *En hora mala*: in an evil hour, unluckily.

287–8 *Valga me el cielo*: heaven help me.

GERRARD. (*apart to* HIPPOLITA) What d'ee mean by't?

DON DIEGO. Hey! They are frolic, a-dancing.

CAUTION. Indeed they are dancing, I think. Why, niece!

DON DIEGO. Nay, hold a little. I'll make 'em dance in the devil's name – but it shall not be la galliarda.

Draws his sword; CAUTION *holds him.*

CAUTION. O niece! Why, niece!

GERRARD. (*apart to* HIPPOLITA) Do you hear her? What do you mean?

HIPPOLITA. Take no notice of them but walk about still and sing a little. Sing a corant.

GERRARD. I can't sing but I'll hum, if you will.

DON DIEGO. Are you so merry? Well, I'll be with you en hora mala.

CAUTION. Oh niece, niece, why, niece, oh!

DON DIEGO. Why, daughter, my dainty daughter, my shame, my ruin, my plague. (*Struggling, gets from* CAUTION, *goes towards 'em with his sword drawn*)

HIPPOLITA. Mind him not but dance and sing on.

GERRARD. A pretty time to dance and sing indeed when I have a Spaniard with naked Toledo at my tail. No, pray excuse me, miss, from fooling any longer.

HIPPOLITA. (*turning about*) O my father! My father, poor father! You are welcome. Pray give me your blessing.

DON DIEGO. My blessing en hora mala.

HIPPOLITA. What, am I not your daughter, sir?

DON DIEGO. My daughter, mi mal, mi muerte.

HIPPOLITA. My name's Hippolita, sir; I don't own your Spanish names. But pray, father, why do you frighten one so? You know I don't love to see a sword. What do you mean to do with that ugly thing out?

DON DIEGO. I'll show you. Traidor, ladrón, demi honra, thou diest. (*Runs at* GERRARD)

GERRARD. (*draws*) Not if I can help it, good don. But

---

295 *la galliarda*: the galliard, a lively dance.
309 *Toledo*: a sword made from the famous Toledo steel.
316 *mi mal, mi muerte*: my plague, my death.
321–2 *Traidor, ladrón, demi honra*: Traitor, thief, give me back my honour. Q1 reads *houra* and Ward suggested that the *n* was turned. *Honra* is the great principle of *public* honour.

by the names you give me I find you mistake your man. I suppose some Spaniard has affronted you.

DON DIEGO. None but thee, ladrón, and thou diest for't.

Fight.

CAUTION. Oh, oh, oh, help, help, help.

HIPPOLITA. (*kneels*) Oh, what, will you kill my poor dancing-master?

DON DIEGO. A dancing-master! He's a fencing-master rather, I think. But is he your dancing-master? Umph.

GERRARD. (*aside*) So much wit and innocency were never together before.

DON DIEGO. (*pausing*) Is he a dancing-master?

CAUTION. Is he a dancing-master? He does not look like a dancing-master.

HIPPOLITA. Pish, you don't know a dancing-master; you have not seen one these threescore years, I warrant.

CAUTION. No matter. But he does not look like a dancing-master.

DON DIEGO. Nay, nay, dancing-masters look like gentlemen enough, sister. But he's no dancing-master by drawing his sword so briskly. Those tripping outsides of gentlemen are like gentlemen enough in everything but in drawing a sword and, since he is a gentleman, he shall die by mine.

Fight again.

HIPPOLITA. Oh hold, hold.

CAUTION. Hold, hold! Pray, brother, let's talk with him a little first. I warrant you I shall trap him and if he confesses you may kill him, for those that confess, they say, ought to be hanged. Let's see.

GERRARD. (*aside*) Poor Hippolita, I wish I had not had this occasion of admiring thy wit. I have increased my love whilst I have lost my hopes – the common fate of poor lovers.

CAUTION. Come, you are guilty by that hanging down of your head. Speak. Are you a dancing-master? Speak, speak. A dancing-master?

GERRARD. Yes, forsooth, I am a dancing-master, ay, ay.

DON DIEGO. How dost it appear?

HIPPOLITA. Why, there is his fiddle, there upon the table, father.

CAUTION. No, busybody, but it is not. That is my nephew's fiddle.

HIPPOLITA. Why, he lent it to my cousin. I tell you it is his.

CAUTION. Nay, it may be indeed, he might lend it to him for ought I know.

DON DIEGO. Ay, ay, but ask him, sister, if he be a dancing-master, where.

CAUTION. Pray, brother, let me alone with him. I know what to ask him, sure!

DON DIEGO. What, will you be wiser than I? Nay, then stand away. Come, if you are a dancing-master, where's your school? Adonde, adonde?

CAUTION. Why, he'll say, maybe, he has ne'er a one.

DON DIEGO. Who asked you, nimble chaps? So, you have put an excuse in his head.

GERRARD. Indeed, sir, 'tis no excuse; I have no school.

CAUTION. Well, but who sent you? How came you thither?

GERRARD. (*aside*) There I am puzzled indeed.

CAUTION. How came you hither, I say? How?

GERRARD. Why, how, how, how should I come hither?

DON DIEGO. Ay, how should he come hither? Upon his legs.

CAUTION. So, so, now you have put an excuse in his head too, that you have, so you have. But stay –

DON DIEGO. Nay, with your favour, mistress, I'll ask him now.

CAUTION. Yfacks but you shan't. I'll ask him and ask you no favour, that I will.

DON DIEGO. Yfackins but you shan't ask him. If you go thereto, look you, you prattlebox you, I'll ask him.

CAUTION. I will ask him, I say. Come.

DON DIEGO. Where?

CAUTION. What?

DON DIEGO. Mine's a shrewd question.

CAUTION. Mine's as shrewd as yours.

DON DIEGO. Nay then, we shall have it. Come, answer me. Where's your lodging? Come, come, sir.

CAUTION. A shrewd question indeed. At the Surgeon's

---

376 *Adonde*: where.
378 *chaps*: jaws.
392, 394 *Yfacks, Yfackins*: in faith.

Arms, I warrant, in –, for 'tis springtime, you know.

DON DIEGO. Must you make lies for him?

CAUTION. But come, sir, what's your name? Answer me to that, come.

DON DIEGO. His name. Why, 'tis an easy matter to tell you a false name, I hope.

CAUTION. So, must you teach him to cheat us?

DON DIEGO. Why did you say my questions were not shrewd questions then?

CAUTION. And why would you not let me ask him the question then? Brother, brother, ever while you live, for all your Spanish wisdom, let an old woman make discoveries. The young fellows cannot cheat us in anything. I'd have you to know. Set your old woman still to grope out an intrigue, because you know the mother found her daughter in the oven. A word to the wise, brother.

DON DIEGO. Come, come, leave this tattling. He has dishonoured my family, debauched my daughter and what if he could excuse himself? The Spanish proverb says 'Excuses neither satisfy creditors nor the injured; the wounds of honour must have blood and wounds.' St Jago para mi. (*Kisses the cross of his sword and runs at* GERRARD)

HIPPOLITA. Oh hold, dear father, and I'll confess all.

GERRARD. (*aside*) She will not, sure, after all.

HIPPOLITA. My cousin sent him because, as he said, he would have me recover my dancing a little before our wedding, having made a vow he would never marry a wife who could not dance a corant. I am sure I was unwilling but he would have him come, saying I was to be his wife as soon as you came and therefore expected obedience from me.

---

404 *in* –: Q1 leaves a gap for the street name.

418–19 *the mother . . . the oven*: proverbial; the woman would never have looked in the oven for her daughter if she had not been there herself. 'Oven' may well have had the modern innuendo of 'womb', as in 'bun in the oven'.

426 *St Jago para mi*: St James for me. James Formal swears by St James the apostle, just as his chosen Spanish name, Diego, is a Spanish form of James.

426 s.d. *the cross*: formed by the hilt-guards and the blade.

DON DIEGO. Indeed the venture is most his and the shame would be most his, for I know here in England 'tis not the custom for the father to be much concerned what the daughter does – but I will be a Spaniard still.

HIPPOLITA. Did not you hear him say last night he would send me one this morning?

CAUTION. No, not I, sure. If I had, he had never come here.

HIPPOLITA. Indeed, aunt, you grow old, I see; your memory fails you very much. Did not you hear him, Prue, say he would send him to me?

PRUE. Yes, I'll be sworn did I.

HIPPOLITA. Look you there, aunt.

CAUTION. I wonder I should not remember it.

DON DIEGO. Come, come, you are a doting old fool.

CAUTION. So, so, the fault will be mine now. But pray, mistress, how did he come in? I am sure I had the keys of the doors which, till your father came in, were not opened today.

HIPPOLITA. He came in just after my father, I suppose.

CAUTION. It might be indeed while the porters brought in the things and I was talking with you.

DON DIEGO. O might he so, forsooth. You are a brave governante, look you, you a duenna, voto – and not know who comes in and out.

CAUTION. So, 'twas my fault, I know.

DON DIEGO. Your maid was in the room with you, was she not, child?

HIPPOLITA. Yes, indeed and indeed, father, all the while.

DON DIEGO. Well, child, I am satisfied then. But I hope he does not use the dancing-masters' tricks of squeezing your hands, setting your legs and feet by handling your thighs and seeing your legs.

HIPPOLITA. No, indeed, father. I'd give him a box on the ear if he should.

DON DIEGO. Poor innocent! Well, I am contented you should learn to dance since, for ought I know, you shall be married tomorrow or the next day at farthest.

---

460 *duenna*: governess.

By that time you may recover a corant, a sarabrand, I would say, and since your cousin too will have a dancing wife it shall be so and I'll see you dance myself. You shall be my charge these two days and then I dare venture you in the hand of any dancing-master, even a saucy French dancing-master, look you.

CAUTION. Well, have a care though, for this man is not dressed like a dancing-master.

DON DIEGO. Go, go, you dote. Are they not, for the most part, better dressed and prouder than many a good gentleman? You would be wiser than I, would you? Cuerno!

CAUTION. Well, I say only look to't, look to't.

DON DIEGO. Hey, hey! Come, friend, to your business; teach her her lesson over again. Let's see.

HIPPOLITA. Come, master.

DON DIEGO. Come, come, let's see your English method. I understand something of dancing myself. Come.

HIPPOLITA. Come, master.

GERRARD. (*apart to* HIPPOLITA) I shall betray you yet, dearest miss, for I know not a step. I could never dance.

HIPPOLITA. [*apart to* GERRARD] No!

DON DIEGO. Come, come, child.

HIPPOLITA. Indeed, I'm ashamed, father.

DON DIEGO. You must not be ashamed, child. You'll never dance well if you are ashamed.

HIPPOLITA. Indeed I can't help it, father.

DON DIEGO. Come, come, I say, go to't.

HIPPOLITA. Indeed I can't father, before you. 'Tis my first lesson and I shall do it so ill. Pray, good father, go into the next room for this once and the next time my master comes I shall be confident enough.

DON DIEGO. Poor, foolish, innocent creature. Well, well, I will, child. Who but a Spanish kind of a father could have so innocent a daughter in England? Well,

---

476 *sarabrand*: Don Diego means saraband, a slow and stately Spanish dance, supposedly introduced to Spain by the Moors; though nothing like the courante, the saraband was a reasonable Spanish approximation for the French dance.

487 *Cuerno*: a very mild expletive, damn.

I would fain see anyone steal or debauch my daughter from me.

HIPPOLITA. Nay, won't you go, father?

DON DIEGO. Yes, yes, I go, child. We will all go but your maid. You can dance before your maid.

HIPPOLITA. Yes, yes, father, a maid at most times with her mistress is nobody.

Exeunt DIEGO *and* MRS CAUTION.

GERRARD. He peeps yet at the door.

HIPPOLITA. Nay, father, you peep; indeed you must not see me. When we have done you shall come in. (*She pulls the door to*)

PRUE. [*apart to* HIPPOLITA] Indeed, little mistress, like the young kitten, you see, you played with your prey till you had almost lost it!

HIPPOLITA. [*apart to* PRUE] 'Tis true. A good old mouser like you had taken it up and run away with it presently.

GERRARD. (*going to embrace her*) Let me adore you, dearest miss, and give you –

HIPPOLITA. No, no embracing, good master. That ought to be the last lesson you are to teach me, I have heard.

GERRARD. Though an after game be the more tedious and dangerous, 'tis won, miss, with the more honour and pleasure, for all that I repent we were put to't. The coming-in of your father as he did was the most unlucky thing that ever befell me.

HIPPOLITA. What, then you think I would have gone with you?

GERRARD. Yes, and will go with me, yet, I hope. Courage, miss. We have yet an opportunity and the gallery window is yet open.

HIPPOLITA. No, no, if I went I would go for good and all. But now my father will soon come in again and may quickly overtake us. Besides, now I think on't, you are a stranger to me. I know not where you live nor whither you might carry me. For ought I know, you might be a spirit and carry me to Barbadoes.

---

528 *taken it*: it taken Q1.

534 *after game*: a second game played to reverse or improve the first result.

549 *spirit*: kidnapper; abductions to the Barbadoes were not uncommon.

GERRARD. No, dear miss, I would carry you to Court, the playhouses and Hyde Park –

HIPPOLITA. Nay, I know 'tis the trick of all you that spirit women away to speak 'em mighty fair at first. But, when you have got 'em in your clutches, you carry 'em into Yorkshire, Wales or Cornwall, which is as bad as to Barbadoes, and, rather than be served so, I would be a prisoner in London still as I am.

GERRARD. I see the air of this town without the pleasures of it is enough to infect women with an aversion for the country. Well, miss, since it seems you have some diffidence in me, give me leave to visit you as your dancing-master, now you have honoured me with the character and, under that, I may have your father's permission to see you, till you may better know me and my heart and have a better opportunity to reward it.

HIPPOLITA. I am afraid to know your heart would require a great deal of time and my father intends to marry me very suddenly to my cousin who sent you hither.

GERRARD. Pray, sweet miss, then let us make the better use of our time if it be short. But how shall we do with that cousin of yours in the meantime? We must needs charm him.

HIPPOLITA. Leave that to me.

GERRARD. But, what's worse, how shall I be able to act a dancing-master who ever wanted inclination and patience to learn myself?

HIPPOLITA. A dancing-school in half an hour will furnish you with terms of the art. Besides, love, as I have heard say, supplies his scholars with all sorts of capacities they have need of, in spite of nature. But what has love to do with you?

GERRARD. Love indeed has made a grave, gouty statesman fight duels, the soldier fly from his colours, a pedant a fine gentleman, nay, and the very lawyer a poet and therefore may make me a dancing-master.

HIPPOLITA. If he were your master.

GERRARD. I'm sure, dearest miss, there is nothing else which I cannot do for you already and therefore may hope to succeed in that.

Enter DON DIEGO.

DON DIEGO. Come, have you done?

HIPPOLITA. [*aside*] O! My father again!

DON DIEGO. Come, now let us see you dance.

HIPPOLITA. Indeed, I am not perfect yet. Pray excuse me till the next time my master comes. But when must he come again, father?

DON DIEGO. Let me see. Friend, you must needs come after dinner again and then at night again and so three times tomorrow too. If she be not married tomorrow (which I am to consider of) she will dance a corant in twice or thrice teaching more, will she not? For 'tis but a twelvemonth since she came from Hackney School.

GERRARD. We will lose no time, I warrant you, sir, if she be to be married tomorrow.

DON DIEGO. Truly I think she may be married tomorrow, therefore I would not have you lose any time, look you.

GERRARD. You need not caution me, I warrant you, sir. Sweet scholar, your humble servant, I will not fail you immediately after dinner.

DON DIEGO. No, no, pray do not and I will not fail to satisfy you very well, look you.

HIPPOLITA. He does not doubt his reward, father, for his pains. If you should not I would make that good to him.

DON DIEGO. Come, let us go in to your aunt. I must talk with you both together, child.

HIPPOLITA. I will follow you, sir.

Exeunt GERRARD, DON DIEGO.

PRUE. Here's the gentlewoman o'th'next house come to see you, mistress.

HIPPOLITA. (*aside*) She's come as if she came expressly to sing the new song she sung last night. I must hear it, for 'tis to my purpose now. –

[*Enter* SINGER.]

Madam, your servant. I dreamt last night of the song you sung last, the new song against delays in love; pray let's hear it again.

---

620 s.d. after line 619 Q1.

[SINGER.] (*sings*)

1.

Since we poor slavish women know
Our men cannot pick and choose,
To him we like why say we no,
And both our time and lover lose?

With feigned repulses and delays
A lover's appetite we pall
And if too long the gallant stays
His stomach's gone for good and all.

2.

Or our impatient am'rous guest,
Unknown to us, away may steal
And, rather than stay for a feast,
Take up with some coarse, ready meal.

When opportunity is kind,
Let prudent woman be so too
And if the man be to your mind,
Till needs you must, ne'er let him go.

3.

The match soon made is happy still,
For only love has there to do.
Let no one marry 'gainst her will
But stand off, when her parents woo,

And only to their suits be coy,
For she whom joynter can obtain
To let a fop her bed enjoy
Is but a lawful wench for gain.

PRUE. (*steps to the door*) Your father calls for you, miss.

HIPPOLITA. I come, I come. I must be obedient as long as I am with him. (*Pausing*)
Our parents who restrain our liberty,
But take the course to make us sooner free,
Though all we gain be but new slavery.
We leave our fathers and to husbands fly.

Exeunt.

---

629 *Song*: the music, by John Bannister, is most conveniently available in Weales's edition, p. 169; it was first published in John Playford, *Choice Songs and Airs* (1673).

650 *joynter*: the jointure was the estate settled on a wife at marriage for the remainder of her life.

ACT III

SCENE I

Don Diego's house.

Enter MONSIEUR, HIPPOLITA *and* PRUE.

MONSIEUR. Serviteur, serviteur, la cousin, your maid told me she watched at the stairfoot for my coming because you had a mind to speak wit me before I saw your fader, it seem.

HIPPOLITA. I would so indeed, cousin.

MONSIEUR. Or ça, or ça, I know your affair; it is to tell me wat recreation you 'ade with Monsieur Gerrard. But did he come? I was afrait he would not come.

HIPPOLITA. Yes, yes, he did come.

MONSIEUR. Ha, ha, ha. And were you not infiniment divertisé and please? Confess.

HIPPOLITA. I was indeed, cousin, I was very well pleased.

MONSIEUR. I do tinke so. I did tinke to come and be divertisé myself this morning with the sight of his reception but I did rancounter last night wit dam company dat keep me up so late I could not rise in de morning. Mal à peste de putains –

HIPPOLITA. Indeed we wanted you here mightily, cousin.

MONSIEUR. To 'elpe you to laugh, for if I 'adde been here I had made such recreation wid dat coxcomb Gerrard.

HIPPOLITA. Indeed, cousin. You need not have any subject or property to make one laugh; you are so pleasant yourself and when you are but alone you would make one burst.

MONSIEUR. Am I so happy, cousin, then in the bon quality of making people laugh?

HIPPOLITA. Mighty happy, cousin.

MONSIEUR. De grâce.

HIPPOLITA. Indeed!

17 *Mal à peste de putains*: a plague on whores.

MONSIEUR. Nay, sans vanitié, I observe wheresoe'er I come I make everybody merry, sans vanitié, da.

HIPPOLITA. I do believe you do.

MONSIEUR. Nay, as I marche in de street, I can make de dull apprenti laugh and sneer.

HIPPOLITA. (*aside*) This fool, I see, is as apt as an ill poet to mistake the contempt and scorn of people for applause and admiration.

MONSIEUR. Ah, cousin, you see wat it is to have been in France. Before I went into France I could get nobody to laugh at me, ma foy.

HIPPOLITA. No? Truly, cousin, I think you deserved it before. But you are improved indeed by going into France.

MONSIEUR. Ay, ay, the Franch education make us propre à tout. Beside, cousin, you must know to play the fool is the science in France and I didde go to the Italian Academy at Paris thrice a week to learn to play de fool of Signior Scaramouche, who is the most excellent personage in the world for dat noble science. Angel is a damn English fool to him.

HIPPOLITA. Methinks now Angel is a very good fool.

MONSIEUR. Nauh, nauh, Nokes is a better fool. But indeed the Englis' are not fit to be fools; here are ver few good fools. 'Tis true you have many a young cavalier who go over into France to learn to be the buffoon but, for all dat, dey return but mauvais buffoon, jarnie.

HIPPOLITA. I'm sure, cousin, you have lost no time there.

MONSIEUR. Auh, le brave Scaramouche!

HIPPOLITA. But is it a science in France, cousin? And is there an Academy for fooling? Sure, none go to it but the players.

---

50 *Signior Scaramouche*: Tiberio Fiorillo, the famous actor of Scaramuccia in commedia dell'arte was playing with the Comédie Italienne at the Hôtel de Bourgogne in Paris at this time. He and his troupe visited London for the first time in April 1673 and were a triumphant success.

52–4 It is almost certain that James Nokes played Monsieur and Edward Angel Don Diego in the first production, thereby adding point to the values Monsieur places on their relative merits as actors. See Additional Note.

MONSIEUR. Dey are comedians dat are de matres but all the beaux monde go to learn, as they do here of Angel and Nokes, for if you did go abroad into company you would find the best almost of de nation conning in all places the lessons which dey have learnt of the fools dere matres, Nokes and Angel.

HIPPOLITA. Indeed?

MONSIEUR. Yes, yes, dey are the gens de quality that practise dat science most and the most ambitieux, for fools and buffoons have been always most welcome to courts and desired in all companies. Auh, to be de fool, de buffoon, is to be de greate personage.

HIPPOLITA. Fools have fortune, they say, indeed.

MONSIEUR. So say old Seneque.

HIPPOLITA. Well, cousin, (not to make you proud) you are the greatest fool in England, I am sure.

MONSIEUR. Non, non, de grâce, non. Nokes de comedian is a pretty man, a pretty man for a comedian, da.

HIPPOLITA. You are modest, cousin. But lest my father should come in presently, which he will do as soon as he knows you are here, I must give you a caution, which 'tis fit you should have before you see him.

MONSIEUR. Well, vel, cousin, vat is dat?

HIPPOLITA. You must know then, as commonly the conclusion of all mirth is sad, after I had a good while pleased myself in jesting and leading the poor gentleman you sent into a fool's paradise and almost made him believe I would go away with him, my father, coming home this morning, came in upon us and caught him with me.

MONSIEUR. Mal à peste.

HIPPOLITA. And drew his sword upon him and would have killed him, for you know my father's Spanish fierceness and jealousy.

MONSIEUR. But how did he come off then? Tête non.

HIPPOLITA. In short, I was fain to bring him off by saying he was my dancing-master.

MONSIEUR. Hah, ha, ha, ver good jeste.

---

66 *matres*: maîtres, masters, but probably pronounced by Monsieur rather more like 'matress'.

78–9 'Fools have fortune' is proverbial but I cannot find Seneca's version of it, nor, I suspect, had Monsieur found it there.

HIPPOLITA. I was unwilling to have the poor man killed, you know, for our foolish frolic with him. But then upon my aunt's and father's inquiry how he came in and who sent him I was forced to say you did, desiring I should be able to dance a corant before our wedding.

MONSIEUR. A ver good jest, da, still bettre as bettre.

HIPPOLITA. Now all that I am to desire of you is to own you sent him, that I may not be caught in a lie.

MONSIEUR. Yes, yes, a ver good jest. Gerrard a mastre de danse, hah, ha, ha.

HIPPOLITA. Nay, the jest is like to be better yet, for my father has obliged him now to come and teach me so that now he must take the dancing-master upon him and come three or four times to me before our wedding lest my father, if he should come no more, should be suspicious I had told him a lie and, for ought I know, if he should know or but guess he were not a dancing-master, in his Spanish strictness and punctilios of honour, he might kill me as the shame and stain of his honour and family which he talks of so much. Now you know the jealous, cruel fathers in Spain serve their poor innocent daughters often so and he is more than a Spaniard.

MONSIEUR. Non, non, fear noting. I warrant you he shall come as often as you will to the house and your father shall never know who he is till we are married. But then I'll tell him all for the jest's sake.

HIPPOLITA. But will you keep my counsel, dear cousin, till we are married?

MONSIEUR. Poor, dear fool, I warrant thee, mon foy.

HIPPOLITA. Nay, what a fool am I indeed, for you would not have me killed. You love me too well, sure, to be an instrument of my death.

Enter DON DIEGO *walking gravely, a little* BLACK *behind him,* [*and*] MRS CAUTION.

But here comes my father – remember.

MONSIEUR. I would no more tell him of it than I would tell you if I had been with a wench, jarnie. (*Aside*) She's afraid to be killed, poor wretch, and he's a capricious, jealous fop enough to do't. But here he comes. – I'll keep thy counsel, I warrant thee, my dear soul, mon petit coeur.

HIPPOLITA. Peace, peace, my father's coming this way.

MONSIEUR. Ay, but by his march he won't be near enough to hear us this half hour, hah, ha, ha.

DON DIEGO *walks leisurely round the* MONSIEUR, *surveying him and shrugging his shoulders whilst* MONSIEUR *makes legs and faces.*

DON DIEGO. (*aside*) Is that thing my cousin, sister?

CAUTION. 'Tis he, sir.

DON DIEGO. Cousin, I'm sorry to see you.

MONSIEUR. Is that a Spanish complement?

DON DIEGO. So much disguised, cousin.

MONSIEUR. (*aside*) Oh, is it out at last, ventre? – Serviteur, serviteur, à monseur mon oncle and I am glad to see you here within doors, most Spanish oncle, ha, ha, ha. But I should be sorry to see you in the streets, tête non.

DON DIEGO. Why soh, would you be ashamed of me, hah? Voto a St Jago, would you? Hauh!

MONSIEUR. Ay, it may be you would be ashamed yourself, monseur mon oncle, of the great train you would get to wait upon your Spanish hose, puh. The boys would follow you and hoot at you, vert et bleu, pardone my Franch franchise, monsieur mon oncle.

HIPPOLITA. (*apart to* PRUE) We shall have sport anon betwixt these two contraries.

DON DIEGO. Dost thou call me monseur, voto a St Jago?

MONSIEUR. No, I did not call you Monseur Voto a St Jago, sir. I know you are my uncle, Mr James Formal, da.

DON DIEGO. But I can hardly know you are my cousin, Mr Nathaniel Paris. But call me Sir Don Diego henceforward, look you, and no Monsieur. Call me Monsieur, guarda!

---

147 s.d. *makes legs*: bows.

152 *aside*: after line 000 Q1.

154 *monseur*: I have preserved the original spelling, since it may well have been that Monsieur and Don Diego pronounce it *monsewer* at this point, though it is more likely to have been the compositor's or Wycherley's mistake.

162 *Spanish hose*: breeches which fitted closely down the thighs; Monsieur's pantaloons (line 180) had vast legs and were pleated to the waist, resembling skirts more than breeches.

164 *Franchise*: frankness.

MONSIEUR. I confess my error, sir, for none but a blind man would call you monsieur, ha, ha, ha. But pray do not call me neder Paris but de Paris, de Paris, si vous plaît, Monseur de Paris! Call me Monseur and welcome, da!

DON DIEGO. Monsieur de Pantalloons then, voto!

MONSIEUR. Monsieur de Pantalloons! A pretty name, a pretty name, ma foy, da. Bien trove, de Pantalloons. How much betre den your de la Fountaines, de la Rivières, de la Roches and all the de's in France, da. Well, but have you not the admiration for my pantaloon, Don Diego mon oncle?

DON DIEGO. I am astonished at them verdaderamente; they are wonderfully ridiculous.

MONSIEUR. Redicule, redicule! Ah, 'tis well you are my uncle, da. Redicule, ah! Is dere anyting in de universe so gentil as de pantaloons? Anyting so ravisaunt as de pantaloons? Auh, I could kneel down and varship a pair of gentil pantaloons. Vat, vat, you would have me have de admiration for dis outward skin of your thigh which you call Spanish hose. Fie, fie, fie, ha, ha, ha.

DON DIEGO. Dost thou deride my Spanish hose, young man, hauh?

MONSIEUR. In comparison of pantaloon I do undervalue 'em indeet, Don Diègue mon oncle, ha, ha, ha.

DON DIEGO. Thou art then a gabacho de malo gusto, look you.

MONSIEUR. You may call me vat you vil, oncle Don Diègue, but I must needs say your Spanish hose are scurvy hose, ugly hose, lousy hose and stinking hose.

DON DIEGO. (*puts his hand to his sword*) Do not provoke me, borracho.

MONSIEUR. Indeet for 'lousy' I recant dat epithet, for dere is scarce room in 'em for dat little animal, ha, ha, ha. But for stinking hose, dat epithet may stand, for how can dey choose but stink since dey are so furieusemente close to your Spanish tail, da.

---

187 *verdaderamente*: (Q1 verde deramentè) indeed.

201 *gabacho*: Q1 reads *gavanho* but Ward's emendation is sensible since *gabacho* means 'frenchified'.

201 *de malo gusto*: of bad taste.

207 *borracho*: wildly angry man.

HIPPOLITA. (*aside*) Ha, ha, ridiculous.

DON DIEGO. (*seems to draw*) Do not provoke me, I say, en hora mala.

MONSIEUR. Nay, oncle, I am sorry you are in de passion but I must live and die for de pantaloon against de Spanish hose, da.

DON DIEGO. You are a rash young man and while you wear pantaloons you are beneath my passion, voto. Auh, they make thee look and waddle, with all those gewgaw ribbons, like a great, old, fat, slovenly water-dog.

MONSIEUR. And your Spanish hose and your nose in the air make you look like a great, grizzled, long, Irish greyhound reaching a crust off from a high shelf, ha, ha, ha.

DON DIEGO. Bueno, bueno.

CAUTION. What, have you a mind to ruin yourself and break off the match?

MONSIEUR. Pshaw, wat do you tell me of de matche? D'ee tink I will not vindicate pantaloons, morbleu?

DON DIEGO. (*aside*) Well, he is a lost man, I see, and desperately far gone in the epidemic malady of our nation, the affectation of the worst of French vanities. But I must be wiser than him as I am a Spaniard, look you, Don Diego, and endeavour to reclaim him by art and fair means, look you, Don Diego. If not he shall never marry my daughter, look you, Don Diego, though he be my own sister's son and has two thousand five hundred seventy three pound sterling twelve shillings and twopence a year penny-rent, segouaramente. – Come, young man, since you are so obstinate, we will refer our difference to arbitration. Your mistress, my daughter, shall be umpire betwixt us concerning Spanish hose and pantaloons.

MONSIEUR. Pantaloons and Spanish hose, si vous plaît.

DON DIEGO. Your mistress is the fittest judge of your dress, sure.

MONSIEUR. I know ver vel dat most of the jeunesse of Englant will not change the ribband upon de crevat

---

242 *penny-rent*: income.
242–3 *segouaramente*: *seguramente*, definitely.

widout the consultation of dere matress but I am no Anglois, da, nor shall I make de reference of my dress to any in the universe, da. I judged by any in England, tête non! I would not be judged by an English looking-glass, jarnie.

DON DIEGO. Be not positivo, young man.

CAUTION. Nay, pray refer it, cousin, pray do.

MONSIEUR. Non, non, your servant, your servant, aunt.

DON DIEGO. But pray be not so positive. Come hither, daughter. Tell me which is best.

HIPPOLITA. Indeed, father, you have kept me in universal ignorance; I know nothing.

MONSIEUR. And do you tink I shall refer an affair of dat consequence to a poor young ting who have not see the varld, da? I am wiser than so, voto.

DON DIEGO. Well, in short, if you will not be wiser and leave off your French dress, stammering and tricks, look you, you shall be a fool and go without my daughter, voto.

MONSIEUR. How, must I leave off my gentil Franch accoutrements and speak base Englis' too or not marry my cousin, mon oncle Don Diego? Do not break off the match, do not, for know I will not leave off my pantaloon and Franch pronunciation for n'er a cousin in Englant, da.

DON DIEGO. I tell you again, he that marries my daughter shall at least look like a wise man, for he shall wear the Spanish habit. I am a Spanish positivo.

MONSIEUR. Ver vel, ver vel! And I am a Franch positivo.

DON DIEGO. Then I am definitivo and, if you do not go immediately into your chamber and put on a Spanish habit I have brought over on purpose for your wedding clothes and put off all these French fopperies and vanidades with all your grimaces, agreeables, adorables, ma foys and jernies, I swear you shall never marry my daughter and by an oath by Spaniard never broken – by my whiskers and snuffbox.

---

252 *matress*: *maîtresse*, mistress.

266 *voto*: intentionally or not, Monsieur borrows Don Diego's favourite word.

286 *vanidades*: vanities.

289 *by my whiskers and snuffbox*: see Additional Note.

MONSIEUR. O hold, do not swear, uncle, for I love your daughter furieusement.

DON DIEGO. If you love her you'll obey me.

MONSIEUR. Auh, wat vil become of me! But have the consideration. Must I leave off all the Franch beautés, graces and embellisements, bot' of my person and language?

Exeunt HIPPOLITA, MRS CAUTION *and* PRUE *laughing.*

DON DIEGO. I will have it so.

MONSIEUR. I am ruine den, undone. Have some consideration for me, for dere is not the least ribbon of my garniture but is as dear to me as your daughter, jernie!

DON DIEGO. Then you do not deserve her and for that reason I will be satisfied you love her better or you shall not have her, for I am positivo.

MONSIEUR. Vil you break mine 'arte? Pray, have de consideration for me.

DON DIEGO. I say again, you shall be dressed before night from top to toe in the Spanish habit or you shall never marry my daughter, look you.

MONSIEUR. If you will not have de consideration for me, have de consideration for your daughter, for she have de passionate amour for me and like me in dis habite betre den in yours, da.

DON DIEGO. What I have said I have said and I am uno positivo.

MONSIEUR. Will you not so mush as allow me one little Franch oat'?

DON DIEGO. No, you shall look like a Spaniard but speak and swear like an Englishman, look you.

MONSIEUR. Hélas, hélas, den I shall take my leave, mort, tête, ventre, jernie, tête bleu, ventre bleu, ma foy, certes.

DON DIEGO. (*calls at the door*) Pedro, Sanchez, wait upon this cavaliero into his chamber with those things I ordered you to take out of the trunks. – I would have you a little accustomed to your clothes before your wedding, for if you comply with me you shall marry my daughter tomorrow, look you.

MONSIEUR. Adieu then dear pantaloon, dear belte,

dear sword, dear peruke and dear chappeaux retrousé and dear shoe garni. Adieu, adieu, adieu, hélas, hélas, hélas. Will you have yet no pitié?

DON DIEGO. I am a Spanish positivo, look you.

MONSIEUR. And more cruel than de Spanish Inquisitiono, to compel a man to a habit against his conscience. Hélas, hélas, hélas. *Exit* MONSIEUR.

Enter PRUE *and* GERRARD.

PRUE. Here is the dancing-master. Shall I call my mistress, sir?

DON DIEGO. Yes.

Exit PRUE.

O, you are as punctual as a Spaniard. I love your punctual men. Nay, I think 'tis before your time something.

GERRARD. Nay, I am resolved your daughter, sir, shall lose no time by my fault.

DON DIEGO. So, so, 'tis well.

GERRARD. I were a very unworthy man if I should not be punctual with her, sir.

DON DIEGO. You speak honestly, very honestly, friend, and I believe a very honest man, though a dancing-master.

GERRARD. I am very glad you think me so, sir.

DON DIEGO. What, you are but a young man. Are you married yet?

GERRARD. No, sir, but I hope I shall, sir, very suddenly, if things hit right.

DON DIEGO. What, the old folks, her friends, are wary and cannot agree with you so soon as the daughter can?

GERRARD. Yes, sir, the father hinders it a little at present but the daughter, I hope, is resolved and then we shall do well enough.

DON DIEGO. What! You do not steal her, according to the laudable custom of some of your brother dancing-masters?

---

330 *chappeaux retrousé*: cocked hat.
331 *shoe garni*: shoe decorated with bows or ribbons.
339 s.d. follows line 338 Q1.

GERRARD. No, no, sir, steal her, sir, steal her! You are pleased to be merry, sir, ha, ha, ha. (*Aside*) I cannot but laugh at that question.

DON DIEGO. No, sir, methinks you are pleased to be merry but you say the father does not consent.

GERRARD. Not yet, sir. But 'twill be no matter whether he does or no.

DON DIEGO. Was she one of your scholars? If she were, 'tis a hundred to ten but you steal her.

GERRARD. (*aside, laughs*) I shall not be able to hold laughing.

DON DIEGO. Nay, nay, I find by your laughing you steal her. She was your scholar, was she not?

GERRARD. Yes, sir, she was the first I ever had and may be the last too, for she has a fortune, if I can get her, will keep me from teaching to dance any more.

DON DIEGO. So, so, then she is your scholar still it seems and she has a good portion. I am glad on't. Nay, I knew you stole her.

GERRARD. (*aside*) My laughing may give him suspicions, yet I cannot hold.

DON DIEGO. What, you laugh, I warrant, to think how the young baggage and you will mump the poor old father. But if all her dependence for a fortune be upon the father, he may chance to mump you both and spoil the jest.

GERRARD. I hope it will not be in his power, sir, ha, ha, ha. (*Aside*) I shall laugh too much anon. – Pray, sir, be pleased to call for your daughter. I am impatient till she comes, for time was never more precious with me and with her too. It ought to be so, sure, since you say she is to be married tomorrow.

DON DIEGO. She ought to bestir her, as you say, indeed. (*Calls at the door*) Wuh, daughter, daughter. Prue, Hippolita. Come away, child. Why do you stay so long?

Enter HIPPOLITA, PRUE *and* CAUTION.

HIPPOLITA. Your servant, master! Indeed, I am ashamed you have stayed for me.

GERRARD. O good madam, 'tis my duty. I know you came as soon as you could.

HIPPOLITA. I knew my father was with you, therefore I did not make altogether so much haste as I might.

But if you had been alone, nothing should have kept me from you; I would not have been so rude as to have made you stay a minute for me, I warrant you.

DON DIEGO. Come, fiddle-faddle, what a deal of ceremony there is betwixt your dancing-master and you, cuerno!

HIPPOLITA. Lord, sir, I hope you'll allow me to show my respect to my master, for I have a great respect for my master.

GERRARD. And I am very proud of my scholar and am a very great honourer of my scholar.

DON DIEGO. Come, come, friend, about your business and honour the king. (*To* MRS CAUTION) Your dancing-masters and barbers are such finical, smooth-tongued, tattling fellows and if you set 'em once a-talking they'll ne'er a done, no more than when you set 'em a-fiddling – indeed, all that deal with fiddles are given to impertinency.

CAUTION. Well, well! This is an impertinent fellow without being a dancing-master. He's no more a dancing-master than I am a maid.

DON DIEGO. What, will you still be wiser than I? Voto. – Come, come about with my daughter, man.

PRUE. So he would, I warrant you, if your worship would let him alone.

DON DIEGO. How now, Mrs Nimble-chaps?

GERRARD. (*aside to* HIPPOLITA) Well, though I have got a little canting at the dancing-school since I was here, yet I do all so bunglingly, he'll discover me.

HIPPOLITA. [*aside*] Try. – Come, take my hand, master.

CAUTION. Look you, brother, the impudent harlotry gives him her hand.

DON DIEGO. Can he dance with her without holding her by the hand?

HIPPOLITA. Here, take my hand, master.

GERRARD. (*aside to her*) I wish it were for good and all.

HIPPOLITA. You dancing-masters are always so hasty, so nimble.

DON DIEGO. Voto a St Jago, not that I can see. About, about with her, man.

---

419 *honour the king*: bow and curtsey before a dance.
442 *for*: for for Q1.

GERRARD. Indeed, sir, I cannot go about with her as I would do, unless you will please to go out a little, sir, for I see she is bashful still before you, sir.

DON DIEGO. Hey, hey, more fooling yet. Come, come, about with her.

HIPPOLITA. Nay, indeed, father, I am ashamed and cannot help it.

DON DIEGO. But you shall help it, for I will not stir. Move her, I say. Begin, hussy, move when he'll have you.

PRUE. (*aside*) I cannot but laugh at that, ha, ha, ha.

GERRARD. (*apart to* HIPPOLITA) Come then, madam, since it must be so, let us try. But I shall discover all. – One, two and coupée.

CAUTION. Nay, d'ee see how he squeezes her hand, brother? O the lewd villain!

DON DIEGO. Come, move, I say, and mind her not.

GERRARD. One, two, three, four and turn around.

CAUTION. D'ee see again? He took her by the bare arm.

DON DIEGO. Come, move on. She's mad.

GERRARD. One, two and a coupée.

DON DIEGO. Come. One, two. Turn out your toes.

CAUTION. There, there, he pinched her by the thigh. Will you suffer it?

GERRARD. One, two, three and fall back.

DON DIEGO. Fall back, fall back, back. Some of you are forward enough to fall back.

GERRARD. Back, madam.

DON DIEGO. Fall back when he bids you, hussy.

CAUTION. How, how! Fall back, fall back! Marry but she shall not fall back when he bids her.

DON DIEGO. I say she shall, huswife. Come.

GERRARD. She will, she will, I warrant you, sir, if you won't be angry with her.

CAUTION. Do you know what he means by that now, you a Spaniard?

DON DIEGO. How's that, I not a Spaniard? Say such a word again.

GERRARD. Come forward, madam, three steps again.

---

460 *coupée*: a step in which the dancer rests on one foot passing the other backward and forward, a bow made in advancing.

473 *to fall back*: to back Q1.

CAUTION. See, see, she squeezes his hand now. O the debauched harlotry!

DON DIEGO. So, so, mind her not. She moves forward pretty well but you must move as well backward as forward or you'll never do anything to purpose.

CAUTION. Do you know what you say, brother, yourself? Now are you at your beastliness before your young daughter?

PRUE. Ha, ha, ha.

DON DIEGO. How now, mistress, are you so merry? Is this your staid maid as you call her, sister impertinent?

GERRARD. (*aside to* HIPPOLITA) I have not much to say to you, miss, but I shall not have an opportunity to do it unless we can get your father out.

DON DIEGO. Come about again with her.

CAUTION. Look you, there she squeezes his hand hard again.

HIPPOLITA. Indeed and indeed, father, my aunt puts me quite out. I cannot dance while she looks on, for my heart. She makes me ashamed and afraid together.

GERRARD. Indeed if you would please to take her out, sir, I am sure I should make my scholar do better than when you are present, sir. Pray, sir, be pleased for this time to take her away. For the next time I hope I shall order it so we shall trouble neither of you.

CAUTION. No, no, brother, stir not. They have a mind to be left alone. Come, there's a beastly trick in't. He's no dancing-master, I tell you.

GERRARD. (*aside to* HIPPOLITA) Damned jade, she'll discover us.

DON DIEGO. What, will you teach me? Nay, then, I will go out and you shall go out too, look you.

CAUTION. I will not go out, look you.

DON DIEGO. Come, come, thou art a censorious, wicked woman and you shall disturb them no longer.

CAUTION. What, will you bawd for your daughter?

DON DIEGO. Ay, ay, come. Go out, out, out.

CAUTION. I will not go out, I will not go out. My conscience will not suffer me, for I know by experience what will follow.

GERRARD. I warrant you, sir, we'll make good use of our time when you are gone.

CAUTION. Do you hear him again? Don't you know what he means?

Exit DON DIEGO *thrusting* CAUTION *out.*

HIPPOLITA. 'Tis very well; you are a fine gentleman to abuse my poor father so.

GERRARD. 'Tis but by your example, miss.

HIPPOLITA. Well, I am his daughter and may make the bolder with him, I hope.

GERRARD. And I am his son-in-law that shall be and therefore may claim my privilege too of making bold with him, I hope.

HIPPOLITA. Methinks you should be contented in making bold with his daughter, for you have made very bold with her, sure.

GERRARD. I hope I shall make bolder with her yet.

HIPPOLITA. I do not doubt your confidence, for you are a dancing-master.

GERRARD. Why, miss, I hope you would not have me a fine, senseless, whining, modest lover, for modesty in a man is as ill as the want of it in a woman.

HIPPOLITA. I thank you for that, sir; now you have made bold with me indeed. But if I am such a confident piece I am sure you made me so. If you had not had the confidence to come in at the window, I had not had the confidence to look upon a man. I am sure I could not look upon a man before.

GERRARD. But that I humbly conceive, sweet miss, was your father's fault because you had not a man to look upon. But, dearest miss, I do not think you confident; you are only innocent, for that which would be called confidence, nay impudence, in a woman of years, is called innocency in one of your age and the more impudent you appear the more innocent you are thought.

HIPPOLITA. Say you so? Has youth such privileges? I do not wonder then most women seem impudent, since it is to be thought younger than they are, it seems. But indeed, master, you are as great an encourager of impudence, I see, as if you were a dancing-master in good earnest.

GERRARD. Yes, yes, a young thing may do anything, may leap out of her window and go away with her dancing-master, if she please.

HIPPOLITA. So, so, the use follows the doctrine very suddenly.

GERRARD. Well, dearest, pray let us make the use we should of it, lest your father should make too bold with us and come in before we would have him.

HIPPOLITA. Indeed old relations are apt to take that ill-bred freedom of pressing into young company at unseasonable hours.

GERRARD. Come, dear miss, let me tell you how I have designed matters, for in talking of anything else we lose time and opportunity. People abroad indeed say the English women are the worst in the world in using an opportunity – they love tittle-tattle and ceremony.

HIPPOLITA. 'Tis because, I warrant, opportunities are not so scarce here as abroad; they have more here than they can use. But let people abroad say what they will of English women, because they do not know 'em – but what say people at home?

GERRARD. Pretty innocent, ha, ha, ha. Well, I say you will not make use of your opportunity.

HIPPOLITA. I say you have no reason to say so yet.

GERRARD. Well then, anon at nine of the clock at night I'll try you, for I have already bespoke a parson and have taken up the three back rooms of the tavern which front upon the gallery window, that nobody may see us escape, and I have appointed, precisely between eight and nine of the clock, when it is dark, a coach and six to wait at the tavern-door for us.

HIPPOLITA. A coach and six, a coach and six, do you say? Nay then, I see you are resolved to carry me away, for a coach and six, though there were not a man but the coachman with it, would carry away any young girl of my age in England. A coach and six!

GERRARD. Then you will be sure to be ready to go with me?

HIPPOLITA. What young woman of the town could ever say no to a coach and six, unless it were going into the country? A coach and six! 'Tis not in the power of fourteen-year-old to resist it.

GERRARD. You will be sure to be ready?

HIPPOLITA. You are sure 'tis a coach and six?

GERRARD. I warrant you, miss.

HIPPOLITA. I warrant you then they'll carry us merrily away. A coach and six?

GERRARD. But have you charmed your cousin, the Monsieur, as you said you would, that he in the meantime say nothing to prevent us?

HIPPOLITA. I warrant you.

Enter to 'em DON DIEGO *and* MRS CAUTION *pressing in.*

CAUTION. I will come in.

DON DIEGO. Well, I hope by this time you have given her full instructions, you have told her what and how to do, you have done all.

GERRARD. We have just done indeed, sir.

HIPPOLITA. Ay, sir, we have just done, sir.

CAUTION. And I fear just undone, sir.

GERRARD. (*aside to* HIPPOLITA) D'ee hear that damned witch?

DON DIEGO. Come, leave your censorious prating. Thou hast been a false right woman thyself in thy youth, I warrant you.

CAUTION. I right! I right! I scorn your words, I'd have you to know, and 'tis well known. I right! No, 'tis your dainty minx, that gillflirt, your daughter here, that is right. Do you see how her handkerchief is ruffled and what a heat she's in?

DON DIEGO. She has been dancing.

CAUTION. Ay, ay, Adam and Eve's dance or the beginning of the world. D'ee see how she pants?

DON DIEGO. She has not been used to motion.

CAUTION. Motion, motion! Motion, d'ee call it? No, indeed, I kept her from motion till now. Motion with a vengeance!

DON DIEGO. You put the poor bashful girl to the blush, you see. Hold your peace.

CAUTION. 'Tis her guilt, not her modesty, marry.

DON DIEGO. Come, come, mind her not, child. Come, master, let me see her dance now the whole dance roundly together. Come, sing to her.

GERRARD. (*aside to* HIPPOLITA) Faith, we shall be discovered after all. You know I cannot sing a note, miss.

---

629 *right*: promiscuous.
634 *gillflirt*: giddy wanton.

DON DIEGO. Come, come, man.

HIPPOLITA. Indeed, father, my master's in haste now. Pray let it alone till anon at night when you say he is to come again and then you shall see me dance it to the violin. Pray stay till then, father.

DON DIEGO. I will not be put off so. Come, begin.

HIPPOLITA. Pray, father.

DON DIEGO. Come, sing to her; come, begin.

GERRARD. Pray, sir, excuse me till anon. I am in some haste.

DON DIEGO. I say begin. I will not excuse you. Come, take her by the hand and about with her.

CAUTION. I say he shall not take her by the hand. He shall touch her no more. While I am here there shall be no more squeezing and tickling her palm, good Mr Dancing-master. Stand off. (*Thrusts* GERRARD *away*)

DON DIEGO. Get you out, Mrs Impertinence. Take her by the hand, I say.

CAUTION. Stand off, I say. He shall not touch her. He has touched her too much already.

DON DIEGO. If patience were not a Spanish virtue, I would lay it aside now. I say let 'em dance.

CAUTION. I say they shall not dance.

HIPPOLITA. Pray, father, since you see my aunt's obstinacy, let us alone till anon when you may keep her out.

DON DIEGO. Well then, friend, do not fail to come.

HIPPOLITA. Nay, if he fail me at last –

DON DIEGO. Be sure you come, for she's to be married tomorrow – do you know it?

GERRARD. Yes, yes, sir. Sweet scholar, your humble servant till night and think in the meantime of the instructions I have given you, that you may be the readier when I come.

DON DIEGO. Ay, girl, be sure you do and do you be sure to come.

CAUTION. You need not be so concerned; he'll be sure to come, I warrant you. But if I could help it he should never set foot again in the house.

DON DIEGO. You would frighten the poor dancing-master from the house. But be sure you come for all her.

GERRARD. Yes, sir. (*Aside*) But this jade will pay me when I am gone.

CAUTION. Hold, hold, sir, I must let you out and I wish I could keep you out. He a dancing-master? He's a chouse, a cheat, a mere cheat and that you'll find.

DON DIEGO. I find any man a cheat! I cheated by any man! I scorn your words. I that have so much Spanish care, circumspection and prudence cheated by a man! Do you think I who have been in Spain, look you, and have kept up my daughter a twelvemonth, for fear of being cheated of her, look you? I cheated of her!

CAUTION. Well, say no more.

Exeunt DON DIEGO, HIPPOLITA, CAUTION *and* PRUE.

GERRARD. Well, old formality, if you had not kept up your daughter, I am sure I had never cheated you of her.
The wary fool is by his care betrayed,
As cuckolds by their jealousy are made. *Exit.*

ACT IV

SCENE I

Enter MONSIEUR DE PARIS *without a peruke, with a Spanish hat, a Spanish doublet, stockings and shoes but in pantaloons, a waist-belt and a Spanish dagger in't and a cravat about his neck. Enter* HIPPOLITA *and* PRUE *behind, laughing.*

MONSIEUR. To see wat a fool love do make of one, jernie! It do metamorphose de brave man into de beast, de sotte, de animal.

HIPPOLITA. Ha, ha, ha.

MONSIEUR. Nay, you may laugh. 'Tis ver vel; I am become as redicule for you as can be, mort bleu. I have deform myself into an ugly Spaniard.

---

710 s.d. *Exit*: *Exeunt* Q1.

s.d. *Spanish hat*: probably the flat-crowned hat, see Additional Note to III i 289.

HIPPOLITA. Why, do you call this disguising yourself like a Spaniard while you wear pantaloons still and the cravat?

MONSIEUR. But is here not the double doublet and the Spanish dagger aussi?

HIPPOLITA. But 'tis as long as the French sword and worn like it. But where's your Spanish beard, the thing of most consequence?

MONSIEUR. Jernie, do you tink beards are as easy to be had as in de playhouses? Non. But if here be no the ugly, long Spanish beard, here are, I am certain, the ugly, long Spanish ear.

HIPPOLITA. That's very true, ha, ha, ha.

MONSIEUR. Auh de ingrate dat de woman is! When we poor men are your gallants you laugh at us yourselves and wen we are your husband you make all the warld laugh at us, jernie. Love, damn love, it make the man more redicule than poverty, poetry or a new title of honneur, jernie.

Enter DON DIEGO *and* CAUTION.

DON DIEGO. What, at your 'jernies' still? Voto.

MONSIEUR. Why, oncle, you are at your 'votos' still.

DON DIEGO. Nay, I'll allow you to be at your votos too but not to make the incongruous match of Spanish doublet and French pantaloons.

MONSIEUR. (*holding his hat before his pantaloons*) Nay, pray, dear oncle, let me unite France and Spain – 'tis the mode of France now, jarnie, voto.

DON DIEGO. Well, I see I must pronounce. I told you if you were not dressed in the Spanish habit tonight you should not marry my daughter tomorrow, look you.

MONSIEUR. Well, am I not habillé in de Spanish habit? My doublet, ear and hat, leg and feet are Spanish, that dey are.

DON DIEGO. I told you I was a Spanish positivo, voto.

---

19 *Spanish ear*: wearing earrings was no longer popular in England and certainly not fashionable in France.

32 s.d. follows line 31 Q1.

32–3 *let me unite . . . now*: war between France and Spain had ended with the Treaty of Aix-la-Chapelle in 1668.

MONSIEUR. Vil you not spare my pantaloon, begar? I will give you one little finger to excuse my pantaloon, da.

DON DIEGO. I have said, look you.

MONSIEUR. Auh, chères pantaloons! Speak for my pantaloons. My poor pantaloons are as dear to me as de scarf to de country capitaine or de new-made officer. Therefore, have de compassion for my pantaloons, Don Diego, mon oncle. Hélas, hélas, hélas. (*Kneels to* DON DIEGO)

DON DIEGO. I have said, look you, your dress must be Spanish and your language English. I am uno positivo.

MONSIEUR. And must speak base good English too? Ah la pitié, hélas!

DON DIEGO. It must be done and I will see this great change ere it be dark, voto. Your time is not long. Look to't, look you.

MONSIEUR. Hélas, hélas, hélas, dat Espagne should conquer la France in England! Hélas, hélas, hélas.

Exit MONSIEUR.

DON DIEGO. You see what pains I take to make him the more agreeable to you, daughter.

HIPPOLITA. But indeed and indeed, father, you wash the blackamoor white in endeavouring to make a Spaniard of a monsieur, nay an English monsieur too – consider that, father. For when once they have taken the French pli, as they call it, they are never to be made so much as Englishmen again, I have heard say.

DON DIEGO. What, I warrant you are like the rest of the young silly baggages of England that like nothing but what is French. You would not have him reformed, you would have a monsieur to your husband, would you? Cuerno.

HIPPOLITA. No, indeed, father, I would not have a monsieur to my husband, not I indeed, and I am sure you'll never make my cousin otherwise.

DON DIEGO. I warrant you.

HIPPOLITA. You can't, you can't, indeed, father, and

---

48 *scarf*: sash worn diagonally to indicate rank.
66 *pli*: from *prendre le pli*, forming unalterable habits, conforming.

you have sworn, you know, he shall never have me if he does not leave off his monsieurship. Now as I told you, 'tis as hard for him to cease being a monsieur as 'tis for you to break a Spanish oath, so that I am not in any great danger of having a monsieur to my husband.

DON DIEGO. Well, but you shall have him for your husband, look you.

HIPPOLITA. Then you will break your Spanish oath.

DON DIEGO. No, I will break him of his French tricks and you shall have him for your husband, cuerno.

HIPPOLITA. Indeed and indeed, father, I shall not have him.

DON DIEGO. Indeed you shall, daughter.

HIPPOLITA. Well, you shall see, father.

CAUTION. No, I warrant you, she will not have him. She'll have her dancing-master rather. I know her meaning, I understand her.

DON DIEGO. Thou malicious, foolish woman, you understand her! But I do understand her. She says I will not break my oath nor he his French customs, so through our difference she thinks she shall not have him. But she shall.

HIPPOLITA. But I shan't.

CAUTION. I know she will not have him, because she hates him.

DON DIEGO. I tell you, if she does hate him, 'tis a sign she will have him for her husband, for 'tis not one of a thousand marries the man she loves, look you. Besides, 'tis all one whether she loves him now or not, for, as soon as she's married, she'd be sure to hate him. That's the reason we wise Spaniards are jealous and only expect, nay, will be sure our wives shall fear us, look you.

HIPPOLITA. Pray, good father and aunt, do not dispute about nothing, for I am sure he will never be my husband to hate.

CAUTION. I am of your opinion indeed. I understand you. I can see as far as another.

DON DIEGO. You, you cannot see so much as through your spectacles! But I understand her. 'Tis her mere desire to marriage makes her say she shall not have him, for your poor young things, when they are once in the teens, think they shall never be married.

HIPPOLITA. Well, father, think what you will but I know what I think.

Enter MONSIEUR *in the Spanish habit entire only with a cravat and followed by the little* BLACKAMOOR *with a golilla in his hand.*

DON DIEGO. Come, did I not tell you you should have him. Look you there; he has complied with me and is a perfect Spaniard.

MONSIEUR. Ay, ay, I am ugly rogue enough now, sure, for my cousin. But 'tis your father's fault, cousin, that you han't the handsomest, best-dressed man in the nation, a man bien mise.

DON DIEGO. Yet again at your French? And a cravat on still, voto a St Jago! Off, off with it.

MONSIEUR. Nay, I will ever hereafter speak clownish good English. Do but spare me my cravat.

DON DIEGO. I am uno positivo, look you.

MONSIEUR. Let me not put on that Spanish yoke but spare me my cravat, for I love cravat furieusement.

DON DIEGO. Again at your 'furieusements'!

MONSIEUR. Indeed I have forgot myself but have some mercy. (*Kneels*)

DON DIEGO. Off, off, off with it, I say. Come, refuse the ornamento principal of the Spanish habit!

Takes him by the cravat, pulls it off and the BLACK *puts on the golilla.*

MONSIEUR. Will you have no mercy, no pity? Alas, alas, alas. Oh, I had rather put on the English pillory than this Spanish golilla, [*takes it off*] for 'twill be all a case, I'm sure, for, when I go abroad, I shall soon have a crowd of boys about me, peppering me with rotten eggs and turnips, hélas, hélas.

DON DIEGO *puts on the golilla.*

DON DIEGO. 'Hélas' again?

MONSIEUR. Alas, alas, alas.

HIPPOLITA. I shall die.
PRUE. I shall burst.
} Ha, ha, ha.

MONSIEUR. Ay, ay, you see what I am come to for your

---

124 s.d. *golilla*: a stiff and restricting collar standing up at the back of the head and shaped with wire, vastly different from Monsieur's loose cravat.

sake, cousin, and, uncle, pray take notice how ridiculous I am grown to my cousin that loves me above all the world. She can no more forbear laughing at me, I vow and swear, than if I were as arrant a Spaniard as yourself.

DON DIEGO. Be a Spaniard like me and ne'er think people laugh at you. There was never a Spaniard that thought anyone laughed at him. But, what, do you laugh at a golilla, baggage? Come, sirrah black, now do you teach him to walk with the verdadero gesto, gracia and gravidad of a true Castilian.

MONSIEUR. Must I have my dancing-master too? Come, little master, then, lead on.

BLACK *struts about the stage. The* MONSIEUR *follows him, imitating awkwardly all he does.*

DON DIEGO. Malo, malo! With your hat on your pole, as if it hung upon a pin! The French and English wear their hats as if their horns would not suffer 'em to come over their foreheads, voto.

MONSIEUR. 'Tis true. There are some well-bred gentlemen have so much reverence for their peruke that they would refuse to be grandees of your Spain, for fear of putting on their hats, I vow and swear.

DON DIEGO. Come, black, teach him now to make a Spanish leg.

MONSIEUR. Ha, ha, ha, your Spanish leg is an English curtsey, I vow and swear, hah, hah, ha.

DON DIEGO. Well, the hood does not make the monk; the ass was an ass still, though he had the lion's skin on. This will be a light French fool in spite of the grave Spanish habit, look you. But, black, do what you can, make the most of him, walk him about.

PRUE *goes to the door and returns.*

PRUE. Here are the people, sir, you sent to speak with about provisions for the wedding and here are your clothes brought home too, mistress.

164–5 *verdadero gesto, gracia and gravidad*: true countenance, grace and seriousness.
168 *pole*: head.
169 *pin*: peg.
170 *horns*: (*a*) the swept-up horns of the wig (*b*) cuckold's horns.

DON DIEGO. Well, I come. Black, do what you can with him; walk him about.

MONSIEUR. Indeed, uncle, if I were as you, I would not have the grave Spanish habit so travestied. I shall disgrace it and my little black master too, I vow and swear.

DON DIEGO. Learn, learn of him, improve yourself by him. And do you walk him, walk him about soundly. Come, sister and daughter, I must have your judgements, though I shall not need 'em, look you. Walk him, see you walk him.

Exeunt DON DIEGO, HIPPOLITA *and* CAUTION.

MONSIEUR. Jernie, he does not only make a Spaniard of me but a Spanish gennet, in giving me to his lackey to walk. But come along, little master.

The BLACK *instructs the* MONSIEUR *on one side of the stage,* PRUE *standing on the other.*

PRUE. (*aside*) O the unfortunate condition of us poor chambermaids, who have all the carking and caring, the watching and sitting up, the trouble and danger of our mistresses' intrigues, whilst they go away with all the pleasure! And if they can get their man in a corner, 'tis well enough; they ne'er think of the poor watchful chambermaid who sits knocking her heels in the cold, for want of better exercise, in some melancholy lobby or entry, when she could employ her time every whit as well as her mistress, for all her quality, if she were but put to't.

BLACK. Hold up your head, hold up your head, sir. A stooping Spaniard, malo!

MONSIEUR. True, a true Spaniard scorns to look upon the ground.

PRUE. (*aside*) We can shift for our mistresses and not for ourselves. Mine has got a handsome proper young man and is just going to make the most of him, whilst I must be left in the lurch here with a couple of ugly little blackamoor boys in bonnets and an old withered Spanish eunuch – not a servant else in the house, nor have I hopes of any comfortable society at all.

BLACK. Now let me see you make your visit-leg thus.

---

203 *carking*: anxious toil.
221 *bonnets*: servants' caps.

MONSIEUR. Auh, tête non, ha, ha, ha.

BLACK. What, a Spaniard and laugh aloud! No, if you laugh, thus only – [*laughs*] so. Now your salutation in the street as you pass by your acquaintance, look you, thus. If to a woman, thus, putting your hat upon your heart. If to a man, thus, with a nod, so – but frown a little more, frown. But if to a woman you would be very ceremonious to, thus – so – your neck nearer your shoulder, so. Now if you would speak contemptibly of any man or thing, do thus with your head – so – and shrug up your shoulders, till they hide your ears.

MONSIEUR *imitating the* BLACK.

Now walk again.

The BLACK *and the* MONSIEUR *walk off the stage.*

PRUE. All my hopes are in that coxcomb there. I must take up with my mistress's leavings, though we chambermaids are wont to be beforehand with them. But he is the dullest, modestest fool – for a Frenchified fool – as ever I saw, for nobody could be more coming to him than I have been (though I say it) and yet I am ne'er the nearer. I have stolen away his handkerchief and told him of it and yet he would never so much as struggle with me to get it again. I have pulled off his peruke, untied his ribbons and have been very bold with him, yet he would never be so with me. Nay, I have pinched him, punched him and tickled him and yet he would never do the like for me.

The BLACK *and* MONSIEUR *return.*

BLACK. Nay, thus, thus, sir.

PRUE. [*aside*] And to make my person more acceptable to him I have used art, as they say, for, every night since he came, I have worn the forehead-piece of beeswax and bog's grease and every morning washed with buttermilk and wild tansy and have put on every day, for his only sake, my Sunday Bow-dye stockings and

---

246 *get it*: get Q1.

255 *forehead-piece*: piece of cloth worn on the face overnight to improve the complexion; Prue's choice of cosmetic substances is by no means the most bizarre.

258 *Bow-dye*: scarlet, from the dye made at Bow.

have new chalked my shoes and's constantly as the morning came. Nay, I have taken an occasion to garter my stockings before him, as if unawares of him, for a good leg and foot with good shoes and stockings are very provoking, as they say. But the devil would he be provoked! But I must think of a way.

BLACK. Thus, thus.

MONSIEUR. What, so? Well, well, I have lessons enow for this time. Little master, I will have no more lest the multiplicity of 'em make me forget 'em, da. Prue, art thou there and so pensive? What art thou thinking of?

PRUE. Indeed I am ashamed to tell your worship.

MONSIEUR. What, ashamed! Wert thou thinking then of my beastliness? Ha, ha, ha.

PRUE. Nay, then, I am forced to tell your worship in my own vindication.

MONSIEUR. Come then.

PRUE. But indeed your worship – I'm ashamed, that I am, though it was nothing but of a dream I had of your sweet worship last night.

MONSIEUR. Of my sweet worship! I warrant it was a sweet dream then. What was it? Ha, ha, ha.

PRUE. Nay, indeed, I have told your worship enough already – you may guess the rest.

MONSIEUR. I cannot guess, ha, ha, ha. What should it be? Prithee, let's know the rest.

PRUE. Would you have me so impudent?

MONSIEUR. Impudent! Ha, ha, ha, nay, prithee tell me, for I can't guess, da.

PRUE. Nay, 'tis always so; for want of the men's guessing the poor women are forced to be impudent. But I am still ashamed.

MONSIEUR. I will know it. Speak.

PRUE. Why, then, methoughts last night you came up into my chamber in your shirt, when I was in bed, and that you might easily do, for I have ne'er a lock to my door. Now I warrant I am as red as my petticoat.

MONSIEUR. No, thou'rt as yellow as e'er thou wert.

PRUE. Yellow, sir!

MONSIEUR. Ay, ay. But let's hear the dream out.

PRUE. Why, can't you guess the rest now?

MONSIEUR. No, not I, I vow and swear. Come, let's hear.

PRUE. But can't you guess in earnest?

MONSIEUR. Not I, the devil eat me.

PRUE. Not guess yet! Why then, methoughts you came to bed to me! Now am I as red as my petticoat again.

MONSIEUR. Ha, ha, ha. Well and what then? Ha, ha, ha.

PRUE. Nay, now I know by your worship's laughing you guess what you did. I'm sure I cried out and waked all in tears with these words in my mouth, 'You have undone me, you have undone me, your worship has undone me!'.

MONSIEUR. Hah, ha, ha. But you waked and found it was but a dream.

PRUE. Indeed it was so lively I know not whether 'twas a dream or no. But if you were not there I'll undertake you may come when you will and do anything to me you will – I sleep so fast.

MONSIEUR. No, no, I don't believe that.

PRUE. Indeed you may, your worship.

MONSIEUR. It cannot be.

PRUE. (*aside*) Insensible beast! He will not understand me yet and one would think I speak plain enough.

MONSIEUR. Well, but Prue, what art thou thinking of?

PRUE. Of the dream, whether it were a dream or no.

MONSIEUR. 'Twas a dream, I warrant thee.

PRUE. Was it? I am hugeous glad it was a dream.

MONSIEUR. Ay, ay, it was a dream and I am hugeous glad it was a dream too.

PRUE. But now I have told your worship my door hath neither lock nor latch to it, if you should be so naughty as to come one night and prove the dream true – I am so afraid on't.

MONSIEUR. Ne'er fear it. Dreams go by the contraries.

PRUE. Then by that I should come into your worship's chamber and come to bed to your worship. Now am I as red as my petticoat again, I warrant.

MONSIEUR. No, thou art no redder than a brick unburnt, Prue.

PRUE. But if I should do such a trick in my sleep, your worship would not censure a poor harmless maid, I hope, for I am apt to walk in my sleep.

MONSIEUR. Well then, Prue, because thou shalt not shame thyself, poor wretch, I'll be sure to lock my door every night fast.

PRUE. [*aside*] So, so, this way I find will not do. I must come roundly and downright to the business, like other women, or –

Enter GERRARD.

MONSIEUR. O, the dancing-master!

PRUE. Dear sir, I have something to say to you in your ear which I am ashamed to speak aloud.

MONSIEUR. Another time, another time, Prue, but now go call your mistress to her dancing-master. Go, go.

PRUE. Nay, pray hear me, sir, first.

MONSIEUR. Another time, another time, Prue. Prithee be gone.

PRUE. Nay, I beseech your worship hear me.

MONSIEUR. No, prithee be gone.

PRUE. [*aside*] Nay, I am e'en well enough served for not speaking my mind when I had an opportunity. Well, I must be playing the modest woman, forsooth. A woman's hypocrisy in this case does only deceive herself. *Exit* PRUE.

MONSIEUR. O, the brave dancing-master, the fine dancing-master, your servant, your servant.

GERRARD. Your servant, sir, I protest I did not know you at first. (*Aside*) I am afraid this fool should spoil all, notwithstanding Hippolita's care and management. Yet I ought to trust her. But a secret is more safe with a treacherous knave than a talkative fool.

MONSIEUR. Come, sir, you must know a little brother dancing-master of yours – walking-master I should have said, for he teaches me to walk and make legs by the by. Pray know him, sir. Salute him, sir. You Christian dancing-masters are so proud.

GERRARD. But, Monsieur, what strange metamorphosis is this? You look like a Spaniard and talk like an Englishman again, which I thought had been impossible.

MONSIEUR. Nothing impossible to love. I must do't or lose my mistress, your pretty scholar, for 'tis I am to have her. You may remember I told you she was to be married to a great man, a man of honour and quality.

GERRARD. But does she enjoin you to this severe penance? Such I am sure it is to you.

MONSIEUR. (*draws him aside*) No, no, 'tis by the compulsion of the starched fop her father, who is so arrant a Spaniard he would kill you and his daughter if he knew who you were, therefore have a special care to dissemble well.

GERRARD. I warrant you.

MONSIEUR. Dear Gerrard. – Go, little master, and call my cousin. Tell her her dancing-master is here.

Exit BLACK.

I say, dear Gerrard, faith, I'm obliged to you for the trouble you have had. When I sent you I intended a jest indeed but did not think it would have been so dangerous a jest. Therefore pray forgive me.

GERRARD. I do, do heartily forgive you.

MONSIEUR. But can you forgive me for sending you, at first, like a fool as I was? 'Twas ill done of me. Can you forgive me?

GERRARD. Yes, yes, I do forgive you.

MONSIEUR. Well, thou art a generous man, I vow and swear, to come and take upon you this trouble, danger and shame, to be thought a paltry dancing-master and all this to preserve a lady's honour and life, who intended to abuse you. But I take the obligation upon me.

GERRARD. Pish, pish, you are not obliged to me at all.

MONSIEUR. Faith but I am strangely obliged to you.

GERRARD. Faith but you are not.

MONSIEUR. I vow and swear but I am.

GERRARD. I swear you are not.

MONSIEUR. Nay, thou art so generous a dancing-master, ha, ha, ha.

Enter DON DIEGO, HIPPOLITA, CAUTION *and* PRUE.

DON DIEGO. You shall not come in, sister.

CAUTION. I will come in.

DON DIEGO. You will not be civil.

CAUTION. I'm sure they will not be civil if I do not come in. I must, I will.

DON DIEGO. Well, honest friend, you are very punctual, which is a rare virtue in a dancing-master. I take notice of it and will remember it. I will, look you.

MONSIEUR. (*aside*) So, silly, damned, politic Spanish uncle, ha, ha, ha.

GERRARD. My fine scholar, sir, there, shall never have reason, as I told you, sir, to say I am not a punctual man, for I am more her servant than to any scholar I ever had.

MONSIEUR. (*aside*) Well said, i'faith, thou dost make a pretty fool of him, I vow and swear. But I wonder people can be made such fools of, ha, ha, ha.

HIPPOLITA. Well, master, I thank you and I hope I shall be a grateful kind scholar to you.

MONSIEUR. (*aside*) Ha, ha, ha, cunning little jilt, what a fool she makes of him too. I wonder people can be made such fools of, I vow and swear, ha, ha, ha.

HIPPOLITA. Indeed it shall go hard but I'll be a grateful kind scholar to you.

CAUTION. As kind as ever your mother was to your father, I warrant.

DON DIEGO. How! Again with your senseless suspicions!

MONSIEUR. Pish, pish, aunt. (*Aside*) Ha, ha, ha, she's a fool another way. She thinks she loves him, ha, ha, ha. Lord, that people should be such fools!

CAUTION. Come, come, I cannot but speak. I tell you beware in time, for he is no dancing-master but some debauched person who will mump you of your daughter.

DON DIEGO. Will you be wiser than I still? Mump me of my daughter! I would I could see anyone mump me of my daughter.

CAUTION. And mump you of your mistress too, young Spaniard.

MONSIEUR. (*to* CAUTION) Ha, ha, ha, will you be wiser than I too, voto? Mump me of my mistress! I would I could see anyone mump me of my mistress. (*Aside to* GERRARD and HIPPOLITA) I am afraid this damned old aunt should discover us, I vow and swear. Be careful and resolute.

CAUTION. He, he does not go about his business like a dancing-master. He'll ne'er teach her to dance but he'll teach her no goodness soon enough, I warrant. He a dancing-master!

MONSIEUR. Ay, the devil eat me if he be not the best dancing-master in England now. (*Aside to* GERRARD *and* HIPPOLITA) Was not that well said, cousin? Was

---

446 *mump*: cheat.

it not? For he's a gentleman dancing-master, you know.

DON DIEGO. You know him, cousin, very well, cousin? You sent him to my daughter?

MONSIEUR. Yes, yes, uncle, know him. (*Aside*) We'll ne'er be discovered, I warrant, ha, ha, ha.

CAUTION. But will you be made a fool of too?

MONSIEUR. Ay, ay, aunt, ne'er trouble yourself.

DON DIEGO. Come, friend, about your business, about with my daughter.

HIPPOLITA. Nay, pray, father, be pleased to go out a little and let us but practise a while and then you shall see me dance the whole dance to the violin.

DON DIEGO. Tittle-tattle, more fooling still! Did not you say when your master was here last I should see you dance to the violin when he came again?

HIPPOLITA. So I did, father, but let me practise a little first before that I may be perfect. Besides, my aunt is here and she will put me out. You know I cannot dance before her.

DON DEIGO. Fiddle-faddle.

MONSIEUR. (*aside*) They're afraid to be discovered by Gerrard's bungling, I see. – Come, come, uncle, turn out. Let 'em practise.

DON DIEGO. I won't, voto a St Jago. What a fooling's here?

MONSIEUR. Come, come, let 'em practise. Turn out, turn out, uncle.

DON DIEGO. Why, can't she practise it before me?

MONSIEUR. Come, dancers and singers are sometimes humoursome. Besides, 'twill be more grateful to you to see it danced all at once to the violin. Come, turn out, turn out, I say.

DON DIEGO. What a fooling's here still amongst you, voto!

MONSIEUR. So there he is with you, voto. Turn out, turn out. I vow and swear you shall turn out. (*Takes him by the shoulder*)

DON DIEGO. Well, shall I see her dance it to the violin at last?

GERRARD. Yes, yes, sir. What do you think I teach her for?

Exit DON DIEGO.

MONSIEUR. Go, go, turn out, and you too, aunt.

CAUTION. Seriously, nephew, I shall not budge. Royally I shall not.

MONSIEUR. Royally you must, aunt. Come.

CAUTION. Pray hear me, nephew.

MONSIEUR. I will not hear you.

CAUTION. 'Tis for your sake I stay. I must not suffer you to be wronged.

MONSIEUR. Come, no wheedling, aunt. Come away.

CAUTION. That slippery fellow will do't.

MONSIEUR. Let him do't.

CAUTION. Indeed he will do't; royally he will.

MONSIEUR. Well let him do't, royally.

CAUTION. He will wrong you.

MONSIEUR. Well, let him, I say. I have a mind to be wronged. What's that to you? I will be wronged, if you go thereto, I vow and swear.

CAUTION. You shall not be wronged.

MONSIEUR. I will.

CAUTION. You shall not.

DON DIEGO *returns.*

DON DIEGO. What's the matter? Won't she be ruled? Come, come away. You shall not disturb 'em.

DON DIEGO *and* MONSIEUR *thrust* CAUTION *out.*

CAUTION. D'ee see how they laugh at you both? Well, go to, the troth-telling Trojan gentlewoman of old was ne'er believed till the town was taken, rummaged and ransacked, even, even so.

MONSIEUR. Hah, hah, ha, turn out.

Exit CAUTION [*and* DON DIEGO].

Lord, that people should be such arrant cuddens, ha, ha, ha. But I may stay, may I not?

HIPPOLITA. No, no, I'd have you go out and hold the door, cousin, or else my father will come in again before his time.

MONSIEUR. I will, I will then, sweet cousin. 'Twas well thought on, that was well thought on indeed for me to hold the door.

---

508 *royally*: positively.

530 *the troth-telling Trojan gentlewoman*: Cassandra, fated to prophesy accurately but never to be believed.

533 s.d. after line 532 Q1.

534 *cuddens*: dolts.

HIPPOLITA. But be sure you keep him out, cousin, till we knock.

MONSIEUR. I warrant you, cousin. Lord, that people should be made such fools of, ha, ha, ha.

Exit MONSIEUR.

GERRARD. So, so, to make him hold the door while I steal his mistress is not unpleasant.

HIPPOLITA. Ay, but would you do so ill a thing, so treacherous a thing? Faith, 'tis not well.

GERRARD. Faith, I can't help it, since 'tis for your sake. Come, sweetest, is not this our way into the gallery?

HIPPOLITA. Yes, but it goes against my conscience to be accessory to so ill a thing. You say you do it for my sake?

GERRARD. Alas, poor miss! 'Tis not against your conscience but against your modesty, you think, to do it frankly.

HIPPOLITA. Nay, if it be against my modesty too, I can't do it indeed.

GERRARD. Come, come, miss, let us make haste. All's ready.

HIPPOLITA. Nay, faith, I can't satisfy my scruple.

GERRARD. Come, dearest, this is not a time for scruples nor modesty. Modesty between lovers is as impertinent as ceremony between friends and modesty is now as unseasonable as on the wedding night. Come away, my dearest.

HIPPOLITA. Whither?

GERRARD. Nay, sure, we have lost too much time already. Is that a proper question now? If you would know come along, for I have all ready.

HIPPOLITA. But I am not ready.

GERRARD. Truly, miss, we shall have your father come in upon us and prevent us again as he did in the morning.

HIPPOLITA. 'Twas well for me he did, for, on my conscience, if he had not come in I had gone clear away with you when I was in the humour.

GERRARD. Come, dearest, you would frighten me as if you were not yet in the same humour. Come, come away. The coach and six is ready.

HIPPOLITA. 'Tis too late to take the air and I am not ready.

GERRARD. You were ready in the morning.

HIPPOLITA. Ay, so I was.

GERRARD. Come, come, miss. Indeed the jest begins to be none.

HIPPOLITA. What, I warrant you think me in jest then?

GERRARD. In jest, certainly, but it begins to be troublesome.

HIPPOLITA. But, sir, you could believe I was in earnest in the morning when I but seemed to be ready to go with you and why won't you believe me now, when I declare to the contrary? I take it unkindly that the longer I am acquainted with you you should have the less confidence in me.

GERRARD. For heaven's sake, miss, lose no more time thus. Your father will come in upon us, as he did –

HIPPOLITA. Let him, if he will.

GERRARD. He'll hinder our design.

HIPPOLITA. No, he will not, for mine is to stay here now.

GERRARD. Are you in earnest?

HIPPOLITA. You'll find it so.

GERRARD. How! Why, you confessed but now you would have gone with me in the morning.

HIPPOLITA. I was in the humour then.

GERRARD. And I hope you are in the same still. You cannot change so soon.

HIPPOLITA. Why, is it not a whole day ago?

GERRARD. What, are you not a day in the same humour?

HIPPOLITA. Lord, that you who know the town, they say, should think any woman could be a whole day together in an humour! Ha, ha, ha.

GERRARD. Hey! This begins to be pleasant. What, won't you go with me then after all?

HIPPOLITA. No, indeed, sir, I desire to be excused.

GERRARD. Then you have abused me all this while?

HIPPOLITA. It may be so.

GERRARD. Could all that so natural innocency be dissembled? Faith, it could not, dearest miss.

HIPPOLITA. Faith, it was, dear master.

GERRARD. Was it, faith?

HIPPOLITA. Methinks you might believe me without an oath. You saw I could dissemble with my father – why should you think I could not with you?

GERRARD. So young a wheedle?

HIPPOLITA. Ay, a mere damned jade I am.

GERRARD. And I have been abused, you say?

HIPPOLITA. 'Tis well you can believe it at last.

GERRARD. And I must never hope for you?

HIPPOLITA. Would you have me abuse you again?

GERRARD. Then you will not go with me?

HIPPOLITA. No, but for your comfort your loss will not be great and, that you may not resent it, for once I'll be ingenuous and disabuse you. I am no heiress, as I told you, to twelve hundred pound a year. I was only a lying jade then. Now you will part with me willingly I doubt not.

GERRARD. (*sighs*) I wish I could.

HIPPOLITA. Come, now I find 'tis your turn to dissemble. But men use to dissemble for money – will you dissemble for nothing?

GERRARD. 'Tis too late for me to dissemble.

HIPPOLITA. Don't you dissemble, faith?

GERRARD. Nay, this is too cruel.

HIPPOLITA. What, would you take me without the twelve hundred pound a year? Would you be such a fool as to steal a woman with nothing?

GERRARD. I'll convince you, for you shall go with me and since you are twelve hundred pound a year the lighter you'll be the easier carried away.

He takes her in his arms; she struggles.

PRUE. What, he takes her away against her will. I find I must knock for my master then. (*She knocks*)

Enter DON DIEGO *and* MRS CAUTION.

HIPPOLITA. My father, my father is here.

GERRARD. Prevented again! (GERRARD *sets her down again*)

DON DIEGO. What, you have done, I hope, now, friend, for good and all?

GERRARD. Yes, yes, we have done for good and all indeed.

DON DIEGO. How now! You seem to be out of humour, friend.

GERRARD. Yes, so I am. I can't help it.

CAUTION. He's a dissembler in his very throat, brother.

HIPPOLITA. (*aside to* GERRARD) Pray do not carry things so as to discover yourself, if it be but for my sake, good master.

GERRARD. (*aside*) She is grown impudent.

CAUTION. See, see, they whisper, brother, to steal a kiss under a whisper! O the harlotry!

DON DIEGO. What's the matter, friend?

HIPPOLITA. (*to* GERRARD) I say, for my sake, be in humour and do not discover yourself but be as patient as a dancing-master still.

DON DIEGO. What, she is whispering to him indeed! What's the matter? I will know it, friend, look you.

GERRARD. Will you know it?

DON DIEGO. Yes, I will know it.

GERRARD. Why, if you will know it, then she would not do as I would have her and whispered me to desire me not to discover it to you.

DON DIEGO. What, hussy, would you not do as he'd have you? I'll make you do as he'd have you.

GERRARD. I wish you would.

CAUTION. 'Tis a lie. She'll do all he'll have her do and more too, to my knowledge.

DON DIEGO. Come, tell me what 'twas then she would not do. Come to it, hussy, or – Come, take her by the hand, friend. Come, begin. Let's see if she will not do anything now I am here.

HIPPOLITA. Come, pray be in humour, master.

GERRARD. I cannot dissemble like you.

DON DIEGO. What, she can't dissemble already, can she?

CAUTION. Yes but she can, but 'tis with you she dissembles, for they are not fallen out, as we think, for I'll be sworn I saw her just now give him the languishing eye, as they call it, that is, the whiting's eye, of old called the sheep's eye. I'll be sworn I saw it with these two eyes, that I did.

HIPPOLITA. (*aside to* GERRARD) You'll betray us. Have a care, good master.

GERRARD. Hold your peace, I say, silly woman.

DON DIEGO. But does she dissemble already? How do you mean?

GERRARD. She pretends she can't do what she should do and that she is not in humour – the common excuse of women for not doing what they should do.

DON DIEGO. Come, I'll put her in humour. Dance, I say. Come, about with her, master.

GERRARD. (*aside*) I am in a pretty humour to dance. (*To* HIPPOLITA) I cannot fool any longer since you have fooled me.

HIPPOLITA. [*aside to* GERRARD] You would not be so ungenerous as to betray the woman that hated you. I do not do that yet. For heaven's sake, for this once be more obedient to my desires than your passion.

DON DIEGO. What, is she humoursome still? But methinks you look yourself as if you were in an ill humour. But about with her.

GERRARD. I am in no good dancing humour indeed.

Enter MONSIEUR.

MONSIEUR. Well, how goes the dancing forward? What, my aunt here to disturb 'em again.

DON DIEGO. Come, come.

GERRARD *leads her about.*

CAUTION. I say stand off. Thou shalt not come near. Avoid, Satan, as they say.

DON DIEGO. Nay then, we shall have it. Nephew, hold her a little, that she may not disturb 'em. Come, now away with her.

GERRARD. One, two and a coupée. (*Aside*) Fooled and abused!

CAUTION. Wilt thou lay violent hands upon thy own natural aunt, wretch?

The MONSIEUR *holding* CAUTION.

DON DIEGO. Come, about with her.

GERRARD. One, two, three, four and turn round. (*Aside*) By such a piece of innocency!

CAUTION. Dost thou see, fool, how he squeezes her hand?

MONSIEUR. That won't do, aunt.

HIPPOLITA. Pray, master, have patience and let's mind our business.

DON DIEGO. Why did you anger him then, hussy, look you?

CAUTION. Do you see how she smiles in his face and squeezes his hand now?

MONSIEUR. Your servant, aunt, that won't do, I say.

HIPPOLITA. Have patience, master.

GERRARD. (*aside*) I am become her sport. – One, two, three, death, hell and the devil.

DON DIEGO. Ay, they are three indeed. But pray have patience.

CAUTION. Do you see how she leers upon him and clings to him? Can you suffer it?

MONSIEUR. Ay, ay.

GERRARD. One, two and a slur. Can you be so unconcerned after all?

DON DIEGO. What, is she unconcerned? Hussy, mind your business.

GERRARD. One, two, three and turn round. One, two, fall back, hell and damnation.

DON DIEGO. Ay, people fall back indeed into hell and damnation, heaven knows.

GERRARD. One, two, three and your honour. I can fool no longer.

CAUTION. Nor will I be withheld any longer like a poor hen in her pen while the kite is carrying away her chicken before her face.

DON DIEGO. What have you done? Well then, let's see her dance it now to the violin.

MONSIEUR. Ay, ay, let's see her dance it to the violin.

GERRARD. Another time, another time.

DON DIEGO. Don't you believe that, friend. These dancing-masters make no bones of breaking their words. Did not you promise just now I should see her dance it to the violin? And that I will too, before I stir.

GERRARD. Let Monsieur play then while I dance with her. She can't dance alone.

MONSIEUR. I can't play at all. I'm but a learner. But if you'll play, I'll dance with her.

GERRARD. I can't play neither.

DON DIEGO. What, a dancing-master and not play!

CAUTION. Ay, you see what a dancing-master he is. 'Tis as I told you, I warrant. A dancing-master and not play upon the fiddle!

DON DIEGO. How!

HIPPOLITA. (*aside to* GERRARD) O you have betrayed us all! If you confess that you undo us for ever.

---

756 *slur*: glide.

GERRARD. [*aside to* HIPPOLITA] I cannot play. What would you have me say?

MONSIEUR. [*aside*] I vow and swear, we are all undone if you cannot play.

DON DIEGO. What, are you a dancing-master and cannot play? Umph!

HIPPOLITA. He is only out of humour, sir. (*She offers* GERRARD *the violin*) Here, master. I know you will play for me yet, for he has an excellent hand.

MONSIEUR. Ay, that he has – (*Aside*) at giving a box on the ear.

DON DIEGO. Why does he not play then?

HIPPOLITA. (*gives* GERRARD *the violin*) Here, master. Pray play for my sake.

GERRARD. [*aside*] What would you have me do with it? I cannot play a stroke.

HIPPOLITA. (*apart to* GERRARD) No, stay then. Seem to tune it and break the strings.

GERRARD. Come then. (*Aside*) Next to the devil's the invention of women. They'll no more want an excuse to cheat a father with than an opportunity to abuse a husband. – But what do you give me such a damned fiddle with rotten strings for? (*Winds up the strings till they break and throws the violin on the ground*)

DON DIEGO. Hey-day, the dancing-master is frantic.

MONSIEUR. [*aside*] Ha, ha, ha, that people should be made such fools of!

CAUTION. He broke the strings on purpose, because he could not play. You are blind, brother.

DON DIEGO. What, will you see further than I, look you?

HIPPOLITA. But pray, master, why in such haste?

GERRARD. Because you have done with me.

DON DIEGO. But don't you intend to come tomorrow again?

GERRARD. Your daughter does not desire it.

DON DIEGO. No matter. I do. I must be your paymaster, I'm sure. I would have you come betimes too, not only to make her perfect but, since you have so good a hand upon the violin, to play your part with half a dozen of musicians more whom I would have you bring with you, for we will have a very merry wedding, though a very private one. You'll be sure to come?

GERRARD. Your daughter does not desire it.

DON DIEGO. Come, come, baggage, you shall desire it of him; he is your master.

HIPPOLITA. My father will have me desire it of you, it seems.

GERRARD. But you'll make a fool of me again if I should come, would you not?

HIPPOLITA. If I should tell you so you'd be sure not to come.

DON DIEGO. Come, come, she shall not make a fool of you, upon my word. I'll secure you, she shall do what you'll have her.

MONSIEUR. (*aside*) Ha, ha, ha, so, so, silly don.

GERRARD. But, madam, will you have me come?

HIPPOLITA. I'd have you to know, for my part, I care not whether you come or no. There are other dancing-masters to be had. It is my father's request to you. All that I have to say to you is a little good advice which, because I will not shame you, I'll give you in private. (*Whispers* GERRARD)

CAUTION. What, will you let her whisper with him too?

DON DIEGO. Nay, if you find fault with it, they shall whisper. Though I did not like it before, I'll ha' nobody wiser than myself. But do you think if 'twere any hurt she would whisper it to him before us?

CAUTION. If it be no hurt, why does she not speak aloud?

DON DIEGO. Because she says she will not put the man out of countenance.

CAUTION. Hey-day, put a dancing-master out of countenance!

DON DIEGO. You say he is no dancing-master.

CAUTION. Yes, for his impudence he may be a dancing-master.

DON DIEGO. Well, well, let her whisper before me as much as she will tonight since she is to be married tomorrow, especially since her husband that shall be stands by consenting too.

MONSIEUR. Ay, ay, let 'em whisper (as you say) as much as they will before we marry. (*Aside*) She's making more sport with him, I warrant. But I wonder how people can be fooled so, ha, ha, ha.

DON DIEGO. Well, a penny for the secret, daughter.

HIPPOLITA. Indeed, father, you shall have it for nothing tomorrow.

DON DIEGO. Well, friend, you will not fail to come?

GERRARD. No, no, sir. (*Aside*) Yet I am a fool if I do.

DON DIEGO. And be sure you bring the fiddlers with you, as I bid you.

HIPPOLITA. Yes, be sure you bring the fiddlers with you, as I bid you.

CAUTION. So, so, he'll fiddle your daughter out of the house. Must you have the fiddles, with a fiddle-faddle?

MONSIEUR. [*aside*] Lord! That people should be made such fools of, hah, hah!

Exeunt DON DIEGO, HIPPOLITA, MONSIEUR, CAUTION *and* PRUE.

GERRARD. Fortune we sooner may than woman trust;
To her confiding gallant she is just,
But falser woman only him deceives
Who to her tongue and eyes most credit gives. *Exit.*

ACT V

SCENE I

Enter MONSIEUR *and* BLACK *stalking over the stage. To them,* MR GERRARD.

MONSIEUR. Good morrow to thee, noble dancing-master, ha, ha, ha. Your little black brother here, my master, I see, is the more diligent man of the two. But why do you come so late? What, you begin to neglect your scholar, do you? Little black master, con licentia, pray get you out of the room.

Exit BLACK.

What, out of humour, man! A dancing-master should be like his fiddle, always in tune. Come, my cousin has made an ass of thee. What then? I know it.

GERRARD. (*aside*) Does he know it?

MONSIEUR. But prithee don't be angry. 'Twas agreed upon betwixt us before I sent you to make a fool of thee, ha, ha, ha.

GERRARD. Was it so?

MONSIEUR. I knew you would be apt to entertain vain hopes from the summons of a lady but, faith, the design was but to make a fool of thee, as you find.

GERRARD. 'Tis very well.

MONSIEUR. But indeed I did not think the jest would have lasted so long and that my cousin would have made a dancing-master of you, ha, ha, ha.

GERRARD. (*aside*) The fool has reason, I find, and I am the coxcomb while I thought him so.

MONSIEUR. Come, I see you are uneasy and the jest of being a dancing-master grows tedious to you. But have a little patience; the parson is sent for and when once my cousin and I are married my uncle may know who you are.

GERRARD. [*aside*] I am certainly abused.

MONSIEUR *listens.*

MONSIEUR. What do you say?

GERRARD. (*aside*) Merely fooled.

MONSIEUR. Why do you doubt it? Ha, ha, ha.

GERRARD. (*aside*) Can it be?

MONSIEUR. Pish, pish, she told me yesterday as soon as you were gone that she had led you into a fool's paradise and made you believe she would go away with you, ha, ha, ha.

GERRARD. (*aside*) Did she so? I am no longer to doubt it then?

MONSIEUR. Ay, ay, she makes a mere fool of thee, I vow and swear. But don't be concerned; there's hardly a man of a thousand but has been made a fool of by some woman or other. I have been made a fool of myself, man, by the women; I have, I vow and swear, I have.

GERRARD. Well, you have, I believe it, for you are a coxcomb.

MONSIEUR. Lord! You need not be so touchy with one. I tell you but the truth for your good, for, though she does, I would not fool you any longer. But prithee don't be troubled at what can't be helped. Women are made on purpose to fool men. When they are children they fool their fathers and when they have taken leave of their hanging-sleeves they fool their gallants or dancing-masters, ha, ha, ha.

GERRARD. Hark you, sir, to be fooled by a woman, you say, is not to be helped but I will not be fooled by a fool.

MONSIEUR. You show your English breeding now. An English rival is so dull and brutish as not to understand raillery. But what is spoken in your passion I'll take no notice of, for I am your friend and would not have you my rival to make yourself ridiculous. Come, prithee, prithee, don't be so concerned, for, as I was saying, women first fool their fathers, then their gallants, and then their husbands, so that it will be my turn to be fooled too (for your comfort) and when they come to be widows they would fool the devil, I vow and swear. Come, come, dear Gerrard, prithee don't be out of humour and look so sillily.

GERRARD. Prithee do not talk so sillily.

MONSIEUR. Nay, faith, I am resolved to beat you out of this ill humour.

GERRARD. Faith, I am afraid I shall first beat you into an ill humour.

MONSIEUR. Ha, ha, ha. That thou shouldst be gulled so by a little gipsy who left off her bib but yesterday. Faith, I can't but laugh at thee.

GERRARD. Faith, then I shall make your mirth (as being too violent) conclude in some little misfortune to you. The fool begins to be tyrannical.

MONSIEUR. Ha, ha, ha, poor angry dancing-master. Prithee match my Spanish pumps and legs with one of your best and newest sarabands. Ha, ha, ha, come.

GERRARD. I will match your Spanish ear thus, sir, and make you dance thus. (*Strikes and kicks him*)

MONSIEUR. How! Sa, sa, sa. Then I'll make you dance thus.

MONSIEUR *draws his sword and runs at him but,* GERRARD *drawing, he retires.*

Hold, hold a little. (*Aside*) A desperate, disappointed lover will cut his own throat; then, sure, he will make nothing of cutting his rival's throat.

---

54 *hanging-sleeves*: loose open sleeves, worn only by children.

GERRARD. Consideration is an enemy to fighting. If you have a mind to revenge yourself your sword's in your hand.

MONSIEUR. Pray, sir, hold your peace. I'll ne'er take my rival's counsel, be't what 'twill. I know what you would be at. You are disappointed of your mistress and could hang yourself and therefore will not fear hanging. But I am a successful lover and need neither hang for you nor my mistress. Nay, if I should kill you I know I should do you a kindness, therefore e'en live to die daily with envy of my happiness. But if you will needs die, kill yourself and be damned for me, I vow and swear.

GERRARD. But won't you fight for your mistress?

MONSIEUR. I tell you, you shall not have the honour to be killed for her. Besides, I will not be hit in the teeth by her as long as I live with the great love you had for her. Women speak well of their dead husbands – what will they do of their dead gallants?

GERRARD. But if you will not fight for her you shall dance for her, since you desired me to teach you to dance too. I'll teach you to dance thus.

Strikes his sword at his legs. MONSIEUR *leaps.*

MONSIEUR. Nay, if it be for the sake of my mistress, there's nothing I will refuse to do.

GERRARD. Nay, you must dance on.

MONSIEUR. Ay, ay, for my mistress and sing too. La, la, la, ra, la.

Enter HIPPOLITA *and* PRUE.

HIPPOLITA. What, swords drawn betwixt you too? What's the matter?

MONSIEUR. (*aside*) Is she here? – Come, put up your sword. You see this is no place for us. But the devil eat me if you shall not eat my sword but –

HIPPOLITA. What's the matter, cousin?

MONSIEUR. Nothing, nothing, cousin. But your presence is a sanctuary for my greatest enemy or else, tête non.

HIPPOLITA. (*to* GERRARD) What, you have not hurt my cousin, sir, I hope?

GERRARD. (*aside*) How she's concerned for him! Nay, then I need not doubt; my fears are true.

MONSIEUR. What was that you said, cousin? Hurt me,

ha, ha, ha, hurt me! If any man hurt me he must do it basely. He shall ne'er do it when my sword's drawn, sa, sa, sa.

HIPPOLITA. Because you will ne'er draw your sword perhaps.

MONSIEUR. (*aside*) Scurvily guessed. – You ladies may say anything. But, cousin, pray do not talk of swords and fighting. Meddle with your guitar and talk of dancing with your dancing-master there, ha, ha, ha.

HIPPOLITA. But I am afraid you have hurt my master, cousin. He says nothing. Can he draw his breath?

MONSIEUR. No, 'tis you have hurt your master, cousin, in the very heart, cousin, and therefore he would hurt me, for love is a disease makes people as malicious as the plague does.

HIPPOLITA. Indeed, poor master, something does ail you.

MONSIEUR. Nay, nay, cousin, faith, don't abuse him any longer. He's an honest gentleman and has been long of my acquaintance and a man of tolerable sense to take him out of his love. But prithee, cousin, don't drive the jest too far for my sake.

GERRARD. He counsels you well, pleasant, cunning, jilting miss for his sake, for, if I am your divertisement, it shall be at his cost, since he's your gallant in favour.

HIPPOLITA. I don't understand you.

MONSIEUR. (*aside*) But I do, a pox take him, and the custom that so orders it, forsooth: that, if a lady abuse or affront a man, presently the gallant must be beaten; nay, what's more unreasonable, if a woman abuse her husband, the poor cuckold must bear the shame as well as the injury.

HIPPOLITA. But what's the matter, master? What was it you said?

GERRARD. I say, pleasant, cunning, jilting lady, though you make him a cuckold it will not be revenge enough for me upon him for marrying you.

HIPPOLITA. How, my surly, huffing, jealous, senseless, saucy master?

MONSIEUR. Nay, nay, faith, give losers leave to speak, losers of mistresses especially, ha, ha, ha. Besides, your anger is too great a favour for him. I scorn to honour him with mine, you see.

HIPPOLITA. I tell you, my saucy master, my cousin shall never be made that monstrous thing you mention by me.

MONSIEUR. Thank you, I vow and swear, cousin. No, no, I never thought I should.

GERRARD. Sure, you marry him by the sage maxim of your sex, which is, 'wittols make the best husbands', that is, cuckolds.

HIPPOLITA. Indeed, master, whatsoever you think, I would sooner choose you for that purpose than him.

MONSIEUR. Ha, ha, ha, there she was with him, i'faith. I thank you for that, cousin, I vow and swear.

HIPPOLITA. Nay, he shall thank me for that too. But how came you two to quarrel? I thought, cousin, you had more wit than to quarrel or more kindness for me than to quarrel here. What if my father, hearing the bustle, should have come in? He would soon have discovered our false dancing-master (for passion unmasks every man) and then the result of your quarrel had been my ruin.

MONSIEUR. Nay, you had both felt his desperate, deadly, daunting dagger. There are your d's for you.

HIPPOLITA. Go, go presently therefore and hinder my father from coming in, whilst I put my master into a better humour, that we may not be discovered, to the prevention of our wedding or worse, when he comes. Go, go.

MONSIEUR. Well, well, I will, cousin.

HIPPOLITA. Be sure you let him not come in this good while.

MONSIEUR. No, no, I warrant you. (MONSIEUR *goes out and returns*) But if he should come before I would have him, I'll come before him and cough and hawk soundly, that you may not be surprised. Won't that do well, cousin?

HIPPOLITA. Very well. Pray be gone.

Exit MONSIEUR.

Well, master, since I find you are quarrelsome and melancholy and would have taken me away without a portion – three infallible signs of a true lover – faith,

---

209 *hawk*: clear the throat.

here's my hand now in earnest, to lead me a dance as long as I live.

GERRARD. How's this? You surprise me as much as when first I found so much beauty and wit in company with so much innocency. But, dearest, I would be assured of what you say and yet dare not ask the question. You – h – do not abuse me again. You – h – will fool me no more, sure.

HIPPOLITA. Yes but I will, sure.

GERRARD. How! Nay, I was afraid on't.

HIPPOLITA. For I say you are to be my husband and you say husbands must be wittols and some strange things to boot.

GERRARD. Well, I will take my fortune.

HIPPOLITA. But have a care, rash man.

GERRARD. I will venture.

HIPPOLITA. At your peril. Remember I wished you to have a care. Forewarned, forearmed.

PRUE. Indeed now, that's fair, for most men are forearmed before they are warned.

HIPPOLITA. Plain-dealing is some kind of honesty, however, and few women would have said so much.

GERRARD. None but those who would delight in a husband's jealousy as the proof of his love and her honour.

HIPPOLITA. Hold, sir, let us have a good understanding betwixt one another at first, that we may be long friends. I differ from you in the point, for a husband's jealousy, which cunning men would pass upon their wives for a compliment, is the worst can be made 'em, for, indeed, it is a compliment to their beauty but an affront to their honour.

GERRARD. But, madam –

HIPPOLITA. So that upon the whole matter I conclude, jealousy in a gallant is humble true love and the height of respect and only an undervaluing of himself to overvalue her but in a husband 'tis arrant sauciness, cowardice and ill-breeding and not to be suffered.

GERRARD. I stand corrected, gracious miss.

HIPPOLITA. Well, have you brought the gentlemen fiddlers with you, as I desired?

GERRARD. They are below.

HIPPOLITA. Are they armed well?

GERRARD. Yes, they have instruments too that are not of wood. But what will you do with them?

HIPPOLITA. What did you think I intended to do with them, when I whispered you to bring gentlemen of your acquaintance instead of fiddlers, as my father desired you to bring? Pray, what did you think I intended?

GERRARD. Faith, e'en to make fools of the gentlemen fiddlers as you had done of your gentleman dancing-master.

HIPPOLITA. I intended 'em for our guard and defence against my father's Spanish and Guinea force, when we were to make our retreat from hence, and to help us to take the keys from my aunt, who has been the watchful porter of this house this twelvemonth, and this design (if your heart do not fail you) we will put in execution, as soon as you have given your friends below instructions.

GERRARD. Are you sure your heart will stand right still? You flinched last night, when I little expected it, I am sure.

HIPPOLITA. The time last night was not so proper for us as now for reasons I will give you. But besides that, I confess I had a mind to try whether your interest did not sway you more than your love, whether the twelve hundred pounds a year I told you of had not made a greater impression in your heart than Hippolita. But finding it otherwise – yet hold, perhaps upon consideration you are grown wiser. Can you yet, as I said, be so desperate, so out of fashion, as to steal a woman with nothing?

GERRARD. With you I can want nothing nor can be made by anything more rich or happy.

HIPPOLITA. Think well again. Can you take me without the twelve hundred pounds a year? The twelve hundred pounds a year?

GERRARD. Indeed, miss, now you begin to be unkind again and use me worse than e'er you did.

HIPPOLITA. Well, though you are so modest a gentleman as to suffer a wife to be put upon you with

270 *Guinea*: not only Spanish Guinea but any part of West Africa.

nothing I have more conscience than to do it. I have the twelve hundred pounds a year, out of my father's power, which is yours and I am sorry it is not the Indies to mend your bargain.

GERRARD. Dear miss, you but increase my fears and not my wealth. Pray, let us make haste away. I desire but to be secure of you. Come, what are you thinking of?

HIPPOLITA. I am thinking, if some little, flinching, inquisitive poet should get my story and represent it on the stage, what those ladies who are never precise but at a play would say of me now; that I were a confident, coming piece, I warrant, and they would damn the poor poet for libelling the sex. But sure, though I give myself and fortune away frankly, without the consent of my friends, my confidence is less than theirs who stand off only for separate maintenance.

GERRARD. They would be widows before their time, have a husband and no husband. But let us be gone, lest fortune should recant my happiness. Now you are fixed my dearest miss. (*He kisses her hand*)

Enter MONSIEUR *coughing and* DON DIEGO.

HIPPOLITA. Oh, here's my father!

DON DIEGO. How now, sir! What, kissing her hand? What means that, friend, ha? Daughter, ha! Do you permit this insolence, ha? Voto a mi honra.

GERRARD. [*aside*] We are prevented again.

HIPPOLITA. Ha, ha, ha, you are so full of your Spanish jealousy, father. Why, you must know he's a city dancing-master and they, forsooth, think it fine to kiss the hand at the honour before the corant.

MONSIEUR. Ay, ay, ay, uncle, don't you know that?

DON DIEGO. Go to, go to, you are an easy French fool. There's more in it than so, look you.

MONSIEUR. I vow and swear there's nothing more in't, if you'll believe one. (*Aside to* HIPPOLITA *and* GERRARD) Did not I cough and hawk? A jealous, prudent husband could not cough and hawk louder at the approach of his wife's chamber in visiting-time and yet you would not hear me. He'll make now ado about nothing and you'll be discovered both.

DON DIEGO. Umph, umph, no, no. I see it plain. He is no dancing-master. Now I have found it out and I think I can see as far into matters as another. I have found it now, look you.

GERRARD. [*aside*] My fear was prophetical.

HIPPOLITA. [*aside*] What shall we do?

GERRARD *offers to go out with her.*

Nay, pray, sir, do not stir yet.

Enter MRS CAUTION.

CAUTION. What's the matter, brother? What's the matter?

DON DIEGO. I have found it out, sister, I have found it out. Sister, this villain here is no dancing-master but a dishonourer of my house and daughter. I caught him kissing her hand.

MONSIEUR. Pish, pish, you are a strange Spanish kind of an uncle, that you are. A dishonourer of your daughter because he kissed her hand! Pray, how could he honour her more? He kissed her hand, you see, while he was making his honour to her.

DON DIEGO. You are an unthinking, shallow, French fop, voto. But I tell you, sister, I have thought of it and have found it out: he is no dancing-master, sister. Do you remember the whispering last night? I have found out the meaning of that too and I tell you, sister, he's no dancing-master. I have found it out.

CAUTION. You found it out, marry come up! Did not I tell you always he was no dancing-master?

DON DIEGO. You tell me, you silly woman! What then? What of that? You tell me! D'ee think I heeded what you told me? But I tell you now I have found it out.

CAUTION. I say I found it out.

DON DIEGO. I say 'tis false, gossip. I found him out.

CAUTION. I say I found him out first – say what you will.

DON DIEGO. Sister, mum, Not such a word again, guarda. You found him out!

CAUTION. Nay, I must submit or dissemble like other prudent women or –

DON DIEGO. Come, come, sister, take it from me, he is no dancing-master.

CAUTION. O yes, he is a dancing-master.

DON DIEGO. What, will you be wiser than I every way? Remember the whispering, I say.

CAUTION. (*aside*) So, he thinks I speak in earnest. Then I'll fit him still. – But what do you talk of their whispering? They would not whisper any ill before us, sure.

DON DIEGO. Will you still be an idiot, a dolt and see nothing?

MONSIEUR. Lord! You'll be wiser than all the world, will you? Are we not all against you? Pshaw, pshaw, I ne'er saw such a donissimo as you are, I vow and swear.

DON DIEGO. No, sister, he's no dancing-master, for, now I think on't too, he could not play upon the fiddle.

CAUTION. Pish, pish, what dancing-master can play upon a fiddle without strings?

DON DIEGO. Again, I tell you, he broke 'em on purpose, because he could not play. I have found it out now, sister.

CAUTION. Nay, you see farther than I, brother.

GERRARD *offers to lead* [HIPPOLITA] *out.*

HIPPOLITA. [*aside to* GERRARD] For heaven's sake, stir not yet.

DON DIEGO. Besides, if you remember, they were perpetually putting me out of the room – that was, sister, because they had a mind to be alone. I have found that out too. Now, sister, look you, he is no dancing-master.

CAUTION. But has he not given her a lesson often before you?

DON DIEGO. Ay, but, sister, he did not go about his business like a dancing-master. But go, go down to the door. Somebody rings.

Exit CAUTION.

MONSIEUR. I vow and swear, uncle, he is a dancing-master. Pray be appeased. Lord, d'ee think I'd tell you a lie?

DON DIEGO. If it prove to be a lie and you do not confess it, though you are my next heir after my daughter, I will disown thee as much as I do her, for thy folly and treachery to thyself as well as me. You may have her but never my estate, look you.

MONSIEUR. (*aside*) How! I must look to my hits then.

DON DIEGO. Look to't.

MONSIEUR. (*aside*) Then I had best confess all before he discover all, which he will soon do.

Enter PARSON.

O, here's the parson too! He won't be in choler nor brandish Toledo before the parson, sure? – Well, uncle, I must confess, rather than lose your favour; he is no dancing-master.

DON DIEGO. No.

GERRARD. What, has the fool betrayed us then at last? Nay then, 'tis time to be gone. Come away, miss. (*Going out*)

DON DIEGO. Nay, sir, if you pass this way, my Toledo will pass that way, look you. (*Thrusts at him with his sword*)

HIPPOLITA. O hold, Mr Gerrard! Hold, father!

MONSIEUR. (*stops his uncle*) I tell you uncle, he's an honest gentleman, means no hurt and came hither but upon a frolic of mine and your daughter's.

DON DIEGO. Ladrón, traidor.

MONSIEUR. I tell you, all's but a jest, a mere jest, I vow and swear.

DON DIEGO. A jest! Jest with my honour, voto! Ha! No family to dishonour but the grave, wise, noble, honourable, illustrious, puissant and right worshipful family of the Formals! Nay, I am contented to reprieve you till you know who you have dishonoured and convict you of the greatness of your crime before you die. We are descended, look you –

MONSIEUR. Nay, pray, uncle, hear me.

DON DIEGO. I say, we are descended –

MONSIEUR. 'Tis no matter for that.

DON DIEGO. And my great-great-great-grandfather was –

MONSIEUR. Well, well, I have something to say more to the purpose.

DON DIEGO. My great-great-great-grandfather, I say, was –

MONSIEUR. Well, a pinmaker in –

---

420 *look to my hits*: look to my chances, attend to my business.

DON DIEGO. But he was a gentleman for all that, fop, for he was a sergeant to a company of the train-bands and my great-great-grandfather was –

MONSIEUR. Was his son. What then? Won't you let me clear this gentleman?

DON DIEGO. He was, he was –

MONSIEUR. He was a feltmaker, his son a wine-cooper, your father a vintner, and so you came to be a Canary merchant.

DON DIEGO. But we were still gentlemen, for our coat was, as the heralds say, was –

MONSIEUR. Was – your sign was the three tuns and the field canary. Now let me tell you, this honest gentleman –

DON DIEGO. Now that you should dare to dishonour this family. By the graves of my ancestors in Great St Ellen's Church –

MONSIEUR. Yard.

DON DIEGO. Thou shalt die for't, ladrón. (*Runs at* GERRARD)

MONSIEUR. Hold, hold, uncle. Are you mad?

HIPPOLITA. Oh, oh.

MONSIEUR. Nay then, by your own Spanish rules of honour, though he be my rival, I must help him, since I brought him into danger. (*Draws his sword. Aside*) Sure, he will not show his valour upon his nephew and son-in-law – otherwise I should be afraid of showing mine. – Here, Mr Gerrard, go in here. Nay, you shall go in, Mr Gerrard. I'll secure you all. And, parson, do you go in too with 'em, for I see you are afraid of a sword and the other world, though you talk of it so familiarly and make it so fine a place.

Opens a door and thrusts GERRARD, HIPPOLITA *and* PARSON *in, then shuts it and guards it with his sword.*

---

457 *train-bands*: the citizen militia.
458 Q1 has one *great* too many.
463–4 *Canary merchant*: a merchant involved in a wide range of West African trade, not only the import of Canary wines.
467 *tuns*: wine barrels.
471–2 *Great St Ellen's Church*: Great St Helen's, Bishopsgate. Only the rich were buried inside church, hence Monsieur's gibe.

DON DIEGO. Tu quoque, Brute.

MONSIEUR. Nay, now, uncle, you must understand reason. What, you are not only a don but you are a Don Quixote too, I vow and swear.

DON DIEGO. Thou spot, sploach of my family and blood! I will have his blood, look you.

MONSIEUR. Pray, good Spanish uncle, have but patience to hear me. Suppose – I say, suppose he had done, done, done the feat to your daughter.

DON DIEGO. How! Done the feat, done the feat, done the feat, en hora mala!

MONSIEUR. I say, suppose, suppose –

DON DIEGO. Suppose –

MONSIEUR. I say, suppose he had, for I do but suppose it. Well, I am ready to marry her however. Now marriage is as good a solder for cracked female honour as blood and can't you suffer the shame but for a quarter of an hour till the parson has married us and then, if there be any shame, it becomes mine. For, here in England, the father has nothing to do with the daughter's business, honour, what-d'ee-call't when once she's married, d'ee see?

DON DIEGO. England! What d'ee tell me of England? I'll be a Spaniard still, voto a mi hora, and I will be revenged. (*Calls at the door*) Pedro, Juan, Sanchez.

Enter MRS CAUTION *followed by* FLIRT *and* FLOUNCE *in vizard masks.*

CAUTION. What's the matter, brother?

DON DIEGO. Pedro, Sanchez, Juan! But who are these, sister? Are they not men in women's clothes? What make they here?

CAUTION. They are relations, they say, of my cousin's, who pressed in when I let in the parson. They say my cousin invited 'em to his wedding.

MONSIEUR. Two of my relations, ha! [*Aside*] They are my cousins indeed of the other night, a pox take 'em. But that's no curse for 'em; a plague take 'em then! But how came they here?

---

491 *sploach*: splotch.
510 *hora*: Don Diego – or Wycherley – means *honra*.

DON DIEGO. (*aside*) Now must I have witnesses too of the dishonour of my family. It were Spanish prudence to dispatch 'em away out of the house before I begin my revenge. – What are you? What make you here? Who would you speak with?

FLIRT. With Monsieur.

DON DIEGO. Here he is.

MONSIEUR. [*aside*] Now will these jades discredit me and spoil my match, just in the coupling minute.

DON DIEGO. Do you know 'em?

MONSIEUR. Yes, sir, sure, I know 'em. (*Aside to 'em*) Pray, ladies, say as I say or you will spoil my wedding, for I am just going to be married and if my uncle or mistress should know who you are it might break off the match.

FLOUNCE. We came on purpose to break the match.

MONSIEUR. How!

FLIRT. Why, d'ee think to marry and leave us so in the lurch?

MONSIEUR. (*aside*) What do the jades mean?

DON DIEGO. Come, who are they? What would they have? If they come to the wedding, ladies, I assure you, there will be none today here.

MONSIEUR. They won't trouble you, sir. They are going again. Ladies, you hear what my uncle says. I know you won't trouble him. (*Aside*) I wish I were well rid of 'em.

FLOUNCE. (*aside*) You shall not think to put us off so.

DON DIEGO. Who are they? What are their names?

FLIRT. We are, sir –

MONSIEUR. (*aside to 'em*) Nay, for heaven's sake, don't tell who you are, for you will undo me and spoil my match infallibly.

FLOUNCE. We care not. 'Tis our business to spoil matches.

MONSIEUR. You need not, for, I believe, married men are your best customers, for greedy bachelors take up with their wives.

DON DIEGO. Come, pray, ladies, if you have no business here, be pleased to retire, for few of us are in humour to be so civil to you as you may deserve.

MONSIEUR. Ay, prithee, dear jades, get you gone.

FLIRT. We will not stir.

DON DIEGO. Who are they, I say, fool, and why don't they go?

FLOUNCE. We are, sir –

MONSIEUR. Hold, hold. – They are persons of honour and quality and –

FLIRT. We are no persons of honour and quality, sir. We are –

MONSIEUR. They are modest ladies and being in a kind of disguise will not own their quality.

FLOUNCE. We modest ladies!

MONSIEUR. (*aside to 'em*) Why, sometimes you are in the humour to pass for women of honour and quality. Prithee, dear jades, let your modesty and greatness come upon you now.

FLIRT. Come, sir, not to delude you, as he would have us, we are –

MONSIEUR. Hold, hold –

FLIRT. The other night at the French house –

MONSIEUR. Hold, I say. [*Aside*] 'Tis even true as Gerrard says: the women will tell, I see.

FLOUNCE. [*aside to him*] If you would have her silent, stop her mouth with that ring.

MONSIEUR. Will that do't? Here, here – (*Takes off his ring and gives it her. Aside*) 'Tis worth one hundred and fifty pounds but I must not lose my match, I must not lose a trout for a fly. That men should live to hire women to silence!

Enter GERRARD, HIPPOLITA, PARSON *and* PRUE.

DON DIEGO. Oh, are you come again? (*Draws his sword and runs at 'em*)

MONSIEUR. Oh, hold, hold, uncle! (MONSIEUR *holds him*) What are you mad, Gerrard, to expose yourself to a new danger? Why would you come out yet?

GERRARD. Because our danger now is over, I thank the parson there. And now we must beg –

GERRARD *and* HIPPOLITA *kneel.*

MONSIEUR. Nay, faith, uncle, forgive him now, since he asks you forgiveness upon his knees and my poor cousin too.

---

588 s.d. follows line 587 Q1.

HIPPOLITA. You are mistaken, cousin. We ask him blessing and you forgiveness.

MONSIEUR. How, how, how! What do you talk of blessing? What, do you ask your father blessing and he asks me forgiveness? But why should he ask me forgiveness?

HIPPOLITA. Because he asks my father blessing.

MONSIEUR. Pish, pish, I don't understand you, I vow and swear.

HIPPOLITA. The parson will expound to you, cousin.

MONSIEUR. Hey! What say you to it, parson?

PARSON. They are married, sir.

MONSIEUR. Married!

CAUTION. Married! So, I told you what 'twould come to.

DON DIEGO. You told us!

MONSIEUR. Nay, she is setting up for the reputation of a witch.

DON DIEGO. Married! Juan, Sanchez, Pedro, arm, arm, arm.

CAUTION. A witch, a witch!

HIPPOLITA. Nay, indeed, father, now we are married you had better call the fiddles. Call 'em, Prue, quickly.

Exit PRUE.

MONSIEUR. Who do you say married, man?

PARSON. Was I not sent for on purpose to marry 'em? Why should you wonder at it?

MONSIEUR. No, no, you were to marry me, man, to her. I knew there was a mistake in't somehow. You were merely mistaken, therefore you must do your business over again for me now. The parson was mistaken, uncle, it seems, ha, ha, ha.

CAUTION. I suppose five or six guineas made him make the mistake, which will not be rectified now, nephew. They'll marry all that come near 'em and for a guinea or two care not what mischief they do, nephew.

DON DIEGO. Married! Pedro, Sanchez!

MONSIEUR. How, and must she be his wife then for ever and ever? Have I held the door then for this, like a fool as I was?

CAUTION. Yes, indeed.

619, 648 *Pedro*: Petro Q1

MONSIEUR. Have I worn golilla here for this? Little breeches for this?

CAUTION. Yes, truly.

MONSIEUR. And put on the Spanish honour with the habit, in defending my rival. Nay then, I'll have another turn of honour in revenge. Come, uncle, I'm of your side now. Sa, sa, sa. But let's stay for our force. Sanchez, Juan, Pedro, arm, arm, arm.

Enter two blacks and the Spaniard, followed by PRUE, MARTIN *and five other gentlemen like fiddlers.*

DON DIEGO. Murder the villain, kill him!

Running all upon GERRARD.

MARTIN. Hold, hold, sir.

DON DIEGO. How now! Who sent for you, friends?

MARTIN. We fiddlers, sir, often come unsent for.

DON DIEGO. And you are often kicked downstairs for't too.

MARTIN. No, sir, our company was never kicked, I think.

DON DIEGO. Fiddlers and not kicked? Then, to preserve your virgin honour, get you downstairs quickly, for we are not at present disposed much for mirth, voto.

MONSIEUR. (*peeping*) A pox, is it you, Martin? Nay, uncle, then 'tis in vain, for they won't be kicked downstairs, to my knowledge. They are gentlemen fiddlers, forsooth. A pox on all gentlemen fiddlers and gentlemen dancing-masters, say I!

DON DIEGO. (*pausing*) How! Ha.

MONSIEUR. Well, Flirt, now I am a match for thee, now I may keep you and there's little difference betwixt keeping a wench and marriage – only marriage is a little the cheaper but the other is the more honourable now, vert et bleu. Nay, now I may swear a French oath too. Come, come, I am thine. Let us strike up the bargain, thine according to the honourable institution of keeping, come.

FLIRT. Nay, hold, sir. Two words to the bargain. First, I have ne'er a lawyer here to draw articles and settlements.

MONSIEUR. How! Is the world come to that? A man cannot keep a wench without articles and settlements? Nay then, 'tis e'en as bad as marriage indeed and there's no difference betwixt a wife and a wench.

FLIRT. Only in cohabitation, for the first article shall be against cohabitation. We mistresses suffer no cohabitation.

MONSIEUR. Nor wives neither now.

FLIRT. Then separate maintenance, in case you should take a wife or I a new friend.

MONSIEUR. How! That too? Then you are every whit as bad as a wife.

FLIRT. Then my house in town and yours in the country, if you will.

MONSIEUR. A mere wife.

FLIRT. Then my coach apart, as well as my bed apart.

MONSIEUR. As bad as a wife still.

FLIRT. But take notice I will have no little, dirty, secondhand chariot new-furbished but a large, sociable, well-painted coach, nor will I keep it till it be as well known as myself and it comes to be called Flirt Coach; nor will I have such pitiful horses as cannot carry me every night to the park, for I will not miss a night in the park, I'd have you to know.

MONSIEUR. 'Tis very well. You must have your great, gilt, fine, painted coaches. I'm sure they are grown so common already amongst you that ladies of quality begin to take up with hackneys again, jarnie. But what else?

FLIRT. Then, that you do not think I will be served by a little dirty boy in a bonnet but a couple of handsome, lusty, cleanly footmen, fit to serve ladies of quality and do their business as they should do.

MONSIEUR. What then?

FLIRT. Then, that you never grow jealous of them.

MONSIEUR. Why, will you make so much of them?

FLIRT. I delight to be kind to my servants.

MONSIEUR. Well, is this all?

FLIRT. No. Then, that when you come to my house you never presume to touch a key, lift up a latch or thrust a door without knocking beforehand and that you ask no questions if you see a stray piece of plate, cabinet or looking-glass in my house.

---

694 *chariot*: a light four-wheeled carriage, less grand and splendid than the coach.

703 *hackneys*: hired coaches.

MONSIEUR. Just a wife in everything. But what else?

FLIRT. Then, that you take no acquaintance with me abroad nor bring me home any when you are drunk whom you will not be willing to see there when you are sober.

MONSIEUR. But what allowance? Let's come to the main business, the money.

FLIRT. Stay, let me think. First, for advance-money, five hundred pounds for pins.

MONSIEUR. A very wife.

FLIRT. Then you must take the lease of my house and furnish it as becomes one of my quality, for don't you think we'll take up with your old Queen Elizabeth furniture, as your wives do.

MONSIEUR. Indeed, there she is least like a wife, as she says.

FLIRT. Then, for housekeeping, servant wages, clothes and the rest, I'll be contented with a thousand pound a year present maintenance and but three hundred pound a year separate maintenance for my life, when our love grows cold. But I am contented with a thousand a year because for pendants, necklaces and all sorts of jewels and such trifles, nay, and some plate, I will shift myself as I can, make shifts, which you shall not take any notice of.

MONSIEUR. A thousand pound a year! What will wenching come to? Time was, a man might have fared as well at a much cheaper rate and a lady of one's affections, instead of a house, would have been contented with a little chamber three pair of stairs backward with a little closet or larder to't and, instead of variety of new gowns and rich petticoats, with her dishabillé or flame-colour gown called Indian and slippers of the same would have been contented for a twelvemonth and, instead of visits and gadding to plays, would have entertained herself at home with *St George for England*, *The Knight of the Sun* or *The*

---

731 *old Queen Elizabeth*: old-fashioned, not necessarily Elizabethan.

751 *flame-colour gown called Indian*: informal, undress gowns, worn only at home.

754–6 *St George . . . Piety*: *St George for England* is presumably

Practice of Piety and, instead of sending her wine and meat from the French houses, would have been contented if you had given her, poor wretch, but credit at the next chandler's and chequered cellar and then, instead of a coach, would have been well satisfied to have gone out and taken the air for three or four hours in the evening in the balcony, poor soul. Well, Flirt, however, we'll agree. 'Tis but three hundred pound a year separate maintenance, you say, when I am weary of thee and the charge.

DON DIEGO. [*aside*] Robbed of my honour, my daughter and my revenge too! Oh my dear honour! Nothing vexes me but that the world should say I had not Spanish policy enough to keep my daughter from being debauched from me. But methinks my Spanish policy might help me yet. I have it so; I will cheat 'em all, for I will declare I understood the whole plot and contrivance and connived at it, finding my cousin a fool and not answering my expectation. Well, but then if I approve of the match I must give this mock dancing-master my estate, especially since half he would have in right of my daughter and in spite of me. Well, I am resolved to turn the cheat upon themselves and give them my consent and estate.

MONSIEUR. Come, come, ne'er be troubled, uncle. 'Twas a combination, you see, of all these heads and your daughter's (you know what I mean, uncle) not to be thwarted or governed by all the Spanish policy in Christendom. I'm sure my French policy would not have governed her. So, since I have scaped her, I am glad to have scaped her, jernie.

Richard Johnson's tremendously popular *The Most Famous History of the Seven Champions of Christendom* (1596 and many subsequent editions); Summers suggested that *The Knight of the Sun* must be the hero of Diego Ortuñez de Calahorra's *The Mirrour of Princely Deedes and Knighthood* (translation published in 1580) but I find no evidence for any particular popularity; Lewis Bayly's *The Practice of Piety* was first published around 1610 and reprinted dozens of times in the century.

759 *chequered cellar*: tavern, from the common inn-sign of the chequered board.

CAUTION. Come, brother, you are wiser than I, you see, ay, ay.

DON DIEGO. No, you think you are wiser than I now in earnest. But know, while I was thought a gull, I gulled you all and made them and you think I knew nothing of the contrivance. Confess. Did you not think, verily, that I knew nothing of it and that I was a gull?

CAUTION. Yes, indeed, brother, I did think verily you were a gull.

HIPPOLITA. (*listening*) How's this?

DON DIEGO. Alas, alas, all the sputter I made was but to make this young man, my cousin, believe, when the thing should be effected, that it was not with my connivance or consent. But, since he is so well satisfied, I own it. For, do you think I would ever have suffered her to marry a monsieur? A monsieur, guarda! Besides, it had been but a beastly, incestuous kind of a match, voto.

CAUTION. Nay then, I see, brother, you were wiser than I indeed.

GERRARD. (*aside*) So, so.

CAUTION. Nay, young man, you have danced a fair dance for yourself royally and now you may go jig it together till you are both weary and, though you were so eager to have him, Mrs Minx, you'll soon have your bellyfull of him, let me tell you, mistress.

PRUE. Hah, ha.

MONSIEUR. How, uncle! What was't you said? Nay, if I had your Spanish policy against me, it was no wonder I missed of my aim, mon foy.

DON DIEGO. I was resolved too my daughter should not marry a coward, therefore made the more ado to try you, sir, but I find you are a brisk man of honour, firm, stiff, Spanish honour and that you may see I deceived you all along and you not me, ay, and am able to deceive you still, for I know now you think that I will give you little or nothing with my daughter (like other fathers) since you have married her without my consent but, I say, I'll deceive you now, for you shall have the most part of my estate in present and the rest at my death. There's for you. I think I have deceived you now, look you.

GERRARD. No, indeed, sir, you have not deceived me,

for I never suspected your love to your daughter nor your generosity.

DON DIEGO. How, sir! Have a care of saying I have not deceived you, lest I deceive you another way – guarda! Pray, gentlemen, do not think any man could deceive me, look you, that any man could steal my daughter, look you, without my connivance.
The less we speak the more we think
And he sees most that seems to wink.

HIPPOLITA. So, so, now I could give you my blessing, father, now you are a good complaisant father, indeed.
When children marry, parents should obey,
Since love claims more obedience far than they.

Exeunt omnes.

EPILOGUE, *spoken by* FLIRT

The ladies first I am to compliment,
Whom, if he could, the poet would content,
But to their pleasure then they must consent.
Most spoil their sport still by their modesty
And, when they should be pleased, cry out 'O fie'
And the least smooty jest will ne'er pass by.
But city damsel ne'er had confidence
At smooty play to take the least offence
But mercy shows to show her innocence.
Yet, lest the merchants' daughters should today
Be scandalised – not at our harmless play
But our Hippolita, since she's like one
Of us bold flirts of t'other end o'th'town –
Our poet, sending to you (though unknown)
His best respects by me, does frankly own
The character to be unnatural.
Hippolita is not like you at all.
You, while your lovers court you, still look grum
And, far from wooing, when they woo, cry 'Mum'
And if some of you e'er were stolen away

---

6 *smooty*: smutty.

Your portion's fault 'twas only, I dare say.
Thus much for him the poet bid me speak.
Now to the men I my own mind will break.
You good men o'th'Exchange, on whom alone
We must depend when sparks to sea are gone,
Into the pit already you are come –
'Tis but a step more to our tiring-room,
Where none of us but will be wondrous sweet
Upon an able love of Lumber Street.
You we had rather see between our scenes
Then spendthrift fops with better clothes and miens;
Instead of laced coats, belts and pantaloons,
Your velvet jumps, gold chains and grave fur gowns;
Instead of periwigs and broad cocked hats,
Your satin caps, small cuffs and vast cravats.
For you are fair and square in all your dealings;
You never cheat your doxies with gilt shillings;
You ne'er will break our windows – then you are
Fit to make love, while our houzas make war,
And, since all gentlemen must pack to sea
Our gallants and our judges must you be.
We therefore and our poet do submit
To all the camlet cloaks now i'the pit.

---

25 With the Dutch war imminent, many gentlemen had already volunteered.
27 *tiring-room*: dressing-room.
29 *Lumber Street*: Lombard Street, famous for its goldsmiths and bankers.
33 *jumps*: short coats.
35 *satin caps*: worn over the natural hair, as opposed to the gentleman's wig.
35 *small cuffs*: the fashion was for vast, open cuffs.
39 *houzas*: rakes.
43 *camlet*: camelhair or, more often, Angora goat hair.

THE

Country-Wife,

A

COMEDY,

Acted at the

THEATRE ROYAL.

Written by Mr. *Wycherley.*

Indignor quicquam reprehendi, non quia crassè
Compositum illepidéve putetur, sed quia nuper:
Nec veniam Antiquis, sed honorem & præmia posci.
Horat.

LONDON,

Printed for *Thomas Dring*, at the *Harrow*, at the Corner of *Chancery-Lane* in *Fleet-street*, 1675.

Title-page of the 1675 Quarto of *The Country Wife*, reproduced by permission of the British Library.

Motto

Horace, *Epistles*, II i 76–8:

'I am angry that any work is criticised, not because it is thought dull or inelegantly written but because it is modern, and that for the ancients they demand not indulgence but honour and rewards'

INTRODUCTORY NOTE

The ultimate source of Horner's stratagem in *The Country Wife* is Terence's *Eunuchus*, in which Chaerea disguises himself as a eunuch in order to gain access to Pamphila. But Wycherley owes nothing more than the disguise to Terence. Wycherley's major source for the Pinchwife plot is Molière. In *L'École des femmes* (1662) Wycherley found Arnolphe, a long-time despiser of marriage, who intends to marry Agnès, a girl brought up in the country apparently in total innocence on Arnolphe's instructions. Like Margery, Agnès admits her love, for Horace, to Arnolphe but he is easily convinced by the complete frankness of her declaration that there is nothing to it. In *L'École des maris* (1661), Isabelle makes Sganarelle carry a letter to Valère by pretending that it is a letter from Valère which she is returning unopened (see Margery's trick with her letter to Horner, carried by Pinchwife, in IV ii); later, Isabelle manages to escape to Valère by pretending to Sganarelle that her sister is planning to do so (see Margery's escape disguised as Alithea in V i). Wycherley's dialogue contains other fragmentary reminiscences of Molière but little of significance. Margery's reasons for not writing to Horner (IV ii 77ff) may derive from Furetière's *Le Roman Bourgeois* (Paris, 1666, translated as *Scarron's City Romance* in 1671).

The Country Wife was first performed by the King's Company at the Theatre Royal, Drury Lane, in January 1675; a performance recorded for 12 January was probably the first. Even though records are fragmentary, the play seems to have been a success, revived at various times for the rest of the century. Between 1700 and 1753 we know of 153 performances of the play and it held a regular place in the repertoire. But after 1753 Wycherley's play in its original form disappears from the stage until the 1920s. In 1765, John Lee turned the play into a two-act farce, performed as an after-piece at various times until the 1780s. In 1766 David Garrick completed the emasculation of Horner by turning him into Belville in *The Country Girl*. Garrick's version retains some of Wycherley's comedy but without any of its satiric bite and also without any sexual improprieties. Only in this sterilised form was Wycherley's play to be performed. Garrick's version was revived in 1979 by Cambridge Theatre Company. In February 1924, the Phoenix Society revived Wycherley's original version at the Regent Theatre; once the audience had got over the 'shock' of seeing Wycherley uncensored, the production was a success. Still in an adapted form, the play was performed at the Everyman Theatre, Hampstead, in December

1926. *The Country Wife* only fully re-established its place with the production by Baliol Holloway at the Ambassadors Theatre in 1934. In 1936 it was performed at the Old Vic, with Michael Redgrave as Horner, Edith Evans as Lady Fidget and Ruth Gordon as Margery. Since then there have been major productions at the Theatre Royal, Stratford East, directed by Tony Richardson (1955), at the Royal Court, directed by George Devine with Joan Plowright as Margery (1956), at Chichester Festival Theatre with Maggie Smith as Margery (1969) and at the National Theatre in a disappointing production directed by Peter Hall with Albert Finney as Horner (1977), as well as countless other productions professional and amateur.

The play was first published in 1675 and there were further quarto editions in 1683, 1688 and 1695 (two). In recent years there have been three editions of the play published separately: Thomas H. Fujimura edited the play for the Regents Restoration Drama Series (1965); John Dixon Hunt's edition with some good annotation and a lively introduction appeared in the New Mermaids series in 1973; David Cook and John Swannell edited the play for the Revels Plays in 1975, but their annotation is often excessive and their introduction disappointingly dull. Scolar Press published a facsimile of the first edition in 1970.

PROLOGUE, *spoken by Mr Hart*

Poets, like cudgelled bullies, never do
At first or second blow submit to you;
But will provoke you still, and ne'er have done,
Till you are weary first with laying on.
The late so baffled scribbler of this day,
Though he stands trembling, bids me boldly say,
What we before most plays are used to do,
For poets out of fear first draw on you;
In a fierce prologue the still pit defy
And ere you speak, like Castril, give the lie.
But though our Bayes's battles oft I've fought,
And with bruised knuckles their dear conquests bought;
Nay, never yet feared odds upon the stage,
In prologue dare not hector with the age,
But would take quarter from your saving hands,
Though Bayes within all yielding countermands,
Says you confederate wits no quarter give,
Therefore his play shan't ask your leave to live.
Well, let the vain rash fop, by huffing so,
Think to obtain the better terms of you;
But we the actors humbly will submit,
Now, and at any time, to a full pit;
Nay, often we anticipate your rage,
And murder poets for you on our stage.
We set no guards upon our tiring-room,
But when with flying colours there you come,
We patiently, you see, give up to you
Our poets, virgins, nay, our matrons too.

---

1 *bullies*: ruffians.
5 A comment on the failure of *The Gentleman Dancing-Master.*
10 *Castril*: the 'angry boy' of Ben Jonson's *The Alchemist* (1610).
11 *Bayes*: the name given by George Villiers, Duke of Buckingham, to his parody of Dryden in *The Rehearsal* (1671). Charles Hart usually played the hero in Dryden's tragedies. The name was also used for any poet, as in line 16 for Wycherley.
19 *huffing*: blustering.
25 *tiring-room*: dressing-room.

THE PERSONS

MR HORNER	*Mr Hart*
MR HARCOURT	*Mr Kynaston*
MR DORILANT	*Mr Lydal*
MR PINCHWIFE	*Mr Mohun*
MR SPARKISH	*Mr Haines*
SIR JASPAR FIDGET	*Mr Cartwright*
MRS MARGERY PINCHWIFE	*Mrs Boutell*
MRS ALITHEA	*Mrs James*
MY LADY FIDGET	*Mrs Knep*
MRS DAINTY FIDGET	*Mrs Corbet*
MRS SQUEAMISH	*Mrs Wyatt*
OLD LADY SQUEAMISH	*Mrs Rutter*
Waiters, servants, and attendants	
A BOY	
A QUACK	*Mr Shatterel*
LUCY, Alithea's maid	*Mrs Corey*
[CLASP]	
[A Parson]	

The Scene: *London*

ACT I

SCENE I

Enter HORNER, *and* QUACK *following him at a distance.*

HORNER. (*aside*) A quack is as fit for a pimp as a midwife for a bawd; they are still but in their way both helpers of nature. – Well, my dear doctor, hast thou done what I desired?

QUACK. I have undone you forever with the women, and reported you throughout the whole town as bad as an eunuch, with as much trouble as if I had made you one in earnest.

HORNER. But have you told all the midwives you know, the orange-wenches at the playhouses, the city husbands, and old fumbling keepers of this end of the town? For they'll be the readiest to report it.

QUACK. I have told all the chambermaids, waiting-women, tire-women and old women of my acquaintance; nay, and whispered it as a secret to 'em, and to the whisperers of Whitehall; so that you need not doubt, 'twill spread, and you will be as odious to the handsome young women as –

HORNER. As the smallpox. Well –

QUACK. And to the married women of this end of the town as –

HORNER. As the great ones; nay, as their own husbands.

QUACK. And to the city dames as aniseed Robin of filthy and contemptible memory; and they will frighten their children with your name, especially their females.

---

10 *orange-wenches*: orange-sellers.
11 *keepers*: men who maintain a mistress.
11–12 *this end of the town*: the fashionable, west, end of London, away from the merchants in the city.
14 *tire-women*: ladies' maids.
16 *Whitehall*: the king's residence and the ideal place for gossip.
22 *great ones*: syphilis.
23 *aniseed Robin*: a famous hermaphrodite; Charles Cotton wrote a burlesque epitaph on him (*Poems*, 1689).

HORNER. And cry, 'Horner's coming to carry you away.' I am only afraid 'twill not be believed. You told 'em 'twas by an English–French disaster and an English–French chirurgeon, who has given me at once, not only a cure, but an antidote for the future against that damned malady, and that worse distemper, love, and all other women's evils.

QUACK. Your late journey into France has made it the more credible and your being here a fortnight before you appeared in public looks as if you apprehended the shame, which I wonder you do not. Well, I have been hired by young gallants to belie 'em t'other way, but you are the first would be thought a man unfit for women.

HORNER. Dear Mr Doctor, let vain rogues be contented only to be thought abler men than they are, generally 'tis all the pleasure they have; but mine lies another way.

QUACK. You take, methinks, a very preposterous way to it and as ridiculous as if we operators in physic should put forth bills to disparage our medicaments, with hopes to gain customers.

HORNER. Doctor, there are quacks in love as well as physic, who get but the fewer and worse patients for their boasting; a good name is seldom got by giving it oneself, and women no more than honour are compassed by bragging. Come, come, doctor, the wisest lawyer never discovers the merits of his cause till the trial; the wealthiest man conceals his riches, and the cunning gamester his play. Shy husbands and keepers, like old rooks, are not to be cheated but by a new unpractised trick; false friendship will pass now no more than false dice upon 'em; nò, not in the city.

Enter BOY.

BOY. There are two ladies and a gentleman coming up. *Exit.*

29–30 *English–French . . . chirurgeon*: the French disease, syphilis, caught by an Englishman from an English whore and cured by an English surgeon specialising in venereal diseases. See Additional Note.

57 *rooks*: cheats, sharpers.

HORNER. A pox! Some unbelieving sisters of my former acquaintance, who, I am afraid, expect their sense should be satisfied of the falsity of the report. No – this formal fool and women!

Enter SIR JASPAR FIDGET, LADY FIDGET *and* MRS DAINTY FIDGET

QUACK. His wife and sister.

SIR JASPAR. My coach breaking just now before your door, sir, I look upon as an occasional reprimand to me, sir, for not kissing your hands, sir, since your coming out of France, sir; and so my disaster, sir, has been my good fortune, sir; and this is my wife, and sister, sir.

HORNER. What then, sir?

SIR JASPAR. My lady, and sister, sir. – Wife, this is Master Horner.

LADY FIDGET. Master Horner, husband!

SIR JASPAR. My lady, my Lady Fidget, sir.

HORNER. So, sir.

SIR JASPAR. Won't you be acquainted with her, sir? (*Aside*) So the report is true, I find, by his coldness or aversion to the sex; but I'll play the wag with him. – Pray salute my wife, my lady, sir.

HORNER. I will kiss no man's wife, sir, for him, sir; I have taken my eternal leave, sir, of the sex already, sir.

SIR JASPAR. (*aside*) Hah, hah, hah! I'll plague him yet. – Not know my wife, sir?

HORNER. I do know your wife, sir; she's a woman, sir, and consequently a monster, sir, a greater monster than a husband, sir.

SIR JASPAR. A husband! How, sir?

HORNER. (*makes horns*) So, sir; but I make no more cuckolds, sir.

SIR JASPAR. Hah, hah, hah! Mercury, Mercury!

LADY FIDGET. Pray, Sir Jaspar, let us be gone from this rude fellow.

---

65 *formal*: pompous.
68 *occasional*: timely.
91 s.d. *makes horns*: the sign of a cuckold, indicated with his fore-fingers on his forehead.
93 *Mercury*: used in the treatment of syphilis.

DAINTY. Who, by his breeding, would think he had ever been in France?

LADY FIDGET. Foh, he's but too much a French fellow, such as hate women of quality and virtue for their love to their husbands, Sir Jaspar; a woman is hated by 'em as much for loving her husband as for loving their money. But pray, let's be gone.

HORNER. You do well, madam, for I have nothing that you came for; I have brought over not so much as a bawdy picture, new postures, nor the second part of the *École des Filles*, nor –

QUACK. (*apart to* HORNER) Hold, for shame, sir! What d'ye mean? You'll ruin yourself forever with the sex –

SIR JASPAR. Hah, hah, hah, he hates women perfectly, I find.

DAINTY. What a pity 'tis he should.

LADY FIDGET. Ay, he's a base, rude fellow for't; but affectation makes not a woman more odious to them than virtue.

HORNER. Because your virtue is your greatest affectation madam.

LADY FIDGET. How, you saucy fellow! Would you wrong my honour?

HORNER. If I could.

LADY FIDGET. How d'ye mean, sir?

SIR JASPAR. Hah, hah, hah! No, he can't wrong your ladyship's honour, upon my honour; he, poor man – hark you in your ear – a mere eunuch.

LADY FIDGET. O filthy French beast, foh, foh! Why do we stay? Let's be gone; I can't endure the sight of him.

SIR JASPAR. Stay but till the chairs come; they'll be here presently.

LADY FIDGET. No, no.

---

105 *new postures*: pornographic engravings like those by Giulio Romano published with Pietro Aretino's notorious *Sonnetti lussuriosi* (1523).

106 *École des filles*: (Q1 *de*) Michel Millot's bawdy dialogues, first published and suppressed in Paris in 1655. Pepys guiltily bought a copy on 8 February 1668.

128 *chairs*: sedan chairs.

129 *presently*: at once.

SIR JASPAR. Nor can I stay longer. 'Tis – let me see, a quarter and a half quarter of a minute past eleven; the Council will be sat, I must away. Business must be preferred always before love and ceremony with the wise, Mr Horner.

HORNER. And the impotent, Sir Jaspar.

SIR JASPAR. Ay, ay, the impotent, Master Horner, hah, ha, ha!

LADY FIDGET. What, leave us with a filthy man alone in his lodgings?

SIR JASPAR. He's an innocent man now, you know. Pray stay, I'll hasten the chairs to you. – Mr Horner, your servant; I should be glad to see you at my house. Pray come and dine with me, and play at cards with my wife after dinner; you are fit for women at that game yet, hah, ha! (*Aside*) 'Tis as much a husband's prudence to provide innocent diversion for a wife as to hinder her unlawful pleasures, and he had better employ her than let her employ herself. – Farewell. *Exit* SIR JASPAR.

HORNER. Your servant, Sir Jaspar.

LADY FIDGET. I will not stay with him, foh!

HORNER. Nay, madam, I beseech you stay, if it be but to see I can be as civil to ladies yet as they would desire.

LADY FIDGET. No, no, foh, you cannot be civil to ladies.

DAINTY. You as civil as ladies would desire?

LADY FIDGET. No, no, no, foh, foh, foh!

Exeunt LADY FIDGET *and* DAINTY.

QUACK. Now, I think, I, or you yourself rather, have done your business with the women.

HORNER. Thou art an ass. Don't you see already, upon the report and my carriage, this grave man of business leaves his wife in my lodgings, invites me to his house and wife, who before would not be acquainted with me out of jealousy?

QUACK. Nay, by this means you may be the more acquainted with the husbands, but the less with the wives.

---

133 *Council*: Privy Council.
161 *done your business*: ruined you.
163 *carriage*: behaviour.

HORNER. Let me alone; if I can but abuse the husbands, I'll soon disabuse the wives. Stay – I'll reckon you up the advantages I am like to have by my stratagem: first, I shall be rid of all my old acquaintances, the most insatiable sorts of duns, that invade our lodgings in a morning. And next to the pleasure of making a new mistress is that of being rid of an old one; and of all old debts, love, when it comes to be so, is paid the most unwillingly.

QUACK. Well, you may be so rid of your old acquaintances; but how will you get any new ones?

HORNER. Doctor, thou wilt never make a good chemist, thou art so incredulous and impatient. Ask but all the young fellows of the town if they do not lose more time, like huntsmen, in starting the game than in running it down; one knows not where to find 'em, who will or will not. Women of quality are so civil, you can hardly distinguish love from good breeding and a man is often mistaken; but now I can be sure, she that shows an aversion to me loves the sport, as those women that are gone, whom I warrant to be right. And then the next thing is, your women of honour, as you call 'em, are only chary of their reputations, not their persons, and 'tis scandal they would avoid, not men. Now may I have, by the reputation of an eunuch, the privileges of one and be seen in a lady's chamber in a morning as early as her husband, kiss virgins before their parents or lovers and may be, in short, the *passe partout* of the town. Now, doctor.

QUACK. Nay, now you shall be the doctor; and your process is so new that we do not know but it may succeed.

HORNER. Not so new neither; *probatum est*, doctor.

QUACK. Well, I wish you luck and many patients whilst I go to mine. *Exit* QUACK.

---

174 *duns*: importunate creditors.
181 *chemist*: alchemist.
190 *right*: game, promiscuous.
198 *passe partout*: one permitted to go anywhere.
202 *probatum est*: tried and tested, used of prescriptions. Perhaps a reference to Wycherley's revival of Terence's stratagem.

Enter HARCOURT *and* DORILANT *to* HORNER.

HARCOURT. Come, your appearance at the play yesterday has, I hope, hardened you for the future against the women's contempt and the men's raillery and now you'll abroad as you were wont.

HORNER. Did I not bear it bravely?

DORILANT. With a most theatrical impudence; nay, more than the orange-wenches show there or a drunken vizard-mask or a great-bellied actress; nay, or the most impudent of creatures, an ill poet; or what is yet more impudent, a secondhand critic.

HORNER. But what say the ladies? Have they no pity?

HARCOURT. What ladies? The vizard-masks, you know, never pity a man when all's gone, though in their service.

DORILANT. And for the women in the boxes, you'd never pity them when 'twas in your power.

HARCOURT. They say, 'tis pity, but all that deal with common women should be served so.

DORILANT. Nay, I dare swear, they won't admit you to play at cards with them, go to plays with 'em, or do the little duties which other shadows of men are wont to do for 'em.

HORNER. Who do you call shadows of men?

DORILANT. Half-men.

HORNER. What, boys?

DORILANT. Ay, your old boys, old *beaux garçons*, who, like superannuated stallions, are suffered to run, feed and whinny with the mares as long as they live, though they can do nothing else.

HORNER. Well, a pox on love and wenching! Women serve but to keep a man from better company; though I can't enjoy them, I shall you the more. Good fellowship and friendship are lasting, rational and manly pleasures.

HARCOURT. For all that, give me some of those pleasures you call effeminate too; they help to relish one another.

---

212 *vizard-mask*: a prostitute, so called from the fashionable masks they wore.

230 *beaux garçons*: ageing gallants.

HORNER. They disturb one another.

HARCOURT. No, mistresses are like books. If you pore upon them too much, they doze you and make you unfit for company; but if used discreetly, you are the fitter for conversation by 'em.

DORILANT. A mistress should be like a little country retreat near the town, not to dwell in constantly, but only for a night and away, to taste the town the better when a man returns.

HORNER. I tell you, 'tis as hard to be a good fellow, a good friend and a lover of women, as 'tis to be a good fellow, a good friend and a lover of money. You cannot follow both, then choose your side. Wine gives you liberty, love takes it away.

DORILANT. Gad, he's in the right on't.

HORNER. Wine gives you joy; love, grief and tortures, besides the chirurgeon's. Wine makes us witty; love, only sots. Wine makes us sleep; love breaks it.

DORILANT. By the world, he has reason, Harcourt.

HORNER. Wine makes –

DORILANT. Ay, wine makes us – makes us princes; love makes us beggars, poor rogues, ygad – and wine –

HORNER. So, there's one converted. – No, no, love and wine, oil and vinegar.

HARCOURT. I grant it; love will still be uppermost.

HORNER. Come, for my part I will have only those glorious, manly pleasures of being very drunk and very slovenly.

Enter BOY.

BOY. Mr Sparkish is below, sir. *Exit.*

HARCOURT. What, my dear friend! A rogue that is fond of me only, I think, for abusing him.

DORILANT. No, he can no more think the men laugh at him than that women jilt him, his opinion of himself is so good.

HORNER. Well, there's another pleasure by drinking I thought not of: I shall lose his acquaintance, because

---

244 *doze*: befuddle.
258 *chirurgeon's. Wine*: Chirurgeon's Wine Q1.
260 *has reason*: is right (from French).
274 *jilt*: deceive.

he cannot drink; and you know 'tis a very hard thing to be rid of him, for he's one of those nauseous offerers at wit, who, like the worst fiddlers, run themselves into all companies.

HARCOURT. One that, by being in the company of men of sense, would pass for one.

HORNER. And may so to the short-sighted world, as a false jewel amongst true ones is not discerned at a distance. His company is as troublesome to us as a cuckold's when you have a mind to his wife's.

HARCOURT. No, the rogue will not let us enjoy one another, but ravishes our conversation, though he signifies no more to't than Sir Martin Mar-all's gaping and awkward thrumming upon the lute does to his man's voice and music.

DORILANT. And to pass for a wit in town shows himself a fool every night to us that are guilty of the plot.

HORNER. Such wits as he are, to a company of reasonable men, like rooks to the gamesters, who only fill a room at the table, but are so far from contributing to the play that they only serve to spoil the fancy of those that do.

DORILANT. Nay, they are used like rooks too, snubbed, checked and abused; yet the rogues will hang on.

HORNER. A pox on 'em, and all that force nature and would be still what she forbids 'em! Affectation is her greatest monster.

HARCOURT. Most men are the contraries to that they would seem. Your bully, you see, is a coward with a long sword; the little, humbly fawning physician, with his ebony cane, is he that destroys men.

DORILANT. The usurer, a poor rogue possessed of mouldy bonds and mortgages, and we they call spendthrifts are only wealthy, who lay out his money upon daily new purchases of pleasure.

HORNER. Ay, your arrantest cheat is your trustee or executor; your jealous man, the greatest cuckold;

---

284 *short-sighted*: short-sighed Q1.

290 *Sir Martin Mar-all*: the foolish hero of Dryden's comedy of that name (1667) who serenades his mistress by miming to the performance of his out-of-sight servant. Sir Martin forgets to stop when his servant does and is found out.

296 *rooks*: here, *fools* rather than *cheats*.

your churchman, the greatest atheist; and your noisy, pert rogue of a wit, the greatest fop, dullest ass and worst company, as you shall see: for here he comes.

Enter SPARKISH *to them.*

SPARKISH. How is't, sparks, how is't? Well, faith, Harry, I must rally thee a little, ha, ha, ha, upon the report in town of thee, ha, ha, ha, I can't hold i'faith; shall I speak?

HORNER. Yes, but you'll be so bitter then.

SPARKISH. Honest Dick and Frank here shall answer for me, I will not be extreme bitter, by the universe.

HARCOURT. We will be bound in ten thousand pound bond, he shall not be bitter at all.

DORILANT. Nor sharp, nor sweet.

HORNER. What, not downright insipid?

SPARKISH. Nay then, since you are so brisk and provoke me, take what follows. You must know, I was discoursing and rallying with some ladies yesterday, and they happened to talk of the fine new signs in town.

HORNER. Very fine ladies, I believe.

SPARKISH. Said I, 'I know where the best new sign is.' 'Where?' says one of the ladies. 'In Covent Garden,' I replied. Said another, 'In what street?' 'In Russell Street,' answered I. 'Lord,' says another, 'I'm sure there was ne'er a fine new sign there yesterday.' 'Yes, but there was,' said I again, 'and it came out of France and has been there a fortnight.'

DORILANT. A pox, I can hear no more, prithee.

HORNER. No, hear him out; let him tune his crowd a while.

HARCOURT. The worst music, the greatest preparation.

SPARKISH. Nay, faith, I'll make you laugh. 'It cannot be,' says a third lady. 'Yes, yes,' quoth I again. Says a fourth lady –

HORNER. Look to't, we'll have no more ladies.

SPARKISH. No – then mark, mark, now. Said I to the fourth, 'Did you never see Mr Horner? He lodges in

---

332 *signs*: hung over shops to indicate the trade.
335 *Covent Garden*: then the most fashionable part of London.
342 *crowd*: fiddle, with a pun on Sparkish's audience.

Russell Street, and he's a sign of a man, you know, since he came out of France.' Heh, hah, he!

HORNER. But the devil take me, if thine be the sign of a jest.

SPARKISH. With that they all fell a-laughing, till they bepissed themselves. What, but it does not move you, methinks? Well, I see one had as good go to law without a witness as break a jest without a laugher on one's side. Come, come, sparks, but where do we dine? I have left at Whitehall an earl to dine with you.

DORILANT. Why, I thought thou hadst loved a man with a title better than a suit with a French trimming to't.

HARCOURT. Go, to him again.

SPARKISH. No, sir, a wit to me is the greatest title in the world.

HORNER. But go dine with your earl, sir; he may be exceptious. We are your friends and will not take it ill to be left, I do assure you.

HARCOURT. Nay, faith, he shall go to him.

SPARKISH. Nay, pray, gentlemen.

DORILANT. We'll thrust you out, if you wo'not. What, disappoint anybody for us?

SPARKISH. Nay, dear gentlemen, hear me.

HORNER. No, no, sir, by no means; pray go, sir.

SPARKISH. Why, dear rogues –

DORILANT. No, no.

They all thrust him out of the room.

ALL. Ha, ha, ha!

SPARKISH *returns.*

SPARKISH. But, sparks, pray hear me. What, d'ye think I'll eat then with gay, shallow fops and silent coxcombs? I think wit as necessary at dinner as a glass of good wine, and that's the reason I never have any stomach when I eat alone. – Come, but where do we dine?

HORNER. Even where you will.

---

357 *I*: Q1 omits.
362 *French trimming*: a pun on Horner's 'state'.
364 see Additional Note.
368 *exceptious*: vexed.

SPARKISH. At Chateline's?

DORILANT. Yes, if you will.

SPARKISH. Or at the Cock?

DORILANT. Yes, if you please.

SPARKISH. Or at the Dog and Partridge?

HORNER. Ay, if you have a mind to't, for we shall dine at neither.

SPARKISH. Pshaw, with your fooling we shall lose the new play; and I would no more miss seeing a new play the first day than I would miss setting in the wits' row. Therefore I'll go fetch my mistress and away.

Exit SPARKISH.

Manent HORNER, HARCOURT, DORILANT.

Enter to them MR PINCHWIFE.

HORNER. Who have we here? Pinchwife?

PINCHWIFE. Gentlemen, your humble servant.

HORNER. Well, Jack, by the long absence from the town, the grumness of thy countenance and the slovenliness of thy habit, I should give thee joy, should I not, of marriage?

PINCHWIFE. (*aside*) Death! Does he know I'm married too? I thought to have concealed it from him at least. – My long stay in the country will excuse my dress and I have a suit of law, that brings me up to town, that puts me out of humour; besides, I must give Sparkish tomorrow five thousand pound to lie with my sister.

HORNER. Nay, you country gentlemen, rather than not purchase, will buy anything; and he is a cracked title, if we may quibble. Well, but am I to give thee joy? I heard thou wert married.

PINCHWIFE. What then?

HORNER. Why, the next thing that is to be heard is thou'rt a cuckold.

---

386 *Chateline's*: a famous French restaurant in Covent Garden.

388 *the Cock*: out of many possible taverns, most probably the one in Bow Street; see *The Plain-Dealer*, Act V Scene ii.

390 *the Dog and Partridge*: a tavern in Fleet Street.

391 *a mind*: mind Q1.

400 *grumness*: sullenness.

408 *five thousand pound*: as a dowry.

411 *cracked title*: an unsound right of ownership; *cracked* also means foolish.

PINCHWIFE. (*aside*) Insupportable name!

HORNER. But I did not expect marriage from such a whoremaster as you, one that knew the town so much and women so well.

PINCHWIFE. Why, I have married no London wife.

HORNER. Pshaw, that's all one; that grave circumspection in marrying a country wife is like refusing a deceitful, pampered Smithfield jade to go and be cheated by a friend in the country.

PINCHWIFE. (*aside*) A pox on him and his simile. – At least we are a little surer of the breed there, know what her keeping has been, whether foiled or unsound.

HORNER. Come, come, I have known a clap gotten in Wales; and there are cozens, justices, clerks and chaplains in the country, I won't say coachmen. But she's handsome and young?

PINCHWIFE. (*aside*) I'll answer as I should do. – No, no, she has no beauty but her youth; no attraction but her modesty; wholesome, homely and housewifely; that's all.

DORILANT. He talks as like a grazier as he looks.

PINCHWIFE. She's too awkward, ill-favoured, and silly to bring to town.

HARCOURT. Then methinks you should bring her, to be taught breeding.

PINCHWIFE. To be taught! No, sir! I thank you. Good wives and private soldiers should be ignorant. [*Aside*] I'll keep her from your instructions, I warrant you.

HARCOURT. (*aside*) The rogue is as jealous as if his wife were not ignorant.

HORNER. Why, if she be ill-favoured, there will be less danger here for you than by leaving her in the country; we have such variety of dainties that we are seldom hungry.

---

419 *whoremaster*: a man experienced in whoring.

424 *Smithfield jade*: a worn-out horse bought at Smithfield Market, a place notorious for sharp practice; *jade* also means a disreputable woman.

428 *foiled*: injured, defective (horse); deflowered, diseased (woman)

429 *clap*: syphilis.

430 *cozens*: cheats.

437 *grazier*: grazer of cattle fattened for market.

441 *breeding*: (*a*) gentility (*b*) pregnancy.

DORILANT. But they have always coarse, constant, swingeing stomachs in the country.

HARCOURT. Foul feeders indeed.

DORILANT. And your hospitality is great there.

HARCOURT. Open house, every man's welcome.

PINCHWIFE. So, so, gentlemen.

HORNER. But, prithee, why wouldst thou marry her? If she be ugly, ill-bred and silly, she must be rich then.

PINCHWIFE. As rich as if she brought me twenty thousand pound out of this town, for she'll be as sure not to spend her moderate portion as a London baggage would be to spend hers, let it be what it would; so 'tis all one. Then, because she's ugly, she's the likelier to be my own; and being ill-bred, she'll have conversation; and since silly and innocent, will not know the difference betwixt a man of one-and-twenty and one of forty.

HORNER. Nine – to my knowledge; but if she be silly, she'll expect as much from a man of forty-nine as from him of one-and-twenty. But methinks wit is more necessary than beauty, and I think no young woman ugly that has it, and no handsome woman agreeable without it.

PINCHWIFE. 'Tis my maxim, he's a fool that marries, but he's a greater that does not marry a fool. What is wit in a wife good for, but to make a man a cuckold?

HORNER. Yes, to keep it from his knowledge.

PINCHWIFE. A fool cannot contrive to make her husband a cuckold.

HORNER. No, but she'll club with a man that can; and what is worse, if she cannot make her husband a cuckold, she'll make him jealous and pass for one, and then 'tis all one.

PINCHWIFE. Well, well, I'll take care for one, my wife shall make me no cuckold, though she had your help, Mr Horner; I understand the town, sir.

DORILANT. (*aside*) His help!

HARCOURT. (*aside*) He's come newly to town, it seems, and has not heard how things are with him.

HORNER. But tell me, has marriage cured thee of whoring, which it seldom does?

---

452 *swingeing stomachs*: enormous appetites.
479 *club*: get together with.

HARCOURT. 'Tis more than age can do.

HORNER. No, the word is, I'll marry and live honest; but a marriage vow is like a penitent gamester's oath and entering into bonds and penalties to stint himself to such a particular small sum at play for the future, which makes him but the more eager and, not being able to hold out, loses his money again and his forfeit to boot.

DORILANT. Ay, ay, a gamester will be a gamester whilst his money lasts, and a whoremaster whilst his vigour.

HARCOURT. Nay, I have known 'em, when they are broke and can lose no more, keep a-fumbling with the box in their hands to fool with only and hinder other gamesters.

DORILANT. That had wherewithal to make lusty stakes.

PINCHWIFE. Well, gentlemen, you may laugh at me, but you shall never lie with my wife; I know the town.

HORNER. But prithee, was not the way you were in better? Is not keeping better than marriage?

PINCHWIFE. A pox on't! The jades would jilt me; I could never keep a whore to myself.

HORNER. So, then you only married to keep a whore to yourself. Well, but let me tell you, women, as you say, are like soldiers, made constant and loyal by good pay rather than by oaths and covenants. Therefore I'd advise my friends to keep rather than marry, since too, I find, by your example, it does not serve one's turn, for I saw you yesterday in the eighteen-penny place with a pretty country wench.

PINCHWIFE. (*aside*) How the devil! Did he see my wife then? I sat there that she might not be seen. But she shall never go to a play again.

HORNER. What, dost thou blush at nine-and-forty, for having been seen with a wench?

DORILANT. No, faith, I warrant 'twas his wife, which he seated there out of sight, for he's a cunning rogue and understands the town.

---

503 *box*: for shaking the dice.

518–19 *eighteen-penny place*: the middle gallery of the theatre, frequented by citizens and whores.

HARCOURT. He blushes. Then 'twas his wife, for men are now more ashamed to be seen with them in public than with a wench.

PINCHWIFE. (*aside*) Hell and damnation! I'm undone, since Horner has seen her and they know 'twas she.

HORNER. But prithee, was it thy wife? She was exceedingly pretty; I was in love with her at that distance.

PINCHWIFE. You are like never to be nearer to her. Your servant, gentlemen. (*Offers to go*)

HORNER. Nay, prithee stay.

PINCHWIFE. I cannot, I will not.

HORNER. Come, you shall dine with us.

PINCHWIFE. I have dined already.

HORNER. Come, I know thou hast not. I'll treat thee, dear rogue; thou shalt spend none of thy Hampshire money today.

PINCHWIFE. (*aside*) Treat me! So, he uses me already like his cuckold.

HORNER. Nay, you shall not go.

PINCHWIFE. I must, I have business at home.

Exit PINCHWIFE.

HARCOURT. To beat his wife; he's as jealous of her as a Cheapside husband of a Covent Garden wife.

HORNER. Why, 'tis as hard to find an old whoremaster without jealousy and the gout, as a young one without fear or the pox.

As gout in age from pox in youth proceeds,
So wenching past, then jealousy succeeds,
The worst disease that love and wenching breeds.

[*Exeunt.*]

---

537 s.d. *Offers*: attempts.

550 *Cheapside . . . wife*: a city merchant of a fashionable wife.

ACT II

SCENE I

MRS MARGERY PINCHWIFE *and* ALITHEA.
MR PINCHWIFE *peeping behind at the door.*

MRS PINCHWIFE. Pray, sister, where are the best fields and woods to walk in, in London?

ALITHEA. A pretty question! Why, sister, Mulberry Garden and St James's Park and, for close walks, the New Exchange.

MRS PINCHWIFE. Pray, sister, tell me why my husband looks so grum here in town and keeps me up so close and will not let me go a-walking, nor let me wear my best gown yesterday.

ALITHEA. Oh, he's jealous, sister.

MRS PINCHWIFE. Jealous? What's that?

ALITHEA. He's afraid you should love another man.

MRS PINCHWIFE. How should he be afraid of my loving another man, when he will not let me see any but himself?

ALITHEA. Did he not carry you yesterday to a play?

MRS PINCHWIFE. Ay, but we sat amongst ugly people; he would not let me come near the gentry, who sat under us, so that I could not see 'em. He told me none but naughty women sat there, whom they toused and moused. But I would have ventured for all that.

ALITHEA. But how did you like the play?

3–4 *Mulberry Garden*: a garden of mulberry trees, now the site of Buckingham Palace, a fashionable meeting-place. *Love in a Wood*, Act V Scene ii, is set in 'the dining-room in Mulberry Garden House'.

4 *St James's Park*: the park near Whitehall, scene of Act II and part of Act V of *Love in a Wood* – and also its subtitle.

4 *close*: covered.

5 *New Exchange*: an arcade with two galleries of shops, situated south of the Strand; it is the setting for Act III Scene ii of *The Country Wife*.

7 *grum*: sullen.

21 *toused and moused*: rumpled and played with, usually sexily.

MRS PINCHWIFE. Indeed, I was a-weary of the play, but I liked hugeously the actors; they are the goodliest, properest men, sister!

ALITHEA. O, but you must not like the actors, sister.

MRS PINCHWIFE. Ay, how should I help it, sister? Pray, sister, when my husband comes in, will you ask leave for me to go a-walking?

ALITHEA. (*aside*) A-walking, hah, ha! Lord, a country gentlewoman's leisure is the drudgery of a foot-post; and she requires as much airing as her husband's horses.

Enter MR PINCHWIFE *to them.*

But here comes your husband; I'll ask, though I'm sure he'll not grant it.

MRS PINCHWIFE. He says he won't let me go abroad for fear of catching the pox.

ALITHEA. Fie! The smallpox you should say.

MRS PINCHWIFE. O my dear, dear bud, welcome home! Why dost thou look so fropish? Who has nangered thee?

PINCHWIFE. You're a fool.

MRS PINCHWIFE *goes aside and cries.*

ALITHEA. Faith, so she is, for crying for no fault, poor tender creature!

PINCHWIFE. What, you would have her as impudent as yourself, as arrant a jill-flirt, a gadder, a magpie and, to say all, a mere notorious town-woman?

ALITHEA. Brother, you are my only censurer; and the honour of your family shall sooner suffer in your wife there than in me, though I take the innocent liberty of the town.

PINCHWIFE. Hark you, mistress, do not talk so before my wife. The innocent liberty of the town!

ALITHEA. Why, pray, who boasts of any intrigue with me? What lampoon has made my name notorious?

---

32 *foot-post*: letter-carrier on foot.

41 *fropish*: peevish.

41 *nangered*: angered.

47 *jill-flirt, a gadder, a magpie*: a wanton girl, a gadabout, an idle chatterer.

56 *lampoon*: scurrilous satire.

What ill women frequent my lodgings? I keep no company with any women of scandalous reputations.

PINCHWIFE. No, you keep the men of scandalous reputations company.

ALITHEA. Where? Would you not have me civil? Answer 'em in a box at the plays? In the drawing room at Whitehall? In St James's Park? Mulberry Gardens? Or –

PINCHWIFE. Hold, hold! Do not teach my wife where the men are to be found! I believe she's the worse for your town documents already. I bid you keep her in ignorance, as I do.

MRS PINCHWIFE. Indeed, be not angry with her, bud; she will tell me nothing of the town, though I ask her a thousand times a day.

PINCHWIFE. Then you are very inquisitive to know, I find!

MRS PINCHWIFE. Not I, indeed, dear; I hate London. Our place-house in the country is worth a thousand of't; would I were there again!

PINCHWIFE. So you shall, I warrant. But were you not talking of plays and players when I came in? [*To* ALITHEA] You are her encourager in such discourses.

MRS PINCHWIFE. No, indeed, dear; she chid me just now for liking the playermen.

PINCHWIFE. (*aside*) Nay, if she be so innocent as to own to me her liking them, there is no hurt in't. – Come, my poor rogue, but thou lik'st none better than me?

MRS PINCHWIFE. Yes, indeed, but I do; the playermen are finer folks.

PINCHWIFE. But you love none better than me?

MRS PINCHWIFE. You are mine own dear bud, and I know you; I hate a stranger.

PINCHWIFE. Ay, my dear, you must love me only and not be like the naughty town-women, who only hate their husbands and love every man else, love plays, visits, fine coaches, fine clothes, fiddles, balls, treats, and so lead a wicked town-life.

---

67 *documents*: information.
75 *place-house*: chief house on an estate.

MRS PINCHWIFE. Nay, if to enjoy all these things be a town-life, London is not so bad a place, dear.

PINCHWIFE. How! If you love me, you must hate London.

ALITHEA. [*aside*] The fool has forbid me discovering to her the pleasures of the town and he is now setting her agog upon them himself.

MRS PINCHWIFE. But, husband, do the town-women love the playermen too?

PINCHWIFE. Yes, I warrant you.

MRS PINCHWIFE. Ay, I warrant you.

PINCHWIFE. Why, you do not, I hope?

MRS PINCHWIFE. No, no, bud; but why have we no playermen in the country?

PINCHWIFE. Ha – Mrs Minx, ask me no more to go to a play.

MRS PINCHWIFE. Nay, why, love? I did not care for going; but when you forbid me, you make me, as 'twere, desire it.

ALITHEA. (*aside*) So 'twill be in other things, I warrant.

MRS PINCHWIFE. Pray let me go to a play, dear.

PINCHWIFE. Hold your peace, I wo'not.

MRS PINCHWIFE. Why, love?

PINCHWIFE. Why, I'll tell you.

ALITHEA. (*aside*) Nay, if he tell her, she'll give him more cause to forbid her that place.

MRS PINCHWIFE. Pray, why, dear?

PINCHWIFE. First, you like the actors and the gallants may like you.

MRS PINCHWIFE. What, a homely country girl? No, bud, nobody will like me.

PINCHWIFE. I tell you, yes, they may.

MRS PINCHWIFE. No, no, you jest – I won't believe you, I will go.

PINCHWIFE. I tell you then that one of the lewdest fellows in town, who saw you there, told me he was in love with you.

MRS PINCHWIFE. Indeed! Who, who, pray, who was't?

PINCHWIFE. (*aside*) I've gone too far and slipped before I was aware. How overjoyed she is!

MRS PINCHWIFE. Was it any Hampshire gallant, any of our neighbours? I promise you, I am beholding to him.

PINCHWIFE. I promise you, you lie, for he would but ruin you, as he has done hundreds. He has no other love for women but that; such as he look upon women, like basilisks, but to destroy 'em.

MRS PINCHWIFE. Ay, but if he loves me, why should he ruin me? Answer me to that. Methinks he should not; I would do him no harm.

ALITHEA. Hah, ha, ha!

PINCHWIFE. 'Tis very well; but I'll keep him from doing you any harm, or me either.

Enter SPARKISH *and* HARCOURT.

But here comes company; get you in, get you in.

MRS PINCHWIFE. But pray, husband, is he a pretty gentleman that loves me?

PINCHWIFE. In, baggage, in. (*Thrusts her in, shuts the door*) What, all the lewd libertines of the town brought to my lodging by this easy coxcomb! 'Sdeath, I'll not suffer it.

SPARKISH. Here, Harcourt, do you approve my choice? [*To* ALITHEA] Dear little rogue, I told you I'd bring you acquainted with all my friends, the wits, and –

HARCOURT *salutes her.*

PINCHWIFE. [*aside*] Ay, they shall know her, as well as you yourself will, I warrant you.

SPARKISH. This is one of those, my pretty rogue, that are to dance at your wedding tomorrow; and him you must bid welcome ever to what you and I have.

PINCHWIFE. (*aside*) Monstrous!

SPARKISH. Harcourt, how dost thou like her, faith? – Nay, dear, do not look down; I should hate to have a wife of mine out of countenance at anything.

PINCHWIFE. [*aside*] Wonderful!

SPARKISH. Tell me, I say, Harcourt, how dost thou like her? Thou hast stared upon her enough to resolve me.

HARCOURT. So infinitely well that I could wish I had a mistress too, that might differ from her in nothing but her love and engagement to you.

ALITHEA. Sir, Master Sparkish has often told me that his acquaintance were all wits and railleurs and now I find it.

---

140 *basilisks*: mythical serpents whose glance was fatal.
173 *railleurs*: witty banterers.

SPARKISH. No, by the universe, madam, he does not rally now; you may believe him. I do assure you, he is the honestest, worthiest, true-hearted gentleman – a man of such perfect honour, he would say nothing to a lady he does not mean.

PINCHWIFE. [*aside*] Praising another man to his mistress!

HARCOURT. Sir, you are so beyond expectation obliging that –

SPARKISH. Nay, ygad, I am sure you do admire her extremely; I see't in your eyes. – He does admire you, madam. – By the world, don't you?

HARCOURT. Yes, above the world, or the most glorious part of it, her whole sex; and till now I never thought I should have envied you, or any man about to marry, but you have the best excuse for marriage I ever knew.

ALITHEA. Nay, now, sir, I'm satisfied you are of the society of the wits and railleurs, since you cannot spare your friend, even when he is but too civil to you; but the surest sign is since you are an enemy to marriage, for that, I hear, you hate as much as business or bad wine.

HARCOURT. Truly, madam, I never was an enemy to marriage till now, because marriage was never an enemy to me before.

ALITHEA. But why, sir, is marriage an enemy to you now? Because it robs you of your friend here? For you look upon a friend married as one gone into a monastery, that is dead to the world.

HARCOURT. 'Tis indeed because you marry him; I see, madam, you can guess my meaning. I do confess heartily and openly, I wish it were in my power to break the match; by heavens I would.

SPARKISH. Poor Frank!

ALITHEA. Would you be so unkind to me?

HARCOURT. No, no, 'tis not because I would be unkind to you.

SPARKISH. Poor Frank! No, gad, 'tis only his kindness to me.

PINCHWIFE. (*aside*) Great kindness to you indeed! Insensible fop, let a man make love to his wife to his face!

SPARKISH. Come, dear Frank, for all my wife there that shall be, thou shalt enjoy me sometimes, dear rogue. By my honour, we men of wit condole for our deceased brother in marriage as much as for one dead in earnest. I think that was prettily said of me, ha, Harcourt? But come, Frank, be not melancholy for me.

HARCOURT. No, I assure you I am not melancholy for you.

SPARKISH. Prithee, Frank, dost think my wife that shall be there a fine person?

HARCOURT. I could gaze upon her till I became as blind as you are.

SPARKISH. How, as I am? How?

HARCOURT. Because you are a lover and true lovers are blind, stock blind.

SPARKISH. True, true; but by the world, she has wit too, as well as beauty. Go, go with her into a corner and try if she has wit; talk to her anything; she's bashful before me.

HARCOURT. Indeed, if a woman wants wit in a corner, she has it nowhere.

ALITHEA. (*aside to* SPARKISH) Sir, you dispose of me a little before your time –

SPARKISH. Nay, nay, madam, let me have an earnest of your obedience, or – go, go, madam –

HARCOURT *courts* ALITHEA *aside.*

PINCHWIFE. How, sir! If you are not concerned for the honour of a wife, I am for that of a sister; he shall not debauch her. Be a pander to your own wife, bring men to her, let 'em make love before your face, thrust 'em into a corner together, then leave 'em in private! Is this your town wit and conduct?

SPARKISH. Hah, ha, ha, a silly wise rogue would make one laugh more than a stark fool, hah, ha! I shall burst. Nay, you shall not disturb 'em; I'll vex thee, by the world. (*Struggles with* PINCHWIFE *to keep him from* HARCOURT *and* ALITHEA)

ALITHEA. The writings are drawn, sir, settlements made; 'tis too late, sir, and past all revocation.

---

222 *not*: not not Q1.
232 *stock blind*: as blind as a log.
241 *earnest*: foretaste.
251 *vex*: stop.

HARCOURT. Then so is my death.

ALITHEA. I would not be unjust to him.

HARCOURT. Then why to me so?

ALITHEA. I have no obligation to you.

HARCOURT. My love.

ALITHEA. I had his before.

HARCOURT. You never had it; he wants, you see, jealousy, the only infallible sign of it.

ALITHEA. Love proceeds from esteem; he cannot distrust my virtue. Besides, he loves me, or he would not marry me.

HARCOURT. Marrying you is no more sign of his love than bribing your woman, that he may marry you, is a sign of his generosity. Marriage is rather a sign of interest than love, and he that marries a fortune covets a mistress, not loves her. But if you take marriage for a sign of love, take it from me immediately.

ALITHEA. No, now you have put a scruple in my head; but, in short, sir, to end our dispute, I must marry him, my reputation would suffer in the world else.

HARCOURT. No, if you do marry him, with your pardon, madam, your reputation suffers in the world and you would be thought in necessity for a cloak.

ALITHEA. Nay, now you are rude, sir. – Mr Sparkish, pray come hither, your friend here is very troublesome, and very loving.

HARCOURT. (*aside to* ALITHEA) Hold, hold! –

PINCHWIFE. D'ye hear that?

SPARKISH. Why, d'ye think I'll seem to be jealous, like a country bumpkin?

PINCHWIFE. No, rather be a cuckold, like a credulous cit.

HARCOURT. Madam, you would not have been so little generous as to have told him.

ALITHEA. Yes, since you could be so little generous as to wrong him.

HARCOURT. Wrong him! No man can do't, he's beneath an injury; a bubble, a coward, a senseless idiot, a

---

277 *necessity for a cloak*: to hide pregnancy, perhaps, as well as other affairs.

286 *cit*: contemptuous term for a citizen, a merchant not a gentleman.

292 *bubble*: gullible fool.

wretch so contemptible to all the world but you that –

ALITHEA. Hold, do not rail at him, for since he is like to be my husband, I am resolved to like him. Nay, I think I am obliged to tell him you are not his friend. – Master Sparkish, Master Sparkish.

SPARKISH. What, what? – Now, dear rogue, has not she wit?

HARCOURT. (*speaks surlily*) Not so much as I thought and hoped she had.

ALITHEA. Mr Sparkish, do you bring people to rail at you?

HARCOURT. Madam –

SPARKISH. How! No, but if he does rail at me, 'tis but in jest, I warrant; what we wits do for one another and never take any notice of it.

ALITHEA. He spoke so scurrilously of you, I had no patience to hear him; besides, he has been making love to me.

HARCOURT. (*aside*) True, damned, telltale woman!

SPARKISH. Pshaw, to show his parts – we wits rail and make love often but to show our parts; as we have no affections, so we have no malice. We –

ALITHEA. He said you were a wretch, below an injury.

SPARKISH. Pshaw!

HARCOURT. [*aside*] Damned, senseless, impudent, virtuous jade! Well, since she won't let me have her, she'll do as good, she'll make me hate her.

ALITHEA. A common bubble.

SPARKISH. Pshaw!

ALITHEA. A coward.

SPARKISH. Pshaw, pshaw!

ALITHEA. A senseless, drivelling idiot.

SPARKISH. How! Did he disparage my parts? Nay, then my honour's concerned; I can't put up that, sir, by the world. Brother, help me to kill him. (*Aside*) I may draw now, since we have the odds of him. 'Tis a good occasion, too, before my mistress – (*Offers to draw*)

ALITHEA. Hold, hold!

SPARKISH. What, what?

ALITHEA. (*aside*) I must not let 'em kill the gentleman neither, for his kindness to me; I am so far from hating him that I wish my gallant had his person and understanding. – Nay, if my honour –

SPARKISH. I'll be thy death.

ALITHEA. Hold, hold! Indeed, to tell the truth, the gentleman said after all that what he spoke was but out of friendship to you.

SPARKISH. How! say I am, I am a fool, that is, no wit, out of friendship to me?

ALITHEA. Yes, to try whether I was concerned enough for you and made love to me only to be satisfied of my virtue, for your sake.

HARCOURT. (*aside*) Kind, however –

SPARKISH. Nay, if it were so, my dear rogue, I ask thee pardon; but why would not you tell me so, faith?

HARCOURT. Because I did not think on't, faith.

SPARKISH. Come, Horner does not come, Harcourt, let's be gone to the new play. – Come, madam.

ALITHEA. I will not go if you intend to leave me alone in the box and run into the pit, as you use to do.

SPARKISH. Pshaw! I'll leave Harcourt with you in the box to entertain you, and that's as good; if I sat in the box, I should be thought no judge but of trimmings. – Come away, Harcourt, lead her down.

Exeunt SPARKISH, HARCOURT *and* ALITHEA.

PINCHWIFE. Well, go thy ways, for the flower of the true town fops, such as spend their estates before they come to 'em and are cuckolds before they're married. But let me go look to my own freehold. – How! –

Enter MY LADY FIDGET, MRS DAINTY FIDGET *and* MRS SQUEAMISH.

LADY FIDGET. Your servant, sir; where is your lady? We are come to wait upon her to the new play.

PINCHWIFE. New play!

LADY FIDGET. And my husband will wait upon you presently.

PINCHWIFE. (*aside*) Damn your civility. – Madam, by no means; I will not see Sir Jaspar here till I have waited upon him at home; nor shall my wife see you till she has waited upon your ladyship at your lodgings.

LADY FIDGET. Now we are here, sir –

PINCHWIFE. No, madam.

DAINTY. Pray, let us see her.

355–6 *trimmings*: clothes.

SQUEAMISH. We will not stir till we see her.

PINCHWIFE. (*aside*) A pox on you all! (*Goes to the door, and returns*) – She has locked the door and is gone abroad.

LADY FIDGET. No, you have locked the door and she's within.

DAINTY. They told us below she was here.

PINCHWIFE. (*aside*) Will nothing do? – Well, it must out then. To tell you the truth, ladies, which I was afraid to let you know before, lest it might endanger your lives, my wife has just now the smallpox come out upon her. Do not be frightened but pray, be gone, ladies; you shall not stay here in danger of your lives. Pray get you gone, ladies.

LADY FIDGET. No, no, we have all had 'em.

SQUEAMISH. Alack, alack.

DAINTY. Come, come, we must see how it goes with her; I understand the disease.

LADY FIDGET. Come.

PINCHWIFE. (*aside*) Well, there is no being too hard for women at their own weapon, lying; therefore I'll quit the field. *Exit* PINCHWIFE.

SQUEAMISH. Here's an example of jealousy.

LADY FIDGET. Indeed, as the world goes, I wonder there are no more jealous, since wives are so neglected.

DAINTY. Pshaw, as the world goes, to what end should they be jealous?

LADY FIDGET. Foh, 'tis a nasty world.

SQUEAMISH. That men of parts, great acquaintance and quality should take up with and spend themselves and fortunes in keeping little playhouse creatures, foh!

LADY FIDGET. Nay, that women of understanding, great acquaintance and good quality should fall a-keeping too of little creatures, foh!

SQUEAMISH. Why, 'tis the men of quality's fault; they never visit women of honour and reputation, as they used to do and have not so much as common civility for ladies of our rank, but use us with the same indifferency and ill-breeding as if we were all married to 'em.

LADY FIDGET. She says true; 'tis an arrant shame women of quality should be so slighted. Methinks birth, birth should go for something. I have known men admired, courted and followed for their titles only.

SQUEAMISH. Ay, one would think men of honour should not love, no more than marry, out of their own rank.

DAINTY. Fie, fie upon 'em! They are come to think crossbreeding for themselves best, as well as for their dogs and horses.

LADY FIDGET. They are dogs and horses for't.

SQUEAMISH. One would think, if not for love, for vanity a little.

DAINTY. Nay, they do satisfy their vanity upon us sometimes and are kind to us in their report, tell all the world they lie with us.

LADY FIDGET. Damned rascals! That we should be only wronged by 'em! To report a man has had a person, when he has not had a person, is the greatest wrong in the whole world that can be done to a person.

SQUEAMISH. Well, 'tis an arrant shame noble persons should be so wronged and neglected.

LADY FIDGET. But still 'tis an arranter shame for a noble person to neglect her own honour and defame her own noble person with little inconsiderable fellows, foh!

DAINTY. I suppose the crime against our honour is the same with a man of quality as with another.

LADY FIDGET. How! No, sure, the man of quality is likest one's husband and therefore the fault should be the less.

DAINTY. But then the pleasure should be the less.

LADY FIDGET. Fie, fie, fie, for shame, sister! Whither shall we ramble? Be continent in your discourse, or I shall hate you.

DAINTY. Besides, an intrigue is so much the more notorious for the man's quality.

SQUEAMISH. 'Tis true, nobody takes notice of a private man and therefore with him 'tis more secret, and the crime's the less when 'tis not known.

LADY FIDGET. You say true; i'faith, I think you are in the right on't. 'Tis not an injury to a husband till it be an injury to our honours; so that a woman of honour loses no honour with a private person; and to say truth –

DAINTY. (*apart to* SQUEAMISH) So, the little fellow is grown a private person – with her –

LADY FIDGET. But still my dear, dear honour.

Enter SIR JASPAR, HORNER, DORILANT.

SIR JASPAR. Ay, my dear, dear of honour, thou hast still so much honour in thy mouth –

HORNER. (*aside*) That she has none elsewhere.

LADY FIDGET. Oh, what d'ye mean to bring in these upon us?

DAINTY. Foh, these are as bad as wits.

SQUEAMISH. Foh!

LADY FIDGET. Let us leave the room.

SIR JASPAR. Stay, stay; faith, to tell you the naked truth –

LADY FIDGET. Fie, Sir Jaspar, do not use that word 'naked'.

SIR JASPAR. Well, well, in short, I have business at Whitehall and cannot go to the play with you, therefore would have you go –

LADY FIDGET. With those two to a play?

SIR JASPAR. No, not with t'other but with Mr Horner; there can be no more scandal to go with him than with Mr Tattle or Master Limberham.

LADY FIDGET. With that nasty fellow! No – no!

SIR JASPAR. Nay, prithee, dear, hear me. (*Whispers to* LADY FIDGET)

HORNER. Ladies –

HORNER, DORILANT *drawing near* SQUEAMISH *and* DAINTY.

DAINTY. Stand off.

SQUEAMISH. Do not approach us.

DAINTY. You herd with the wits, you are obscenity all over.

SQUEAMISH. And I would as soon look upon a picture of Adam and Eve, without fig leaves, as any of you, if I could help it; therefore keep off and do not make us sick.

---

482 *Mr Tattle or Master Limberham*: the 'old civil gentlemen' of line 557; Tattle was later used by Congreve for the fop in *Love for Love* (1695) and Limberham by Dryden for the title character in *The Kind Keeper* (1678).

DORILANT. What a devil are these?

HORNER. Why, these are pretenders to honour, as critics to wit, only by censuring others; and as every raw, peevish, out-of-humoured, affected, dull, tea-drinking, arithmetical fop sets up for a wit by railing at men of sense, so these for honour by railing at the Court and ladies of as great honour as quality.

SIR JASPAR. Come, Mr Horner, I must desire you to go with these ladies to the play, sir.

HORNER. I, sir!

SIR JASPAR. Ay, ay, come, sir.

HORNER. I must beg your pardon, sir, and theirs; I will not be seen in women's company in public again for the world.

SIR JASPAR. Ha, ha, strange aversion!

SQUEAMISH. No, he's for women's company in private.

SIR JASPAR. He – poor man – he! Hah, ha, ha!

DAINTY. 'Tis a greater shame amongst lewd fellows to be seen in virtuous women's company than for the women to be seen with them.

HORNER. Indeed, madam, the time was I only hated virtuous women, but now I hate the other too; I beg your pardon, ladies.

LADY FIDGET. You are very obliging, sir, because we would not be troubled with you.

SIR JASPAR. In sober sadness, he shall go.

DORILANT. Nay, if he wo'not, I am ready to wait upon the ladies; and I think I am the fitter man.

SIR JASPAR. You, sir, no, I thank you for that – Master Horner is a privileged man amongst the virtuous ladies; 'twill be a great while before you are so; heh, he, he! He's my wife's gallant, heh, he, he! No, pray withdraw, sir, for as I take it, the virtuous ladies have no business with you.

DORILANT. And I am sure he can have none with them. 'Tis strange a man can't come amongst virtuous women now but upon the same terms as men are admitted into the Great Turk's seraglio; but heavens

---

498 *arithmetical*: precise.
531 *the Great Turk's seraglio*: the Turkish Sultan's harem.

keep me from being an ombre player with 'em! But where is Pinchwife? *Exit* DORILANT.

SIR JASPAR. Come, come, man; what, avoid the sweet society of womankind? that sweet, soft, gentle, tame, noble creature, woman, made for man's companion –

HORNER. So is that soft, gentle, tame and more noble creature a spaniel, and has all their tricks: can fawn, lie down, suffer beating and fawn the more; barks at your friends when they come to see you; makes your bed hard; gives you fleas, and the mange sometimes. And all the difference is, the spaniel's the more faithful animal and fawns but upon one master.

SIR JASPAR. Heh, he, he!

SQUEAMISH. Oh, the rude beast!

DAINTY. Insolent brute!

LADY FIDGET. Brute! Stinking, mortified, rotten French wether, to dare –

SIR JASPAR. Hold, an't please your ladyship. – For shame, Master Horner, your mother was a woman. (*Aside*) Now shall I never reconcile 'em. [*Aside to* LADY FIDGET] Hark you, madam, take my advice in your anger. You know you often want one to make up your drolling pack of ombre players; and you may cheat him easily, for he's an ill gamester and consequently loves play. Besides, you know, you have but two old civil gentlemen, with stinking breaths too, to wait upon you abroad; take in the third into your service. The other are but crazy; and a lady should have a supernumerary gentleman-usher, as a supernumerary coach-horse, lest sometimes you should be forced to stay at home.

LADY FIDGET. But are you sure he loves play and has money?

SIR JASPAR. He loves play as much as you and has money as much as I.

LADY FIDGET. Then I am contented to make him pay for his scurrility; money makes up in a measure all

---

532 *ombre*: a card game and a pun on *hombre* (man).
548 *French wether*: castrated ram.
554 *drolling*: ridiculous.
559 *crazy*: decrepit.

other wants in men. (*Aside*) Those whom we cannot make hold for gallants, we make fine.

SIR JASPAR. (*aside*) So, so; now to mollify, to wheedle him. – Master Horner, will you never keep civil company? Methinks 'tis time now, since you are only fit for them. Come, come, man, you must e'en fall to visiting our wives, eating at our tables, drinking tea with our virtuous relations after dinner, dealing cards to 'em, reading plays and gazettes to 'em, picking fleas out of their shocks for 'em, collecting receipts, new songs, women, pages and footmen for 'em.

HORNER. I hope they'll afford me better employment, sir.

SIR JASPAR. Heh, he, he! 'Tis fit you know your work before you come into your place; and since you are unprovided of a lady to flatter and a good house to eat at, pray frequent mine and call my wife mistress and she shall call you gallant, according to the custom.

HORNER. Who, I?

SIR JASPAR. Faith, thou shalt for my sake; come, for my sake only.

HORNER. For your sake –

SIR JASPAR. [*to* LADY FIDGET] Come, come, here's a gamester for you; let him be a little familiar sometimes. Nay, what if a little rude? Gamesters may be rude with ladies, you know.

LADY FIDGET. Yes, losing gamesters have a privilege with women.

HORNER. I always thought the contrary, that the winning gamester had most privilege with women, for when you have lost your money to a man, you'll lose anything you have, all you have, they say, and he may use you as he pleases.

SIR JASPAR. Heh, he, he! Well, win or lose, you shall have your liberty with her.

LADY FIDGET. As he behaves himself; and for your sake I'll give him admittance and freedom.

---

570 *fine*: pay; particularly appropriate here, since the word was used in cases where a man paid to avoid the duties of an office.

578 *shocks*: poodles.

578 *receipts*: recipes.

HORNER. All sorts of freedom, madam?

SIR JASPAR. Ay, ay, ay, all sorts of freedom thou canst take, and so go to her, begin thy new employment; wheedle her, jest with her and be better acquainted one with another.

HORNER. (*aside*) I think I know her already, therefore may venture with her, my secret for hers.

HORNER *and* LADY FIDGET *whisper.*

SIR JASPAR. Sister, cuz, I have provided an innocent playfellow for you there.

DAINTY. Who, he!

SQUEAMISH. There's a playfellow indeed!

SIR JASPAR. Yes, sure; what, he is good enough to play at cards, blindman's buff, or the fool with sometimes.

SQUEAMISH. Foh, we'll have no such playfellows.

DAINTY. No, sir, you shan't choose playfellows for us, we thank you.

SIR JASPAR. Nay, pray hear me. (*Whispering to them*)

LADY FIDGET. [*aside to* HORNER] But, poor gentleman, could you be so generous, so truly a man of honour, as for the sakes of us women of honour, to cause yourself to be reported no man? No man! And to suffer yourself the greatest shame that could fall upon a man, that none might fall upon us women by your conversation? But indeed, sir, as perfectly, perfectly the same man as before your going into France, sir? As perfectly, perfectly, sir?

HORNER. As perfectly, perfectly, madam. Nay, I scorn you should take my word; I desire to be tried only, madam.

LADY FIDGET. Well, that's spoken again like a man of honour; all men of honour desire to come to the test. But, indeed, generally you men report such things of yourselves, one does not know how or whom to believe and it is come to that pass we dare not take your words, no more than your tailors, without some staid servant of yours be bound with you. But I have so strong a faith in your honour, dear, dear, noble sir, that I'd forfeit mine for yours at any time, dear sir.

---

640 *tailors*: tailors could not trust a gentleman's word about payment.

HORNER. No, madam, you should not need to forfeit it for me; I have given you security already to save you harmless, my late reputation being so well known in the world, madam.

LADY FIDGET. But if upon any future falling out or upon a suspicion of my taking the trust out of your hands to employ some other, you yourself should betray your trust, dear sir? I mean, if you'll give me leave to speak obscenely, you might tell, dear sir.

HORNER. If I did, nobody would believe me; the reputation of impotency is as hardly recovered again in the world as that of cowardice, dear madam.

LADY FIDGET. Nay then, as one may say, you may do your worst, dear, dear sir.

SIR JASPAR. Come, is your ladyship reconciled to him yet? Have you agreed on matters? For I must be gone to Whitehall.

LADY FIDGET. Why, indeed, Sir Jaspar, Master Horner is a thousand, thousand times a better man than I thought him. Cousin Squeamish, Sister Dainty, I can name him now; truly, not long ago, you know, I thought his very name obscenity and I would as soon have lain with him as have named him.

SIR JASPAR. Very likely, poor madam.

DAINTY. I believe it.

SQUEAMISH. No doubt on't.

SIR JASPAR. Well, well – that your ladyship is as virtuous as any she, I know, and him all the town knows – heh, he, he! Therefore, now you like him, get you gone to your business together; go, go to your business, I say, pleasure, whilst I go to my pleasure, business.

LADY FIDGET. Come then, dear gallant.

HORNER. Come away, my dearest mistress.

SIR JASPAR. So, so. Why, 'tis as I'd have it.

Exit SIR JASPAR.

HORNER. And as I'd have it.

LADY FIDGET. Who for his business from his wife will run,
Takes the best care to have her business done.

Exeunt omnes.

ACT III

SCENE I

ALITHEA *and* MRS PINCHWIFE.

ALITHEA. Sister, what ails you? You are grown melancholy.

MRS PINCHWIFE. Would it not make anyone melancholy to see you go every day fluttering about abroad, whilst I must stay at home like a poor, lonely, sullen bird in a cage?

ALITHEA. Ay, sister, but you came young and just from the nest to your cage, so that I thought you liked it and could be as cheerful in't as others that took their flight themselves early and are hopping abroad in the open air.

MRS PINCHWIFE. Nay, I confess I was quiet enough till my husband told me what pure lives the London ladies live abroad, with their dancing, meetings and junketings, and dressed every day in their best gowns, and, I warrant you, play at ninepins every day of the week, so they do.

Enter MR PINCHWIFE.

PINCHWIFE. Come, what's here to do? You are putting the town pleasures in her head and setting her a-longing.

ALITHEA. Yes, after ninepins; you suffer none to give her those longings, you mean, but yourself.

PINCHWIFE. I tell her of the vanities of the town like a confessor.

ALITHEA. A confessor! Just such a confessor as he that, by forbidding a silly ostler to grease the horse's teeth, taught him to do't.

PINCHWIFE. Come, Mistress Flippant, good precepts are lost when bad examples are still before us; the liberty

---

13 *pure*: fine

24–6 unscrupulous ostlers would grease a horse's teeth, which supposedly stopped it eating, but still charge the horse's owner for the uneaten feed; see *King Lear*, II iv 123–4.

25 *silly*: ignorant.

you take abroad makes her hanker after it, and out of humour at home, poor wretch! She desired not to come to London; I would bring her.

ALITHEA. Very well.

PINCHWIFE. She has been this week in town and never desired, till this afternoon, to go abroad.

ALITHEA. Was she not at a play yesterday?

PINCHWIFE. Yes, but she ne'er asked me; I was myself the cause of her going.

ALITHEA. Then, if she ask you again, you are the cause of her asking, and not my example.

PINCHWIFE. Well, tomorrow night I shall be rid of you and the next day, before 'tis light, she and I'll be rid of the town, and my dreadful apprehensions. [*To* MRS PINCHWIFE] Come, be not melancholy, for thou shalt go into the country after tomorrow, dearest.

ALITHEA. Great comfort!

MRS PINCHWIFE. Pish, what d'ye tell me of the country for?

PINCHWIFE. How's this! What, pish at the country!

MRS PINCHWIFE. Let me alone, I am not well.

PINCHWIFE. Oh, if that be all – what ails my dearest?

MRS PINCHWIFE. Truly I don't know; but I have not been well since you told me there was a gallant at the play in love with me.

PINCHWIFE. Ha –

ALITHEA. That's by my example too!

PINCHWIFE. Nay, if you are not well, but are so concerned because a lewd fellow chanced to lie and say he liked you, you'll make me sick too.

MRS PINCHWIFE. Of what sickness?

PINCHWIFE. O, of that which is worse than the plague, jealousy.

MRS PINCHWIFE. Pish, you jeer! I'm sure there's no such disease in our receipt-book at home.

PINCHWIFE. No, thou never met'st with it, poor innocent. (*Aside*) Well, if thou cuckold me, 'twill be my own fault – for cuckolds and bastards are generally makers of their own fortune.

MRS PINCHWIFE. Well, but pray, bud, let's to go a play tonight.

PINCHWIFE. 'Tis just done, she comes from it. But why are you so eager to see a play?

MRS PINCHWIFE. Faith, dear, not that I care one pin for their talk there; but I like to look upon the playermen and would see, if I could, the gallant you say loves me; that's all, dear bud.

PINCHWIFE. Is that all, dear bud?

ALITHEA. This proceeds from my example.

MRS PINCHWIFE. But if the play be done, let's go abroad, however, dear bud.

PINCHWIFE. Come, have a little patience and thou shalt go into the country on Friday.

MRS PINCHWIFE. Therefore I would see first some sights, to tell my neighbours of. Nay, I will go abroad, that's once.

ALITHEA. I'm the cause of this desire too.

PINCHWIFE. But now I think on't, who was the cause of Horner's coming to my lodging today? That was you.

ALITHEA. No, you, because you would not let him see your handsome wife out of your lodging.

MRS PINCHWIFE. Why, O Lord! Did the gentleman come hither to see me indeed?

PINCHWIFE. No, no. – You are not cause of that damned question too, Mistress Alithea? (*Aside*) Well, she's in the right of it. He is in love with my wife – and comes after her – 'tis so – but I'll nip his love in the bud, lest he should follow us into the country and break his chariot-wheel near our house on purpose for an excuse to come to't. But I think I know the town.

MRS PINCHWIFE. Come, pray, bud, let's go abroad before 'tis late, for I will go, that's flat and plain.

PINCHWIFE. (*aside*) So! the obstinacy already of a town-wife, and I must, whilst she's here, humour her like one. – Sister, how shall we do, that she may not be seen or known?

ALITHEA. Let her put on her mask.

PINCHWIFE. Pshaw, a mask makes people but the more inquisitive and is as ridiculous a disguise as a stage-beard; her shape, stature, habit will be known and if we should meet with Horner, he would be sure to take acquaintance with us, must wish her joy, kiss her, talk to her, leer upon her, and the devil and all. No, I'll

84 *once*: once and for all.

not use her to a mask, 'tis dangerous, for masks have made more cuckolds than the best faces that ever were known.

ALITHEA. How will you do then?

MRS PINCHWIFE. Nay, shall we go? The Exchange will be shut, and I have a mind to see that.

PINCHWIFE. So – I have it – I'll dress her up in the suit we are to carry down to her brother, little Sir James; nay, I understand the town tricks. Come, let's go dress her. A mask! No – a woman masked, like a covered dish, gives a man curiosity and appetite, when, it may be, uncovered, 'twould turn his stomach; no, no.

ALITHEA. Indeed your comparison is something a greasy one. But I had a gentle gallant used to say, 'A beauty masked, like the sun in eclipse, gathers together more gazers than if it shined out.'

Exeunt.

SCENE II

The scene changes to the New Exchange.

Enter HORNER, HARCOURT, DORILANT.

DORILANT. Engaged to women, and not sup with us?

HORNER. Ay, a pox on 'em all!

HARCOURT. You were much a more reasonable man in the morning and had as noble resolutions against 'em as a widower of a week's liberty.

DORILANT. Did I ever think to see you keep company with women in vain?

HORNER. In vain! No – 'tis, since I can't love 'em, to be revenged on 'em.

HARCOURT. Now your sting is gone, you looked in the box amongst all those women, like a drone in the hive, all upon you, shoved and ill-used by 'em all, and thrust from one side to t'other.

DORILANT. Yet he must be buzzing amongst 'em still,

---

125 *greasy*: filthy, vulgar.
127 *like*: lik'd Q1.

like other old beetle-headed, liquorish drones. Avoid 'em, and hate 'em as they hate you.

HORNER. Because I do hate 'em, and would hate 'em yet more, I'll frequent 'em; you may see by marriage, nothing makes a man hate a woman more than her constant conversation. In short, I converse with 'em, as you do with rich fools, to laugh at 'em and use 'em ill.

DORILANT. But I would no more sup with women, unless I could lie with 'em, than sup with a rich coxcomb, unless I could cheat him.

HORNER. Yes, I have known thee sup with a fool for his drinking; if he could set out your hand that way only, you were satisfied, and if he were a wine-swallowing mouth 'twas enough.

HARCOURT. Yes, a man drinks often with a fool, as he tosses with a marker, only to keep his hand in ure. But do the ladies drink?

HORNER. Yes, sir, and I shall have the pleasure at least of laying 'em flat with a bottle, and bring as much scandal that way upon 'em as formerly t'other.

HARCOURT. Perhaps you may prove as weak a brother amongst 'em that way as t'other.

DORILANT. Foh, drinking with women is as unnatural as scolding with 'em; but 'tis a pleasure of decayed fornicators, and the basest way of quenching love.

HARCOURT. Nay, 'tis drowning love instead of quenching it. But leave us for civil women too!

DORILANT. Ay, when he can't be the better for 'em. We hardly pardon a man that leaves his friend for a wench, and that's a pretty lawful call.

HORNER. Faith, I would not leave you for 'em, if they would not drink.

DORILANT. Who would disappoint his company at Lewis's for a gossiping?

---

15 *beetle-headed*: stupid.
15 *liquorish*: lecherous.
27 *set out your hand*: furnish you with food and drink.
31 *tosses with a marker*: plays dice with a score-keeper.
31 *ure*: practice.
49 *Lewis's*: an unidentified London eating-house, perhaps the one in Bread Street, Cheapside.

HARCOURT. Foh, wine and women, good apart, together as nauseous as sack and sugar. But hark you, sir, before you go, a little of your advice; an old maimed general, when unfit for action, is fittest for counsel. I have other designs upon women than eating and drinking with them. I am in love with Sparkish's mistress, whom he is to marry tomorrow. Now how shall I get her?

Enter SPARKISH, *looking about.*

HORNER. Why, here comes one will help you to her.

HARCOURT. He! He, I tell you, is my rival, and will hinder my love.

HORNER. No, a foolish rival and a jealous husband assist their rival's designs, for they are sure to make their women hate them, which is the first step to their love for another man.

HARCOURT. But I cannot come near his mistress but in his company.

HORNER. Still the better for you, for fools are most easily cheated when they themselves are accessories; and he is to be bubbled of his mistress, as of his money, the common mistress, by keeping him company.

SPARKISH. Who is that, that is to be bubbled? Faith, let me snack, I han't met with a bubble since Christmas. Gad, I think bubbles are like their brother woodcocks, go out with the cold weather.

HARCOURT. (*apart to* HORNER) A pox! He did not hear all, I hope.

SPARKISH. Come, you bubbling rogues you, where do we sup? – Oh, Harcourt, my mistress tells me you have been making fierce love to her all the play long, hah, ha! But I –

---

51 *sack and sugar*: sack was any white wine from Spain or the Canary Islands and was often drunk with sugar at this time (as Falstaff said 'If sack and sugar be a fault, God help the wicked': *1 Henry IV*, II iv 454–5). It was often an invalid's drink, hence perhaps Harcourt's distaste.

69 *bubbled*: cheated, gulled.

73 *snack*: share.

75 *woodcocks*: simpletons.

HARCOURT. I make love to her?

SPARKISH. Nay, I forgive thee, for I think I know thee, and I know her, but I am sure I know myself.

HARCOURT. Did she tell you so? I see all women are like these of the Exchange, who, to enhance the price of their commodities, report to their fond customers offers which were never made 'em.

HORNER. Ay, women are as apt to tell before the intrigue as men after it, and so show themselves the vainer sex. But hast thou a mistress, Sparkish? 'Tis as hard for me to believe it as that thou ever hadst a bubble, as you bragged just now.

SPARKISH. Oh, your servant, sir; are you at your raillery, sir? But we were some of us beforehand with you today at the play. The wits were something bold with you, sir; did you not hear us laugh?

HORNER. Yes, but I thought you had gone to plays to laugh at the poet's wit, not at your own.

SPARKISH. Your servant, sir; no, I thank you. Gad, I go to a play as to a country treat; I carry my own wine to one and my own wit to t'other, or else I'm sure I should not be merry at either. And the reason why we are so often louder than the players is because we think we speak more wit and so become the poet's rivals in his audience. For to tell you the truth, we hate the silly rogues, nay, so much that we find fault even with their bawdy upon the stage, whilst we talk nothing else in the pit as loud.

HORNER. But why shouldst thou hate the silly poets? Thou hast too much wit to be one, and they, like whores, are only hated by each other – and thou dost scorn writing, I'm sure.

SPARKISH. Yes, I'd have you to know I scorn writing; but women, women, that make men do all foolish things, make 'em write songs too. Everybody does it. 'Tis even as common with lovers as playing with fans; and you can no more help rhyming to your Phyllis than drinking to your Phyllis.

HARCOURT. Nay, poetry in love is no more to be avoided than jealousy.

DORILANT. But the poets damned your songs, did they?

SPARKISH. Damn the poets! They turned 'em into burlesque, as they call it. That burlesque is a hocus-pocus trick they have got, which, by virtue of *hictius doctius*, *topsy-turvy*, they make a wise and witty man in the world a fool upon the stage, you know not how; and 'tis therefore I hate 'em too, for I know not but it may be my own case, for they'll put a man into a play for looking asquint. Their predecessors were contented to make serving-men only their stage-fools, but these rogues must have gentlemen, with a pox to 'em, nay, knights; and, indeed, you shall hardly see a fool upon the stage but he's a knight and, to tell you the truth, they have kept me these six years from being a knight in earnest, for fear of being knighted in a play, and dubbed a fool.

DORILANT. Blame 'em not; they must follow their copy, the age.

HARCOURT. But why shouldst thou be afraid of being in a play, who expose yourself every day in the playhouses and as public places?

HORNER. 'Tis but being on the stage, instead of standing on a bench in the pit.

DORILANT. Don't you give money to painters to draw you like? And are you afraid of your pictures at length in a playhouse, where all your mistresses may see you?

SPARKISH. A pox! Painters don't draw the smallpox or pimples in one's face. Come, damn all your silly authors whatever, all books and booksellers, by the world, and all readers, courteous or uncourteous.

HARCOURT. But who comes here, Sparkish?

Enter MR PINCHWIFE *and his wife in man's clothes,* ALITHEA, LUCY *her maid.*

SPARKISH. Oh, hide me! There's my mistress too. (SPARKISH *hides himself behind* HARCOURT)

HARCOURT. She sees you.

SPARKISH. But I will not see her. 'Tis time to go to Whitehall and I must not fail the drawing room.

HARCOURT. Pray, first carry me, and reconcile me to her.

125–6 *hictius doctius*: a piece of jugglers' patter.
142 *as*: equally.

SPARKISH. Another time; faith, the King will have supped.

HARCOURT. Not with the worse stomach for thy absence; thou art one of those fools that think their attendance at the King's meals as necessary as his physicians', when you are more troublesome to him than his doctors, or his dogs.

SPARKISH. Pshaw, I know my interest, sir. Prithee hide me.

HORNER. Your servant, Pinchwife. – What, he knows us not!

PINCHWIFE. (*to his wife aside*) Come along.

MRS PINCHWIFE. Pray, have you any ballads? Give me sixpenny worth.

CLASP. We have no ballads.

MRS PINCHWIFE. Then give me *Covent Garden Drollery*, and a play or two – Oh, here's *Tarugo's Wiles*, and *The Slighted Maiden*; I'll have them.

PINCHWIFE. (*apart to her*) No, plays are not for your reading. Come along; will you discover yourself?

HORNER. Who is that pretty youth with him, Sparkish?

SPARKISH. I believe his wife's brother, because he's something like her, but I never saw her but once.

HORNER. Extremely handsome; I have seen a face like it too. Let us follow 'em.

Exeunt PINCHWIFE, MRS PINCHWIFE, ALITHEA, LUCY; HORNER, DORILANT *following them.*

HARCOURT. Come, Sparkish, your mistress saw you and will be angry you go not to her. Besides, I would fain be reconciled to her, which none but you can do, dear friend.

SPARKISH. Well, that's a better reason, dear friend, I would not go near her now, for hers or my own sake, but I can deny you nothing, for though I have known

---

174 *Covent Garden Drollery*: a miscellany of songs, poems, prologues and epilogues by various writers, including Wycherley, published in 1672.

175–6 *Tarugo's Wiles, and The Slighted Maiden*: *Tarugo's Wiles*, a comedy by Sir Thomas St Serfe (1668), best remembered for its scene of coffeehouse talk; *The Slighted Maiden*, a tragicomedy by Sir Robert Stapylton (1663). Margery's taste in plays is out-of-date.

thee a great while, never go, if I do not love thee as well as a new acquaintance.

HARCOURT. I am obliged to you indeed, dear friend. I would be well with her, only to be well with thee still, for these ties to wives usually dissolve all ties to friends. I would be contented she should enjoy you a-nights, but I would have you to myself a-days, as I have had, dear friend.

SPARKISH. And thou shalt enjoy me a-days, dear, dear friend, never stir, and I'll be divorced from her sooner than from thee. Come along.

HARCOURT. (*aside*) So, we are hard put to't when we make our rival our procurer; but neither she nor her brother would let me come near her now. When all's done, a rival is the best cloak to steal to a mistress under, without suspicion, and when we have once got to her as we desire, we throw him off like other cloaks.

Exit SPARKISH, *and* HARCOURT *following him.*

Re-enter MR PINCHWIFE, MRS PINCHWIFE *in man's clothes.*

PINCHWIFE. (*to* ALITHEA [*off-stage*]) Sister, if you will not go, we must leave you. (*Aside*) The fool her gallant and she will muster up all the young saunterers of this place, and they will leave their dear seamstresses to follow us. What a swarm of cuckolds and cuckold-makers are here! – Come, let's be gone, Mistress Margery.

MRS PINCHWIFE. Don't you believe that; I han't half my bellyful of sights yet.

PINCHWIFE. Then walk this way.

MRS PINCHWIFE. Lord, what a power of brave signs are here! Stay – the Bull's-Head, the Ram's-Head and the Stag's-Head, dear –

PINCHWIFE. Nay, if every husband's proper sign here were visible, they would be all alike.

MRS PINCHWIFE. What d'ye mean by that, bud?

PINCHWIFE. 'Tis no matter – no matter, bud.

MRS PINCHWIFE. Pray tell me; nay, I will know.

---

191 *never go*: like *never stir* (line 200), it means little more than *don't worry*.

221 *proper sign*: a cuckold's horns.

PINCHWIFE. They would be all bulls', stags' and rams' heads.

Exeunt MR PINCHWIFE, MRS PINCHWIFE.

Re-enter SPARKISH, HARCOURT, ALITHEA, LUCY, *at t'other door.*

SPARKISH. Come, dear madam, for my sake you shall be reconciled to him.

ALITHEA. For your sake I hate him.

HARCOURT. That's something too cruel, madam, to hate me for his sake.

SPARKISH. Ay indeed, madam, too, too cruel to me, to hate my friend for my sake.

ALITHEA. I hate him because he is your enemy; and you ought to hate him too, for making love to me, if you love me.

SPARKISH. That's a good one! I hate a man for loving you! If he did love you, 'tis but what he can't help and 'tis your fault, not his, if he admires you. I hate a man for being of my opinion! I'll ne'er do't by the world.

ALITHEA. Is it for your honour or mine, to suffer a man to make love to me, who am to marry you tomorrow?

SPARKISH. Is it for your honour or mine, to have me jealous? That he makes love to you is a sign you are handsome and that I am not jealous is a sign you are virtuous. That, I think, is for your honour.

ALITHEA. But 'tis your honour too I am concerned for.

HARCOURT. But why, dearest madam, will you be more concerned for his honour than he is himself? Let his honour alone, for my sake and his. He, he has no honour –

SPARKISH. How's that?

HARCOURT. But what my dear friend can guard himself.

SPARKISH. O ho – that's right again.

HARCOURT. Your care of his honour argues his neglect of it, which is no honour to my dear friend here;

---

227 s.d. *t'other door*: there were two doors on each side of the forestage; this entrance is through the other door on the same side as the one the Pinchwifes used to leave by.

therefore once more, let his honour go which way it will, dear madam.

SPARKISH. Ay, ay, were it for my honour to marry a woman whose virtue I suspected and could not trust her in a friend's hands?

ALITHEA. Are you not afraid to lose me?

HARCOURT. He afraid to lose you, madam! No, no – you may see how the most estimable and most glorious creature in the world is valued by him. Will you not see it?

SPARKISH. Right, honest Frank, I have that noble value for her that I cannot be jealous of her.

ALITHEA. You mistake him, he means you care not for me, nor who has me.

SPARKISH. Lord, madam, I see you are jealous. Will you wrest a poor man's meaning from his words?

ALITHEA. You astonish me, sir, with your want of jealousy.

SPARKISH. And you make me giddy, madam, with your jealousy and fears and virtue and honour. Gad, I see virtue makes a woman as troublesome as a little reading or learning.

ALITHEA. Monstrous!

LUCY. (*behind*) Well, to see what easy husbands these women of quality can meet with; a poor chambermaid can never have such lady-like luck. Besides, he's thrown away upon her; she'll make no use of her fortune, her blessing. None to a gentleman for a pure cuckold, for it requires good breeding to be a cuckold.

ALITHEA. I tell you then plainly, he pursues me to marry me.

SPARKISH. Pshaw!

HARCOURT. Come, madam, you see you strive in vain to make him jealous of me; my dear friend is the kindest creature in the world to me.

SPARKISH. Poor fellow.

HARCOURT. But his kindness only is not enough for me, without your favour; your good opinion, dear madam, 'tis that must perfect my happiness. Good

---

275 *jealous*: vehement, wrought. Alithea puns on its other meaning, line 278.

288 *None*: there is no one like.

gentleman, he believes all I say – would you would do so. Jealous of me! I would not wrong him nor you for the world.

SPARKISH. Look you there; hear him, hear him, and do not walk away so.

ALITHEA *walks carelessly to and fro.*

HARCOURT. I love you, madam, so –

SPARKISH. How's that! Nay – now you begin to go too far indeed.

HARCOURT. So much, I confess, I say I love you, that I would not have you miserable and cast yourself away upon so unworthy and inconsiderable a thing as what you see here. (*Clapping his hand on his breast, points at* SPARKISH)

SPARKISH. No, faith, I believe thou wouldst not; now his meaning is plain. But I knew before thou wouldst not wrong me nor her.

HARCOURT. No, no, heavens forbid the glory of her sex should fall so low as into the embraces of such a contemptible wretch, the last of mankind – my dear friend here – I injure him! (*Embracing* SPARKISH)

ALITHEA. Very well.

SPARKISH. No, no, dear friend, I knew it. – Madam, you see he will rather wrong himself than me, in giving himself such names.

ALITHEA. Do not you understand him yet?

SPARKISH. Yes, how modestly he speaks of himself, poor fellow.

ALITHEA. Methinks he speaks impudently of yourself, since – before yourself too; insomuch that I can no longer suffer his scurrilous abusiveness to you, no more than his love to me. (*Offers to go*)

SPARKISH. Nay, nay, madam, pray stay – his love to you! Lord, madam, he has not spoke yet plain enough?

ALITHEA. Yes, indeed, I should think so.

SPARKISH. Well then, by the world, a man can't speak civilly to a woman now but presently she says he makes love to her. Nay, madam, you shall stay, with your pardon, since you have not yet understood

---

304 s.d. *carelessly*: unconcernedly.

him, till he has made an éclaircissement of his love to you, that is, what kind of love it is. [*To* HARCOURT] Answer to thy catechism. Friend, do you love my mistress here?

HARCOURT. Yes, I wish she would not doubt it.

SPARKISH. But how do you love her?

HARCOURT. With all my soul.

ALITHEA. I thank him; methinks he speaks plain enough now.

SPARKISH. (*to* ALITHEA) You are out still. – But with what kind of love, Harcourt?

HARCOURT. With the best and truest love in the world.

SPARKISH. Look you there then, that is with no matrimonial love, I'm sure.

ALITHEA. How's that? Do you say matrimonial love is not best?

SPARKISH. Gad, I went too far ere I was aware. But speak for thyself, Harcourt; you said you would not wrong me nor her.

HARCOURT. No, no, madam, e'en take him for heaven's sake –

SPARKISH. Look you there, madam.

HARCOURT. Who should in all justice be yours, he that loves you most. (*Claps his hand on his breast*)

ALITHEA. Look you there, Mr Sparkish, who's that?

SPARKISH. Who should it be? – Go on, Harcourt.

HARCOURT. Who loves you more than women titles or fortune fools. (*Points at* SPARKISH)

SPARKISH. Look you there, he means me still, for he points at me.

ALITHEA. Ridiculous!

HARCOURT. Who can only match your faith and constancy in love.

SPARKISH. Ay.

HARCOURT. Who knows, if it be possible, how to value so much beauty and virtue.

SPARKISH. Ay.

HARCOURT. Whose love can no more be equalled in the world than that heavenly form of yours.

SPARKISH. No.

---

338 *éclaircissement*: full explanation.

HARCOURT. Who could no more suffer a rival than your absence, and yet could no more suspect your virtue than his own constancy in his love to you.

SPARKISH. No.

HARCOURT. Who, in fine, loves you better than his eyes that first made him love you.

SPARKISH. Ay – nay, madam, faith, you shan't go till –

ALITHEA. Have a care, lest you make me stay too long –

SPARKISH. But till he has saluted you, that I may be assured you are friends, after his honest advice and declaration. Come, pray, madam, be friends with him.

Enter MR PINCHWIFE, MRS PINCHWIFE

ALITHEA. You must pardon me, sir, that I am not yet so obedient to you.

PINCHWIFE. What, invite your wife to kiss men? Monstrous! Are you not ashamed? I will never forgive you.

SPARKISH. Are you not ashamed that I should have more confidence in the chastity of your family than you have? You must not teach me. I am a man of honour, sir, though I am frank and free; I am frank, sir –

PINCHWIFE. Very frank, sir, to share your wife with your friends.

SPARKISH. He is an humble, menial friend, such as reconciles the differences of the marriage bed. You know man and wife do not always agree; I design him for that use, therefore would have him well with my wife.

PINCHWIFE. A menial friend! – you will get a great many menial friends by showing your wife as you do.

SPARKISH. What then? It may be I have a pleasure in't, as I have to show fine clothes at a playhouse the first day and count money before poor rogues.

PINCHWIFE. He that shows his wife or money will be in danger of having them borrowed sometimes.

SPARKISH. I love to be envied and would not marry a wife that I alone could love; loving alone is as dull as

---

382 *in fine*: to conclude.
397 *frank*: candid, open, generous.
401 *menial*: domestic.

eating alone. Is it not a frank age? And I am a frank person. And to tell you the truth, it may be I love to have rivals in a wife; they make her seem to a man still but as a kept mistress. And so good night, for I must to Whitehall. – Madam, I hope you are now reconciled to my friend and so I wish you a good night, madam, and sleep if you can, for tomorrow you know I must visit you early with a canonical gentleman. Good night, dear Harcourt. *Exit* SPARKISH.

HARCOURT. Madam, I hope you will not refuse my visit tomorrow, if it should be earlier, with a canonical gentleman, than Mr Sparkish's.

PINCHWIFE. (*coming between* ALITHEA *and* HARCOURT) This gentlewoman is yet under my care; therefore you must yet forbear your freedom with her, sir.

HARCOURT. Must, sir!

PINCHWIFE. Yes, sir, she is my sister.

HARCOURT. 'Tis well she is, sir – for I must be her servant, sir. – Madam –

PINCHWIFE. Come away, sister; we had been gone, if it had not been for you, and so avoided these lewd rakehells, who seem to haunt us.

Enter HORNER, DORILANT *to them.*

HORNER. How now, Pinchwife?

PINCHWIFE. Your servant.

HORNER. What, I see a little time in the country makes a man turn wild and unsociable and only fit to converse with his horses, dogs and his herds.

PINCHWIFE. I have business, sir, and must mind it; your business is pleasure, therefore you and I must go different ways.

HORNER. Well, you may go on, but this pretty young gentleman – (*Takes hold of* MRS PINCHWIFE)

HARCOURT. The lady –

DORILANT. And the maid –

HORNER. Shall stay with us, for I suppose their business is the same with ours, pleasure.

435–6 *rakehells*: rakes, ruffians.

PINCHWIFE. (*aside*) 'Sdeath, he know her, she carries it so sillily! Yet if he does not, I should be more silly to discover it first.

ALITHEA. Pray, let us go, sir.

PINCHWIFE. Come, come –

HORNER. (*to* MRS PINCHWIFE) Had you not rather stay with us? – Prithee, Pinchwife, who is this pretty young gentleman?

PINCHWIFE. One to whom I'm a guardian. (*Aside*) I wish I could keep her out of your hands.

HORNER. Who is he? I never saw anything so pretty in all my life.

PINCHWIFE. Pshaw, do not look upon him so much. He's a poor bashful youth, you'll put him out of countenance. – Come away, brother. (*Offers to take her away*)

HORNER. Oh, your brother!

PINCHWIFE. Yes, my wife's brother. – Come, come, she'll stay supper for us.

HORNER. I thought so, for he is very like her I saw you at the play with, whom I told you I was in love with.

MRS PINCHWIFE. (*aside*) O jeminy! Is this he that was in love with me? I am glad on't, I vow, for he's a curious fine gentleman, and I love him already too. (*To* MR PINCHWIFE) Is this he, bud?

PINCHWIFE. (*to his wife*) Come away, come away.

HORNER. Why, what haste are you in? Why won't you let me talk with him?

PINCHWIFE. Because you'll debauch him; he's yet young and innocent and I would not have him debauched for anything in the world. (*Aside*) How she gazes on him! The devil!

HORNER. Harcourt, Dorilant, look you here; this is the likeness of that dowdy he told us of, his wife. Did you ever see a lovelier creature? The rogue has reason to be jealous of his wife since she is like him, for she would make all that see her in love with her.

HARCOURT. And as I remember now, she is as like him here as can be.

DORILANT. She is indeed very pretty, if she be like him.

---

483 *dowdy*: a plain, dull woman.

HORNER. Very pretty? A very pretty commendation! She is a glorious creature, beautiful beyond all things I ever beheld.

PINCHWIFE. So, so.

HARCOURT. More beautiful than a poet's first mistress of imagination.

HORNER. Or another man's last mistress of flesh and blood.

MRS PINCHWIFE. Nay, now you jeer, sir; pray don't jeer me.

PINCHWIFE. Come, come. (*Aside*) By heavens, she'll discover herself!

HORNER. I speak of your sister, sir.

PINCHWIFE. Ay, but saying she was handsome, if like him, made him blush. (*Aside*) I am upon a rack!

HORNER. Methinks he is so handsome he should not be a man.

PINCHWIFE. [*aside*] Oh, there 'tis out! He has discovered her! I am not able to suffer any longer. (*To his wife*) Come, come away, I say.

HORNER. Nay, by your leave, sir, he shall not go yet. – (*To them*) Harcourt, Dorilant, let us torment this jealous rogue a little.

HARCOURT.
DORILANT. } How?

HORNER. I'll show you.

PINCHWIFE. Come, pray, let him go, I cannot stay fooling any longer. I tell you his sister stays supper for us.

HORNER. Does she? Come then, we'll all go sup with her and thee.

PINCHWIFE. No, now I think on't, having stayed so long for us, I warrant she's gone to bed. (*Aside*) I wish she and I were well out of their hands. – Come, I must rise early tomorrow, come.

HORNER. Well, then, if she be gone to bed, I wish her and you a good night. But pray, young gentleman, present my humble service to her.

MRS PINCHWIFE. Thank you heartily, sir.

PINCHWIFE. (*aside*) 'Sdeath! she will discover herself yet in spite of me. – He is something more civil to you, for your kindness to his sister, than I am, it seems.

HORNER. Tell her, dear sweet little gentleman, for all

your brother there, that you have revived the love I had for her at first sight in the playhouse.

MRS PINCHWIFE. But did you love her indeed, and indeed?

PINCHWIFE. (*aside*) So, so. – Away, I say.

HORNER. Nay, stay. Yes, indeed, and indeed, pray do you tell her so, and give her this kiss from me. (*Kisses her*)

PINCHWIFE. (*aside*) O heavens! What do I suffer! Now 'tis too plain he knows her, and yet –

HORNER. And this, and this – (*Kisses her again*)

MRS PINCHWIFE. What do you kiss me for? I am no woman.

PINCHWIFE. (*aside*) So – there, 'tis out. – Come, I cannot, nor will stay any longer.

HORNER. Nay, they shall send your lady a kiss too. Here, Harcourt, Dorilant, will you not?

They kiss her.

PINCHWIFE. (*aside*) How! Do I suffer this? Was I not accusing another just now for this rascally patience, in permitting his wife to be kissed before his face? Ten thousand ulcers gnaw away their lips! – Come, come.

HORNER. Good night, dear little gentleman. Madam, good night. Farewell, Pinchwife. (*Apart to* HARCOURT *and* DORILANT) Did not I tell you I would raise his jealous gall?

Exeunt HORNER, HARCOURT *and* DORILANT.

PINCHWIFE. So, they are gone at last; stay, let me see first if the coach be at this door. *Exit.*

HORNER, HARCOURT, DORILANT *return.*

HORNER. What, not gone yet? Will you be sure to do as I desired you, sweet sir?

MRS PINCHWIFE. Sweet sir, but what will you give me then?

HORNER. Anything. Come away into the next walk.

Exit HORNER, *haling away* MRS PINCHWIFE.

ALITHEA. Hold, hold! What d'ye do?

LUCY. Stay, stay, hold –

HARCOURT. Hold, madam, hold! Let him present him,

---

567 *present*: give a present to.

he'll come presently. Nay, I will never let you go till you answer my question.

LUCY. For God's sake, sir, I must follow 'em.

DORILANT. No, I have something to present you with too; you shan't follow them.

ALITHEA, LUCY *struggling with* HARCOURT *and* DORILANT.

PINCHWIFE *returns.*

PINCHWIFE. Where? – how? – what's become of? – gone! – whither?

LUCY. He's only gone with the gentleman, who will give him something, an't please your worship.

PINCHWIFE. Something – give him something, with a pox! – where are they?

ALITHEA. In the next walk only, brother.

PINCHWIFE. Only, only! Where, where?

Exit PINCHWIFE *and returns presently, then goes out again.*

HARCOURT. What's the matter with him? Why so much concerned? But dearest madam –

ALITHEA. Pray let me go, sir; I have said and suffered enough already.

HARCOURT. Then you will not look upon nor pity my sufferings?

ALITHEA. To look upon 'em, when I cannot help 'em, were cruelty, not pity; therefore I will never see you more.

HARCOURT. Let me then, madam, have my privilege of a banished lover, complaining or railing, and giving you but a farewell reason why, if you cannot condescend to marry me, you should not take that wretch, my rival.

ALITHEA. He only, not you, since my honour is engaged so far to him, can give me a reason why I should not marry him; but if he be true and what I think him to me, I must be so to him. Your servant, sir.

HARCOURT. Have women only constancy when 'tis a vice and, like fortune, only true to fools?

DORILANT. (*to* LUCY, *who struggles to get from him*) Thou shalt not stir, thou robust creature; you see I can deal with you, therefore you should stay the rather, and be kind.

Enter PINCHWIFE.

PINCHWIFE. Gone, gone, not to be found! Quite gone! Ten thousand plagues go with 'em! Which way went they?

ALITHEA. But into t'other walk, brother.

LUCY. Their business will be done presently sure, an't please your worship; it can't be long in doing, I'm sure on't.

ALITHEA. Are they not there?

PINCHWIFE. No; you know where they are, you infamous wretch, eternal shame of your family, which you do not dishonour enough yourself, you think, but you must help her to do it too, thou legion of bawds!

ALITHEA. Good brother –

PINCHWIFE. Damned, damned sister!

ALITHEA. Look you here, she's coming.

Enter MRS PINCHWIFE *in man's clothes, running, with her hat under her arm, full of oranges and dried fruit;* HORNER *following.*

MRS PINCHWIFE. O dear bud, look you here what I have got, see!

PINCHWIFE. (*aside, rubbing his forehead*) And what I have got here too, which you can't see.

MRS PINCHWIFE. The fine gentleman has given me better things yet.

PINCHWIFE. Has he so? (*Aside*) Out of breath and coloured! I must hold yet.

HORNER. I have only given your little brother an orange, sir.

PINCHWIFE. (*to* HORNER) Thank you, sir. (*Aside*) You have only squeezed my orange, I suppose, and given it me again; yet I must have a city patience. (*To his wife*) Come, come away.

MRS PINCHWIFE. Stay, till I have put up my fine things, bud.

Enter SIR JASPAR FIDGET.

---

631 *city patience*: the patience of a city husband cuckolded by a gallant.

SIR JASPAR. O Master Horner, come, come, the ladies stay for you; your mistress, my wife, wonders you make not more haste to her.

HORNER. I have stayed this half hour for you here and 'tis your fault I am not now with your wife.

SIR JASPAR. But pray, don't let her know so much; the truth on't is, I was advancing a certain project to his Majesty about – I'll tell you.

HORNER. No, let's go and hear it at your house. – Good night, sweet little gentleman. One kiss more, you'll remember me now, I hope. (*Kisses her*)

DORILANT. What, Sir Jaspar, will you separate friends? He promised to sup with us; and if you take him to your house, you'll be in danger of our company too.

SIR JASPAR. Alas, gentlemen, my house is not fit for you; there are none but civil women there, which are not fit for your turn. He, you know, can bear with the society of civil women now, ha, ha, ha! Besides, he's one of my family – he's – heh, heh, heh!

DORILANT. What is he?

SIR JASPAR. Faith, my eunuch, since you'll have it, heh, he, he!

Exeunt SIR JASPAR FIDGET, *and* HORNER.

DORILANT. I rather wish thou wert his, or my cuckold. Harcourt, what a good cuckold is lost there for want of a man to make him one! Thee and I cannot have Horner's privilege, who can make use of it.

HARCOURT. Ay, to poor Horner 'tis like coming to an estate at threescore, when a man can't be the better for't.

PINCHWIFE. Come.

MRS PINCHWIFE. Presently, bud.

DORILANT. Come, let us go too. (*To* ALITHEA) Madam, your servant. (*To* LUCY) Good night, strapper.

HARCOURT. Madam, though you will not let me have a good day or night, I wish you one; but dare not name the other half of my wish.

---

656 s.d. *Exeunt*: *Exit* Q1.

668 *strapper*: strapping wench, tall and robust.

ALITHEA. Good night, sir, forever.

MRS PINCHWIFE. I don't know where to put this here, dear bud; you shall eat it; nay, you shall have part of the fine gentleman's good things, or treat as you call it, when we come home.

PINCHWIFE. Indeed, I deserve it, since I furnished the best part of it. (*Strikes away the orange*)
The gallant treats, presents, and gives the ball
But 'tis the absent cuckold pays for all.

[*Exeunt.*]

ACT IV

SCENE I

In PINCHWIFE*'s house in the morning.*

LUCY, ALITHEA *dressed in new clothes.*

LUCY. Well – madam, now have I dressed you and set you out with so many ornaments and spent upon you ounces of essence and pulvilio; and all this for no other purpose but as people adorn and perfume a corpse for a stinking secondhand grave – such or as bad I think as Master Sparkish's bed.

ALITHEA. Hold your peace.

LUCY. Nay, madam, I will ask you the reason why you would banish poor Master Harcourt forever from your sight. How could you be so hardhearted?

ALITHEA. 'Twas because I was not hardhearted.

LUCY. No, no, 'twas stark love and kindness, I warrant.

ALITHEA. It was so; I would see him no more because I love him.

LUCY. Hey-day, a very pretty reason!

ALITHEA. You do not understand me.

LUCY. I wish you may yourself.

---

3 *essence and pulvilio*: scent and perfumed powder.

ALITHEA. I was engaged to marry, you see, another man, whom my justice will not suffer me to deceive or injure.

LUCY. Can there be a greater cheat or wrong done to a man than to give him your person without your heart? I should make a conscience of it.

ALITHEA. I'll retrieve it for him after I am married a while.

LUCY. The woman that marries to love better will be as much mistaken as the wencher that marries to live better. No, madam, marrying to increase love is like gaming to become rich; alas, you only lose what little stock you had before.

ALITHEA. I find by your rhetoric you have been bribed to betray me.

LUCY. Only by his merit, that has bribed your heart, you see, against your word and rigid honour. But what a devil is this honour! 'Tis sure a disease in the head, like the megrim, or falling sickness, that always hurries people away to do themselves mischief. Men lose their lives by it; women what's dearer to 'em, their love, the life of life.

ALITHEA. Come, pray talk you no more of honour, nor Master Harcourt. I wish the other would come to secure my fidelity to him and his right in me.

LUCY. You will marry him then?

ALITHEA. Certainly. I have given him already my word and will my hand too, to make it good when he comes.

LUCY. Well, I wish I may never stick pin more if he be not an arrant natural to t'other fine gentleman.

ALITHEA. I own he wants the wit of Harcourt, which I will dispense withal for another want he has, which is want of jealousy, which men of wit seldom want.

LUCY. Lord, madam, what should you do with a fool to your husband? You intend to be honest, don't you? Then that husbandly virtue, credulity, is thrown away upon you.

ALITHEA. He only that could suspect my virtue should

---

36 *megrim*: migraine.
36 *falling sickness*: epilepsy.
47 *natural*: simpleton.

have cause to do it; 'tis Sparkish's confidence in my truth that obliges me to be so faithful to him.

LUCY. You are not sure his opinion may last.

ALITHEA. I am satisfied 'tis impossible for him to be jealous after the proofs I have had of him. Jealousy in a husband – Heaven defend me from it! It begets a thousand plagues to a poor woman, the loss of her honour, her quiet and her –

LUCY. And her pleasure.

ALITHEA. What d'ye mean, impertinent?

LUCY. Liberty is a great pleasure, madam.

ALITHEA. I say, loss of her honour, her quiet, nay, her life sometimes, and what's as bad almost, the loss of this town; that is, she is sent into the country, which is the last ill usage of a husband to a wife, I think.

LUCY. (*aside*) Oh, does the wind lie there? – Then, of necessity, madam, you think a man must carry his wife into the country, if he be wise. The country is as terrible, I find, to our young English ladies as a monastery to those abroad, and, on my virginity, I think they would rather marry a London gaoler than a high sheriff of a county, since neither can stir from his employment. Formerly women of wit married fools for a great estate, a fine seat, or the like, but now 'tis for a pretty seat only in Lincoln's Inn Fields, St James's Fields or the Pall Mall.

Enter to them SPARKISH *and* HARCOURT *dressed like a parson.*

SPARKISH. Madam, your humble servant, a happy day to you, and to us all.

HARCOURT. Amen.

ALITHEA. Who have we here?

SPARKISH. My chaplain, faith. O madam, poor Harcourt remembers his humble service to you and, in obedience to your last commands, refrains coming into your sight.

80–1 *Lincoln's Inn . . . Pall Mall*: fashionable areas to live in. Lincoln's Inn Fields is a square west of Lincoln's Inn; St James's Fields had been built over and become St James's Square; Pall Mall, the 'Old Pell Mell' in which Act IV Scene ii of *Love in a Wood* is set, is near St James's Palace and was then the home of Nell Gwynn, among others.

ALITHEA. Is not that he?

SPARKISH. No, fie, no; but to show that he ne'er intended to hinder our match, has sent his brother here to join our hands. When I get me a wife, I must get her a chaplain, according to the custom; this is his brother, and my chaplain.

ALITHEA. His brother?

LUCY. (*aside*) And your chaplain, to preach in your pulpit then.

ALITHEA. His brother!

SPARKISH. Nay, I knew you would not believe it. – I told you, sir, she would take you for your brother Frank.

ALITHEA. Believe it!

LUCY. (*aside*) His brother! hah, ha, he! He has a trick left still, it seems.

SPARKISH. Come, my dearest, pray let us go to church before the canonical hour is past.

ALITHEA. For shame, you are abused still.

SPARKISH. By the world, 'tis strange now you are so incredulous.

ALITHEA. 'Tis strange you are so credulous.

SPARKISH. Dearest of my life, hear me. I tell you this is Ned Harcourt of Cambridge; by the world, you see he has a sneaking college look. 'Tis true he's something like his brother Frank and they differ from each other no more than in their age, for they were twins.

LUCY. Hah, ha, he!

ALITHEA. Your servant, sir; I cannot be so deceived, though you are. But come, let's hear; how do you know what you affirm so confidently?

SPARKISH. Why, I'll tell you all. Frank Harcourt coming to me this morning, to wish me joy and present his service to you, I asked him if he could help me to a parson, whereupon he told me he had a brother in town who was in orders and he went straight away and sent him you see there to me.

ALITHEA. Yes, Frank goes and puts on a black coat, then tells you he is Ned; that's all you have for't.

SPARKISH. Pshaw, pshaw, I tell you by the same token,

---

107 *canonical hour*: marriages could only be celebrated in church between 8 a.m. and noon.

the midwife put her garter about Frank's neck to know 'em asunder, they were so like.

ALITHEA. Frank tells you this too.

SPARKISH. Ay, and Ned there too; nay, they are both in a story.

ALITHEA. So, so; very foolish!

SPARKISH. Lord, if you won't believe one, you had best try him by your chambermaid there, for chambermaids must needs know chaplains from other men, they are so used to 'em.

LUCY. Let's see; nay, I'll be sworn he has the canonical smirk and the filthy, clammy palm of a chaplain.

ALITHEA. Well, most reverend doctor, pray let us make an end of this fooling.

HARCOURT. With all my soul, divine, heavenly creature, when you please.

ALITHEA. He speaks like a chaplain indeed.

SPARKISH. Why, was there not 'soul', 'divine', 'heavenly', in what he said?

ALITHEA. Once more, most impertinent black coat, cease your persecution and let us have a conclusion of this ridiculous love.

HARCOURT. (*aside*) I had forgot. I must suit my style to my coat, or I wear it in vain.

ALITHEA. I have no more patience left; let us make once an end of this troublesome love, I say.

HARCOURT. So be it, seraphic lady, when your honour shall think it meet and convenient so to do.

SPARKISH. Gad, I'm sure none but a chaplain could speak so, I think.

ALITHEA. Let me tell you, sir, this dull trick will not serve your turn; though you delay our marriage, you shall not hinder it.

HARCOURT. Far be it from me, munificent patroness, to delay your marriage. I desire nothing more than to marry you presently, which I might do, if you yourself would, for my noble, good-natured and thrice generous patron here would not hinder it.

SPARKISH. No, poor man, not I, faith.

137–9 a standard Restoration joke on the promiscuity of clergymen – and chambermaids.

HARCOURT. And now, madam, let me tell you plainly, nobody else shall marry you; by heavens, I'll die first, for I'm sure I should die after it.

LUCY. [*aside*] How his love has made him forget his function, as I have seen it in real parsons!

ALITHEA. That was spoken like a chaplain too! Now you understand him, I hope.

SPARKISH. Poor man, he takes it heinously to be refused. I can't blame him; 'tis putting an indignity upon him not to be suffered. But you'll pardon me, madam, it shan't be, he shall marry us. Come away, pray, madam.

LUCY. [*aside*] Hah, ha, he! More ado! 'Tis late.

ALITHEA. Invincible stupidity! I tell you he would marry me as your rival, not as your chaplain.

SPARKISH. (*pulling her away*) Come, come, madam.

LUCY. Ay, pray, madam, do not refuse this reverend divine the honour and satisfaction of marrying you, for I dare say he has set his heart upon't, good doctor.

ALITHEA. What can you hope or design by this?

HARCOURT. [*aside*] I could answer her, a reprieve for a day only often revokes a hasty doom; at worst, if she will not take mercy on me and let me marry her, I have at least the lover's second pleasure, hindering my rival's enjoyment, though but for a time.

SPARKISH. Come, madam, 'tis e'en twelve o'clock, and my mother charged me never to be married out of the canonical hours. Come, come. Lord, here's such a deal of modesty, I warrant, the first day.

LUCY. Yes, an't please your worship, married women show all their modesty the first day, because married men show all their love the first day.

Exeunt SPARKISH, ALITHEA, HARCOURT *and* LUCY.

170–1 *die . . . die*: the traditional pun on *orgasm* and *death*.

SCENE II

The scene changes to a bedchamber, where appear PINCHWIFE, MRS PINCHWIFE.

PINCHWIFE. Come, tell me, I say.

MRS PINCHWIFE. Lord, han't I told it an hundred times over?

PINCHWIFE. (*aside*) I would try if, in the repetition of the ungrateful tale, I could find her altering it in the least circumstance, for if her story be false, she is so too. – Come, how was't, baggage?

MRS PINCHWIFE. Lord, what pleasure you take to hear it, sure!

PINCHWIFE. No, you take more in telling it, I find; but speak, how was't?

MRS PINCHWIFE. He carried me up into the house next to the Exchange.

PINCHWIFE. So, and you two were only in the room.

MRS PINCHWIFE. Yes, for he sent away a youth that was there, for some dried fruit and China oranges.

PINCHWIFE. Did he so? Damn him for it – and for –

MRS PINCHWIFE. But presently came up the gentlewoman of the house.

PINCHWIFE. O, 'twas well she did; but what did he do whilst the fruit came?

MRS PINCHWIFE. He kissed me an hundred times and told me he fancied he kissed my fine sister, meaning me, you know, whom he said he loved with all his soul and bid me be sure to tell her so and to desire her to be at her window by eleven of the clock this morning and he would walk under it at that time.

PINCHWIFE. (*aside*) And he was as good as his word, very punctual – a pox reward him for't.

MRS PINCHWIFE. Well, and he said if you were not within, he would come up to her, meaning me, you know, bud, still.

PINCHWIFE. (*aside*) So – he knew her certainly; but for this confession, I am obliged to her simplicity. – But what, you stood very still when he kissed you?

---

16 *China oranges*: the sweet orange, *citrus sinensis*, supposedly from China; a delicacy at this time.

MRS PINCHWIFE. Yes, I warrant you; would you have had me discovered myself?

PINCHWIFE. But you told me he did some beastliness to you, as you called it; what was't?

MRS PINCHWIFE. Why, he put –

PINCHWIFE. What?

MRS PINCHWIFE. Why, he put the tip of his tongue between my lips and so mousled me – and I said, I'd bite it.

PINCHWIFE. An eternal canker seize it, for a dog!

MRS PINCHWIFE. Nay, you need not be so angry with him neither, for to say truth, he has the sweetest breath I ever knew.

PINCHWIFE. The devil! – you were satisfied with it then, and would do it again.

MRS PINCHWIFE. Not unless he should force me.

PINCHWIFE. Force you, changeling! I tell you no woman can be forced.

MRS PINCHWIFE. Yes, but she may, sure, by such a one as he, for he's a proper, goodly strong man; 'tis hard, let me tell you, to resist him.

PINCHWIFE. So, 'tis plain she loves him, yet she has not love enough to make her conceal it from me; but the sight of him will increase her aversion for me and love for him and that love instruct her how to deceive me and satisfy him, all idiot as she is. Love! 'Twas he gave women first their craft, their art of deluding; out of nature's hands they came plain, open, silly and fit for slaves, as she and Heaven intended 'em; but damned love – well – I must strangle that little monster whilst I can deal with him. – Go fetch pen, ink and paper out of the next room.

MRS PINCHWIFE. Yes, bud. *Exit* MRS PINCHWIFE.

PINCHWIFE. (*aside*) Why should women have more invention in love than men? It can only be because they have more desires, more soliciting passions, more lust, and more of the devil.

MRS PINCHWIFE *returns.*

Come, minx, sit down and write.

---

43 *mousled*: rumpled.
65–6 *little monster*: Cupid.

MRS PINCHWIFE. Ay, dear bud, but I can't do't very well.

PINCHWIFE. I wish you could not at all.

MRS PINCHWIFE. But what should I write for?

PINCHWIFE. I'll have you write a letter to your lover.

MRS PINCHWIFE. O Lord, to the fine gentleman a letter!

PINCHWIFE. Yes, to the fine gentleman.

MRS PINCHWIFE. Lord, you do but jeer; sure, you jest.

PINCHWIFE. I am not so merry. Come, write as I bid you.

MRS PINCHWIFE. What, do you think I am a fool?

PINCHWIFE. [*aside*] She's afraid I would not dictate any love to him, therefore she's unwilling. – But you had best begin.

MRS PINCHWIFE. Indeed, and indeed, but I won't, so I won't.

PINCHWIFE. Why?

MRS PINCHWIFE. Because he's in town; you may send for him if you will.

PINCHWIFE. Very well, you would have him brought to you; is it come to this? I say, take the pen and write, or you'll provoke me.

MRS PINCHWIFE. Lord, what d'ye make a fool of me for? Don't I know that letters are never writ but from the country to London and from London into the country? Now he's in town and I am in town too; therefore I can't write to him, you know.

PINCHWIFE. (*aside*) So, I am glad it is no worse; she is innocent enough yet. – Yes, you may, when your husband bids you, write letters to people that are in town.

MRS PINCHWIFE. O, may I so? Then I'm satisfied.

PINCHWIFE. Come, begin. – (*Dictates*) 'Sir' –

MRS PINCHWIFE. Shan't I say, 'Dear Sir'? You know one says always something more than bare 'Sir'.

PINCHWIFE. Write as I bid you, or I will write 'whore' with this penknife in your face.

MRS PINCHWIFE. Nay, good bud – (*She writes*) 'Sir' –

PINCHWIFE. 'Though I suffered last night your nauseous, loathed kisses and embraces' – Write.

MRS PINCHWIFE. Nay, why should I say so? You know I told you he had a sweet breath.

PINCHWIFE. Write.

MRS PINCHWIFE. Let me but put out 'loathed'.

PINCHWIFE. Write, I say.

MRS PINCHWIFE. Well then. (*Writes*)

PINCHWIFE. Let's see, what have you writ? (*Takes the paper and reads*) 'Though I suffered last night your kisses and embraces' – Thou impudent creature, where is 'nauseous' and 'loathed'?

MRS PINCHWIFE. I can't abide to write such filthy words.

PINCHWIFE. Once more write as I'd have you, and question it not, or I will spoil thy writing with this. (*Holds up the penknife*) I will stab out those eyes that cause my mischief.

MRS PINCHWIFE. O Lord, I will!

PINCHWIFE. So – so – let's see now! (*Reads*) 'Though I suffered last night your nauseous, loathed kisses and embraces' – go on – 'yet I would not have you presume that you shall ever repeat them' – So –

She writes.

MRS PINCHWIFE. I have writ it.

PINCHWIFE. On then. – 'I then concealed myself from your knowledge to avoid your insolencies' –

She writes.

MRS PINCHWIFE. So –

PINCHWIFE. 'The same reason, now I am out of your hands' –

She writes.

MRS PINCHWIFE. So –

PINCHWIFE. 'Makes me own to you my unfortunate, though innocent, frolic, of being in man's clothes' –

She writes.

MRS PINCHWIFE. So –

PINCHWIFE. 'That you may for evermore cease to pursue her, who hates and detests you' –

She writes on.

MRS PINCHWIFE. So – h – (*Sighs*)

PINCHWIFE. What, do you sigh? – 'detests you – as much as she loves her husband and her honour'.

MRS PINCHWIFE. I vow, husband, he'll ne'er believe I should write such a letter.

PINCHWIFE. What, he'd expect a kinder from you? Come, now your name only.

MRS PINCHWIFE. What, shan't I say, 'Your most faithful, humble servant till death'?

PINCHWIFE. No, tormenting fiend! (*Aside*) Her style, I find, would be very soft. – Come, wrap it up now, whilst I go fetch wax and a candle, and write on the backside, 'For Mr Horner.' *Exit* PINCHWIFE.

MRS PINCHWIFE. 'For Mr Horner.' – So, I am glad he has told me his name. Dear Mr Horner! But why should I send thee such a letter that will vex thee and make thee angry with me? – Well, I will not send it – Ay, but then my husband will kill me – for I see plainly he won't let me love Mr Horner – but what care I for my husband? – I won't, so I won't send poor Mr Horner such a letter – But then my husband – But oh – What if I writ at bottom, my husband made me write it? – Ay, but then my husband would see't – Can one have no shift? Ah, a London woman would have had a hundred presently. Stay – what if I should write a letter, and wrap it up like this, and write upon't too? Ay, but then my husband would see't – I don't know what to do – But yet y'vads I'll try, so I will – for I will not send this letter to poor Mr Horner, come what will on't. (*She writes, and repeats what she hath writ*)
'Dear, sweet Mr Horner' – so – 'my husband would have me send you a base, rude, unmannerly letter – but I won't' – so – 'and would have me forbid you loving me – but I won't' – so – 'and would have me say to you, I hate you, poor Mr Horner – but I won't tell a lie for him' – there – 'for I'm sure if you and I were in the country at cards together' – so – 'I could not help treading on your toe under the table' – so – 'or rubbing knees with you and staring in your face till you saw me' – very well – 'and then looking down and blushing for an hour together' – so – 'but I must make haste before my husband comes; and now he has taught me to write letters, you shall have longer ones from me, who am,

Dear, dear, poor, dear Mr Horner,

Your most humble friend, and servant
to command till death,
Margery Pinchwife.'

---

171 *shift*: stratagem.
175 *y'vads*: in faith.

Stay, I must give him a hint at bottom – so – now wrap it up just like t'other – so – now write, 'For Mr Horner' – But, oh now, what shall I do with it? For here comes my husband.

Enter PINCHWIFE.

PINCHWIFE. (*aside*) I have been detained by a sparkish coxcomb, who pretended a visit to me; but I fear 'twas to my wife. – What, have you done?

MRS PINCHWIFE. Ay, ay, bud, just now.

PINCHWIFE. Let's see't. What d'ye tremble for? What, you would not have it go?

MRS PINCHWIFE. Here. (*Aside*) No, I must not give him that; so I had been served if I had given him this.

PINCHWIFE. (*He opens, and reads the first letter*) Come, where's the wax and seal?

MRS PINCHWIFE. (*aside*) Lord, what shall I do now? Nay, then, I have it. – Pray let me see't. Lord, you think me so arrant a fool I cannot seal a letter. I will do't, so I will. (*Snatches the letter from him, changes it for the other, seals it and delivers it to him*)

PINCHWIFE. Nay, I believe you will learn that, and other things too, which I would not have you.

MRS PINCHWIFE. So, han't I done it curiously? (*Aside*) I think I have; there's my letter going to Mr Horner, since he'll needs have me send letters to folks.

PINCHWIFE. 'Tis very well; but I warrant you would not have it go now?

MRS PINCHWIFE. Yes, indeed, but I would, bud, now.

PINCHWIFE. Well, you are a good girl then. Come, let me lock you up in your chamber, till I come back, and be sure you come not within three strides of the window when I am gone, for I have a spy in the street.

Exit MRS PINCHWIFE. PINCHWIFE *locks the door.*

At least, 'tis fit she think so. If we do not cheat women, they'll cheat us, and fraud may be justly used with secret enemies, of which a wife is the most dangerous, and he that has a handsome one to keep, and a frontier town, must provide against treachery rather than open force. Now I have secured all within, I'll deal with the foe without with false intelligence.

Holds up the letter. Exit PINCHWIFE.

---

216 *curiously*: skilfully.

SCENE III

The scene changes to HORNER*'s lodging.*

QUACK *and* HORNER.

QUACK. Well, sir, how fadges the new design? Have you not the luck of all your brother projectors, to deceive only yourself at last?

HORNER. No, good domine doctor, I deceive you, it seems, and others too, for the grave matrons and old, rigid husbands think me as unfit for love as they are but their wives, sisters and daughters know some of 'em better things already.

QUACK. Already!

HORNER. Already, I say. Last night I was drunk with half a dozen of your civil persons, as you call 'em, and people of honour, and so was made free of their society and dressing-rooms forever hereafter, and am already come to the privileges of sleeping upon their pallats, warming smocks, tying shoes and garters, and the like, doctor, already, already, doctor.

QUACK. You have made use of your time, sir.

HORNER. I tell thee, I am now no more interruption to 'em when they sing or talk bawdy than a little squab French page who speaks no English.

QUACK. But do civil persons and women of honour drink and sing bawdy songs?

HORNER. O, amongst friends, amongst friends. For your bigots in honour are just like those in religion; they fear the eye of the world more than the eye of Heaven and think there is no virtue but railing at vice and no sin but giving scandal. They rail at a poor, little, kept player and keep themselves some young, modest pulpit comedian to be privy to their sins in their closets, not to tell 'em of them in their chapels.

---

1 *fadges*: succeeds.
2 *projectors*: schemers, promoters of hare-brained and often fraudulent projects.
4 *domine*: master.
15 *pallats*: mattresses.
19 *squab*: short and plump.
29 *pulpit comedian*: chaplain.

QUACK. Nay, the truth on't is, priests among the women now have quite got the better of us lay confessors, physicians.

HORNER. And they are rather their patients, but –

Enter MY LADY FIDGET, *looking about her.*

Now we talk of women of honour, here comes one. Step behind the screen there and but observe if I have not particular privileges with the women of reputation already, doctor, already.

[QUACK *steps behind screen.*]

LADY FIDGET. Well, Horner, am not I a woman of honour? You see I'm as good as my word.

HORNER. And you shall see, madam, I'll not be behindhand with you in honour and I'll be as good as my word too, if you please but to withdraw into the next room.

LADY FIDGET. But first, my dear sir, you must promise to have a care of my dear honour.

HORNER. If you talk a word more of your honour, you'll make me incapable to wrong it. To talk of honour in the mysteries of love is like talking of heaven or the deity in an operation of witchcraft, just when you are employing the devil; it makes the charm impotent.

LADY FIDGET. Nay, fie, let us not be smooty. But you talk of mysteries and bewitching to me; I don't understand you.

HORNER. I tell you, madam, the word 'money' in a mistress's mouth, at such a nick of time, is not a more disheartening sound to a younger brother than that of 'honour' to an eager lover like myself.

LADY FIDGET. But you can't blame a lady of my reputation to be chary.

HORNER. Chary! I have been chary of it already, by the report I have caused of myself.

LADY FIDGET. Ay, but if you should ever let other women know that dear secret, it would come out. Nay, you must have a great care of your conduct, for my acquaintance are so censorious (oh, 'tis a

---

53 *smooty*: smutty.

56–8 younger brothers were traditionally impecunious.

wicked, censorious world, Mr Horner!), I say, are so censorious and detracting that perhaps they'll talk, to the prejudice of my honour, though you should not let them know the dear secret.

HORNER. Nay, madam, rather than they shall prejudice your honour, I'll prejudice theirs, and, to serve you, I'll lie with 'em all, make the secret their own, and then they'll keep it. I am a Machiavel in love, madam.

LADY FIDGET. Oh, no, sir, not that way.

HORNER. Nay, the devil take me if censorious women are to be silenced any other way.

LADY FIDGET. A secret is better kept, I hope, by a single person than a multitude; therefore pray do not trust anybody else with it, dear, dear Mr Horner. (*Embracing him*)

Enter SIR JASPAR FIDGET.

SIR JASPAR. How now!

LADY FIDGET. (*aside*) Oh, my husband – prevented – and what's almost as bad, found with my arms about another man – that will appear too much – what shall I say? – Sir Jaspar, come hither, I am trying if Mr Horner were ticklish, and he's as ticklish as can be; I love to torment the confounded toad. Let you and I tickle him.

SIR JASPAR. No, your ladyship will tickle him better without me, I suppose. But is this your buying china? I thought you had been at the china house.

HORNER. (*aside*) China house! That's my cue, I must take it. – A pox, can't you keep your impertinent wives at home? Some men are troubled with the husbands, but I with the wives. But I'd have you to know, since I cannot be your journeyman by night, I will not be your drudge by day, to squire your wife about and be your man of straw, or scarecrow, only to pies and jays, that would be nibbling at your forbidden fruit; I shall be shortly the hackney gentleman-usher of the town.

---

92 *china house*: place where china is exhibited and sold, notorious as places of assignation.

97 *journeyman*: one who labours for another.

99–100 *pies and jays*: fops.

101 *hackney*: hired.

SIR JASPAR. (*aside*) Heh, heh, he! Poor fellow, he's in the right on't, faith; to squire women about for other folks is as ungrateful an employment as to tell money for other folks. – Heh, he, he! Ben't angry, Horner –

LADY FIDGET. No, 'tis I have more reason to be angry, who am left by you to go abroad indecently alone; or, what is more indecent, to pin myself upon such ill-bred people of your acquaintance as this is.

SIR JASPAR. Nay, prithee, what has he done?

LADY FIDGET. Nay, he has done nothing.

SIR JASPAR. But what d'ye take ill, if he has done nothing?

LADY FIDGET. Hah, hah, hah! Faith, I can't but laugh, however; why d'ye think the unmannerly toad would not come down to me to the coach? I was fain to come up to fetch him, or go without him, which I was resolved not to do, for he knows china very well and has himself very good, but will not let me see it lest I should beg some. But I will find it out and have what I came for yet.

Exit LADY FIDGET *and locks the door, followed by* HORNER *to the door.*

HORNER. (*apart to* LADY FIDGET) Lock the door, madam. – So, she has got into my chamber, and locked me out. Oh, the impertinency of womankind! Well, Sir Jaspar, plain-dealing is a jewel; if ever you suffer your wife to trouble me again here, she shall carry you home a pair of horns, by my Lord Mayor she shall; though I cannot furnish you myself, you are sure, yet I'll find a way.

SIR JASPAR. (*aside*) Hah, ha, he! At my first coming in and finding her arms about him, tickling him it seems, I was half jealous, but now I see my folly. – Heh, he, he! Poor Horner.

HORNER. Nay, though you laugh now, 'twill be my turn ere long. Oh, women, more impertinent, more cunning and more mischievous than their monkeys, and to me almost as ugly! Now is she throwing my things about and rifling all I have, but I'll get into her the back way and so rifle her for it.

SIR JASPAR. Hah, ha, ha, poor angry Horner.

---

105 *tell*: count.

HORNER. Stay here a little; I'll ferret her out to you presently, I warrant. *Exit* HORNER *at t'other door.*

SIR JASPAR. Wife! My Lady Fidget! Wife! He is coming into you the back way.

SIR JASPAR *calls through the door to his wife; she answers from within.*

LADY FIDGET. Let him come, and welcome, which way he will.

SIR JASPAR. He'll catch you and use you roughly and be too strong for you.

LADY FIDGET. Don't you trouble yourself; let him if he can.

QUACK. (*behind*) This indeed I could not have believed from him, nor any but my own eyes.

Enter MRS SQUEAMISH.

SQUEAMISH. Where's this woman-hater, this toad, this ugly, greasy, dirty sloven?

SIR JASPAR. (*aside*) So, the women all will have him ugly; methinks he is a comely person, but his wants make his form contemptible to 'em and 'tis e'en as my wife said yesterday, talking of him, that a proper handsome eunuch was as ridiculous a thing as a gigantic coward.

SQUEAMISH. Sir Jaspar, your servant. Where is the odious beast?

SIR JASPAR. He's within in his chamber, with my wife; she's playing the wag with him.

SQUEAMISH. Is she so? And he's a clownish beast, he'll give her no quarter; he'll play the wag with her again, let me tell you. Come, let's go help her. – What, the door's locked?

SIR JASPAR. Ay, my wife locked it.

SQUEAMISH. Did she so? Let us break it open then.

SIR JASPAR. No, no, he'll do her no hurt.

SQUEAMISH. No. (*Aside*) But is there no other way to get in to 'em? Whither goes this? I will disturb 'em. *Exit* SQUEAMISH *at another door.*

Enter OLD LADY SQUEAMISH.

OLD LADY SQUEAMISH. Where is this harlotry, this impudent baggage, this rambling tomrig? O Sir Jaspar, I'm glad to see you here. Did you not see my vild grandchild come in hither just now?

SIR JASPAR. Yes.

OLD LADY SQUEAMISH. Ay, but where is she then? Where is she? Lord, Sir Jaspar, I have e'en rattled myself to pieces in pursuit of her. But can you tell what she makes here? They say below, no woman lodges here.

SIR JASPAR. No.

OLD LADY SQUEAMISH. No! What does she here then? Say, if it be not a woman's lodging, what makes she here? But are you sure no woman lodges here?

SIR JASPAR. No, nor no man neither; this is Mr Horner's lodging.

OLD LADY SQUEAMISH. Is it so, are you sure?

SIR JASPAR. Yes, yes.

OLD LADY SQUEAMISH. So then there's no hurt in't, I hope. But where is he?

SIR JASPAR. He's in the next room with my wife.

OLD LADY SQUEAMISH. Nay, if you trust him with your wife, I may with my Biddy. They say he's a merry harmless man now, e'en as harmless a man as ever came out of Italy with a good voice, and as pretty harmless company for a lady as a snake without his teeth.

SIR JASPAR. Ay, ay, poor man.

Enter MRS SQUEAMISH.

SQUEAMISH. I can't find 'em. – Oh, are you here, Grandmother? I followed, you must know, my Lady Fidget hither; 'tis the prettiest lodging and I have been staring on the prettiest pictures.

Enter LADY FIDGET *with a piece of china in her hand, and* HORNER *following.*

---

176 *tomrig*: tomboy, strumpet.
177 *vild*: archaic form of *vile*.
197 *Biddy*: abbreviation of Bridget.
198–9 *a man . . . voice*: a castrato singer.

LADY FIDGET. And I have been toiling and moiling for the prettiest piece of china, my dear.

HORNER. Nay, she has been too hard for me, do what I could.

SQUEAMISH. O Lord, I'll have some china too. Good Mr Horner, don't think to give other people china and me none; come in with me too.

HORNER. Upon my honour, I have none left now.

SQUEAMISH. Nay, nay, I have known you deny your china before now, but you shan't put me off so. Come –

HORNER. This lady had the last there.

LADY FIDGET. Yes, indeed, madam, to my certain knowledge he has no more left.

SQUEAMISH. O, but it may be he may have some you could not find.

LADY FIDGET. What, d'ye think if he had had any left, I would not have had it too? For we women of quality never think we have china enough.

HORNER. Do not take it ill. I cannot make china for you all, but I will have a roll-wagon for you too, another time.

SQUEAMISH. Thank you, dear toad.

LADY FIDGET. (*to* HORNER *aside*) What do you mean by that promise?

HORNER. (*apart to* LADY FIDGET) Alas, she has an innocent, literal understanding.

OLD LADY SQUEAMISH. Poor Mr Horner, he has enough to do to please you all, I see.

HORNER. Ay, madam, you see how they use me.

OLD LADY SQUEAMISH. Poor gentleman, I pity you.

HORNER. I thank you, madam. I could never find pity but from such reverend ladies as you are; the young ones will never spare a man.

SQUEAMISH. Come, come, beast, and go dine with us, for we shall want a man at ombre after dinner.

HORNER. That's all their use of me, madam, you see.

---

207 *moiling*: labouring.

227 *roll-wagon*: 'the cylindrical-bodied vase of the type frequently found in Transitional and K'ang Hsi blue-and-white' (R.J. Charleston, writing in *Apollo*, vol. 65, 1957, p. 251; a picture accompanying the article shows the phallic shape that provides Horner's double meaning).

SQUEAMISH. Come, sloven, I'll lead you, to be sure of you. (*Pulls him by the cravat*)

OLD LADY SQUEAMISH. Alas, poor man, how she tugs him! Kiss, kiss her; that's the way to make such nice women quiet.

HORNER. No, madam, that remedy is worse than the torment; they know I dare suffer anything rather than do it.

OLD LADY SQUEAMISH. Prithee, kiss her and I'll give you her picture in little, that you admired so last night; prithee do.

HORNER. Well, nothing but that could bribe me; I love a woman only in effigy and good painting, as much as I hate them. I'll do't, for I could adore the devil well painted. (*Kisses* MRS SQUEAMISH)

SQUEAMISH. Foh, you filthy toad! Nay, now I've done jesting.

OLD LADY SQUEAMISH. Ha, ha, ha, I told you so.

SQUEAMISH. Foh, a kiss of his –

SIR JASPAR. Has no more hurt in't than one of my spaniel's.

SQUEAMISH. Nor no more good neither.

QUACK. (*behind*) I will now believe anything he tells me.

Enter MR PINCHWIFE.

LADY FIDGET. O Lord, here's a man! Sir Jaspar, my mask, my mask! I would not be seen here for the world.

SIR JASPAR. What, not when I am with you?

LADY FIDGET. No, no, my honour – let's be gone.

SQUEAMISH. Oh, Grandmother, let us be gone; make haste, make haste, I know not how he may censure us.

LADY FIDGET. Be found in the lodging of anything like a man! Away!

Exeunt SIR JASPAR, LADY FIDGET, OLD LADY SQUEAMISH, MRS SQUEAMISH.

QUACK. (*behind*) What's here? Another cuckold? He looks like one, and none else sure have any business with him.

HORNER. Well, what brings my dear friend hither?

---

247 *nice*: fastidious.
253 *picture in little*: miniature.

PINCHWIFE. Your impertinency.

HORNER. My impertinency! – Why, you gentlemen that have got handsome wives think you have a privilege of saying anything to your friends and are as brutish as if you were our creditors.

PINCHWIFE. No, sir, I'll ne'er trust you any way.

HORNER. But why not, dear Jack? Why diffide in me thou knowest so well?

PINCHWIFE. Because I do know you so well.

HORNER. Han't I been always thy friend, honest Jack, always ready to serve thee, in love or battle, before thou wert married, and am so still?

PINCHWIFE. I believe so; you would be my second now indeed.

HORNER. Well then, dear Jack, why so unkind, so grum, so strange to me? Come, prithee kiss me, dear rogue. Gad, I was always, I say, and am still as much thy servant as –

PINCHWIFE. As I am yours, sir. What, you would send a kiss to my wife, is that it?

HORNER. So, there 'tis – a man can't show his friendship to a married man but presently he talks of his wife to you. Prithee, let thy wife alone and let thee and I be all one, as we were wont. What, thou art as shy of my kindness as a Lombard Street alderman of a courtier's civility at Locket's.

PINCHWIFE. But you are overkind to me, as kind as if I were your cuckold already; yet I must confess you ought to be kind and civil to me, since I am so kind, so civil to you, as to bring you this. Look you there, sir. (*Delivers him a letter*)

HORNER. What is't?

PINCHWIFE. Only a love-letter, sir.

HORNER. From whom? – how! this is from your wife – hum – and hum – (*Reads*)

PINCHWIFE. Even from my wife, sir. Am I not wondrous kind and civil to you now too? (*Aside*) But you'll not think her so.

---

286 *diffide in*: distrust.
304 *Lombard Street*: famous for goldsmiths, hence *wealthy*.
305 *Locket's*: a fashionable restaurant in Charing Cross.
304–5 The moneylender suspects the gentleman is about to ask for a loan or to renege on the repayment of one.

HORNER. (*aside*) Ha, is this a trick of his or hers?

PINCHWIFE. The gentleman's surprised, I find. What, you expected a kinder letter?

HORNER. No, faith, not I, how could I?

PINCHWIFE. Yes, yes, I'm sure you did; a man so well made as you are must needs be disappointed if the women declare not their passion at first sight or opportunity.

HORNER. [*aside*] But what should this mean? Stay, the postscript. (*Reads aside*) 'Be sure you love me, whatsoever my husband says to the contrary, and let him not see this, lest he should come home and pinch me, or kill my squirrel.' (*Aside*) It seems he knows not what the letter contains.

PINCHWIFE. Come, ne'er wonder at it so much.

HORNER. Faith, I can't help it.

PINCHWIFE. Now, I think, I have deserved your infinite friendship and kindness and have showed myself sufficiently an obliging kind friend and husband; am I not so, to bring a letter from my wife to her gallant?

HORNER. Ay, the devil take me, art thou the most obliging, kind friend and husband in the world, ha, ha!

PINCHWIFE. Well, you may be merry, sir; but in short I must tell you, sir, my honour will suffer no jesting.

HORNER. What dost thou mean?

PINCHWIFE. Does the letter want a comment? Then know, sir, though I have been so civil a husband as to bring you a letter from my wife, to let you kiss and court her to my face, I will not be a cuckold, sir, I will not.

HORNER. Thou art mad with jealousy. I never saw thy wife in my life but at the play yesterday, and I know not if it were she or no. I court her, kiss her!

PINCHWIFE. I will not be a cuckold, I say; there will be danger in making me a cuckold.

HORNER. Why, wert thou not well cured of thy last clap?

PINCHWIFE. I wear a sword.

HORNER. It should be taken from thee lest thou shouldst do thyself a mischief with it; thou art mad, man.

PINCHWIFE. As mad as I am, and as merry as you are, I must have more reason from you ere we part. I say again, though you kissed and courted last night my wife in man's clothes, as she confesses in her letter –

HORNER. (*aside*) Ha!

PINCHWIFE. Both she and I say, you must not design it again, for you have mistaken your woman, as you have done your man.

HORNER. (*aside*) Oh – I understand something now. – Was that thy wife? Why wouldst thou not tell me 'twas she? Faith, my freedom with her was your fault, not mine.

PINCHWIFE. (*aside*) Faith, so 'twas.

HORNER. Fie, I'd never do't to a woman before her husband's face, sure.

PINCHWIFE. But I had rather you should do't to my wife before my face than behind my back, and that you shall never do.

HORNER. No – you will hinder me.

PINCHWIFE. If I would not hinder you, you see by her letter, she would.

HORNER. Well, I must e'en acquiesce then and be contented with what she writes.

PINCHWIFE. I'll assure you 'twas voluntarily writ; I had no hand in't, you may believe me.

HORNER. I do believe thee, faith.

PINCHWIFE. And believe her too, for she's an innocent creature, has no dissembling in her; and so fare you well, sir.

HORNER. Pray, however, present my humble service to her and tell her I will obey her letter to a tittle and fulfill her desires, be what they will, or with what difficulty soever I do't, and you shall be no more jealous of me, I warrant her and you.

PINCHWIFE. Well, then, fare you well, and play with any man's honour but mine, kiss any man's wife but mine, and welcome. *Exit* MR PINCHWIFE.

HORNER. Ha, ha, ha, doctor.

QUACK. It seems he has not heard the report of you, or does not believe it.

HORNER. Ha, ha! Now, doctor, what think you?

QUACK. Pray let's see the letter – hum – (*Reads the letter*) 'for – dear – love you – '

HORNER. I wonder how she could contrive it! What say'st thou to't? 'Tis an original.

QUACK. So are your cuckolds, too, originals, for they are like no other common cuckolds, and I will henceforth believe it not impossible for you to cuckold the Grand Signior amidst his guards of eunuchs, that I say.

HORNER. And I say for the letter, 'tis the first love-letter that ever was without flames, darts, fates, destinies, lying and dissembling in't.

Enter SPARKISH, *pulling in* MR PINCHWIFE.

SPARKISH. Come back, you are a pretty brother-in-law, neither go to church, nor to dinner with your sister bride!

PINCHWIFE. My sister denies her marriage and you see is gone away from you dissatisfied.

SPARKISH. Pshaw, upon a foolish scruple, that our parson was not in lawful orders and did not say all the Common Prayer; but 'tis her modesty only, I believe. But let women be never so modest the first day, they'll be sure to come to themselves by night, and I shall have enough of her then. In the meantime, Harry Horner, you must dine with me; I keep my wedding at my aunt's in the Piazza.

HORNER. Thy wedding! What stale maid has lived to despair of a husband, or what young one of a gallant?

SPARKISH. Oh, your servant, sir – this gentleman's sister then – no stale maid.

HORNER. I'm sorry for't.

PINCHWIFE. (*aside*) How comes he so concerned for her?

SPARKISH. You sorry for't? Why, do you know any ill by her?

HORNER. No, I know none but by thee; 'tis for her sake, not yours, and another man's sake that might have hoped, I thought.

SPARKISH. Another man, another man! What is his name?

HORNER. Nay, since 'tis past he shall be nameless. (*Aside*) Poor Harcourt, I am sorry thou hast missed her.

---

407 *Grand Signior*: the Sultan of Turkey.
423 *Piazza*: an open arcade on two sides of Covent Garden, designed by Inigo Jones; see Act V Scene iii.

INCHWIFE. (*aside*) He seems to be much troubled at the match.

PARKISH. Prithee tell me – nay, you shan't go, brother.

INCHWIFE. I must of necessity, but I'll come to you to dinner. *Exit* PINCHWIFE.

PARKISH. But, Harry, what, have I a rival in my wife already? But with all my heart, for he may be of use to me hereafter, for though my hunger is now my sauce and I can fall on heartily without, but the time will come when a rival will be as good sauce for a married man to a wife as an orange to veal.

ORNER. O thou damned rogue! Thou hast set my teeth on edge with thy orange.

PARKISH. Then let's to dinner – there I was with you again. Come.

ORNER. But who dines with thee?

PARKISH. My friends and relations, my brother Pinchwife, you see, of your acquaintance.

ORNER. And his wife?

PARKISH. No, gad, he'll ne'er let her come amongst us good fellows. Your stingy country coxcomb keeps his wife from friends, as he does his little firkin of ale for his own drinking, and a gentleman can't get a smack on't; but his servants, when his back is turned, broach it at their pleasures and dust it away, ha, ha, ha! Gad, I am witty, I think, considering I was married today, by the world. But come –

ORNER. No, I will not dine with you, unless you can fetch her too.

PARKISH. Pshaw, what pleasure canst thou have with women now, Harry?

ORNER. My eyes are not gone; I love a good prospect yet and will not dine with you unless she does too. Go fetch her, therefore, but do not tell her husband 'tis for my sake.

PARKISH. Well, I'll try what I can do. In the meantime come away to my aunt's lodging; 'tis in the way to Pinchwife's.

---

462 *firkin*: cask.
463 *smack*: taste.
465 *dust it away*: polish it off.

HORNER. The poor woman has called for aid and stretched forth her hand, doctor; I cannot but help her over the pale out of the briars.

Exeunt SPARKISH, HORNER, QUACK.

SCENE IV

The scene changes to PINCHWIFE*'s house.*

MRS PINCHWIFE *alone, leaning on her elbow. A table, pen, ink and paper.*

MRS PINCHWIFE. Well, 'tis e'en so, I have got the London disease they call love; I am sick of my husband and for my gallant. I have heard this distemper called a fever, but methinks 'tis liker an ague, for when I think of my husband, I tremble and am in a cold sweat and have inclinations to vomit but when I think of my gallant, dear Mr Horner, my hot fit comes and I am all in a fever, indeed, and as in other fevers my own chamber is tedious to me and I would fain be removed to his and then methinks I should be well. Ah, poor Mr Horner! Well, I cannot, will not stay here; therefore I'd make an end of my letter to him, which shall be a finer letter than my last, because I have studied it like anything. O, sick, sick! (*Takes the pen and writes*)

Enter MR PINCHWIFE, *who, seeing her writing, steals softly behind her and, looking over her shoulder, snatches the paper from her.*

PINCHWIFE. What, writing more letters?

MRS PINCHWIFE. O Lord, bud, why d'ye fright me so?

She offers to run out; he stops her and reads.

PINCHWIFE. How's this! Nay, you shall not stir, madam. 'Dear, dear, dear Mr Horner' – very well – I have taught you to write letters to good purpose – but let's see't.

'First, I am to beg your pardon for my boldness in writing to you, which I'd have you to know I would not have done had not you said first you loved me so extremely, which if you do, you will never suffer me to lie in the arms of another man, whom I loathe, nauseate and detest.' – Now you can write these filthy words. But what follows? – 'Therefore I hope you will speedily find some way to free me from this unfortunate match, which was never, I assure you, of my choice, but I'm afraid 'tis already too far gone. However, if you love me, as I do you, you will try what you can do, but you must help me away before tomorrow, or else, alas, I shall be forever out of your reach, for I can defer no longer our – our' (*The letter concludes*) – What is to follow 'our'? – Speak, what? Our journey into the country, I suppose – Oh, woman, damned woman and love, damned love, their old tempter! For this is one of his miracles; in a moment he can make all those blind that could see and those see that were blind, those dumb that could speak and those prattle who were dumb before; nay, what is more than all, make these dough-baked, senseless, indocile animals, women, too hard for us, their politic lords and rulers, in a moment. But make an end of your letter and then I'll make an end of you thus, and all my plagues together. (*Draws his sword*)

MRS PINCHWIFE. O Lord, O Lord, you are such a passionate man, bud!

Enter SPARKISH.

SPARKISH. How now, what's here to do?

PINCHWIFE. This fool here now!

SPARKISH. What, drawn upon your wife? You should never do that but at night in the dark, when you can't hurt her. This is my sister-in-law, is it not? (*Pulls aside her handkerchief*) Ay, faith, e'en our country Margery; one may know her. Come, she and you must go dine with me; dinner's ready, come. But where's my wife? Is she not come home yet? Where is she?

PINCHWIFE. Making you a cuckold; 'tis that they all do, as soon as they can.

SPARKISH. What, the wedding day? No, a wife that designs to make a cully of her husband will be sure to

---

42 *dough-baked*: half-baked, foolish.
43 *indocile*: perhaps with the sense 'difficult to teach'.
61 *cully*: dupe, cuckold.

let him win the first stake of love, by the world. But come, they stay dinner for us. Come, I'll lead down our Margery.

PINCHWIFE. No – sir, go, we'll follow you.

SPARKISH. I will not wag without you.

PINCHWIFE. [*aside*] This coxcomb is a sensible torment to me amidst the greatest in the world.

SPARKISH. Come, come, Madam Margery.

PINCHWIFE. No, I'll lead her my way. What, would you treat your friends with mine, for want of your own wife? (*Leads her to t'other door and locks her in and returns. Aside*) I am contented my rage should take breath.

SPARKISH. [*aside*] I told Horner this.

PINCHWIFE. Come now.

SPARKISH. Lord, how shy you are of your wife! But let me tell you, brother, we men of wit have amongst us a saying that cuckolding, like the smallpox, comes with a fear, and you may keep your wife as much as you will out of danger of infection but if her constitution incline her to't, she'll have it sooner or later, by the world, say they.

PINCHWIFE. (*aside*) What a thing is a cuckold, that every fool can make him ridiculous! – Well, sir – but let me advise you, now you are come to be concerned, because you suspect the danger, not to neglect the means to prevent it, especially when the greatest share of the malady will light upon your own head, for –

Hows'e'er the kind wife's belly comes to swell,
The husband breeds for her and first is ill.

[*Exeunt* PINCHWIFE *and* SPARKISH.]

---

65 s.p. *Pinchwife*: Mrs Pinchwife Q1.
66 *wag*: stir.
67 *sensible*: acutely felt.
77 *shy*: suspicious.
92 *breeds for*: grows cuckold's horns on her behalf.

ACT V

SCENE I

Mr Pinchwife's house.

Enter MR PINCHWIFE *and* MRS PINCHWIFE. *A table and candle.*

PINCHWIFE. Come, take the pen and make an end of the letter, just as you intended; if you are false in a tittle, I shall soon perceive it and punish you with this as you deserve. (*Lays his hand on his sword*) Write what was to follow – let's see – 'You must make haste and help me away before tomorrow, or else I shall be forever out of your reach, for I can defer no longer our – ' What follows 'our'?

MRS PINCHWIFE. Must all out then, bud? (MRS PINCHWIFE *takes the pen and writes*) Look you there then.

PINCHWIFE. Let's see – 'For I can defer no longer our – wedding – Your slighted Alithea.' – What's the meaning of this? My sister's name to't. Speak, unriddle!

MRS PINCHWIFE. Yes, indeed, bud.

PINCHWIFE. But why her name to't? Speak – speak, I say!

MRS PINCHWIFE. Ay, but you'll tell her then again; if you would not tell her again –

PINCHWIFE. I will not – I am stunned, my head turns round. Speak.

MRS PINCHWIFE. Won't you tell her, indeed, and indeed?

PINCHWIFE. No, speak, I say.

MRS PINCHWIFE. She'll be angry with me, but I had rather she should be angry with me than you, bud; and to tell you the truth, 'twas she made me write the letter and taught me what I should write.

PINCHWIFE. (*aside*) Ha! I thought the style was some-

30 s.d. *aside*: not in Q1.

what better than her own. – But how could she come to you to teach you, since I had locked you up alone?

MRS PINCHWIFE. O, through the keyhole, bud.

PINCHWIFE. But why should she make you write a letter for her to him, since she can write herself?

MRS PINCHWIFE. Why, she said because – for I was unwilling to do it.

PINCHWIFE. Because what – because?

MRS PINCHWIFE. Because, lest Mr Horner should be cruel and refuse her or vain afterwards and show the letter, she might disown it, the hand not being hers.

PINCHWIFE. (*aside*) How's this? Ha! – then I think I shall come to myself again. This changeling could not invent this lie; but if she could, why should she? She might think I should soon discover it – stay – now I think on't too, Horner said he was sorry she had married Sparkish, and her disowning her marriage to me makes me think she has evaded it for Horner's sake. Yet why should she take this course? But men in love are fools; women may well be so. – But hark you, madam, your sister went out in the morning and I have not seen her within since.

MRS PINCHWIFE. Alackaday, she has been crying all day above, it seems, in a corner.

PINCHWIFE. Where is she? Let me speak with her.

MRS PINCHWIFE. (*aside*) O Lord, then he'll discover all! – Pray hold, bud. What, d'ye mean to discover me? She'll know I have told you then. Pray, bud, let me talk with her first.

PINCHWIFE. I must speak with her, to know whether Horner ever made her any promise and whether she be married to Sparkish or no.

MRS PINCHWIFE. Pray, dear bud, don't, till I have spoken with her and told her that I have told you all, for she'll kill me else.

PINCHWIFE. Go then, and bid her come out to me.

MRS PINCHWIFE. Yes, yes, bud.

PINCHWIFE. Let me see –

MRS PINCHWIFE. [*aside*] I'll go, but she is not within to come to him. I have just got time to know of Lucy her maid, who first set me on work, what lie I shall tell next, for I am e'en at my wit's end.

Exit MRS PINCHWIFE.

PINCHWIFE. Well, I resolve it; Horner shall have her. I'd

rather give him my sister than lend him my wife and such an alliance will prevent his pretensions to my wife, sure. I'll make him of kin to her and then he won't care for her.

MRS PINCHWIFE *returns.*

MRS PINCHWIFE. O Lord, bud, I told you what anger you would make me with my sister.

PINCHWIFE. Won't she come hither?

MRS PINCHWIFE. No, no, alackaday, she's ashamed to look you in the face, and she says, if you go in to her, she'll run away downstairs and shamefully go herself to Mr Horner, who has promised her marriage, she says, and she will have no other, so she won't –

PINCHWIFE. Did he so – promise her marriage – then she shall have no other. Go tell her so, and if she will come and discourse with me a little concerning the means, I will about it immediately. Go.

Exit MRS PINCHWIFE.

His estate is equal to Sparkish's, and his extraction as much better than his as his parts are; but my chief reason is, I'd rather be of kin to him by the name of brother-in-law than that of cuckold.

Enter MRS PINCHWIFE.

Well, what says she now?

MRS PINCHWIFE. Why, she says she would only have you lead her to Horner's lodging – with whom she first will discourse the matter before she talk with you, which yet she cannot do, for alack, poor creature, she says she can't so much as look you in the face, therefore she'll come to you in a mask, and you must excuse her if she make you no answer to any question of yours, till you have brought her to Mr Horner, and if you will not chide her, nor question her, she'll come out to you immediately.

PINCHWIFE. Let her come. I will not speak a word to her, nor require a word from her.

MRS PINCHWIFE. Oh, I forgot; besides, she says, she cannot look you in the face though through a mask, therefore would desire you to put out the candle.

PINCHWIFE. I agree to all; let her make haste – there, 'tis out. (*Puts out the candle*)

Exit MRS PINCHWIFE.

My case is something better. I'd rather fight with Horner for not lying with my sister than for lying with my wife, and of the two I had rather find my sister too forward than my wife; I expected no other from her free education, as she calls it, and her passion for the town. Well – wife and sister are names which make us expect love and duty, pleasure and comfort, but we find 'em plagues and torments, and are equally, though differently, troublesome to their keeper, for we have as much ado to get people to lie with our sisters as to keep 'em frm lying with our wives.

Enter MRS PINCHWIFE *masked and in hoods and scarves, and a nightgown and petticoat of* ALITHEA*'s, in the dark.*

What, are you come, sister? Let us go then – but first let me lock up my wife. – Mrs Margery, where are you?

MRS PINCHWIFE. Here, bud.

PINCHWIFE. Come hither, that I may lock you up; get you in. (*Locks the door*) Come, sister, where are you now?

MRS PINCHWIFE *gives him her hand but, when he lets her go, she steals softly on t'other side of him, and is led away by him for his sister* ALITHEA.

SCENE II

The scene changes to HORNER*'s lodging.*

QUACK, HORNER.

QUACK. What, all alone? Not so much as one of your cuckolds here, nor one of their wives! They use to take their turns with you, as if they were to watch you.

HORNER. Yes, it often happens that a cuckold is but his wife's spy and is more upon family duty when he is with her gallant abroad, hindering his pleasure, than when he is at home with her, playing the gallant. But

---

124 s.d. *nightgown*: a loose gown, usually but not necessarily worn at home.

the hardest duty a married woman imposes upon a lover is keeping her husband company always.

QUACK. And his fondness wearies you almost as soon as hers.

HORNER. A pox, keeping a cuckold company, after you have had his wife, is as tiresome as the company of a country squire to a witty fellow of the town, when he has got all his money.

QUACK. And as at first a man makes a friend of the husband to get the wife, so at last you are fain to fall out with the wife to be rid of the husband.

HORNER. Ay, most cuckold-makers are true courtiers; when once a poor man has cracked his credit for 'em, they can't abide to come near him.

QUACK. But at first, to draw him in, are so sweet, so kind, so dear, just as you are to Pinchwife. But what becomes of that intrigue with his wife?

HORNER. A pox, he's as surly as an alderman that has been bit and, since he's so coy, his wife's kindness is in vain, for she's a silly innocent.

QUACK. Did she not send you a letter by him?

HORNER. Yes, but that's a riddle I have not yet solved. Allow the poor creature to be willing, she is silly too, and he keeps her up so close –

QUACK. Yes, so close that he makes her but the more willing and adds but revenge to her love, which two, when met, seldom fail of satisfying each other one way or other.

HORNER. What, here's the man we are talking of, I think.

Enter MR PINCHWIFE, *leading in his wife masked, muffled and in her sister's gown.*

Pshaw!

QUACK. Bringing his wife to you is the next thing to bringing a love-letter from her.

HORNER. What means this?

PINCHWIFE. The last time, you know, sir, I brought you a love-letter; now, you see, a mistress. I think you'll say I am a civil man to you.

---

26 *bit*: tricked.

HORNER. Ay, the devil take me, will I say thou art the civilest man I ever met with, and I have known some! I fancy I understand thee now better than I did the letter. But hark thee, in thy ear –

PINCHWIFE. What?

HORNER. Nothing but the usual question, man: is she sound, on thy word?

PINCHWIFE. What, you take her for a wench and me for a pimp?

HORNER. Pshaw, wench and pimp, paw words. I know thou art an honest fellow and hast a great acquaintance among the ladies and perhaps hast made love for me rather than let me make love to thy wife –

PINCHWIFE. Come, sir, in short, I am for no fooling.

HORNER. Nor I neither; therefore, prithee, let's see her face presently. Make her show, man. Art thou sure I don't know her?

PINCHWIFE. I am sure you do know her.

HORNER. A pox, why dost thou bring her to me then?

PINCHWIFE. Because she's a relation of mine.

HORNER. Is she, faith, man? Then thou art still more civil and obliging, dear rogue.

PINCHWIFE. Who desired me to bring her to you.

HORNER. Then she is obliging, dear rogue.

PINCHWIFE. You'll make her welcome for my sake, I hope.

HORNER. I hope she is handsome enough to make herself welcome. Prithee, let her unmask.

PINCHWIFE. Do you speak to her; she would never be ruled by me.

HORNER. Madam –

MRS PINCHWIFE *whispers to* HORNER.

She says she must speak with me in private. Withdraw, prithee.

PINCHWIFE. (*aside*) She's unwilling, it seems, I should know all her undecent conduct in this business. – Well then, I'll leave you together and hope when I am gone you'll agree; if not, you and I shan't agree, sir.

HORNER. [*aside*] What means the fool? – If she and I agree, 'tis no matter what you and I do.

---

51 *sound*: free from the pox.
54 *paw*: naughty, improper.

Whispers to MRS PINCHWIFE, *who makes signs with her hand for him* [PINCHWIFE] *to be gone.*

PINCHWIFE. In the meantime, I'll fetch a parson and find out Sparkish and disabuse him. You would have me fetch a parson, would you not? Well then – now I think I am rid of her, and shall have no more trouble with her. Our sisters and daughters, like usurers' money, are safest when put out; but our wives, like their writings, never safe but in our closets under lock and key. *Exit* MR PINCHWIFE.

Enter BOY.

BOY. Sir Jaspar Fidget, sir, is coming up. [*Exit.*]

HORNER. Here's the trouble of a cuckold, now, we are talking of. A pox on him! Has he not enough to do to hinder his wife's sport but he must other women's too? – Step in here, madam.

Exit MRS PINCHWIFE.

Enter SIR JASPAR.

SIR JASPAR. My best and dearest friend.

HORNER. [*aside to* QUACK] The old style, doctor. – Well, be short, for I am busy. What would your impertinent wife have now?

SIR JASPAR. Well guessed, i'faith, for I do come from her.

HORNER. To invite me to supper. Tell her I can't come; go.

SIR JASPAR. Nay, now you are out, faith, for my lady and the whole knot of the virtuous gang, as they call themselves, are resolved upon a frolic of coming to you tonight in a masquerade and are all dressed already.

HORNER. I shan't be at home.

SIR JASPAR. [*aside*] Lord, how churlish he is to women! – Nay, prithee don't disappoint 'em; they'll think 'tis my fault. Prithee don't. I'll send in the banquet and the fiddles. But make no noise on't, for the poor virtuous rogues would not have it known for the world that they go a-masquerading, and they would come to no man's ball but yours.

---

90 *writings*: deeds, documents.

HORNER. Well, well – get you gone and tell 'em, if they come, 'twill be at the peril of their honour and yours.

SIR JASPAR. Heh, he, he! – we'll trust you for that; farewell. *Exit* SIR JASPAR.

HORNER. Doctor, anon you too shall be my guest,
But now I'm going to a private feast.

[*Exeunt.*]

SCENE III

The scene changes to the Piazza of Covent Garden.

SPARKISH, PINCHWIFE.

SPARKISH. (*with the letter in his hand*) But who would have thought a woman could have been false to me? By the world, I could not have thought it.

PINCHWIFE. You were for giving and taking liberty; she has taken it only, sir, now you find in that letter. You are a frank person and so is she you see there.

SPARKISH. Nay, if this be her hand – for I never saw it.

PINCHWIFE. 'Tis no matter whether that be her hand or no; I am sure this hand, at her desire, led her to Mr Horner, with whom I left her just now, to go fetch a parson to 'em, at their desire too, to deprive you of her forever, for it seems yours was but a mock marriage.

SPARKISH. Indeed, she would needs have it that 'twas Harcourt himself in a parson's habit that married us, but I'm sure he told me 'twas his brother Ned.

PINCHWIFE. Oh, there 'tis out, and you were deceived, not she, for you are such a frank person – but I must be gone. You'll find her at Mr Horner's; go and believe your eyes. *Exit* MR PINCHWIFE.

SPARKISH. Nay, I'll to her and call her as many crocodiles, sirens, harpies and other heathenish names as a poet would do a mistress who had refused to hear his suit, nay more, his verses on her. – But stay, is not

---

1 s.d. *letter*: the one written by Mrs Pinchwife as though from Alithea.

that she following a torch at t'other end of the Piazza? And from Horner's certainly – 'tis so.

Enter ALITHEA, *following a torch, and* LUCY *behind.*

You are well met, madam, though you don't think so. What, you have made a short visit to Mr Horner, but I suppose you'll return to him presently; by that time the parson can be with him.

ALITHEA. Mr Horner, and the parson, sir!

SPARKISH. Come, madam, no more dissembling, no more jilting, for I am no more a frank person.

ALITHEA. How's this?

LUCY. (*aside*) So, 'twill work, I see.

SPARKISH. Could you find out no easy country fool to abuse? None but me, a gentleman of wit and pleasure about the town? But it was your pride to be too hard for a man of parts, unworthy false woman, false as a friend that lends a man money to lose, false as dice who undo those that trust all they have to 'em.

LUCY. (*aside*) He has been a great bubble by his similes, as they say.

ALITHEA. You have been too merry, sir, at your wedding dinner, sure.

SPARKISH. What, d'ye mock me too?

ALITHEA. Or you have been deluded.

SPARKISH. By you.

ALITHEA. Let me understand you.

SPARKISH. Have you the confidence – I should call it something else, since you know your guilt – to stand my just reproaches? You did not write an impudent letter to Mr Horner, who I find now has clubbed with you in deluding me with his aversion for women, that I might not, forsooth, suspect him for my rival.

LUCY. (*aside*) D'ye think the gentleman can be jealous now, madam?

ALITHEA. I write a letter to Mr Horner!

SPARKISH. Nay, madam, do not deny it; your brother showed it me just now and told me likewise he left you at Horner's lodging to fetch a parson to marry

---

25 *torch*: a linkboy with a torch.

you to him, and I wish you joy, madam, joy, joy, and to him too, much joy, and to myself more joy for not marrying you.

ALITHEA. (*aside*) So, I find my brother would break off the match, and I can consent to't, since I see this gentleman can be made jealous. – O Lucy, by his rude usage and jealousy, he makes me almost afraid I am married to him. Art thou sure 'twas Harcourt himself and no parson that married us?

SPARKISH. No, madam, I thank you. I suppose that was a contrivance too of Mr Horner's and yours, to make Harcourt play the parson; but I would as little as you have him one now, no, not for the world, for shall I tell you another truth? I never had any passion for you till now, for now I hate you. 'Tis true I might have married your portion, as other men of parts of the town do sometimes, and so your servant, and to show my unconcernedness, I'll come to your wedding and resign you with as much joy as I would a stale wench to a new cully, nay, with as much joy as I would after the first night, if I had been married to you. There's for you, and so your servant, servant.

Exit SPARKISH.

ALITHEA. How was I deceived in a man!

LUCY. You'll believe, then, a fool may be made jealous now? For that easiness in him that suffers him to be led by a wife will likewise permit him to be persuaded against her by others.

ALITHEA. But marry Mr Horner! My brother does not intend it, sure; if I thought he did, I would take thy advice and Mr Harcourt for my husband. And now I wish that if there be any over-wise woman of the town who, like me, would marry a fool for fortune, liberty or title; first, that her husband may love play and be a cully to all the town but her and suffer none but fortune to be mistress of his purse; then, if for liberty, that he may send her into the country under the conduct of some housewifely mother-in-law, and, if for title, may the world give 'em none but that of cuckold.

LUCY. And for her greater curse, madam, may he not deserve it.

ALITHEA. Away, impertinent! – Is not this my old Lady Lanterlu's?

LUCY. Yes, madam. (*Aside*) And here I hope we shall find Mr Harcourt.

Exeunt ALITHEA, LUCY.

SCENE IV

The scene changes again to HORNER*'s lodging.*

HORNER, LADY FIDGET, MRS DAINTY FIDGET, MRS SQUEAMISH. *A table, banquet, and bottles.*

HORNER. (*aside*) A pox! They are come too soon – before I have sent back my new – mistress. All I have now to do is to lock her in, that they may not see her.

LADY FIDGET. That we may be sure of our welcome, we have brought our entertainment with us and are resolved to treat thee, dear toad.

DAINTY. And that we may be merry to purpose, have left Sir Jaspar and my old Lady Squeamish quarrelling at home at backgammon.

SQUEAMISH. Therefore let us make use of our time, lest they should chance to interrupt us.

LADY FIDGET. Let us sit then.

HORNER. First, that you may be private, let me lock this door and that, and I'll wait upon you presently.

LADY FIDGET. No, sir, shut 'em only and your lips forever, for we must trust you as much as our women.

HORNER. You know all vanity's killed in me; I have no occasion for talking.

LADY FIDGET. Now, ladies, supposing we had drank each of us our two bottles, let us speak the truth of our hearts.

DAINTY.
SQUEAMISH. } Agreed.

LADY FIDGET. By this brimmer, for truth is nowhere

---

104 *Lanterlu's*: the card game, lanterloo or loo.

23 *brimmer*: a full glass.

else to be found. (*Aside to* HORNER) Not in thy heart, false man!

HORNER. (*aside to* LADY FIDGET) You have found me a true man, I'm sure.

LADY FIDGET. (*aside to* HORNER) Not every way. – But let us sit and be merry. (LADY FIDGET *sings*)

1

Why should our damned tyrants oblige us to live
On the pittance of pleasure which they only give?
We must not rejoice
With wine and with noise.
In vain we must wake in a dull bed alone,
Whilst to our warm rival, the bottle, they're gone.
They lay aside charms
And take up these arms.* *The glasses.

2

'Tis wine only gives 'em their courage and wit;
Because we live sober, to men we submit.
If for beauties you'd pass,
Take a lick of the glass;
'Twill mend your complexions and, when they are gone,
The best red we have is the red of the grape.
Then, sisters, lay't on,
And damn a good shape.

DAINTY. Dear brimmer! Well, in token of our openness and plain-dealing, let us throw our masks over our heads.

HORNER. So, 'twill come to the glasses anon.

SQUEAMISH. Lovely brimmer! Let me enjoy him first.

LADY FIDGET. No, I never part with a gallant till I've tried him. Dear brimmer, that mak'st our husbands shortsighted.

DAINTY. And our bashful gallants bold.

SQUEAMISH. And for want of a gallant, the butler lovely in our eyes. – Drink, eunuch.

LADY FIDGET. Drink, thou representative of a husband. Damn a husband!

DAINTY. And, as it were a husband, an old keeper.

SQUEAMISH. And an old grandmother.

HORNER. And an English bawd and a French chirurgeon.

---

62 The causes of Horner's 'state'; see I i 29–30.

LADY FIDGET. Ay, we have all reason to curse 'em.

HORNER. For my sake, ladies?

LADY FIDGET. No, for our own, for the first spoils all young gallants' industry.

DAINTY. And the other's art makes 'em bold only with common women.

SQUEAMISH. And rather run the hazard of the vile distemper amongst them than of a denial amongst us.

DAINTY. The filthy toads choose mistresses now as they do stuffs, for having been fancied and worn by others.

SQUEAMISH. For being common and cheap.

LADY FIDGET. Whilst women of quality, like the richest stuffs, lie untumbled and unasked for.

HORNER. Ay, neat and cheap and new often they think best.

DAINTY. No, sir, the beasts will be known by a mistress longer than by a suit.

SQUEAMISH. And 'tis not for cheapness neither.

LADY FIDGET. No, for the vain fops will take up druggets and embroider 'em. But I wonder at the depraved appetites of witty men; they use to be out of the common road and hate imitation. Pray tell me, beast, when you were a man, why you rather chose to club with a multitude in a common house for an entertainment than to be the only guest at a good table.

HORNER. Why, faith, ceremony and expectation are unsufferable to those that are sharp bent; people always eat with the best stomach at an ordinary, where every man is snatching for the best bit.

LADY FIDGET. Though he get a cut over the fingers. – But I have heard people eat most heartily of another man's meat, that is, what they do not pay for.

HORNER. When they are sure of their welcome and freedom, for ceremony in love and eating is as ridiculous as in fighting; falling on briskly is all should be done in those occasions.

LADY FIDGET. Well, then, let me tell you, sir, there is nowhere more freedom than in our houses and we

---

83 *druggets*: cheap woollen material.
87 *common house*: (*a*) an ordinary, a restaurant (*b*) a brothel.
91 *sharp bent*: hungry.

take freedom from a young person as a sign of good breeding, and a person may be as free as he pleases with us, as frolic, as gamesome, as wild as he will.

HORNER. Han't I heard you all declaim against wild men?

LADY FIDGET. Yes, but for all that, we think wildness in a man as desirable a quality as in a duck or rabbit; a tame man, foh!

HORNER. I know not, but your reputations frightened me, as much as your faces invited me.

LADY FIDGET. Our reputation! Lord, why should you not think that we women make use of our reputation, as you men of yours, only to deceive the world with less suspicion? Our virtue is like the statesman's religion, the Quaker's word, the gamester's oath and the great man's honour – but to cheat those that trust us.

SQUEAMISH. And that demureness, coyness and modesty that you see in our faces in the boxes at plays is as much a sign of a kind woman as a vizard-mask in the pit.

DAINTY. For, I assure you, women are least masked when they have the velvet vizard on.

LADY FIDGET. You would have found us modest women in our denials only.

SQUEAMISH. Our bashfulness is only the reflection of the men's.

DAINTY. We blush when they are shamefaced.

HORNER. I beg your pardon, ladies; I was deceived in you devilishly. But why that mighty pretence to honour?

LADY FIDGET. We have told you. But sometimes 'twas for the same reason you men pretend business often, to avoid ill company, to enjoy the better and more privately those you love.

HORNER. But why would you ne'er give a friend a wink then?

LADY FIDGET. Faith, your reputation frightened us as much as ours did you, you were so notoriously lewd.

HORNER. And you so seemingly honest.

LADY FIDGET. Was that all that deterred you?

HORNER. And so expensive – you allow freedom, you say –

LADY FIDGET. Ay, ay.

HORNER. That I was afraid of losing my little money, as well as my little time, both which my other pleasures required.

LADY FIDGET. Money, foh! You talk like a little fellow now; do such as we expect money?

HORNER. I beg your pardon, madam; I must confess, I have heard that great ladies, like great merchants, set but the higher prizes upon what they have, because they are not in necessity of taking the first offer.

DAINTY. Such as we make sale of our hearts?

SQUEAMISH. We bribed for our love? Foh!

HORNER. With your pardon, ladies, I know, like great men in offices, you seem to exact flattery and attendance only from your followers; but you have receivers about you and such fees to pay, a man is afraid to pass your grants. Besides, we must let you win at cards, or we lose your hearts, and if you make an assignation, 'tis at a goldsmith's, jeweller's or china house, where, for your honour you deposit to him, he must pawn his to the punctual cit, and so paying for what you take up, pays for what he takes up.

DAINTY. Would you not have us assured of our gallant's love?

SQUEAMISH. For love is better known by liberality than by jealousy.

LADY FIDGET. For one may be dissembled, the other not. (*Aside*) But my jealousy can be no longer dissembled, and they are telling ripe. – Come, here's to our gallants in waiting, whom we must name, and I'll begin. This is my false rogue. (*Claps him on the back*)

SQUEAMISH. How!

HORNER. So all will out now.

SQUEAMISH. (*aside to* HORNER) Did you not tell me, 'twas for my sake only you reported yourself no man?

---

154 *prizes*: prices.

160 *receivers*: servants to be bribed.

162 *pass your grants*: accept your favours.

165–7 *for your honour . . . he takes up*: for trusting your honour to your gallant, he must in turn pawn his to the citizen, who will be punctual about demanding repayment, and so, in paying for your purchases, your gallant pays for getting you.

174 *telling ripe*: ready to be told.

DAINTY. (*aside to* HORNER) Oh, wretch! Did you not swear to me, 'twas for my love and honour you passed for that thing you do?

HORNER. So, so.

LADY FIDGET. Come, speak, ladies; this is my false villain.

SQUEAMISH. And mine too.

DAINTY. And mine.

HORNER. Well then, you are all three my false rogues too, and there's an end on't.

LADY FIDGET. Well then, there's no remedy; sister sharers, let us not fall out, but have a care of our honour. Though we get no presents, no jewels of him, we are savers of our honour, the jewel of most value and use, which shines yet to the world unsuspected, though it be counterfeit.

HORNER. Nay, and is e'en as good as if it were true, provided the world think so, for honour, like beauty now, only depends on the opinion of others.

LADY FIDGET. Well, Harry Common, I hope you can be true to three. Swear – but 'tis to no purpose to require your oath, for you are as often forsworn as you swear to new women.

HORNER. Come, faith, madam, let us e'en pardon one another, for all the difference I find betwixt we men and you women, we forswear ourselves at the beginning of an amour, you as long as it lasts.

Enter SIR JASPAR FIDGET *and* OLD LADY SQUEAMISH.

SIR JASPAR. Oh, my Lady Fidget, was this your cunning, to come to Mr Horner without me? But you have been nowhere else, I hope.

LADY FIDGET. No, Sir Jaspar.

OLD LADY SQUEAMISH. And you came straight hither, Biddy?

SQUEAMISH. Yes, indeed, Lady Grandmother.

SIR JASPAR. 'Tis well, 'tis well; I knew when once they were thoroughly acquainted with poor Horner,

---

200 *Harry Common*: Harry Horner is shared by them all.

they'd ne'er be from him. You may let her masquerade it with my wife and Horner and I warrant her reputation safe.

Enter BOY.

BOY. Oh, sir, here's the gentleman come whom you bid me not suffer to come up without giving you notice, with a lady too, and other gentlemen –

HORNER. Do you all go in there, whilst I send 'em away, and, boy, do you desire 'em to stay below till I come, which shall be immediately.

Exeunt SIR JASPAR, [OLD] LADY SQUEAMISH, LADY FIDGET, MRS DAINTY, SQUEAMISH.

BOY. Yes, sir. *Exit.*

Exit HORNER *at t'other door and returns with* MRS PINCHWIFE.

HORNER. You would not take my advice to be gone home before your husband came back; he'll now discover all. Yet pray, my dearest, be persuaded to go home and leave the rest to my management. I'll let you down the back way.

MRS PINCHWIFE. I don't know the way home, so I don't.

HORNER. My man shall wait upon you.

MRS PINCHWIFE. No, don't you believe that I'll go at all. What, are you weary of me already?

HORNER. No, my life, 'tis that I may love you long, 'tis to secure my love, and your reputation with your husband; he'll never receive you again else.

MRS PINCHWIFE. What care I? D'ye think to frighten me with that? I don't intend to go to him again; you shall be my husband now.

HORNER. I cannot be your husband, dearest, since you are married to him.

MRS PINCHWIFE. Oh, would you make me believe that? Don't I see every day, at London here, women leave their first husbands and go and live with other men as their wives? Pish, pshaw, you'd make me angry, but that I love you so mainly.

HORNER. So, they are coming up – in again, in, I hear 'em.

---

249 *mainly*: strongly.

Exit MRS PINCHWIFE.

Well, a silly mistress is like a weak place, soon got, soon lost, a man has scarce time for plunder; she betrays her husband first to her gallant and then her gallant to her husband.

Enter PINCHWIFE, ALITHEA, HARCOURT, SPARKISH, LUCY *and a Parson.*

PINCHWIFE. Come, madam, 'tis not the sudden change of your dress, the confidence of your asseverations and your false witness there, shall persuade me I did not bring you hither just now; here's my witness, who cannot deny it, since you must be confronted. – Mr Horner, did not I bring this lady to you just now?

HORNER. (*aside*) Now must I wrong one woman for another's sake, but that's no new thing with me, for in these cases I am still on the criminal's side, against the innocent.

ALITHEA. Pray, speak, sir.

HORNER. (*aside*) It must be so – I must be impudent and try my luck; impudence uses to be too hard for truth.

PINCHWIFE. What, you are studying an evasion or excuse for her. Speak, sir.

HORNER. No, faith, I am something backward only to speak in women's affairs or disputes.

PINCHWIFE. She bids you speak.

ALITHEA. Ay, pray, sir, do; pray satisfy him.

HORNER. Then truly, you did bring that lady to me just now.

PINCHWIFE. O ho!

ALITHEA. How, sir!

HARCOURT. How, Horner!

ALITHEA. What mean you, sir? I always took you for a man of honour.

HORNER. (*aside*) Ay, so much a man of honour that I must save my mistress, I thank you, come what will on't.

SPARKISH. So, if I had had her, she'd have made me believe the moon had been made of a Christmas pie.

LUCY. (*aside*) Now could I speak, if I durst, and 'solve

---

288 *'solve*: dissolve.

the riddle, who am the author of it.

ALITHEA. O unfortunate woman! A combination against my honour, which most concerns me now, because you share in my disgrace, sir, and it is your censure, which I must now suffer, that troubles me, not theirs.

HARCOURT. Madam, then have no trouble, you shall now see 'tis possible for me to love too, without being jealous; I will not only believe your innocence myself, but make all the world believe it. (*Apart to* HORNER) Horner, I must now be concerned for this lady's honour.

HORNER. And I must be concerned for a lady's honour too.

HARCOURT. This lady has her honour and I will protect it.

HORNER. My lady has not her honour but has given it me to keep and I will preserve it.

HARCOURT. I understand you not.

HORNER. I would not have you.

MRS PINCHWIFE. (*peeping in behind*) What's the matter with 'em all?

PINCHWIFE. Come, come, Mr Horner, no more disputing. Here's the parson; I brought him not in vain.

HARCOURT. No, sir, I'll employ him, if this lady please.

PINCHWIFE. How! What d'ye mean?

SPARKISH. Ay, what does he mean?

HORNER. Why, I have resigned your sister to him; he has my consent.

PINCHWIFE. But he has not mine, sir; a woman's injured honour, no more than a man's, can be repaired or satisfied by any but him that first wronged it; and you shall marry her presently, or – (*Lays his hand on his sword*)

Enter to them MRS PINCHWIFE.

MRS PINCHWIFE. [*aside*] O Lord, they'll kill poor Mr Horner! Besides, he shan't marry her whilst I stand by and look on; I'll not lose my second husband so.

PINCHWIFE. What do I see?

---

313 s.p. *Harcourt*: Horner Q1.

ALITHEA. My sister in my clothes!

SPARKISH. Ha!

MRS PINCHWIFE. (*to* MR PINCHWIFE) Nay, pray now don't quarrel about finding work for the parson; he shall marry me to Mr Horner, for now, I believe, you have enough of me.

HORNER. Damned, damned, loving changeling!

MRS PINCHWIFE. Pray, sister, pardon me for telling so many lies of you.

HARCOURT. I suppose the riddle is plain now.

LUCY. No, that must be my work. Good sir, hear me.

Kneels to MR PINCHWIFE, *who stands doggedly, with his hat over his eyes.*

PINCHWIFE. I will never hear woman again, but make 'em all silent, thus – (*Offers to draw upon his wife*)

HORNER. No, that must not be.

PINCHWIFE. You then shall go first; 'tis all one to me.

Offers to draw on HORNER*; stopped by* HARCOURT.

HARCOURT. Hold!

Enter SIR JASPAR FIDGET, LADY FIDGET, [OLD] LADY SQUEAMISH, MRS DAINTY FIDGET, MRS SQUEAMISH.

SIR JASPAR. What's the matter, what's the matter, pray, what's the matter, sir? I beseech you communicate, sir.

PINCHWIFE. Why, my wife has communicated, sir, as your wife may have done too, sir, if she knows him, sir.

SIR JASPAR. Pshaw, with him? Ha, ha, he!

PINCHWIFE. D'ye mock me, sir? A cuckold is a kind of a wild beast; have a care, sir.

SIR JASPAR. No, sure, you mock me, sir – he cuckold you! It can't be, ha, ha, he! Why, I tell you, sir – (*Offers to whisper*)

PINCHWIFE. I tell you again, he has whored my wife, and yours too, if he knows her, and all the women he comes near; 'tis not his dissembling, his hypocrisy can wheedle me.

---

345 *communicated*: had sex.

SIR JASPAR. How! does he dissemble? Is he a hypocrite? Nay, then – how – wife – sister, is he an hypocrite?

OLD LADY SQUEAMISH. An hypocrite, a dissembler! Speak, young harlotry, speak, how?

SIR JASPAR. Nay, then – O, my head too! – O thou libidinous lady!

OLD LADY SQUEAMISH. O thou harloting harlotry! Hast thou done't then?

SIR JASPAR. Speak, good Horner, art thou a dissembler, a rogue? Hast thou –

HORNER. Soh –

LUCY. (*apart to* HORNER) I'll fetch you off, and her too, if she will but hold her tongue.

HORNER. (*apart to* LUCY) Canst thou? I'll give thee –

LUCY. (*to* MR PINCHWIFE) Pray have but patience to hear me, sir, who am the unfortunate cause of all this confusion. Your wife is innocent, I only culpable, for I put her upon telling you all these lies concerning my mistress, in order to the breaking off the match between Mr Sparkish and her, to make way for Mr Harcourt.

SPARKISH. Did you so, eternal rotten tooth? Then, it seems, my mistress was not false to me, I was only deceived by you. – Brother that should have been, now man of conduct, who is a frank person now? To bring your wife to her lover – ha!

LUCY. I assure you, sir, she came not to Mr Horner out of love, for she loves him no more –

MRS PINCHWIFE. Hold, I told lies for you, but you shall tell none for me, for I do love Mr Horner with all my soul, and nobody shall say me nay. Pray, don't you go to make poor Mr Horner believe to the contrary; 'tis spitefully done of you, I'm sure.

HORNER. (*aside to* MRS PINCHWIFE) Peace, dear idiot.

MRS PINCHWIFE. Nay, I will not peace.

PINCHWIFE. Not till I make you.

Enter DORILANT, QUACK.

---

362 *libidinous*: libinous Q1.
367 *Soh*: a sigh.

DORILANT. Horner, your servant; I am the doctor's guest, he must excuse our intrusion.

QUACK. But what's the matter, gentlemen? For heaven's sake, what's the matter?

HORNER. Oh, 'tis well you are come. 'Tis a censorious world we live in; you may have brought me a reprieve, or else I had died for a crime I never committed, and these innocent ladies had suffered with me. Therefore pray satisfy these worthy, honourable, jealous gentlemen – that – (*Whispers*)

QUACK. O, I understand you; is that all? (*Whispers to* SIR JASPAR) Sir Jaspar, by heavens and upon the word of a physician, sir –

SIR JASPAR. Nay, I do believe you truly. – Pardon me, my virtuous lady and dear of honour.

OLD LADY SQUEAMISH. What, then all's right again?

SIR JASPAR. Ay, ay, and now let us satisfy him too.

They whisper with MR PINCHWIFE.

PINCHWIFE. An eunuch! Pray, no fooling with me.

QUACK. I'll bring half the chirurgeons in town to swear it.

PINCHWIFE. They! – they'll swear a man that bled to death through his wounds died of an apoplexy.

QUACK. Pray hear me, sir – why, all the town has heard the report of him.

PINCHWIFE. But does all the town believe it?

QUACK. Pray inquire a little, and first of all these.

PINCHWIFE. I'm sure when I left the town he was the lewdest fellow in't.

QUACK. I tell you, sir, he has been in France since; pray, ask but these ladies and gentlemen, your friend Mr Dorilant. – Gentlemen and ladies, han't you all heard the late sad report of poor Mr Horner?

ALL THE LADIES. Ay, ay, ay.

DORILANT. Why, thou jealous fool, dost thou doubt it? He's an arrant French capon.

MRS PINCHWIFE. 'Tis false, sir, you shall not disparage poor Mr Horner, for to my certain knowledge –

LUCY. Oh, hold!

414–15 useful because duelling was illegal.

428 *capon*: castrated cock, hence an impotent person.

SQUEAMISH. (*aside to* LUCY) Stop her mouth!

LADY FIDGET. (*to* PINCHWIFE) Upon my honour, sir, 'tis as true –

DAINTY. D'ye think we would have been seen in his company?

SQUEAMISH. Trust our unspotted reputations with him!

LADY FIDGET. (*aside to* HORNER) This you get, and we too, by trusting your secret to a fool.

HORNER. Peace, madam. (*Aside to* QUACK) Well, doctor, is not this a good design, that carries a man on unsuspected and brings him off safe?

PINCHWIFE. (*aside*) Well, if this were true, but my wife –

DORILANT *whispers with* MRS PINCHWIFE.

ALITHEA. Come, brother, your wife is yet innocent, you see; but have a care of too strong an imagination, lest like an overconcerned, timorous gamester, by fancying an unlucky cast, it should come. Women and fortune are truest still to those that trust 'em.

LUCY. And any wild thing grows but the more fierce and hungry for being kept up and more dangerous to the keeper.

ALITHEA. There's doctrine for all husbands, Mr Harcourt.

HARCOURT. I edify, madam, so much that I am impatient till I am one.

DORILANT. And I edify so much by example I will never be one.

SPARKISH. And because I will not disparage my parts I'll ne'er be one.

HORNER. And I, alas, can't be one.

PINCHWIFE. But I must be one – against my will, to a country wife, with a country murrain to me.

MRS PINCHWIFE. (*aside*) And I must be a country wife still too, I find, for I can't, like a city one, be rid of my musty husband and do what I list.

HORNER. Now, sir, I must pronounce your wife innocent, though I blush whilst I do it, and I am the only man by her now exposed to shame, which I will straight

---

432, 438 s.p. *Lady Fidget*: Old Lady Fidget Q1.
458 s.p. *Sparkish*: Eew Q1 (inexplicably).
462 *murrain*: cattle plague.

drown in wine, as you shall your suspicion, and the ladies' troubles we'll divert with a ballet. – Doctor, where are your maskers?

LUCY. Indeed, she's innocent, sir, I am her witness; and her end of coming out was but to see her sister's wedding and what she has said to your face of her love to Mr Horner was but the usual innocent revenge on a husband's jealousy – was it not, madam? Speak.

MRS PINCHWIFE. (*aside to* LUCY *and* HORNER)
Since you'll have me tell more lies – Yes, indeed, bud.

PINCHWIFE. For my own sake fain I would all believe;
Cuckolds, like lovers, should themselves deceive.
But – (*Sighs*)
His honour is least safe, too late I find,
Who trusts it with a foolish wife or friend.

A dance of cuckolds.

HORNER. Vain fops but court and dress and keep a puther,
To pass for women's men with one another,
But he who aims by women to be priz'd,
First by the men, you see, must be despis'd.

---

473 *end of*: aim in.

482 s.d. *A dance of cuckolds*: the music must have made the point; presumably it was 'Cuckolds all a row' which Pepys saw the King dance on 31 December 1662 (see John Playford's *The Dancing Master*, published five times between 1652 and 1675).

483 *puther*: pother, turmoil.

EPILOGUE, *spoken by* MRS KNEP

Now, you the vigorous, who daily here
O'er vizard-mask in public domineer,
And what you'd do to her if in place where,
Nay, have the confidence to cry, 'Come out',
Yet when she says 'Lead on', you are not stout,
But to your well-dressed brother straight turn round
And cry, 'Pox on her, Ned, she can't be sound',
Then slink away, a fresh one to engage,
With so much seeming heat and loving rage,
You'd frighten listening actress on the stage,
Till she at last has seen you huffing come
And talk of keeping in the tiring-room,
Yet cannot be provok'd to lead her home.
Next, you Falstaffs of fifty, who beset
Your buckram maidenheads, which your friends get,
And whilst to them you of achievements boast,
They share the booty and laugh at your cost.
In fine, you essenced boys, both old and young,
Who would be thought so eager, brisk and strong,
Yet do the ladies, not their husbands, wrong,
Whose purses for your manhood make excuse,
And keep your Flanders mares for show, not use:
Encourag'd by our woman's man today,
A Horner's part may vainly think to play
And may intrigues so bashfully disown
That they may doubted be by few or none,
May kiss the cards at picquet, ombre, loo,
And so be thought to kiss the lady too;
But, gallants, have a care, faith, what you do.
The world, which to no man his due will give,
You by experience know you can deceive
And men may still believe you vigorous,
But then we women – there's no cozening us.

Mrs Knep: Mr Hart Q1 (but clearly spoken by a woman, corrected by Q2).

15 *buckram*: stiff but also, like Falstaff's buckram rogues (*1 Henry IV*, II iv), illusory.

22 *Flanders mares*: Flemish horses were primarily imported for breeding.

27 *picquet*: a card game, like ombre and loo.

THE

PLAIN-DEALER.

A

COMEDY.

As it is Acted at the

Theatre Royal.

Written by Mr WYCHERLEY.

HORAT.

—— *Ridiculum acre*

Fortius & melius magnas plerumque secat res.

Licensed *Jan.* 9. 1676.

ROGER L'ESTRANGE.

LONDON,

Printed by T: N. for *James Magnes* and *Rich. Bentley* in *Russel-Street* in *Covent-garden* near the *Piazza's*.

M. DC. LXXVII.

Title-page of the 1677 Quarto of *The Plain-Dealer*, reproduced by permission of the Master and Fellows, Trinity College, Cambridge.

Motto
Horace, *Satires*, I x 14–15:
'Ridicule usually decides great matters more forcefully and better than severity'

INTRODUCTORY NOTE

Wycherley made use of more sources for *The Plain-Dealer* than for any of his other plays. Some are comparatively straightforward. Olivia's discussion with Eliza about the merits of Wycherley's previous play, *The Country Wife*, in Act II stems from Molière's *Critique de l'école des femmes* (1663). Manly's display of the way to get rid of importunate acquaintances at the end of Act III derives ultimately from the traditions of formal verse satire but may also owe something to Molière's *Les Fâcheux*. When Fidelia, disguised as a man, has her place taken in the assignation with Olivia by Manly, is surprised by Olivia's husband and nearly raped by him when her sex is discovered, Wycherley is making use of Marie-Catherine Desjardins's *Memoires de la vie de Henriette-Sylvie de Molière* (Paris, 1671) and the aftermath of the chaos, when Vernish cannot understand why Olivia should have run away and Olivia cannot understand why Vernish should have taken her lover for a woman, stems from the same source. Wycherley used Furetière's *Le Roman Bourgeois* (Paris, 1666, translated as *Scarron's City Romance* in 1671) as the source for Oldfox's argument with Widow Blackacre over who should read their papers (IV 255–98); he may also have taken a hint for his dedication from Mythophilacte's dedication of his work to the public executioner later in Furetière's work. It has been suggested that Manly was intended as a portrait of John Sheffield, Earl of Mulgrave, but the parallels are not convincing. Wycherley's father, Daniel, has traditionally been held to be the source for Widow Blackacre; they have only their litigiousness in common.

The other two sources are sources of an entirely different nature. Fidelia is a heroine derived from a long tradition of dramatic romance but the peculiar situation in which she finds herself is deliberately reminiscent of *Twelfth Night*; like Viola, she is ordered by the man she loves to woo Olivia (in both cases), who loves her. Wycherley wants his audience to recall Shakespeare's play, for it is Olivia, not the misanthropic Malvolio, who leaves the stage at the end. Even more complex is *The Plain-Dealer*'s relation to its most important source, Molière's *Le Misanthrope* (1666). Certain passages from Molière are imitated quite closely: Alceste's opening conversation with Philinte on friendship becomes Manly's with Plausible and Freeman (Act I); Olivia's gossiping with Novel (Act II) is patterned on the dissection of absent friends performed by Celimène and Acaste; the letters written by Olivia to Novel and Plausible parallel Celimène's to Clitandre and

Acaste. But Wycherley alters the structure of Molière's play in numerous ways: Alceste rushes off to the wilderness at the end of Molière's play while Manly returns from such an expedition at the beginning of Wycherley's; Philinte and Éliante agree to marry in Molière but Freeman and Eliza never speak to each other in Wycherley. The more Wycherley's audience knew *Le Misanthrope* the more they would have appreciated *The Plain-Dealer.*

The performance of *The Plain-Dealer* on 11 December 1676 at the Theatre Royal, Drury Lane, by the King's Company is probably the first. As John Dennis recorded in 1725, the audience were bemused and 'appeared doubtful what judgement to form of it' until a group including Rochester, Buckingham, Mulgrave and others 'by their loud approbation of it gave it both a sudden and a lasting reputation' (*The Critical Works*, vol. II, p. 277). The play was frequently performed until the end of the century, including the court performance in 1685 that helped Wycherley to be released from the Fleet prison. It was performed fairly frequently between 1715 and 1743 and there were occasional performances later in the century. In 1765 Isaac Bickerstaffe revised it in a version that was performed on odd occasions throughout the 1770s. In 1796 John Philip Kemble attempted to revive it in a new revised version but it was a flop. In this century it was performed by the Renaissance Theatre Company at the Scala Theatre in November 1925 but it still awaits a full-scale professional revival.

The play was first published in 1677 and there were numerous subsequent editions (1681, 1686, 1691, 1694, 1700 and 1709). Of modern editions, Leo Hughes edited the play for the Regents Restoration Drama Series in 1967 and James L. Smith for the New Mermaids in 1979. A facsimile of the first edition was published by Scolar Press in 1971.

TO MY LADY *B*–

Madam,

Though I never had the honour to receive a favour from you, nay, or be known to you, I take the confidence of an author to write to you a *billet doux* dedicatory; which is no new thing, for by most dedications it appears that authors, though they praise their patrons from top to toe and seem to turn 'em inside out, know 'em as little as sometimes their patrons their books, though they read 'em out; and if the poetical daubers did not write the name of the man or woman on top of the picture, 'twere impossible to guess whose it were. But you, madam, without the help of a poet, have made yourself known and famous in the world and, because you do not want it, are therefore most worthy of an epistle dedicatory. And this play claims naturally your protection, since it has lost its reputation with the ladies of stricter lives in the playhouse; and (you know) when men's endeavours are discountenanced and refused by the nice coy women of honour, they come to you, to you the great and noble patroness of rejected and bashful men, of which number I profess myself to be one, though a poet, a dedicating poet; to you, I say, madam, who have as discerning a judgement, in what's obscene or not, as any quick-sighted civil person of 'em all, and can make as much of a double-meaning saying as the best of 'em; yet would not, as some do, make nonsense of a poet's jest, rather than not make it bawdy; by which they show they as little value wit in a play as in a lover, provided they can bring t'other thing about. Their sense indeed lies all one way, and therefore are only for that in a poet which is moving, as they say. But what do they mean by that word 'moving'? Well, I must not put 'em to the blush, since I find I can do't. In short, madam, you would not be one of those who ravish a poet's innocent words and make 'em guilty of their own naughtiness (as 'tis termed) in spite of his teeth; nay, nothing is secure from the power of their imaginations, no, not their husbands, whom they cuckold with themselves by thinking of other men and so make the lawful matrimonial embraces adultery; wrong husbands and

1 *Lady B*–: Mother Bennet, a famous London bawd.

poets in thought and word, to keep their own reputations. But your ladyship's justice, I know, would think a woman's arraigning and damning a poet for her own obscenity, like her crying out a rape and hanging a man for giving her pleasure, only that she might be thought not to consent to't; and so, to vindicate her honour forfeits her modesty. But you, madam, have too much modesty to pretend to't, though you have as much to say for your modesty as many a nicer she, for you never were seen at this play, no, not the first day; and 'tis no matter what people's lives have been, they are unquestionably modest who frequent not this play. For, as Mr Bayes says of his, that it is the only touchstone of men's wit and understanding, mine is, it seems, the only touchstone of women's virtue and modesty. But hold, that touchstone is equivocal and by the strength of a lady's imagination may become something that is not civil; but your ladyship, I know, scorns to misapply a touchstone. And, madam, though you have not seen this play, I hope (like other nice ladies) you will the rather read it. Yet, lest the chambermaid or page should not be trusted and their indulgence could gain no further admittance for it than to their ladies' lobbies or outward rooms, take it into your care and protection, for, by your recommendation and procurement, it may have the honour to get into their closets; for what they renounce in public often entertains 'em there, with your help especially. In fine, madam, for these and many other reasons, you are the fittest patroness or judge of this play, for you show no partiality to this or that author. For from some many ladies will take a broad jest as cheerfully as from the watermen and sit at some downright filthy plays (as they call 'em) as well satisfied and

---

54 *Mr Bayes*: the name given by George Villiers, Duke of Buckingham, to his parody of Dryden in *The Rehearsal* (1671). Bayes comments in Act III, 'I know you have wit by the judgement you make of this play, for that's the measure I go by; my play is my touchstone.'

56 *touchstone*: (*a*) a stone to test gold, a criterion, a standard (*b*) a penis.

69 *In fine*: in short, to conclude.

73 *watermen*: the Thames boatmen, notorious for their inventive language of abuse.

as still as a poet could wish 'em elsewhere. Therefore it must be the doubtful obscenity of my plays alone they take exceptions at, because it is too bashful for 'em, and indeed most women hate men for attempting to halves on their chastity, and bawdy I find, like satire, should be home, not to have it taken notice of. But, now I mention satire, some there are who say, 'tis the plain-dealing of the play, not the obscenity, 'tis taking off the ladies' masks, not offering at their petticoats, which offends 'em. And generally they are not the handsomest, or most innocent, who are the most angry at being discovered:

– *Nihil est audacius illis*
Deprehensis; iram, atque animos a crimine sumunt.

Pardon, madam, the quotation, for a dedication can no more be without ends of Latin than flattery; and 'tis no matter for whom it is writ to, for an author can as easily (I hope) suppose people to have more understanding and languages than they have, as well as more virtues. But why the devil should any of the few modest and handsome be alarmed? (For some there are who as well as any deserve those attributes, yet refrain not from seeing this play, nor think it any addition to their virtue to set up for it in a playhouse, lest there it should look too much like acting.) But why, I say, should any at all of the truly virtuous be concerned, if those who are not so are distinguished from 'em? For by that mask of modesty which women wear promiscuously in public, they are all alike, and you can no more know a kept wench from a woman of honour by her looks than by her dress. For those who are of quality without honour (if any such there are), they have their quality to set off their false modesty, as well as their false jewels, and you must no more suspect their countenances for counterfeit than their pendants, though, as the Plain-dealer Montaigne

87–8 *Nihil . . . sumunt*: Juvenal, *Satires*, VI 284–5: 'Nothing is bolder than these when found out; they put on anger and passion from their guilt.'

says, *Elles envoyent leur conscience au bordel et tiennent leur contenance en règle*. But those who act as they look ought not to be scandalised at the reprehension of others' faults, lest they tax themselves with 'em and by too delicate and quick an apprehension not only make that obscene which I meant innocent but that satire on all which was intended only on those who deserved it. But, madam, I beg your pardon for this digression to civil women and ladies of honour, since you and I shall never be the better for 'em; for a comic poet and a lady of your profession make most of the other sort, and the stage and your houses, like our plantations, are propagated by the least nice women; and, as with the ministers of justice, the vices of the age are our best business. But, now I mention public persons, I can no longer defer doing you the justice of a dedication and telling you your own, who are, of all public-spirited people, the most necessary, most communicative, most generous and hospitable. Your house has been the house of the people, your sleep still disturbed for the public, and when you arose 'twas that others might lie down and you waked that others might rest. The good you have done is unspeakable. How many young unexperienced heirs have you kept from rash, foolish marriages and from being jilted for their lives by the worst sort of jilts, wives? How many bewitched widowers' children have you preserved from the tyranny of stepmothers? How many old dotards from cuckoldage and keeping other men's wenches and children? How many adulteries and unnatural sins have you prevented? In fine, you have been a constant scourge to the old lecher, and often a terror to the young. You have made concupiscence its own punishment and extinguished lust with lust, like blowing up of houses to stop the fire.

110–11 *Elles . . . règle*: Montaigne, *Essays*, Book III chapter 5: 'They send their conscience to the stews and keep their countenance in order' (Florio's translation, 1603).

110 *Elles envoyent*: Els envoy Q1.

110 *tiennent*: teinnent Q1.

122 *nice*: (*a*) fastidious (*b*) shy, unwilling.

134 *jilted*: deceived, cheated.

Nimirum propter continentiam, incontinentia
Necessaria est, incendium ignibus extinguitur.

There's Latin for you again, madam; I protest to you, as I am an author, I cannot help it. Nay, I can hardly keep myself from quoting Aristotle and Horace and talking to you of the rules of writing (like the French authors) to show you and my readers I understand 'em, in my epistle, lest neither of you should find it out by the play; and, according to the rules of dedication, 'tis no matter whether you understand or no what I quote or say to you of writing, for an author can as easily make anyone a judge or critic in an epistle as an hero in his play. But, madam, that this may prove to the end a true epistle dedicatory, I'd have you know 'tis not without a design upon you, which is in the behalf of the fraternity of Parnassus, that songs and sonnets may go at your houses and in your liberties for guineas and half guineas, and that wit, at least with you, as of old, may be the price of beauty; and so you will prove a true encourager of poetry, for love is a better help to it than wine and poets, like painters, draw better after the life than by fancy. Nay, in justice, madam, I think a poet ought to be as free of your houses as of the playhouses, since he contributes to the support of both and is as necessary to such as you as a ballad-singer to the pick-purse, in convening the cullies at the theatres, to be picked up and carried to supper and bed at your houses. And, madam, the reason of this motion of mine is because poor poets can get no favour in the tiring-rooms, for they are no keepers, you know; and folly and money,

---

144–5 *Nimirum . . . extinguitur*: Tertullian, *De Pudicitia*, I 16, quoted by Montaigne in the same essay: 'Belike we must be incontinent that we may be continent; burning is quenched by fire' (Florio's translation).

149–50 *French authors*: Corneille, for example, who prefaced his collected plays with *Discours* and *Examens*.

160 *liberties*: districts outside the city but under municipal control, as well as a pun on *freedoms*.

165–6 *a poet . . . playhouses*: playwrights were allowed free admission to the theatres.

169 *cullies*: dupes, often cuckolds.

172 *tiring-rooms*: dressing-rooms at the theatres.

173 *keepers*: men who maintain mistresses.

the old enemies of wit, are even too hard for it on its own dunghill. And for other ladies, a poet can least go to the price of them. Besides, his wit, which ought to recommend him to 'em, is as much an obstruction to his love as to his wealth or preferment, for most women nowadays apprehend wit in a lover as much as in a husband. They hate a man that knows 'em; they must have a blind, easy fool whom they can lead by the nose and, as the Scythian women of old, must baffle a man and put out his eyes ere they will lie with him, and then too, like thieves, when they have plundered and stripped a man, leave him. But if there should be one of an hundred of those ladies generous enough to give herself to a man that has more wit than money (all things considered) he would think it cheaper coming to you for a mistress though you made him pay his guinea, as a man in a journey (out of good husbandry) had better pay for what he has in an inn than lie on freecost at a gentleman's house.

In fine, madam, like a faithful dedicator I hope I have done myself right in the first place, then you and your profession, which in the wisest and most religious government of the world is honoured with the public allowance and in those that are thought the most uncivilised and barbarous is protected and supported by the ministers of justice. And of you, madam, I ought to say no more here, for your virtues deserve a poem rather than an epistle, or a volume entire to give the world your memoirs or life at large, and which (upon the word of an author that has a mind to make an end of his dedication) I promise to do, when I write the annals of our British love, which shall be dedicated to the ladies concerned, if they will not think them something too obscene too, when your life, compared with many that are thought innocent, I doubt not may vindicate you, and me, to the world for the confidence I have taken in this address to you, which then may be thought neither impertinent, nor immodest. And, whatsoever your amorous mis-

---

179 *apprehend*: fear.
182–3 *Scythian women . . . lie with him*: taken from Montaigne, *Essays*, Book III chapter 5.
182 *baffle*: humiliate.

fortunes have been, none can charge you with that heinous and worst of women's crimes, hypocrisy. Nay, in spite of misfortunes or age you are the same woman still, though most of your sex grow Magdalens at fifty and, as a solid French author has it,

Après le plaisir, vient la peine,
Après la peine la vertu.

But sure an old sinner's continency is much like a gamester's forswearing play when he has lost all his money; and modesty is a kind of a youthful dress, which as it makes a young woman more amiable makes an old one more nauseous. A bashful old woman is like an hopeful old man, and the affected chastity of antiquated beauties is rather a reproach than an honour to 'em, for it shows the men's virtue only, not theirs. But you, in fine, madam, are no more an hypocrite than I am when I praise you, therefore, I doubt not, will be thought (even by yours and the play's enemies, the nicest ladies) to be the fittest patroness for,

Madam,
Your ladyship's most obedient,
faithful, humble servant, and
The Plain-Dealer.

217–18 *Après . . . vertu*: 'After pleasure comes pain, after pain virtue' (source unknown).

PROLOGUE, *spoken by the Plain-Dealer*

I the Plain-Dealer am to act today
And my rough part begins before the play.
First, you who scribble, yet hate all that write,
And keep each other company in spite,
As rivals in your common mistress, fame,
And with faint praises one another damn;
'Tis a good play (we know) you can't forgive,
But grudge yourselves the pleasure you receive:
Our scribbler therefore bluntly bid me say,
He would not have the wits pleased here today.
Next, you, the fine, loud gentlemen o'th'pit,
Who damn all plays; yet if y'ave any wit,
'Tis but what here you sponge and daily get;
Poets, like friends to whom you are in debt,
You hate, and so rooks laugh, to see undone
Those pushing gamesters whom they live upon.
Well, you are sparks and still will be i'th'fashion;
Rail then at plays to hide your obligation.
Now, you shrewd judges who the boxes sway,
Leading the ladies' hearts and sense astray,
And, for their sakes, see all and hear no play,
Correct your cravats, foretops, lock behind,
The dress and breeding of the play ne'er mind;
Plain-dealing is, you'll say, quite out of fashion;
You'll hate it here, as in a dedication;
And your fair neighbours, in a limning poet,
No more than in a painter will allow it.
Pictures too like, the ladies will not please;
They must be drawn too here, like goddesses.
You, as at Lely's too, would truncheon wield,
And look like heroes in a painted field;
But the coarse dauber of the coming scenes
To follow life and nature only means,
Displays you as you are, makes his fine woman

---

13 *sponge*: by soaking up the poet's wit and using it as their own.
15 *rooks*: cheats, con-men.
17 *sparks*: fashionable and often foppish gallants.
22 *foretops*: a lock of hair ornamenting the forehead.
26 *limning poet*: a writer who draws portraits.
30 *Lely's*: Sir Peter Lely (1618–80), the fashionable portrait painter.
30 *truncheon*: officer's staff of authority.

A mercenary jilt, and true to no man;
His men of wit and pleasure of the age
Are as dull rogues as ever cumbered stage;
He draws a friend, only to custom just,
And makes him naturally break his trust.
I, only, act a part like none of you –
And yet, you'll say, it is a fool's part too –
An honest man, who, like you, never winks
At faults but, unlike you, speaks what he thinks,
The only fool who ne'er found patron yet,
For truth is now a fault, as well as wit.
And where else, but on stages, do we see
Truth pleasing or rewarded honesty?
Which our bold poet does this day in me.
If not to th'honest, be to th'prosperous kind;
Some friends at court let the Plain-Dealer find.

THE PERSONS

MANLY, of an honest, surly, nice humour, supposed first in the time of the Dutch War to have procured the command of a ship out of honour, not interest, and choosing a sea life only to avoid the world.	*Mr Hart*
FREEMAN, Manly's lieutenant, a gentleman well educated, but of a broken fortune, a complier with the age	*Mr Kynaston*
VERNISH, Manly's bosom and only friend	*Mr Griffin*
NOVEL, a pert, railing coxcomb and an admirer of novelties, makes love to Olivia	*Mr Clark*
MAJOR OLDFOX, an old impertinent fop, given to scribbling, makes love to the Widow Blackacre	*Mr Cartwright*
MY LORD PLAUSIBLE, a ceremonious, supple, commending coxcomb, in love with Olivia	*Mr Haines*
JERRY BLACKACRE, a true raw squire, under age and his mother's government, bred to the law	*Mr Charlton*
OLIVIA, Manly's mistress	*Mrs Marshall*
FIDELIA, in love with Manly and followed him to sea in man's clothes	*Mrs Boutell*
ELIZA, cousin to Olivia	*Mrs Knep*
LETTICE, Olivia's woman	*Mrs Knight*
THE WIDOW BLACKACRE, a petulant, litigious widow, always in law, and mother to Squire Jerry	*Mrs Corey*

LAWYERS, KNIGHTS OF THE POST, BAILIFFS, an ALDERMAN, a BOOKSELLER'S PRENTICE, a FOOT-BOY, SAILORS, WAITERS and attendants

The Scene: *London*

1–2 *nice humour*: punctilious disposition.
3 *Dutch War*: either the second war of 1664–7 or the third of 1672–4.
18 *Blackacre*: a legal phrase for a fictitious parcel of land.
30 *Knights of the Post*: professional perjurers and false witnesses.

THE PLAIN-DEALER

ACT I

SCENE I

Captain Manly's lodging.

Enter CAPTAIN MANLY, *surlily, and* MY LORD PLAUSIBLE *following him, and two* SAILORS *behind.*

MANLY. Tell not me, my good Lord Plausible, of your decorums, supercilious forms and slavish ceremonies, your little tricks, which you the spaniels of the world do daily over and over for and to one another, not out of love or duty, but your servile fear.

LORD PLAUSIBLE. Nay, i'faith, i'faith, you are too passionate, and I must humbly beg your pardon and leave to tell you, they are the arts, and rules, the prudent of the world walk by.

MANLY. Let 'em. But I'll have no leading-strings; I can walk alone. I hate a harness and will not tug on in a faction, kissing my leader behind, that another slave may do the like to me.

LORD PLAUSIBLE. What, will you be singular then, like nobody? Follow, love, and esteem nobody?

MANLY. Rather than be general, like you, follow everybody, court and kiss everybody, though perhaps at the same time you hate everybody.

LORD PLAUSIBLE. Why, seriously, with your pardon, my dear friend –

MANLY. With your pardon, my no friend, I will not, as you do, whisper my hatred or my scorn, call a man fool or knave by signs or mouths over his shoulder whilst you have him in your arms. For such as you, like common whores and pickpockets, are only dangerous to those you embrace.

LORD PLAUSIBLE. Such as I! Heavens defend me – upon my honour –

MANLY. Upon your title, my lord, if you'd have me believe you.

15 *follow, love*: follow Love Q1.

LORD PLAUSIBLE. Well then, as I am a person of honour, I never attempted to abuse or lessen any person in my life.

MANLY. What, you were afraid?

LORD PLAUSIBLE. No; but seriously, I hate to do a rude thing. No, faith, I speak well of all mankind.

MANLY. I thought so; but know that speaking well of all mankind is the worst kind of detraction, for it takes away the reputation of the few good men in the world by making all alike. Now I speak ill of most men, because they deserve it, I that can do a rude thing rather than an unjust thing.

LORD PLAUSIBLE. Well, tell not me, my dear friend, what people deserve; I ne'er mind that. I, like an author in a dedication, never speak well of a man for his sake but my own. I will not disparage any man to disparage myself, for to speak ill of people behind their backs is not like a person of honour, and truly to speak ill of 'em to their faces is not like a complaisant person. But if I did say or do an ill thing to anybody, it should be sure to be behind their backs out of pure good manners.

MANLY. Very well; but I, that am an unmannerly sea-fellow, if I ever speak well of people (which is very seldom indeed), it should be sure to be behind their backs, and if I would say or do ill to any, it should be to their faces. I would justle a proud, strutting, overlooking coxcomb at the head of his sycophants rather than put out my tongue at him when he were past me, would frown in the arrogant, big, dull face of an overgrown knave of business rather than vent my spleen against him when his back were turned, would give fawning slaves the lie whilst they embrace or commend me, cowards whilst they brag, call a rascal by no other title though his father had left him a duke's, laugh at fools aloud before their mistresses, and must desire people to leave me when their visits grow at last as troublesome as they were at first impertinent.

LORD PLAUSIBLE. I would not have my visits troublesome.

MANLY. The only way to be sure not to have 'em troublesome is to make 'em when people are not at home, for your visits, like other good turns, are most obliging when made or done to a man in his absence. A pox, why should anyone, because he has nothing to do, go and disturb another man's business?

LORD PLAUSIBLE. I beg your pardon, my dear friend. What, you have business?

MANLY. If you have any, I would not detain your lordship.

LORD PLAUSIBLE. Detain me, dear sir! I can never have enough of your company.

MANLY. I'm afraid I should be tiresome. I know not what you think.

LORD PLAUSIBLE. Well, dear sir, I see you would have me gone.

MANLY. (*aside*) But I see you won't.

LORD PLAUSIBLE. Your most faithful –

MANLY. God be w'ye, my lord.

LORD PLAUSIBLE. Your most humble –

MANLY. Farewell.

LORD PLAUSIBLE. And eternally –

MANLY. And eternally ceremony – (*Aside*) Then the devil take thee eternally.

LORD PLAUSIBLE. You shall use no ceremony, by my life.

MANLY. I do not intend it.

LORD PLAUSIBLE. Why do you stir then?

MANLY. Only to see you out of doors, that I may shut 'em against more welcomes.

LORD PLAUSIBLE. Nay, faith, that shan't pass upon your most faithful, humble servant.

MANLY. (*aside*) Nor this any more upon me.

LORD PLAUSIBLE. Well, you are too strong for me.

MANLY. (*aside*) I'd sooner be visited by the plague, for that only would keep a man from visits and his doors shut. *Exit, thrusting out* MY LORD PLAUSIBLE.

Manent SAILORS.

FIRST SAILOR. Here's a finical fellow, Jack! What a brave fair-weather captain of a ship he would make!

SECOND SAILOR. He a captain of a ship! It must be when she's in the dock then, for he looks like one of

---

109 *finical*: affectedly fastidious.

those that get the King's Commissions for Hulls to sell a king's ship, when a brave fellow has fought her almost to a longboat.

FIRST SAILOR. On my conscience then, Jack, that's the reason our bully tar sunk our ship: not only that the Dutch might not have her, but that the courtiers, who laugh at wooden legs, might not make her prize.

SECOND SAILOR. A pox of his sinking, Tom; we have made a base, broken, short voyage of it.

FIRST SAILOR. Ay, your brisk dealers in honour always make quick returns with their ship to the dock and their men to the hospitals. 'Tis, let me see, just a month since we set out of the river, and the wind was almost as cross to us as the Dutch.

SECOND SAILOR. Well, I forgive him sinking my own poor truck, if he would but have given me time and leave to have saved black Kate of Wapping's small venture.

FIRST SAILOR. Faith, I forgive him since, as the purser told me, he sunk the value of five or six thousand pound of his own with which he was to settle himself somewhere in the Indies, for our merry lieutenant was to succeed him in his commission for the ship back, for he was resolved never to return again for England.

SECOND SAILOR. So it seemed by his fighting.

FIRST SAILOR. No, but he was a-weary of this side of the world here, they say.

SECOND SAILOR. Ay, or else he would not have bid so fair for a passage into t'other.

FIRST SAILOR. Jack, thou think'st thyself in the fore-castle, thou'rt so waggish; but I tell you then, he had a mind to go live and bask himself on the sunny side of the globe.

SECOND SAILOR. What, out of any discontent? For

113–14 the common practice of selling off out-of-commission ships.
115 *longboat*: the largest rowing-boat belonging to a sailing ship.
117 *bully*: fine fellow.
128 *truck*: odds and ends, goods of little value.
129 *Wapping*: a suburb of London beside the Thames, downriver from the Tower, frequented by sailors.
134 *Indies*: East Indies.

he's always as dogged as an old tarpaulin when hindered of a voyage by a young pantaloon captain.

FIRST SAILOR. 'Tis true, I never saw him pleased but in the fight, and then he looked like one of us coming from the pay-table, with a new lining to our hats under our arms.

SECOND SAILOR. A pox, he's like the Bay of Biscay, rough and angry, let the wind blow where 'twill.

FIRST SAILOR. Nay, there's no more dealing with him than with the land in a storm, no-near –

SECOND SAILOR. 'Tis a hurry-durry blade. Dost thou remember after we had tugged hard the old leaky longboat to save his life, when I welcomed him ashore, he gave me a box on the ear and called me fawning water-dog?

Enter MANLY *and* FREEMAN.

FIRST SAILOR. Hold thy peace, Jack, and stand by; the foul weather's coming.

MANLY. You rascals, dogs, how could this tame thing get through you?

FIRST SAILOR. Faith, to tell your honour the truth, we were at hob in the hall and, whilst my brother and I were quarrelling about a cast, he slunk by us.

SECOND SAILOR. He's a sneaking fellow I warrant for't.

MANLY. Have more care for the future, you slaves. Go and with drawn cutlasses stand at the stair foot and keep all that ask for me from coming up. Suppose you were guarding the scuttle to the powder room. Let none enter here at your and their peril.

FIRST SAILOR. No, for the danger would be the same; you would blow them and us up if we should.

148–9 the quarrel between the professional seamen and the gentlemen captains was long and acrimonious, especially in times of war.

148 *tarpaulin*: waterproof cloth, hence sailor, particularly a professional naval officer.

149 *pantaloon*: fashionable breeches.

157 *no-near*: a command to the helmsman to come no closer to the wind, hence to keep away from Manly's dangerous shores.

158 *hurry-durry*: rough weather (sailor's slang).

168 *hob*: a coin-tossing game.

174 *scuttle*: hatchway.

SECOND SAILOR. Must no one come to you, sir?

MANLY. No man, sir.

FIRST SAILOR. No man, sir, but a woman then, an't like your honour –

MANLY. No woman neither, you impertinent dog. Would you be pimping? A sea pimp is the strangest monster she has.

SECOND SAILOR. Indeed, an't like your honour, 'twill be hard for us to deny a woman anything since we are so newly come on shore.

FIRST SAILOR. We'll let no old woman come up, though it were our trusting landlady at Wapping.

MANLY. Would you be witty, you brandy casks you? You become a jest as ill as you do a horse. Be gone, you dogs, I hear a noise on the stairs.

Exeunt SAILORS.

FREEMAN. Faith, I am sorry you would let the fop go. I intended to have had some sport with him.

MANLY. Sport with him! A pox, then why did you not stay? You should have enjoyed your coxcomb and had him to yourself for me.

FREEMAN. No, I should not have cared for him without you neither, for the pleasure which fops afford is like that of drinking, only good when 'tis shared, and a fool, like a bottle, which would make you merry in company, will make you dull alone. But how the devil could you turn a man of his quality downstairs? You use a lord with very little ceremony, it seems.

MANLY. A lord! What, thou art one of those who esteem men only by the marks and value fortune has set upon 'em and never consider intrinsic worth. But counterfeit honour will not be current with me; I weigh the man, not his title. 'Tis not the king's stamp can make the metal better or heavier: your lord is a leaden shilling which you may bend every way, and debases the stamp he bears, instead of being raised by't. – Here again, you slaves?

Enter SAILORS.

FIRST SAILOR. Only to receive farther instructions, an't like your honour: what if a man should bring you money? Should we turn him back?

MANLY. All men, I say. Must I be pestered with you too? You dogs, away.

SECOND SAILOR. Nay, I know one man your honour would not have us hinder coming to you, I'm sure.

MANLY. Who's that? Speak quickly, slaves.

SECOND SAILOR. Why, a man that should bring you a challenge, for, though you refuse money, I'm sure you love fighting too well to refuse that.

MANLY. Rogue, rascal, dog.

Kicks the SAILORS *out.*

FREEMAN. Nay, let the poor rogues have their forecastle jests; they cannot help 'em in a fight, scarce when a ship's sinking.

MANLY. Damn their untimely jests. A servant's jest is more sauciness than his counsel.

FREEMAN. But what, will you see nobody? Not your friends?

MANLY. Friends – I have but one, and he, I hear, is not in town; nay, can have but one friend, for a true heart admits but of one friendship as of one love. But in having that friend I have a thousand, for he has the courage of men in despair, yet the diffidency and caution of cowards, the secrecy of the revengeful and the constancy of martyrs, one fit to advise, to keep a secret, to fight and die for his friend. Such I think him, for I have trusted him with my mistress in my absence, and the trust of beauty is sure the greatest we can show.

FREEMAN. Well, but all your good thoughts are not for him alone, I hope. Pray, what d'ye think of me for a friend?

MANLY. Of thee! Why, thou art a latitudinarian in friendship, that is, no friend; thou dost side with all mankind but will suffer for none. Thou art indeed like your Lord Plausible, the pink of courtesy, therefore hast no friendship, for ceremony and great professing renders friendship as much suspected as it does religion.

FREEMAN. And no professing, no ceremony at all in friendship were as unnatural and as undecent as in

---

247 *latitudinarian*: one who accepts as Christian anyone who accepts the Apostles' Creed, allowing many different concepts of God; Freeman has too many different friends for Manly.

religion; and there is hardly such a thing as an honest hypocrite, who professes himself to be worse than he is, unless it be yourself, for though I could never get you to say you were my friend, I know you'll prove so.

MANLY. I must confess I am so much your friend I would not deceive you, therefore must tell you, not only because my heart is taken up but according to your rules of friendship, I cannot be your friend.

FREEMAN. Why, pray?

MANLY. Because he that is, you'll say, a true friend to a man is a friend to all his friends. But you must pardon me, I cannot wish well to pimps, flatterers, detractors and cowards, stiff nodding knaves and supple, pliant, kissing fools. Now, all these I have seen you use like the dearest friends in the world.

FREEMAN. Hah, hah, hah – What, you observed me, I warrant, in the galleries at Whitehall doing the business of the place! Pshaw! Court professions, like court promises, go for nothing, man. But, faith, could you think I was a friend to all those I hugged, kissed, flattered, bowed to? Hah, ha –

MANLY. You told 'em so and swore it too; I heard you.

FREEMAN. Ay, but when their backs were turned did I not tell you they were rogues, villains, rascals whom I despised and hated?

MANLY. Very fine! But what reason had I to believe you spoke your heart to me since you professed deceiving so many?

FREEMAN. Why, don't you know, good captain, that telling truth is a quality as prejudicial to a man that would thrive in the world as square play to a cheat, or true love to a whore! Would you have a man speak truth to his ruin? You are severer than the law, which requires no man to swear against himself. You would have me speak truth against myself, I warrant, and tell my promising friend, the courtier, he has a bad memory?

MANLY. Yes.

---

272 *galleries at Whitehall*: the popular gathering-place in the king's residence, a place for gossip, rumour, seeking preferment.

276 *to*: too Q1.

FREEMAN. And so make him remember to forget my business. And I should tell the great lawyer too that he takes oftener fees to hold his tongue than to speak?

MANLY. No doubt on't.

FREEMAN. Ay, and have him hang or ruin me, when he should come to be a judge and I before him. And you would have me tell the new officer who bought his employment lately that he is a coward?

MANLY. Ay.

FREEMAN. And so get myself cashiered, not him, he having the better friends though I the better sword. And I should tell the scribbler of honour that heraldry were a prettier and fitter study for so fine a gentleman than poetry?

MANLY. Certainly.

FREEMAN. And so find myself mauled in his next hired lampoon. And you would have me tell the holy lady too she lies with her chaplain?

MANLY. No doubt on't.

FREEMAN. And so draw the clergy upon my back and want a good table to dine at sometimes. And by the same reason too, I should tell you that the world thinks you a madman, a brutal, and have you cut my throat, or worse, hate me! What other good success of all my plain-dealing could I have than what I've mentioned?

MANLY. Why, first your promising courtier would keep his word, out of fear of more reproaches or at least would give you no more vain hopes. Your lawyer would serve you more faithfully, for he, having no honour but his interest, is truest still to him he knows suspects him. The new officer would provoke thee to make him a coward and so be cashiered, that thou or some other honest fellow, who had more courage than money, might get his place. The noble sonneteer would trouble thee no more with his madrigals. The praying lady would leave off railing at wenching before thee and not turn away her chambermaid for her own known frailty with thee. And I, instead of hating thee, should love thee for thy plain-dealing

---

316 *brutal*: a short space after the word in Q1 may indicate that a word has dropped out.

and, in lieu of being mortified, am proud that the world and I think not well of one another.

FREEMAN. Well, doctors differ. You are for plain-dealing, I find; but against your particular notions I have the practice of the whole world. Observe but any morning what people do when they get together on the Exchange, in Westminster Hall, or the galleries in Whitehall.

MANLY. I must confess, there they seem to rehearse Bayes's grand dance: here you see a bishop bowing low to a gaudy atheist, a judge to a doorkeeper, a great lord to a fishmonger or a scrivener with a jack-chain about his neck, a lawyer to a sergeant-at-arms, a velvet physician to a threadbare chemist and a supple gentleman usher to a surly beefeater, and so tread round in a preposterous huddle of ceremony to each other, whilst they can hardly hold their solemn false countenances.

FREEMAN. Well, they understand the world.

MANLY. Which I do not, I confess.

FREEMAN. But, sir, pray believe the friendship I promise you real, whatsoever I have professed to others. Try me at least.

MANLY. Why, what would you do for me?

FREEMAN. I would fight for you.

MANLY. That you would do for your own honour. But what else?

FREEMAN. I would lend you money, if I had it.

MANLY. To borrow more of me another time. That were but putting your money to interest; a usurer would be as good a friend. But what other piece of friendship?

---

340 *Exchange*: either the New Exchange, the arcade of shops near the Strand, the location of Act III Scene ii of *The Country Wife*, or the Royal Exchange, the meeting-place of merchants and bankers.

340 *Westminster Hall*: part of the Palace of Westminster, site of the law-courts and also a number of shops; see Act III.

343 *Bayes's grand dance*: a ridiculous dance of the two Kings of Brentford in *The Rehearsal*, Act V.

345 *scrivener with a jack-chain*: a notary wearing his chain of office.

347 *chemist*: alchemist.

FREEMAN. I would speak well of you to your enemies.

MANLY. To encourage others to be your friends by a show of gratitude. But what else?

FREEMAN. Nay, I would not hear you ill spoken of behind your back by my friend.

MANLY. Nay, then thou'rt a friend indeed. But it were unreasonable to expect it from thee as the world goes now, when new friends, like new mistresses, are got by disparaging old ones.

Enter FIDELIA.

But here comes another will say as much at least. Dost not thou love me devilishly too, my little volunteer, as well as he or any man can?

FIDELIA. Better than any man can love you, my dear captain.

MANLY. Look you there. I told you so.

FIDELIA. As well as you do truth or honour, sir, as well.

MANLY. Nay, good young gentleman, enough, for shame. Thou hast been a page, by thy flattering and lying, to one of those praying ladies who love flattery so well they are jealous of it, and wert turned away for saying the same things to the old housekeeper for sweetmeats as you did to your lady; for thou flatterest everything and everybody alike.

FIDELIA. You, dear sir, should not suspect the truth of what I say of you, though to you. Fame, the old liar, is believed when she speaks wonders of you. You cannot be flattered, sir; your merit is unspeakable.

MANLY. Hold, hold, sir, or I shall suspect worse of you, that you have been a cushion-bearer to some state hypocrite and turned away by the chaplains for outflattering their probation sermons for a benefice.

FIDELIA. Suspect me for anything, sir, but the want of love, faith and duty to you, the bravest, worthiest of mankind. Believe me, I could die for you, sir.

MANLY. Nay, there you lie, sir. Did I not see thee more afraid in the fight than the chaplain of the ship or the purser that bought his place?

---

396 *probation sermons*: sermons preached by candidates for appointment to a living.

FIDELIA. Can he be said to be afraid that ventures to sea with you?

MANLY. Fie, fie, no more. I shall hate thy flattery worse than thy cowardice, nay, than thy bragging.

FIDELIA. Well, I own then I was afraid, mightily afraid; yet for you I would be afraid again, an hundred times afraid. Dying is ceasing to be afraid, and that I could do sure for you and you'll believe me one day. (*Weeps*)

FREEMAN. Poor youth! Believe his eyes if not his tongue; he seems to speak truth with them.

MANLY. What, does he cry? A pox on't, a maudlin flatterer is as nauseously troublesome as a maudlin drunkard. No more, you little milksop, do not cry. I'll never make thee afraid again, for of all men, if I had occasion, thou shouldst not be my second and, when I go to sea again, thou shalt venture thy life no more with me.

FIDELIA. Why, will you leave me behind then? (*Aside*) If you would preserve my life, I'm sure you should not.

MANLY. Leave thee behind! Ay, ay, thou art a hopeful youth for the shore only. Here thou wilt live to be cherished by fortune and the great ones, for thou may'st easily come to out-flatter a dull poet, out-lie a coffeehouse or gazette writer, out-swear a knight of the post, out-watch a pimp, out-fawn a rook, out-promise a lover, out-rail a wit and out-brag a sea-captain. All this thou canst do, because thou'rt a coward, a thing I hate; therefore thou'lt do better with the world than with me and these are the good courses you must take in the world. There's good advice, at least, at parting. Go and be happy with't.

FIDELIA. Parting, sir! O let me not hear that dismal word.

MANLY. If my words frighten thee, be gone the sooner, for, to be plain with thee, cowardice and I cannot dwell together.

FIDELIA. And cruelty and courage never dwelt together, sure, sir. Do not turn me off to shame and misery, for I am helpless and friendless.

MANLY. Friendless! There are half a score friends for thee then. (*Offers her gold*) I leave myself no more. They'll help thee a little. Be gone, go; I must be cruel to thee (if thou call'st it so) out of pity.

FIDELIA. If you would be cruelly pitiful, sir, let it be with your sword, not gold. *Exit.*

Enter FIRST SAILOR.

FIRST SAILOR. We have with much ado turned away two gentlemen who told us forty times over their names were Mr Novel and Major Oldfox.

MANLY. Well, to your post again.

Exit SAILOR.

But how come those puppies coupled always together?

FREEMAN. O, the coxcombs keep each other company to show each other, as Novel calls it, or, as Oldfox says, like two knives to whet one another.

MANLY. And set other people's teeth an edge.

Enter SECOND SAILOR.

SECOND SAILOR. Here is a woman, an't like your honour, scolds and bustles with us to come in, as much as a seaman's widow at the Navy Office. Her name is Mrs Blackacre.

MANLY. That fiend too!

FREEMAN. The Widow Blackacre, is it not? That litigious she-pettifogger, who is at law and difference with all the world; but I wish I could make her agree with me in the church. They say she has fifteen hundred pounds a year jointure and the care of her son, that is, the destruction of his estate.

MANLY. Her lawyers, attornies and solicitors have fifteen hundred pound a year whilst she is contented to be poor to make other people so, for she is as vexatious as her father was, the great attorney, nay, as a dozen Norfolk attornies, and as implacable an adversary as a wife suing for alimony or a parson for his tithes, and she loves an Easter term, or any term, not as other country ladies do, to come up to be fine, cuckold their husbands, and take their pleasure, for

---

460 *a seaman's widow . . . Office*: trying to collect her widow's pension.

464 *pettifogger*: a lawyer adept at chicanery.

467 *jointure*: the estate held by a wife or widow for the remainder of her life.

473 *Norfolk*: traditionally a litigious county.

475 *Easter term*: one of the four terms of the law-courts.

she has no pleasure but in vexing others and is usually clothed and daggled like a bawd in disguise, pursued through alleys by sergeants. When she is in town she lodges in one of the Inns of Chancery, where she breeds her son and is herself his tutoress in law-French, and for her country abode, though she has no estate there, she chooses Norfolk. But bid her come in, with a pox to her. She is Olivia's kinswoman and may make me amends for her visit by some discourse of that dear woman.

Exit SAILOR.

Enter WIDOW BLACKACRE *with a mantle and a green bag and several papers in the other hand,* JERRY BLACKACRE, *her son, in a gown, laden with green bags, following her.*

WIDOW. I never had so much to do with a judge's door-keeper, as with yours, but –

MANLY. But the incomparable Olivia, how does she since I went?

WIDOW. Since you went, my suit –

MANLY. Olivia, I say, is she well?

WIDOW. My suit, if you had not returned –

MANLY. Damn your suit. How does your cousin Olivia?

WIDOW. My suit, I say, had been quite lost, but now –

MANLY. But now, where is Olivia? In town? For –

WIDOW. For tomorrow we are to have a hearing.

MANLY. Would you'd let me have a hearing today.

WIDOW. But why won't you hear me?

MANLY. I am no judge and you talk of nothing but suits. But, pray tell me, when did you see Olivia?

WIDOW. I am no visitor but a woman of business, or if I ever visit 'tis only the Chancery Lane ladies, ladies towards the law and not any of your lazy, good-for-

---

479 *daggled*: muddy, bespattered.

481 *Inns of Chancery*: residences for law students in which they learnt the rudiments of law before being admitted to the Inns of Court.

482 *law-French*: the corrupted Norman French used in English law.

487 s.d. *green bags*: carried by barristers for documents and papers.

504 *Chancery Lane*: the street runs close to the Inns of Court in Holborn.

nothing flirts, who cannot read law-French, though a gallant writ it. But, as I was telling you, my suit –

MANLY. Damn these impertinent, vexatious people of business, of all sexes. They are still troubling the world with the tedious recitals of their lawsuits, and one can no more stop their mouths than a wit's when he talks of himself, or an intelligencer's when he talks of other people.

WIDOW. And a pox of all vexatious, impertinent lovers. They are still perplexing the world with the tedious narrations of their love-suits and discourses of their mistresses. You are as troublesome to a poor widow of business as a young coxcombly rithming lover.

MANLY. And thou art as troublesome to me as a rook to a losing gamester or a young putter of cases to his mistress and sempstress, who has love in her head for another.

WIDOW. Nay, since you talk of putting of cases and will not hear me speak, hear our Jerry a little. Let him put our case to you, for the trial's tomorrow and, since you are my chief witness, I would have your memory refreshed and your judgement informed, that you may not give your evidence improperly. Speak out, child.

JERRY. Yes, forsooth. Hemh! Hemh! John-a-Stiles –

MANLY. You may talk, young lawyer, but I shall no more mind you than a hungry judge does a cause after the clock has struck one.

FREEMAN. Nay, you'll find him as peevish too.

WIDOW. No matter. Jerry, go on. Do you observe it then, sir, for I think I have seen you in a gown once. Lord, I could hear our Jerry put cases all day long! Mark him, sir.

JERRY. John-a-Stiles – no – There are first Fitz, Pere and Ayle – No, no, Ayle, Pere and Fitz. Ayle is seised

---

512 *intelligencer*: newsmonger.

518 *rithming*: rhyming.

530 *John-a-Stiles*: a fictitious name for one of the parties in a legal action.

540 *Fitz, Pere and Ayle*: son, father and grandfather (Fr. *fils, père* and *aieul*), law-French equivalents to John-a-Stiles.

in fee of Blackacre; John-a-Stiles disseises Ayle; Ayle makes claim and the disseisor dies; then the Ayle – no, the Fitz.

WIDOW. No, the Pere, sirrah.

JERRY. O, the Pere. Ay, the Pere, sir, and the Fitz – no, the Ayle; no, the Pere and the Fitz, sir, and –

MANLY. Damn Pere, Mere and Fitz, sir.

WIDOW. No, you are out, child. Hear me, captain, then. There are Ayle, Pere and Fitz; Ayle is seised in fee of Blackacre and, being so seised, John-a-Stiles disseises the Ayle; Ayle makes claim and the disseisor dies. And then the Pere re-enters, (*to* JERRY) the Pere sirrah, the Pere – And the Fitz enters upon the Pere, and the Ayle brings his writ of disseisin in the *post*, and the Pere brings his writ of disseisin in the *per* and –

MANLY. Can'st thou hear this stuff, Freeman? I could as soon suffer a whole noise of flatterers at a great man's levy in a morning but thou hast servile complacency enough to listen to a quibbling statesman in disgrace, nay, and be beforehand with him in laughing at his dull no-jest. But I – (*Offering to go out*)

WIDOW. Nay, sir, hold. Where's the subpoena, Jerry? I must serve you, sir. You are required by this to give your testimony –

MANLY. I'll be forsworn to be revenged on thee.

Exit MANLY, *throwing away the subpoena.*

WIDOW. Get you gone for a lawless companion. Come, Jerry. I had almost forgot we were to meet at the Master's at three. Let us mind our business still, child.

JERRY. Ay, forsooth, e'en so let's.

FREEMAN. Nay, madam, now I would beg you to hear me a little, a little of my business.

WIDOW. I have business of my own calls me away, sir.

---

541 *Blackacre*: not the widow's lands but a legal phrase for a fictitious parcel of land.

548–56 See Additional Note.

555 *per*: Pere Q1.

562 s.d. *Offering*: Attempting.

569 *Master's*: either one of the twelve Masters in Ordinary of the Court of Chancery, assistants to the Lord Chancellor, or a member of the governing body of one of the Inns of Court.

FREEMAN. My business would prove yours too, dear madam.

WIDOW. Yours would be some sweet business, I warrant. What, 'tis no Westminster Hall business? Would you have my advice?

FREEMAN. No, faith, 'tis a little Westminster Abbey business: I would have your consent.

WIDOW. O fie, fie, sir, to me such discourse before my dear minor there!

JERRY. Ay, ay, mother, he would be taking livery and seisin of your jointure by digging the turf, but I'll watch your waters, bully, ifac. Come away, mother.

Exit JERRY, *haling away his mother.*

Manet FREEMAN. *Enter to him* FIDELIA.

FIDELIA. Dear sir, you have pity. Beget but some in our captain for me.

FREEMAN. Where is he?

FIDELIA. Within, swearing as much as he did in the great storm and cursing you and sometimes sinks into calms and sighs and talks of his Olivia.

FREEMAN. He would never trust me to see her. Is she handsome?

FIDELIA. No, if you'll take my word, but I am not a proper judge.

FREEMAN. What is she?

FIDELIA. A gentlewoman, I suppose, but of as mean a fortune as beauty, but her relations would not suffer her to go with him to the Indies, and his aversion to this side of the world, together with the late opportunity of commanding the convoy, would not let him stay here longer, though to enjoy her.

FREEMAN. He loves her mightily then.

FIDELIA. Yes, so well that the remainder of his fortune (I hear about five or six thousand pounds) he has left

---

583–4 *livery and seisin*: livery of seisin, delivery of possession of freehold estates by the handing over of a symbolic piece of turf, strictly by the widow to Freeman, though that would ruin Jerry's double meaning.

585 *watch your waters*: keep an eye on, derived from checking urine for diagnosis and hence associated with the kind of digging Freeman has in mind.

585 *ifac*: in faith.

her in case he had died by the way or before she could prevail with her friends to follow him, which he expected she should do, and has left behind him his great bosom friend to be her convoy to him.

FREEMAN. What charms has she for him if she be not handsome?

FIDELIA. He fancies her, I suppose, the only woman of truth and sincerity in the world.

FREEMAN. No common beauty I confess.

FIDELIA. Or else sure he would not have trusted her with so great a share of his fortune in his absence; I suppose (since his late loss) all he has.

FREEMAN. Why, has he left it in her own custody?

FIDELIA. I am told so.

FREEMAN. Then he has showed love to her indeed in leaving her, like an old husband that dies as soon as he has made his wife a good jointure. But I'll go in to him and speak for you and know more from him of his Olivia. *Exit.*

Manet FIDELIA *sola.*

FIDELIA. His Olivia indeed, his happy Olivia,
Yet she was left behind, when I was with him;
But she was ne'er out of his mind or heart.
She has told him she loved him; I have showed it
And durst not tell him so till I had done,
Under this habit, such convincing acts
Of loving friendship for him that through it
He first might find out both my sex and love,
And, when I'd had him from his fair Olivia
And this bright world of artful beauties here,
Might then have hoped he would have looked on me
Amongst the sooty Indians; and I could,
To choose, there live his wife, where wives are forced
To live no longer when their husbands die,
Nay, what's yet worse, to share them whil'st they live
With many rival wives. But here he comes,
And I must yet keep out of his sight, not
To lose it forever. *Exit.*

Enter MANLY *and* FREEMAN.

FREEMAN. But, pray, what strange charms has she that could make you love?

MANLY. Strange charms indeed! She has beauty enough to call in question her wit or virtue, and her form would make a starved hermit a ravisher; yet her virtue and conduct would preserve her from the subtle lust of a pampered prelate. She is so perfect a beauty that art could not better it nor affectation deform it; yet all this is nothing. Her tongue, as well as face, ne'er knew artifice; nor ever did her words or looks contradict her heart. She is all truth and hates the lying, masking, daubing world as I do, for which I love her and for which I think she dislikes not me. For she has often shut out of her conversation for mine the gaudy, fluttering parrots of the town, apes and echoes of men only, and refused their commonplace pert chat, flattery and submissions, to be entertained with my sullen bluntness and honest love. And, last of all, swore to me, since her parents would not suffer her to go with me, she would stay behind for no other man but follow me without their leave, if not to be obtained. Which oath –

FREEMAN. Did you think she would keep?

MANLY. Yes, for she is not (I tell you) like other women but can keep her promise, though she has sworn to keep it. But that she might the better keep it I left her the value of five or six thousand pound, for women's wants are generally their most importunate solicitors to love or marriage.

FREEMAN. And money summons lovers more than beauty, and augments but their importunity and their number, so makes it the harder for a woman to deny 'em. For my part, I am for the French maxim; if you would have your female subjects loyal, keep 'em poor. But, in short, that your mistress may not marry, you have given her a portion.

MANLY. She had given me her heart first and I am satisfied with the security; I can never doubt her truth and constancy.

FREEMAN. It seems you do since you are fain to bribe it with money. But how come you to be so diffident of the man that says he loves you and not doubt the woman that says it?

MANLY. I should, I confess, doubt the love of any other woman but her, as I do the friendship of any other man but him I have trusted, but I have such proofs of their faith as cannot deceive me.

FREEMAN. Cannot!

MANLY. Not but I know that generally no man can be a great enemy but under the name of friend; and if you are a cuckold, it is your friend only that makes you so, for your enemy is not admitted to your house; if you are cheated in your fortune, 'tis your friend that does it, for your enemy is not made your trustee; if your honour or good name be injured, 'tis your friend that does it still, because your enemy is not believed against you. Therefore I rather choose to go where honest, downright barbarity is professed, where men devour one another like generous hungry lions and tigers, not like crocodiles, where they think the devil white, of our complexion, and I am already so far an Indian. But if your weak faith doubts this miracle of a woman, come along with me and believe and thou wilt find her so handsome that thou, who art so much my friend, wilt have a mind to lie with her and so will not fail to discover what her faith and thine is to me.
When we're in love, the great adversity,
Our friends and mistresses at once we try.

ACT II

SCENE I

Olivia's lodging.

Enter OLIVIA, ELIZA, LETTICE.

OLIVIA. Ah, cousin, what a world 'tis we live in! I am so weary of it.

ELIZA. Truly, cousin, I can find no fault with it but that we cannot always live in't, for I can never be weary of it.

OLIVIA. O hideous! You cannot be in earnest, sure, when you say you like the filthy world.

ELIZA. You cannot be in earnest, sure, when you say you dislike it.

OLIVIA. You are a very censorious creature, I find.

ELIZA. I must confess I think we women as often discover where we love by railing, as men when they lie by their swearing, and the world is but a constant keeping gallant, whom we fail not to quarrel with when anything crosses us, yet cannot part with't for our hearts.

LETTICE. A gallant indeed, madam, whom ladies first make jealous and then quarrel with it for being so, for if, by her indiscretion, a lady be talked of for a man, she cries presently, ''Tis a censorious world'; if by her vanity the intrigue be found out, ''Tis a prying, malicious world'; if by her over-fondness the gallant proves unconstant, ''Tis a false world'; and if by her niggardliness the chambermaid tells, ''Tis a perfidious world' – but that, I'm sure, your ladyship cannot say of the world yet, as bad as 'tis.

OLIVIA. But I may say, ''Tis a very impertinent world.' Hold your peace. And, cousin, if the world be a gallant, 'tis such an one as is my aversion. Pray name it no more.

ELIZA. But is it possible the world, which has such variety of charms for other women, can have none for you? Let's see – first, what d'ye think of dressing and fine clothes?

OLIVIA. Dressing! Fie, fie, 'tis my aversion. But come hither, you dowdy, methinks you might have opened this toure better. O hideous! I cannot suffer it! D'ye see how't sits?

ELIZA. Well enough, cousin, if dressing be your aversion.

OLIVIA. 'Tis so, and for variety of rich clothes, they are more my aversion.

LETTICE. Ay, 'tis because your ladyship wears 'em too long, for indeed a gown, like a gallant, grows one's aversion by having too much of it.

OLIVIA. Insatiable creature! I'll be sworn I have had this not above three days, cousin, and within this month have made some six more.

ELIZA. Then your aversion to 'em is not altogether so great.

OLIVIA. Alas! 'Tis for my woman only I wear 'em, cousin.

---

36 *dowdy*: plain creature.

37 *toure*: usually *taure*, a forehead fringe of curls.

LETTICE. If it be for me only, madam, pray do not wear 'em.

ELIZA. But what d'ye think of visits – balls –

OLIVIA. O, I detest 'em.

ELIZA. Of plays?

OLIVIA. I abominate 'em: filthy, obscene, hideous things!

ELIZA. What say you to masquerading in the winter and Hyde Park in the summer?

OLIVIA. Insipid pleasures I taste not.

ELIZA. Nay, if you are for more solid pleasure, what think you of a rich, young husband?

OLIVIA. O horrid! Marriage! What a pleasure you have found out! I nauseate it of all things.

LETTICE. But what does your ladyship think then of a liberal, handsome young lover?

OLIVIA. A handsome young fellow, you impudent! Be gone, out of my sight. Name a handsome young fellow to me! Foh, a hideous, handsome young fellow I abominate. (*Spits*)

ELIZA. Indeed! But let's see – will nothing please you? What d'ye think of the court?

OLIVIA. How? The court! The court, cousin! My aversion, my aversion, my aversion of all aversions.

ELIZA. How? The court! Where –

OLIVIA. Where sincerity is a quality as out of fashion and as unprosperous as bashfulness. I could not laugh at a quibble, though it were a fat privy councillor's, nor praise a lord's ill verses, though I were myself the subject, nor an old lady's young looks, though I were her woman, nor sit to a vain young simile-maker, though he flattered me. In short, I could not gloat upon a man when he comes into a room and laugh at him when he goes out; I cannot rail at the absent to flatter the standers-by; I –

ELIZA. Well, but railing now is so common that 'tis no more malice but the fashion, and the absent think they are no more the worse for being railed at than the present think they are the better for being flattered. And for the court –

---

60 *Hyde Park*: a fashionable place for promenading.
83–4 *gloat upon*: feast my eyes on, admire.

OLIVIA. Nay, do not defend the court, for you'll make me rail at it, like a trusting citizen's widow.

ELIZA. Or like a Holborn lady, who could not get into the last ball or was out of countenance in the drawing-room the last Sunday of her appearance there; for none rail at the court but those who cannot get into it or else who are ridiculous when they are there, and I shall suspect you were laughed at when you were last there or would be a Maid of Honour.

OLIVIA. I a Maid of Honour! To be a Maid of Honour were yet of all things my aversion.

ELIZA. In what sense am I to understand you? But in fine by the word aversion I'm sure you dissemble, for I never knew woman yet that used it who did not. Come, our tongues belie our hearts more than our pocket-glasses do our faces; but methinks we ought to leave off dissembling, since 'tis grown of no use to us, for all wise observers understand us nowadays as they do dreams, almanacs and Dutch gazettes, by the contrary. And a man no more believes a woman when she says she has an aversion for him than when she says she'll cry out.

OLIVIA. O filthy, hideous! Peace, cousin, or your discourse will be my aversion, and you may believe me.

ELIZA. Yes, for if anything be a woman's aversion 'tis plain-dealing from another woman and perhaps that's your quarrel to the world, for that will talk, as your woman says.

OLIVIA. Talk not of me sure, for what men do I converse with? What visits do I admit?

Enter BOY.

BOY. Here's the gentleman to wait upon you, madam.

OLIVIA. On me! You little, unthinking fop, d'ye know what you say?

BOY. Yes, madam, 'tis the gentleman that comes every day to you, who –

---

94 *Holborn lady*: a citizen's wife. Holborn leads towards the city.

95–6 *drawing-room*: at Whitehall.

110 *Dutch gazettes*: the enemy's newspapers, of course, appeared to be inaccurate.

OLIVIA. Hold your peace, you heedless little animal, and get you gone. This country boy, cousin, takes my dancing-master, tailor or the spruce milliner for visitors.

Exit BOY.

LETTICE. No, madam, 'tis Mr Novel, I'm sure, by his talking so loud. I know his voice too, madam.

OLIVIA. You know nothing, you buffle-headed, stupid creature you. You would make my cousin believe I receive visits. But if it be Mr – what did you call him?

LETTICE. Mr Novel, madam, he that –

OLIVIA. Hold your peace, I'll hear no more of him. But if it be your Mr – (I can't think of his name again) I suppose he has followed my cousin hither.

ELIZA. No, cousin, I will not rob you of the honour of the visit; 'tis to you, cousin, for I know him not.

OLIVIA. Nor did I ever hear of him before, upon my honour, cousin. Besides, han't I told you that visits and the business of visits, flattery and detraction, are my aversion? D'ye think then I would admit such a coxcomb as he is, who rather than not rail will rail at the dead whom none speak ill of, and rather than not flatter will flatter the poets of the age, whom none will flatter, who affects novelty as much as the fashion and is as fantastical as changeable and as well known as the fashion, who likes nothing but what is new, nay, would choose to have his friend or his title a new one. In fine, he is my aversion.

ELIZA. I find you do know him, cousin, at least have heard of him.

OLIVIA. Yes, now I remember, I have heard of him.

ELIZA. Well, but since he is such a coxcomb, for heaven's sake let him not come up. Tell him, Mrs Lettice, your lady is not within.

OLIVIA. No, Lettice, tell him my cousin is here and that he may come up, for, notwithstanding I detest the sight of him, you may like his conversation and, though I would use him scurvily, I will not be rude to you in my own lodging. Since he has followed you hither, let him come up, I say.

---

133 *buffle-headed*: blockheaded, simpleton.

ELIZA. Very fine! Pray let him go to the devil, I say, for me. I know him not nor desire it. Send him away, Mrs Lettice.

OLIVIA. Upon my word, she shan't. I must disobey your commands, to comply with your desires. Call him up, Lettice.

ELIZA. Nay, I'll swear she shall not stir on that errand. (*Holds* LETTICE)

OLIVIA. Well then, I'll call him myself for you, since you will have it so. (*Calls out at the door*) Mr Novel, sir, sir.

Enter NOVEL.

NOVEL. Madam, I beg your pardon; perhaps you were busy. I did not think you had company with you.

ELIZA. (*aside*) Yet he comes to me, cousin!

OLIVIA. – Chairs there.

They sit. [*Exit* LETTICE.]

NOVEL. Well, but, madam, d'ye know whence I come now?

OLIVIA. From some melancholy place I warrant, sir, since they have lost your good company.

ELIZA. So.

NOVEL. From a place where they have treated me, at dinner, with so much civility and kindness, a pox on 'em, that I could hardly get away to you, dear madam.

OLIVIA. You have a way with you so new and obliging, sir.

ELIZA. (*apart to* OLIVIA) You hate flattery, cousin!

NOVEL. Nay, faith, madam, d'ye think my way new? Then you are obliging, madam. I must confess I hate imitation, to do anything like other people; all that know me do me the honour to say I am an original, faith. But, as I was saying, madam, I have been treated today with all the ceremony and kindness imaginable at my Lady Autum's, but the nauseous old woman at the upper end of her table –

OLIVIA. Revives the old Grecian custom of serving in a death's head with their banquets.

199–200 Weales suggests that Olivia is misremembering Herodotus's comments on Egyptian feasts.

NOVEL. Hah, ha! Fine, just, i'faith, nay, and new. 'Tis like eating with the ghost in *The Libertine*; she would frighten a man from her dinner with her hollow invitations and spoil one's stomach –

OLIVIA. To meat or women. I detest her hollow cherry cheeks; she looks like an old coach new painted, affecting an unseemly smugness whilst she is ready to drop in pieces.

ELIZA. (*apart to* OLIVIA) You hate detraction I see, cousin!

NOVEL. But the silly old fury, whilst she affects to look like a woman of this age, talks –

OLIVIA. Like one of the last, and as passionately as an old courtier who has outlived his office.

NOVEL. Yes, madam, but pray let me give you her character. Then, she never counts her age by the years but –

OLIVIA. By the masques she has lived to see.

NOVEL. Nay then, madam, I see you think a little harmless railing too great a pleasure for any but yourself and therefore I've done.

OLIVIA. Nay, faith, you shall tell me who you had there at dinner.

NOVEL. If you would hear me, madam.

OLIVIA. Most patiently. Speak, sir.

NOVEL. Then, we had her daughter –

OLIVIA. Ay, her daughter, the very disgrace to good clothes, which she always wears but to heighten her deformity, not mend it, for she is still most splendidly, gallantly ugly and looks like an ill piece of daubing in a rich frame.

NOVEL. So! But have you done with her, madam? And can you spare her to me a little now?

OLIVIA. Ay, ay, sir.

NOVEL. Then, she is like –

OLIVIA. She is, you'd say, like a city bride, the greater fortune but not the greater beauty for her dress.

NOVEL. Well, yet have you done, madam? Then, she –

OLIVIA. Then she bestows as unfortunately on her face all the graces in fashion, as the languishing eye, the

---

202 *The Libertine*: Shadwell's play on the Don Juan theme (1675).

hanging or pouting lip; but as the fool is never more provoking than when he aims at wit, the ill-favoured of our sex are never more nauseous than when they would be beauties, adding to their natural deformity the artificial ugliness of affectation.

ELIZA. So, cousin, I find one may have a collection of all one's acquaintances' pictures as well at your house as at Mr Lely's. Only the difference is, there we find 'em much handsomer than they are and like; here, much uglier and like. And you are the first of the profession of picture-drawing I ever knew without flattery.

OLIVIA. I draw after the life, do nobody wrong, cousin.

ELIZA. No, you hate flattery and detraction!

OLIVIA. But, Mr Novel, who had you besides at dinner?

NOVEL. Nay, the devil take me if I tell you, unless you will allow me the privilege of railing in my turn; but, now I think on't, the women ought to be your province, as the men are mine. And you must know, we had him whom –

OLIVIA. Him whom –

NOVEL. What? Invading me already? And giving the character before you know the man?

ELIZA. No, that is not fair, though it be usual.

OLIVIA. I beg your pardon, Mr Novel. Pray, go on.

NOVEL. Then, I say, we had that familiar coxcomb, who is at home wheresoe'er he comes.

OLIVIA. Ay, that fool –

NOVEL. Nay then, madam, your servant. I'm gone. Taking a fool out of one's mouth is worse than taking the bread out of one's mouth.

OLIVIA. I've done. Your pardon, Mr Novel, pray proceed.

NOVEL. I say, the rogue, that he may be the only wit in the company, will let nobody else talk and –

OLIVIA. Ay, those fops who love to talk all themselves are of all things my aversion.

NOVEL. Then you'll let me speak, madam, sure. The rogue, I say, will force his jest upon you, and I hate a jest that's forced upon a man as much as a glass.

ELIZA. Why, I hope, sir, he does not expect a man of your temperance in jesting should do him reason?

---

281 *do him reason*: do him justice, keep up with his jesting.

NOVEL. What, interruption from this side too! I must then –

Offers to rise; OLIVIA *holds him.*

OLIVIA. No, sir – You must know, cousin, that fop he means, though he talks only to be commended, will not give you leave to do't.

NOVEL. But, madam –

OLIVIA. He a wit! Hang him, he's only an adopter of straggling jests and fatherless lampoons, by the credit of which he eats at good tables and so, like the barren beggar-woman, lives by borrowed children.

NOVEL. Madam –

OLIVIA. And never was author of anything but his news, but that is still all his own.

NOVEL. Madam, pray –

OLIVIA. An eternal babbler, and makes no more use of his ears than a man that sits at a play by his mistress or in fop-corner. He's, in fine, a base, detracting fellow, and is my aversion. But who else prithee, Mr Novel, was there with you? Nay, you shan't stir.

NOVEL. I beg your pardon, madam, I cannot stay in any place where I'm not allowed a little Christian liberty of railing.

OLIVIA. Nay, prithee, Mr Novel, stay, and, though you should rail at me, I would hear you with patience. Prithee, who else was there with you?

NOVEL. Your servant, madam.

OLIVIA. Nay, prithee tell us, Mr Novel, prithee do.

NOVEL. We had nobody else.

OLIVIA. Nay, faith I know you had. Come, my Lord Plausible was there too, who is, cousin, a –

ELIZA. You need not tell me what he is, cousin, for I know him to be a civil, good-natured, harmless gentleman, that speaks well of all the world and is always in good humour and –

OLIVIA. Hold, cousin, hold. I hate detraction, but I must tell you, cousin, his civility is cowardice, his good nature want of wit, and has neither courage or sense to rail. And for his being always in humour, 'tis because he is never dissatisfied with himself. In fine,

---

298 *fop-corner*: the part of the playhouse favoured by self-styled wits.

he is my aversion, and I never admit his visits beyond my hall.

NOVEL. No, he visit you! Damn him, cringing, grinning rogue. If I should see him coming up to you, I would make bold to kick him down again. Ha! –

Enter MY LORD PLAUSIBLE

My dear lord, your most humble servant. (*Rises and salutes* PLAUSIBLE *and kisses him*)

ELIZA. (*aside*) So! I find kissing and railing succeed each other with the angry men as well as with the angry women, and their quarrels are like love-quarrels, since absence is the only cause of them, for, as soon as the man appears again, they are over.

LORD PLAUSIBLE. Your most faithful, humble servant, generous Mr Novel, and, madam, I am your eternal slave and kiss your fair hands, which I had done sooner, according to your commands, but –

OLIVIA. No excuses, my lord.

ELIZA. (*apart*) What, you sent for him then, cousin?

NOVEL. (*aside*) Ha! Invited!

OLIVIA. I know you must divide yourself, for your good company is too general a good to be engrossed by any particular friend.

LORD PLAUSIBLE. O Lord, madam, my company! Your most obliged, faithful, humble servant, but I could have brought you good company indeed, for I parted at your door with two of the worthiest, bravest men –

OLIVIA. Who were they, my lord?

NOVEL. Who do you call the worthiest, bravest men, pray?

LORD PLAUSIBLE. O the wisest, bravest gentlemen! Men of such honour and virtue! Of such good qualities! Ah –

ELIZA. (*aside*) This is a coxcomb that speaks ill of all people a different way and libels everybody with dull praise and commonly in the wrong place, so makes his panegyrics abusive lampoons.

OLIVIA. But pray let me know who they were.

LORD PLAUSIBLE. Ah! Such patterns of heroic virtue! Such –

NOVEL. Well, but who the devil were they?

LORD PLAUSIBLE. The honour of our nation, the glory of our age. Ah! I could dwell a twelvemonth on their praise, which indeed I might spare by telling their names: Sir John Current and Sir Richard Court-Title.

NOVEL. Court-Title! Hah, ha.

OLIVIA. And Sir John Current! Why will you keep such a wretch company, my lord?

LORD PLAUSIBLE. Oh, madam, seriously you are a little too severe, for he is a man of unquestioned reputation in everything.

OLIVIA. Yes, because he endeavours only with the women to pass for a man of courage and with the bullies for a wit, with the wits for a man of business and with the men of business for a favourite at court and at court for good city security.

NOVEL. And for Sir Richard, he –

LORD PLAUSIBLE. He loves your choice, picked company, persons that –

OLIVIA. He loves a lord indeed, but –

NOVEL. Pray, dear madam, let me have but a bold stroke or two at his picture. He loves a lord, as you say, though –

OLIVIA. Though he borrowed his money and ne'er paid him again.

NOVEL. And would bespeak a place three days before at the back end of a lord's coach to Hyde Park.

LORD PLAUSIBLE. Nay, i'faith, i'faith, you are both too severe.

OLIVIA. Then, to show yet more his passion for quality, he makes love to that fulsome coach-load of honour, my Lady Goodly, for he is always at her lodging.

LORD PLAUSIBLE. Because it is the conventicle-gallant, the meetinghouse of all the fair ladies and glorious, superfine beauties of the town.

NOVEL. Very fine ladies! There's first –

OLIVIA. Her honour, as fat as an hostess.

LORD PLAUSIBLE. She is something plump indeed, a goodly, comely, graceful person.

---

393 *conventicle-gallant*: meeting-place *à la mode.*

NOVEL. Then there's my Lady Frances What-d'ye-call-'er? As ugly –

OLIVIA. As a citizen's lawfully begotten daughter.

LORD PLAUSIBLE. She has wit in abundance and the handsomest heel, elbow and tip of an ear you ever saw.

NOVEL. Heel and elbow! Hah, ha! And there's my Lady Betty you know –

OLIVIA. As sluttish and slatternly as an Irishwoman bred in France.

LORD PLAUSIBLE. Ah, all she has hangs with a loose air indeed and becoming negligence.

ELIZA. You see all faults with lover's eyes, I find, my lord.

LORD PLAUSIBLE. Ah, madam, your most obliged, faithful, humble servant to command! But you can say nothing sure against the superfine mistress –

OLIVIA. I know who you mean. She is as censorious and detracting a jade as a superannuated sinner.

LORD PLAUSIBLE. She has a smart way of raillery, 'tis confessed.

NOVEL. And then, for Mrs Grideline.

LORD PLAUSIBLE. She I'm sure is –

OLIVIA. One that never spoke ill of anybody, 'tis confessed, for she is as silent in conversation as a country lover and no better company than a clock or a weather-glass, for if she sounds 'tis but once an hour to put you in mind of the time of day or to tell you 'twill be cold or hot, rain or snow.

LORD PLAUSIBLE. Ah, poor creature! She's extremely good and modest.

NOVEL. And for Mrs Bridlechin, she's –

OLIVIA. As proud as a churchman's wife.

LORD PLAUSIBLE. She's a woman of great spirit and honour and will not make herself cheap, 'tis true.

NOVEL. Then Mrs Hoyden, that calls all people by their surnames and is –

OLIVIA. As familiar a duck –

NOVEL. As an actress in the tiring-room. There I was once beforehand with you, madam.

---

421 *Grideline*: *gris de lin*, flax-grey, pale purple.

LORD PLAUSIBLE. Mrs Hoyden! A poor, affable, good-natured soul! But the divine Mrs Trifle comes thither too; sure her beauty, virtue and conduct you can say nothing to.

OLIVIA. No!

NOVEL. No! – Pray let me speak, madam.

OLIVIA. First, can anyone be called beautiful that squints?

LORD PLAUSIBLE. Her eyes languish a little, I own.

NOVEL. Languish! Hah, ha.

OLIVIA. Languish! Then for her conduct she was seen at *The Country Wife* after the first day. There's for you, my lord.

LORD PLAUSIBLE. But, madam, she was not seen to use her fan all the play long, turn aside her head, or by a conscious blush discover more guilt than modesty.

OLIVIA. Very fine! Then you think a woman modest that sees the hideous *Country Wife* without blushing or publishing her detestation of it? D'ye hear him, cousin?

ELIZA. Yes, and am, I must confess, something of his opinion and think that as an over-conscious fool at a play, by endeavouring to show the author's want of wit, exposes his own to more censure, so may a lady call her modesty in question by publicly cavilling with the poets, for all those grimaces of honour and artificial modesty disparage a woman's real virtue as much as the use of white and red does the natural complexion, and you must use very, very little if you would have it thought your own.

OLIVIA. Then you would have a woman of honour with passive looks, ears and tongue undergo all the hideous obscenity she hears at nasty plays?

ELIZA. Truly, I think a woman betrays her want of modesty by showing it publicly in a playhouse as much as a man does his want of courage by a quarrel there, for the truly modest and stout say least and are least exceptious, especially in public.

---

443 *to*: too Q1.

451 *after the first day*: after the first performance, when she had no excuse for not knowing what kind of play it was.

477 *stout*: brave.

OLIVIA. O hideous! Cousin, this cannot be your opinion, but you are one of those who have the confidence to pardon the filthy play.

ELIZA. Why, what is there of ill in't, say you?

OLIVIA. O fie, fie, fie, would you put me to the blush anew? Call all the blood into my face again? But to satisfy you then, first, the clandestine obscenity in the very name of Horner.

ELIZA. Truly, 'tis so hidden I cannot find it out, I confess.

OLIVIA. O horrid! Does it not give you the rank conception or image of a goat, a town-bull or a satyr? Nay, what is yet a filthier image than all the rest, that of an eunuch?

ELIZA. What then? I can think of a goat, a bull or satyr without any hurt.

OLIVIA. Ay, but, cousin, one cannot stop there.

ELIZA. I can, cousin.

OLIVIA. O no, for when you have those filthy creatures in your head once, the next thing you think is what they do, as their defiling of honest men's beds and couches, rapes upon sleeping and waking country virgins under hedges and on haycocks. Nay, farther –

ELIZA. Nay, no farther, cousin. We have enough of your comment on the play, which will make me more ashamed than the play itself.

OLIVIA. O, believe me, 'tis a filthy play, and you may take my word for a filthy play as soon as another's, but the filthiest thing in that play, or any other play, is –

ELIZA. Pray keep it to yourself, if it be so.

OLIVIA. No, faith, you shall know it. I'm resolved to make you out of love with the play. I say, the lewdest, filthiest thing is his china; nay, I will never forgive the beastly author his china. He has quite taken away the reputation of poor china itself and sullied the most innocent and pretty furniture of a lady's chamber,

---

490 *town-bull*: a bull for the use of the town, hence a rake.
492 *an eunuch*: Horner's disguise in *The Country Wife*.
501 *haycocks*: conical haystacks.
512 *china*: see *The Country Wife*, Act IV Scene iii.

insomuch that I was fain to break all my defiled vessels. You see I have none left; nor you, I hope.

ELIZA. You'll pardon me, I cannot think the worse of my china for that of the playhouse.

OLIVIA. Why, you will not keep any now sure! 'Tis now as unfit an ornament for a lady's chamber as the pictures that come from Italy and other hot countries, as appears by their nudities, which I always cover or scratch out, wheresoe'er I find 'em. But china! Out upon't, filthy china, nasty, debauched china!

ELIZA. All this will not put me out of conceit with china nor the play, which is acted today or another of the same beastly author's, as you call him, which I'll go see.

OLIVIA. You will not, sure! Nay, you sha'not venture your reputation by going and mine by leaving me alone with two men here. Nay, you'll disoblige me for ever, if – (*Pulls her back*)

ELIZA. I stay! – your servant. *Exit* ELIZA.

OLIVIA. Well – but my lord, though you justify everybody, you cannot in earnest uphold so beastly a writer, whose ink is so smutty, as one may say.

LORD PLAUSIBLE. Faith, I dare swear the poor man did not think to disoblige the ladies by any amorous, soft, passionate, luscious saying in his play.

OLIVIA. Foy, my lord, but what think you, Mr Novel, of the play? Though I know you are a friend to all that are new.

NOVEL. Faith, madam, I must confess the new plays would not be the worse for my advice but I could never get the silly rogues, the poets, to mind what I say; but I'll tell you what counsel I gave the surly fool you speak of.

OLIVIA. What was't?

NOVEL. Faith, to put his play into rithme, for rithme, you know, often makes mystical nonsense pass with the critics for wit and a double-meaning saying with the ladies for soft, tender and moving passion. But, now I talk of passion, I saw your old lover this morning – Captain – (*Whispers*)

---

541 *Foy*: *ma foi*, faith.

Enter CAPTAIN MANLY, FREEMAN *and* FIDELIA *standing behind.*

OLIVIA. Whom? – Nay, you need not whisper.

MANLY. We are luckily got hither unobserved. – How! In a close conversation with these supple rascals, the outcasts of sempstresses' shops?

FREEMAN. Faith, pardon her, captain, that, since she could no longer be entertained with your manly bluntness and honest love, she takes up with the pert chat and commonplace flattery of these fluttering parrots of the town, apes and echoes of men only.

MANLY. Do not you, sir, play the echo too, mock me, dally with my own words and show yourself as impertinent as they are.

FREEMAN. Nay, captain –

FIDELIA. Nay, lieutenant, do not excuse her. Methinks she looks very kindly upon 'em both and seems to be pleased with what that fool there says to her.

MANLY. You lie, sir, and hold your peace that I may not be provoked to give you a worse reply.

OLIVIA. Manly returned, d'ye say! And is he safe?

NOVEL. My lord saw him too. (*Whispers to* PLAUSIBLE) Hark you, my lord.

MANLY. (*aside*) She yet seems concerned for my safety and perhaps they are admitted now here but for their news of me, for intelligence indeed is the common passport of nauseous fools when they go their round of good tables and houses.

OLIVIA. I heard of his fighting only, without particulars, and confess I always loved his brutal courage because it made me hope it might rid me of his more brutal love.

MANLY. (*apart*) What's that?

OLIVIA. But is he at last returned, d'ye say, unhurt?

NOVEL. Ay faith, without doing his business, for the rogue has been these two years pretending to a wooden leg, which he would take from fortune as kindly as the staff of a marshal of France and rather read his name in a gazette –

---

579 *intelligence*: news.
592 *gazette*: war report.

OLIVIA. Than in the entail of a good estate.
MANLY. (*aside*) So! –
NOVEL. I have an ambition, I must confess, of losing my heart before such a fair enemy as yourself, madam, but that silly rogues should be ambitious of losing their arms and –
OLIVIA. Looking like a pair of compasses.
NOVEL. But he has no use of his arms but to set them on kimbow, for he never pulls off his hat, at least not to me, I'm sure, for you must know, madam, he has a fanatical hatred to good company: he can't abide me.
LORD PLAUSIBLE. O, be not so severe to him as to say he hates good company, for I assure you he has a great respect, esteem and kindness for me.
MANLY. [*aside*] That kind, civil rogue has spoken yet ten thousand times worse of me than t'other.
OLIVIA. Well, if he be returned, Mr Novel, then shall I be pestered again with his boisterous sea love, have my alcove smell like a cabin, my chamber perfumed with his tarpaulin Brandenburgh, and hear vollies of brandy sighs, enough to make a fog in one's room. Foh! I hate a lover that smells like Thames Street!
MANLY. (*aside*) I can bear no longer and need hear no more. – But, since you have these two pulvillio boxes, these essence bottles, this pair of musk-cats here, I hope I may venture to come yet nearer you.
OLIVIA. Overheard us then?
NOVEL. (*aside*) I hope he heard me not.
LORD PLAUSIBLE. Most noble and heroic captain, your most obliged, faithful, humble servant.
NOVEL. Dear tar, thy humble servant.
MANLY. Away – madam. (*Thrusts* NOVEL *and* PLAUSIBLE *on each side*)
OLIVIA. Nay, I think I have fitted you for listening.

---

593 *entail*: the prescribed and often highly restrictive rules under which future ownership of an estate is determined.
601 *on kimbow*: akimbo.
612 *Brandenburgh*: morning gown.
614 *Thames Street*: a notoriously smelly street along the north bank of the river.
616 *pulvillio*: scented powder.
617 *essence*: perfume.
624 s.d. After line 625 in Q1.

MANLY. You have fitted me for believing you could not be fickle though you were young, could not dissemble love though 'twas your interest, nor be vain though you were handsome, nor break your promise though to a parting lover, nor abuse your best friend though you had wit. But I take not your contempt of me worse than your esteem or civility for these things here though you know 'em.

NOVEL. Things!

LORD PLAUSIBLE. Let the captain rally a little.

MANLY. Yes, things. Can'st thou be angry, thou thing? (*Coming up to* NOVEL)

NOVEL. No, since my lord says you speak in raillery, for, though your sea-raillery be something rough, yet I confess we use one another to as bad every day at Locket's and never quarrel for the matter.

LORD PLAUSIBLE. Nay, noble captain, be not angry with him. A word with you, I beseech you – (*Whispers to* MANLY)

OLIVIA. (*aside*) Well, we women, like the rest of the cheats of the world, when our cullies or creditors have found us out and will or can trust no longer, pay debts and satisfy obligations with a quarrel, the kindest present a man can make to his mistress when he can make no more presents, for oftentimes in love as at cards we are forced to play foul, only to give over the game, and use our lovers, like the cards, when we can get no more by 'em, throw 'em up in a pet upon the first dispute.

MANLY. My lord, all that you have made me know by your whispering, which I knew not before, is that you have a stinking breath: there's a secret for your secret.

LORD PLAUSIBLE. Pshaw! Pshaw!

MANLY. But, madam, tell me, pray, what was't about this spark could take you? Was it the merit of his fashionable impudence, the briskness of his noise, the wit of his laugh, his judgement or fancy in his garniture? Or was it a well-trimmed glove or the scent of it that charmed you?

---

628 *vain*: in vain Q1.

640 *Locket's*: famous restaurant in Charing Cross.

NOVEL. Very well, sir. Gad, these sea-captains make nothing of dressing. But let me tell you, sir, a man by his dress, as much as by anything, shows his wit and judgement, nay, and his courage too.

FREEMAN. How his courage, Mr Novel?

NOVEL. Why, for example, by red breeches, tucked-up hair or peruke, a greasy broad belt and nowadays a short sword.

MANLY. Thy courage will appear more by thy belt than thy sword, I dare swear. Then, madam, for this gentle piece of courtesy, this man of tame honour, what could you find in him? Was it his languishing affected tone? His mannerly look? His secondhand flattery, the refuse of the playhouse tiring-rooms? Or his slavish obsequiousness in watching at the door of your box at the playhouse for your hand to your chair? Or his janty way of playing with your fan? Or was it the gunpowder spot on his hand or the jewel in his ear that purchased your heart?

OLIVIA. Good jealous captain, no more of your –

LORD PLAUSIBLE. No, let him go on, madam, for perhaps he may make you laugh, and I would contribute to your pleasure any way.

MANLY. Gentle rogue!

OLIVIA. No, noble captain, you cannot sure think anything could take me more than that heroic title of yours, captain, for you know we women love honour inordinately.

NOVEL. Hah, ha, faith, she is with thee, bully, for thy raillery.

MANLY. (*aside to* NOVEL) Faith, so shall I be with you, no bully, for your grinning.

OLIVIA. Then, that noble lion-like mien of yours, that soldier-like, weather-beaten complexion and that manly rougliness of your voice, how can they otherwise than charm us women who hate effeminacy!

NOVEL. Hah, ha! Faith, I can't hold from laughing.

669–71 Novel describes military dress as usually worn, there being no prescribed uniform.

680 *janty*: genteel (Fr. *gentil*).

681 *gunpowder spot*: a beauty spot made by using gunpowder.

MANLY. (*aside to* NOVEL) Nor shall I from kicking anon.

OLIVIA. And then, that captain-like carelessness in your dress, but especially your scarf; 'twas just such another, only a little higher tied, made me in love with my tailor as he passed by my window the last training day, for we women adore a martial man, and you have nothing wanting to make you more one, or more agreeable, but a wooden leg.

LORD PLAUSIBLE. Nay, i'faith there your ladyship was a wag, and it was fine, just and well rallied.

NOVEL. Ay, ay, madam, with you ladies too, martial men must needs be very killing.

MANLY. Peace, you Bartholomew-Fair buffoons, and be not you vain that these laugh on your side, for they will laugh at their own dull jests. But no more of 'em, for I will only suffer now this lady to be witty and merry.

OLIVIA. You would not have your panegyric interrupted. I go on then to your humour. Is there anything more agreeable than the pretty sullenness of that? Than the greatness of your courage? – which most of all appears in your spirit of contradiction, for you dare give all mankind the lie and your opinion is your only mistress, for you renounce that too when it becomes another man's.

NOVEL. Hah, ha! I cannot hold. I must laugh at thee, tar, faith!

LORD PLAUSIBLE. And i'faith, dear captain, I beg your pardon and leave to laugh at you too, though I protest I mean you no hurt, but when a lady rallies, a stander-by must be complaisant and do her reason in laughing. Hah, ha.

MANLY. Why, you impudent, pitiful wretches, you presume sure upon your effeminacy to urge me, for you are in all things so like women that you may think it in me a kind of cowardice to beat you.

---

706 *tailor*: tailors were notoriously cowardly.

706–7 *training day*: for the train-bands, the citizen militia.

714 *Bartholomew-Fair*: the very popular fair held in Smithfield at the end of August, famous for its drolls, puppets and other such entertainments.

OLIVIA. No hectoring, good captain.

MANLY. Or perhaps you think this lady's presence secures you. But have a care, she has talked herself out of all the respect I had for her, and by using me ill before you has given me a privilege of using you so before her. But if you would preserve your respect to her and not be beaten before her, go, be gone immediately.

NOVEL. Be gone! What?

LORD PLAUSIBLE. Nay, worthy, noble, generous captain.

MANLY. Be gone, I say.

NOVEL. Be gone again! To us be gone!

MANLY. No chattering, baboons, instantly be gone. Or –

MANLY *puts 'em out of the room:*
NOVEL *struts,* PLAUSIBLE *cringes.*

NOVEL. Well, madam, we'll go make the cards ready in your bedchamber. Sure you will not stay long with him.

Exeunt PLAUSIBLE, NOVEL.

OLIVIA. Turn hither your rage, good Captain Swaggerhuff, and be saucy with your mistress, like a true captain; but be civil to your rivals and betters and do not threaten anything but me here, no, not so much as my windows, nor do not think yourself in the lodgings of one of your suburb mistresses beyond the Tower.

MANLY. Do not give me cause to think so, for those less infamous women part with their lovers, just as you did from me, with unforced vows of constancy and floods of willing tears, but the same winds bear away their lovers and their vows; and for their grief, if the credulous, unexpected fools return, they find new comforters, fresh cullies, such as I found here. The mercenary love of those women too suffers shipwrack with their gallants' fortunes. Now you have heard chance has used me scurvily, therefore you do too. Well, persevere in your ingratitude, falsehood and disdain; have constancy in something and I promise you to be as just to your real scorn as I was to your feigned love and henceforward will despise, contemn, hate loathe and detest you, most faithfully.

Enter LETTICE.

OLIVIA. Get the ombre cards ready in the next room, Lettice, and –

Whispers to LETTICE [*who goes out*].

FREEMAN. Bravely resolved, captain.

FIDELIA. And you'll be sure to keep your word, I hope, sir.

MANLY. I hope so too.

FIDELIA. Do you but hope it, sir? If you are not as good as your word, 'twill be the first time you ever bragged, sure.

MANLY. She has restored my reason with my heart.

FREEMAN. But, now you talk of restoring, captain, there are other things which, next to one's heart, one would not part with: I mean your jewels and money, which it seems she has, sir.

MANLY. What's that to you, sir?

FREEMAN. Pardon me, whatsoever is yours, I have a share in't, I'm sure, which I will not lose for asking, though you may be too generous, or too angry now to do't yourself.

FIDELIA. Nay, then I'll make bold to make my claim too.

Both going towards OLIVIA.

MANLY. Hold, you impertinent, officious fops! (*Aside*) How have I been deceived!

FREEMAN. Madam, there are certain appurtenances to a lover's heart, called jewels, which always go along with it.

FIDELIA. And which, with lovers, have no value in themselves but from the heart they come with; our captain's, madam, it seems you scorn to keep and much more will those worthless things without it, I am confident.

OLIVIA. A gentleman so well made as you are may be confident – us easy women could not deny you anything you ask, if'twere for yourself; but, since 'tis for another, I beg your leave to give him my answer. (*Aside*) An agreeable young fellow this! – And would not be my aversion! (*Aside to* MANLY) Captain, your young friend here has a very persuading face, I con-

---

777 *ombre*: a card game.

fess; yet you might have asked me yourself for those trifles you left with me, which (hark you a little, for I dare trust you with the secret; you are a man of so much honour, I'm sure), I say then, not expecting your return, or hoping ever to see you again, I have delivered your jewels to –

MANLY. Whom?

OLIVIA. My husband.

MANLY. Your husband!

OLIVIA. Ay, my husband, for, since you could leave me, I am lately and privately married to one who is a man of so much honour and experience in the world that I dare not ask him for your jewels again to restore 'em to you, lest he should conclude you never would have parted with 'em to me, on any other score but the exchange of my honour, which rather than you'd let me lose, you'd lose, I'm sure, yourself those trifles of yours.

MANLY. Triumphant impudence! But married too!

OLIVIA. O, speak not so loud; my servants know it not. I am married; there's no resisting one's destiny, or love, you know.

MANLY. Why, did you love him too?

OLIVIA. Most passionately, nay, love him now, though I have married him, and he me; which mutual love, I hope, you are too good, too generous a man to disturb by any future claim or visits to me. 'Tis true he is now absent in the country but returns shortly. Therefore, I beg of you, for your own ease and quiet, and my honour, you will never see me more.

MANLY. I wish I never had seen you.

OLIVIA. But if you should ever have anything to say to me hereafter, let that young gentleman there be your messenger.

MANLY. You would be kinder to him; I find he should be welcome.

OLIVIA. Alas, his youth would keep my husband from suspicions and his visits from scandal, for we women may have pity for such as he but no love. And I already think you do not well to spirit him away to sea, and the sea is already but too rich with the spoils of the shore.

MANLY. (*aside*) True perfect woman! If I could say anything more injurious to her now, I would, for I could out-rail a bilked whore or a kicked coward, but, now I think on't, that were rather to discover my love than hatred, and I must not talk, for something I must do.

OLIVIA. (*aside*) I think I have given him enough of me now never to be troubled with him again.

Enter LETTICE.

Well, Lettice, are the cards and all ready within? I come then. Captain, I beg your pardon; you will not make one at ombre?

MANLY. No, madam, but I'll wish you a little good luck before you go.

OLIVIA. No, if you would have me thrive, curse me, for that you'll do heartily, I suppose.

MANLY. Then, if you will have it so, may all the curses light upon you women ought to fear and you deserve: first, may the curse of loving play attend your sordid covetousness and fortune cheat you by trusting to her as you have cheated me; the curse of pride or a good reputation fall on your lust; the curse of affectation on your beauty; the curse of your husband's company on your pleasures; and the curse of your gallant's disappointments in his absence; and the curse of scorn, jealousy or despair on your love – and then the curse of loving on.

OLIVIA. And, to requite all your curses, I will only return you your last. May the curse of loving me still fall upon your proud, hard heart that could be so cruel to me in these horrid curses, but heaven forgive you. *Exit* OLIVIA.

MANLY. Hell and the devil reward thee.

FREEMAN. Well, you see now mistresses, like friends, are lost by letting 'em handle your money, and most women are such kind of witches, who can have no power over a man unless you give 'em money; but when once they have got any from you, they never leave you, till they have all; therefore I never dare give a woman a farthing.

MANLY. Well, there is yet this comfort by losing one's money with one's mistress: a man is out of danger of

---

859 *bilked*: cheated out of payment.

getting another, of being made prize again by love, who, like a pirate, takes you by spreading false colours, but when once you have run your ship aground, the treacherous picaroon loofs, so by your ruin you save yourself from slavery at least.

Enter BOY.

BOY. Mrs Lettice, here's Madam Blackacre come to wait upon her honour.

[*Exeunt* BOY *and* LETTICE.]

MANLY. D'ye hear that? Let us be gone before she comes, for henceforward I'll avoid the whole damned sex forever and woman as a sinking ship.

Exeunt MANLY *and* FIDELIA.

FREEMAN. And I'll stay to revenge on her your quarrel to the sex, for out of love to her jointure and hatred to business I would marry her, to make an end of her thousand suits and my thousand engagements, to the comfort of two unfortunate sorts of people: my plaintiffs and her defendants, my creditors and her adversaries.

Enter WIDOW BLACKACRE *led in by* MAJOR OLDFOX, *and* JERRY BLACKACRE *following, laden with green bags.*

WIDOW. 'Tis an arrant sea-ruffian, but I am glad I met with him at last to serve him again, major, for the last service was not good in law. Boy, duck, Jerry, where is my paper of memorandums? Give me, child. So. Where is my cousin Olivia now, my kind relation?

FREEMAN. Here is one that would be your kind relation, madam.

WIDOW. What mean you, sir?

FREEMAN. Why, faith (to be short) to marry you, widow.

WIDOW. Is not this the wild, rude person we saw at Captain Manly's?

JERRY. Ay, forsooth, an't please.

899–900 *spreading false colours*: flying false flags.
901 *picaroon*: pirate.
901 *loofs*: luffs, changes course nearer the wind.
917 *service*: delivery of the subpoena.

WIDOW. What would you? What are you? Marry me!

FREEMAN. Ay, faith, for I am a younger brother and you are a widow.

WIDOW. You are an impertinent person, and go about your business.

FREEMAN. I have none but to marry thee, widow.

WIDOW. But I have other business, I'd have you to know.

FREEMAN. But you have no business anights, widow, and I'll make you pleasanter business than any you have; for anights, I assure you, I am a man of great business, for the business –

WIDOW. Go, I'm sure you're an idle fellow.

FREEMAN. Try me but, widow, and employ me as you find my abilities and industry.

OLDFOX. Pray be civil to the lady, Mr –. She's a person of quality, a person that is no person –

FREEMAN. Yes, but she's a person that is a widow. Be you mannerly to her because you are to pretend only to be her squire, to arm her to her lawyer's chambers; but I will be impudent and bawdy, for she must love and marry me.

WIDOW. Marry come up, you saucy familiar Jack! You think with us widows, 'tis no more than up and ride. Gad forgive me, nowadays every idle, young, hectoring, roaring companion with a pair of turned red breeches and a broad back thinks to carry away any widow of the best degree, but I'd have you to know, sir, all widows are not got, like places at court, by impudence and importunity only.

OLDFOX. No, no, soft, soft. You are a young man and not fit –

FREEMAN. For a widow? Yes, sure, old man, the fitter.

OLDFOX. Go to, go to, if others had not laid in their claims before you –

FREEMAN. Not you, I hope.

OLDFOX. Why not I, sir? Sure, I am a much more proportionable match for her than you, sir, I, who am an elder brother, of a comfortable fortune and of equal years with her.

---

952 *roaring*: roistering.

952–3 *turned red breeches*: unclear, either 'well-cut' or 'military trousers dyed' or 're-used'.

WIDOW. How's that? You unmannerly person, I'd have you to know, I was born but in *ann' undec' Caroli prim'*.

OLDFOX. Your pardon, lady, your pardon. Be not offended with your very servant. – But I say, sir, you are a beggarly younger brother, twenty years younger than her, without any land or stock but your great stock of impudence. Therefore what pretension can you have to her?

FREEMAN. You have made it for me; first, because I am a younger brother.

WIDOW. Why, is that a sufficient plea to a relict? How appears it, sir? By what foolish custom?

FREEMAN. By custom time out of mind only. Then, sir, because I have nothing to keep me after her death, I am the likelier to take care of her life. And, for my being twenty years younger than her and having a sufficient stock of impudence, I leave it to her whether they will be valid exceptions to me in her widow's law or equity.

OLDFOX. Well, she has been so long in Chancery that I'll stand to her equity and decree between us. Come, lady, pray snap up this young snap at first or we shall be troubled with him. Give him a city widow's answer (*aside to the* WIDOW) that is, with all the ill breeding imaginable. – Come, madam.

WIDOW. Well then, to make an end of this foolish wooing, for nothing interrupts business more. First, for you, major –

OLDFOX. You declare in my favour then?

FREEMAN. What, direct the court? (*To* JERRY) Come, young lawyer, thou shalt be a counsel for me.

JERRY. Gad, I shall betray your cause then as well as an older lawyer, never stir.

969–70 *ann' undec' Caroli prim'*: the eleventh year of Charles I's reign, 1636; the form of dating used in law.

978 *relict*: widow.

986 *equity*: the parallel system of law to common law and having authority over it to correct defects, based on general principles of law and justice; equity was administered by the Courts of Chancery in particular.

989 *snap up . . . snap*: shut up this young rogue.

WIDOW. First, I say, for you, major, my walking hospital of an ancient foundation, thou bag of mummy that wouldst fall asunder if 'twere not for thy cerecloths –

OLDFOX. How, lady?

FREEMAN. Hah, ha –

JERRY. Hey, brave mother! Use all suitors thus, for my sake.

WIDOW. Thou withered, hobbling, distorted cripple; nay, thou art a cripple all over. Wouldst thou make me the staff of thy age, the crutch of thy decrepitness? Me –

FREEMAN. Well said, widow! Faith, thou wouldst make a man love thee now without dissembling.

WIDOW. Thou senseless, impertinent, quibbling, drivelling, feeble, paralytic, impotent, fumbling, frigid nincompoop.

JERRY. Hey, brave mother for calling of names, ifac!

WIDOW. Wouldst thou make a caudlemaker, a nurse of me? Can't you be bedrid without a bedfellow? Won't your swanskins, furs, flannels and the scorched trencher keep you warm there? Would you have me your Scotch warming-pan, with a pox to you? Me! –

OLDFOX. O heavens!

FREEMAN. I told you I should be thought the fitter man, major.

JERRY. Ay, you old fobus, and you would have been my guardian, would you? To have taken care of my estate, that half of't should never come to me, by letting long leases at peppercorn rents.

WIDOW. If I would have married an old man, 'tis well known I might have married an earl, nay, what's more, a judge and been covered the winter nights with the lambskins which I prefer to the ermines of nobles. And dost thou think I would wrong my poor minor there for you?

1003 *cerecloths*: winding-sheets for a corpse.
1017 *caudlemaker*: maker of drinks for invalids.
1020 *trencher*: platter, here used to heat the bed.
1021 *Scotch warming-pan*: a woman to take to bed.
1025 *fobus*: fool, perhaps from 'to fob', to trick.
1028 *peppercorn rents*: nominal, token payments of rent.
1032 *lambskins*: used in judges' robes.

FREEMAN. Your minor is a chopping minor, God bless him. (*Strokes* JERRY *on the head*)

OLDFOX. Your minor may be a major of horse or foot for his bigness, and it seems you will have the cheating of your minor to yourself.

WIDOW. Pray, sir, bear witness. Cheat my minor! I'll bring my action of the case for the slander.

FREEMAN. Nay, I would bear false witness for thee now, widow, since you have done me justice and have thought me the fitter man for you.

WIDOW. Fair and softly, sir. 'Tis my minor's case more than my own, and I must do him justice now on you.

FREEMAN. How?

OLDFOX. So then.

WIDOW. You are first, I warrant, some renegado from the Inns of Court and the law, and thou'lt come to suffer for't by the law, that is, be hanged.

JERRY. Not about your neck, forsooth, I hope.

FREEMAN. But, madam –

OLDFOX. Hear the court.

WIDOW. Thou art some debauched, drunken, lewd, hectoring, gaming companion and want'st some widow's old gold to nick upon; but, I thank you sir, that's for my lawyers.

FREEMAN. Faith, we should ne'er quarrel about that, for guineas would serve my turn. But, widow –

WIDOW. Thou art a foul-mouthed boaster of thy lust, a mere braggadocio of thy strength for wine and women and wilt belie thyself more than thou dost women and art every way a base deceiver of women; and would deceive me too, would you?

FREEMAN. Nay, faith, widow, this is judging without seeing the evidence.

WIDOW. I say, you are a worn-out whoremaster at five

1035 *chopping*: strapping.

1041 *action of the case*: usually 'action on the case', a common-law claim for damages for loss or injury resulting only indirectly from the act complained of.

1057 *nick upon*: gamble with.

1060 *guineas*: first minted in 1663 and therefore newer than the 'old gold' of line 1057.

1062 *braggadocio*: braggart.

1068 *whoremaster*: one experienced in whoring.

and twenty both in body and fortune, and cannot be trusted by the common wenches of the town, lest you should not pay 'em, nor by the wives of the town, lest you should pay 'em; so you want women and would have me your bawd, to procure 'em for you.

FREEMAN. Faith, if you had any good acquaintance, widow, 'twould be civilly done of thee, for I am just come from sea.

WIDOW. I mean, you would have me keep you that you might turn keeper, for poor widows are only used like bawds by you; you go to church with us but to get other women to lie with. In fine, you are a cheating, chousing spendthrift and, having sold your own annuity, would waste my jointure.

JERRY. And make havoc of our estate personal and all our old gilt plate. I should soon be picking up all our mortgaged apostle-spoons, bowls and beakers out of most of the alehouses betwixt Hercules' Pillars and the Boatswain in Wapping; nay, and you'd be scouring amongst my trees and make 'em knock down one another, like routed, reeling watchmen at midnight. Would you so, bully?

FREEMAN. Nay, prithee, widow, hear me.

WIDOW. No, sir. I'd have you to know, thou pitiful, paltry, lath-backed fellow, if I would have married a young man, 'tis well known I could have had any young heir in Norfolk, nay, the hopefullest young man this day at the King's Bench Bar, I that am a relict and executrix of known plentiful assets and

---

1071–2 *lest you should pay 'em*: presumably by passing on venereal disease.

1081 *chousing*: cheating.

1085 *apostle-spoons*: silver spoons with figures of the apostles on the handles.

1086–7 *Hercules' Pillars . . . Wapping*: Hercules' Pillars was an inn in Fleet Street, close to the Inns of Court; the Boatswain is not known but Wapping was at the opposite end of the city.

1096 *King's Bench Bar*: the highest of the three common-law courts at Westminster Hall, originally dealing with cases involving the Crown. The other two were Common Pleas (for cases of subject against subject) and Exchequer (for revenue cases). In practice, the jurisdiction of each court was not clearly defined.

parts, who understand myself and the law. And would you have me under covert baron again? No, sir, no covert baron for me.

FREEMAN. But, dear widow, hear me. I value you only, not your jointure.

WIDOW. Nay, sir, hold there. I know your love to a widow is covetousness of her jointure. And a widow a little stricken in years with a good jointure is like an old mansion house in a good purchase, never valued, but take one, take t'other. And perhaps when you are in possession you'd neglect it, let it drop to the ground for want of necessary repairs or expenses upon't.

FREEMAN. No, widow, one would be sure to keep all tight when one is to forfeit one's lease by dilapidation.

WIDOW. Fie, fie, I neglect my business with this foolish discourse of love. Jerry, child, let me see the list of the jury; I'm sure my cousin Olivia has some relations amongst 'em. But where is she?

FREEMAN. Nay, widow, but hear me one word only.

WIDOW. Nay, sir, no more, pray. I will no more hearken again to your foolish love motions than to offers of arbitration.

Exeunt WIDOW *and* JERRY.

FREEMAN. Well, I'll follow thee yet, for he that has a pretension at court or to a widow must never give over for a little ill usage.

OLDFOX. Therefore I'll get her by assiduity, patience and long-sufferings, which you will not undergo, for you idle young fellows leave off love when it comes to be business, and industry gets more women, than love.

FREEMAN. Ay, industry, the fool's and old man's merit; but I'll be industrious too and make a business on't and get her by law, wrangling and contests and not by sufferings. And, because you are no dangerous rival, I'll give thee counsel, major:
If you litigious widow e'er would gain,
Sigh not to her but by the law complain;
To her, as to a bawd, defendant sue
With statutes and make justice pimp for you.

Exeunt.

1099 *covert baron*: under a husband's protection.

ACT III

SCENE I

Westminster Hall.

Enter MANLY *and* FREEMAN, *two* SAILORS *behind.*

MANLY. I hate this place, worse than a man that has inherited a chancery suit. I wish I were well out on't again.

FREEMAN. Why, you need not be afraid of this place, for a man without money needs no more fear a crowd of lawyers than a crowd of pickpockets.

MANLY. This, the reverend of the law would have thought the palace or residence of justice; but, if it be, she lives here with the state of a Turkish Emperor, rarely seen, and beseiged, rather than defended, by her numerous black guard here.

FREEMAN. Methinks 'tis like one of their own halls in Christmas time, whither from all parts fools bring their money to try by the dice – not the worst judges – whether it shall be their own or no. But after a tedious fretting and wrangling they drop away all their money on both sides and, finding neither the better, at last go emptily and lovingly away together to the tavern, joining their curses against the young lawyers' box, that sweeps all like the old ones.

MANLY. Spoken like a revelling Christmas lawyer.

FREEMAN. Yes, I was one, I confess, but was fain to leave the law out of conscience and fall to making

1–2 the delays in Chancery were notorious even then.
7 *the reverend*: (= *reverent*) those who revere.
11 *black*: the colour of lawyers' gowns.
12–15 gambling was permitted in the Inns of Court at Christmas.
19–20 *the young lawyers' . . . the old ones*: the box which takes the house's cut during the gambling takes all the money, just as the old lawyers' cash-box does in litigation.

false musters, rather chose to cheat the king than his subjects, plunder rather than take fees.

MANLY. Well, a plague and a purse famine light on the law, and that female limb of it who dragged me hither today. But prithee go see if in that crowd of daggled gowns there thou canst find her. (*Pointing to a crowd of lawyers at the end of the stage*)

Exit FREEMAN.
Manet MANLY.

How hard it is to be an hypocrite!
At least to me, who am but newly so.
I thought it once a kind of knavery,
Nay, cowardice, to hide one's faults; but now
The common frailty, love, becomes my shame.
He must not know I love th'ungrateful still,
Lest he contemn me more than she, for I,
It seems, can undergo a woman's scorn
But not a man's –

Enter to him FIDELIA.

FIDELIA. Sir, good sir, generous captain.

MANLY. Prithee, kind impertinence, leave me. Why shouldst thou follow me, flatter my generosity now, since thou know'st I have no money left? If I had it, I'd give it thee, to buy my quiet.

FIDELIA. I never followed yet, sir, reward or fame but you alone, nor do I now beg anything but leave to share your miseries. You should not be a niggard of 'em, since methinks you have enough to spare. Let me follow you now because you hate me, as you have often said.

MANLY. I ever hated a coward's company, I must confess.

FIDELIA. Let me follow you till I am none then, for you, I'm sure, will through such worlds of dangers that I shall be inured to 'em; nay, I shall be afraid of your anger more than danger and so turn valiant out of fear. Dear captain, do not cast me off till you have

---

24 *false musters*: by claiming to have more soldiers than they had, officers could claim subsistence money for the non-existent troops.

tried me once more. Do not, do not go to sea again without me.

MANLY. Thou to sea! To court, thou fool. Remember the advice I gave thee: thou art a handsome spaniel and canst fawn naturally. Go, busk about and run thyself into the next great man's lobby; first fawn upon the slaves without and then run into the lady's bedchamber; thou may'st be admitted at last to tumble her bed. Go seek, I say, and lose me, for I am not able to keep thee; I have not bread for myself.

FIDELIA. Therefore I will not go, because then I may help and serve you.

MANLY. Thou!

FIDELIA. I warrant you, sir, for at worst I could beg or steal for you.

MANLY. Nay, more bragging! Dost thou not know there's venturing your life in stealing? Go, prithee, away. Thou art as hard to shake off as that flattering effeminating mischief, love.

FIDELIA. Love, did you name? Why, you are not so miserable as to be yet in love, sure!

MANLY. No, no, prithee away, be gone, on – (*Aside*) I had almost discovered my love and shame. Well, if I had? That thing could not think the worse of me – or if he did? – No – yes, he shall know it – he shall – but then I must never leave him, for they are such secrets that make parasites and pimps lords of their masters, for any slavery or tyranny is easier than love's. – Come hither. Since thou art so forward to serve me, hast thou but resolution enough to endure the torture of a secret? For such to some is insupportable.

FIDELIA. I would keep it as safe as if your dear precious life depended on't.

MANLY. Damn your dearness. It concerns more than my life, my honour.

FIDELIA. Doubt it not, sir.

MANLY. And do not discover it by too much fear of discovering it, but have a great care you let not Freeman find it out.

---

61 *busk about*: change course.

FIDELIA. I warrant you, sir. I am already all joy with the hopes of your commands and shall be all wings in the execution of 'em. Speak quickly, sir.

MANLY. You said you would beg for me.

FIDELIA. I did, sir.

MANLY. Then you shall beg for me.

FIDELIA. With all my heart, sir.

MANLY. That is, pimp for me.

FIDELIA. How, sir?

MANLY. D'ye start! Thinkst thou thou couldst do me any other service? Come, no dissembling honour. I know you can do it handsomely; thou wert made for't. You have lost your time with me at sea; you must recover it.

FIDELIA. Do not, sir, beget yourself more reasons for your aversion to me and make my obedience to you a fault. I am the unfittest in the world to do you such a service.

MANLY. Your cunning arguing against it shows but how fit you are for it. No more dissembling. Here, I say, you must go use it for me to Olivia.

FIDELIA. To her, sir?

MANLY. Go flatter, lie, kneel, promise, anything to get her for me. I cannot live unless I have her. Didst thou not say thou wouldst do anything to save my life? And she said you had a persuading face.

FIDELIA. But did not you say, sir, your honour was dearer to you than your life? And would you have me contribute to the loss of that and carry love from you to the most infamous, most false and –

MANLY. And most beautiful! (*Sighs aside*)

FIDELIA. Most ungrateful woman that ever lived, for sure she must be so that could desert you so soon, use you so basely, and so lately too. Do not, do not forget it, sir, and think –

MANLY. No, I will not forget it but think of revenge. I will lie with her, out of revenge. Go, be gone, and prevail for me or never see me more.

FIDELIA. You scorned her last night.

MANLY. I know not what I did last night. I dissembled last night.

FIDELIA. Heavens!

MANLY. Be gone, I say, and bring me love or compliance

back, or hopes at least, or I'll never see thy face again. By –

FIDELIA. O do not swear, sir. First hear me.

MANLY. I am impatient. Away. You'll find me here till twelve. (*Turns away*)

FIDELIA. Sir –

MANLY. Not one word, no insinuating argument more or soothing persuasion; you'll have need of all your rhetoric with her. Go, strive to alter her, not me. Be gone. *Exit* MANLY *at the end of the stage.*

Manet FIDELIA.

FIDELIA. Should I discover to him now my sex
And lay before him his strange cruelty,
'Twould but incense it more. – No, 'tis not time.
For his love, must I then betray my own?
Were ever love or chance, till now, severe?
Or shifting woman posed with such a task?
Forced to beg that which kills her if obtained
And give away her lover not to lose him.

Exit FIDELIA.

Enter WIDOW BLACKACRE *in the middle of half a dozen lawyers, whispered to by a fellow in black,* JERRY BLACKACRE *following the crowd.*

WIDOW. Offer me a reference, you saucy companion you! D'ye know who you speak to? Art thou a solicitor in Chancery and offer a reference? A pretty fellow! Mr Serjeant Ploddon, here's a fellow has the impudence to offer me a reference.

SERJEANT PLODDON. Who's that has the impudence to offer a reference within these walls?

WIDOW. Nay, for a splitter of causes to do't!

SERJEANT PLODDON. No, madam, to a lady learned in the law as you are the offer of a reference were to impose upon you.

---

158 *reference*: submitting a matter to be decided by the Masters in Ordinary of the Court of Chancery, a kind of arbitration to speed up litigation and hence unacceptable to Widow Blackacre.

161 *Serjeant*: officer of the court.

165 *splitter of causes*: lawyer.

WIDOW. No, no, never fear me for a reference, Mr Serjeant. But, come, have you not forgot your brief? Are you sure you shan't make the mistake of – hark you – (*Whispers*) Go then, go to your Court of Common Pleas and say one thing over and over again. You do it so naturally, you'll never be suspected for protracting time.

SERJEANT PLODDON. Come, I know the course of the court, and your business.

Exit SERJEANT PLODDON.

WIDOW. Let's see, Jerry, where are my minutes? Come, Mr Quaint, pray, go talk a great deal for me in Chancery. Let your words be easy and your sense hard; my cause requires it. Branch it bravely and deck my cause with flowers that the snake may lie hidden. Go, go, and be sure you remember the decree of my Lord Chancellor *tricesimo quart'* of the Queen.

QUAINT. I will, as I see cause, extenuate or examplify matter of fact, baffle truth with impudence, answer exceptions with questions, though never so impertinent, for reasons give 'em words, for law and equity, tropes and figures; and so relax and enervate the sinews of their argument with the oil of my eloquence. But when my lungs can reason no longer, and not being able to say anything more for our cause, say everything of our adversary, whose reputation, though never so clear and evident in the eye of the world, yet with sharp invectives –

WIDOW. (Alias Billingsgate.)

QUAINT. With poignant and sour invectives, I say, I will deface, wipe out and obliterate his fair reputation, even as a record with the juice of lemons, and tell such a story – for the truth on't is, all that we can do for our client in Chancery is telling a story – a fine story, a long story, such a story –

WIDOW. Go, save thy breath for the cause; talk at the bar, Mr Quaint. You are so copiously fluent you can weary anyone's ears sooner than your own tongue.

---

181 *branch*: embroider.
184 *tricesimo quart' of the Queen*: the thirty-fourth year of Elizabeth's reign, 1592.
196 *Billingsgate*: the London fish market's famous style of abuse.

Go, weary our adversary's counsel and the court. Go, thou art a fine-spoken person. Adad, I shall make thy wife jealous of me if you can but court the court into a decree for us. Go, get you gone, and remember – (*Whispers*)

Exit QUAINT.

Come, Mr Blunder, pray bawl soundly for me at the King's Bench, bluster, sputter, question, cavil, but be sure your argument be intricate enough to confound the court, and then you do my business. Talk what you will but be sure your tongue never stand still, for your own noise will secure your sense from censure – 'tis like coughing or hemming when one has got the bellyache, which stifles the unmannerly noise. Go, dear rogue, and succeed and I'll invite thee, ere it be long, to more soused venison.

BLUNDER. I'll warrant you, after your verdict your judgement shall not be arrested upon ifs and ands.

[*Exit* BLUNDER.]

WIDOW. Come, Mr Petulant, let me give you some new instructions for our cause in the Exchequer. Are the barons sat?

PETULANT. Yes, no. May be they are, may be they are not. What know I? What care I?

WIDOW. Hey-day! I wish you would but snap up the counsel on t'other side anon, at the bar, as much and have a little more patience with me that I might instruct you a little better.

PETULANT. You instruct me! What is my brief for, mistress?

WIDOW. Ay, but you seldom read your brief but at the bar, if you do it then.

PETULANT. Perhaps I do, perhaps I don't, and perhaps 'tis time enough. Pray hold yourself contented, mistress.

WIDOW. Nay, if you go there too, I will not be contented, sir. Though you, I see, will lose my cause for want of speaking, I won't. You shall hear me and shall be instructed. Let's see your brief.

---

219 *soused*: pickled.
224 *barons*: the judges in the Court of Exchequer.

PETULANT. Send your solicitor to me. Instructed by a woman! I'd have you to know, I do not wear a bar-gown –

WIDOW. By a woman! And I'd have you to know, I am no common woman but a woman conversant in the laws of the land, as well as yourself, though I have no bar-gown.

PETULANT. Go to, go to, mistress. You are impertinent, and there's your brief for you. Instruct me! (*Flings her breviate at her*)

WIDOW. Impertinent to me, you saucy Jack you! You return my breviate but where's my fee? You'll be sure to keep that and scan that so well that if there chance to be but a brass halfcrown in't, one's sure to hear on't again. Would you would but look on your breviate half so narrowly. But pray give me my fee too as well as my brief.

PETULANT. Mistress, that's without precedent. When did a counsel ever return his fee, pray? And you are impertinent, and ignorant, to demand it.

WIDOW. Impertinent again and ignorant to me! Gadsbodikins, you puny upstart in the law, to use me so, you green bag carrier, you murderer of unfortunate causes. The clerk's ink is scarce off of your fingers, you that newly come from lamp-blacking the judge's shoes and are not fit to wipe mine. You call me impertinent and ignorant! I would give thee a cuff on the ear, sitting the courts, if I were ignorant. Marry gep, if it had not been for me, thou hadst been yet but a hearing counsel at the bar.

Exit PETULANT.

Enter MR BUTTONGOWN *crossing the stage in haste.*

Mr Buttongown, Mr Buttongown, whither so fast? What, won't you stay till we are heard?

---

265 *lamp-blacking*: smearing with lamp-soot, polishing.

268 *sitting the courts*: the penalty for assault in Westminster Hall while the courts were in session was life imprisonment and confiscation of one's goods.

268–9 *Marry gep*: a corruption of 'By Mary Gipsey', i.e. 'By St Mary of Egypt'.

270 *hearing counsel*: a barrister without a case.

BUTTONGOWN. I cannot, Mrs Blackacre, I must be at the Council; my lord's cause stays there for me.

WIDOW. And mine suffers here.

BUTTONGOWN. I cannot help it.

WIDOW. I'm undone.

BUTTONGOWN. What's that to me?

WIDOW. Consider the five pound fee if not my cause – that was something to you.

BUTTONGOWN. Away, away, pray be not so troublesome, mistress. I must be gone.

WIDOW. Nay, but consider a little. I am your old client, my lord but a new one; or, let him be what he will, he will hardly be a better client to you than myself. I hope you believe I shall be in law as long as I live, therefore am no despicable client. Well, but go to your lord. I know you expect he should make you a judge one day; but I hope his promise to you will prove a true lord's promise. But that he might be sure to fail you I wish you had his bond for't.

BUTTONGOWN. But, what, will you yet be thus impertinent, mistress?

WIDOW. Nay, I beseech you, sir, stay, if it be but to tell me my lord's case. Come, in short.

BUTTONGOWN. Nay then – *Exit* BUTTONGOWN.

WIDOW. Well, Jerry, observe, child, and lay it up for hereafter: these are those lawyers who by being in all causes are in none; therefore if you would have 'em for you, let your adversary fee 'em, for he may chance to depend upon 'em, and so in being against thee they'll be for thee.

JERRY. Ay, mother, they put me in mind of the unconscionable wooers of widows, who undertake briskly their matrimonial business for their money, but when they have got it once, let who's will drudge for them; therefore have a care of 'em, forsooth. There's advice for your advice.

WIDOW. Well said, boy. Come, Mr Splitcause, pray go see when my cause in Chancery comes on; and go speak with Mr Quillet in the King's Bench and Mr Quirk in the Common Pleas and see how our matters go there.

Enter MAJOR OLDFOX.

OLDFOX. Lady, a good and propitious morning to you, and may all your causes go as well as if I myself were judge of 'em.

WIDOW. Sir, excuse me, I am busy and cannot answer compliments in Westminster Hall. Go, Mr Splitcause, and come to me again to that bookseller's – there I'll stay for you that you may be sure to find me.

OLDFOX. No, sir, come to the other bookseller's, I'll attend your ladyship thither.

Exit SPLITCAUSE.

WIDOW. Why to the other?

OLDFOX. Because he is my bookseller, lady.

WIDOW. What, to sell you lozenges for your catarrh? Or medicines for your corns? What else can a major deal with a bookseller for?

OLDFOX. Lady, he prints for me.

WIDOW. Why, are you an author?

OLDFOX. Of some few essays. Deign you, lady, to peruse 'em. (*Aside*) She is a woman of parts and I must win her by showing mine.

BOOKSELLER'S BOY. Will you see Culpepper, mistress? Aristotle's *Problems*? *The Compleat Midwife*?

WIDOW. No, let's see Dalton, Hughes, Shepherd, Wingate.

BOY. We have no lawbooks.

WIDOW. No? You are a pretty bookseller then.

OLDFOX. Come, have you e'er a one of my essays left?

BOY. Yes, sir, we have enough, and shall always have 'em.

OLDFOX. How so?

333–4 *Culpepper . . . Midwife*: Nicholas Culpepper was a medical writer, best known for *The English Physician* (1652 and many later editions); *The Problems of Aristotle* (1595, editions in 1666 and 1670), 'wherein are contained divers questions, with their answers, touching the estate of man's body', not by Aristotle at all; *The Compleat Midwifes Practice* (1656) probably by Thomas Chamberlayne.

335 *Dalton . . . Wingate*: all lawbooks: Michael Dalton, *The Country Justice* (1618, editions in 1661, 1666); William Hughes wrote many lawbooks, e.g. *The Parson's Law* (1641, third edition 1673); William Sheppard was highly prolific – the most frequently reprinted of his works was *The Court-Keeper's Guide* (1649, sixth edition 1676); Edmund Wingate, *The Body of the Common Law* (1655, third edition 1670). Both Hughes and Sheppard had published new works in 1675.

BOY. Why, they are good, steady, lasting ware.

OLDFOX. Nay, I hope they will live. Let's see. Be pleased, madam, to peruse the poor endeavours of my pen, for I have a pen, though I say it, that – (*Gives her a book*)

JERRY. Pray let me see *St George for Christendom* or *The Seven Champions of England.*

WIDOW. No, no, give him *The Young Clerk's Guide.* What, we shall have you read yourself into a humour of rambling and fighting and studying military discipline and wearing red breeches!

OLDFOX. Nay, if you talk of military discipline, show him my treatise of *The Art Military.*

WIDOW. Hold, I would as willingly he should read a play.

JERRY. O pray, forsooth, mother, let me have a play.

WIDOW. No, sirrah, there are young students of the law enough spoiled already by plays; they would make you in love with your laundress or, what's worse, some queen of the stage that was a laundress, and so turn keeper before you are of age.

Several crossing the stage.

But stay, Jerry, is not that Mr What-d'y'call-him that goes there, he that offered to sell me a suit in Chancery for five hundred pound, for a hundred down and only paying the clerks' fees?

JERRY. Ay, forsooth, 'tis he.

WIDOW. Then stay here and have a care of the bags whilst I follow him. Have a care of the bags, I say.

JERRY. And do you have a care, forsooth, of the statute against champerty, I say.

Exit WIDOW.

Enter FREEMAN *to them.*

345–6 *St George . . . England*: probably Richard Johnson's extraordinarily popular *The Most Famous History of the Seven Champions of Christendom* (1596, editions in 1660, 1670 and 1675).

347 *The Young Clerk's Guide*: by Sir Richard Hutton (1649, fourteenth edition 1673).

368 *champerty*: an illegal agreement for someone not involved in a case to receive part of the lands or money in dispute in exchange for payment of the costs.

FREEMAN. (*aside*) So, there's a limb of my widow which was wont to be inseparable from her. She can't be far. – How now, my pretty son-in-law that shall be, where's my widow?

JERRY. My mother, but not your widow, will be forthcoming presently.

FREEMAN. Your servant, major. What, are you buying furniture for a little sleeping closet which you miscall a study? For you do only by your books as by your wenches, bind 'em up neatly and make 'em fine, for other people to use 'em; and your bookseller is properly your upholster, for he furnishes your room rather than your head.

OLDFOX. Well, well, good sea-lieutenant, study you your compass – that's more than your head can deal with. (*Aside*) I will go find out the widow to keep her out of his sight, or he'll board her whilst I am treating a peace. *Exit* OLDFOX.

Manent FREEMAN, JERRY.

JERRY. Nay, prithee, friend, now let me have but the *Seven Champions*. You shall trust me no longer than till my mother's Mr Splitcause comes, for I hope he'll lend me wherewithal to pay for't.

FREEMAN. Lend thee! Here, I'll pay him. Do you want money, squire? I'm sorry a man of your estate should want money.

JERRY. Nay, my mother will ne'er let me be at age. And till then she says –

FREEMAN. At age! Why, you are at age already to have spent an estate, man; there are younger than you have kept their women these three years, have had half a dozen claps, and lost as many thousand pounds at play.

JERRY. Ay, they are happy sparks! Nay, I know some of my schoolfellows who when we were at school were two years younger than me but now, I know not how, are grown men before me and go where they will and look to themselves, but my curmudgeonly mother won't allow me wherewithal to be a man of myself with.

FREEMAN. Why, there 'tis. I knew your mother was in

---

371 *son-in-law*: stepson.
399 *claps*: doses of syphilis.

the fault. Ask but your schoolfellows what they did to be men of themselves.

JERRY. Why, I know they went to law with their mothers, for they say there's no good to be done upon a widow-mother till one goes to law with her, but mine is as plaguey a lawyer as any's of our Inn. Then would she marry too and cut down my trees. Now I should hate, man, to have my father's wife kissed and slapped and t'other thing too (you know what I mean) by another man, and our trees are the purest, tall, even, shady twigs, by my fa –

FREEMAN. Come, squire, let your mother and your trees fall as she pleases rather than wear this gown and carry green bags all thy life and be pointed at for a tony. But you shall be able to deal with her yet the common way; thou shalt make false love to some lawyer's daughter, whose father, upon the hopes of thy marrying her, shall lend the money, and law, to preserve thy estate and trees, and thy mother is so ugly nobody will have her if she cannot cut down thy trees.

JERRY. Nay, if I had but anybody to stand by me, I am as stomachful as another.

FREEMAN. That will I. I'll not see any hopeful young gentleman abused.

BOY. (*aside*) By any but yourself.

JERRY. The truth on't is, mine's as arrant a widow-mother to her poor child as any's in England: she won't so much as let one have sixpence in one's pocket to see a motion or the dancing of the ropes or –

FREEMAN. Come, you shan't want money. There's gold for you.

JERRY. O Lurd, sir, two guineas! D'ye lend me this? Is there no trick in't? Well, sir, I'll give you my bond for security.

FREEMAN. No, no, thou hast given me thy face for security. Anybody would swear thou dost not look like a cheat. You shall have what you will of me and,

---

418 *purest*: finest.
422 *tony*: simpleton.
430 *stomachful*: brave.
437 *motion*: puppet-play.

if your mother will not be kinder to you, come to me, who will.

JERRY. (*aside*) By my fa – he's a curious fine gentleman! – But, will you stand by one?

FREEMAN. If you can be resolute.

JERRY. Can be resolved! Gad, if she gives me but a cross word, I'll leave her tonight and come to you. But now I have got money I'll go to Jack of All Trades, at t'other end of the Hall, and buy the neatest, purest things –

FREEMAN. [*aside*] And I'll follow the great boy and my blow at his mother. Steal away the calf and the cow will follow you.

Exit JERRY, *followed by* FREEMAN.

Enter, on the other side, MANLY, WIDOW BLACKACRE *and* OLDFOX.

MANLY. Damn your cause; can't you lose it without me? Which you are like enough to do if it be, as you say, an honest one. I will suffer no longer for't.

WIDOW. Nay, captain, I tell you, you are my prime witness and the cause is just now coming on, Mr Splitcause tells me. Lord, methinks you should take a pleasure in walking here as half you see now do, for they have no business here, I assure you.

MANLY. Yes, but I'll assure you then, their business is to persecute me. But d'ye think I'll stay any longer, to have a rogue, because he knows my name, pluck me aside and whisper a newsbook-secret to me with a stinking breath? A second come piping angry from the court and sputter in my face his tedious complaints against it? A third law-coxcomb, because he saw me once at a Reader's dinner, come and put me a long lawcase, to make discovery of his indefatigable dullness and my wearied patience? A fourth, a most barbarous civil rogue, who will keep a man half an hour in the crowd with a bowed body and a hat off,

---

470 *newsbook-secret*: no secret because already published in the newspapers.

474 *Reader's dinner*: feast given at the end of his term by one of the two lecturers appointed annually at the Inns.

acting the reformed sign of the Salutation Tavern, to hear his bountiful professions of service and friendship, whilst he cares not if I were damned and I am wishing him hanged out of my way? I'd as soon run the gauntlet as walk t'other turn.

Enter to them JERRY BLACKACRE *without his bags but laden with trinkets, which he endeavours to hide from his mother, and followed at a distance by* FREEMAN.

WIDOW. O, are you come, sir? But where have you been, you ass? And how come you thus laden?

JERRY. Look here, forsooth mother, now here's a duck, here's a boar-cat and here's an owl. (*Making a noise with catcalls and other suchlike instruments*)

WIDOW. Yes, there is an owl, sir.

OLDFOX. He's an ungracious bird, indeed.

WIDOW. But go, thou trangame, and carry back those trangames which thou hast stolen or purloined, for nobody would trust a minor in Westminster Hall, sure.

JERRY. Hold yourself contented, forsooth. I have these commodities by a fair bargain and sale, and there stands my witness and creditor.

WIDOW. How's that! What, sir, d'ye think to get the mother by giving the child a rattle? But where are my bags, my writings, you rascal?

JERRY. (*aside*) O law! Where are they indeed?

WIDOW. How, sirrah? Speak, come –

MANLY. (*apart to him*) You can tell her, Freeman, I suppose?

FREEMAN. (*apart to him*) 'Tis true, I made one of your salt-water sharks steal 'em, whilst he was eagerly choosing his commodities, as he calls 'em, in order to my design upon his mother.

WIDOW. Won't you speak? Where were you, I say, you son of a – an unfortunate woman? O major, I'm undone. They are all that concern my estate, my

---

479 *reformed . . . Tavern*: the sign which originally showed the Annunciation by the Angel Gabriel to Mary was changed to two men bowing. There were a number of Salutation Taverns in London.

487 s.d. *catcalls*: squeaking whistles.

490 *trangame*: trinket, toy; originally a fictitious law term.

jointure, my husband's deed of gift, my evidences for all my suits now depending! What will become of them?

FREEMAN. (*aside*) I'm glad to hear this. – They'll be safe, I warrant you, madam.

WIDOW. O where? Where? Come, you villain, along with me and show me where.

Exeunt WIDOW, JERRY, OLDFOX.
Manent MANLY, FREEMAN.

MANLY. Thou hast taken the right way to get a widow, by making her great boy rebel, for when nothing will make a widow marry she'll do't to cross her children. But canst thou in earnest marry this harpy, this volume of shrivelled, blurred parchments and law, this attorney's desk?

FREEMAN. Ay, ay, I'll marry and live honestly, that is, give my creditors, not her, due benevolence, pay my debts.

MANLY. Thy creditors, you see, are not so barbarous as to put thee in prison; and wilt thou commit thyself to a noisome dungeon for thy life, which is the only satisfaction thou canst give thy creditors by this match?

FREEMAN. Why, is not she rich?

MANLY. Ay, but he that marries a widow for her money will find himself as much mistaken as the widow that marries a young fellow for due benevolence, as you call it.

FREEMAN. Why, d'ye think I shan't deserve wages? I'll drudge faithfully.

MANLY. I tell thee again, he that is the slave in the mine has the least propriety in the ore. You may dig and dig, but if thou wouldst have her money rather get to be her trustee than her husband, for a true widow will make over her estate to anybody and cheat herself rather than be cheated by her children or a second husband.

Enter to them JERRY, *running in a fright.*

JERRY. O law! I'm undone, I'm undone, My mother will kill me. You said you'd stand by one.

FREEMAN. So I will, my brave squire, I warrant thee.

JERRY. Ay, but I dare not stay till she comes, for she's

as furious, now she has lost her writings, as a bitch when she has lost her puppies.

MANLY. The comparison's handsome!

JERRY. O, she's here!

Enter WIDOW BLACKACRE *and* OLDFOX.

FREEMAN. (*to the* SAILOR) Take him, Jack, and make haste with him to your master's lodging; and be sure you keep him up till I come.

Exeunt JERRY *and* SAILOR.

WIDOW. O my dear writings! Where's this heathen rogue, my minor?

FREEMAN. Gone to drown or hang himself.

WIDOW. No, I know him too well, he'll ne'er be *felo de se* that way; but he may go and choose a guardian of his own head and so be *felo de ses biens*: for he has not yet chosen one.

FREEMAN. (*aside*) Say you so? And he shan't want one.

WIDOW. But, now I think on't, 'tis you, sir, have put this cheat upon me; for there is a saying, 'Take hold of a maid by her smock and a widow by her writings and they cannot get from you.' But I'll play fast and loose with you yet, if there be law; and my minor and writings are not forthcoming, I'll bring my action of detinue or trover. But first I'll try to find out this guardianless, graceless villain. Will you jog, major?

MANLY. If you have lost your evidence, I hope your causes cannot go on and I may be gone?

WIDOW. O no, stay but a making-water while, as one may say, and I'll be with you again.

Exeunt WIDOW *and* OLDFOX.

Manent MANLY, FREEMAN.

---

555 *keep him up*: keep him locked in.

555 s.d. *Exeunt*: *Exit* Q1. There is no entrance for the sailor in Q1 and I have deliberately not added one for him. He was presumably one of the crowd passing to and fro throughout this act.

559–60 *felo de se*: suicide, in which case the goods were forfeit to the state.

561 *felo de ses biens*: murderer of his goods.

570 *detinue or trover*: action to recover property lawfully obtained but unlawfully detained or action to recover the value of such property when used by the detainor.

FREEMAN. Well, sure I am the first man that ever began a love intrigue in Westminster Hall.

MANLY. No, sure, for the love to a widow generally begins here. And as the widow's cause goes against the heir or executors, the jointure rivals commence their suit to the widow.

FREEMAN. Well, but how, pray, have you passed your time here since I was forced to leave you alone? You have had a great deal of patience.

MANLY. Is this a place to be alone or have patience in? But I have had patience indeed, for I have drawn upon me, since I came, but three quarrels and two lawsuits.

FREEMAN. Nay, faith, you are too cursed to be let loose in the world; you should be tied up again in your sea-kennel called a ship. But how could you quarrel here?

MANLY. How could I refrain? A lawyer talked peremptorily and saucily to me and as good as gave me the lie.

FREEMAN. They do it so often to one another at the bar that they make no bones on't elsewhere.

MANLY. However, I gave him a cuff on the ear; whereupon he jogs two men, whose backs were turned to us, for they were reading at a bookseller's, to witness I struck him, sitting the courts, which office they so readily promised that I called 'em rascals and knights of the post. One of 'em presently calls two other absent witnesses who were coming towards us at a distance, whilst the other with a whisper desires to know my name that he might have satisfaction by way of challenge as t'other by way of writ; but if it were not rather to direct his brother's writ than his own challenge. There you see is one of my quarrels and two of my lawsuits.

FREEMAN. So – and the other two?

MANLY. For advising a poet to leave off writing and turn lawyer because he is dull and impudent and says or writes nothing now but by precedent.

FREEMAN. And the third quarrel?

MANLY. For giving more sincere advice to a handsome, well-dressed young fellow (who asked it too) not to marry a wench that he loved and I had lain with.

FREEMAN. Nay, if you will be giving your sincere advice to lovers and poets you will not fail of quarrels.

MANLY. Or if I stay in this place, for I see more quarrels crowding upon me. Let's be gone and avoid 'em.

Enter NOVEL, *at a distance, coming towards them.*

A plague on him, that sneer is ominous to us; he is coming upon us and we shall not be rid of him.

NOVEL. Dear bully, don't look so grum upon me; you told me just now you had forgiven me a little harmless raillery upon wooden legs last night.

MANLY. Yes, yes, pray be gone. I am talking of business.

NOVEL. Can't I hear it? I love thee and will be faithful and always –

MANLY. Impertinent! 'Tis business that concerns Freeman only.

NOVEL. Well, I love Freeman too and would not divulge his secret. Prithee speak, prithee, I must –

MANLY. Prithee, let me be rid of thee. I must be rid of thee.

NOVEL. Faith, thou canst hardly, I love thee so. Come, I must know the business.

MANLY. (*aside*) So, I have it now. – Why, if you needs will know it, he has a quarrel and his adversary bids him bring two friends with him. Now, I am one and we are thinking who we shall have for a third.

Several crossing the stage.

NOVEL. A pox, there goes a fellow owes me an hundred pound and goes out of town tomorrow. I'll speak with him and come to you presently. *Exit* NOVEL.

MANLY. No but you won't.

FREEMAN. You are dextrously rid of him.

Enter OLDFOX.

MANLY. To what purpose, since here comes another as impertinent? I know by his grin he is bound hither.

OLDFOX. Your servant, worthy, noble captain. Well, I have left the widow because she carried me from your

---

625 *grum*: sullen.

company, for, faith, captain, I must needs tell thee thou art the only officer in England who was not an Edgehill officer that I care for.

MANLY. I'm sorry for't.

OLDFOX. Why, wouldst thou have me love them?

MANLY. Anybody rather than me.

OLDFOX. What, you are modest, I see! Therefore too I love thee.

MANLY. No, I am not modest but love to brag myself and can't patiently hear you fight over the last civil war; therefore go look out the fellow I saw just now here, that walks with his stockings and his sword out at heels, and let him tell you the history of that scar on his cheek, to give you occasion to show yours, got in the field at Bloomsbury, not that of Edgehill. Go to him, poor fellow. He is fasting and has not yet the happiness this morning to stink of brandy and tobacco; go, give him some to hear you. I am busy.

OLDFOX. Well, ygad, I love thee now, boy, for thy surliness. Thou art no tame captain, I see, that will suffer –

MANLY. An old fox.

OLDFOX. All that shan't make me angry. I consider thou art peevish and fretting at some ill success at law. Prithee tell me what ill luck you have met with here.

MANLY. You.

OLDFOX. Do I look like the picture of ill luck? Gadsnouns, I love thee more and more; and shall I tell thee what made me love thee first?

MANLY. Do, that I may be rid of that damned quality and thee.

OLDFOX. 'Twas thy wearing that broad sword there.

MANLY. Here, Freeman, let's change. I'll never wear it more.

OLDFOX. How! You won't sure. Prithee don't look like

---

654 *Edgehill*: the first major battle of the Civil War, October 1642; it seems from line 699 that Oldfox was for Parliament, not the King.

666 *Bloomsbury*: probably the fields behind Southampton House in London, popular for duels.

678–9 *Gadsnouns*: by God's wounds.

one of our holiday captains nowadays, with a bodkin by your side, your Martinet rogues.

MANLY. (*aside*) O, then there's hopes. – What, d'ye find faults with Martinet? Let me tell you, sir, 'tis the best exercise in the world, the most ready, most easy, most graceful exercise that ever was used and the most –

OLDFOX. Nay, nay, sir, no more, sir, your servant. If you praise Martinet once, I have done with you, sir. Martinet! Martinet! *Exit* OLDFOX.

FREEMAN. Nay, you have made him leave you as willingly as ever he did an enemy, for he was truly for the king and parliament: for the parliament in their list and for the king in cheating 'em of their pay and never hurting the king's party in the field.

Enter a LAWYER *towards them.*

MANLY. A pox! This way; here's a lawyer I know threatening us with another greeting.

LAWYER. Sir, sir, your very servant. I was afraid you had forgotten me.

MANLY. I was not afraid you had forgotten me.

LAWYER. No, sir, we lawyers have pretty good memories.

MANLY. You ought to have, by your wits.

LAWYER. O, you are a merry gentleman, sir. I remember you were merry when I was last in your company.

MANLY. I was never merry in your company, Mr Lawyer, sure.

LAWYER. Why, I'm sure you joked upon me and shammed me all night long.

MANLY. Shammed! Prithee, what barbarous law-term is that?

LAWYER. Shamming! Why, don't you know that? 'Tis all our way of wit, sir.

MANLY. I am glad I do not know it then. Shamming! What does he mean by't, Freeman?

FREEMAN. Shamming is telling you an insipid, dull lie, with a dull face, which the sly wag the author only

---

688 *Martinet*: the system of drill developed by Lt.-Col. Jean Martinet and an integral part of the modernisation of the French army in the 1660s.

laughs at himself, and making himself believe 'tis a good jest, puts the sham only upon himself.

MANLY. So, your lawyer's jest, I find, like his practice, has more knavery than wit in't. I should make the worst shammer in England. I must always deal ingeniously, as I will with you, Mr Lawyer, and advise you to be seen rather with attornies and solicitors then such fellows as I am; they will credit your practice more.

LAWYER. No, sir, your company's an honour to me.

MANLY. No, faith, go this way, there goes an attorney; leave me for him. Let it be never said a lawyer's civility did him hurt.

LAWYER. No, worthy, honoured sir, I'll not leave you for any attorney, sure.

MANLY. Unless he had a fee in his hand.

LAWYER. Have you any business here, sir? Try me. I'd serve you sooner than any attorney breathing.

MANLY. Business! (*Aside*) So, I have thought of a sure way. – Yes, faith, I have a little business.

LAWYER. Have you so, sir? In what court, sir? What is't, sir? Tell me but how I may serve you and I'll do't, sir, and take it for as great an honour –

MANLY. Faith, 'tis for a poor orphan of a sea-officer of mine that has no money; but if it could be followed *in forma pauperis*, and when the legacy's recovered –

LAWYER. *Forma pauperis*, sir!

MANLY. Ay, sir.

Several crossing the stage.

LAWYER. Mr Bumblecase, Mr Bumblecase, a word with you. – Sir, I beg your pardon at present, I have a little business –

MANLY. Which is not *in forma pauperis*.

Exit LAWYER.

FREEMAN. So, you have now found a way to be rid of people without quarrelling.

Enter ALDERMAN.

---

729 *ingeniously*: ingenuously.

749 *in forma pauperis*: free of court costs and legal fees, for a pauper.

MANLY. But here's a city rogue will stick as hard upon us as if I owed him money.

ALDERMAN. Captain, noble sir, I am yours heartily, d'ye see. Why should you avoid your old friends?

MANLY. And why should you follow me? I owe you nothing.

ALDERMAN. Out of my hearty respects to you, for there is not a man in England –

MANLY. Thou wouldst save from hanging with the expense of a shilling only.

ALDERMAN. Nay, nay, but captain, you are like enough to tell me –

MANLY. Truth, which you won't care to hear; therefore you had better go talk with somebody else.

ALDERMAN. No, I know nobody can inform me better of some young wit or spendthrift that has a good dipped seat and estate in Middlesex, Hertfordshire, Essex or Kent – any of these would serve my turn. Now, if you knew of such an one and would but help –

MANLY. You to finish his ruin.

ALDERMAN. I'faith, you should have a snip –

MANLY. Of your nose. You thirty in the hundred rascal, would you make me your squire setter, your bawd for manors? (*Takes him by the nose*)

ALDERMAN. Oh!

FREEMAN. Hold or here will be your third lawsuit.

ALDERMAN. Gad's precious, you hectoring person you, are you wild? I meant you no hurt, sir. I begin to think, as things go, land security best and have, for a convenient mortgage, some ten, fifteen or twenty thousand pound by me.

MANLY. Then go lay it out upon an hospital and take a mortgage of heaven according to your city custom, for you think by laying out a little money to hook in that too hereafter. Do, I say, and keep the poor you've made by taking forfeitures that heaven may not take yours.

---

774 *dipped seat*: mortgaged country estate.
778 *snip*: share.
779 *thirty in the hundred*: charging 30% interest on loans; the highest leval rate was 6%.
780 *setter*: pimp.

ALDERMAN. No, to keep the cripples you make this war; this war spoils our trade.

MANLY. Damn your trade; 'tis the better for't.

ALDERMAN. What, will you speak against our trade?

MANLY. And dare you speak against the war, our trade?

ALDERMAN. (*aside*) Well, he may be a convoy of ships I am concerned in. – Come, captain, I will have a fair correspondency with you, say what you will.

MANLY. Then prithee be gone.

ALDERMAN. No, faith, prithee, captain, let's go drink a dish of laced coffee and talk of the times. Come, I'll treat you. Nay, you shall go, for I have no business here.

MANLY. But I have.

ALDERMAN. To pick up a man to give thee a dinner? Come, I'll do thy business for thee.

MANLY. Faith, now I think on't, so you may, as well as any man, for 'tis to pick up a man to be bound with me to one who expects city security, for –

ALDERMAN. Nay, then your servant, captain. Business must be done.

MANLY. Ay, if it can, but hark you, alderman, without you –

ALDERMAN. Business, sir, I say, must be done, and there's an officer of the Treasury I have an affair with –

Several crossing the stage. Exit ALDERMAN.

MANLY. You see now what the mighty friendship of the world is, what all ceremony, embraces and plentiful professions come to. You are no more to believe a professing friend than a threatening enemy and, as no man hurts you that tells you he'll do you a mischief, no man, you see, is your servant who says he is so. Why the devil, then, should a man be troubled with the flattery of knaves, if he be not a fool or cully, or with the fondness of fools, if he be not a knave or cheat?

FREEMAN. Only for his pleasure, for there is some in laughing at fools and disappointing knaves.

MANLY. That's a pleasure, I think, would cost you too dear, as well as marrying your widow to disappoint

806 *laced*: with brandy.

her; but, for my part, I have no pleasure by 'em, but in despising 'em, wheresoe'er I meet 'em, and then the pleasure of hoping so to be rid of 'em. But now my comfort is, I am not worth a shilling in the world, which all the world shall know; and then I'm sure I shall have none of 'em come near me.

FREEMAN. A very pretty comfort, which I think you pay too dear for. But is the twenty pound gone since the morning?

MANLY. To my boat's crew. Would you have the poor, honest, brave fellows want?

FREEMAN. Rather than you or I.

MANLY. Why, art thou without money? Thou who art a friend to everybody?

FREEMAN. I ventured my last stake upon the squire, to nick him of his mother and cannot help you to a dinner, unless you will go dine with my lord –

MANLY. No, no, the ordinary is too dear for me, where flattery must pay for my dinner; I am no herald, or poet.

FREEMAN. We'll go then to the bishop's –

MANLY. There you must flatter the old philosophy. I cannot renounce my reason for a dinner.

FREEMAN. Why, then let's go to your alderman's.

MANLY. Hang him, rogue! That were not to dine, for he makes you drunk with lees of sack before dinner to take away your stomach and there you must call usury and extortion, God's blessings or the honest turning of the penny; hear him brag of the leather breeches in which he trotted first to town, and make a greater noise with his money in his parlour than his cashiers do in his counting-house, without hopes of borrowing a shilling.

FREEMAN. Ay, a pox on't, 'tis like dining with the great gamesters and, when they fall to their common dessert, see the heaps of gold drawn on all hands, without going to twelve. Let us go to my Lady Goodly's.

---

850 *nick*: cheat, defraud.
852 *ordinary*: eating-house.
860 *lees of sack*: dregs of sherry.
871 *without going to twelve*: gambler's slang whose meaning is lost; here it seems to mean 'without joining the game'.

MANLY. There to flatter her looks you must mistake her grandchildren for her own, praise her cook that she may rail at him and feed her dogs, not yourself.

FREEMAN. What d'ye think of eating with your lawyer then?

MANLY. Eat with him! Damn him, to hear him employ his barbarous eloquence in a reading upon the two and thirty good bits in a shoulder of veal and be forced yourself to praise the cold bribe pie that stinks and drink law-French wine as rough and harsh as his law-French. A pox on him, I'd rather dine in the Temple Rounds or Walks, with the knights without noses, or the knights of the post, who are honester fellows and better company. But let us home and try our fortune, for I'll stay no longer here for your damned widow.

FREEMAN. Well, let us go home then, for I must go for my damned widow and look after my new damned charge. Three or four hundred year ago a man might have dined in this hall.

MANLY. But now, the lawyer only here is fed
And, bullylike, by quarrels gets his bread.

Exeunt.

ACT IV

SCENE I

Manly's lodging.

Enter MANLY *and* FIDELIA.

MANLY. Well, there's success in thy face. Hast thou prevailed? Say.

879–80 *two and thirty good bits*: a garbled version of the saying: there are thirty bits but only two good ones.

889–90 *knights without noses*: decayed statues of the Knights Templar in the Round Church belonging to the Middle and Inner Temples, two of the Inns of Court.

891–2 Westminster Hall had been a royal banqueting-hall.

FIDELIA. As I could wish, sir.

MANLY. So, I told thee what thou wert fit for and thou wouldst not believe me. Come, thank me for bringing thee acquainted with thy genius. Well, thou hast mollified her heart for me?

FIDELIA. No, sir, not so, but what's better.

MANLY. How? What's better!

FIDELIA. I shall harden your heart against her.

MANLY. Have a care, sir. My heart is too much in earnest to be fooled with and my desire at heighth and needs no delays to incite it. What, you are too good a pimp already and know how to endear pleasure by withholding it? But leave off your page's bawdyhouse tricks, sir, and tell me; will she be kind?

FIDELIA. Kinder than you could wish, sir.

MANLY. So then. Well, prithee what said she?

FIDELIA. She said –

MANLY. What? Thou'rt so tedious. Speak comfort to me. What?

FIDELIA. That, of all things, you were her aversion.

MANLY. How?

FIDELIA. That she would sooner take a bedfellow out of an hospital and diseases into her arms than you.

MANLY. What?

FIDELIA. That she would rather trust her honour with a dissolute, debauched hector, nay worse, with a finical, baffled coward, all over loathsome with affectation of the fine gentleman.

MANLY. What's all this you say?

FIDELIA. Nay, that my offers of your love to her were more offensive than when parents woo their virgin daughters to the enjoyment of riches only and that you were in all circumstances as nauseous to her as a husband on compulsion.

MANLY. Hold, I understand you not.

FIDELIA. (*aside*) So, 'twill work, I see.

MANLY. Did not you tell me –

FIDELIA. She called you ten thousand ruffians.

MANLY. Hold, I say.

FIDELIA. Brutes –

MANLY. Hold.

---

29 *baffled*: disgraced.

FIDELIA. Sea-monsters –

MANLY. Damn your intelligence. Hear me a little now.

FIDELIA. Nay, surly coward she called you too.

MANLY. Won't you hold yet? Hold, or –

FIDELIA. Nay, sir, pardon me. I could not but tell you she had the baseness, the injustice, to call you coward, sir, coward, coward, sir.

MANLY. Not yet?

FIDELIA. I've done. Coward, sir.

MANLY. Did not you say she was kinder than I could wish her?

FIDELIA. Yes sir.

MANLY. How then? – O – I understand you now. At first she appeared in rage and disdain, the truest sign of a coming woman, but at last you prevailed, it seems; did you not?

FIDELIA. Yes, sir.

MANLY. So then, let's know that only. Come, prithee, without delays. I'll kiss thee for that news beforehand.

FIDELIA. (*aside*) So, the kiss, I'm sure, is welcome to me, whatsoe'er the news will be to you.

MANLY. Come, speak, my dear volunteer.

FIDELIA. (*aside*) How welcome were that kind word too, if it were not for another woman's sake!

MANLY. What, won't you speak? You prevailed for me at last, you say?

FIDELIA. No, sir.

MANLY. No more of your fooling, sir; it will not agree with my impatience or temper.

FIDELIA. Then, not to fool you, sir, I spoke to her for you but prevailed for myself. She would not hear me when I spoke in your behalf but bid me say what I would in my own – though she gave me no occasion, she was so coming – and so was kinder, sir, than you could wish, which I was only afraid to let you know without some warning.

MANLY. How's this? Young man, you are of a lying age, but I must hear you out, and if –

FIDELIA. I would not abuse you and cannot wrong her by any report of her, she is so wicked.

---

77 *coming*: eager, willing.

MANLY. How, wicked! Had she the impudence, at the second sight of you only –

FIDELIA. Impudence, sir! O, she has impudence enough to put a court out of countenance and debauch a stews.

MANLY. Why, what said she?

FIDELIA. Her tongue, I confess, was silent, but her speaking eyes gloated such things, more immodest and lascivious than ravishers can act or women under a confinement think.

MANLY. I know there are whose eyes reflect more obscenity than the glasses in alcoves, but there are others too who use a little art with their looks to make 'em seem more beautiful, not more loving, which vain young fellows like you are apt to interpret in their own favour and to the lady's wrong.

FIDELIA. Seldom, sir. Pray have you a care of gloating eyes, for he that loves to gaze upon 'em will find at last a thousand fools and cuckolds in 'em, instead of cupids.

MANLY. Very well, sir. But, what, you had only eye-kindness from Olivia?

FIDELIA. I tell you again, sir, no woman sticks there. Eye-promises of love they only keep; nay, they are contracts which make you sure of 'em. In short, sir, she, seeing me with shame and amazement dumb, unactive and resistless, threw her twisting arms about my neck and smothered me with a thousand tasteless kisses – believe me, sir, they were so to me.

MANLY. Why did you not avoid 'em then?

FIDELIA. I fenced with her eager arms as you did with the grapples of the enemy's fireship and nothing but cutting 'em off could have freed me.

MANLY. Damned, damned woman, that could be so false and infamous! And damned, damned heart of mine, that cannot yet be false, though so infamous! What easy, tame, suffering, trampled things does that little god of talking cowards make of us! But –

FIDELIA. (*aside*) So! It works I find as I expected.

---

88 *stews*: brothel.

115 *fireship*: Fidelia puns on the meaning 'whore'.

MANLY. But she was false to me before. She told me so herself, and yet I could not quite believe it. But she was, so that her second falseness is a favour to me, not an injury, in revenging me upon the man that wronged me first of her love. Her love! – A whore's, a witch's love! – But, what, did she not kiss well, sir? I'm sure I thought her lips – but I must not think of 'em more – but yet they are such I could still kiss – grow to – and then tear off with my teeth, grind 'em into mammocks and spit 'em into her cuckold's face.

FIDELIA. (*aside*) Poor man, how uneasy he is! I have hardly the heart to give him so much pain, though withal I give him a cure and to myself new life.

MANLY. But, what, her kisses sure could not but warm you into desire at last or a compliance with hers at least?

FIDELIA. Nay, more, I confess –

MANLY. What more? Speak.

FIDELIA. All you could fear had passed between us, if I could have been made to wrong you, sir, in that nature.

MANLY. Could have been made! You lie, you did.

FIDELIA. Indeed, sir, 'twas impossible for me; besides, we were interrupted by a visit. But, I confess, she would not let me stir till I promised to return to her again within this hour, as soon as it should be dark, by which time she would dispose of her visit and her servants and herself for my reception, which I was fain to promise to get from her.

MANLY. Ha!

FIDELIA. But if ever I go near her again, may you, sir, think me as false to you as she is, hate and renounce me, as you ought to do her and I hope will do now.

MANLY. Well, but now I think on't, you shall keep your word with your lady. What, a young fellow and fail the first, nay, so tempting an assignation!

FIDELIA. How, sir?

MANLY. I say you shall go to her when 'tis dark and shall not disappoint her.

FIDELIA. I, sir! I should disappoint her more by going, for –

---

132 *mammocks*: shreds.

MANLY. How so?

FIDELIA. Her impudence and injustice to you will make me disappoint her love, loathe her.

MANLY. Come, you have my leave and, if you disgust her, I'll go with you and act love whilst you shall talk it only.

FIDELIA. You, sir! Nay, then I'll never go near her. You act love, sir! You must but act it indeed after all I have said to you. Think of your honour, sir. Love –

MANLY. Well, call it revenge and that is honourable. I'll be revenged on her and thou shalt be my second.

FIDELIA. Not in a base action, sir, when you are your own enemy. O, go not near her, sir, for heaven's sake, for your own, think not of it.

MANLY. How concerned you are! I thought I should catch you. What, you are my rival at last and are in love with her yourself and have spoken ill of her out of your love to her, not me, and therefore would not have me go to her!

FIDELIA. Heaven witness for me, 'tis because I love you only I would not have you go to her.

MANLY. Come, come, the more I think on't, the more I'm satisfied you do love her. Those kisses, young man, I knew were irresistible; 'tis certain.

FIDELIA. There is nothing certain in the world, sir, but my truth and your courage.

MANLY. Your servant, sir. Besides, false and ungrateful as she has been to me, and though I may believe her hatred to me as great as you report it, yet I cannot think you are so soon and at that rate beloved by her, though you may endeavour it.

FIDELIA. Nay, if that be all and you doubt it still, sir, I will conduct you to her and, unseen, your ears shall judge of her falseness and my truth to you, if that will satisfy you.

MANLY. Yes, there is some satisfaction in being quite out of doubt: because 'tis that alone withholds us from the pleasure of revenge.

FIDELIA. Revenge! What revenge can you have, sir? Disdain is best revenged by scorn, and faithless love

---

166 *disgust*: dislike.

by loving another and making her happy with the other's losings, which, if I might advise –

Enter FREEMAN.

MANLY. Not a word more.

FREEMAN. What, are you talking of love yet, captain? I thought you had done with't.

MANLY. Why, what did you hear me say?

FREEMAN. Something imperfectly of love, I think.

MANLY. I was only wondering why fools, rascals and desertless wretches should still have the better of men of merit with all women, as much as with their own common mistress, Fortune!

FREEMAN. Because most women, like Fortune, are blind, seem to do all things in jest and take pleasure in extravagant actions. Their love deserves neither thanks or blame, for they cannot help it; 'tis all sympathy. Therefore the noisy, the finical, the talkative, the cowardly and effeminate have the better of the brave, the reasonable and man of honour, for they have no more reason in their love or kindness than Fortune herself.

MANLY. Yes, they have their reason. First, honour in a man they fear too much to love and sense in a lover upbraids their want of it and they hate anything that disturbs their admiration of themselves; but they are of that vain number who had rather show their false generosity in giving away profusely to worthless flatterers than in paying just debts. And, in short, all women, like Fortune, as you say, and rewards, are lost by too much meriting.

FIDELIA. All women, sir! Sure, there are some who have no other quarrel to a lover's merit but that it begets their despair of him.

MANLY. Thou art young enough to be credulous, but we –

Enter FIRST SAILOR.

FIRST SAILOR. Here are now below the scolding, daggled gentlewoman and that Major Old – old – Fop, I think you call him.

FREEMAN. Oldfox. Prithee, bid 'em come up, with your leave, captain, for now I can talk with her upon the square, if I shall not disturb you.

MANLY. No, for I'll be gone. Come, volunteer.

FREEMAN. Nay, pray stay. The scene between us will not be so tedious to you as you think. Besides, you shall see how I have rigged my squire out with the remains of my shipwracked wardrobe. He is under your sea *valet de chambre*'s hands and by this time dressed and will be worth your seeing. Stay and I'll fetch my fool.

MANLY. No, you know I cannot easily laugh; besides, my volunteer and I have business abroad.

Exeunt MANLY, FIDELIA, *on one side,* FREEMAN *on t'other.*

Enter MAJOR OLDFOX *and* WIDOW BLACKACRE.

WIDOW. What, nobody here! Did not the fellow say he was within?

OLDFOX. Yes, lady, and he may be perhaps a little busy at present, but if you think the time long till he comes, (*unfolding papers*) I'll read you here some of the fruits of my leisure, the overflowings of my fancy and pen. (*Aside*) To value me right, she must know my parts. – Come –

WIDOW. No, no, I have reading work enough of my own in my bag, I thank you.

OLDFOX. Ay, law, madam, but here is a poem in blank verse which I think a handsome declaration of one's passion.

WIDOW. O! If you talk of declarations, I'll show you one of the prettiest penned things which I mended too myself you must know.

OLDFOX. Nay, lady, if you have used yourself so much to the reading of harsh law that you hate smooth poetry, here is a character for you of –

WIDOW. A character! Nay, then I'll show you my bill in Chancery here that gives you such a character of my adversary, makes him as black –

OLDFOX. Pshaw, away, away, lady. But if you think the character too long, here is an epigram not above

---

271 *character*: a short, often satirical prose sketch of a person or type, developed from those by Theophrastus.

twenty lines, upon a cruel lady who decreed her servant should hang himself to demonstrate his passion.

WIDOW. Decreed! If you talk of decreeing, I have such a decree here, drawn by the finest clerk –

OLDFOX. O lady, lady, all interruption and no sense between us, as if we were lawyers at the bar! But I had forgot, Apollo and Littleton never lodge in a head together. If you hate verses, I'll give you a cast of my politics in prose: 'tis a letter to a friend in the country, which is now the way of all such sober, solid persons as myself, when they have a mind to publish their disgust to the times, though perhaps, between you and I, they have no friend in the country. And, sure, a politic, serious person may as well have a feigned friend in the country to write to as well as an idle poet a feigned mistress to write to. And so here is my letter to a friend, or no friend, in the country concerning the late conjuncture of affairs in relation to coffeehouses, or the Coffeeman's Case.

WIDOW. Nay, if your letter have a case in't, 'tis something, but first I'll read you a letter of mine to a friend in the country, called a letter of attorney.

Enter to them FREEMAN *and* JERRY BLACKACRE *in a gaudy suit and red breeches of Freeman's.*

OLDFOX. (*aside*) What, interruption still? O the plague of interruption, worse to an author than the plague of critics!

WIDOW. What's this I see, Jerry Blackacre, my minor, in red breeches! What, hast thou left the modest, seemly garb of gown and cap for this? And have I lost all my good Inns of Chancery breeding upon thee then? And thou wilt go a-breeding thyself, from our Inn of Chancery and Westminster Hall, at coffeehouses and ordinaries, playhouses, tennis courts and bawdyhouses.

---

283 *Apollo and Littleton*: art and the law; Sir Thomas Littleton (1422–81) was a jurist famous for his treatise on tenure.

294–5 *the late . . . coffeehouses*: in an attempt to suppress seditious talk, a royal proclamation, never enforced, announced the closure of the coffeehouses in January 1676.

298 *letter of attorney*: a document empowering a person to act on another's behalf.

JERRY. Ay, ay, what then? Perhaps I will. But what's that to you? Here's my guardian and tutor now, forsooth, that I am out of your huckster's hands.

WIDOW. How? Thou hast not chosen him for thy guardian yet?

JERRY. No, but he has chosen me for his charge and that's all one; and I'll do anything he'll have me and go all the world over with him, to ordinaries and bawdyhouses, or anywhere else.

WIDOW. To ordinaries and bawdyhouses! Have a care, minor. Thou wilt infeeble there thy estate and body. Do not go to ordinaries and bawdyhouses, good Jerry.

JERRY. Why, how come you to know any ill by bawdyhouses? You never had any hurt by 'em, had you, forsooth? Pray hold yourself contented. If I do go where money and wenches are to be had, you may thank yourself, for you used me so unnaturally, you would never let me have a penny to go abroad with nor so much as come near the garret where your maidens lay; nay, you would not so much as let me play at hotcockles with 'em nor have any recreation with 'em, though one should have kissed you behind, you were so unnatural a mother, so you were.

FREEMAN. Ay, a very unnatural mother, faith, squire.

WIDOW. But Jerry, consider thou art yet but a minor. However, if thou wilt go home with me again and be a good child, thou shalt see –

FREEMAN. Madam, I must have a better care of my heir under age than so. I would sooner trust him alone with a stale waiting-woman and a parson than with his widow-mother and her lover or lawyer.

WIDOW. Why, thou villain, part mother and minor! Rob me of my child and my writings! But thou shalt find there's law, and as in the case of ravishment of guard – Westminster the second.

---

311 *huckster's*: mercenary.

330 *hotcockles*: (*a*) an innocent game of blindfolding (*b*) a less innocent game of sex-play.

343–4 *ravishment . . . the second*: the statute known as Westminster 2, 1285, includes sections covering the abduction of wards and minors.

OLDFOX. Young gentleman, squire, pray be ruled by your mother and your friends.

JERRY. Yes, I'll be ruled by my friends, therefore not by my mother, so I won't. I'll choose him for my guardian till I am of age, nay, maybe for as long as I live.

WIDOW. Wilt thou so, thou wretch? And when thou'rt of age, thou wilt sign, seal and deliver too, wilt thou?

JERRY. Yes, marry will I, if you go there too.

WIDOW. O do not squeeze wax, son. Rather go to ordinaries and bawdyhouses than squeeze wax. If thou dost that, farewell the goodly manor of Blackacre with all its woods, underwoods and appurtenances whatever. Oh, Oh! (*Weeps*)

FREEMAN. Come, madam, in short, you see I am resolved to have a share in the estate, yours or your son's: if I cannot get you, I'll keep him, who is less coy you find; but if you would have your son again, you must take me too. Peace or war? Love or law? You see my hostage is in my hand. I'm in possession.

WIDOW. Nay, if one of us must be ruined, e'en let it be him. By my body, a good one! Did you ever know yet a widow marry or not marry for the sake of her child? I'd have you to know, sir, I shall be hard enough for you both yet without marrying you, if Jerry won't be ruled by me. What say you, booby, will you be ruled? Speak.

JERRY. Let one alone, can't you?

WIDOW. Wilt thou choose him for guardian whom I refuse for husband?

JERRY. Ay, to choose, I thank you.

WIDOW. And are all my hopes frustrated? Shall I never hear thee put cases again to John the butler or our vicar? Never see thee amble the circuit with the judges and hear thee in our town hall louder than the crier?

JERRY. No, for I have taken my leave of lawyering and pettifogging.

WIDOW. Pettifogging! Thou profane villain, hast thou so? Pettifogging! – Then you shall take your leave of me and your estate too. Thou shalt be an alien to me and it forever. Pettifogging!

JERRY. O, but if you go there too, mother, we have the

deeds and settlements, I thank you. Would you cheat me of my estate, ifac?

WIDOW. No, no, I will not cheat your little brother Bob, for thou wert not born in wedlock.

FREEMAN. How's that?

JERRY. How? What quirk has she got in her head now?

WIDOW. I say thou canst not, shalt not inherit the Blackacres' estate.

JERRY. Why? Why, forsooth? What d'ye mean, if you go there too?

WIDOW. Thou art but my base child and according to the law canst not inherit it; nay, thou art not so much as bastard eigne.

JERRY. What, what? Am I then the son of a whore, mother?

WIDOW. The law says –

FREEMAN. Madam, we know what the law says, but have a care what you say. Do not let your passion to ruin your son ruin your reputation.

WIDOW. Hang reputation, sir. Am not I a widow? Have no husband nor intend to have any? Nor would you, I suppose, now have me for a wife. So I think now I'm revenged on my son and you, without marrying, as I told you.

FREEMAN. But consider, madam.

JERRY. What, have you no shame left in you, mother?

WIDOW. (*aside to* OLDFOX) Wonder not at it, major. 'Tis often the poor pressed widow's case, to give up her honour to save her jointure and seem to be a light woman rather than marry, as some young men, they say, pretend to have the filthy disease and lose their credit with most women to avoid the importunities of some.

FREEMAN. But one word with you, madam.

WIDOW. No, no, sir. Come, major, let us make haste now to the Prerogative Court.

OLDFOX. But, lady, if what you say be true, will you stigmatise your reputation on record? And, if it be not true, how will you prove it?

---

400 *bastard eigne*: the elder of two bastards (eigne = Fr. *aîné*).
423 *Prerogative Court*: the archbishop's court for probate of wills and cases caused by wills.

WIDOW. Pshaw! I can prove anything and, for my reputation, know, major, a wise woman will no more value her reputation in disinheriting a rebellious son of a good estate than she would in getting him to inherit an estate.

Exeunt WIDOW *and* OLDFOX.

FREEMAN. Madam – We must not let her go so, squire.

JERRY. Nay, the devil can't stop her though if she has a mind to't. But come, bully guardian, we'll go and advise with three attornies, two proctors, two solicitors and a shrewd man of Whitefriars, neither attorney, proctor or solicitor but as pure a pimp to the law as any of 'em; and, sure, all they will be hard enough for her, for I fear, bully guardian, you are too good a joker to have any law in your head.

FREEMAN. Thou'rt in the right on't, squire; I understand no law, especially that against bastards, since I'm sure the custom is against that law, and more people get estates by being so than lose 'em.

Exeunt.

SCENE II

The scene changes to Olivia's lodgings.

Enter LORD PLAUSIBLE *and* BOY *with a candle.*

LORD PLAUSIBLE. Little gentleman, your most obedient, faithful, humble servant; where, I beseech you, is that divine person, your noble lady?

BOY. Gone out, my lord, but commanded me to give you this letter. (*Gives him a letter*)

Enter to him NOVEL.

LORD PLAUSIBLE. (*aside*) Which he must not observe. (*Puts it up*)

NOVEL. Hey, boy, where is thy lady?

---

436 *Whitefriars*: an area of the East End which was a sanctuary for debtors and other criminals.

6 s.d. *Puts it up*: set as part of speech Q1.

BOY. Gone out, sir, but I must beg a word with you.

Gives him a letter and exit.

NOVEL. For me? So. (*Puts up the letter*) Servant, servant, my lord. You see the lady knew of your coming, for she is gone out.

LORD PLAUSIBLE. Sir, I humbly beseech you not to censure the lady's good breeding. She has reason to use more liberty with me than with any other man.

NOVEL. How, viscount, how?

LORD PLAUSIBLE. Nay, I humbly beseech you, be not in choler. Where there is most love there may be most freedom.

NOVEL. Nay, then 'tis time to come to an éclaircissement with you and to tell you you must think no more of this lady's love.

LORD PLAUSIBLE. Why, under correction, dear sir?

NOVEL. There are reasons, reasons, viscount.

LORD PLAUSIBLE. What, I beseech you, noble sir?

NOVEL. Prithee, prithee, be not impertinent, my lord. Some of you lords are such conceited, well-assured, impertinent rogues.

LORD PLAUSIBLE. And you noble wits are so full of shamming and drolling one knows not where to have you, seriously.

NOVEL. Well, you shall find me in bed with this lady one of these days.

LORD PLAUSIBLE. Nay, I beseech you, spare the lady's honour, for hers and mine will be all one shortly.

NOVEL. Prithee, my lord, be not an ass. Dost thou think to get her from me? I have had such encouragements –

LORD PLAUSIBLE. I have not been thought unworthy of 'em.

NOVEL. What, not like mine! Come to an éclaircissement, as I said.

LORD PLAUSIBLE. Why, seriously then, she has told me viscountess sounded prettily.

NOVEL. And me that Novel was a name she would sooner change hers for than for any title in England.

19–20 *éclaircissement*: clarification.

LORD PLAUSIBLE. She has commended the softness and respectfulness of my behaviour.

NOVEL. She has praised the briskness of my raillery of all things, man.

LORD PLAUSIBLE. The sleepiness of my eyes she liked.

NOVEL. Sleepiness! Dullness, dullness. But the fierceness of mine she adored.

LORD PLAUSIBLE. The brightness of my hair she liked.

NOVEL. The brightness! No, the greasiness, I warrant. But the blackness and lustre of mine she admires.

LORD PLAUSIBLE. The gentleness of my smile.

NOVEL. The subtlety of my leer.

LORD PLAUSIBLE. The clearness of my complexion.

NOVEL. The redness of my lips.

LORD PLAUSIBLE. The whiteness of my teeth.

NOVEL. My janty way of picking them.

LORD PLAUSIBLE. The sweetness of my breath.

NOVEL. Hah, ha! – Nay then she abused you, 'tis plain, for you know what Manly said; the sweetness of your pulvillio she might mean, but for your breath! Ha, ha, ha. Your breath is such, man, that nothing but tobacco can perfume, and your complexion nothing could mend but the smallpox.

LORD PLAUSIBLE. Well, sir, you may please to be merry, but, to put you out of all doubt, sir, she has received some jewels from me of value.

NOVEL. And presents from me, besides what I presented her jantily by way of ombre, of three or four hundred pound value, which, I'm sure, are the earnest pence for our love bargain.

LORD PLAUSIBLE. Nay then, sir, with your favour and to make an end of all your hopes, look you there, sir, she has writ to me. –

NOVEL. How! How! Well, well, and so she has to me: look you there. –

Deliver to each other their letters.

LORD PLAUSIBLE. What's here!

NOVEL. How's this? (*Reads out*)

My Dear Lord,

You'll excuse me for breaking my word with you since 'twas to oblige, not to offend you, for I am only

---

81 s.d. after line 79 Q1.

gone abroad but to disappoint Novel and meet you in the drawing-room, where I expect you with as much impatience as when I used to suffer Novel's visits, the most impertinent fop that ever affected the name of a wit, therefore not capable, I hope, to give you jealousy, for, for your sake alone, you saw, I renounced an old lover and will do all the world. Burn the letter but lay up the kindness of it in your heart, with your

Olivia

Very fine! But pray let's see mine.

LORD PLAUSIBLE. I understand it not but, sure, she cannot think so of me.

NOVEL. (*reads the other letter*) Humh! – Ha! – meet – for your sake – umh – quitted an old lover – world – burn – in your heart, with your

Olivia

Just the same, the names only altered.

LORD PLAUSIBLE. Surely there must be some mistake, or somebody has abused her, and us.

NOVEL. Yes, you are abused, no doubt on't, my lord, but I'll to Whitehall and see.

LORD PLAUSIBLE. And I, where I shall find you are abused.

NOVEL. Where, if it be so, for our comfort we cannot fail of meeting with fellow-sufferers enough, for, as Freeman said of another, she stands in the drawing-room like the glass, ready for all comers to set their gallantry by her, and, like the glass too, lets no man go from her unsatisfied with himself.

Exeunt ambo.

Enter OLIVIA *and* BOY.

OLIVIA. Both here and just gone?

BOY. Yes, madam.

OLIVIA. But are you sure neither saw you deliver the other a letter?

BOY. Yes, yes, madam, I am very sure.

OLIVIA. Go then to the Old Exchange, to Westminster, Holborn and all the other places I told you of; I

88 *drawing-room*: at the palace at Whitehall.

121–2 *Old Exchange . . . Holborn*: widely spread all over London.

shall not need you these two hours. Be gone and take the candle with you and be sure you leave word again below, I am gone out to all that ask.

BOY. Yes, madam. *Exit.*

OLIVIA. And my new lover will not ask I'm sure. He has his lesson and cannot miss me here, though in the dark, which I have purposely designed as a remedy against my blushing gallant's modesty, for young lovers like gamecocks are made bolder by being kept without light.

Enter her husband VERNISH *as from a journey.*

VERNISH. (*softly*) Where is she? Darkness everywhere!

OLIVIA. What, come before your time? My soul! My life! Your haste has augmented your kindness and let me thank you for it thus and thus – (*Embracing and kissing him*) And though, my soul, the little time since you left me has seemed an age to my impatience, sure it is yet but seven –

VERNISH. How! Who's that you expected after seven?

OLIVIA. [*aside*] Ha! My husband returned! And have I been throwing away so many kind kisses on my husband and wronged my lover already?

VERNISH. Speak, I say, who was't you expected after seven?

OLIVIA. (*aside*) What shall I say? – O – Why, 'tis but seven days, is it, dearest, since you went out of town? And I expected you not so soon.

VERNISH. No, sure, 'tis but five days since I left you.

OLIVIA. Pardon my impatience, dearest, I thought 'em seven at least.

VERNISH. Nay then –

OLIVIA. But, my life, you shall never stay half so long from me again, you shan't, indeed, by this kiss, you shan't.

VERNISH. No, no, but why alone in the dark?

OLIVIA. Blame not my melancholy in your absence – But, my soul, since you went, I have strange news to tell you: Manly is returned.

VERNISH. Manly returned! Fortune forbid.

OLIVIA. Met with the Dutch in the Channel, fought, sunk his ship and all he carried with him. He was here with me yesterday.

VERNISH. And did you own our marriage to him?

OLIVIA. I told him I was married, to put an end to his love and my trouble, but to whom is yet a secret kept from him and all the world. And I have used him so scurvily his great spirit will ne'er return to reason it farther with me. I have sent him to sea again, I warrant.

VERNISH. 'Twas bravely done. And sure he will now hate the shore more than ever after so great a disappointment. Be you sure only to keep awhile our great secret till he be gone. In the meantime I'll lead the easy, honest fool by the nose as I used to do and, whilst he stays, rail with him at thee and, when he's gone, laugh with thee at him. But have you his cabinet of jewels safe? Part not with a seed pearl to him to keep him from starving.

OLIVIA. Nor from hanging.

VERNISH. He cannot recover 'em and, I think, will scorn to beg 'em again.

OLIVIA. But, my life, have you taken the thousand guineas he left in my name out of the goldsmith's hands?

VERNISH. Ay, ay, they are removed to another goldsmith's.

OLIVIA. Ay but, my soul, you had best have a care he find not where the money is, for his present wants, as I'm informed, are such as will make him inquisitive enough.

VERNISH. You say true and he knows the man too, but I'll remove it tomorrow.

OLIVIA. Tomorrow! O do not stay till tomorrow. Go tonight, immediately.

VERNISH. Now I think on't, you advise well and I will go presently.

OLIVIA. Presently! Instantly! I will not let you stay a jot.

VERNISH. I will then, though I return not home till twelve.

OLIVIA. Nay, though not till morning with all my heart. Go, dearest, I am impatient till you are gone –

Thrusts him out.

So, I have at once now brought about those two grateful businesses which all prudent women do together, secured money and pleasure, and now all interruptions of the last are removed. Go husband

and come up friend, just the buckets in the well: the absence of one brings the other but I hope, like them too, they will not meet in the way, justle and clash together.

Enter FIDELIA, *and* MANLY *treading softly and staying behind at some distance.*

So, are you come? (But not the husband-bucket, I hope, again.) Who's there? My dearest? (*Softly*)

FIDELIA. My life –

OLIVIA. Right, right. Where are thy lips? Here, take the dumb and best welcomes, kisses and embraces; 'tis not a time for idle words. In a duel of love, as in others, parleying shows basely. Come, we are alone, and now the word is only satisfaction and defend not thyself.

MANLY. (*aside*) How's this? Wuh, she makes love like a devil in a play and, in this darkness, which conceals her angel's face, if I were apt to be afraid I should think her a devil.

OLIVIA. What, you traverse ground, young gentleman.

FIDELIA *avoiding her.*

FIDELIA. I take breath only.

MANLY. (*aside*) Good heavens! How was I deceived!

OLIVIA. Nay, you are a coward. What, are you afraid of the fierceness of my love?

FIDELIA. Yes, madam, lest its violence might presage its change and I must needs be afraid you would leave me quickly who could desert so brave a gentleman as Manly.

OLIVIA. O! Name not his name, for in a time of stolen joys, as this is, the filthy name of husband were not a more allaying sound.

MANLY. (*aside*) There's some comfort yet.

FIDELIA. But did you not love him?

OLIVIA. Never. How could you think it?

FIDELIA. Because he thought it, who is a man of that sense, nice discerning and diffidency that I should think it hard to deceive him.

OLIVIA. No, he that distrusts most the world trusts

---

225 *traverse ground*: move from side to side (fencing term).

most to himself and is but the more easily deceived because he thinks he can't be deceived. His cunning is like the coward's sword by which he is oftener worsted than defended.

FIDELIA. Yet, sure, you used no common art to deceive him.

OLIVIA. I knew he loved his own singular moroseness so well as to dote upon any copy of it; wherefore I feigned an hatred to the world too that he might love me in earnest. But if it had been hard to deceive him I'm sure 'twere much harder to love him. A dogged, ill-mannered –

FIDELIA. (*aside to* MANLY) D'ye hear her, sir? Pray hear her.

OLIVIA. Surly, untractable, snarling brute! He! A masty dog were as fit a thing to make a gallant of.

MANLY. (*aside*) Ay, a goat or monkey were fitter for thee.

FIDELIA. I must confess for my part, though my rival, I cannot but say he has a manly handsomeness in's face and mien.

OLIVIA. So has a Saracen in the sign.

FIDELIA. Is proper and well made.

OLIVIA. As a drayman.

FIDELIA. Has wit.

OLIVIA. He rails at all mankind.

FIDELIA. And undoubted courage.

OLIVIA. Like the hangman's, can murder a man when his hands are tied. He has cruelty indeed, which is no more courage than his railing is wit.

MANLY. (*aside*) Thus women, and men like women, are too hard for us when they think we do not hear 'em and reputation, like other mistresses, is never true to a man in his absence.

FIDELIA. He is –

OLIVIA. Prithee no more of him. I thought I had satisfied you enough before that he could never be a rival for you to apprehend; and you need not be more assured of my aversion to him but by the last testi-

---

258 *masty*: mastiff.

265 *Saracen in the sign*: the large and ugly face of a Saracen used on street signs.

mony of my love to you which I am ready to give you. Come, my soul, this way – (*Pulls* FIDELIA)

FIDELIA. But, madam, what could make you dissemble love to him, when 'twas so hard a thing for you, and flatter his love to you?

OLIVIA. That which makes all the world flatter and dissemble; 'twas his money – I had a real passion for that. Yet I loved not that so well as for it to take him, for as soon as I had his money I hastened his departure like a wife who, when she has made the most of a dying husband's breath, pulls away the pillow.

MANLY. [*aside*] Damned money! Its master's potent rival still and like a saucy pimp corrupts itself the mistress it procures for us.

OLIVIA. But I did not think with you, my life, to pass my time in talking. Come hither, come. Yet stay till I have locked a door in the other room that might chance to let us in some interruption, which reciting poets or losing gamesters fear not more than I at this time do. *Exit* OLIVIA.

FIDELIA. Well, I hope you are now satisfied, sir, and will be gone to think of your revenge.

MANLY. No, I am not satisfied and must stay to be revenged.

FIDELIA. How, sir? You'll use no violence to her, I hope, and forfeit your own life to take away hers? That were no revenge.

MANLY. No, no, you need not fear; my revenge shall only be upon her honour, not her life.

FIDELIA. How, sir? Her honour? O heavens! Consider, sir, she has no honour. D'ye call that revenge? Can you think of such a thing? But reflect, sir, how she hates and loathes you.

MANLY. Yes, so much she hates me that it would be a revenge sufficient to make her accessory to my pleasure and then let her know it.

FIDELIA. No, sir, no, to be revenged on her now were to disappoint her. Pray, sir, let us be gone. (*Pulls* MANLY)

MANLY. Hold off. What, you are my rival then and therefore you shall stay and keep the door for me whilst I go in for you. But when I'm gone, if you dare to stir off from this very board or breathe the least murmuring accent, I'll cut her throat first and if you love her you will not venture her life; nay, then I'll cut your throat too and I know you love your own life at least.

FIDELIA. But, sir, good sir.

MANLY. Not a word more, lest I begin my revenge on her by killing you.

FIDELIA. But are you sure 'tis revenge that makes you do this? How can it be?

MANLY. Whist.

FIDELIA. 'Tis a strange revenge indeed.

MANLY. If you make me stay, I shall keep my word and begin with you. No more.

Exit MANLY *at the same door* OLIVIA *went.* *Manet* FIDELIA.

FIDELIA. O heavens! Is there not punishment enough
In loving well, if you will have't a crime,
But you must add fresh torments daily to't
And punish us like peevish rivals still,
Because we fain would find a heaven here?
But did there never any love like me,
That, untried tortures, you must find me out?
Others, at worst, you force to kill themselves,
But I must be self-murderess of my love,
Yet will not grant me power to end my life,
My cruel life, for, when a lover's hopes
Are dead and gone, life is unmerciful. (*Sits down and weeps*)

Enter MANLY *to her.*

MANLY. I have thought better on't; I must not discover myself now; I am without witnesses, for if I barely should publish it, she would deny it with as much impudence as she would act it again with this young fellow here. Where are you?

FIDELIA. Here – oh – now I suppose we may be gone.

MANLY. I will, but not you; you must stay and act the second part of a lover, that is, talk kindness to her.

FIDELIA. Not I, sir.

MANLY. No disputing, sir, you must; 'tis necessary to my design of coming again tomorrow night.

---

341 *peevish*: spiteful.

FIDELIA. What, can you come again then hither?

MANLY. Yes, and you must make the appointment and an apology for your leaving her so soon, for I have said not a word to her but have kept your counsel, as I expect you should do mine. Do this faithfully and I promise you here you shall run my fortune still and we will never part as long as we live, but if you do not do it expect not to live.

FIDELIA. 'Tis hard, sir, but such a consideration will make it easier. You won't forget your promise, sir?

MANLY. No, by heavens. But I hear her coming. *Exit.*

Enter OLIVIA *to* FIDELIA.

OLIVIA. Where is my life? Run from me already! You do not love me, dearest; nay, you are angry with me, for you would not so much as speak a kind word to me within. What was the reason?

FIDELIA. I was transported too much.

OLIVIA. That's kind; but come, my soul, what make you here? Let us go in again. We may be surprised in this room, 'tis so near the stairs.

FIDELIA. No, we shall hear the better here if anybody should come up.

OLIVIA. Nay, I assure you, we shall be secure enough within. Come, come –

FIDELIA. I am sick and, troubled with a sudden dizziness, cannot stir yet.

OLIVIA. Come, I have spirits within.

FIDELIA. Oh! – don't you hear a noise madam?

OLIVIA. No, no, there is none. Come, come. (*Pulls her*)

FIDELIA. Indeed there is, and I love you so much I must have a care of your honour, if you won't, and go, but to come to you tomorrow night if you please.

OLIVIA. With all my soul, but you must not go yet. Come, prithee.

FIDELIA. Oh! – I am now sicker and am afraid of one of my fits.

OLIVIA. My fits?

FIDELIA. Of the falling sickness, and I lie generally an hour in a trance; therefore pray consider your honour

---

397 *falling sickness*: epilepsy.

for the sake of my love and let me go that I may return to you often.

OLIVIA. But you will be sure then to come tomorrow night?

FIDELIA. Yes.

OLIVIA. Swear.

FIDELIA. By our past kindness.

OLIVIA. Well, go your ways then, if you will, you naughty creature you.

Exit FIDELIA.

These young lovers with their fears and modesty make themselves as bad as old ones to us and I apprehend their bashfulness more than their tattling.

FIDELIA *returns.*

FIDELIA. O, madam, we're undone! There was a gentleman upon the stairs, coming up, with a candle, which made me retire. Look you, here he comes!

Enter VERNISH *and his man with a light.*

OLIVIA. How! My husband! Oh, undone indeed! This way. *Exit.*

VERNISH. Ha! You shall not scape me so, sir. (*Stops* FIDELIA)

FIDELIA. (*aside*) O heavens! More fears, plagues and torments yet in store!

VERNISH. Come, sir, I guess what your business was here, but this must be your business now. Draw. (*Draws*)

FIDELIA. Sir –

VERNISH. No expostulations. I shall not care to hear of't. Draw.

FIDELIA. Good sir. –

VERNISH. How, you rascal! Not courage to draw yet durst do me the greatest injury in the world? Thy cowardice shall not save thy life. (*Offers to run at* FIDELIA)

FIDELIA. O hold, sir, and send but your servant down and I'll satisfy you, sir, I could not injure you as you imagine.

---

410 *tattling*: telling the secret.

VERNISH. Leave the light and be gone.

Exit SERVANT.

Now quickly, sir, what you've to say, or –

FIDELIA. I am a woman, sir, a very unfortunate woman.

VERNISH. How! A very handsome woman, I'm sure, then. Here are witnesses of't too, I confess – (*Pulls off her peruke and feels her breasts. Aside*) Well, I'm glad to find the tables turned, my wife in more danger of cuckolding than I was.

FIDELIA. Now, sir, I hope you are so much a man of honour as to let me go now I have satisfied you, sir.

VERNISH. When you have satisfied me, madam, I will.

FIDELIA. I hope, sir, you are too much a gentleman to urge those secrets from a woman which concern her honour. You may guess my misfortune to be love by my disguise; but a pair of breeches could not wrong you, sir.

VERNISH. I may believe love has changed your outside, which could not wrong me, but why did my wife run away?

FIDELIA. I know not, sir. Perhaps because she would not be forced to discover me to you or to guide me from your suspicions that you might not discover me yourself, which ungentlemanlike curiosity I hope you will cease to have and let me go.

VERNISH. Well, madam, if I must not know who you are, 'twill suffice for me only to know certainly what you are, which you must not deny me. Come, there is a bed within, the proper rack for lovers, and if you are a woman, there you can keep no secrets; you'll tell me there all unasked. Come. (*Pulls her*)

FIDELIA. Oh! What d'ye mean? Help, oh –

VERNISH. I'll show you, but 'tis in vain to cry out. No one dares help you, for I am lord here.

FIDELIA. Tyrant here. But if you are master of this house, which I have taken for a sanctuary, do not violate it yourself.

VERNISH. No, I'll preserve you here and nothing shall hurt you and will be as true to you as your disguise, but you must trust me then. Come, come.

FIDELIA. Oh, oh! Rather than you shall drag me to a death so horrid and so shameful I'll die here a thousand deaths; but you do not look like a ravisher, sir.

VERNISH. Nor you like one would put me to't but if you will –

FIDELIA. Oh! Oh! Help, help –

Enter SERVANT.

VERNISH. You saucy rascal, how durst you come in when you heard a woman squeak? That should have been your cue to shut the door.

SERVANT. I come, sir, to let you know the alderman, coming home immediately after you were at his house, has sent his cashier with the money, according to your note.

VERNISH. Damn his money! Money never came to any, sure, unseasonably till now. Bid him stay.

SERVANT. He says he cannot a moment.

VERNISH. Receive it you then.

SERVANT. He says he must have your receipt for it. He is in haste, for I hear him coming up, sir.

VERNISH. Damn him. Help me in here then with this dishonourer of my family.

FIDELIA. Oh! Oh!

SERVANT. You say she is a woman, sir.

VERNISH. No matter, sir. Must you prate?

FIDELIA. O heavens! Is there –

They thrust her in and lock the door.

VERNISH. Stay there, my prisoner. You have a short reprieve.

I'll fetch the gold and that she can't resist,
For with a full hand 'tis we ravish best.

Exeunt.

ACT V

SCENE I

Eliza's lodging.

Enter OLIVIA *and* ELIZA.

OLIVIA. Ah, cousin, nothing troubles me but that I have

given the malicious world its revenge and reason now to talk as freely of me as I used to do of it.

ELIZA. Faith, then, let not that trouble you, for, to be plain, cousin, the world cannot talk worse of you than it did before.

OLIVIA. How, cousin? I'd have you to know, before this faux pas, this trip of mine, the world could not talk of me.

ELIZA. Only that you mind other people's actions so much that you take no care of your own but to hide 'em, that, like a thief, because you know yourself most guilty you impeach your fellow criminals first to clear yourself.

OLIVIA. O wicked world!

ELIZA. That you pretend an aversion to all mankind in public only that their wives and mistresses may not be jealous and hinder you of their conversation in private.

OLIVIA. Base world!

ELIZA. That abroad you fasten quarrels upon innocent men for talking of you, only to bring 'em to ask you pardon at home and to become dear friends with 'em who were hardly your acquaintance before.

OLIVIA. Abominable world!

ELIZA. That you condemn the obscenity of modern plays only that you may not be censured for never missing the most obscene of the old ones.

OLIVIA. Damned world!

ELIZA. That you deface the nudities of pictures and little statues only because they are not real.

OLIVIA. O fie, fie, fie. Hideous, hideous, cousin! The obscenity of their censures makes me blush.

ELIZA. The truth of 'em, the naughty world would say now.

Enter LETTICE *hastily.*

LETTICE. O! Madam, here is that gentleman coming up who now you say is my master.

OLIVIA. O! Cousin, whither shall I run? Protect me, or – (OLIVIA *runs away and stands at a distance*)

Enter VERNISH.

VERNISH. Nay, nay, come –

OLIVIA. O, sir, forgive me.

VERNISH. Yes, yes, I can forgive you being alone in the dark with a woman in man's clothes, but have a care of a man in woman's clothes.

OLIVIA. (*aside*) What does he mean? He dissembles only to get me into his power. Or has my dear friend made him believe he was a woman? My husband may be deceived by him but I'm sure I was not.

VERNISH. Come, come, you need not have lain out of your house for this, but perhaps you were afraid, when I was warm with suspicions, you must have discovered who she was; and prithee may I not know it?

OLIVIA. She was – (*Aside*) I hope he has been deceived, and since my lover has played the card I must not renounce.

VERNISH. Come, what's the matter with thee? If I must not know who she is, I'm satisfied without. Come hither.

OLIVIA. Sure you do know her. She has told you herself, I suppose.

VERNISH. No, I might have known her better but that I was interrupted by the goldsmith, you know, and was forced to lock her into your chamber to keep her from his sight but when I returned I found she was got away by tying the window-curtains to the balcony, by which she slid down into the street, for, you must know, I jested with her and made her believe I'd ravish her, which she apprehended, it seems, in earnest.

OLIVIA. Then she got from you?

VERNISH. Yes.

OLIVIA. And is quite gone?

VERNISH. Yes.

OLIVIA. I'm glad on't – otherwise you had ravished her, sir? But how dar'st you go so far as to make her believe you would ravish her? Let me understand that, sir. What! There's guilt in your face; you blush too – nay, then you did ravish her, you did, you base fellow. What, ravish a woman in the first month of our

---

50 *discovered*: revealed.

54 *renounce*: fail to follow suit though an appropriate card is held, revoke.

marriage! 'Tis a double injury to me, thou base ungrateful man. Wrong my bed already, villain! I could tear out those false eyes, barbarous, unworthy wretch.

ELIZA. So, so! –

VERNISH. Prithee hear, my dear.

OLIVIA. I will never hear you, my plague, my torment.

VERNISH. I swear – prithee hear me.

OLIVIA. I have heard already too many of your false oaths and vows, especially your last in the church. O wicked man! And wretched woman that I was! I wish I had then sunk down into a grave rather than to have given you my hand to be led to your loathsome bed. Oh – oh – (*Seems to weep*)

VERNISH. So, very fine! Just a marriage quarrel! Which, though it generally begins by the wife's fault, yet in the conclusion it becomes the husband's and, whosoever offends at first, he only is sure to ask pardon at last. My dear –

OLIVIA. My devil –

VERNISH. Come, prithee be appeased and go home. I have bespoken our supper betimes, for I could not eat till I found you. Go, I'll give you all kind of satisfactions and one which uses to be a reconciling one, two hundred of those guineas I received last night, to do what you will with.

OLIVIA. What, would you pay me for being your bawd?

VERNISH. Nay, prithee no more. Go, and I'll thoroughly satisfy you when I come home, and then too we will have a fit of laughter at Manly, whom I am going to find at the Cock in Bow Street, where, I hear, he dined. Go, dearest, go home.

ELIZA. (*aside*) A very pretty turn indeed, this!

VERNISH. Now, cousin, since by my wife I have that honour and privilege of calling you so, I have something to beg of you too, which is not to take notice of our marriage, to any whatever, yet awhile for some reasons very important to me; and next, that you will do my wife the honour to go home with her

---

108 *Cock . . . Street*: a famous tavern where events like those of the next scene were not unexpected.

and me the favour to use that power you have with her in our reconcilement.

ELIZA. That, I dare promise, sir, will be no hard matter. Your servant.

Exit VERNISH.

Well, cousin, this I confess was reasonable hypocrisy. You were the better for't.

OLIVIA. What hypocrisy?

ELIZA. Why, this last deceit of your husband was lawful since in your own defence.

OLIVIA. What deceit? I'd have you to know I never deceived my husband.

ELIZA. You do not understand me, sure. I say, this was an honest come-off and a good one. But 'twas a sign your gallant had had enough of your conversation since he could so dextrously cheat your husband in passing for a woman!

OLIVIA. What d'ye mean, once more, with 'my gallant' and 'passing for a woman'?

ELIZA. What do you mean? You see your husband took him for a woman.

OLIVIA. Whom?

ELIZA. Hey-day! Why, the man he found you with, for whom last night you were so much afraid and who you told me –

OLIVIA. Lord, you rave sure!

ELIZA. Why, did not you tell me last night –

OLIVIA. I know not what I might tell you last night, in a fright.

ELIZA. Ay, what was that fright for? For a woman? Besides, were you not afraid to see your husband just now? I warrant, only for having been found with a woman! Nay, did you not just now too own your false step, or trip, as you called it? Which was with a woman too! Fie, this fooling is so insipid, 'tis offensive.

OLIVIA. And fooling with my honour will be more offensive. Did you not hear my husband say he found me with a woman in man's clothes? And d'ye think he does not know a man from a woman?

ELIZA. Not so well, I'm sure, as you do; therefore I'd rather take your word.

OLIVIA. What, you grow scurrilous and are, I find, more censorious than the world! I must have a care of you, I see.

ELIZA. No, you need not fear yet; I'll keep your secret.

OLIVIA. My secret! I'd have you to know I have no need of confidants, though you value yourself upon being a good one.

ELIZA. O admirable confidence! You show more in denying your wickedness than other people in glorying in't.

OLIVIA. Confidence, to me! To me such language! Nay, then I'll never see your face again. (*Aside*) I'll quarrel with her that people may never believe I was in her power but take for malice all the truth she may speak against me. – Lettice, where are you? Let us be gone from this censorious, ill woman.

ELIZA. (*aside*) Nay, thou shalt stay a little to damn thyself quite. – One word first, pray, madam. Can you swear that whom your husband found you with –

OLIVIA. Swear! Ay, that whosoever 'twas that stole up, unknown, into my room when 'twas dark, I know not whether man or woman, by heavens, by all that's good or may I never more have joys here or in the other world; nay, may I eternally –

ELIZA. Be damned. So, so, you are damned enough already by your oaths, and I enough confirmed, and now you may please to be gone. Yet take this advice with you, in this plain-dealing age, to leave off forswearing yourself; for, when people hardly think the better of a woman for her real modesty, why should you put that great constraint upon yourself to feign it?

OLIVIA. O hideous! Hideous advice! Let us go out of the hearing of it. She will spoil us, Lettice.

Exeunt OLIVIA *and* LETTICE *at one door,*
ELIZA *at t'other.*

SCENE II

The scene changes to the Cock in Bow Street. A table and bottles.

MANLY *and* FIDELIA.

MANLY. How! Saved her honour by making her husband believe you were a woman! 'Twas well, but hard enough to do sure.

FIDELIA. We were interrupted before he could contradict me.

MANLY. But can't you tell me, d'ye say, what kind of man he was?

FIDELIA. I was so frightened, I confess, I can give no other account of him but that he was pretty tall, round-faced and one I'm sure I ne'er had seen before.

MANLY. But she, you say, made you swear to return tonight?

FIDELIA. But I have since sworn never to go near her again, for the husband would murder me, or worse, if he caught me again.

MANLY. No, I'll go with you and defend you tonight and then I'll swear too never to go near her again.

FIDELIA. Nay, indeed sir, I will not go to be accessory to your death too. Besides, what should you go again, sir, for?

MANLY. No disputing or advice, sir. You have reason to know I am unalterable. Go therefore presently and write her a note to inquire if her assignation with you holds and, if not to be at her own house, where else. And be importunate to gain admittance to her tonight. Let your messenger, ere he deliver your letter, inquire first if her husband be gone out. Go, 'tis now almost six of the clock. I expect you back here before seven with leave to see her again. Go, do this dextrously and expect the performance of my last night's promise, never to part with you.

FIDELIA. Ay, sir, but will you be sure to remember that?

MANLY. Did I ever break my word? Go, no more replies or doubts.

Exit FIDELIA.

Enter FREEMAN *to* MANLY.

Where hast thou been?

FREEMAN. In the next room with my Lord Plausible and Novel.

MANLY. Ay, we came hither because 'twas a private house, but with thee indeed no house can be private, for thou hast that pretty quality of the familiar fops of the town who in an eating-house always keep company with all people in't but those they came with.

FREEMAN. I went into their room but to keep them and my own fool the squire out of your room; but you shall be peevish now because you have no money. But why the devil won't you write to those we were speaking of? Since your modesty or your spirit will not suffer you to speak to 'em to lend you money, why won't you try 'em at last that way?

MANLY. Because I know 'em already and can bear want better than denials, nay, than obligations.

FREEMAN. Deny you! They cannot. All of 'em have been your intimate friends.

MANLY. No, they have been people only I have obliged particularly.

FREEMAN. Very well, therefore you ought to go to 'em the rather, sure.

MANLY. No, no. Those you have obliged most, most certainly avoid you when you can oblige 'em no longer and they take your visits like so many duns. Friends, like mistresses, are avoided for obligations past.

FREEMAN. Pshaw! But most of 'em are your relations, men of great fortune and honour.

MANLY. Yes, but relations have so much honour as to think poverty taints the blood and disown their wanting kindred, believing, I suppose, that, as riches at first makes a gentleman, the want of 'em degrades him. But, damn 'em, now I'm poor I'll anticipate their contempt and disown them.

FREEMAN. But you have many a female acquaintance whom you have been liberal to who may have a heart to refund to you a little if you would ask it. They are not all Olivias.

MANLY. Damn thee! How couldst thou think of such a thing? I would as soon rob my footman of his wages. Besides, 'twere in vain too, for a wench is like a box in an ordinary, receives all people's money easily but there's no getting, nay, shaking any out again and he that fills it is sure never to keep the key.

78–9 *box in an ordinary*: the box which receives the house share in gambling; ordinaries were often gambling houses as well as eating-houses.

FREEMAN. Well, but noble captain, would you make me believe that you who know half the town, have so many friends and have obliged so many can't borrow fifty or an hundred pound?

MANLY. Why, noble lieutenant, you who know all the town and call all you know friends methinks should not wonder at it, since you find ingratitude too; for how many lords' families (though descended from blacksmiths or tinkers) hast thou called great and illustrious? How many ill tables called good eating? How many noisy coxcombs wits? How many pert, cocking cowards stout? How many tawdry, affected rogues well-dressed? How many perukes admired? And how many ill verses applauded? And yet canst not borrow a shilling. Dost thou expect I, who always spoke truth, should?

FREEMAN. Nay, now you think you have paid me; but hark you, captain, I have heard of a thing called grinning honour but never of starving honour.

MANLY. Well, but it has been the fate of some brave men; and if they won't give me a ship again I can go starve anywhere with a musket on my shoulder.

FREEMAN. Give you a ship! Why, you will not solicit it?

MANLY. If I have not solicited it by my services, I know no other way.

FREEMAN. Your servant, sir. Nay, then I'm satisfied I must solicit my widow the closer and run the desperate fortune of matrimony on shore. *Exit.*

Enter, to MANLY, VERNISH.

MANLY. How! – Nay, here is a friend indeed, and he that has him in his arms can know no wants. (*Embraces* VERNISH)

VERNISH. Dear sir! And he that is in your arms is secure from all fears whatever. Nay, our nation is secure by your defeat at sea and the Dutch that fought against you have proved enemies to themselves only, in bringing you back to us.

MANLY. Fie, fie! This from a friend? And yet from any

---

91 *called good*: call good Q1.
93 *cocking*: coaching Q1 (some copies only).

other 'twere unsufferable. I thought I should never have taken anything ill from you.

VERNISH. A friend's privilege is to speak his mind though it be taken ill.

MANLY. But your tongue need not tell me you think too well of me. I have found it from your heart, which spoke in actions, your unalterable heart. But Olivia is false, my friend, which I suppose is no news to you.

VERNISH. (*aside*) He's in the right on't.

MANLY. But couldst thou not keep her true to me?

VERNISH. Not for my heart, sir.

MANLY. But could you not perceive it at all before I went? Could she so deceive us both?

VERNISH. I must confess, the first time I knew it was three days after your departure when she received the money you had left in Lombard Street in her name, and her tears did not hinder her it seems from counting that. You would trust her with all, like a true, generous lover!

MANLY. And she, like a mean jilting –

VERNISH. Traitorous –

MANLY. Base –

VERNISH. Damned –

MANLY. Covetous –

VERNISH. Mercenary whore – (*Aside*) I can hardly hold from laughing.

MANLY. Ay, a mercenary whore indeed, for she made me pay her before I lay with her.

VERNISH. How! – Why, have you lain with her?

MANLY. Ay, ay.

VERNISH. Nay, she deserves you should report it at least, though you have not.

MANLY. Report it! By heaven, 'tis true.

VERNISH. How! Sure not.

MANLY. I do not use to lie, nor you to doubt me.

VERNISH. When?

MANLY. Last night about seven or eight of the clock.

VERNISH. (*aside*) Ha! – Now I remember, I thought

---

134 *Lombard Street*: street in the city known for its bankers and goldsmiths.

she spake as if she expected some other rather than me. A confounded whore indeed!

MANLY. But, what, thou wonderest at it! Nay, you seem to be angry too.

VERNISH. I cannot but be enraged against her for her usage of you, damned, infamous, common jade.

MANLY. Nay, her cuckold, who first cuckolded me in my money, shall not laugh all himself. We will do him reason, shan't we?

VERNISH. Ay, ay.

MANLY. But thou dost not, for so great a friend, take pleasure enough in your friend's revenge, methinks.

VERNISH. Yes, yes, I'm glad to know it since you have lain with her.

MANLY. Thou canst not tell me who that rascal, her cuckold, is?

VERNISH. No.

MANLY. She would keep it from you, I suppose.

VERNISH. Yes, yes –

MANLY. Thou wouldst laugh if thou knewest but all the circumstances of my having her. Come, I'll tell thee.

VERNISH. Damn her. I care not to hear any more of her.

MANLY. Faith, thou shalt. You must know –

Enter FREEMAN, *backwards, endeavouring to keep out* NOVEL, LORD PLAUSIBLE, JERRY *and* OLDFOX, *who all press in upon him.*

FREEMAN. I tell you he has a wench with him and would be private.

MANLY. Damn 'em! A man can't open a bottle in these eating-houses but presently you have these impudent, intruding, buzzing flies and insects in your glass. – Well, I'll tell thee all anon. In the meantime, prithee go to her, but not from me, and try if you can get her to lend me but an hundred pound of my money to supply my present wants, for I suppose there is no recovering any of it by law.

VERNISH. Not any. Think not of it, nor by this way neither.

MANLY. Go, try, at least.

VERNISH. I'll go, but I can satisfy you beforehand, 'twill be to no purpose. You'll no more find a refunding wench –

MANLY. Than a refunding lawyer; indeed their fees alike scarce ever return. However, try her, put it to her.

VERNISH. Ay, ay, I'll try her, put it to her home, with a vengeance. *Exit* VERNISH.

Manent caeteri.

NOVEL. Nay, you shall be our judge, Manly. Come, major, I'll speak it to your teeth. If people provoke me to say bitter things to their faces, they must take what follows, though, like my Lord Plausible, I'd rather do't civilly behind their backs.

MANLY. Nay, thou art a dangerous rogue, I've heard, behind a man's back.

LORD PLAUSIBLE. You wrong him sure, noble captain. He would do a man no more harm behind his back than to his face.

FREEMAN. I am of my lord's mind.

MANLY. Yes, a fool, like a coward, is the more to be feared behind a man's back, more than a witty man, for as a coward is more bloody than a brave man a fool is more malicious than a man of wit.

NOVEL. A fool, tar – a fool! Nay, thou art a brave sea-judge of wit! A fool! Prithee, when did you ever find me want something to say, as you do often?

MANLY. Nay, I confess, thou art always talking, roaring or making a noise; that I'll say for thee.

NOVEL. Well, and is talking a sign of a fool?

MANLY. Yes, always talking, especially too if it be loud and fast, is the sign of a fool.

NOVEL. Pshaw! Talking is like fencing, the quicker the better; run 'em down, run 'em down, no matter for parrying, push on still, sa, sa, sa. No matter whether you argue in form, push in guard or no.

MANLY. Or hit or no. I think thou always talkest without thinking, Novel.

NOVEL. Ay, ay, studied play's the worse, to follow the allegory, as the old pedant says.

OLDFOX. A young fop!

MANLY. I ever thought the man of most wit had been like him of most money, who has no vanity in show-

---

199 s.d. *manent caeteri*: the others remain.
225 *sa, sa, sa*: fencing cry when delivering a thrust (Fr. *ça*).
226 *push in guard*: thrust inside the defence.

ing it everywhere, whilst the beggarly pusher of his fortune has all he has about him still, only to show.

NOVEL. Well, sir, and makes a very pretty show in the world, let me tell you, nay, a better than your close hunks. A pox, give me ready money in play. What care I for a man's reputation? What are we the better for your substantial, thrifty curmudgeon in wit, sir?

OLDFOX. Thou art a profuse young rogue indeed.

NOVEL. So much for talking, which I think I have proved a mark of wit, and so is railing, roaring and making a noise, for railing is satire, you know, and roaring and making a noise, humour.

Enter to them FIDELIA, *taking* MANLY *aside and showing him a paper.*

FIDELIA. The hour is betwixt seven and eight exactly. 'Tis now half an hour after six.

MANLY. Well, go then to the Piazza and wait for me; as soon as it is quite dark I'll be with you. I must stay here yet awhile for my friend. But is railing satire, Novel?

Exit FIDELIA.

FREEMAN. And roaring and making a noise humour?

NOVEL. What, won't you confess there's humour in roaring and making a noise?

FREEMAN. No.

NOVEL. Nor in cutting napkins and hangings?

MANLY. No, sure.

NOVEL. Dull fops!

OLDFOX. O rogue, rogue, insipid rogue! Nay, gentlemen, allow him those things for wit, for his parts lie only that way.

NOVEL. Peace, old fool, I wonder not at thee, but that young fellows should be so dull as to say there's no humour in making a noise and breaking windows! I tell you, there's wit and humour too in both. And a wit is as well known by his frolic as by his simile.

OLDFOX. Pure rogue! There's your modern wit for you!

---

238 *hunks*: miser.

248 *Piazza*: arcade on two sides of Covent Garden, scene of Act V Scene iii of *The Country Wife*.

Wit and humour in breaking of windows! There's mischief if you will but no wit or humour.

NOVEL. Prithee, prithee peace, old fool. I tell you, where there is mischief there's wit. Don't we esteem the monkey a wit amongst beasts only because he's mischievous? And let me tell you, as good nature is a sign of a fool, being mischievous is a sign of wit.

OLDFOX. O rogue, rogue! Pretend to be a wit by doing mischief and railing!

NOVEL. Why, thou, old fool, hast no other pretence to the name of a wit but by railing at new plays.

OLDFOX. Thou by railing at that facetious, noble way of wit, quibbling.

NOVEL. Thou call'st thy dullness, gravity and thy dozing, thinking.

OLDFOX. You, sir, your dullness, spleen. And you talk much and say nothing.

NOVEL. Thou readest much and understand'st nothing, sir.

OLDFOX. You laugh loud and break no jest.

NOVEL. You rail and nobody hangs himself. And thou hast nothing of the satyr but in thy face.

OLDFOX. And you have no jest but your face, sir.

NOVEL. Thou art an illiterate pedant.

OLDFOX. Thou art a fool with a bad memory.

MANLY. Come, a pox on you both. You have done like wits now, for you wits, when you quarrel, never give over till you prove one another fools.

NOVEL. And you fools have never any occasion of laughing at us wits but when we quarrel; therefore let us be friends, Oldfox.

MANLY. They are such wits as thou art who make the name of a wit as scandalous as that of a bully and signify a loud-laughing, talking, incorrigible coxcomb, as bully a roaring, hardened coward.

FREEMAN. And would have his noise and laughter pass for wit, as t'other his huffing and blustering for courage.

Enter VERNISH.

---

289 *satyr*: (*a*) satire (*b*) the half-man, half-goat figure of Greek mythology, lustful, drunken companions of Bacchus.

MANLY. Gentlemen, with your leave, here is one I would speak with and I have nothing to say to you.

Pulls 'em out of the room. Manent MANLY, VERNISH.

VERNISH. I told you 'twas in vain to think of getting money out of her. She says, if a shilling would do't, she would not save you from starving or hanging or what you would think worse, begging or flattering, and rails so at you one would not think you had lain with her.

MANLY. O friend, never trust for that matter a woman's railing, for she is no less a dissembler in her hatred than her love. And as her fondness of her husband is a sign he's a cuckold, her railing at another man is a sign she lies with him.

VERNISH. (*aside*) He's in the right on't. I know not what to trust to.

MANLY. But you did not take any notice of it to her, I hope?

VERNISH. (*aside*) So! Sure he is afraid I should have disproved him, by an inquiry of her. All may be well yet.

MANLY. What hast thou in thy head that makes thee seem so unquiet?

VERNISH. Only this base, impudent woman's falseness; I cannot put her out of my head.

MANLY. O my dear friend, be not you too sensible of my wrongs, for then I shall feel 'em too, with more pain, and think 'em unsufferable. Damn her, her money and that ill-natured whore, too, Fortune herself; but if thou wouldst ease a little my present trouble prithee go borrow me somewhere else some money. I can trouble thee.

VERNISH. You trouble me indeed, most sensibly, when you command me anything I cannot do. I have lately lost a great deal of money at play, more than I can yet pay, so that not only my money but my credit too is gone and I know not where to borrow; but could rob a church for you. (*Aside*) Yet would rather end your wants, by cutting your throat.

MANLY. Nay, then I doubly feel my poverty since I'm incapable of supplying thee. (*Embraces* VERNISH)

---

338 *at play*: gambling.

VERNISH. But methinks she that granted you the last favour (as they call it) should not deny you anything.

NOVEL. Hey, tarpaulin, have you done?

NOVEL *looks in and retires again.*

VERNISH. I understand not that point of kindness, I confess.

MANLY. No, thou dost not understand it and I have not time to let you know all now, for these fools, you see, will interrupt us; but anon, at supper, we'll laugh at leisure together at Olivia's cuckold, who took a young fellow that goes between his wife and me for a woman.

VERNISH. Ha!

MANLY. Senseless, easy rascal! 'Twas no wonder she chose him for a husband, but she thought him, I thank her, fitter than me for that blind, bearing office.

VERNISH. (*aside*) I could not be deceived in that long woman's hair tied up behind nor those infallible proofs, her pouting, swelling breasts; I have handled too many sure not to know 'em.

MANLY. What, you wonder the fellow could be such a blind coxcomb!

VERNISH. Yes, yes –

NOVEL. Nay, prithee come to us, Manly. Gad, all the fine things one says in their company are lost without thee.

NOVEL *looks in again and retires.*

MANLY. Away, fop, I'm busy yet. – You see we cannot talk here at our ease; besides, I must be gone immediately in order to meeting with Olivia again tonight.

VERNISH. Tonight! It cannot be, sure –

MANLY. I had an appointment just now from her.

VERNISH. For what time?

MANLY. At half an hour after seven precisely.

VERNISH. Don't you apprehend the husband?

MANLY. He! Snivelling gull! He a thing to be feared! A husband, the tamest of creatures!

VERNISH. (*aside*) Very fine!

MANLY. But, prithee, in the meantime go try to get me some money. Though thou art too modest to borrow for thyself, thou canst do anything for me, I know. Go, for I must be gone to Olivia. Go and meet me here anon. – Freeman, where are you? *Exit* MANLY.

Manet VERNISH.

VERNISH. Ay, I'll meet with you, I warrant, but it shall

be at Olivia's. Sure it cannot be. She denies it so calmly and with that honest, modest assurance, it can't be true – and he does not use to lie – but belying a woman when she won't be kind is the only lie a brave man will least scruple. But then the woman in man's clothes, whom he calls a man! Well but by her breasts I know her to be a woman. – But then again his appointment from her to meet with him tonight! I am distracted more with doubt than jealousy. Well, I have no way to disabuse or revenge myself but by going home immediately, putting on a riding suit, and pretending to my wife the same business which carried me out of town last requires me again to go post to Oxford tonight. Then, if the appointment he boasts of be true, it's sure to hold and I shall have an opportunity either of clearing her or revenging myself on both. Perhaps she is his wench of an old date and I am his cully whilst I think him mine and he has seemed to make his wench rich only that I might take her off of his hands; or if he has but lately lain with her, he must needs discover, by her, my treachery to him, which I'm sure he will revenge with my death and which I must prevent with his, if it were only but for fear of his too just reproaches, for, I must confess, I never had till now any excuse but that of interest for doing ill to him. *Exit* VERNISH.

Re-enter MANLY *and* FREEMAN.

MANLY. Come hither, only I say be sure you mistake not the time. You know the house exactly where Olivia lodges; 'tis just hard by.

FREEMAN. Yes, yes.

MANLY. Well then, bring 'em all, I say, thither, and all you know that may be then in the house, for the more witnesses I have of her infamy the greater will be my revenge. And be sure you come straight up to her chamber without more ado. Here, take the watch. You see 'tis above a quarter past seven. Be there in half an hour exactly.

FREEMAN. You need not doubt my diligence or dexterity. I am an old scourer and can naturally beat up a

---

424 *scourer*: late night roisterer.

wench's quarters that won't be civil. Shan't we break her windows too?

MANLY. No, no. Be punctual only.

Exeunt ambo.

Enter WIDOW BLACKACRE *and two* KNIGHTS OF THE POST; *a* WAITER *with wine.*

WIDOW. Sweetheart, are you sure the door was shut close, that none of those roisters saw us come in?

WAITER. Yes, mistress, and you shall have a privater room above instantly. *Exit* WAITER.

WIDOW. You are safe enough, gentlemen, for I have been private in this house ere now upon other occasions when I was something younger. Come, gentlemen, in short, I leave my business to your care and fidelity and so, here's to you.

FIRST KNIGHT. We were ungrateful rogues if we should not be honest to you, for we have had a great deal of your money.

WIDOW. And you have done me many a good job for't, and so, here's to you again.

SECOND KNIGHT. Why, we have been perjured but six times for you.

FIRST KNIGHT. Forged but four deeds with your husband's last deed of gift.

SECOND KNIGHT. And but three wills.

FIRST KNIGHT. And counterfeited hands and seals to some six bonds. I think that's all, brother.

WIDOW. Ay, that's all, gentlemen, and so, here's to you again.

SECOND KNIGHT. Nay, 'twould do one's heart good to be forsworn for you. You have a conscience in your ways and pay us well.

FIRST KNIGHT. You are in the right on't, brother; one would be damned for her with all one's heart.

SECOND KNIGHT. But there are rogues who make us forsworn for 'em and when we come to be paid they'll be forsworn too and not pay us our wages which they promised with oaths sufficient.

FIRST KNIGHT. Ay, a great lawyer, that shall be nameless, bilked me too.

WIDOW. That was hard, methinks, that a lawyer should use gentlemen witnesses no better.

SECOND KNIGHT. A lawyer! D'ye wonder a lawyer should do't? I was bilked by a reverend divine that preaches twice on Sundays and prays half an hour still before dinner.

WIDOW. How? A conscientious divine and not pay people for damning themselves! Sure then, for all his talking he does not believe damnation. But come, to our business. Pray be sure to imitate exactly the flourish at the end of this name. (*Pulls out a deed or two*)

FIRST KNIGHT. O he's the best in England at untangling a flourish, madam.

WIDOW. And let not the seal be a jot bigger. Observe well the dash too at the end of this name.

SECOND KNIGHT. I warrant you, madam.

WIDOW. Well, these and many other shifts poor widows are put to sometimes, for everybody would be riding a widow, as they say, and breaking into her jointure. They think marrying a widow an easy business, like leaping the hedge where another has gone over before; a widow is a mere gap, a gap with them.

Enter to them MAJOR OLDFOX *with two waiters. The* KNIGHTS OF THE POST *huddle up the writings.*

What, he here! Go then, go, my hearts, you have your instructions.

Exeunt KNIGHTS OF THE POST.

OLDFOX. Come, madam, to be plain with you, I'll be fobbed off no longer. (*Aside*) I'll bind her and gag her but she shall hear me. – Look you, friends, there's the money I promised you and now do you what you promised me. Here are my garters and here's a gag. You shall be acquainted with my parts, lady, you shall.

WIDOW. Acquainted with your parts! A rape, a rape – What, will you ravish me?

The waiters tie her to the chair and gag her and exeunt.

OLDFOX. Yes, lady, I will ravish you, but it shall be through the ear, lady, the ear only, with my well-penned acrostics.

---

496 *acrostics*: a short poem in which the initial letters of the lines spell out a word, often a name.

Enter to them FREEMAN, JERRY BLACKACRE, *three* BAILIFFS, *a constable and his assistants, with the two* KNIGHTS OF THE POST.

What, shall I never read my things undisturbed again?

JERRY. O law! My mother bound hand and foot and gaping as if she rose before her time today!

FREEMAN. What means this, Oldfox? But I'll release you from him. You shall be no man's prisoner but mine. Bailiffs, execute your writ. (FREEMAN *unties her*)

OLDFOX. Nay, then I'll be gone for fear of being bail and paying her debts without being her husband.

Exit OLDFOX.

FIRST BAILIFF. We arrest you, in the King's name at the suit of Mr Freeman, guardian to Jeremiah Blackacre, Esquire, in an action of ten thousand pounds.

WIDOW. How! How! In a choke-bail action! What, and the pen-and-ink gentlemen taken too! Have you confessed, you rogues?

FIRST KNIGHT. We needed not to confess, for the bailiffs dogged us hither to the very door and overheard all that you and we said.

WIDOW. Undone, undone then! No man was ever too hard for me till now. O, Jerry, child, wilt thou vex again the womb that bore thee?

JERRY. Ay, for bearing me before wedlock, as you say. But I'll teach you to call a Blackacre a bastard, though you were never so much my mother.

WIDOW. (*aside*) Well, I'm undone. not one trick left? No law-meush imaginable? – Cruel sir, a word with you I pray.

FREEMAN. In vain, madam, for you have no other way to release yourself but by the bonds of matrimony.

WIDOW. How, sir, how! That were but to sue out an *habeas corpus* for a removal from one prison to another. Matrimony!

---

508 *choke-bail action*: a suit in which bail is not allowed.
521 *law-meush*: legal loophole.
526 *habeas corpus*: a writ requiring an individual under restraint to be brought before a judge in order to establish the legality of the restraint.

FREEMAN. Well, bailiffs, away with her.

WIDOW. O stay, sir, can you be so cruel as to bring me under covert baron again and put it out of my power to sue in my own name? Matrimony, to a woman, is worse than excommunication in depriving her of the benefit of the law and I would rather be deprived of life. But hark you, sir, I am contented you should hold and enjoy my person by lease or patent but not by the spiritual patent called a licence, that is, to have the privileges of a husband without the dominion, that is, *durante beneplacito*; in consideration of which I will, out of my jointure, secure you an annuity of three hundred pounds a year and pay your debts, and that's all you younger brothers desire to marry a widow for, I'm sure.

FREEMAN. Well, widow, if –

JERRY. What, I hope, bully guardian, you are not making agreements without me?

FREEMAN. No, no. First, widow, you must say no more that he is the son of a whore; have a care of that. And then he must have a settled exhibition of forty pounds a year and a nag of assizes, kept by you, but not upon the common, and have free ingress, egress and regress to and from your maids' garret.

WIDOW. Well, I can grant all that too.

JERRY. Ay, ay, fair words butter no cabbage; but, guardian, make her sign, sign and seal, for otherwise, if you knew her as well as I, you would not trust her word for a farthing.

FREEMAN. I warrant thee, squire. Well, widow, since thou art so generous, I will be generous too, and if you'll secure me four hundred pound a year but during your life and pay my debts, not above a thousand pound, I'll bate you your person to dispose of as you please.

---

531 *is*: Q1 omits.
538 *durante beneplacito*: so long as one is satisfactory (term used of tenure of judges).
548 *exhibition*: gift for maintenance.
549 *nag of assizes*: a horse of good quality, as prescribed by the ordinances governing weights and measures.

WIDOW. Have a care, sir, a settlement without a consideration is void in law. You must do something for't.

FREEMAN. Prithee then, let the settlement on me be called alimony and the consideration our separation. Come, my lawyer, with writings ready drawn, is within and in haste. Come.

WIDOW. But, what, no other kind of consideration, Mr Freeman? Well, a widow, I see, is a kind of a *sine cure*, by custom of which the unconscionable incumbent enjoys the profits without any duty but does that still elsewhere.

Exeunt omnes.

SCENE III

The scene changes to Olivia's lodging.

Enter OLIVIA *with a candle in her hand.*

OLIVIA. So, I am now prepared once more for my timorous young lover's reception; my husband is gone and go thou out too, thou next interrupter of love. (*Puts out the candle*) Kind darkness that frees us lovers from scandal and bashfulness, from the censure of our gallants and the world. So, are you there?

Enter to OLIVIA, FIDELIA, *followed softly by* MANLY.

Come, my dear punctual lover, there is not such another in the world; thou hast beauty and youth to please a wife, address and wit to amuse and fool a husband; nay, thou hast all things to be wished in a lover but your fits. I hope, my dear, you won't have one tonight and, that you may not, I'll lock the door though there be no need of it but to lock out your fits, for my husband is just gone out of town again. Come, where are you? (*Goes to the door and locks it*)

MANLY. (*aside*) Well, thou hast impudence enough to

563–4 *consideration*: an action undertaken by the one who is to gain by the settlement and for which settlement is made.

give me fits too and make revenge itself impotent, hinder me from making thee yet more infamous, if it can be.

OLIVIA. Come, come, my soul, come.

FIDELIA. Presently, my dear. We have time enough sure.

OLIVIA. How! Time enough! True lovers can no more think they ever have time enough than love enough. You shall stay with me all night, but that is but a lover's moment. Come.

FIDELIA. But won't you let me give you and myself the satisfaction of telling you how I abused your husband last night?

OLIVIA. Not when you can give me and yourself too the satisfaction of abusing him again tonight. Come.

FIDELIA. Let me but tell you how your husband –

OLIVIA. O name not his or Manly's more loathsome name, if you love me. I forbid 'em last night, and you know I mentioned my husband but once and he came. No talking, pray; 'twas ominous to us. You make me fancy a noise at the door already, but I'm resolved not to be interrupted.

A noise at the door.

Where are you? Come, for rather than lose my dear expectation now, though my husband were at the door and the bloody ruffian Manly here in the room with all his awful insolence, I would give myself to this dear hand, to be led away to heavens of joy which none but thou canst give. But what's this noise at the door? So, I told you what talking would come to.

The noise at the door increases.

Ha! – O heavens, my husband's voice! – (OLIVIA *listens at the door*)

MANLY. (*aside*) Freeman is come too soon.

OLIVIA. O 'tis he! – Then here is the happiest minute lost that ever bashful boy or trifling woman fooled away! I'm undone! My husband's reconcilement too was false, as my joy, all delusion. But, come this way. Here's a back door. (*Exit and returns*) The officious jade has locked us in instead of locking others out; but let us then escape your way, by the balcony, and, whilst you pull down the curtains, I'll fetch from my closet what next will best secure our escape. I have left my key in the door and 'twill not suddenly be broke open. *Exit.*

A noise as it were people forcing the door.

MANLY. Stir not, yet fear nothing.

FIDELIA. Nothing but your life, sir.

MANLY. We shall now know this happy man she calls husband.

OLIVIA *re-enters.*

OLIVIA. O, where are you? What, idle with fear? Come, I'll tie the curtains if you will hold. Here, take this cabinet and purse, for it is thine if we escape.

MANLY *takes from her the cabinet and purse.*

Therefore let us make haste. *Exit* OLIVIA.

MANLY. 'Tis mine indeed now again and it shall never escape more from me, to you at least.

The door broken open, enter VERNISH *alone with a dark lanthorn and a sword, running at* MANLY, *who draws, puts by the thrust and defends himself, whilst* FIDELIA *runs at* VERNISH *behind.*

VERNISH. (*with a low voice*) So, there I'm right, sure –

MANLY. (*softly*) Sword and dark lanthorn, villain, are some odds, but –

VERNISH. (*with a low voice*) Odds! I'm sure I find more odds than I expected. What, has my insatiable two seconds at once? But –

Whilst they fight, OLIVIA *re-enters, tying two curtains together.*

OLIVIA. Where are you now? – What, is he entered then and are they fighting? O do not kill one that can make no defence.

MANLY *throws* VERNISH *down and disarms him.*

How! But I think he has the better on't. Here's his scarf; 'tis he. So keep him down still. I hope thou hast no hurt, my dearest? (*Embraces* MANLY)

---

69 s.d. *lanthorn*: lantern.

Enter to them FREEMAN, LORD PLAUSIBLE, NOVEL, JERRY BLACKACRE *and the* WIDOW BLACKACRE, *lighted in by the two* SAILORS *with torches.*

Ha! – What? – Manly! And have I been thus concerned for him, embracing him? And has he his jewels again too? What means this? O 'tis too sure, as well as my shame, which I'll go hide for ever!

Offers to go out; MANLY *stops her.*

MANLY. No, my dearest, after so much kindness as has passed between us, I cannot part with you yet. Freeman, let nobody stir out of the room, for, notwithstanding your lights, we are yet in the dark till this gentleman please to turn his face. – (*Pulls* VERNISH *by the sleeve*) How! Vernish! Art thou the happy man then? Thou! Thou! Speak, I say. But thy guilty silence tells me all. – Well, I shall not upbraid thee, for my wonder is striking me as dumb as thy shame has made thee. But, what? My little volunteer hurt and fainting!

FIDELIA. My wound, sir, is but a slight one, in my arm. 'Tis only my fear of your danger, sir, not yet well over.

MANLY. (*observing* FIDELIA*'s hair untied behind and without a peruke, which she lost in the scuffle*) But what's here? More strange things! What means this long woman's hair? And face, now all of it appears, too beautiful for a man? Which I still thought womanish indeed! What, you have not deceived me too, my little volunteer?

OLIVIA. (*aside*) Me she has I'm sure.

MANLY. Speak.

Enter ELIZA *and* LETTICE.

ELIZA. What, cousin, I am brought hither by your woman, I suppose, to be a witness of the second vindication of your honour?

OLIVIA. Insulting is not generous. You might spare me; I have you.

ELIZA. Have a care, cousin. You'll confess anon too much and I would not have your secrets.

MANLY. (*to* FIDELIA) Come, your blushes answer me sufficiently and you have been my volunteer in love.

FIDELIA. I must confess I needed no compulsion to follow you all the world over, which I attempted in this habit, partly out of shame to own my love to you and fear of a greater shame, your refusal of it, for I knew of your engagement to this lady and the constancy of your nature, which nothing could have altered but herself.

MANLY. Dear madam, I desired you to bring me out of confusion and you have given me more. I know not what to speak to you or how to look upon you. The sense of my rough, hard and ill usage of you, though chiefly your own fault, gives me more pain now 'tis over than you had when you suffered it; and if my heart, the refusal of such a woman (*pointing to* OLIVIA), were not a sacrifice to profane your love and a greater wrong to you than ever yet I did you, I would beg of you to receive it, though you used it as she had done, for though it deserved not from her the treatment she gave it, it does from you.

FIDELIA. Then it has had punishment sufficient from her already and needs no more from me, and, I must confess, I would not be the only cause of making you break your last night's oath to me of never parting with me, if you do not forget or repent it.

MANLY. Then, take forever my heart and this with it (*gives her the cabinet*), for 'twas given to you before and my heart was before your due. I only beg leave to dispose of these few – Here, madam, I never yet left my wench unpaid.

Takes some of the jewels and offers 'em to OLIVIA. *She strikes 'em down.*
PLAUSIBLE *and* NOVEL *take 'em up.*

OLIVIA. So it seems, by giving her the cabinet.

LORD PLAUSIBLE. These pendants appertain to your most faithful, humble servant.

NOVEL. And this locket is mine, my earnest for love, which she never paid, therefore my own again.

WIDOW. By what law, sir, pray? Cousin Olivia, a word. What, do they make a seizure on your goods and chattels, *vi et armis*? Make your demand, I say, and

152 *vi et armis*: by force of arms.

bring your trover, bring your trover. I'll follow the law for you.

OLIVIA. And I my revenge. *Exit* OLIVIA.

MANLY. (*to* VERNISH) But 'tis, my friend, in your consideration most that I would have returned part of your wife's portion, for 'twere hard to take all from thee, since thou hast paid so dear for't in being such a rascal. Yet thy wife is a fortune without a portion and thou art a man of that extraordinary merit in villainy, the world and fortune can never desert thee, though I do; therefore be not melancholy. Fare you well, sir.

Exit VERNISH *doggedly*.

Now, madam, I beg your pardon (*turning to* FIDELIA), for lessening the present I made you, but my heart can never be lessened. This, I confess, was too small for you before, for you deserve the Indian world and I would now go thither out of covetousness for your sake only.

FIDELIA. Your heart, sir, is a present of that value I can never make any return to't. (*Pulling* MANLY *from the company*) But I can give you back such a present as this, which I got by the loss of my father, a gentleman of the North, of no mean extraction, whose only child I was, therefore left me in the present possession of two thousand pounds a year, which I left, with multitudes of pretenders, to follow you, sir, having in several public places seen you and observed your actions throughly, with admiration, when you were too much in love to take notice of mine, which yet was but too visible. The name of my family is Grey, my other Fidelia. The rest of my story you shall know when I have fewer auditors.

MANLY. Nay, now, madam, you have taken from me all power of making you any compliment on my part, for I was going to tell you that for your sake only I would quit the unknown pleasure of a retirement and stay in this ill world of ours still, though odious to me, than give you more frights again at sea and make again too great a venture there in you alone. But if I

---

164 s.d. *doggedly*: sullenly.

should tell you now all this and that your virtue (since greater than I thought any was in this world) had now reconciled me to't, my friend here would say, 'tis your estate that has made me friends with the world.

FREEMAN. I must confess I should, for I think most of our quarrels to the world are just such as we have to a handsome woman, only because we cannot enjoy her as we would do.

MANLY. Nay, if thou art a plain-dealer too, give me thy hand, for now I'll say I am thy friend indeed. And, for your two sakes, though I have been so lately deceived in friends of both sexes,
I will believe there are now in the world
Good-natured friends who are not prostitutes,
And handsome women worthy to be friends.
Yet for my sake let no one e'er confide
In tears or oaths, in love or friend untried.

Exeunt omnes.

EPILOGUE, *spoken by the* WIDOW BLACKACRE

To you, the judges learned in stage laws,
Our poet now, by me, submits his cause,
For with young judges, such as most of you,
The men by women best their business do;
And, truth on't is, if you did not sit here,
To keep for us a term throughout the year,
We could not live by'r tongues; nay, but for you,
Our chamber-practice would be little too.
And 'tis not only the stage practiser
Who, by your meeting, gets her living here,
For, as in Hall of Westminster,
Sleek sempstress vents, amidst the courts, her ware,
So, while we bawl, and you in judgement sit,
The visor-mask sells linen too i'th'pit.
O many of your friends, besides us here,
Do live by putting off their several ware.
Here's daily done the great affair o'th'nation;

14 *visor-mask sells linen*: prostitute solicits customers.

Let love, and us then, ne'er have long vacation.
But hold; like other pleaders, I have done
Not my poor client's business, but my own.
Spare me a word then, now, for him. First know,
Squires of the long robe, he does humbly show
He has a just right in abusing you
Because he is a brother Templar too,
For, at the bar, you rally one another,
And fool, and knave, is swallowed from a brother;
If not the poet here, the Templar spare;
And maul him, when you catch him at the bar.
From you, our common modish censurers,
Your favour, not your judgement, 'tis he fears;
Of all love begs you then to rail, find fault,
For plays, like women, by the world are thought
(When you speak kindly of 'em) very naught.

---

22 *Squires . . . robe*: law students at the Inns of Court.
24 *brother Templar*: fellow member of Middle or Inner Temple.

NOTES

TEXTUAL NOTE

The Gentleman Dancing-Master

For every editor of Wycherley the greatest nightmare is Monsieur's French. It is difficult to tell how many of the disasters are Monsieur's, Wycherley's or the compositor's. As it stands, the first quarto scatters grave accents over everything with gay profusion. I have tried to modernise consistently in order to reflect what was actually heard on stage and what a modern actor would speak. Monsieur learnt his French from hearing it spoken, not from reading it, and then exaggerated it. I have therefore eliminated 's' where it is printed but not voiced in the 1670s (e.g. *teste* becomes *tête*), but I have conserved spellings that may reflect Monsieur's pronunciation (*foy* rather than *foi*). Monsieur plainly sounded all final 'e' forms and the grave accents frequently indicate that; I suspect this was over-emphasised in French and English words (*cousine*, *ventre* but also *drunke*, *speake*, etc.) but I have not put in an accent, leaving it instead for the reader to put in the sound, in a suitably ridiculous tone. The compositor's grave accents are used in one peculiar way that I have changed, that is, to indicate a genuine acute accent: *disobligeè* changes to *disobligé*. Monsieur's French is, of course, comic; I hope my modernisation has not obscured any of Wycherley's jokes.

ADDITIONAL NOTES

Love in A Wood

Dedication. John Dennis describes Wycherley's encounter with Barbara Villiers as follows: 'Upon the writing of his first play . . . he became acquainted with several of the most celebrated wits both of the court and town. The writing of that play was likewise the occasion of his becoming acquainted with one of King Charles's mistresses after a very particular manner. As Mr Wycherley was going through Pall Mall towards St James's in his chariot he met the foresaid lady in hers, who, thrusting half her body out of the chariot, cried aloud to him 'You, Wycherley, you are a son of a whore', at the same time laughing aloud and heartily. Perhaps, sir, if you never heard of this passage before, you may be surprised at so strange a greeting from one of the most beautiful and best bred ladies in the world. Mr Wycherley was certainly very much surprised at it, yet not so much but he soon apprehended it was spoke with allusion to the latter end of a song in the forementioned play.

When parents are slaves
Their brats cannot be any other.
Great wits and great braves
Have always a punk to their mother.

As, during Mr Wycherley's surprise, the chariots drove different ways, they were soon at a considerable distance from each other when Mr Wycherley, recovering from his surprise, ordered his coachman to drive back and to overtake the lady. As soon as he got over against her he said to her 'Madam, you have been pleased to bestow a title on me which generally belongs to the fortunate. Will your ladyship be at the play tonight?' 'Well', she replied, 'What if I am there?' 'Why, then I will be there to wait on your ladyship, though I disappoint a very fine woman who has made me an assignation.' 'So', said she, 'you are sure to disappoint a woman who has favoured you for one who has not.' 'Yes', he replied, 'if she who has not favoured me is the finer woman of the two. But he who will be constant to your ladyship till he can find a finer woman is sure to die your captive.' The lady blushed and bade her coachman drive away. As she was then in all her bloom and the most celebrated beauty that was then in England or perhaps that has been in England since, she was touched with the gallantry of that compliment. In short, she was that night in the first row of the King's Box in Drury Lane and Mr Wycherley in the pit under her, where he entertained her during the whole play. And this, sir, was the beginning of a correspondence between these two persons, which afterwards made a great noise in the town' (*The Critical Works*, II 409–10).

The Gentleman Dancing-Master

II i s.d. Antoine de Brunel in *A Journey into Spain* (1670) offers this description of Spanish costume: 'The Spaniards wear a cassock with deep skirts which sits very close to the body from the neck to the haunches, a black leather girdle which buckles on the breast or towards the navel; their breeches are so straight that for more easy putting them on and off they are buttoned at the sides towards the bottom; their shoes are shaped exactly to their feet, with narrow soles, and a little foot and large calf of the leg are in such request that gallants bind their feet about with riband, to their no small torment, whilst by quilted stockings they put themselves perfectly in the mode. Their silk stockings are knit very open, almost like net-work, which they stretch very straight upon white that is seen through them' (p. 57)

III i 52–4. John Downes describes Nokes's acting a French fop in a famous story: 'Our company were commanded to Dover in May, 1670, the King with ali his court meeting his sister, the Duchess of Orleans, there . . . The French court wearing then excessive short laced coats, some scarlet, some blue, with broad waist belts, Mr Nokes having at that time one shorter than the French fashion to act Sir Arthur Addle in [in John Caryll's *Sir Salomon*], the Duke of Monmouth gave Mr Nokes his sword and belt from his side and buckled it on himself on purpose to ape the French, that Mr Nokes looked more like a dressed-up ape than a Sir Arthur, which, upon his first entrance on the stage, put the King and court to an excessive laughter, at which the French looked very shaggrin to see themselves aped by such a buffoon as Sir Arthur. Mr Nokes kept the Duke's sword to his dying day' (*Roscius Anglicanus* (1708), p. 29).

III i 289. Ned Ward's comments are irresistible: 'We were got amongst a parcel of lank-haired formalists, in flat-crowned hats and short cloaks, walking with as much state and gravity as a snail o'er the leaf of a cabbage, with a box of tobacco dust in one hand, the other employed in charging their nostrils, from whence it drops into their mustachoes which were always as full of snuff as a beau's wig is full of powder . . . These, my friend told me, were Spaniards' (*The London Spy*, quoted by Weales, p. 246).

The Country Wife

I i 29–30. Commentators have been unsure of the nationality of both whore and surgeon. Since Horner has been in France we could expect the whore to be French and the English–French disaster to be Horner's making love to her. But at V iv 62 Horner blames 'an English Bawd' and therefore the whore may well have been English with a French disease. As to the doctor, the 'English–French chiruregon' becomes 'a French chirurgeon' at V iv 62; however, I think the latter means an English doctor specialising in syphilis (cf. 'horse-doctor') – though in that case it is not clear why Horner has been in France at all!

I i 364. Most editors follow Q2 and later editions and read 'Go to him again', assuming that Harcourt is telling Sparkish to go back to his earl. But Q1 could mean that Harcourt is speaking to Dorilant, encouraging him to tease Sparkish further.

The Plain-Dealer

I i 548–56. Once Widow Blackacre straightens out Jerry's mistake, the case does make sense. For those who worry about such things, it concerns suit and countersuit over dispossession: 'Ayle owns Black-acre as a freeholder. John-a-Stiles dispossesses and evicts Ayle. Ayle files a claim for repossession and John-a-Stiles dies. Pere takes possession of the land and Fitz dispossesses Pere. Ayle brings an action for recovery in the *post* (because the current holder is distant from the original dispossessor) and Pere brings an action for recovery in the *per* (against the heir to the dispossessor).' Either Pere, Widow Blackacre or Wycherley is at this point making a mistake. Some editors have further confused matters by mistaking post-disseisin and entry in the *post*, which has not helped their explanations.